The
Ultimate
DVD Guide

TITAN BOOKS

DVD REVIEW PRESENTS THE ULTIMATE DVD GUIDE
ISBN 1 84023 290 0

Published by
Titan Books
A division of
Titan Publishing Group Ltd
144 Southwark St
London, SE1 0UP

First edition November 2000
10 9 8 7 6 5 4 3 2 1

FRONT COVER IMAGES
Austin Powers The Spy Who Shagged Me © 2000 Entertainment in Video; *The Matrix* and *Eyes Wide Shut* © 2000 Warner Home Video; *Men in Black* © 2000 Columbia TriStar; *The World is Not Enough* © 2000 MGM Home Entertainment

ACKNOWLEDGEMENTS
The Publishers would like to thank Damian Butt, Andy McDermott and Kevin Petley at Paragon Publishing for their help and support on this project. We would also like to thank the team who put this book together, especially Stephen Jones for his invaluable help at a crucial time.

CONTRIBUTORS
The reviews within these pages were written by Ross Andrews, Mark Anniss, Scott Anthony, Neil Armstrong, James Beech, Adam Boussada, Simon Brew, Elaine Brown, Graeme Brown, Damian Butt, Ryan Butt, Simon Byron, Andy Connor, Nerys Coward, Gideon Daly, Ian Dean, Mark Eveleigh, Sarah Ginger, Conor Hamill, Geoff Harris, Mark Hattersley, Nina Hicks, Karen Hollocks, Robert Irvine, Russell Jackson, Mark Kendrick, Roy Kimber, Kendall Lacey, Ben Lawrence, Matt Leppard, Paul Malinowski, Martin Mathers, Danny McAleer, Tim McCann, Andy McDermott, Stuart Messham, Sarah Moran, Paul Morgan, Russell Murray, Graeme Nicholson, Sney Noorani, Simon Phillips, Mark Pickavance, Nev Pierce, Mike Richardson, Jem Roberts, Nick Roberts, Paul Roland, Guy Rowland, Tom Sargent, Geoff Spick, Jason Spiller, Stuart Taylor, Adrian Tankard, Andrea Thompson, Lou Wells, Mark Wynne and Stuart Wynne.

NOTE:
The Publishers have endeavoured to ensure that all the information contained within this book is correct at the time of going to press, but inaccuracies are possible in a book of this nature and we would therefore advise readers to also check all details for themselves before purchasing any of the discs reviewed.

Did you enjoy this book? We love to hear from our readers. Please e-mail us at: readerfeedback@titanemail.com or write to Reader Feedback at the address above.

All Titan Books are available through most good bookshops or direct from our mail order service. For a free catalogue or to order, telephone 01858 433169 with your credit card details, e-mail asmltd@btinternet.com or contact Titan Books Mail Order, Bowden House, 36 Northampton Road, Market Harborough, Leics, LE16 9HE. Please quote reference DVD/MO.

A CIP catalogue record for this title is available from the British Library.

Printed and bound in Great Britain by Cox and Wyman Ltd, Reading, Berkshire.

CONTENTS

If you studiously avoid all forms of news, advertising, popular culture and entertainment in general, you may not be aware of DVD. In which case, I hope you're happy in your mountain-top cave, and look forward to the day when you start to appreciate the wonders of electricity and the nutritional advantages of a moss-free diet. On the other hand, if you've heard of some amazing new home entertainment format called DVD, or even if you're well aware of exactly what DVD is and what it offers, then I bid you a cheery "Welcome!" to the 21st century and assure you that this book is just what you're after.

So, what is DVD? DVD stands for Digital Versatile Disc, a rather awkward phrase that nevertheless perfectly describes the format. It's definitely digital, it's extremely versatile, and you probably won't be surprised to learn that it is indeed round and flat in shape. In fact, it looks a lot like a CD, but can hold a lot more than the latest Britney Spears album.

DVD movies are just the beginning, but even this most visible face of DVD tramples old-fashioned technology like the humble VHS cassette into the dirt. Where VHS offers only a feeble 250 lines of resolution at best (well under half of what your television is capable of showing) and wears out just a little more every time you watch it, DVD provides a level of detail almost indistinguishable from a TV broadcast, never wears out no matter how often you rewind to watch your favourite moments and even provides six (or more) channel surround sound that is as good as – or in some cases, better than – you'll find in your local cinema. DVD even beats other, more recent, formats like laserdisc and video CD, and since it has the full support of all the major film companies around the world, it's guaranteed not to end up dropping into the dustbin of history like Betamax or CD-I when the next big thing comes along. DVD is here to stay.

DVD can actually bring a new lease of life to your favourite films, because the discs have so much storage space on them that they can contain not only the film itself, but literally hours of extra features as well. You can watch the film with a running commentary from the stars and director about how it was made, watch documentaries that take you behind the scenes, or even choose between different versions of a movie, such as the original cinema release or a later director's cut, and have the disc seamlessly switch between each version. Then there are more prosaic benefits such as multiple-language subtitles and soundtracks, the ability to skip straight to your favourite scene at the push of a button, and best of all, no more rewinding tapes!

Since its successful launch in the UK in 1998, DVD has proven to be the fastest-growing consumer format of all time, taking only two years to sell ten million discs – audio CD took more than twice as long to achieve the same level of sales. By the time you read this, there will be over a million DVD players sitting in UK homes, and that doesn't even include the ever-growing number of PCs and Apple Macintoshes that come with built-in DVD-ROM drives, meaning you can write a letter or do your accounts, then start watching a movie with no more effort than clicking a mouse button. Even more amazingly, Britain has become the country that leads the world in actually buying films on DVD – we buy more than twice as many discs per head than even the Americans!

The benefits of DVD are easy to see – you just need to start watching one. As well as offering a much more detailed picture than VHS can manage, if you have a widescreen television, DVD also lets you watch films as their makers intended. 'Anamorphic' or 'widescreen enhanced' films take full advantage of DVD's huge storage capacity to cram in widescreen films that automatically stretch themselves out like a cat on a fireside rug to fill the extra width of a 16:9 TV set. DVD also has much better colour reproduction than VHS, with none of those blurry, smeared effects that we've all had to become used to ever since VCRs appeared in the Seventies. Once you've experienced DVD, going back to watching films on video is about as appealing a prospect as living in a mud hut and eating rats.

Of course, as the middle initial of its name suggests, there's more to DVD than just showing movies in the best possible light. The 'versatile' tag is no idle boast. Starting in 2001, DVD machines will gain a new talent – the ability to record as well as play back! Recordable DVD will mean that the days of having to wind through the thousands of adverts you caught whilst taping *The Simpsons*, or of missing the revelation of the murderer's identity in the latest murder mystery because you ran out of tape five minutes before the end, are well and truly over. Instead of shelves of chunky brick-sized cassettes, you'll be able to fit all your recordings neatly into a CD rack, and even chop out and erase adverts at the touch of a button. And because recordable DVD uses the same technology as the discs you can buy in the shops, the picture quality will be every bit as good as it was when it was broadcast.

Slightly muddying the waters of recordable DVD is the fact that, at the moment, there are three different recording formats, all of which – in typical VHS/Beta style – are incompatible with each other. The three rival formats are DVD-RW (supported by Pioneer, Sanyo, Sharp and LG), DVD-RAM (backed by Panasonic, Samsung, Hitachi and Toshiba) and RVD+RW (from Philips). The biggest brand in consumer electronics, Sony, has actually at one time or another dipped its toes into all three pools, but at the time of writing seemed to be leaning towards DVD-RW. Which format will win out will largely depend on who is the first to get a player on sale at a consumer-friendly price, though other factors like the price and capacity of recordable DVDs will play a part. The more timid will probably want to hold back for a while to see which of the three takes the lead, but for many the prospect of being able to bin the VHS and record everything in a quality digital format will no doubt prove irresistible!

The DVD-RAM format is, of course, already in use in the computer market – numerous high-end PCs and Macs come with built-in DVD-RAM drives, allowing users to record huge amounts of data to disk, then edit and delete it whenever they feel like. But DVD-ROM – the read-only DVD format – is growing in popularity as a replacement for CD-ROMs. Games manufacturers in particular have started to see the advantages of the format; instead of having to cram ten CD-ROMs into a box in order to contain the latest mega-game, a single DVD-ROM will do the trick. Sony is taking full advantage of this with its new PlayStation2 console (which also doubles as a DVD player) to create games of previously unimaginable complexity and realism. A lot of DVD-Video discs come with DVD-ROM features included as extras, so after watching the film you can pop the disc into your computer and watch extra featurettes, visit websites and even play games.

The latest bit of versatility provided by DVD is the DVD-Audio format, intended first to complement, then eventually replace, CD. DVD-Audio uses DVD's far greater storage capacity than CD to allow music to be recorded at a much higher sample rate, putting an end to all those "music on disc sounds too clean and too tinny" moans from beardy types who mourn the death of vinyl LPs (and probably wax cylinders too) because it is much closer to the sound of live music. DVD-Audio naturally supports all the same full surround sound formats as its video cousin, so instead of just sitting listening to a performance, it'll seem as though you're in the middle of it! Several companies, such as Panasonic and Technics, are already offering players that combine DVD-Video and DVD-Audio technology, so you'll be able to have one single machine that plays all your DVD movies, your new DVD-Audio discs and your old CDs into the bargain.

So that's DVD in a nutshell – it's not just the format of the future, with every major entertainment company in the world now supporting it, but it's the format of the present too. Every week sees more and more new (and classic) films and TV shows being released on DVD, and the chances are that if your all-time favourite film isn't on DVD already, it will be soon. If you want to keep up with the latest news, then *DVD Review* magazine, Britain's biggest and best-selling DVD title, is the obvious choice, but what if you're just entering the world of DVD and you want to know what's already out there?

Easy enough – just carry on reading this book! It contains a healthy selection of reviews from past issues, and will help you sort the best of what DVD has to offer from the not-so-good (yes, I'm afraid that even DVD has a few dogs on disc!). The reviews also tell you what you can expect from a particular disc in terms of extras and special features – if you just want a DVD for the film and nothing else that's fine, but many people want to take advantage of everything that the digital format can offer.

All you have to do now is decide exactly which DVDs you're going to buy!

Andy McDermott
Editor
DVD Review

ABSOLUTE POWER

Price: £15.99
Supplied by: Warner Home Video
Type of disc: Dual layer, single-sided
No of chapters: 35
Film format(s)/length: 2.35:1 anamorphic / 116 mins
Audio format: Dolby Digital 5.1
Director: Clint Eastwood
Starring: Clint Eastwood, Gene Hackman, Ed Harris
Year made: 1996
Extras: Scene access; soundtrack in English, French and Italian; subtitles in 10 languages; subtitles for the hearing impaired in English and Italian.

This is a film which might have given Bill Clinton a few ideas pre-Monica Lewinsky! Gene Hackman is the US President who kills his lover in a fit of rage thus ensuring that she won't be confessing all on *Entertainment Tonight*. There is still one likely blabbermouth, though – career thief Luther Whitney (Eastwood) was burgling the President's home at the time and witnessed the whole thing. How will it unravel and is anyone likely to believe the word of a thief over that of the President? *Absolute Power* is a gripping thriller showing another unscrupulous power-hungry politician losing control. As a DVD presentation it has fairly average picture quality and – unless you're into languages – not much else, which is a shame because this movie deserves better packaging. Probably better to wait until it gets released on a budget label...

FINAL VERDICT

Picture ☆☆☆ Sound ☆☆☆☆
Entertainment ☆☆☆ Extras ☆☆ Value ☆☆
OVERALL ☆☆☆

ACE VENTURA, PET DETECTIVE

Price: £15.99
Supplied by: Warner Home Video
Type of disc: Dual layer, single-sided
No of chapters: 31
Film format(s)/length: 1.85:1 widescreen / 83 mins
Audio format: Dolby Surround
Director: Tom Shadyac
Starring: Jim Carrey, Courteney Cox, Dan Marino
Year made: 1994
Extras: Scene access; soundtrack in English, French and Italian; subtitles in 9 languages; subtitles for the hearing impaired in English and Italian.

For film fans, Jim Carrey is an acquired taste – you either love him to pieces or want to punch him repeatedly in the face. Thankfully, *Ace Ventura, Pet Detective* is one of those films that puts him in a much better light as it's actually quite funny...especially compared to some of the other rubbish he's made over the years. If you've never seen it before, you're missing out on a treat because it never seems to let up on the slapstick comedy. Watch as the madcap pet 'detective' hunts down a missing dolphin and runs into a man-eating shark, chases the Miami Dolphins around for a bit and then goes one-on-one with a transsexual retired pro-footballer out for revenge. Oh, how we laughed. No, really we did. Mind you, we laughed even harder when we saw the DVD version of this great film...because it really, really sucks. Talk about stripping things to the bare bone – apart from the obvious sound quality that you get from a DVD, there's *nothing here*. No theatrical trailer, no behind-the-scenes coverage, nothing. Even the picture looks like someone's rubbed sandpaper all over it! Unless you're looking to find out the Bulgarian translation of the phrase 'Like a glove!' there's absolutely no reason to buy it. At all. When film companies bring out things like this, it makes you wonder why on earth they bother with DVD in the first place. Save your money – you might as well go out and buy the VHS version. Sorry.

FINAL VERDICT

Picture ☆☆ Sound ☆☆☆
Entertainment ☆☆☆ Extras ☆ Value ☆
OVERALL ☆☆

ACE VENTURA: WHEN NATURE CALLS

Price: £15.99
Supplied by: Warner Home Video
Type of disc: Single layer, single-sided
No of chapters: 36
Film format(s)/length: 2.35:1 widescreen enhanced / 89 mins
Audio format: Dolby Digital 5.1
Director: Steve Oedekerk
Starring: Jim Carrey, Ian McNeice, Simon Callow
Year made: 1995
Extras: Scene access; subtitles in 4 languages.

When Ace Ventura fails to save a raccoon from falling to its death, his guilt drives him to take refuge in a Tibetan monastery. However, the world's wackiest animal lover is lured out of hiding by the search for a sacred white bat, which leads to Africa and more taste-less fart jokes than you can imagine! This follow-up benefits from a bigger budget than its predecessor, and a rip-roaring African adventure results. Crass, oddball and grossly exaggerated, Ace Ventura's quirky humour comes not only from his affinity with animals, but his lack of affinity with humans. Jim

Carrey plays the reckless goofball hero to everyone else's straight men with hilarious results. The extras for the DVD release amount to little more than scene access and subtitles which is a real shame, but the clarity of the sound effects (mainly produced by Carrey himself) and visual gags make this an entertaining and at times outrageously funny movie.

FINAL VERDICT

Picture ☆☆☆☆ Sound ☆☆☆

Entertainment ☆☆☆☆ Extras ☆ Value ☆☆☆

OVERALL ☆☆☆

THE ACID HOUSE

Price: £19.99
Supplied by: VCI
Type of disc: Single layer, single-sided
No of chapters: 18
Film format(s)/length: 16:9 anamorphic widescreen / 106 mins
Audio format: Dolby Surround
Director: Paul McGuigan
Starring: Ewen Bremner, Kevin McKidd, Martin Clunes
Year made: 1998
Extras: Scene access; theatrical trailer; picture library containing stills from the film.

Irvine Welsh's *Trainspotting* as a book and on film received equal amounts of praise and derision. Some applauded its honest and visceral portrayal of the junkie lifestyle, whilst the moral majority wailed that it glamourised heroin, and somehow made it fashionable. However, anyone who has seen the film will probably laugh at the latter assumption, as *Trainspotting* is many things, but what it certainly isn't is glamourous. So, now that FilmFour has released *The Acid House* (the second Irvine Welsh novel-to-film adaptation) onto DVD, how does the subject matter hold up against the recently released *Trainspotting*? Fans will be pleased to know that *The Acid House* is another slice of foul language, chemical abuse and largely pathetic people with little or no real qualities worthy of note. However, that doesn't make this collection of 3 separate stories any less compelling, entertaining, disturbing, and in most cases, downright hilarious than its motion picture predecessor. From the story of layabout Boab Coyle who loses his girlfriend, job, place on the local football team and gets booted out of home all in one day; to the soft touch Johnny, who in a pathetic attempt to keep the peace lets his neighbour use not only his electricity but his wife as well; through to acid-tripping Coco Bryce who ends up mind-swapping with a middle-class family's baby; *The Acid House* is full of unforget-

table moments. It's a pity that the DVD couldn't be the same. The picture and sound quality are good, with the acid trip sequence in the third story proving to be a disturbing experience if played through a decent home cinema set-up. You know that you are going to get a theatrical trailer bundled in with the DVD, so it's not really worth mentioning. The photo library is a nice addition, but hardly worthy of the DVD format. It would have been more interesting if we could have had Welsh talking about the film's production, its relation to *Trainspotting*, and also discussing the differences between writing the novel and the screenplay. A behind-the-scenes piece wouldn't have gone amiss either, and considering the commercial and critical success of *Trainspotting*, FilmFour appears to have missed a golden opportunity to turn the 'chemical generation' onto DVD.

FINAL VERDICT

Picture ☆☆☆☆ Sound ☆☆☆

Entertainment ☆☆☆ Extras ☆☆ Value ☆☆

OVERALL ☆☆

THE ADVENTURES OF BARON MUNCHAUSEN

Price: £19.99
Supplied by: Columbia TriStar Home Video
Type of disc: Single layer, single-sided
No of chapters: 28
Film format(s)/length: 6:9 widescreen enhanced / 121 mins
Audio format: Dolby Surround
Director: Terry Gilliam
Starring: John Neville, Uma Thurman, Robin Williams
Year made: 1989
Extras: Scene access; theatrical trailer; 4 filmographies; biographies of Gilliam and Idle; soundtrack in French, German ; mono soundtrack in Spanish; subtitles in 19 languages.

Having famously endured an out-of-control production team who were unable even to speak a common language, this film went on to became one of the biggest box office flops of all time. It is therefore worth remembering that the end result is as audaciously funny and weird as anyone could wish for – pure, 100 per cent Terry Gilliam. During The Age of Reason (and on a Wednesday), a war is in progress. The hitherto-assumed-to-be mythical Baron Munchausen decides to get help in order to end the carnage he himself claims to have been responsible for. Enter his amazing old companions – one can run at 200,000mph, another can throw ships around and so on. As the team regroups, they journey from the centre of the Earth (where they meet an appropriately cast Uma Thurman as Venus), all the way to the surface of the Moon (whose King is Robin Williams, sporting a fine detachable head). And, don't forget, it's all true. The DVD of this lavish, exuberant production is, sadly, a real disappointment. If this disc were partnered by a candid documentary or commentary featuring Gilliam, it would achieve must-buy status instantly. As it is, it merely contains a poor-by-Columbia-standards picture transfer, complete with pops, scratches, Pro-logic sound which is basically the same as on the VHS, a mildly amusing trailer, and a couple of biogs. Columbia has proved itself more than capable of producing first rate discs – it's a real shame that this isn't one of them.

FINAL VERDICT

Picture ☆☆ Sound ☆☆☆

Entertainment ☆☆☆☆ Extras ☆☆ Value ☆

OVERALL ☆☆☆

THE ADVENTURES OF PRISCILLA, QUEEN OF THE DESERT

Price: £19.99
Supplied by: Columbia TriStar Home Video
Type of disc: Single layer, single-sided
No of chapters: 20
Film format(s)/length: 1:1.85 letterbox / 99 mins
Audio format: Dolby Digital
Director: Stephan Elliott
Starring: Terence Stamp, Hugo Weaving, Guy Pearce
Year made: 1994
Extras: 9 TV clips; filmographies and biographies; teaser trailer; trailer.

This oddly-titled film is a kind of gay Australian *Summer Holiday*. Aborigines dance to Abba, opera comes to the outback and trannies get to wear cork hats. As Bernadette (Stamp) says early on, "What this country needs is a cock in a frock, on a rock." So say g'day Mel Gibson and Crocodile Dundee; in this film, Mike from *Neighbours* (Pearce) gets to fulfil his real ambition. Namely, to climb to the top of King's Canyon in a Gaultier frock, tiara and heels. Not that Stephan Elliott's film is all sex dolls over Ayer's Rock; the basic story is more like *Withnail and I* in the land of Oz. These are performers whose paths are about to diverge. The previously married Mitzi (Weaving, very different to *The Matrix*'s Agent Smith!) must face up to his responsibility as a parent, while the grieving Bernadette ends up in a somewhat conventional romance. However, where *Withnail and I* was weak-kneed, *Priscilla* is pouting and Elliott's film remains both optimistic and gay. Like all the best contemporary

Australian cinema, the insignificance of people before an imposing landscape is used to generate some spectacular images. The DVD captures the film's incredible imagery wonderfully. Brian J Breheny gets full marks for his cinematography, which is good as anything in *The Piano* or *Picnic at Hanging Rock*. The sound quality is also top drawer, although not everyone will enjoy an hour-and-a-half of the Village People, Gloria Gaynor and Ce Ce Peniston. Overall, *Priscilla*'s an attractive film, although arguably not much more than an extended pop video. Enjoyable, but not something you can imagine watching frequently. Decent extras would have really helped keep up your interest, but instead you get fobbed off with some truly feeble postcard-size filmographies and loads of near-identical trailers. What a tart!

FINAL VERDICT

Picture ☆☆☆☆ Sound ☆☆☆☆

Entertainment ☆☆☆☆ Extras ☆☆ Value ☆☆☆☆

OVERALL ☆☆☆☆

AIR FORCE ONE

Price: £15.99
Supplied by: DVD World (01705 796662)
Type of disc: Single layer, double-sided (flipper)
No of chapters: 16 (side A), 19 (side B)
Film format(s)/length: 2.35:1 widescreen / 120 mins
Audio format: Dolby Digital 5.1
Director: Wolfgang Petersen
Starring: Harrison Ford, Gary Oldman, Glenn Close
Year made: 1997
Extras: Widescreen TV enhanced; Dolby Digital 5.1; chapter access; English/French/Italian soundtracks; multilingual subtitles.

Wouldn't it be great if real American Presidents were like Harrison Ford in *Air Force One?* No senile old duffers, dodgy former CIA spooks or Monica-molesting lardarses here; instead, you get a two-fisted tough guy who deals personally with terrorists by punching them on the nose. *Air Force One* is the latest film from Wolfgang Petersen, a director who of late has specialised in films that, despite their pretensions to serious themes, are really just rip-roaring Big Dumb Action Movies. In this airborne example, the titular Presidential 747 is hijacked by eye-rolling communist Korshunov (Oldman) in order to force the release of an imprisoned Russian general. President Marshall (Ford) is supposed to eject in an escape pod, but as his family are hostages he chooses to stay and rescue them in true Bruce Willis-style. While the Vice-President (Close) attempts to negotiate from the ground, Ford scurries around below decks, picking off the bad guys one by one. Petersen plays the set-pieces – the initial hijacking, an abortive landing, Ford dangling from a cargo ramp at 15,000 feet and an attack by Russian MiGs – for all they're worth, skillfully disguising the implausibility of the whole thing (for a start, how come not one of the thousands of rounds fired blows a hole in the plane's hull?) with old-school thrills and tension. You're never in doubt for a moment about who will win, but Ford's heroic President makes you wish that there were real politicians like this. Some hope. DVDs have now overcome any teething troubles, so *Air Force One* looks and sounds as good as we've come to expect – crisp, colourful pictures and neighbour-annoying 5.1 audio. The problem is, it's a Disney disc, so…yes, it's yet another flipper! Apparently Disney signed a contract with a pressing plant that can't make dual-layer discs (or something). What, so their millions of lawyers couldn't work out a way to get out of the deal? In the meantime, we have to suffer this second-rate format and Disney does a fantastic job of shooting itself in the foot.

FINAL VERDICT

Picture ☆☆☆☆ Sound ☆☆☆☆

Entertainment ☆☆☆☆ Extras ☆ Value ☆☆

OVERALL ☆☆☆

ALIEN

Price: £19.99

Supplied by: 20th Century Fox Home Entertainment

Type of disc: Dual layer, single-sided

No of chapters: 20

Film format(s)/length: 2.35:1 widescreen enhanced / 112 mins

Audio format: Dolby Digital 5.1, Dolby Surround

Director: Ridley Scott

Starring: Tom Skerritt, Sigourney Weaver, John Hurt

Year made: 1979

Extras: Scene access; deleted scenes; outtakes; audio commentary by *Alien* director Ridley Scott; artwork and photo galleries; original storyboards; isolated original music score; alternate music track; original theatrical trailers; subtitles in 10 languages; subtitles available for the hearing impaired in English.

The opening chapter of what has become an incredible saga first introduced us to the awe-inspiring resilience of Ellen Ripley (Weaver) and her battles against the perfect killing organism. Regarded by many as the pinnacle of the series, *Alien* terrified audiences worldwide with its classic blend of science fiction and horror. In the future, the crew of the space tug *Nostromo* receive an extraterrestrial transmission that originates from a desolate planet. Reluctantly investigating (if they don't, they'll lose their pay) they find the tattered ruins of an ancient alien spacecraft. The investigating team discovers first a huge fossilised creature, seemingly the ship's pilot, with a hole in its stomach, and soon after Kane (Hurt) makes the mistake of looking too closely at a strange egg. From then on, the nightmare never ends as one of cinema's most memorable evening meals ends with the bloody arrival of an uninvited guest, and a rapidly dwindling band of survivors is forced into a life-or-death struggle against a monster that kills to live – and lives to kill… What the film achieves in suspense and horror, the DVD matches in picture and sound, as the digitally remastered THX audio does exactly what it says on the tin! Anamorphically enhanced, the 112 minutes of exceptional horror is, er…exceptional. But if the glorious visual acuity isn't enough, the special features strike like lightning with a hugely varying and interesting array of extras. The audio commentary reunited Ridley Scott with his own legacy at Shepperton Studios. This exclusive recording for DVD is one of the finest examples of commentary to date, and the inclusion of a topic search is a marvellous idea. Skipping past the traditional ingredient of theatrical trailers, the deleted scenes (of which there are ten) provide clues and answers to many scenes throughout the film – including a rare and much talked-about scene regarding the Alien's life-cycle, which James Cameron must be thankful was never used as it would have made the ending of *Aliens* impossible! The out-takes, although interesting, are just two more short scenes that were omitted from the theatrical release. One of the most unusual special features on the DVD is the alternate music track and isolated original score, with the latter telling a story without the need for words. The artwork (including H R Giger), photo galleries and original storyboards complete the enjoyment in this DVD marvel, making this a must-buy for fans of the film and DVD owners alike.

FINAL VERDICT

Picture ☆☆☆☆ Sound ☆☆☆☆

Entertainment ☆☆☆☆☆ Extras ☆☆☆☆☆

Value ☆☆☆☆☆

OVERALL ☆☆☆☆☆

ALIENS

Price: £19.99

Supplied by: 20th Century Fox Home Entertainment

Type of disc: Dual layer, single-sided

No of chapters: 34

Film format(s)/length: 1.85:1 widescreen enhanced / 148 mins
Audio format: Dolby Digital 5.1
Director: James Cameron
Starring: Sigourney Weaver, Michael Biehn, Lance Henricksen
Year made: 1986
Extras: Scene access; trailer; James Cameron interview; behind-the-scenes footage; photo gallery; subtitles in 10 languages; subtitles available for the hearing impaired in English.

As *Scream 2* proved, people can argue endlessly about which was the better film – Ridley Scott's *Alien* or James Cameron's *Aliens*. The truth is they're different kinds of film – *Alien* is a suspense/horror movie, while *Aliens* is intense action and thrills. Besides, it's *Aliens*. Ripley (Weaver) is woken from a 57-year nap to find that nobody believes a word of her story about stomach-ripping monsters. Unfortunately, while she was sleeping a colony was established on the very planet where Ripley and crew first encountered the Alien, and before long contact is lost. Ripley and a squad of Marines are sent to investigate, and the nightmare begins all over again… The film is without a doubt one of the most exhilarating ever made, as the battles against the Aliens escalate to the final conflict – a one-on-one brawl between the Alien Queen and a power-suited Ripley. The picture quality is superb, allowing you to spot small details previously hidden in a VHS haze. The DVD of *Aliens* is also the extended Special Edition, 17 minutes longer than the original. While the film worked superbly without the deleted scenes, their restoration makes it even better than before. Disappointingly, *Aliens* is yet another James Cameron DVD for which the frequently-married one hasn't provided a commentary track. While you do get an interview recorded at the time he made the film, it's no substitute for being talked through each scene as it unfolds. Still, though the DVD is nowhere near as packed as *Alien*, there's enough here to keep fans happy – and there's more on the disc than *Alien³* and *Alien Resurrection* combined.

FINAL VERDICT
Picture ☆☆☆☆☆ Sound ☆☆☆☆
Entertainment ☆☆☆☆☆ Extras ☆☆☆☆
Value ☆☆☆☆
OVERALL ☆☆☆☆☆

ALIEN RESURRECTION

Price: £19.99
Supplied by: 20th Century Fox Home Entertainment
Type of disc: Dual layer, single-sided

No of chapters: 27
Film format(s)/length: 2.35:1 widescreen enhanced / 108 mins
Audio format: Dolby Digital 5.1
Director: Jean-Pierre Jeunet
Starring: Sigourney Weaver, Winona Ryder
Year made: 1997
Extras: Theatrical trailer; pitiful featurette.

A sinewy Sigourney Weaver leads yet another band of mercenary cyberpunks through a few levels from *Quake*. The action builds with the ferocity of a BBC shipping forecast climaxing in battle with a glistening fleshy alien hybrid: Mick Hucknall right out of the shower. An outrageously unnecessary sequel. The anamorphic transfer is mostly clean, if not terrifically sharp. Sound is actually the disc's best feature, with the impossibly clear high-end and expansive roomy bass that only comes with the THX stamp. Things are less impressive in the extras department. The 'featurette' is 3 minutes 45 seconds of crudely over-exposed talking heads offering insightful gems like, "I think people are gonna really like this movie," and the always popular, "There are things in this movie that have never been done before." Only those who are determined to have the whole series need apply.

FINAL VERDICT
Picture ☆☆☆☆ Sound ☆☆☆☆
Entertainment ☆☆ Extras ☆☆ Value ☆☆
OVERALL ☆☆

ALIEN ³

Price: £19.99
Supplied by: 20th Century Fox Home Entertainment
Type of disc: Dual layer, single-sided
No of chapters: 29
Film format(s)/length: 2.35:1 widescreen enhanced / 110 mins
Audio format: Dolby Digital 5.1
Director: David Fincher
Starring: Sigourney Weaver, Charles Dutton, Charles Dance
Year made: 1992
Extras: Scene access; behind-the-scenes documentary covering all 3 *Alien* movies; cinema trailer; subtitles in 10 languages; subtitles available for the hearing impaired in English.

Not content with scaring us all witless twice, Sigourney Weaver co-produced the third instalment of the *Alien* series herself, with the movie directed by David Fincher, who went on to direct *Se7en*. *Alien³* has a dark and gloomy feel to it, far removed from the shiny metal and moulded plastic view of the future that many sci-fi movies portray. Ripley, played again by Weaver, is rudely woken from hypersleep when her escape pod crashlands on a prison planet populated solely by shaven-headed sociopaths. There's also a slimy surprise in store – inside Ripley herself… Compared to the first two films *Alien³* is disappointing, but it's worth re-watching because it *is* so downbeat and different. It's good to see so many English actors, like Brian Glover and Paul McGann, appearing in the movie too. Some of the effects leave a bit to be desired – the SFX guys were obviously getting to grips with the technology around 1992, as you can spot where the Alien has been superimposed onto a scene from a mile off! Compared to the first two films, *Alien³* is lacking in extras, but there are items of interest here. You get a mini-documentary on the making of the first 3 *Alien* movies that includes a fascinating look at the creature effects. In addition, there's a selection of cinema trailers. It's grim, brown and hardly uplifting to watch, but *Alien³* deserves a repeat viewing – and it's a DVD that's actually got something more than just the movie!

FINAL VERDICT

Picture ☆☆☆ Sound ☆☆☆
Entertainment ☆☆☆ Extras ☆☆☆ Value ☆☆☆
OVERALL ☆☆☆

ALL ABOUT MY MOTHER

Price: £19.99
Supplied by: Pathé Distribution Ltd
Type of disc: Single layer, single-sided
No of chapters: 14
Film format(s)/length: 2.35:1 letterbox / 97 mins
Audio format: Dolby Digital 5.1
Director: Pedro Almodóvar
Starring: Cecilia Roth, Marisa Paredes, Candela Peña
Year made: 1999
Extras: Scene access; original theatrical trailer; subtitles in English.

Stylish like Picasso, Rioja and Ibiza, this eccentric Spanish flick has to be one of the best films made in the past few years. It's a film which deals with the 'big issues' of loss, AIDS, death and poverty unflinchingly. Yet it's anything but miserable. Pedro Almodóvar is a gifted director, and doesn't make dull pictures. Instead, *All About My Mother* is a carnival of emotions, a camp and colourful film bursting with beautiful women, witty transvestites, down-and-outs and drug addicts. It's a quite brilliant melodrama and has the Globes, BAFTAs, Oscars and Cannes awards to prove it. It's also in Spanish. This means that you've probably never heard of it and that you're not going

to buy it, as the market for foreign language films in this country is woefully small. Don't be put off though, because this is a wonderful film and the subtitles look great in digital! It's really good to see interesting independent films becoming more available on the format, a long overdue development. The only criticism possible is that while Hollywood will dump a whole load of extras onto a DVD to flog a dodgy film, the marketing people who put 'highbrow' DVDs together don't make an effort. In terms of extras here you get…a trailer. In this day and age that's not good enough. Still, lay this grumble aside and you have an enjoyable movie from one of the few true originals working in the cinema today. What more could you want?

FINAL VERDICT

Picture ☆☆☆ Sound ☆☆☆☆
Entertainment ☆☆☆ Extras ☆☆ Value ☆☆☆
OVERALL ☆☆☆

AMERICAN HISTORY X

Price: £19.99
Supplied by: Entertainment in Video
Type of disc: Dual layer, single-sided
No of chapters: 33
Film format(s)/length: 16:9 widescreen / 114 mins
Audio format: Dolby Digital 5.1
Director: Tony Kaye
Starring: Edward Norton, Edward Furlong, Fairuza Balk
Year made: 1998
Extras: Scene access; 3 deleted scenes; theatrical trailer; cast and crew biogs; subtitles in English.

Before his mainstream success in the subversive visual showcase that is *Fight Club*, Edward Norton gave the performance of his career in 1998's little-known *American History X*. This disturbing insight into a white power movement group in middle-America does not rely on excessive violence to get its point across, the most disturbing scenes come from the in-depth character moments. Schoolboy Danny Vinyard (played by *Terminator 2*'s Edward Furlong) is making inroads to a local white power group that his older brother, Derek (Norton) used to front. The latter is due out of prison following a 3-year sentence for killing two black youths, and Danny is asked by his history teacher to write an essay about the effect his older brother has had on his life. *American History X* is told from the point of view of Danny, with his narration taking us from the present, to the harrowing events of the past – which are stylistically presented in black and white. We see that the root of the brothers' racism comes from their late father, who insidiously enforces his beliefs upon Derek. These extremist beliefs are eventually echoed by Derek following his father's tragic death. Entertainment in Video has put together a decent package for the DVD release of *American History X*. Whilst it skimps on content – there's only a theatrical trailer, biographies on cast and crew, and deleted scenes – the quality of the goods provided at least make an attempt to do the film some justice. Aural addicts will also be pleased to note that Entertainment in Video has seen fit to present *American History X* in Dolby Digital 5.1 – admittedly, this is not the kind of film that goes all out on the audio special effects, but it is a worthy gesture nonetheless. In all, this is a dark but interesting flick with excellent presentation on DVD and a fair smattering of extras.

FINAL VERDICT

Picture ☆☆☆☆ Sound ☆☆☆☆☆

Entertainment ☆☆☆☆ Extras ☆☆☆ Value ☆☆☆

OVERALL ☆☆☆

AMERICAN PIE

Price: £19.99

Supplied by: Columbia TriStar Home Video

Type of disc: Single layer, single-sided

No of chapters: 18

Film format(s)/length: 16:9 widescreen enhanced / 91 mins

Audio format: Dolby Digital 5.1

Director: Paul Weitz

Starring: Jason Biggs, Chris Klein, Natasha Lyonne

Year made: 1999

Extras: Spotlight on location featurette (10 mins); outtakes (2 mins); feature commentary with director, producer, writer and cast members; US theatrical trailer; interactive DVD-ROM options; classic quotes; production notes; cast and film-makers' notes; subtitles in English.

Only in America. Just when you thought all areas of crudeness and vulgarity had been covered by the likes of *South Park: Bigger, Longer and Uncut* and *There's Something About Mary*, moviegoers from both sides of the pond packed out cinemas last year to see one of the year's funniest and grossest comedies – *American Pie*. The story follows the exploits of 4 high school friends desperate to lose their virginity before prom night. After a disastrous party, Jim, Oz, Kevin and Finch (Biggs, Klein, Thomas Ian Nicholas and Eddie Kaye Thomas respectively) make a secret pact that no longer will their todgers remain flaccid and unused. Cue copious amounts of strong sexuality, crude sexual dialogue, language and drinking – some of which, unfortunately, was cut for the UK release.

As the 4 plan the popping of their cherries, hilarious situations and indescribable embarrassments soon ensue. One of the most infamous incidents associated with the film is the crumbling of an unlucky apple pie, which was triggered after a short but sweet description of what 'third base' feels like – strangely, McDonald's reported an increase of American teens buying apple pies around the same time (hot filling – ouch)! Annoyingly, our over-protective nannies at the BBFC felt the original crust-busting on the kitchen table was slightly too politically incorrect, which is why we see Jim standing upright! Fortunately, the scenes gradually become more risqué, with instant classics such as the protein-filled pale ale and the 'Internet scene', which comprises Jim, a selection of porn magazines and a masturbating foreign student! The special features included on the disc are every bit as impressive as the coarseness of the movie's humour, with a variety of outtakes from the film and a ten-minute *Spotlight on Location* featurette including interviews with the cast and crew. The audio commentary for *American Pie* is significantly better than most, too. Rather than chaining the director in front of a screen and microphone and forcing him at gunpoint to attempt puerile humour, the commentary for *American Pie* features many a witty pun and lewd comment from director Paul Weitz, producer Chris Weitz, writer Adam Herz and cast members Eddie Kaye Thomas, Jason Biggs and Seann William Scott. The obligatory theatrical trailer (albeit the US one) has also been included, along with classic quotes, production notes and cast and film-makers' notes. Interactive DVD-ROM options are also present for those with access to a PC. As for your eyes and ears, the anamorphic picture quality looks great and the Dolby Digital 5.1 sound transfer is equally striking. *American Pie* is truly a fresh wake-up call about the extreme measures that some guys will go to for sex. The jokes often come thick and fast, and most are downright filthy – in the very best of ways. As comedies goes, this one of the best yet to feature so impressively on DVD. A must buy.

FINAL VERDICT

Picture ☆☆☆☆☆ Sound ☆☆☆☆

Entertainment ☆☆☆☆☆ Extras ☆☆☆☆

Value ☆☆☆☆☆

OVERALL ☆☆☆☆☆

THE AMERICAN PRESIDENT

Price: £19.99

Supplied by: Columbia TriStar Home Video

Type of disc: Single layer, single-sided

No of chapters: 33
Film format(s)/length: 2.35:1 widescreen / 109 mins
Audio format: Dolby Digital 5.1
Director: Rob Reiner
Starring: Michael Douglas, Annette Bening, Martin Sheen
Year made: 1995
Extras: Scene access; trailer; production notes; soundtrack in German, French, Dutch, Portuguese, Swedish, Norwegian, Finnish and Danish; multilingual subtitles.

You can't beat irony. Go back a few years and Hollywood was saturated with films professing their love for thinly-disguised versions of Bill Clinton. Of course, that was all before a girl called Monica hit the headlines and cigars became famous for something other than being smoked... Director Reiner is best known for the likes of *This Is Spinal Tap* and *Misery*, but sentiment can strike at any time, and *The American President* is all gooey on the inside. Not only is it a liberal wish-fulfilment fantasy (Douglas' single-parent President gets to hammer the Republicans, save the environment and ban handguns all at the same time), but it also has a love story that rivals *You've Got Mail*. When the professional relationship between Douglas and political lobbyist Bening gets personal, it's an excuse for lots of soft-focus sweetness and nervous romance – the only things that save it from terminal sugar overdose are Sheen's gently mocking turn as the President's top adviser, and Michael J Fox as an overstressed spin doctor. *Spin City* anyone? It's probably not a real surprise that a lightweight film like *The American President* isn't exactly staggering under the weight of extras. Thrill to the trailer! Gasp at the several pages of production notes! Or not. There's nothing in the picture or sound that pushes the DVD format at all, so you're left with an uninvolving slushy romance. What goes on in the real White House is so much more interesting...

FINAL VERDICT

Picture ☆☆☆ Sound ☆☆☆
Entertainment ☆☆ Extras ☆☆ Value ☆☆☆
OVERALL ☆☆

AMITYVILLE II: THE POSSESSION

Price: £15.99
Supplied by: DVDplus (www.dvdplus.co.uk)
Type of disc: Single layer, single-sided
No of chapters: 19
Film format(s)/length: 16:9 widescreen / 104 mins
Audio format: PCM Stereo
Director: Damiano Damiani
Starring: James Olson, Burt Young, Diane Franklin

Year made: 1982
Extras: Scene access; photo gallery.

Set before the initial Amityville horror, this prequel details the events that befell the original occupants of the same misbegotten house. Soon after moving in, the Catholic family become severely dysfunctional, with the eldest son becoming the focus of the inherent evil occupying the basement. Things spiral out of control, with the sinister house provoking the violent father and disturbed son to excessive psychotic behaviour, both towards each other and the rest of the family. Based loosely on a true story, the film is very disturbing. Dealing with such topics as incest and child abuse, the director has definitely set out to shock the audience, with more care and sensitivity than the usual rent-a-monster approach. The bloody massacre of the entire family is incredibly disturbing. Even with the demonic subtext to justify the son's actions, you're still left with a bitter taste in your mouth. You'll definitely need a strong constitution to watch this through to the end. Picture quality is very high. The sound effects and atmospheric music could have done with a 5.1 transfer, but make the hairs stand up on the back of your neck even in stereo. Sadly, in terms of extras, the DVD is as empty as the Amityville house itself, with nought but a photo gallery and basic scene selection to shout about. So much more could have been done. An interview with the Lutz family, crime scene reports or maybe even footage of the actual house could have made this DVD a macabre collector's item. Overall, the disturbing nature of this DVD makes it one for the horror connoisseur only.

FINAL VERDICT

Picture ☆☆☆ Sound ☆☆☆
Entertainment ☆☆☆☆ Extras ☆ Value ☆☆
OVERALL ☆☆☆

AMY FOSTER SWEPT FROM THE SEA

Price: £19.99
Supplied by: DVD Net (020 8890 2520)
Type of disc: Single layer, single-sided
No of chapters: 28
Film format(s)/length: 1.85:1 widescreen / 109 mins
Audio format: Dolby Digital 5.1
Director: Beeban Kidron
Starring: Vincent Pérez, Rachel Weisz, Ian McKellen
Year made: 1997
Extras: Theatrical trailer; filmographies of all leading actors; DVD trailer of forthcoming titles.

With beautiful locations, excellent acting and a gripping story *Amy Foster Swept From the Sea* is a fascinating tale of love against all odds. Starring *City of Angels* lead Vincent Pérez along with Rachel Weisz, who's movies include *Stealing Beauty*, and classic British actors Sir Ian McKellen and Joss Ackland, the story is slow to start, but soon has you completely engrossed. Amy Foster is branded a witch by the local people because she refuses to conform to their small town ways. When a ship is wrecked off the windswept coastline she's accused of causing it, and only one man survives the tragedy – a Russian who immediately takes to Amy and they fall deeply in love, but things aren't that simple. Based on a story by Joseph Conrad, this movie is a surprise hit. Extras are pretty mundane with nothing to shout about, but add that extra dimension that VHS can't offer.

FINAL VERDICT

Picture ☆☆☆☆ Sound ☆☆☆☆

Entertainment ☆☆☆ Extras ☆☆ Value ☆☆☆

OVERALL ☆☆☆

ANACONDA

Price: £19.99

Supplied by: DVD Net (020 8890 2520)

Type of disc: Single layer, single-sided

No of chapters: 19

Film format(s)/length: 2.35:1 widescreen / 86 mins

Director: Luis Llosa

Starring: Jennifer Lopez, Ice Cube, Jon Voight

Year made: 1997

Extras: Multilingual subtitles; scene access.

"I don't know if you know, but this film was supposed to be my big break. It's turned out to be a big disaster." Jennifer Lopez may have been speaking as her character, Terri Flores, about the documentary she set out to make in this movie, but she couldn't have been more accurate if she had spoken those exact words at an *Anaconda* press interview. If you've been lucky enough to avoid it at the cinema, on video rental and on pay-per-view television, imagine *Jaws* in the jungle but without a single likeable character or a true moment of tension. It's hard to tell which is more artificial, Jon Voight with his comic book sneer and wandering Portuguese accent, or the starring snake that looks like a dolled up sock puppet. The encoding may be faultless on this pressing of the movie and it was very selfless of Lopez to attempt to save the project by running through each scene in a damp vest, but *Anaconda* is 86 minutes of completely unengaging viewing.

FINAL VERDICT

Picture ☆☆☆☆ Sound ☆☆☆

Entertainment ☆ Extras ☆ Value ☆

OVERALL ☆

ANALYZE THIS

Price: £19.99

Supplied by: Warner Home Video

Type of disc: Single layer, double-sided

No of chapters: 34

Film format(s)/length: 4:3 regular & 1.85:1 anamorphic / 99 mins

Audio format: Dolby Digital 5.1

Director: Harold Ramis

Starring: Robert De Niro, Billy Crystal, Lisa Kudrow

Year made: 1999

Extras: Scene access; commentary by Billy Crystal and Robert De Niro; gag reel; outtakes; subtitles in 4 languages; subtitles in English for the hearing impaired.

If you're going to give your movie a title like this then, to be honest, you're just asking for criticism. *Analyze This*. Fair enough. Fortunately for Crystal, De Niro and Ramis, everything in this movie worth analysing deserves praise. Mixing the Mafia with laugh-out-loud comedy is rarely a wise decision (anyone who's been subjected to *Jane Austen's Mafia* will probably be wise to this fact), but this neatly-executed tale of the head of a New York crime family, who seeks psychotherapy when he loses his grip, works a treat. Basically this is a one-gag movie, but so many one-liners are tossed out so fast that you'll never be able to keep a straight face so long as this movie is playing. It should have been Crystal's movie. He puts in an excellent performance as Ben Sobel, a family (as opposed to Family) psychiatrist, and he is the crux of the entire plot. Still it's De Niro's turn as weepy mobster Paul Vitti that firmly steals the show. De Niro gets to breeze round the movie, leaving Crystal to clean up the mess. None of the cast has had to stray beyond their realm, particularly De Niro, who just revisits roles he's done so many times before in *Goodfellas* and *Casino*. Fortunately he still gets a worthwhile, self-mocking performance out of it. This is Mafia paint-by-numbers stuff (and it's nowhere near as good as *The Sopranos*), but thankfully no-one's gone over the lines and there's a hilarious little homage to *The Godfather*, which is just priceless. As for the disc, you've got the option for regular or widescreen depending which way up you put the disc in your machine. The added gag reel is just a collection of outtakes, which are fun, albeit usually only once. The most compelling feature is the added commentary by Crystal and De Niro. Both of the stars give very different perspectives into how they approached the movie. The secondary Region 1 commentary from

Ramis is sorely missed, but even without it it's a disc you should welcome with a kiss on both cheeks.

FINAL VERDICT

Picture ☆☆☆☆☆ Sound ☆☆☆☆☆
Entertainment ☆☆☆☆☆ Extras ☆☆☆
Value ☆☆☆☆
OVERALL ☆☆☆☆

ANGELA'S ASHES

Price: £19.99
Supplied by: Columbia TriStar Home Video
Type of disc: Dual layer, single-sided
No of chapters: 30
Film format(s)/length: 1.85:1 anamorphic / 140 mins
Audio format: Dolby Digital 5.1
Director: Alan Parker
Starring: Robert Carlyle, Emily Watson, Joe Breen
Year made: 1999
Extras: Scene access; 2 trailers; behind-the-scenes featurette; cast/crew interviews; Alan Parker interview; Frank McCourt interview; subtitles in English.

Angela's Ashes, the moving tale of how author Frank McCourt survived childhood in the Limerick slums to prosper in America, became one of the bestsellers of the Nineties. Alan Parker has turned this tough rites-of-passage tale into a superb movie, so good that even McCourt praises it to the skies – which makes a refreshing change from snooty authors distancing themselves from film adaptations of their work. The movie has now made a triumphant transfer to DVD. Rather confusingly, *Angela's Ashes* begins in New York, where the alcoholic McCourt senior is struggling to eke out a living. The death of a baby is the last straw, so he moves the whole family back to the Emerald Isle. Life's no easier back home, however, especially when the McCourts move to Limerick. Two more children die from malnourishment and disease, and McCourt's unemployable father drowns his sorrows in booze – one of the saddest scenes in *Angela's Ashes* shows him using the little boy's coffin as a pub table. Things get really bad when the father buggers off to England, forcing McCourt's mother to beg for money and grant sexual favours to a cousin. Somehow, young Frank gets through his schooldays and scrapes together enough money to return to the States. Fast forward 50 years and you've got Frank McCourt the author, now very rich from writing about his hungry youth… While the plot won't have you falling off the sofa with mirth, *Angela's Ashes* reaffirms your faith in the human spirit, and lots of other mushy stuff. There's loads of humour and love here, without too much sentimental Oirish

blarney, and the transfer to widescreen DVD is flawless. The movie looks great on disc, with the greys, blues and browns of the Limerick slums creating a convincingly claustrophobic, foreboding atmosphere. It's hard to forget the faces of the actors either, especially Watson (McCourt's mother, Angela, who ends up as – yup – ashes) and Breen, who plays the young Frank. Robert Carlyle delivers a captivating performance, too, as the deadbeat dad whose spirit collapses under the weight of poverty and bereavement. And we haven't even mentioned the DVD extras yet. There are two trailers for the movie, a fascinating mini-documentary on how it was made, plus illuminating commentaries from Frank McCourt, Alan Parker and the cast. This really is DVD at its best. If you enjoyed the book, or think you might, *Angela's Ashes* is an essential buy.

FINAL VERDICT

Picture ☆☆☆☆☆ Sound ☆☆☆☆
Entertainment ☆☆☆☆☆ Extras ☆☆☆☆
Value ☆☆☆☆
OVERALL ☆☆☆☆☆

ANNIE HALL

Price: £19.99
Supplied by: MGM Home Entertainment
Type of disc: Dual layer, single-sided
No of chapters: 32
Film format(s)/length: 1.85:1 letterbox / 133 mins
Audio format: Mono
Director: Woody Allen
Starring: Woody Allen, Diane Keaton, Tony Roberts
Year made: 1977
Extras: Scene access; collectible booklet; original theatrical trailer; soundtrack in English, French, German, Italian and Spanish; subtitles in 12 languages; subtitles for the hard of hearing in English and German.

It may be a cliché, but it's an undeniable fact that when it comes to Woody Allen movies, you either love them or you hate them. The one-man nervous banter, the New York Jewish twitchiness, the almost stand-up comedian-like quality to his onscreen persona. If you don't get the man, you won't get his movies. *Annie Hall* differs little from most of Allen's work from the late Seventies theme-wise, focusing on relationships and love in the Big Apple. Allen plays Alvy Singer, a successful New York comedian who manages to correlate every relationship he's been to a great Jewish joke. He doesn't take his love life seriously until he meets Annie Hall (Keaton), the larger than life, ditzy nightclub singer who charms the hectic Allen into loving submission. Plagued by his own downfalls, it's Allen's insecurities and hung-up anxiety (the character traits he was born to play) that initially entrance and engage Annie, but ultimately alienate her into starting a new life on the other side of the country. It sounds like dramatic stuff, but throughout the movie Allen reminds us that he was a comedian before he was a film-maker, and his script, despite often being overly reliant on his neuroses, constantly puts a smile on your face. *Annie Hall* might lack the magnitude of *Manhattan*, but Allen's movies have never been about trying to impress. It's still insightful, original, and gleefully entertaining. There are some nice inventive interludes, such as total strangers on the street offering responses to the questions he's asking himself in his internal monologue, and breaking into animation as he fondly remembers his attraction to the wicked stepmother in Disney's *Snow White*. Unfortunately, the disc fails to be as lively as the movie it contains. The picture is fine, and even the menu provides a little fun. However, the fact that the disc has 5 soundtracks does not make up for the fact that they are all in mono. Other films of the era (and earlier) have been remixed for modern systems, so why not this? Being the passionate director that he is, DVD would seem the ultimate forum for Allen to discuss his methods and processes in a director's commentary, but with the inclusion of only a theatrical trailer and a semi-insightful booklet to its credit, this really is a wasted DVD opportunity.

FINAL VERDICT

Picture ☆☆☆☆ Sound ☆☆

Entertainment ☆☆☆☆☆ Extras ☆☆ Value ☆☆

OVERALL ☆☆☆

ANOTHER DAY IN PARADISE

Price: £15.99

Supplied by: Metrodome Distribution

Type of disc: Dual layer, single-sided

No of chapters: 18

Film format(s)/length: 4:3 regular / 100 mins

Audio format: Dolby Digital 2.0

Director: Larry Clark

Starring: James Woods, Melanie Griffith, Vincent Kartheiser

Year made: 1998

Extras: Scene access; James Woods interview; cast and crew information.

Imagine *True Romance* with a pair of leads barely into their teens, and you've got some idea of what this movie is about. Director Larry Clark got his 15 minutes of infamy with *Kids*, an arthouse flick that dealt with teen sex, and the kids in this film are the

most startling aspect here. Kartheiser is shot like a Calvin Klein model, a lithe heroin chic gangster who makes Leonardo DiCaprio look like Bruce Willis. Which isn't to say he's not robustly heterosexual; his couplings with the equally young Natasha Gregson Wagner are startlingly raw and believable. Despite an enthusiasm for drugs and armed robbery, they have an innocence and energy that makes their plight involving. It also makes them vulnerable to James Woods and Melanie Griffith, who initially seem like ideal wish-fulfilment parents, promising to feed up their accomplices and treating Natasha to a clothes-buying spree. However, the film soon tightens into a horrific roller coaster as drug-dealing capers begin to go very wrong. Although the soundtrack is only two-channel, it's effective enough and some classic songs provide plenty of vitality. Picture encoding is good, while the usual filmographies and 'exclusive' star interview are transformed by James Woods. Rather than give the usual bland promo-spiel, he talks for 20 minutes in incomparably blunt fashion. He praises Griffith for her brave performance, but also talks about her whining during production; "She's an actress, what do you expect? No offence." And he's no less direct about the director being comatose during post-production due to his heroin addiction!

FINAL VERDICT

Picture ☆☆☆☆ Sound ☆☆☆

Entertainment ☆☆☆☆ Extras ☆☆☆ Value ☆☆☆

OVERALL ☆☆☆☆

APOLLO 13

Price: £19.99

Supplied by: Columbia TriStar Home Video

Type of disc: Dual layer, single-sided

No of chapters: 57

Film format(s)/length: 2.35: widescreen / 135 mins

Audio format: Dolby Digital 5.1

Director: Ron Howard

Starring: Tom Hanks, Kevin Bacon, Bill Paxton

Year made: 1995

Extras: Scene access; multilingual soundtracks; multilingual subtitles; production notes; trailer; cast and filmmakers' notes; director's commentary; Jim and Marilyn Lovell's commentary.

As understatements go, "Houston, we have a problem" has to be one of the best, especially when said problem is a vital part of your spaceship exploding. Ron Howard's 1995 docu-drama tells the true story of the ill-fated Apollo 13 lunar mission, the heroism and ingenuity of the 3 astronauts aboard (played by Hanks, Paxton and Bacon) and the big brains at Mission Control, led by Ed Harris, in bringing the stricken ship safely back to Earth. *Apollo 13* is a great showcase for home cinema, since in terms of spectacle and noise it's probably hard to beat the launch of 360 feet of Saturn V rocket, and the whole film is made in a suitably grand style. James Horner's score might sound like he's getting some practice in for *Titanic*, but even though much of the film takes place in the cramped confines of the crippled spaceship it still gets across the size and hostility of the empty space separating the astronauts from home. Although this Region 2 disc doesn't contain the same weight of extras as its American counterpart, it's still well above average. The best of the extras are the commentaries. The first is by director Howard, who amiably recounts technical details and filming anecdotes, a lot of them to do with the cast and crew's trips aboard NASA's 'vomit comet' zero-gravity training aircraft. For the most part Howard's commentary is interesting, though he does eventually spend a bit too much time pointing out exactly which shots were filmed aboard the NASA aircraft in zero-g and which were done on a soundstage. The second commentary is by real-life astronaut Jim Lovell, upon whose book the movie is based, and his wife Marilyn. This is the more compelling of the two audio tracks, and Lovell clearly relishes the chance to tell the story his way while Hanks portrays him on screen. Perhaps not surprisingly, Lovell concentrates more on the nuts-and-bolts aspects of the mission (any time there's even the slightest scientific or technical inaccuracy, he's straight in there pointing it out) while Marilyn, who though an important character in the film doesn't get that much screen time, fills in what it felt like to look on helplessly as her husband went around the dark side of the Moon in a leaking tin can. The other extras are a little disappointing, being trailers and the like - no hour-long documentaries for us Brits – but it's almost churlish to complain. If *Armageddon*'s ludicrous comic-book vision of space travel isn't your thing, *Apollo 13* more than compensates – and it's a true story!

FINAL VERDICT

Picture ☆☆☆☆☆ Sound ☆☆☆☆☆

Entertainment ☆☆☆☆ Extras ☆☆☆☆

Value ☆☆☆☆

OVERALL ☆☆☆☆

ARLINGTON ROAD

Price: £17.99
Supplied by: DVDplus (www.dvdplus.co.uk)
Distibutor: Universal

Type of disc: Dual layer, single-sided
No of chapters: 18
Film format(s)/length: 16:9 widescreen enhanced/.113 mins
Audio format: Dolby Digital 5.1
Director: Mark Pellington
Starring: Jeff Bridges, Tim Robbins, Joan Cusack
Year made: 1999
Extras: Scene access; soundtrack (5.1) in German; subtitles in German and Dutch; subtitles for the hard of hearing in English.

The dark side of suburbia and the nightmare counterpart of the American dream are the subjects of *Arlington Road.* The film (costing $35 million to make) only made a paltry $24 million at the US box office. It's easy to work out once viewed — but it's not because this is a bad movie. Jeff Bridges is history professor Michael Faraday, a specialist in the study of American terrorist incidents who lost his wife, an FBI agent, in a botched militia investigation a few years earlier. After saving the life of an injured boy (in a surrealistic pre-credit sequence) Faraday gets to know the boy's parents, neighbours Oliver and Cheryl Lang (Robbins and Cusack). Faraday quickly starts to suspect that there's something suspicious going on in the bland house across the street, especially when he digs into Oliver's past and reveals some very odd facts. But are Faraday's suspicions genuine, or has the death of his wife and the subject of his findings filled his head with worry and paranoia? *Arlington Road* makes a mistake in storytelling terms by dragging on the 'are they or aren't they?' game for too long, despite it becoming clear very quickly that the chubby-yet-intense Oliver and smilingly sinister Cheryl have something to hide behind their perfect suburban façade. Once this slightly plodding middle section is out of the way the film steps up a gear: Bridges gets increasingly desperate to derail the Langs' mysterious plot and get back his son, who has become an unknowing hostage on a scout trip run by men who'll put you off woggles for life. What most likely wrecked *Arlington Road*'s bix office chances in the States is the ending, which defies thriller convention by being one of the most ironic in years. And that's not irony in an Alanis Morissette minor inconvenience sense, but rather the kind of horribly twisted tragedy that Alfred Hitchcock would probably have appreciated. Small wonder the American audience, who like their heroes clean-cut and their flashing red LED timers to be stopped with one second to spare, looked elsewhere for their feel-good entertainment. In actual fact, this daring reversal of expectations is what helps lift *Arlington Road* above average, and after you've seen it once you can then go back into the film and look for all the bits that foreshadow the grim CCN-style coda. On the downside there are no extras. None. Not even a trailer. You get a booklet with cast biographies, but nothing on the disc itself. This is a film where a director's commentary would have been ideal, but the chance was missed. *Arlington Road* turns out to be a decent thriller, but like so many DVDs, no effort was put into added value, which could have made it much, much better.

FINAL VERDICT

Picture ☆☆☆ Sound ☆☆☆

Entertainment ☆☆☆ Extras ☆ Value ☆☆

OVERALL ☆☆☆

ARMAGEDDON

Price: £15.99

Supplied by: Buena Vista

Type of disc: Single layer, double-sided

No of chapters: 27 (14 on side A, 13 on side B)

Film format(s)/length: Widescreen 2.35:1 / 144 mins

Audio format: Dolby Digital 5.1

Director: Michael Bay

Starring: Bruce Willis, Billy Bob Thornton, Liv Tyler

Year made: 1998

Extras: Scene access/interactive menus; English subtitles, close captioned.

A mere 6 minutes, 41 seconds into this latest Bruckheimer-buster we see that favourite disaster movie target, New York, totally decimated by rogue meteors in a cataclysmic sequence that makes the pyrotechnics of *Independence Day* look like a misfire at a bonfire party! Movies don't come more extravagant, explosive and downright clichéd, and that makes *Armageddon* the most exciting UK DVD prospect yet. After *Deep Impact's* frankly embarrassing touchy-feely approach to the modern disaster flick, hooray for the good old-fashioned "Mine's bigger than yours," special effects bonanza. *Armageddon* is all about an asteroid, a global killer "nothing would survive, not even bacteria," the size of Texas and it's hurtling towards an imminent embrace with the Earth at over 22,000mph. With NASA all out of ideas there's only one guy on the planet who can possibly save mankind – roughneck deep core driller Harry Stamper (Willis) and his dysfunctional crew, including the hilarious Rockhound (Buscemi), rebellious daughter Grace (Tyler) and wild card AJ (Affleck). *Armageddon* is essentially a film of two halves – the carnage on Earth and the training of the crew at NASA, and the asteroid drilling itself which makes up the final hour. It also follows the genre's

rulebook to the letter. First you get the trailer-friendly property damage scenes to illustrate what will happen when the asteroid eventually hits, and it's a good excuse for the CGI jockeys to go to town rendering exploding skyscrapers, falling Chrysler buildings and Grand Central Station biting the big one. All of which is shudderingly realistic when listened to through a sound system capable of Dolby Digital. Then there's the improbable hero and a bit of interpersonal friction which you just know is going to come into play during the final reel. And finally you get a shuttle-load of special effects and the explosive climax. All this complemented by a continuous stream of one-liners from Buscemi fulfilling a kind of weightless Groucho Marx role. As entertainment, *Armageddon* is top notch and the best money can buy. Those initial impacts coupled with the dazzling launch sequences are even more realistic when viewed with the crystal clarity of DVD, and despite some misgivings about the format being able to handle the strobe-laden shuttle chase and resultant crash landings, there is no evidence of picture break-up and the entire film is a stunning example of how enhanced digital picture and sound quality can transform movies in the home. Or at least it would be if you didn't have to change the flippin' disc over just before the climax. Yes, they've done it again. *Armageddon* is by far the most significant recent Region 2 DVD and yet Buena Vista has slapped it onto a puny single layered disc which cannot handle the entire film on one side. This is undoubtedly a major flaw in the package and a bitter pill to swallow when you consider that the Region 1 DVD (available in America) managed it, and even included worthwhile extras such as Aerosmith's 'Don't Want to Miss a Thing' video; sadly lacking (among other things) from this offering. Although *Armageddon* is the sort of film that DVD was created for, and is a perfectly entertaining, if corny space adventure (just check out that tear from Bruce – 51:30), it's hard to heartily recommend something which has obviously been rushed out to coincide with the video rental. With a few more extras and a proper dual layer disc, this would have been an essential purchase.

FINAL VERDICT

Picture ☆☆☆☆☆ Sound ☆☆☆☆☆

Entertainment ☆☆☆☆ Extras ☆ Value ☆☆☆

OVERALL ☆☆☆

ARTHUR

Price: £15.99

Supplied by: DVD World (01705 796662)

Type of disc: Single layer, single-sided
No of chapters: 30
Film format(s)/length: 16:9 widescreen / 93 mins
Audio format: Mono
Director: Steve Gordon
Starring: Dudley Moore, Liza Minnelli, John Gielgud
Year made: 1981
Extras: Scene access; mono soundtrack in English, French and Italian; multiple language subtitles; English and Italian subtitles for the hearing impaired.

Dudley Moore plays Arthur Bach, a man who's very, very rich and very, very drunk – at least most of thetime. Arthur's happy but he's got a problem: if he doesn't marry Susan, a girl he doesn't love, then he stands to lose his $750 million inheritance. And he's also just met the girl of his dreams... *Arthur* is a highly amusing comedy which helped Dudley Moore to achieve superstar status. The jokes are clever and the feel-good-factor is very high. Unfortunately, as seems to be the way of things these days, *Arthur* the DVD isn't quite so amusing. The list of special features would be laughable if it wasn't so pitiful and what should be a highly desirable package has little too offer. This is particularly annoying when you consider the fact that you can watch it fairly regularly on TV.

FINAL VERDICT
Picture ☆☆☆☆ Sound ☆☆☆☆
Entertainment ☆☆☆☆ Extras ☆ Value ☆
OVERALL ☆

As Good As It Gets

Price: £19.99
Supplied by: Columbia TriStar Home Video
Type of disc: Dual layer, single-sided
No of chapters: 28
Film format(s)/length: 1.85:1 widescreen / 133 mins
Director: James L Brooks
Starring: Jack Nicholson, Helen Hunt, Greg Kinnear
Year made: 1997
Extras: Chapter access; multilingual subtitles; English/German soundtracks; trailer; cast/crew filmographies; director and stars' commentary.

Novelist Melvin Udell (Nicholson) is an Alf Garnett for the Nineties, hating everyone except waitress Carol (Hunt). Melvin is an obsessive-compulsive who has to have everything just so, but when gay neighbour Simon (Kinnear) gets hospitalised, landing Melvin with his dog, and Carol wants to quit to look after her sick son, his life gets turned upside down and he becomes (surprise!) a better person. Brooks co-created *The Simpsons*, so there's little of the usual romantic comedy soppiness, but once Melvin starts to soften he becomes a lot less fun. Despite his Oscar, Nicholson is just doing the Best of Jaaaack. The commentary is the only real extra, and much of it is, 'We had a good time' stuff rather than anything insightful. The most interesting bit comes right at the end, where Nicholson acidly remarks, "We're sitting here being renumerated for what is ultimately the cancer of film – playing love above all else." Funny how he didn't say that before the Oscars...

FINAL VERDICT
Picture ☆☆☆ Sound ☆☆☆
Entertainment ☆☆☆ Extras ☆☆☆ Value ☆☆☆
Overall ☆☆☆

The Assassin

Price: £15.99
Supplied by: DVD World (01705 796662)
Type of disc: Single layer, single-sided
No of chapters: 30
Film format(s)/length: 2.35:1 widescreen / 101 mins
Audio format: Dolby Digital 5.1
Director: John Badham
Starring: Bridget Fonda, Gabriel Byrne, Harvey Keitel
Year made: 1993
Extras: Scene access; multiple languages; multilingual subtitles.

Bridget Fonda is Maggie, a convicted murderer sentenced to die by lethal injection who is 'recruited' to work for a top secret government agency as an assassin. They chose her because they needed a cold-blooded killer. The only problem is: she's not. A remake of the Luc Besson film *Nikita*, *The Assassin* was bound to suffer criticism from purists that it 'wasn't as good as the original French version.' But then not everyone speaks French and this version is still a cracking film with a drop-dead gorgeous star. But... (and there's always a but) this is yet another Region 2 DVD which suffers from a serious lack of interesting extras. Aside from scene access all we get is multiple languages – 3 to be exact – and multilingual subtitles. Presumably the only reason we get these is because making one version of a disc with several language options is cheaper than producing a different disc for each country. Another great film which falls short of being a good DVD because of the poor special features.

FINAL VERDICT
Picture ☆☆☆☆ Sound ☆☆☆☆
Entertainment ☆☆☆☆ Extras ☆ Value ☆
OVERALL ☆☆

THE ASTRONAUT'S WIFE

Price: £19.99
Supplied by: Entertainment in Video
Type of disc: Dual layer, single-sided
No of chapters: 20
Film format(s)/length: 16:9 anamorphic / 104 mins
Audio format: Dolby Digital 5.1
Director: Rand Ravich
Starring: Johnny Depp, Charlize Theron
Year made: 1999
Extras: Alternative ending; trailer; cast biographies; subtitles in English.

Don't you hate it when you're performing a vital EVA in Earth's orbit and an alien consciousness hijacks your mind? It's just plain rude. Probably the best thing to do is yield to the overpowering mental pressure and subject your wife to repeated forced sexual intercourse until you're sure she's pregnant with space babies. That'll shift it like whisky does a head cold. Such is the life of astronaut Spencer (Depp) and his wife Jillian (Theron) in this exceptionally dull paranoia picture that owes all of the good and none of the bad to *Rosemary's Baby*. Theron's limitless pouty close-ups almost make the thing watchable, especially with the zing of a pin-sharp anamorphic image, and you can dial up an alternative ending to avoid the overtly cheesy CGI horror of the theatrical version. Along with the trailer and biographies, you've got more than the Americans were given – it's just a shame it's a rotten film.

FINAL VERDICT

Picture ☆☆☆☆ Sound ☆☆☆☆
Entertainment ☆ Extras ☆☆☆ Value ☆☆☆
OVERALL ☆☆

AT FIRST SIGHT

Price: £19.99
Supplied by: MGM Home Entertainment
Type of disc: Dual layer, single-sided
No of chapters: 32
Film format(s)/length: 16:9 widescreen enhanced / 123 mins
Audio format: Dolby Digital 5.1
Director: Irwin Winkler
Starring: Val Kilmer, Mira Sorvino, Kelly McGillis
Year made: 1999
Extras: Scene access; theatrical trailer; soundtrack in French, German, Italian and Spanish; subtitles in 12 languages; subtitles for hearing impaired in English and German.

The similarities between this movie and *Awakenings* go beyond sharing the same source material – they basically share the same script. It's the same old story of someone with a disability being given a fulfilling shot at fully able life, only to have it taken away from them and put back to square one. The disability this time round is blindness, and it is Val Kilmer who takes on the role of Virgil, a blind masseur who falls in love with architect Amy (Sorvino) and accepts the chance to regain his sight through a cataract operation. Kilmer portrays his character convincingly, but the script trundles along at such a slow rate and the directing is so un-inspirational, the film only just manages to be engaging. The DVD also lacks anything to hook any interest, offering only a trailer, which is surprisingly more entertaining than the movie.

FINAL VERDICT

Picture ☆☆☆ Sound ☆☆☆☆
Entertainment ☆☆ Extra. ☆ Value ☆☆
OVERALL ☆☆

AUSTIN POWERS INTERNATIONAL MAN OF MYSTERY

Price: £24.99
Supplied by: Pathé Distribution
Type of disc: Single layer, double-sided
No of chapters: 24
Film format(s)/length: 2.35:1 widescreen / 91 mins
Audio format: Dolby Digital 5.1
Director: Jay Roach
Starring: Mike Myers, Elizabeth Hurley, Robert Wagner
Year made: 1997
Extras: Scene access; 2 alternative endings; director's commentary by Mike Myers and Jay Roach; extra scenes; special cameo menu; original theatrical trailer; cast biographies and filmographies; interactive moving menus; English subtitles.

The film's success was guaranteed. Well-developed characters, a humour that rests somewhere between clever parody and fart gags, and the words Mike Myers written all over the project. *Austin Powers: International Man of Mystery* had to become a comedy classic. A warm reception at the box office brought it notoriety, but it was on video that the film really rocketed into popularity and ended up landing somewhere in the land of cult. Indeed, the perfect gentleman spy has become a cultural icon in the last 3 years. *International Man of Mystery* gets a timely Region 2 DVD release as the nation's still Austin Powered-up from the sequel's huge success. Writer, producer and star Mike Myers, plays both Austin Powers as well as his arch enemy Dr Evil. These are carbon copies of the basic hero and villain characters that can be found in any Sixties spy movie, who, through the process of cryogenic freezing, are brought forward in time from their secure comfort of the Sixties, to the unpredictably fast paced Nineties. This is where the main joke of the film lies, and is one which finds itself being spread out over the entire film. Austin finds that his loud, free loving, chauvinistic, gun-toting ways of spying are outdated in a reserved, politically correct Nineties environment. Dr Evil must come to terms with the fact that world domination consists of a simple case of corporate buyouts rather than holding the population hostage to a nuclear threat. There's no real plot to speak of, but plot is not what this movie is about. This is a joke-based film, and when the jokes work, they work brilliantly. Admittedly many of them are based in the Sixties/Nineties rift. However, as Myers develops his scripts, there's also plenty of character-driven humour in the film. In particular, Dr Evil's relationship with his son, Scott Evil, who has no intention of following in his father's footsteps as world dominator. These types of intimate humour can stand up to several repeat viewings. Parody is a strong virtue in this film, and even the most devoted Bond fan can't help but laugh at the jokes made at the spy flick genre. The whole movie is a testament to its star and creator. The script is good at highlighting the dramatic swerve that Western culture has taken since the self-indulgent, caution-free, decadent days of the Sixties, to the stark cynicism we've come to expect from the Nineties. He pays neither decade any compliments or insults, but instead just sifts through the mire and pulls out the comic gems Just watching this film is an event, and that's why it really needed to be dropped onto a good DVD. Fortunately, it has. Okay, this might not have as much as the Region 1 version, but for a Region 2 disc it's head, shoulders and nearly every other body part above the previous effort for European DVDs. But that doesn't matter, for what you are left with on the Region 2 disc are some juicy tit bits that are worth several viewings. The commentary by Roach and Myers about the movie was as much fun to make as it is to watch. You're not listening to an artist talk about his art; you're listening to two fans laughing at their favourite scenes in a movie. Also, a definite bonus for DVD owners over VHS are deleted scenes. The two alternative endings are very entertaining, though you can see why they weren't used for the final version. However, what is hard to believe is that some of the deleted scenes were taken out at all. It definitely wasn't due to their lack of humour. Along with the extended biographies of all the major cast – even the cameos – as well as the original theatrical trailer, the selection of extras to be found on this disc actually serve as a compliment to the movie, instead of just a reason for a company to charge £20. *Austin Powers* isn't really the sort of film that you can just like. You might be completely obsessed by the concept; you might just find it damn funny. Unless you absolutely hate it, you will surely love it, and if that's the case, then this DVD is the only way to watch it.

FINAL VERDICT

Picture ☆☆☆☆ Sound ☆☆☆☆

Entertainment ☆☆☆☆☆

Extras ☆☆☆☆ Value ☆☆☆☆

OVERALL ☆☆☆☆

AUSTIN POWERS: THE SPY WHO SHAGGED ME

Price: £24.99

Supplied by: Entertainment in Video

Type of disc: Dual layer, single-sided

No of chapters: 27

Film format(s)/length: 16:9 widescreen / 91 mins

Audio format: Dolby Digital 5.1

Director: Jay Roach

Starring: Mike Myers, Heather Graham, Michael York

Year made: 1999

Extras: Scene access; feature length audio commentary by star, co-producer and creator Mike Myers, director Jay Roach and co-writer Michael McCullers; 7 deleted scenes (20 mins); behind-the-scenes documentary; Dr Evil's hidden special features menu accessing his Evil songs and desriptions of famous cinematic evil schemes; cast and crew biographies and filmographies; two teaser trailers; theatrical trailer for *The Spy Who Shagged Me*; theatrical trailer for *International Man of Mystery*; animated, music-accompanied menus; access to 8 cameo scenes and filmographies; 3 music videos: Madonna's 'Beautiful Stranger', Lenny Kravitz' 'American Woman', Mel G's 'Word Up'; DVD-ROM features: sample round of Austin Powers Operation: Trivia computer game; subtitles in English.

While *The Matrix* took special effects and Keanu Reeves to new levels in terms of the expectations of cinema going masses, and *The Blair Witch Project* gave Hollywood executives a heart attack, *Austin Powers: The Spy Who Shagged Me* not only grabbed the *zeitgeist*, it pushed its humour buttons until it was rolling around on the floor, screaming for more. Now on Digital Versatile Disc, Mike Myer's comic book fantasy has taken on a new life beyond the multiplex to become one of the definitive DVD's of the Nineties. There's no brain-troublingly complex plot to speak of, but just enough to hang more visual jokes, pop culture references, cinematic homages, juvenile gags and instant catchphrases than any other film since, um...the first *Austin Powers* movie. When we last left swinging London's famous gentleman spy, fashion photographer and all round sexual dynamo, he was embracing marital bliss and Elizabeth Hurley after defeating arch nemesis Dr Evil. But the doctor is back with a cunning plan and flanked by Frau Farbissina (Mindy Sterling), Number Two (Rob Lowe), Scott Evil (Seth Green) and his scene-stealing one eighth-sized clone Mini-Me (Verne Troyer) he 'time travels' to 1967 to steal Austin's mojo, the source of the superspy's prowess with the ladies. Our man in crushed velvet must go back to the past and team up with CIA agent Felicity Shagwell (Graham – a vision in hotpants) to reclaim his powers, save the world and get the girl. But as Basil Exposition (York) says: "I suggest you don't worry about this sort of thing and just enjoy yourself." If future historians need a snapshot of the Nineties, they'd do well to start here. The Internet Movie Database identifies no less than 67 homages, references, connections, spoofs and downright steals from cinematic history – and part of the fun of watching this again is spotting them all! Look out for a glimpse of California's mountains as Austin and Felicity skip across Carnaby Street. *The Spy Who Shagged Me*'s promotion played up its cult underdog status in the face of George Lucas' *Star Wars: Episode 1: The Phantom Menace*, released around the same time. Expectations will be too high next time for this conceit to happen again. Myers' trademark asides to camera – a hangover from *Wayne's World* – and the film's constant and outrageously blatant product placements all serve to deconstruct film-making to its basic elements – and then laugh at them – making it the first post-modernist comedy. There's no doubt that Myers is a fan of DVDs. He features heavily in the 'Making of' documentary, participates in the audio commentary, stars in the new live menu footage and cleared the deleted scenes for our enjoyment. Lucas, Scorsese, Spielberg, stop counting your money and start taking notes! Entertainment in Video have gone the extra mile to make this disc as complete and competitive as possible. Although shattering the glass ceiling of selling DVDs for no more than £19.99, the contents are worth those extra pennies. The documentary is lovingly made, truly revealing and not at all padded out by clips of the movie we've just seen. Featuring all key cast and crew members, director Roach explains why *Our Man Flint* was such

an influence while writers Myers and McCullers describe how they knew Austin's world so much better this time and consequently could pack as many laughs into it as possible. Make sure you explore the menu thoroughly to access the 'hidden extras' that belong to Dr Evil; his crowd pleasing turns on the piano for 'If God Was One of Us' and the pick-yourself-up-off-the-floor cover of 'Just the Two of Us' are instantly accessed plus summaries are given of the evil schemes of James Bond, Matt Helm and others thwarted before Austin. In comes the only blight on this edition: The Region 1 disc contains a fantastic spoof *This is Your Life*-style mockumentary that examines why Dr Evil became evil in the first place and uncovers the reason why the bad doctor and Austin battle each other so determinedly. Sadly this is absent on the Region 2 disc, which is no doubt down to more tedious copyright wrangles. Despite that relatively minor quibble, *Austin Powers: The Spy Who Shagged Me* has joined that rare breed of Region 2 discs – it's become an essential DVD purchase.

FINAL VERDICT

Picture ☆☆☆☆☆ Sound ☆☆☆☆☆

Entertainment ☆☆☆☆☆ Extras ☆☆☆☆☆

Value ☆☆☆☆

OVERALL ☆☆☆☆☆

THE AVENGERS

Price: £15.99

Supplied by: Warner Home Video

Type of disc: Single layer, single-sided

No of chapters: 31

Film format(s)/length: 1.85:1 widescreen / 86 mins

Audio format: Dolby Digital 5.1

Director: Jeremiah S Chechik

Starring: Ralph Fiennes, Uma Thurman, Sean Connery

Year made: 1998

Extras: Production notes; scene access; English and Arabic subtitles.

Considering I was (and still am) a fan of the original *Avengers* TV series you'd have thought I'd be the ideal target audience for this Nineties remake. Yet disappointingly, I squirmed with embarrassment throughout the whole 86 minutes. People who didn't like the Sixties version would need to be heavily bound (to stop them leaving the room) and dosed up with caffeine (to stop them falling asleep) just to make them sit through this diabolical retake of what used to be quite a slick series. Fiennes makes a poor Steed, Thurman can't deliver lines with the same panache as Diana Rigg, and even Eddie Izzard's brief appearances fail to raise a smile. To top it all, there aren't even any extras to shout about. The picture quality and special effects are *The Avengers'* only redeeming factors. You'll be pushed to find better in terms of razor-sharp definition, but it's still a sinking ship with a delightful paintjob. Don't buy it – you'd have more fun watching one of the original episodes on a 12 inch black and white portable.

FINAL VERDICT

Picture ☆☆☆☆ Sound ☆☆☆

Entertainment ☆ Extras ☆ Value ☆

OVERALL ☆

AWAKENINGS

Price: £19.99

Supplied by: Columbia TriStar Home Video

Type of disc: Single layer, single-sided

No of chapters: 28

Film format(s)/length: 1.85:1 widescreen / 116 mins

Audio format: Stereo

Director: Penny Marshall

Starring: Robin Williams, Robert De Niro, Julie Kavner

Year made: 1990

Extras: Scene access; featurette (approx 6 minutes); theatrical trailer; filmographies; soundtrack in French, German, Italian and Spanish; subtitles in 19 languages including English, French, Polish, Hungarian and Czech.

Leonard (De Niro) has been a human statue for 30 years, and is assumed to be incurable. Interest is roused in a medical research student, Williams, when he detects signs of consciousness and he challenges the diagnosis despite a distinct lack of enthusiasm from his superiors. Undeterred, Williams prescribes a drug for Parkinson's disease which wakes not just Leonard but a whole ward full of patients from their 30-year sleep, but is everything as rosy as it appears? This is a genuinely moving tale (screenplay by *Schindler's List* scribe Steven Zaillian) whose humour is never forced and sentiment rarely overblown. While the sound is suspiciously quiet and lacking in atmosphere, image quality is appropriately muted and very clean. Williams fans will want to check out the accompanying featurette, which contains an outtake where De Niro crumbles with laughter thanks to Williams's antics. However, it's a real shame that there is no extra insight into the true story behind the movie itself. Such an explanation would have been a blessing.

FINAL VERDICT

Picture ☆☆☆☆ Sound ☆☆

Entertainment ☆☆☆☆ Extras ☆☆ Value ☆☆

OVERALL ☆☆☆

BABE

Price: £19.99

Supplied by: PolyGram

Type of disc: Dual layer, single-sided

No of chapters: 16

Film format(s)/length: 1.85:1 widescreen / 92 mins

Audio format: Dolby Digital 5.1

Directors: Chris Noonan and George Miller

Starring: James Cromwell, Magda Szubanski, a pig

Year made: 1995

Extras: Scene access; multilingual subtitles.

There are many things I'd like to know about *Babe*. You could probably get a whole series of *How Do They Do That?* out of its production – though keep that to yourselves lest TV rent-a-host Vorderman catches wind – such are the extraordinary digital effects and animatronics on show. The animals act and talk with such authenticity that you'll find it difficult tucking into a bacon sandwich or Sunday roast without feeling a twang of remorse. It's clever stuff, and deserving of an extra special DVD showcase. Sadly – go on, admit you're not surprised – the film doesn't get the disc it deserves. Set in a Yorkshire village where it's not just the animals that have interesting dialect – for some reason the locals display curious American accents – Babe is the story of a young piglet made good. Won by a farmer in a 'guess the weight of the pig' competition (presumably they don't have TVs, let alone DVD players, up north), the eponymous runt must adapt to life on a farm, culminating in his – or her, you're never too sure, as Babe sounds like a cross between Marge Simpson and Michael Jackson – attempt to become the world's first sheep-pig. Obviously. However, the plot is not *Babe's raison d'être*, uneventfully charming though it is. The film exists for the sole purpose of making children and women giggle and coo, which it does better than a gurgling baby in a sailor's outfit. Shift your brain out of gear and there's a moderately entertaining time to be had for the chaps, too, provided you're prepared to forego excessive pyrotechnics in favour of a more emotive cinematic experience. When the credits roll and the menu button is depressed, you're left feeling depressingly unfulfilled. Aside from a static image of the film's hero, there's bugger-all in the way of supplementary material – an absolute crime, considering the wealth of behind-the-scenes documentation that surely exists. An interview with the head honchos at Jim Henson's Creature Workshop, who've put in such a sterling effort that it's almost impossible to distinguish between the real animals and puppets, would have been perfect. Presumably, if the committee that put this disc together saw Elvis Presley riding Shergar emerge from a UFO in the back garden, they wouldn't bother reaching for the camera, such is lack of factual documentation with which this DVD has been assembled. This is another classic example of a distributor doing the bare minimum in bringing a film it knows will sell well. *Babe*'s a fine movie while it lasts, there's no doubting that, and the format's natural advantages – the crystal clear image and spectral sonics – are, thankfully, evident. But in terms of a proper reason to own it, there isn't much to recommend.

FINAL VERDICT
Picture ☆☆☆☆ Sound ☆☆☆☆
Entertainment ☆☆☆ Extras ☆ Value ☆☆
OVERALL ☆☆

BABE PIG IN THE CITY

Price: £19.99
Supplied by: Columbia TriStar Home Video
Type of disc: Single layer, single-sided
No of chapters: 18
Film format(s)/length: 1.85:1 widescreen / 92 mins
Audio format: Dolby Digital 5.1
Director: George Miller
Starring: Magda Szubanski, James Cromwell, Mickey Rooney
Year made: 1998
Extras: Scene access; production notes giving a detailed account of *Babe* from the original novel; filmography and biography of the main characters; Universal Studios weblink; Babe screensaver and wallpapers for the PC; German soundtrack; multilingual subtitles.

Our cute and very talkative 4-legged friend with the trotters returns for another adventure in *Babe Pig in the City*. In a similar vein to the original story, Babe attempts to turn his accident-prone deeds into heroic achievements. Many of Babe's friends accompany him to the city where the bright lights in the concrete jungle turn an innocent cute squealer into a street-smart oinker. Many new loveable characters are revealed throughout Babe's journey into the unknown, giving an overall entertaining sequel for younger viewers. Extra features include the usual language and subtitle selections and a fully animated chapter access menu, with each chapter displaying a sneak clip of the film through a small preview window. Under the 'Bonus' section there are several other goodies, including Production Notes which tell the 'tail' of how our little pink movie star was catapulted from the text pages within a novel called *The Sheep Pig* to stardom after being discovered by director George Miller and made into a fabulous farmyard

hero. The cast and film-makers section provides filmographies and biographies of the main human stars of the film. There is also a theatrical trailer of the film, as well as a Web link to Universal Studios. For the PC owners who have access to a DVD-ROM drive, *Babe Pig in the City* can be accessed through Windows where you can then open and interact with the *Babe* screensaver. There are 5 pictures to use as a screensaver or set as wallpaper, all of which come with a simple 'point and click' interface. The film itself isn't a patch on the original, but it will still delight tiny minds everywhere (and a few grown up ones as well).

FINAL VERDICT
Picture ☆☆☆☆ Sound ☆☆☆
Entertainment ☆☆☆ Extras ☆☆☆☆
Value ☆☆☆
OVERALL ☆☆☆

BACKDRAFT

Price: £19.99
Supplied by: Columbia TriStar
Type of disc: Dual layer, single-sided
No of chapters: 16
Film format(s)/length: 2.35:1 widescreen / 132 mins
Audio format: Dolby Digital 5.1
Director: Ron Howard
Starring: Kurt Russell, William Baldwin, Robert De Niro
Year made: 1991
Extras: Scene selection; production notes.

In spite of the ensemble cast and stunning fire-based set pieces, *Backdraft* is an over-long and ultimately tedious film. Kurt Russell and William Baldwin play rival firefighter brothers, Stephen and Brian McCaffrey, who attempt to bury the sibling hatchet whilst also uncovering a deep-rooted conspiracy behind a series of apparently random arson attacks. Columbia TriStar has opted to supply the very basics in the DVD extras department. The uninspired menu screen only offers you a choice of foreign language subtitles and brief production notes and biographies on the film's main stars. The latter are standard text pieces which in themselves are hardly showcases for the new technology delights of DVD. Ron Howard is a well respected director, and it would have been a worthwhile addition, particularly for film buffs, to at least have his commentary on the making of *Backdraft*. Without it, *Backdraft* is yet another half-baked DVD release.

FINAL VERDICT
Picture ☆☆☆ Sound ☆☆☆☆
Entertainment ☆☆☆
Extras ☆☆ Value ☆☆☆

OVERALL ☆☆

BAD BOYS

Price: £19.99

Supplied by: Columbia TriStar Home Video

Type of disc: Dual layer, single-sided

No of chapters: 28

Film format(s)/length: 1.85:1 widescreen enhanced / 114 mins

Audio format: Dolby Digital 5.1

Director: Michael Bay

Starring: Will Smith, Martin Lawrence, Téa Leoni

Year made: 1995

Extras: Scene access; multilingual soundtracks; multilingual subtitles; trailer; behind-the-scenes featurette; 2 music videos ; cast filmographies; DVD trailer.

Although Martin Lawrence gets top billing, this is the film that first moved Will Smith from being just the Fresh Prince into genuine movie star status. Smith and Lawrence are two Miami narcotics cops – mismatched, of course, with Lawrence being the highly-strung family man and Smith the smooth, wealthy playboy – who have just 4 days to recover $100 million of heroin stolen from their own police station before Internal Affairs shuts them down for incompetence. The plot is nothing that hasn't been done before a thousand times, and is full of holes anyway, so *Bad Boys* depends on the charisma of its stars and the style of its director to succeed. Fortunately, it does on both counts. Bay uses every photographic trick in the book to create a neon-lit, orange-skied Miami populated solely by people who are either implausibly attractive or sneeringly sleazy, and Smith and Lawrence keep the laughs coming as the bickering detectives, setting new records for swearing along the way (181 times – we counted!) Most of the humour comes from a contrived yet entertaining piece of role-reversal. Murder witness Julie (Leoni) will only talk to Smith, but since he's not around when she calls, the jittery, hypertense Lawrence is forced to pretend to be the ultimate ladies' man. Smith therefore has to pretend to be Lawrence (still with me?) which ultimately results in Lawrence's paranoia getting the better of him when Smith seems to be getting along with his wife just a little too well… Mixed in with the jokes are several action sequences, as Euro-villain Tcheky Karyo and his sweaty henchmen try to silence the future Mrs Duchovny before they sell their stolen heroin. The best piece of action is the dazzlingly-done robbery that kickstarts the plot, all blue lights, slo-mo and more cuts than a barber's shop, but if you like to see bloody gun battles, car chases and people having their heads slammed into swilling urinals – and what action movie fan doesn't? – then *Bad Boys* won't disappoint. It doesn't disappoint as a DVD, either. While *Bad Boys* may not be up to the level of *Ghostbusters* or *Contact* with its extras, there's enough to show that Columbia-TriStar is making an effort. (Cue Disney with fingers in its Mickey Mouse ears, going "I'm not listening! Tralalalala!") Both picture and sound are excellent, not even the strobe lights in the nightclub sequence cause any trouble, and you also get the American trailer (which features a scene not in the final movie, of Smith waking up in bed with two women), a short behind-the-scenes feature that interviews all the main cast and crew, a pair of music videos and a rather threadbare set of filmographies of the 3 stars. In an ideal world, this amount of extras would be the rule rather than the exception, so let's hope other companies see sense and start to compile more supplementary material in the future.

FINAL VERDICT

Picture ☆☆☆☆☆ Sound ☆☆☆☆

Entertainment ☆☆☆☆

Extras ☆☆☆ Value ☆☆☆☆

OVERALL ☆☆☆☆

BATMAN

Price: £15.99

Supplied by: DVD World (01705 796662)

Type of disc: Single layer, single-sided

No of chapters: 31

Film format(s)/length: 16:9 widescreen / 121mins

Director: Tim Burton

Starring: Michael Keaton, Jack Nicholson, Kim Basinger

Year made: 1989

Extras: Production/cast notes; scene access; multiple languages.

"A Gotham City which looks as if hell had erupted out of the sidewalk and just kept growing…" Anton Furst's production design is as much a star of *Batman* as Nicholson or Keaton. While the script was rushed due to an impending writer's strike, the look and feel of the finished movie shows just what could be accomplished by a late Eighties mega-budget… and an artistically minded director such as Tim Burton. On VHS, so much of the fine detailing of the Gotham sets have been lost in such a blur that the DVD version comes as a revelation – it's like wiping a fine coating of dust from the TV screen. The soundscape is no less impressive, Danny Elfman's score, some fine songs by Prince and excellent sound effects provide a constantly involving aural backdrop. For salesmen trying to shift Dolby Digital sound systems, the first scene is the perfect demonstration piece with all manner of effect which totally wraps the viewer in sound. Unfortunately, while the movie itself is a near-perfect DVD product, the accompanying material is not. Of course, there's an instant scene access function, but the producers have seen fit to highlight only 9 of the 31 chapters. Odd. By way of contrast, the Production Notes run to some 8 pages of interesting information, nicely illustrated with appropriate pictures. There's also brief biographies and filmographies for the all the cast's principals, plus director Tim Burton, but sadly no theatrical trailer. Something called 'Film Flash' is simply a page of recommended films, but this aside, Batman is a superb movie brilliantly translated to DVD.

FINAL VERDICT

Picture ☆☆☆☆☆ Sound ☆☆☆☆☆

Entertainment ☆☆☆☆

Extras ☆☆☆ Value ☆☆☆☆☆

OVERALL ☆☆☆☆

BATMAN & ROBIN

Price: £15.99

Supplied by: Warner Home Video

Type of disc: Single layer, single-sided

No of chapters: 42

Film format(s)/length: 2.35:1 anamorphic / 120 mins

Director: Joel Schumacher

Starring: George Clooney, Arnold Schwarzenegger, Uma Thurman

Year made: 1997

Extras: Widescreen TV enhanced; chapter select; multi-lingual subtitles; muson on main menu; cast and crew biographies; production notes; list of similar films on DVD

George Clooney must be a really good sport, since in press interviews he's practically single-handedly accepted the blame for *Batman & Robin*. In reality though, blame should go to director Schumacher and writer Akiva Goldsman, for creating one of the most horrid, embarrassing wastes of time and money in cinematic history. Villains Mr Freeze (Ah-nold) and Poison Ivy (an annoying Thurman) want to destroy Gotham City, yadda yadda. Batman (Clooney) aided by Robin (stroppy Chris O'Donnell) and Batgirl (Alicia Silverstone) stop them. Along the way, many hateful puns are ground out and any tough situation is escaped by using a Bat-hook thing. Oh, and Schumacher gets in lots of shots of buttocks clad in rubber. Each new *Batman* film somehow

manages to make its predecessor seem coherent and smart, to the extent that Tim Burton's original is practically *Citizen Kane* by comparison to *Batman & Robin*. If you have a random chapter select function on your player, use it – the story will make just as much sense. DVD shows off Schumacher's vomitous colour scheme far better than it deserves, and the score (practically a note-for-note repeat of *Batman Forever*) and sound effects could crack glass. Sadly, special features are limited to a few pages of totally uninformative and oddly pretentious production notes. If you keep half your brain in a jar by the bed, *Batman & Robin* might be enjoyable. Anyone else should avoid it. Otherwise, it'll encourage them to make another one.

FINAL VERDICT

Picture ☆☆☆☆☆ Sound ☆☆☆☆

Entertainment ☆ Extras ☆☆ Value ☆☆☆

OVERALL ☆☆

BATMAN FOREVER

Price: £15.99

Supplied by: Warner Home Video

Type of disc: Single layer, single-sided

No of chapters: 39

Film format(s)/length:1.85:1 widescreen / 115 mins

Audio format: Dolby Digital 5.1

Director: Joel Schumacher

Starring: Val Kilmer, Tommy Lee Jones, Jim Carrey, Nicole Kidman

Year made: 1995

Extras: Widescreen TV enhanced; English/Arabic subtitles; production notes.

After the S&M homage to German Expressionism that was *Batman Returns*, Warner Bros decided to take a slightly more family-friendly tack with the third film in the *Batman* series. Out went Tim Burton and his rubber-clad characters, in came Joel Schumacher and day-glo colours. Top villain is ostensibly Jones's Two-Face, but it's Carrey's Riddler who steals the show as a geek who gets a brain boost and resolves to destroy Bruce Wayne (Kilmer). Romance is provided by Nicole Kidman as bat-fixated shrink Dr Chase Meridan, but the way things are filmed, you'd be forgiven for thinking that Chris O'Donnell's Robin was the real love interest. *Batman Forever* isn't a patch on Burton's Bat-flicks, but in its favour it's a hundred times better than *Batman & Robin*. The DVD transfer is superb for both sound and vision – check out the final Claw Island battle – but the extras are limited in scope and not very interesting. Watchable, but not memorable.

FINAL VERDICT
Picture ☆☆☆☆☆ Sound ☆☆☆☆☆
Entertainment ☆☆☆ Extras ☆ Value ☆☆
OVERALL ☆☆☆

BATMAN RETURNS

Price: £15.99
Supplied by: Warner Home Video
Type of disc: Dual layer, single-sided
No of chapters: 39
Film format(s)/length: 1.85:1 widescreen / 121 mins
Audio format: Dolby Digital 5.1
Director: Tim Burton
Starring: Michael Keaton, Danny De Vito, Michelle Pfeiffer
Year made: 1992
Extras: Interactive menus; production notes; Arabic subtitles.

Warner's curious handling of its *Batman* franchise continues on DVD with *Batman Returns*, the second Bat-flick, released after parts one and 4. Whether a strange coincidence, the fact remains that that Tim Burton's direction and sets are rendered beautifully on the DVD format. In a nutshell, it's Batman versus Catwoman and The Penguin. But where that fool Joel Schumacher directed *Batman Forever* and *Batman & Robin* with nauseating rapidity, Tim Burton demonstrates restraint; allowing the Gothic architecture to play as much a role as the film's trio of stars. Though written with a mainstream audience in mind, the screenplay is as close to the spirit of *Batman* as its big budget allows, offering both Bat aficionados and newcomers equal entertainment. On VHS, the film loses definition right from the opening sequence. Here, the crisp picture retains pin-sharp clarity throughout even the darkest moments, and contrasting layers thankfully lack artifacts. Danny Elfman's score is one of cinema's most memorable, and with the soundtrack coming on snazzy Dolby Digital, the film will probably sound better in your lounge than it would have done in a 1992 cinema. But Warner has again shown lack of consideration for DVD owners, with virtually no extras to speak of. Aside from production notes, the only additional joy to be gleaned from *Batman Returns* on DVD is watching the subtitles in Arabic. But that's only to be recommended to those that have run out of straws to clutch. An essential purchase *Batman Returns* is not. If you're a biased Bat-fan, it's worth the cash. For those of you that aren't, there's probably a disc on the shelves that's more deserving of your funds.
FINAL VERDICT

Picture ☆☆☆☆☆ Sound ☆☆☆☆☆
Entertainment ☆☆☆☆ Extras ☆ Value ☆☆
OVERALL ☆☆☆

BEAN: THE DISASTER MOVIE

Price: £17.99
Supplied by: PolyGram
Type of disc: Single layer, double-sided
No of chapters: 20
Film format(s)/length: 4:3, 16:9 widescreen / 86 mins
Audio format: Dolby Digital 5.1
Director: Mel Smith
Starring: Rowan Atkinson, Peter MacNicol, Pamela Reed
Year made: 1997
Extras: Scene selection; coming DVD attractions; cast and film maker biographies.

When the Royal National Gallery is asked to send their finest scholar to oversee the unveiling of Whistler's 'Mother' in California, they send their most inept and detested employee, Mr Bean (Atkinson). Atkinson's visual genius is once again exemplified, whilst writer Richard Curtis keeps the tomfoolery coming thick and fast as comedian Mel Smith directs. The picture quality is sharp and colourful although the sound is never really tested. As for the extras, this movie can be viewed in two video aspect ratios: 4:3 and 16:9; whereas you would normally have to purchase two VHS videos for this choice. Yet even DVDs are susceptible to errors, with the widescreen side reporting a fault for this review. You also get coming attractions of future DVD titles plus cast and film makers' biographies. The British comedy of '97 will make you laugh out loud at the benefits of DVD.
FINAL VERDICT
Picture ☆☆☆☆ Sound ☆☆☆
Entertainment ☆☆☆ Extras ☆☆ Value ☆☆☆
OVERALL ☆☆☆

BEAUTY AND THE BEAST: THE ENCHANTED CHRISTMAS

Price: £15.99
Supplied by: Warner Home Video
Type of disc: Single layer, single-sided
No of chapters: 17
Film format(s)/length: 1:33:1 regular / 68 mins
Audio format: Dolby Digital 5.1
Director: Andy Knight
Starring the voices of: Paige O'Hara, Tim Curry, Robby Benson
Year made: 1997
Extras: Scene access; soundtrack (surround only) in

French, Italian, Dutch, Polish, Hungarian, Hebrew and Icelandic; subtitles for the hearing impaired in English and Dutch.

From Disney comes this tie-in to their earlier offering – *Beauty and the Beast*. You remember the original film? Belle (Beauty), an innocent young girl, has to fall in love with the Beast in his present state so that a spell which has been put upon the Beast and his entire fairy-tale castle – servants and all – can be lifted and everyone can live happily ever after. This second offering could at first be mistaken for a sequel, but on watching it you realise it is just a flashback to a time when Belle was falling in love with the Beast, which was not even referred to in the first film. As ever, the cartoon is beautifully translated to DVD and the mixture of animation and the CGI of the pipe organ come together well. The Dolby Digital 5.1 crisply captures the Disney-famous songs and sound effects, although there are no sing-a-long extras for the children. Disney probably considered that if the subtitles are turned on, then all the words are there anyway! As usual there are only the standard subtitles and language options as extras – will Disney ever get the message?

FINAL VERDICT

Picture ☆☆☆☆ Sound ☆☆☆☆

Entertainment ☆☆ Extras ☆ Value ☆☆

OVERALL ☆☆

BEAVIS AND BUTT-HEAD DO AMERICA

Price: £19.99
Supplied by: Paramount
Type of disc: Single layer, single-sided
No of chapters: 30
Film format(s)/length: 1.78: 1 anamorphic / 78 mins
Audio format: Dolby Digital 5.1
Director: Mike Judge
Starring: Mike Judge, Bruce Willis, Demi Moore
Year made: 1996
Extras: Scene access; 2 trailers; soundtrack in English and German; subtitles in 8 languages.

Could anybody sum up the Nineties better than Beavis and Butt-head? The two animated cretins snickered their way through the culturally bankrupt wasteland that is America, seeing the world in absolutes – things are either 'cool' or they 'suck', with no grey areas – and passing mocking commentary on the world around them in amongst all the fart jokes and games of frog baseball. Transferring short MTV cartoons (if you take out the all music videos they insult, a typical *Beavis And Butt-head* episode is less than ten minutes long) to a full-length film could

have produced a disaster, but *Beavis and Butt-head Do America* turns out to be a triumph, thanks to one man. Creator Mike Judge not only co-wrote and directed the film, but also provides the voices for his two skinny anti-heroes, as well as several of the other characters. Trey Parker and Matt Stone may get all the publicity, but Judge was a regular animation mogul and managed to get Isaac Hayes to do a theme song before the *South Park* twosome had even killed Kenny for the first time. Beavis and Butt-head would both agree that complicated plots suck, so the movie keeps things simple – the two teenage tossers have their precious television stolen, and in the process of trying to recover it they set out on a hilarious road trip across America, along the way being mistaken for hitmen, becoming joint Public Enemy #1, meeting President Clinton and arousing the wrath of God himself. In any other film this kind of odyssey would result in the heroes learning from their experiences and becoming better people, but to Beavis and Butt-head it's just a long list of stuff that didn't help them score and got in the way of their TV viewing. Like most of Paramount's titles, while the movie gets a good DVD transfer, no advantage is taken of the format's many possibilities – you only get the movie, trailers and assorted subtitles, nothing more. This sucks, but luckily the film compensates for such shortcomings. Cool!

FINAL VERDICT

Picture ☆☆☆ Sound ☆☆☆☆

Entertainment ☆☆☆☆

Extras ☆☆ Value ☆☆☆

OVERALL ☆☆☆

BEETLEJUICE

Price: £15.99
Supplied by: Warner Home Video
Type of disc: Single layer, double-sided,
No of chapters: 28
Film format(s)/length: 16:9 widescreen / 92 mins
Director: Tim Burton
Starring: Michael Keaton, Geena Davis, Alec Baldwin
Year made: 1988
Extras: Both regular and widescreen versions of the film; production notes; cast info; English (DD), French and Italian (surround); multilingual subtitles.

After making a surprise hit out of *Pee Wee's Big Adventure*, *Beetlejuice* sees director Tim Burton slipping into more characteristically Gothic subject matter. The concept of a sweet, ghostly couple seeking help in exorcising their house of ghastly, albeit living new owners is inspired. Yet while always enjoyable, the film only truly comes alive with the presence of a truly manic Michael Keaton as Beetlejuice himself. Warner Bros has really tried with the DVD version with both widescreen and normal versions of the movie on either side of the disc, plus an option to select a music-only soundtrack. Aside from instant scene access, there's background material on the stars, 9 pages of interesting and well laid out production notes, plus the theatrical trailer. All that said, the film stock seems a little grainy and you don't always get the pinsharp resolution that is DVD's main selling point. Given that you never get as much of Keaton's performance as you want, it might be worth dusting off an old VHS copy of the film before you decide to buy.

FINAL VERDICT

Picture ☆☆☆ Sound ☆☆☆☆

Entertainment ☆☆☆☆ Extras ☆☆☆ Value ☆☆☆

OVERALL ☆☆☆

BEING JOHN MALKOVICH

Price: £19.99
Supplied by: Columbia TriStar Home Video
Type of disc: Dual layer, single-sided
No of chapters: 32
Film format(s)/length: 1.85:1 anamorphic / 112 mins
Audio format: Dolby Digital 5.1
Director: Spike Jonze
Starring: John Cusack, Cameron Diaz, Catherine Keener
Year made: 1999
Extras: Scene access; *American Arts & Culture Presents: John Horatio Malkovich*; Spike Jonze interview; *7 1/2 Floor Orientation*; Spike's Photo Album; 4 TV spots; original theatrical trailer; filmographies; soundtrack in English and German; subtitles in 7 languages.

You could never see the likes of this again. Movies like this come along once in a lifetime. And it's a sad fact, because *Being John Malkovich* is a precision machine that takes the indie concept and repackages it up for the mass audience, trimmed with a beautiful Hollywood bow. Respectfully 'in your face', this is the love child of first-time scriptwriter Charlie Kaufman, and the motion picture directorial debut of music video deity, Spike Jonze. The combining of these two elements is like nuclear fusion, and the end result is a biting Rottweiler of a movie that refuses to let go. Helped by some sublime performances, instantly likeable dialogue, and the appearance of Malkovich himself, the real attraction for this totally satisfying movie is the inconceivable concept. Maintaining both absurdity and simplicity at the same time, the basic idea is 'what would you do if

you could be someone else for 15 minutes?' In this case that question equals an obligatory 15 minutes of fame; as the title suggests, the opportunity to spend quarter of an hour hiding in the mind of Hollywood's thespian of thesps is on offer. Down on his luck, part-time puppeteer, full-time beatnik, Craig Schwartz (the always entertaining Cusack) decides to supplement his income by taking a job as a filing clerk at a company named Lester Corp, located on the 7 1/2 floor of a New York office block. While going about his business Craig stumbles upon a doorway hidden behind some filing cabinets which turns out to be the world's one and only portal into the brain of John Malkovich. After spending 15 minutes inside the head of the star (prior to being spat out on to the shoulder of the New Jersey turnpike) Craig realises that he can actually have an influence over Malkovich. Thus, the plot thickens, and along with work colleague Maxine (Keener), whom Craig has fallen for, he starts charging members of the public $200 dollars to step inside the mind of Malkovich. Craig's winning roll comes to an ugly end when Maxine starts a simultaneous affair with Craig's wife Lotte (a frumpy beyond belief Diaz) and Malkovich himself. Lotte begins using Malkovich's body so that she can 'be' with Maxine, Craig finds out, discovers a way where he can stay inside Malkovich indefinitely, and the whole thing begins to spiral way beyond any realm of predictability. Spiral it may, but the whole concept is never allowed to get out of control, and in the hands of Jonze, fresh from his screen-stealing turn in *Three Kings*, there is a constant air of stylised vibrancy, adding a pleasing coat of sugar to a script that would be harder to swallow in the hands of any other director. It's amazing how this first time script got greenlighted by Universal. It's a stroke of genius that it got sent Jonze's way. Hopefully the critical success, and the big name banners that this film is able to carry, will open the floodgates for other major studios to put their money on the more obscure, less high concept, summer blockbuster movies. What is a shame is that Columbia TriStar weren't able to reproduce the American version for a Region 2 release. Okay, to be fair it's mostly the gimmicky stuff that's gone from the Region 1 disc, but the likes of 'A Page With Nothing on It' and 'An Intimate Portrait of the Art of Background Driving' added something to the ambience of the disc. However, what is left is nothing to be sniffed at. The interview with Jonze is nothing if not hilarious, and the featurette detailing a portrait of John Horatio Malkovich (in reality his middle name is Gavin!) is an unpredictable treat. Picture and soundwise, it's the usual above-the-call-of-duty treatment from Columbia; but this only emphasises the fact that it's a shame it doesn't live up to the Region 1 disc in terms of extra features. There are those who will not like this DVD, finding it too spicy for their taste, but considering that movies such as this come along once in a blue moon, you'd be out of your head not to give it a try.

FINAL VERDICT
Picture ☆☆☆☆ Sound ☆☆☆☆
Entertainment ☆☆☆☆☆
Extras ☆☆☆ Value ☆☆☆☆
OVERALL ☆☆☆☆

BELOVED

Price: £15.99
Supplied by: Warner Home Video
Type of disc: Dual layer, single-sided
No of chapters: 33
Film format(s)/length: 1:85:1 widescreen / 164 mins
Audio format: Dolby Digital 5:1
Director: Jonathan Demme
Starring: Oprah Winfrey, Danny Glover, Thandie Newton
Year made: 1998
Extras: Scene access; subtitles in 7 languages.

Oprah Winfrey isn't an actress. A TV host, celebrity weight-watcher and civil rights campaigner, certainly, but not an actress. But that doesn't stop her trying. A reasonably good cameo in *The Color Purple* landed her this weighty role as the lead woman in the movie adaptation of Toni Morrison's age-of-slavery novel. *Beloved* is an epic tale about one woman's search for freedom and hope set against the American age of slavery. Although well performed by the principal actors, it is slow, overly-epic for its own sake and at times thoroughly confusing. Director Demme attempts to make something great, but struggles with a complex and at times deathly dull plot. Glover is great as Winfrey's ageing, rediscovered childhood friend Paul D. Winfrey is pretty good though her tendency to overact is annoying. In truth, *Beloved* isn't a bad film. It will appeal to serious drama fans and historians. Being a big budget epic, it transfers to DVD fairly well, though the lack of extras is seriously disappointing. The film lends itself to all manner of extra features – a 'Making of' documentary or a short historical background would have been good. But all you get here is disappointing scene access and multi-language subtitles. A reasonable, if slow film, but a poor DVD. There's nothing really here to make you want to buy it, especially if you already own the video.

FINAL VERDICT
Picture ☆☆ Sound ☆☆☆
Entertainment ☆☆ Extras ☆ Value ☆☆
OVERALL ☆☆

A BETTER TOMORROW

Price: £19.99
Supplied by: MIA
Type of disc: Dual layer, single-sided
No of chapters: 17
Film format(s)/length: 16:9 widescreen / 94 mins
Audio format: Stereo
Director: John Woo
Starring: Chow Yun Fat, Leslie Cheung, Ti Lung
Year made: 1986
Extras: Scene access; trailer; English subtitles composited on picture; soundtrack in Cantonese.

Although John Woo is best known for the balletic ultra-violence, which reached its apotheosis with *Face/Off*, this Hong Kong classic shows a more complete picture of the man's ability. Written and directed by Woo, *A Better Tomorrow* won Hong Kong Oscars for Best Film and Best Actor (Chow Yun Fat). It was also a huge box office hit, spawned numerous sequels and a whole new movie genre. Ironically, prior to this breakthrough success, Woo had been best known for his comedies, something which comes through in the opening 20 minutes – with the most lethal weapon being a cello! The clumsy, musically minded girlfriend of Kit (Leslie Cheung) brings a very human introduction to the central family: while her boyfriend is an ambitious cop, brother Ho turns out to be a gangster. His secret profession is exposed when a Taiwanese counterfeiting deal goes spectacularly wrong. This gory shoot-out serves only as a prelude to two even more shocking scenes. A domestic assassination is startlingly fresh in its realism and energy, while Ho's associate Mark (Yun Fat) kicks off a famous revenge attack with plenty of Woo's trademark two-pistol gunplay. According to Woo, inspiration for the attack came from Westerns and simple practicality: "How else could the Chow character kill so many people without having two guns?" However, unlike *Face/Off*, action is only another facet of the film, not the whole point, with the grittily realistic violence pushing the characters to explore their various relationships. Brother is set against brother, and gangster against gangster. That said, the sentimentality that centres around Kit and Ho is somewhat cloying. After so many films seeming to celebrate gangsters, Kit's crisis of conscience seems overwrought – particularly as Ho soon repents. In truth, fully appreciating the movie is difficult with a DVD conversion severely damaged by the quality of the film stock, which is notably grainy. Worse, from about half way in, defects in the film become apparent which, combined with occasionally unclear captions, makes this a disappointing release. On the positive side, an excellent 4-page booklet provides plenty of background on the film, which is credited with creating the Heroic Bloodshed genre. Rick Baker, who actually coined the phrase, provides a comprehensive overview of the genre and reveals that many still believe *A Better Tomorrow* is both first and best of the genre. There's also a fascinating interview with Woo, which concludes with the tantalising promise of a Hollywood collaboration between Woo and Chow Yun Fat, with a script by Tarantino. Now that would be something to see!

FINAL VERDICT

Picture ☆☆ Sound ☆☆

Entertainment ☆☆☆ Extras ☆ Value ☆☆

OVERALL ☆☆

BICENTENNIAL MAN

Price: £19.99
Supplied by: Columbia TriStar Home Video
Type of disc: Dual layer, single-sided
No of chapters: 30
Film format(s)/length: 1.85:1 anamorphic / 126 mins
Audio format: Dolby Digital 5.1
Director: Chris Columbus
Starring: Robin Williams, Sam Neill, Embeth Davidtz
Year made: 1999
Extras: Scene access; filmographies; behind-the-scenes featurette; 3 trailers (theatrical release, *Jumanji* and *Hook*); subtitles in 16 languages.

You'd get the impression that Robin Williams has a contractual obligation to make at least 3 movies a year. As long as it's whimsical, sentimental, and gives him at least one scene where he can go nuts, he'll be as happy as a 5 year-old in Disneyland. This isn't to say that he always turns in under-par performances, but it could be argued that his choice in roles has become a little stale since the days of *Good Morning Vietnam* or *The Fisher King*. Here Williams again fails to expand to his full potential, but still seems to have fun in the role of Andrew, a robotic manservant to the Martin family. Headed by the ever-charming (and inexplicably wise) Sam Neill, the Martins are happy to let Andrew just be another household appliance, until they discover that he has a talent for carpentry, from which point on they allow him to explore his artistic tendencies. Not content with making a living,

Andrew sets his sights on bigger goals and to ultimately achieve his ambition of becoming a human being. 200 years and 3 generations of the Martin family later and Andrew has achieved love, notoriety, fortune and despair, but he still lives in a restrictive society that won't allow him to join its club of human endeavour. Ultimately, *Bicentennial Man* isn't the movie it wants to be. It tries to tell an epic, intelligent and moralistic tale, but clings too tightly to the Disney school of movie making. Like a child failing to avoid the cracks in the pavement, this movie has a blatant problem deciding who its audience really is. One moment Oliver Platt is teaching Andrew to say "shit", then the film spouts dialogue full of sentimental schmaltz that only a 7 year-old would be able to stand. The movie is really nothing more than a sophisticated kids' flick, but if you can hurdle the few major stumbling blocks, then *Bicentennial Man* proves to be quite interesting. The DVD is standard stuff, but the Columbia TriStar logo means that this is no bad thing. The picture quality is pinprick sharp, and the 5.1 sound allows you to hear every bleep and whirring noise coming from within Andrew. The featurette is only a disappointing 5 minutes long, but it, like the movie, is enough for kids to happily swallow.

FINAL VERDICT

Picture ☆☆☆☆☆ Sound ☆☆☆☆

Entertainment ☆☆☆

Extras ☆☆☆ Value ☆☆☆☆

OVERALL ☆☆☆

THE BIG BLUE

Price: £19.99
Supplied by: 20th Century Fox Home Video
Type of disc: Dual layer, single-sided
No of chapters: 69
Film format(s)/length: 2.35:1 anamorphic / 160 mins
Audio format: Dolby Surround
Director: Luc Besson
Starring: Roseanna Arquette, Jean-Marc Barr, Jean Reno
Year made: 1988
Extras: Scene access; theatrical trailer; soundtrack in English and French; subtitles in Dutch and French; subtitles for the hearing impaired in English.

Enzo (Reno) and Jacques (Barr) are best friends and rivals ever since their Mediterranean childhood. Flash forward to today and the two are estranged but still share their common love, diving…but Jacques' swimming skills and ability to hold his breath for long durations gives him the edge. By the time Johanna (Arquette) meets and becomes enchanted by the man-fish, he's working for deep sea diving scientists and Enzo is the reigning diving world champion. An Italian tournament ignites the rivalry between the two men once more. *Le Grand Bleu* is distinguished by some of the best sub-aqua footage yet committed to DVD. The adequate picture quality comes into its own when the cameras follow Barr beneath the waves to swim with the dolphins and fish. Despite getting only third billing, this is really Jean Reno's show, deftly switching between the dramatic and comedic. *The Big Blue* suffers whenever he's absent from the screen. It's easy to see why director and actor struck up a Scorsese/De Niro style partnership. A joint audio commentary from Besson and Reno would have bolstered the disc considerably, but the extras are watered down to a single poor quality trailer. Though the film is indulgently overlong (69 chapters!), for those in the right frame of mind to let Gallic humour and beautiful underwater photography wash over them this is the movie for you. However, it's the familiar story of the disc's content failing to add anything to our home entertainment experience.

FINAL VERDICT

Picture ☆☆☆ Sound ☆☆
Entertainment ☆☆☆ Extras ☆ Value ☆☆
OVERALL ☆☆

THE BIG CHILL

Price: £19.99
Supplied by: Columbia TriStar
Type of disc: Single layer, single-sided
No of chapters: 28
Film format(s)/length: 1.85:1 widescreen / 101 mins
Audio format: 2-Channel or Dolby Digital 5.1
Director: Lawrence Kasdan
Starring: Tom Berenger, Glenn Close, Jeff Goldblum
Year made: 1983
Extras: Hour long documentary with subtitles; deleted footage; original theatrical trailer; filmographies; DVD trailer.

When an old friend dies, it brings together people who may not otherwise have met up in a long while. The conversation isn't up to much but it's one of the best ways to organise a reunion. That is exactly what happens to a gang of idealistic Sixties kids, meeting again 20 years later under sad circumstances with their hair braids and sunflowers replaced by briefcases and careers. *The Big Chill's* release on DVD coincides with its 15th anniversary and a superb job has been done on picture restoration. The quality is brilliantly crisp and sharp, helping to capture the cold, harsh environment under which the old pals

meet. The digital sound is also tremendously clear, showing an expert job in restoration, bringing to life the classic vocals of the artists committed to the soundtrack. Lawrence Kasdan also goes into depth with nearly an hour's worth of meandering documentary about struggling to bring *The Big Chill* to life. It's well executed, but too long. Out-takes and cut scenes add further sense to how the characters cope with their disillusioned lives and the fans of this film should take a peek at some intriguing previously unseen moments, most of them elaborating on minor relationships and trivial plot points. With the almost bog standard fair of trailers and filmographies supporting the lengthy commentary, *The Big Chill* is therefore a pleasing package, exploring sentimentality and friendship beyond the boundaries of the film with the use of the documentary. Not only this but you're also rewarded with a touchingly warm story.

FINAL VERDICT

Picture ☆☆☆☆ Sound ☆☆☆☆
Entertainment ☆☆☆ Extras ☆☆☆ Value ☆☆☆
OVERALL ☆☆☆

BIG DADDY

Price: £19.99
Supplied by: Columbia TriStar Home Video
Type of disc: Dual layer, single-sided
No of chapters: 28
Film format(s)/length: 1.85:1 widescreen / 89 mins
Audio format: Dolby Digital 5.1
Director: Dennis Dugan
Starring: Adam Sandler, Rob Schneider Joey Lauren Adams
Year made: 1999
Extras Scene access; filmographies; theatrical trailer; interviews with Adam Sandler, Rob Schneider and Dennis Dugan; music videos by Sheryl Crow and Garbage; soundtrack in English and German; subtitles in 15 languages.

Adam Sandler can't put a foot wrong, probably because he's treading over the same path again and again. Still, as the wise old proverb goes, if it ain't broke, then don't fix it. For now the Sandler movie routine definitely ain't broke. Here's the drill: Sandler plays a gross, loud-mouthed dropout with a half-hearted approach to life who loses his girlfriend, but goes through some sort of worldly-wise experience in order to resolve everything by the end of the picture. In *Big Daddy*, the formula is changed slightly as there's a cute kid thrown into the mix. Sandler plays Sonny Koufax, a fully-trained lawyer who prefers to spend his time working one day a week as a toll booth operator, for which Sonny's girlfriend dumps him. In a vain effort to win her back, Sonny decides that he must take drastic actions, the most drastic of which is to adopt a son as a demonstration of renewed responsibility. In fact, it's the 5 year-old son of his roommate who has gone to China for 6 weeks. Hence the perfect chance arises for a comedic display of a father-son bonding relationship in the true Sandler style. It's here where most of the laughs are found. *Big Daddy* is, as every Adam Sandler vehicle before, a chance for the man to steal the laughs from every member of the cast. If you don't like Adam Sandler's brand of humour you won't like *Big Daddy*, as basically it's just one big Sandler joke with a soppy ending for the final 20 minutes. However, if the sight of a man teaching a 5 year-old child how to trip up rollerbladers (and who among us can honestly say the idea doesn't appeal?) makes you laugh then *Big Daddy* provides the goods. Painfully funny at moments, and quite endearing at times, it's the winning blend of one very funny man, and one very cute kid that makes *Big Daddy* another sturdy step in Sandler's bid for Hollywood megastardom. The disc itself doesn't fare too badly, either. Though not quite the same calibre as most Columbia TriStar attempts, the inclusion of the music videos as well as the now obligatory HBO (Home Box Office) interviews still make for a nice, tidy package.

FINAL VERDICT

Picture ☆☆☆☆ Sound ☆☆☆☆
Entertainment ☆☆☆☆ Extras ☆☆☆ Value ☆☆☆
OVERALL ☆☆☆☆

BIG HIT

Price: £19.99
Supplied by: Columbia TriStar Home Video
Type of disc: Single layer, single-sided
No of chapters: 28
Film format(s)/length: 16:9 widescreen enhanced / 88 mins
Audio format: Dolby Digital 5.1
Director: Kirk Wong
Starring: Mark Wahlberg, China Chow, Lou Diamond Phillips
Year made: 1998
Extras: Scene access; director's commentary; 3 grainy deleted scenes; theatrical trailer; DVD trailer; filmographies; soundtrack in German (DD 5.1); subtitles in 15 languages.

Life is what you might call over-complicated for Mel, played by Mark 'Prosthetic Todger' Wahlberg. He's got two high maintenance women on the go,

he's a professional hitman, and he's two weeks over-due for returning *King Kong Lives* back to the video store. Mel inevitably pays for these sins one day. While his prospective in-laws visit for dinner, his assassin squad friends show up to do him in and his current hostage keeps breaking free. Though generous with the acrobatic shooting action and unexpected comedy, *The Big Hit* certainly fails to live up to its name for entertainment. It has the feel of one of those diet action movies that's shot on the cheap in Canada and funnily enough that's exactly what it is. The unending and grotesquely blatant exploitation of Japanese schoolgirl Keiko does little to remedy this, and in fact brings the film down to perverted levels. Always in cotton-socks and pleated mini skirt school uniform, she's alternately handcuffed, gagged, knocked out, forcibly molested, smeared in gravy and uses the toilet on screen. Scrumptious actress China Chow really needs to join the union. Technically, *The Big Hit* looks richly colourful in its clean anamorphic glory, though the same cannot be said for the quivering over-compressed (and frankly boring) deleted scenes, of which there are 3. Director Kirk Wong takes a very good-natured but senselessly rambling approach to his commentary duties, often getting lost in bizarre analogies of the movie business when you'd actually like to know about the key scene you're watching. Consequently, even with its features, this ten-a-penny gun flick is not recommended.

FINAL VERDICT

Picture ☆☆☆☆☆ Sound ☆☆☆☆
Entertainment ☆☆ Extras ☆☆ Value ☆☆
OVERALL ☆☆

THE BIG LEBOWSKI

Price: £17.99
Company: PolyGram
Type of disc: Dual layer, single-sided
No of chapters: 22
Film format(s)/length: 1.85:1 anamorphic / 112 mins
Audio format: Dolby Digital 5.1
Director: Joel Coen
Starring: Jeff Bridges, John Goodman, Julianne Moore
Year made: 1998
Extras: Widescreen TV enhanced; scene selection; booklet with interviews/production info; English and French soundtrack; multilingual subtitles option.

The Coen brothers follow up their Oscar-winning *Fargo* with arguably their best film to date. Meet 'The Dude' (aka, Jeff Bridges) as he is drawn into a web of deceit, kidnapping, inept German nihilists, disembodied toes and...ten-pin bowling. Profoundly funny, with some classic performances from the likes of Bridges, John Goodman, and the always dependable, Steve Buscemi. Surprisingly, for a film of this calibre, the DVD extras package is somewhat lacking. Whilst PolyGram may have saved itself some money by including both the English and French language versions of the movie on one DVD, this doesn't offer any real benefit to the lone consumer on either side of the English Channel (unless, of course, you're currently considering taking up another language). The scene selection menu is nicely designed though, and plays up the film's ten-pin bowling theme, but where's the director's commentary, PolyGram? While it is all well and good including a finely packaged booklet which interviews the stars and provides background info on the film's production, surely this should have been incorporated onto the DVD itself?

FINAL VERDICT

Picture ☆☆☆☆ Sound ☆☆☆☆
Entertainment ☆☆☆☆☆ Extras ☆ Value ☆☆☆
OVERALL ☆☆☆

THE BIRDCAGE

Price: £19.99
Supplied by: DVDplus (www.dvdplus.co.uk)
Type of disc: Dual layer, single-sided
No of chapters: 24
Film format(s)/length: 1.85:1 widescreen enhanced / 159 mins
Audio format: Dolby Digital 5.1
Director: Mike Nichols
Starring: Robin Williams, Gene Hackman, Calista Flockhart
Year made: 1996
Extras: Scene access; theatrical trailer; 8-page booklet featuring a revealing insight into the creation of *The Birdcage*; German, French, Italian and Spanish soundtracks; subtitles in 10 languages.

After the success of children's comedy *Jumanji*, Williams followed the CGI box office hit with another film to gross the $100 million mark: *The Birdcage*. This witty remake of the French film *La Cage Aux Folles* re-establishes Williams as one of the great movie comics of our time. Unusually Williams plays the more restrained role, while Nathan Lane takes the honours as his outrageous lover, the pair must put on a show as a happily married couple to impress the parents of the future wife (Flockhart) of Williams' son. Translation? An excuse for a camp comedy that provides plenty of laughs as Williams once again demonstrates his talent as a comedian that won him many acting accolades in the past. The disc is the standard MGM affair – overpriced, well produced and bundled with an interesting, if predominantly sales orientated 8-page booklet. But let's not sell short its merits. The film is widescreen enhanced (anamorphic) which is unusual for a film of this nature. And whilst there are no big explosions, the Dolby Digital mix enhances the film's musical score, resulting in a tremendous quality of sound. Unfortunately the extras are limited. The only two features of note are the aforementioned booklet and theatrical trailer, but neither will divert your attention for more than a few minutes. However, it could be argued that this is another title on the shelves and that can't be a bad thing. Fans of Williams will not be disappointed, but there are better and cheaper DVDs available.

FINAL VERDICT

Picture ☆☆☆☆ Sound ☆☆☆
Entertainment ☆☆☆ Extras ☆ Value ☆☆
OVERALL ☆☆

BIRD ON A WIRE

Price: £19.99
Supplied by: Columbia TriStar Home Entertainment
Type of disc: Single layer, single-sided
No of chapters: 16
Film format(s)/length: 2.35:1 anamorphic / 106 mins
Audio format: Dolby Digital 5.1
Director: John Badham
Starring: Mel Gibson, Goldie Hawn, David Carradine
Year made: 1990
Extras: Chapter access; theatrical trailer; production notes; cast and crew filmographies; soundtrack in English, French, German, Italian and Spanish; subtitles in 11 languages.

By the time *Bird On A Wire* appeared, gone were the days when director John Badham could churn out light-hearted action/comedies like *Short Circuit* and *Stakeout* and still expect a reasonable welcome. In this bland, by-the-numbers chase caper, Gibson is on the run from crime bosses and the law, and only the bewildered Hawn can help him clear his name. After half an hour you'll have slogged through the pair's 3 facial expressions – surprise, anger and confusion – only to realise the script goes no deeper. It's good to find that Columbia has included some padding with the extras, including detailed production notes that manage to flesh out the absurd final shootout set in a zoo. But with little else, save a low-key filmography and a remarkably grainy picture quality, this DVD offers little a VHS wouldn't deliver. Ill-conceived and uninteresting, *Bird On A Wire* has few laughs beyond Gibson's mullet.

FINAL VERDICT

Picture ☆☆ Sound ☆☆

Entertainment ☆☆ Extras ☆☆ Value ☆☆

OVERALL ☆☆

BLADE

Price: £19.99

Supplied by: DVDplus (www.dvdplus.co.uk)

Type of disc: Dual layer, single-sided

No of chapters: 38

Film format(s)/length: 16:9 widescreen / 115 mins

Audio format: Dolby Digital 5.1

Director: Stephen Norrington

Starring: Wesley Snipes, Stephen Dorff, Kris Kristofferson

Year made: 1998

Extras: 'La Magra' alternate ending; alternate ending; cinematic trailer; cast and crew soundbites, text and stills; *Designing Blade* 25-minute documentary; behind-the-scenes footage (6 minutes); scene access.

The US version of *Blade* should come with an additional warning. Sure, the FBI threatens to claim our children for breach of copyright and all the rest of it, but the real danger comes from watching the thing. You see, once you've witnessed the amazing menus – featuring more animation than most Saturday morning kids' cartoons – and marvelled not just at the film but at the wealth of extras, you'll know there is no going back. DVDs will never be the same. Which is why we're so harsh on the lazy discs that we frequently suffer. There really is no excuse for sloppy encoding and pathetic extras when *Blade* has shown us exactly what is possible with a little bit of TLC. Of course, it's a different story here in Region 2 and all the more frustrating when films like *Armageddon* and *Starship Troopers* are stripped of their glorious commentaries, behind-the-scenes documentaries and deleted scenes. So, in truth, we held out little hope for our old friend *Blade*, fearing the journey across the Atlantic would leave the modern-day vampire looking tired and anaemic. Oh how wrong we were. This is one New Line release that delivers what it promises. The UK cut of the film has lost 5 minutes, but what lies on the cutting room floor doesn't detract from the feature. It remains a gory, violent and stylish tale with some stunning fight scenes and a fair amount of shocks. Blade retains the comic-book violence that made the graphic novels such a success and had it featured nothing extra it would remain a justified purchase. While the menus aren't as impressive as its US cousin, dumbed-down slightly to simple animations, it's the subject matter that, well, mat-

ters. Bizarrely not listed on the box, Region 2 viewers are graced with the audio commentary, though this proves heavy on the waffle and light on facts. A documentary on vampires and a couple of static info screens are absent – though these were essentially fillers in the first place. Thankfully, the alternate ending is included, as is the 25-minute documentary on the design and special effects. Both are excellent. But there's an unexpected bonus for us Europeans. Unusually, New Line has included footage unique to Region 2, which more than makes up for what's missing from the US version. The first of these is a 6-minute behind-the-scenes section which, though raw in presentation, shows some of the fight scenes being rehearsed prior to the special effects being dropped in – something that was so obviously lacking on the Region 1 disc. Also, the cast and crew section here contains a series of soundbites from the 4 leads rather than a couple of pages of text. *Blade* is an extremely worthy DVD – one of the best UK discs out there. Send this to the top of the charts and send a clear message to the other packagers that this is what we want.

FINAL VERDICT

Picture ☆☆☆☆☆ Sound ☆☆☆☆☆

Entertainment ☆☆☆

Extras ☆☆☆☆☆ Value ☆☆☆☆☆

OVERALL ☆☆☆☆

BLADE RUNNER: THE DIRECTOR'S CUT BOX SET

Price: £49.99

Supplied by: Metrodome

Supplied by: Dual layer, single-sided

No of chapters: 42

Film format(s) / length: 2.35:1 anamorphic / 112 mins

Audio format: Dolby Surround

Director: Ridley Scott

Starring: Harrison Ford, Rutger Hauer, Sean Young

Year made: 1982

Extras: Scene access; production notes; cast and crew bios; soundtrack in English, French and Dutch; subtitles in 10 languages.

It almost seems tragic to call this a seminal film. The fact that Scott is one of the most talented directors of his generation, Ford is a Hollywood icon, and it is possibly the best sci fi of its era (only *Star Wars* and *Close Encounters of the Third Kind* stand as competition) only adds fuel to the smoke ridden 'director's cut/original cut' inferno. But underneath it all, *Blade Runner* is one of the best detective thrillers that you're ever likely to see. Almost drowned in a landscape of stark metal, artificial light, and continuous rain, Rick Deckard (Ford) is drafted back to the LA police force to track down and 'retire' 4 replicants (near-perfect androids). The plot is simple, but the execution and the outcome are staggering. *Blade Runner*'s influence can still be found in the sci-fi genre almost 20 years on, and rarely has such a 'Hollywood' movie been used to debate the artistic integrity of the director. It's a wonder then, why Warner Bros chose to lend this landmark movie only half-hearted respect. Wrapped up in a box set so sturdy that it could have been used as a shelter during WWII, the DVD is accompanied by a whole host of extra material that will appeal to any die hard fan, but possibly not to anyone else. There is a reprint of the original poster, a collection of promotional stills, and a limit edition Senitype (a film frame copied from the original print). In addition, there is a copy of the screenplay which appears to be printed on tracing paper. In fact, the most interesting aspect of the entire lot are the notes printed on the back of the screenplay, written by screenwriters Hampton Fancher and David Peoples in May 2000. Though insightful, it reveals only a fragment of the information that should have been included as extras on this rather bland DVD.

FINAL VERDICT

Picture ☆☆☆☆ Sound ☆☆☆

Entertainment ☆☆☆☆☆

Extras ☆☆☆ Value ☆☆☆

OVERALL ☆☆☆

THE BLAIR WITCH PROJECT

Price: £19.99

Supplied by: Pathé Distribution Ltd

Type of disc: Dual layer, single-sided

No of chapters: 18

Film format(s)/length: 4:3 regular / 77 mins

Audio format: Dolby Surround

Directors: Daniel Myrick and Eduardo Sanchez

Starring: Heather Donahue, Joshua Leonard, Michael Williams

Year made: 1999

Extras: Scene access; commentary by the directors/producers; *The Blair Witch Phenomenon* feature; 'The Blair Witch Legacy' notes; interviews with the directors; 'newly-discovered' footage; cast and crew biographies; 9 'Fear Sections'; 3 theatrical trailers; 7 TV spots; DVD-ROM content with web links; subtitles for the hearing impaired in English.

In January of 1999, two film students appeared at the Sundance Film Festival near Park City, Utah carrying a revolutionary quasi-documentary horror movie about 3 kids getting lost in the woods. Just over a year later and more than $224 million worth of box office tickets sold, their footage has found its way onto one of the most extraordinary and content-packed DVDs of the year. *The Blair Witch Project* was the lo-fi, high-concept, word-of-mouse indie film that became a phenomenon without the traditional pulls of star power, big name directors or multi-million dollar production values. Cannily set in 1994 so no mobile phones can get in the way and cut the narrative short, 3 film students travel to the small New England town of Burkittsville to shoot a documentary investigating the legend of the Blair Witch, an evil supernatural entity credited with butchering townsfolk at 40 year intervals...and are never seen again. The movie is made out of their 'recovered' tapes. Filmed on a budget that equals Schwarzenegger's cigar allowance, the 3 stars shot the bulk of the footage and interviewed a variety of genuine townspeople and pre-briefed actors. They then ventured into the Black Hills Woods (in reality the Seneca Creek State Park, Maryland) where the film-makers were waiting for them with sticks and stones and freaking-out equipment. The movie brilliantly uses the old rule of horror movies, forgotten in recent times in favour of expensive CGI monsters: what you don't see lets your imagination run riot. Pathé has bettered Artisan's already impressive Region 1 disc, matching everything that Americans enjoy and encoding more besides, such as the comprehensive interview with the key film-makers. It's in this interview that Sanchez and Myrick reveal that originally the film would contain the students' black and white footage, but also professionally shot (and faked) interviews, news reports and even a Seventies TV show called *Mystic Occurrences*. This dropped material now constitutes the bulk of *The Curse of the Blair Witch* mockumentary, a theme the UK disc continues with 9 diverting 'Fear Sections' in which the effects and topics are discussed by a cast of actors. The self-titled 'Haxan Five' – Myrick, Sanchez plus producers Robin Cowie, Gregg Hale and Michael Monello – record the amusing commentary. Not taking their film all that seriously, they spend most of the time bantering, acknowledging Heather's impressive mucus-making abilities and proudly pointing out which stickmen and rock piles they are credited for. The only thing missing from the disc are testimonies from the 3 people at the sharp end of the film. What is their take on it all and what effect has the film had on their real lives?

Perhaps because the film-makers didn't want to break the spell, we're unfortunately left to ponder in the dark. *The Blair Witch Project* is a film that demands you suspend disbelief just like all other horror films. Read the mythology, visit the Web site, buy the DVD and allow yourself to be absorbed by the intense drama played out before you. Anyone who goes in with a 'Well, I'm waiting to be scared' attitude cheats themselves out of one of the most frightening, engrossing and entertaining rides ever made.

FINAL VERDICT

Picture ☆☆☆☆ Sound ☆☆☆☆
Entertainment ☆☆☆☆
Extras ☆☆☆☆☆ Value ☆☆☆☆☆
OVERALL ☆☆☆☆☆

BLAST FROM THE PAST

Price: £19.99
Supplied by: Entertainment in Video
Type of disc: Dual layer, single-sided
No of chapters: 24
Film format(s)/length: 16:9 widescreen / 99 mins
Audio format: Dolby Digital 5.1
Director: Hugh Wilson
Starring: Brendan Fraser, Alicia Silverstone, Christopher Walken
Year made: 1999
Extras: Scene access; trailers; cast notes and mini-interviews; deleted scenes; out-takes; subtitles in English.

In between *The Mummy* and *George of the Jungle*, Brendan Fraser's rise to stardom made a detour through this amiable romantic comedy. Hot from *George*'s $100m box office take, you can see why *Blast* appealed to him as another fish out of water comedy. The story begins with the Cuban Missile Crisis and an aircraft crash – the latter fooling Walken into believing the Cold War has blown hot, so he and wife Sissy Spacek take refuge in their bomb shelter for 35 years. The passing of time is conveyed by the diner built overhead, a business which radically changes over the years. By the Nineties, the diner's become a neo-gothic pit that perfectly resembles the post-apocalypse horror Walken expects. However, the Fifties live on in an underground bubble that has given family son Adam (Fraser) a very idiosyncratic upbringing. When Adam is sent out for supplies, 35 years of bad luck are abruptly ended by a chance encounter with Eve (Silverstone) – a cynical, tough talking woman with a heart of gold. It's a romance with a difference…without ever being all that surprising. There are amusing moments, and director Wilson ably sus-

tains a whimsical atmosphere, but it doesn't quite live up to all the rave reviews plastered over the box. As a DVD, picture quality is beyond reproach, although there are moments when the audio seems to slip out of synch. It's a Disney film in all but name, directed by the creator of *WKRP in Cinncinati*. Now *there's* a recommendation for you!

FINAL VERDICT

Picture ☆☆☆☆ Sound ☆☆☆
Entertainment ☆☆☆☆ Extras ☆☆☆☆
Value ☆☆☆
OVERALL ☆☆☆☆

BLAZING SADDLES

Price: £15.99
Company: Warner Home Video
Type of disc: Single layer, single-sided
No of chapters: 25
Film format(s)/length: 2.35:1 anamorphic / 89 mins
Director: Mel Brooks
Starring: Cleavon Little, Gene Wilder, David Huddleston
Year made: 1974
Extras: Chapter access; English/French/Italian soundtrack; multilingual subtitles; production notes; trailer; 55 minute interview with Mel Brooks.

You thought bad taste in the cinema started with the Farrelly Brothers? Shame on you. Mel Brooks was doing it a quarter of a century ago. The tragedy is that he hasn't managed to match it since. Flash back 25 years, however, and Brooks had followed up his early success with *The Producers* (crooked creatives put on a Nazi-themed musical with the aim of deliberately losing money) by releasing *Young Frankenstein* (riotous spoof of the old horror classics) and *Blazing Saddles* in the same year. *Blazing Saddles* has a token plot, with sleazy politician Hedley Lamarr (Huddleston) trying to drive the inhabitants of Rock Ridge from their town so he can build a railway; his masterstroke is to assign the racist rednecks a black sheriff (Little). However, by the time a huge fight breaks out of the set and into neighbouring soundstages, you've long since forgotten about this. As Brooks explains in his commentary, the studio executives were appalled by *Blazing Saddles'* deliberately outrageous tastelessness, and if not for a successful screening for studio employees, it might never have been released. Farting cowboys, people punching horses and endless distinctly un-PC jokes might have put the suits into a cold sweat…but they're still funny, even now. Brooks' commentary lasts for 55 minutes and is interesting, though rather rambling. The original trailer is also interesting, as whoever edited it just didn't have the guts to include a single tasteless punchline. Quite a change from today's 'give it all away' previews...

FINAL VERDICT

Picture ☆☆☆☆ Sound ☆☆☆
Entertainment ☆☆☆☆ Extras ☆☆☆ Value ☆☆☆
OVERALL ☆☆☆☆

Blue Juice

Price: £19.99
Supplied by: VCI
Type of disc: Single layer, single-sided
No of chapters: 16
Film format(s)/length: 16:9 widescreen enhanced / 96 mins
Audio format: Stereo
Director: Carl Prechezer
Starring: Sean Pertwee, Catherine Zeta-Jones, Ewan McGregor
Year made: 1995
Extras: Scene access; key cast, director and screenwriter interviews; theatrical trailer; 3 filmographies in booklet booklet; soundtrack in English.

This British film is a landmark in more ways than one. For starters, it's a fresh, funny and feel-good movie that's set in contemporary Britain, but doesn't feature criminals or jobbing American actresses. And for a main course, the cast is a virtual 'Who's Who' of British talent before they all made it HUGE! JC (Pertwee) is a man who loves his surfing, his gorgeous long suffering girlfriend Chloe (Zeta-Jones) and hanging out with his wave-chasing mates. But when his childhood pals from London show up on his Cornish doorstep (McGregor, *Lock, Stock*'s Mackintosh and *Brassed Off*'s Peter Gunn) all of them realise they have to face up to life's responsibilities – whether they're ready or not. It's interesting to note how this newly designed sleeve pastes Catherine's name above the title, demonstrating just how much of a star the Valley girl has become. A special mention has to be made for Smuggler FM's hilarious provincial superstar DJs (not in the Paul Oakenfold sense of the word) Dan and Gordon – a sort of Cornish Jay and Silent Bob but without the cussin'. The widescreen package on offer for your twenty quid is a respectable effort: the trailer is present and correct and the disc also serves up interview clips of the stars, writer and director. On the down side, the chance to hear the crashing waves and eclectic soundtrack in 5.1 Dolby Digital has been missed. But in all it's a bright and breezy DVD and a film you'll want to see again and again.

FINAL VERDICT

Picture ☆☆☆☆ Sound ☆
Entertainment ☆☆☆☆ Extras ☆☆☆ Value ☆☆☆
OVERALL ☆☆☆

Blue Streak

Price: £19.99
Supplied by: Columbia TriStar Home Video
Type of disc: Single layer, single-sided
No of chapters: 28
Film format(s)/length: 1.85:1 anamorphic / 90 mins
Audio format: Dolby Digital 5.1
Director: Les Mayfield
Starring: Martin Lawrence, Luke Wilson, William Forsythe
Year made: 1999
Extras: Scene access; *Setting Up The Score* featurette (22 mins); HBO First Look: *Inside And Undercover* featurette (23 mins);3 music videos: 'Girl's Best Friend' by Jay-Z, 'Criminal Mind' by Tyrese and 'Damn (Should've Treated U Right)' by So Plush; trailer; filmographies; soundtrack in English, German and Hungarian; subtitles in 16 languages.

Poacher turned gamekeeper? In this case it's crook turned cop. Lawrence plays Miles Logan, a master jewel thief who, just before being caught, hides a $17 million diamond in a building under construction. Two years later, Miles is released from prison and hurries to reclaim his prize – only to find the building is now a police station! Using his underworld connections he fakes a police ID to gain entrance, but the diamond proves a bit harder to retrieve than he initially planned, and before he knows it, 'detective Malone' is now leading the war against crime with a unique insider's knowledge of illegal behaviour. *Blue Streak* is an action/comedy in the vein of *Bad Boys* – so much so that Lawrence might as well be playing the same character, and if you believe the box, he actually is. Lawrence alternates between being funny and irritating, but luckily for the film the balance is in favour of the former. He's at his best when he's not completely clowning it up, but unfortunately everybody involved in the film thought otherwise, so the story frequently nips off for a fag while Lawrence is pratting about in a sub-Eddie Murphy way. Comparisons with *Bad Boys* are inevitable, so here goes – *Blue Streak* isn't as good. While it's more biased towards the comedy side of things than the action, *Bad Boys* was still funnier. Having Will Smith to bounce jokes off just made Lawrence all the more entertaining, but here all the other characters are basically his stooges as he goes through his manic routine. *Bad Boys* also benefited from Michael Bay's zappy fast-cut direction, whereas Mayfield is rather more pedestrian. That said, *Blue Streak* is still entertaining (there's a really great joke involving a tube of ointment) and is definitely worth an evening of your time if there's nothing on the box – and, let's face it, during summer is there ever? The extras package (the same as the R1 disc) is up to Columbia's usual standards – two made-for-TV featurettes, one of which shows parts of some deleted scenes (why weren't these included as well?), a trio of music videos and the expected trailer and filmographies. The DVD as a whole is excellently presented, picture and sound are both beyond reproach, and while it's not the greatest film ever it's still a lot of cop.

FINAL VERDICT

Picture ☆☆☆☆ Sound ☆☆☆☆

Entertainment ☆☆☆

Extras ☆☆☆ Value ☆☆☆

OVERALL ☆☆☆

BLUE THUNDER

Price: £19.99

Supplied by: Columbia TriStar Home Video

Type of disc: Single layer, single-sided

No of chapters: 28

Film format(s)/length: 2.35:1 anamorphic / 105 mins

Audio format: Dolby Digital 5.1

Director: John Badham

Starring: Roy Scheider, Daniel Stern, Malcolm McDowell

Year made: 1982

Extras: Scene access; trailer; soundtrack in English, French, German, Spanish and Italian; subtitles in 20 languages.

Here's a blast from the past – a very Eighties 'supermachine' movie where the star of the show is definitely the hardware. Scheider gets top billing, but we all know better. Scheider is LAPD helicopter pilot Murphy, who is assigned to test Blue Thunder, an experimental attack helicopter designed for urban use. Murphy soon learns that dodgy guvmint spooks led by McDowell (played as an upper-class twit for no good reason) are stirring up ethnic trouble as an excuse to use their new toy, so he hijacks Blue Thunder and tries to expose the truth while avoiding destruction. What seemed cool back then is now revealed to have *Scooby-Doo*-level plotting ("Hey! This looks like a clue!") and lifeless pacing until the final dogfight is joined. The disc has strong audio and good reproduction of its murky photography, but lacks extras beyond a trailer. Because of this, the whole package never achieves takeoff.

FINAL VERDICT

Picture ☆☆☆ Sound ☆☆☆☆☆

Entertainment ☆☆ Extras ☆☆ Value ☆☆

OVERALL ☆☆

BLUE VELVET

Price: £19.99

Supplied by: Castle Home Video

Type of disc: Single layer, single-sided

No of chapters: 20

Film format(s)/length: 4:3 regular / 115 mins

Audio format: Stereo

Director: David Lynch

Starring: Kyle MacLachlan, Isabella Rossellini, Dennis Hopper

Year made: 1986

Extras: Scene access; picture library.

Oh, dear. David Lynch's nightmarish tale of voyeurism and depravity has here been transformed into an absolute dog of a DVD. Centred around a trio of striking performances: MacLachlan as the strait-laced hero; Isabella Rossellini as a tortured nightclub singer; and particularly Hopper as the barking mad villain, *Blue Velvet* is a superb examination of the dark underbelly of smalltown life. The discovery of a severed ear draws MacLachlan's character into a bizarre web of intrigue, involving kidnap, violent sex and a gas-guzzling psychopath with a penchant for Roy Orbison songs. Self-consciously stylish, with a powerful sense of menace, this is a masterpiece. Unfortunately, the brilliance of the film is undermined by a decidedly substandard digital transfer, which renders the picture grainy throughout, and the colours washed out and often muddy. For a piece that relies so heavily on its cinematography to emphasise the contrast between the safe, bright surfaces of the day, and the dark and dangerous depths of the night, this is unforgivable, making it look almost like a student film. Not only that, the film is presented only in pan-and-scan format, effectively chopping Lynch's carefully crafted shots in half. As far as extras go, there's a picture library featuring promotional stills (one of which is merely a blue swirling image), but nothing else. If you've already got the video, there's no point whatsoever in wasting your money on this overpriced DVD – whoever threw it together should be, if you'll pardon the pun, lynched.

FINAL VERDICT

Picture ☆☆ Sound ☆☆

Entertainment ☆☆☆☆☆ Extras ☆ Value ☆

OVERALL ☆☆

BODY DOUBLE

Price: £19.99
Supplied by: Columbia-TriStar Home Video
Type of disc: Single layer, single-sided
No of chapters: 28
Film format(s)/length: 16:9 widescreen enhanced / 109 mins
Audio format: Dolby Surround
Director: Brian De Palma
Starring: Craig Wasson, Gregg Henry, Melanie Griffith
Year made: 1984
Extras: Scene access; brief filmographies; trailer; soundtrack in German, French, Italian and Spanish; subtitles available in 19 languages.

Brian De Palma reportedly gets very annoyed when critics accuse him of ripping off Alfred Hitchcock. However, it's something he brings on himself – *Body Double* tries so hard to mimic the 'Master of the Macabre' that you expect a walk-on appearance by the man himself. Combining the plots of *Vertigo* and *Rear Window*, but not very well, *Body Double* sees jobless actor Jake Scully (Wasson) housesitting for a friend and peeping on an exhibitionist neighbour. When said neighbour is gruesomely murdered, Jake tries to find out what happened, with the trail eventually leading to porn star Holly Body (Melanie Griffith). The sex really isn't that sexy, the suspense isn't gripping at all, the plot isn't believable in the slightest and the film retires with a final 'twist' you can spot from Neptune. Even De Palma's usual gimmicky camera work is in tragically short supply. With only feeble extras on offer, *Body Double* is no match for the genuine Hitchcock article.

FINAL VERDICT
Picture ☆ Sound ☆☆
Entertainment ☆☆ Extras ☆ Value ☆
OVERALL ☆☆

THE BODYGUARD

Price: £15.99
Supplied by: DVDplus (www.dvdplus.co.uk)
Type of disc: Dual layer, single-sided
No of chapters: 38
Film format(s)/length: 1.85:1 widescreen / 124 mins
Audio format: Dolby Digital 5.1
Director: Mick Jackson
Starring: Kevin Costner, Whitney Houston, Gary Kemp
Year made: 1992
Extras: Scene access; multilingual subtitles; subtitles for the hearing impaired in English.

Sentimental mush, perhaps, right down to a cop-out *Casablanca* ending, but there's no doubt *The Bodyguard* is a very effective piece of Hollywood machinery. Costner is always at his most charismatic playing low-key characters, with an ex-Secret Service bodyguard suiting him just fine. Whitney Houston is, well, a singer and the best thing you can say about her acting is not to say anything. Brit Mick Jackson balances action and romance effectively, while Laurence Kasdan's script keeps you guessing about who's plotting against who. It was a box office smash, of course, and a romance guys can enjoy, so you'd expect first class treatment on DVD. In fact, the film is packaged with zero extras, while picture quality is variable. Sound is reasonable, but unexceptional although stereo's all you really need for the main sonic set-pieces, which are Houston's songs. Sooner or later, there's bound to be a collector's edition, so give this miserly release a miss.

FINAL VERDICT
Picture ☆☆ Sound ☆☆☆
Entertainment ☆☆☆☆ Extras ☆ Value ☆☆☆
OVERALL ☆☆☆

THE BONE COLLECTOR

Price: £19.99
Supplied by: Universal
Type of disc: Dual layer, single-sided
No of chapters: 20
Film format(s)/length: 2.35:1 anamorphic / 113 mins
Audio format: Dolby Digital 5.1
Director: Phillip Noyce
Starring: Denzel Washington, Angelina Jolie, Michael Rooker
Year made: 1999
Extras: Scene access; director's commentary; theatrical trailer; 22-minute behind-the-scenes featurette; talent files; isolated music score; trailer for *Devil In A Blue Dress*; soundtrack in English and German; subtitles in 17 languages.

Washington stars in this movie as ex-forensic cop Lincoln Rhyme, now a quadriplegic after a horrific accident damaged his spine. Jolie is Amelia Donaghy, a fairly experienced beat cop who's just achieved her ambition of a transfer to youth services, but who then gets bullied into working with Rhyme because he believes that she'll make a great forensics expert and can help bring down the vicious serial killer on the loose. Together, this unlikely partnership is up against a murderer who seems to take his victims at random and has a nasty habit of cutting bones from them while they're still alive – hence his nickname. This is quite a spooky movie which keeps you guessing – at least to begin with – although it does get a bit bogged down in the subtext of Rhyme's hatred of his bed-ridden life and his desire to commit suicide. Some of the characters are fairly stereotypical, like the surly police chief who doesn't want a rookie working on *his* case, but Washington and Jolie play well off one another, and the fact that Washington's character has to talk Jolie's through everything provides a neat way of explaining technical details to the audience. Where *The Bone Collector* really comes into its own is in the extras department. In addition to a very informative commentary from director Phillip Noyce, you also get a selection of trailers, detailed filmographies, an isolated musical score and a 22-minute documentary on the making of the movie. Everything is packaged very nicely with some incredibly spooky animated menus that set the scene perfectly for the tone of the movie. *The Bone Collector* is also one of those fortunate DVDs that loads straight to the menu screen without you having to sit through all the numerous adverts and corporate logos which so many companies are sticking on their discs (*cough* BuenaVista *cough*) and this means you can get straight into the movie without any messing about. If you like thrillers and you've got a DVD player, then you really should take a look at this serial chiller!

FINAL VERDICT

Picture ☆☆☆☆ Sound ☆☆☆☆
Entertainment ☆☆☆☆
Extras ☆☆☆☆ Value ☆☆☆☆
OVERALL ☆☆☆☆

THE BONFIRE OF THE VANITIES

Price: £15.99
Supplied by: Warner Home Video
Type of disc: Single layer, single-sided
No of chapters: 35
Film format(s)/length: 1.85:1 widescreen / 120 mins
Audio format: Dolby Surround
Director: Brian De Palma
Starring: Tom Hanks, Bruce Willis, Melanie Griffith
Year made: 1990
Extras: Scene access; soundtrack in English, French and Italian; subtitles in 10 languages; subtitles for the hearing impaired in English and Italian.

There's a certain amount of poetic justice that a novel *about* hubris ended up being made into a film that *exemplified* hubris. Flushed with the success of *Batman*, the top executives at Warner Bros thought they had the golden touch and any film they made would be a success. *The Bonfire Of The Vanities* proved them wrong – in a big way. Tom Wolfe's deeply satirical novel was a story of arrogance, race and greed set in the heyday of Eighties yuppiedom,

where the pride of the people at the very top of Wall Street ended up destroying them. Since the novel was a best-seller, a film was inevitable…but everything that could be done wrong, was. The antihero of the novel was Sherman McCoy, a callous, ruthless, deceitful and downright unpleasant millionaire stockbroker. Who better to play him than Tom Hanks, the epitome of niceness? Similarly, McCoy's downfall was engineered by his mistress, the irresistible ultimate sexual predator, and a sleazy, alcoholic British tabloid journalist. Step forth Melanie Griffith and Bruce Willis, respectively. All you need to completely remove the point of the novel is a happy ending, and – oh, whaddya know? Brian De Palma tried his best to capture some of the twisted feel of Wolfe's novel with his usual extreme camera angles and visual trickery, but Michael Cristofer's script – with the full backing of the suits – chopped Wolfe's cruel attack on the Reagan era into a flaccid tale of 'man gets knocked down, becomes a better person and gets back up again'. What's left is a grotesquely over-budget and badly acted farce that sees several of Hollywood's biggest stars (including Morgan Freeman, in a role originally written as white and Jewish) completely adrift and clearly wishing that they were somewhere else entirely. Perhaps not surprisingly, nobody involved has stepped up to provide a commentary track. However, this doesn't excuse the total absence of any extras on the disc. It's about time a law was passed banning 'interactive menus' and 'scene access' from ever being listed as 'special features' again!

FINAL VERDICT

Picture ☆☆☆ Sound ☆☆
Entertainment ☆☆ Extras ☆ Value ☆☆
OVERALL ☆☆

BOOGIE NIGHTS

Price: £19.99
Supplied by: DVD World
Type of disc: Dual layer, single-sided
No of chapters: 26
Film format(s)/length: 16:9 widescreen / 148 mins
Audio format: Dolby Surround
Director: Paul Thomas Anderson
Starring: Mark Wahlberg, Burt Reynolds, Heather Graham
Year made: 1997
Extras: Scene access; interviews with director and cast.

Marky Mark Wahlberg is Dirk Diggler, aka Eddy Adams. He's a young bus-boy dreaming of movie stardom until he's spotted by 'adult feature' director Jack Horner (Burt Reynolds) and catapulted into a prolific career as a porn star. The sets, music and acting in this movie are superb – Burt Reynolds is perfectly cast as the kind-hearted porn mogul – and it has some excellent comic-tragic moments. That said, at well over two hours it's excessively long and the drama of the last hour or so is undermined by the happy ending for all the characters (apart from the dead ones). The interviews which are promised on the packaging are actually a huge let down when you watch them. Of the 8, none last much longer than a minute and they all take the form of an answer to a question which is never heard. The problem is, they haven't all been asked the same question and so most of the time, it's difficult to work out exactly what they're talking about. For instance, a lot of the time it's not clear whether the actors are talking about themselves, their character, another member of the cast or the director! Aside from the interviews, there's the solitary English language subtitles but that's all you get as far as extras goes. As such, this has to be one of the worst DVDs for extra features with not even a movie trailer in sight. About the only feature that makes it better than the video is the fact that you can get a crystal-clear pause of the shot where the gorgeous Rollergirl (Heather Graham) strips off!

FINAL VERDICT

Picture ☆☆☆☆ Sound ☆☆☆

Entertainment ☆☆☆ Extras ☆☆ Value ☆☆

OVERALL ☆☆

DAS BOOT: THE DIRECTOR'S CUT

Price: £19.99
Supplied by: Columbia TriStar
Type of disc: Dual layer, double-sided
No of chapters: 66
Film length/format(s): 16:9 widescreen / 200 mins
Director: Wolfgang Peterson
Starring: Jurgan Prochnow, Herbert Gronmeyer, Klaus Wennemann
Year made: 1985 (original 1981)
Extras: Scene access; interactive menus; director's commentary; trailer; featurette.

Though Wolfgang Peterson established a worldwide name with *In the Line of Fire* and, subsequently, *Air Force One*, it was this German opus with which he first attracted the attention of the Hollywood big boys. *Das Boot* is a claustrophobic and gripping account of the Second World War told from a rare perspective – a patrolling U-Boat. Sure there have been sub flicks before, but none has captured fear, confusion and anger – usually at the same time – like this, making it an often unsettling tale. It's an assault

on the senses, too, having been beefed up for its DVD debut. Though the original runs forever (it was originally made as a 6-hour TV series) this version boasts additional footage not seen on the typical home or broadcast formats. The image clarity shows off the crew's innovative approach to making the film and it truly blossoms in surround sound, with pulsating use of mechanical effects. The choice of native German language with subtitles is much preferred to the dubbed English version, if you want to soak up the intensity of the original. Peterson's commentary track is awesome – the man's passion for the picture clearly obvious. As a study into film making, it's invaluable; as a source for anecdotal material with which to impress your mates it's unbeatable. The trailer is just that – but the featurette further demonstrates how remarkable a film *Das Boot* is, rightly asserting its acclaim as one of the best war films ever made.

FINAL VERDICT

Picture ☆☆☆☆☆ Sound ☆☆☆☆☆

Entertainment ☆☆☆☆☆ Extras ☆☆☆☆☆

Value ☆☆☆☆☆

OVERALL ☆☆☆☆☆

BORN ON THE FOURTH OF JULY

Price: £19.99
Supplied by: Columbia TriStar Home Video
Type of disc: Dual layer, single-sided
No of chapters: 16
Film format(s)/length: 2.31:1 widescreen enhanced / 138 mins
Audio format: Dolby Digital 5.1
Director: Oliver Stone
Starring: Tom Cruise, Willem Dafoe, Bryan Larkin
Year made: 1989
Extras: Scene access; theatrical trailer; production notes; cast and film-makers' notes; soundtrack in German, French, Italian, Spanish, Polish and Czech; subtitles in 9 languages.

Oliver Stone's feelings about the Vietnam conflict obviously run very deep. In *Platoon* he relived the horror of a war he fought in and returned to tell the tale. In *Born on the Fourth of July* he faces the trauma of coming home to an anti-Vietnam America. The latter is based on the true story of Ron Kovic, a Veteran who returned paralysed from the chest down and became a voice for disenchanted patriots in the Seventies. Like many of Stone's best films, this is a hard-hitting and uncomfortably raw analysis of the human condition, with Tom Cruise giving by far his best performance to date. Given such a strong film, it's ironic that Columbia chose to make such a poor attempt at putting it onto DVD. At best the picture lacks distinction in both contrast and colour. Many of Oliver Stone's films have a 'grainy' appearance, but surely being blurry and faded isn't a deliberate move? Unfortunately, the low quality of the transfer isn't the only disappointing aspect to this disc. The 'extras' are limited to a single trailer and a few pages of production notes. Where's the 'Making of' documentary or the lost scenes? Probably got lost amongst the budget for *The Mask of Zorro*, that's where. It seems most of the disc has been taken up with the 6 soundtracks. Only English is in Dolby 5.1, with 4 others in Surround and a further two in mono! Faced with such a huge selection of soundtracks but no decent visuals, our best advice is to turn the TV off and pump up the hi-fi. This is a disappointing re-hash of the Region 1 release, and an insult to the excellent work of Oliver Stone and Tom Cruise. In fact, it's such a bad DVD it deserves to be napalmed!

FINAL VERDICT

Picture ☆ Sound ☆☆☆

Entertainment ☆☆☆ Extras ☆ Value ☆

OVERALL ☆

THE BORROWERS

Price: £17.99
Supplied by: PolyGram
Type of disc: Single layer, double sided
No of chapters: 15
Film format(s)/length: 4:3 regular, 16:9 widescreen / 87 mins
Audio format: Dolby Digital 5.1
Director: Peter Hewitt
Starring: John Goodman, Jim Broadbent, Mark Williams
Year made: 1997
Extras: Scene access; adverts for other titles; English, German and Dutch soundtracks; multilingual subtitles.

When Mary Norton first created the minuscule world of *The Borrowers* over 40 years ago, there was no way she could have foreseen that one day a major Hollywood studio would film her novel with state of the art CGI effects, and release it on DVD. The movie follows the exploits of the diminutive but determined Clock family – Pod, Homily, Arrietty and Peagreen – as they battle to save their home from the dastardly clutches of odious lawyer Ocious P Potter (played with expert comedy gusto by Goodman). Setting out armed only with pins for swords, the instantly likeable children foil all of Potter's devious plans to destroy them with the aid of exterminator Jeff, played by *Fast Show* regular Williams. The cast,

including Broadbent, Celia Imrie, Ruby Wax, Doon Mackighan and the always perfect Hugh Laurie are the main reason to buy this disc, while the bizarre futuristic setting (that lies somewhere between wartime London and Fifties America) prove this to be well more than your usual kid's flick. Which makes it all the more surprising that the extras given on the DVD are more practical than fun. You are given a choice of 3 languages: English, Danish and German, and subtitles for each, plus scene select and a list of other titles available. This makes *The Borrowers* a little less desirable as a fun family DVD, but if you've got Germans or Netherlanders in your family, it's ideal.

FINAL VERDICT

Picture ☆☆☆☆☆ Sound ☆☆☆☆☆

Entertainment ☆☆☆☆ Extras ☆☆☆ Value ☆☆☆

OVERALL ☆☆☆

BOUND

Price: £19.99
Supplied by: Pathé Distribution
Type of disc: Dual layer, single-sided
No of chapters: 14
Film format(s)/length: 16:9 widescreen enhanced / 104 mins
Audio format: Dolby Digital 5.1
Directors: Larry and Andy Wachowski
Starring: Jennifer Tilly, Gina Gershon, Joe Pantoliano
Year made: 1996
Extras: Scene access ; cast and directors' commentary; 3 trailers; cast and crew biographies; production featurette; subtitles in English; subtitles for the hearing impaired in English.

While it might have the most explicit two-girl action you're likely to see in a mainstream release, *Bound* is a world away from the direct-to-video exploitation flicks (or worse) normally associated with same-sex rumpo. Written and directed by the Wachowski brothers, the men behind *The Matrix* (a fact surprisingly not plugged to death on the sleeve), *Bound* is a modern-day *film noir*, only done with such style and wit that it's almost as much a black comedy as it is a thriller. Twitchy mobster Caesar (Pantoliano) has been given the task of laundering – literally, as it's covered in blood – over two million dollars of stolen money. However, his girlfriend Violet (Tilly) has just experienced lust at first sight with thief-turned-decorator Corky (Gershon), and the sapphic pair quickly come up with a plan to separate Caesar from the cash. This being a thriller, of course, things spin out of control… *Bound* is a great and very tense film, that even comes with some decent extras. The production featurette is so short it's just an 'ette', but you also get biographies, 3 different trailers and an entertaining commentary track featuring the Wachowskis and the 3 stars, among others, where a good time was clearly had by all. The Wachowskis use all kinds of camera tricks to keep a story largely set in two rooms looking interesting, and the end result is a polished, exciting and cruelly funny twist on macho gangster movies. Well worth getting, and not just because it's the 'full, uncut version'!

FINAL VERDICT

Picture ☆☆☆☆ Sound ☆☆☆
Entertainment ☆☆☆☆☆ Extras ☆☆☆
Value ☆☆☆
OVERALL ☆☆☆☆

BOWFINGER

Price: £19.99
Supplied by: Columbia TriStar Home Video
Type of disc: Dual layer, single-sided
No of chapters: 18
Film format(s)/length: 1.85:1 anamorphic / 93 mins
Audio format: Dolby Digital 5.1
Director: Frank Oz
Starring: Steve Martin, Eddie Murphy, Heather Graham
Year made: 1999
Extras: Scene access; director's commentary; *Spotlight on Location* featurette (24 mins); deleted scenes (5 mins); outtakes (3 mins); trailer; DVD-ROM features; production notes; cast and film-makers' notes; soundtrack in English and German; subtitles in 11 languages.

What do you do if you're an aspiring film-maker with a script, a crew and a cast – but no major Hollywood star? If you're Bobby Bowfinger (Martin), there's only one choice – you film the world's biggest movie star, Kit Ramsey (Murphy), without his knowledge…and if you drive him insane in the process, who cares? A common problem with Hollywood films about Hollywood films is that even if they're supposedly attacking the industry, they become nothing more than narcissistic navel-gazing exercises – witness *The Muse* or the horribly overrated *The Player*. Fortunately, despite the occasional fluffy edge *Bowfinger* manages to maintain a healthy cynicism throughout, and even the one moment where Martin's shifty (hell, outright criminal) producer appears to be growing a heart is quickly and firmly stepped on. *Bowfinger* is a clever and sharp comedy with some good scenes for Martin, who's been in danger of turning into the next Leslie Nielsen of late. Better yet, the Region 2 DVD has all the extras found on the American disc, which adds up to a quite extensive selection. The *Spotlight on Location* featurette is rather blah, but the deleted scenes include a different version of the sequence where Bowfinger gathers his colleagues, and the outtakes see Murphy and Martin vying for ad-lib supremacy. Oz's commentary is one of the better examples of the form, with the former *Muppets* man detailing the ins and outs of making a film with two superstar comics on top form. The only annoyance is that he makes frequent references to alternate takes and deleted scenes that don't appear on the DVD. Since some were already included, it's a shame Columbia TriStar didn't go the whole hog and put all of them on the disc. *Bowfinger* is a welcome return to edgy comic form for Martin, and thankfully also pulls Murphy away from the cheesy family comedies he's been concentrating on. Pull your finger out and give it a look.

FINAL VERDICT

Picture ☆☆☆☆ Sound ☆☆☆
Entertainment ☆☆☆☆ Extras ☆☆☆☆
Value ☆☆☆☆
OVERALL ☆☆☆☆

BRAM STOKER'S DRACULA

Price: £19.99
Supplied by: Columbia TriStar
Type of disc: Dual layer, single-sided
No of chapters: 24
Film format(s)/length: 1.85:1 widescreen / 123 mins
Audio format: Dolby Digital 5.1
Director: Francis Ford Coppola
Starring: Gary Oldman, Winona Ryder, Anthony Hopkins
Year made: 1992
Extras: multi-lingual subtitles; English Dolby Digital 5.1; French, German, Italian and Spanish Dolby Surround soundtrack; *The Man, The Myth, The Legend* documentary; theatrical trailer; filmographies; DVD trailer.

Francis Ford Coppola's *Bram Stoker's Dracula* suffered with a cruel blessing. On the one hand the patronage of leading lady Winona Ryder brought in a major league budget, allowing for undoubtedly the most lavish retelling of the vampire myth to date. On the other hand, it demanded 'hot' stars such as Ryder herself and, notoriously, Keanu Reeves, to reassure the accountants. The one undermines the other, Ryder lacks presence as the subject of Dracula's obsession while Reeves turns in a performance which would make a woodworm choke. That said, this is still a very worthwhile film dating from the (pre-*Jack*) time when Coppola was incapable of making a dull movie. The script is flawed, but nonetheless ambitious in making Dracula and Van Helsing moral equivalents. Dracula is seen sympathetically in a gorgeous-looking production wherein Coppola's decision to eschew state-of-the-art CGI in favour of more traditional special effects really pays off. There's a unique, picture-book quality to the film's look and flamboyant touches such as Dracula's eyes appearing in the night-sky all add to the operatic style of the tale. It's a movie wherein almost every frame seems a work of art and DVD really brings that to the fore; it's a simply a treat to watch. In terms of DVD extras, *Dracula* is yet more evidence that at last European productions are catching up with the quality of American offerings. It's dual layer – so the whole film and more fits on a single side with no *Starship Troopers*-style mid-movie flip-over required – and there's plenty of extras. Costume design not only provides background text on Eiko Ishioka's Academy Award-winning work, but also illustrates it with her original sketches. Filmographies on the leading players and director are the usual, simplistic listing of career highlights, but it's good to see the theatrical trailer is included. The real bonus, however, is a 30 minute documentary which, while not breath-takingly original, still serves its promotional purpose. Director, scriptwriter and the actors themselves all get to expound on their ambitions for the film. It also makes everyone involved so much more interesting. A 3-second clip of Reeves enthusing over Dracula's fangs contains more charisma than the entirety of his on-screen performance. Oldman quotes Richard Burton on his deathbed – exclaiming "She still fascinates me," about estranged lover Elizabeth Taylor – to explain his take on eternal love. You're reminded anew how talented these people are. And this is what DVD is all about: reproducing films in breathtaking quality and surrounding them with additions by which to further extend the movie-watching experience. After being disenchanted with this film after buying the VHS version, DVD has renewed my respect for what is a flawed but still beautiful and fascinating movie.

FINAL VERDICT

Picture ☆☆☆☆☆ Sound ☆☆☆☆☆

Entertainment ☆☆☆☆☆ Extras ☆☆☆☆

Value ☆☆☆☆

OVERALL ☆☆☆☆

Brassed Off

Price: £19.99
Supplied by: VCI
Type of disc: Single layer, single-sided
No of chapters: 26

Film format(s)/length: 16:9 widescreen / 103 mins
Director: Mark Herman
Starring: Ewan McGregor, Tara Fitzgerald, Pete Postlethwaite
Year made: 1996
Exrtras: Interactive menus; scene index; sub-plots; trailer; interviews; biographies; photo library.

You'd be forgiven for thinking *Brassed Off* has very little going for it. Admit it: you've often picked the box up and read that it's a tale of Grimley Colliery Band's struggle to stay together through the adversity of the miners' strike. Then you've put the box down and bought *Con Air* or *Face/Off* instead. That's your loss. Written and directed with obvious passion, *Brassed Off* is a true gem of a movie. In many ways more of a British movie triumph than *Four Weddings and a Funeral*, it wisely shuns the combination of crowd-pulling stars and recording artists in favour of a much more understated cast, stronger plot and genuinely moving soundtrack. Hilarious in parts and tragic in others, *Brassed Off* is better suited to the DVD format than you would imagine. It's when you hit 'Menu' that the disc surprises, with much more content than you'd expect. Besides the obvious, the DVD features a sub-plots menu, interviews, biographies and a photo library. Not a massive choice – but proof, once again, that the smaller film companies try much much harder than many of the big boys.

FINAL VERDICT

Picture ☆☆☆☆☆ Sound ☆☆☆☆☆

Entertainment ☆☆☆☆☆ Extras ☆☆☆

Value ☆☆☆☆

OVERALL ☆☆☆☆

Bride of Chucky

Price: £19.99
Supplied by: VCI
Type of disc: Single layer, single-sided
No of chapters: 18
Film format(s)/length: 16:9 widescreen / 85 mins
Audio format: Dolby Digital 5.1
Director: Ronny Yu
Starring: Jennifer Tilly, Brad Dourif, Katherine Heigl
Year made: 1998
Extras: Scene access; introduction by Jennifer Tilly; photo library; 4 UK TV spots; *History of Chucky* – synopsis of the first 3 *Child's Play* movies; theatrical trailer; production notes; Jennifer Tilly's location diary; cast and crew biographies and filmographies; commentary by Jennifer Tilly, Brad Dourif and screenwriter Don Mancini; second commentary by director Ronny Yu; *Chucky & Tiffany Do London: International Murder & Mayhem* –

spoof documentary; soundtrack in English.

Of all the franchises in movie history, the story of a child's toy possessed by a serial killer's spirit seems the least likely to run for 4 sequels. Yet here it is, over twelve years after Chucky's first outing in *Child's Play*, he resurfaces (with a bird on his arm) in *Bride of Chucky*. After being sliced, diced and flambéed several times over, serial killer Charles Lee Ray once more inhabits the hideous body of a Chucky doll, all thanks to his new moll Tiffany (Tilly) who is hellbent on getting hitched to the mad midget. Meanwhile, Jade (Heigl) and Jesse (Nick Stabile) are two lovers trying to escape the clutches of Jade's unhinged cop uncle, John Ritter. When the Romeo and Juliet duo agree to take Satan's Ken and Barbie to Ray's grave, it triggers a road movie that lurches between wickedly funny shocks and so-bad-they're-good one liners. The *Scream* factor haunts this film constantly – everything from the poster artwork through the smart tips of the hat to other vintage horror and cute pop culture references. The major laughs come from the pair's murderous bickering, and the blackly comic methods they go to in order to bump off the rest of the cast. By far the better film of the series this time it's clear no-one involved was taking it entirely seriously and the film's all the more entertaining for it. For this Region 2 DVD, Universal and VCI deserve a standing ovation. The sheer amount of material – and great material to boot – they've fitted onto this single-sided, single layer DVD-5 is a revelation and a perfect example to other penny-pinching studios of what can be done. Not one, but two audio commentaries are included: the first from director, Ronny Yu, and the second by the goddess Jennifer Tilly, creepy Brad Dourif and the brains behind the script, Don Mancini. *The History of Chucky* contextualises this movie by summarising the previous 3 films. In a wonderfully fresh idea, star Jennifer Tilly's account of making the film is presented in diary form and lifts the lid on her on-set experiences. Her involvement in this project was huge, including recording a special introduction for the film that showcases her ironic, deadpan wit. *Bride of Chucky* is the best Friday-night-beers-and-pizza movie yet to arrive on DVD and surpasses the efforts made by more 'respectable' film-makers by a long way.

FINAL VERDICT

Picture ☆☆☆☆ Sound ☆☆☆☆
Entertainment ☆☆☆☆ Extras ☆☆☆☆☆
Value ☆☆☆☆
OVERALL ☆☆☆☆

BRIEF ENCOUNTER

Price: £19.99
Supplied by: Carlton Home Entertainment
Type of disc: Single layer, single-sided
No of chapters: 7
Film format(s)/length: 4:3 only (b/w) / 83 mins
Director: David Lean
Starring: Celia Johnson, Trevor Howard
Year made: 1945
Extras: Scene access; in-depth biographies; forthcoming trailers.

Two married people (Johnson and Howard) meet by chance at Milford Junction. Affection turns to love that can never flourish. Quaintly clipped, plummy or cor' blimey cockney accents aside, from polite acquaintance to passionate love, the story remains author Noel Coward's most enduring film. Those accustomed to the clinical DVD reproduction of more recent films will be in for a shock as no attempt has been made to renovate this venerable old lady. She's etched with age, popping, farting and juddering from scene to scene on a Zimmer frame. The signs of age are extenuated with DVD. Blemishes that are barely detectable at the Sunday matinee are outed with the harsh perfection of the format. You also only get the pan and scan 4:3 version and not the original widescreen. The sound is heavy on the treble – a measure taken in the Thirties and Forties to make voices audible in the crummy old picture houses of the day – but as a collectible treasure it's hard to fault this release from Carlton. On this DVD you get lengthy biographies of the 4 key people involved (Howard, Johnson, Coward and Lean) and a look at forthcoming titles (wow!) but it is for the original classic film that people will buy it. Putting classic films of this age onto DVD format without a serious face lift is like shining an arc light on your granny, not a pretty sight. Time is harsh and unforgiving, but fortunately the story remains irresistible. Bit expensive, though.

FINAL VERDICT

Picture ☆☆ Sound ☆ Entertainment ☆☆☆☆
Extras ☆☆ Value ☆☆
OVERALL ☆☆☆

BRINGING OUT THE DEAD

Price: £15.99
Supplied by: Warner Home Video
Type of disc: Dual layer, single-sided
No of chapters: 30
Film format(s)/length: 2.35:1 anamorphic / 121 mins
Audio format: Dolby Digital 5.1

Director: Martin Scorsese
Starring: Nicolas Cage, Patricia Arquette, John Goodman
Year made: 1999
Extras: Scene access; featurette (11 mins); soundtrack in English, French and Italian; subtitles in 9 languages including French, Dutch, Italian, Swedish and Danish.

Here is yet another chapter in the book by Martin Scorsese entitled *Reasons Why I'm the Greatest Director Working in Hollywood Today*. This movie is a simple showcase for a man who has honed his skills by turning out some of the most spectacular movies of the last 30 years, and here Scorsese shows just what spending years making the likes of *Raging Bull* and *Goodfellas* can do for a director. His sleek, stylish and soft perfection screams the question, why can't every Hollywood director be this good? Telling the tale of New York paramedic Frank Pierce (Cage), *Bringing Out The Dead* is a fierce look at how playing God can be the undoing of a man. Pierce is a man who has touched euphoria by knowing he's responsible for saving peoples' lives. But recently Frank has been unable to obtain this emotion. Haunted by the ghost of a girl he could not save, and the fact that he hasn't helped anyone for far too long, Frank's boundaries begin to blur and he must decide if the ultimate redemption comes in saving someone, or allowing them to die. There are some outstanding displays of talent going on here, in particular from the principal cast. Cage has a gentle believability that could have flopped in the hands of any other actor, and Ving Rhames proves that he is a law unto himself when it comes to producing the goods. Paul Schrader's script is really *Diet Taxi Driver*, lacking much of the steely intensity found in his 1976 script, but the real praise should go to Scorsese. He keeps the pace fast without being frantic, and the visuals sensational without stinging the eyes. The whole thing works because the right elements are in place. Another director could have taken this inspiring but ultimately depressing plot to the wrong level, but Scorsese keeps the pot boiling, and serves up a delicious treat. On basic DVD levels of sound and vision, then the job is well taken care of; yet this is a Warner disc, and so it's something of a wonder that there are any extras at all. An 11-minute featurette is your lot, and while this is vaguely informative, you still can't help but wish that one of these days Scorsese would get around to doing a DVD commentary.

FINAL VERDICT

Picture ☆☆☆☆☆ Sound ☆☆☆☆☆
Entertainment ☆☆☆☆☆ Extras ☆☆ Value ☆☆☆

OVERALL ☆☆☆☆

BROKEN ARROW

Price: £19.99
Supplied by: 20th Century Fox Home Entetainment
Type of disc: Dual layer, single-sided
No of chapters: 22
Film format(s)/length: 16:9 widescreen enhanced / 104 mins
Audio format: Dolby Digital 5.1
Director: John Woo
Starring: John Travolta, Christian Slater, Samantha Mathis
Year made: 1996
Extras: Scene access; theatrical trailer; soundtrack in English, German and French; subtitles in 11 languages; subtitles for the hearing impaired in English.

Take two of Hollywood's sexiest leading men, throw in the most influential action director alive what you get is nothing short of dynamite. *Broken Arrow* is a high-octane action flick that is carried off in style. Amidst the impressive gun-fights and explosions, the struggle between US Air Force pilots Vic Deakins (Travolta) and Riley Hale (Slater) is the forefront of the entertainment. Both rivals and partners, the two are given the task of test running a B3 Stealth bomber carrying live nuclear missiles. Halfway through the mission, Travolta has other plans; turning rogue and sabotaging the mission. To prevent Hale from interfering, he ejects him from the plane, before crashing it so that his partners can collect the 'broken arrows'. Deakin is now in a position to blackmail the US government…that is unless they pay him, 'millions of dollars' – you can just picture Travolta's pinkie at the corner of his mouth, *à la* Dr Evil. However, Hale survives and subsequently teams up with Utah ranger Terry Carmichael (Samantha Mathis), the token female and love interest for Slater. The script is basically an excuse for large amounts of gunplay, action and pure adrenalin adventure – which Woo expertly delivers and does so by the bucket load. As for the disc, the picture quality is excellent and so is sound, but the DVD suffers from a poor showing of extras. Aside from the obligatory subtitles there is little else to choose from. Considering the calibre of the actors and that the director is a living legend, this is inexcusable. If you already have this on video then you might want to think twice before buying the DVD too.

FINAL VERDICTICT

Picture ☆☆☆☆ Sound ☆☆☆☆
Entertainment ☆☆☆☆ Extras ☆ Value ☆☆

OVERALL ☆☆☆

THE BRYLCREAM BOYS

Price: £15.99
Supplied by: Guerilla Films
Type of disc: Single layer, single-sided
No of chapters: 12
Film format(s)/length: 4:3 regular / 102 mins
Audio format: Dolby Surround
Director: Terence Ryan
Starring: Gabriel Byrne, Bill Campbell, John Gordon
Sinclair **Year made:** 1996
Extras: Scene access; documentary *From Past to Present* (32 mins); theatrical trailer.

When Bill Campbell's WWII plane is shot down by the Germans, he and his crew land in enemy territory. Imagine their surprise when they discover that: a) they are in neutral Ireland, not France; and b) they are imprisoned anyway. Worse still, the camp is shared between the Allies and the Germans… Released in the UK 3 years ago and having struggled to find a distributor, *The Brylcream Boys* surprisingly reveals itself to be a small gem of a film, with a great cast and plenty of gentle humour. It's a tragedy that the DVD is not widescreen – unlike the clips used in the essential accompanying 32-minute documentary. Although the source print looks great, it is somewhat marred by heavy digital compression. Meanwhile, Dolby Digital users should make sure they switch their amps manually, this is because sound which is okay defaults to stereo – but it is infact coded in Prologic, so you should get something out of more than two speakers if you make the effort!

FINAL VERDICT
Picture ☆☆ Sound ☆☆ Entertainment ☆☆☆☆
Extras ☆☆☆☆ Value ☆☆☆☆
OVERALL ☆☆☆

BUENA VISTA SOCIAL CLUB

Price: £19.99
Supplied by: VCI
Type of disc: Dual layer, single-sided
No of chapters: 25
Film format(s)/length: 16:9 widescreen enhanced / 100 mins
Audio format: Dolby Digital 5.1
Director: Wim Wenders
Starring: Ry Cooder, Ibrahim Ferrer, Reuben Gonzales
Year made: 1999
Extras: Scene access; director's commentary; deleted scene; theatrical trailer.

In 1998, Ry Cooder travelled to his native Cuba to record an album with Ibrahim Ferrer and the members of the Buena Vista Social Club. Along with a small film crew, director Wim Wenders documented the recording of the album as well as an international tour that ended in Carnegie Hall, New York. It doesn't really matter whether Cuban music is your thing, as *BVSC* is a superb document of young life under communist rule. Interspersed with performance footage as well as filming of the actual recording session, Wenders's film manages to capture an essence of Havana which is long since gone, and tell a story about both human endeavour and musical growth. Both the music and the narrative support one another perfectly. The director's commentary is one of the most heartfelt you could find, though the few other special features pale in comparison.

FINAL VERDICT
Picture ☆☆☆ Sound ☆☆☆☆☆
Entertainment ☆☆☆☆ Extras ☆☆☆
Value ☆☆☆
OVERALL ☆☆☆☆

A BUG'S LIFE

Price: £19.99
Supplied by: Disney Home Video
Type of disc: Single layer, double-sided
No of chapters: 37
Film format(s)/length: 1.33.1 regular (side A) and 2.35:1 widescreen (side B) / 91 mins
Audio format: Dolby Digital 5.1
Director: John Lasseter
Starring the voices of: David Foley, Kevin Spacey, Mike McShane
Year made: 1998
Extras: Scene access; 2 sets of side-splitting 'outtakes'; 1997 Academy Award-winning short *Geri's Game*; English subtitles and English closed captions.

From the moment the first leaf of spring falls into the stream, you can tell that with *A Bug's Life* you're in for a piece of spectacular entertainment unlike anything you've seen before. In fact, you haven't been able to appreciate just what the real benefits of watching films on Digital Versatile Disc are until you've watched this. That's because *A Bug's Life* is the world's first DVD movie created directly from the digital source. This means that, instead of converting the picture and sound information from film, the creators went back to the original computer data and transferred it directly onto CD. They even converted the original format to full-screen, which meant re-animating whole scenes to give each frame in full. So this is a very special disc to own indeed. However, if all this technical gobbledegook means nothing to you, and you just want to be wowed from your sofa, all you need to know is that the latest offering from Pixar is one hell of a cool cartoon. *A Bug's Life* is basically a 6-legged version of *The Magnificent Seven*. Flik is an ant who dares to stand up for himself when the colony is raided by a gang of grasshoppers. An over-enthusiastic but clumsy inventor, (very handy with a blade of grass and a drop of dew) he accidentally ruins the colony's annual offering to Hopper, and is forced out to the city to round up a vicious gang of warriors to fight their oppressors before the last leaf of autumn falls. Unfortunately, he returns with a raddled band of circus performers, including Heimlich the greedy German caterpillar, Francis the violently male lady-bird, (voiced by Dennis Leary), Rosie the caring Black Widow and best of all, the two mental earwigs, Tuck and Roll, voiced almost unrecognisably by *Whose Line is it Anyway* regular Mike McShane. Without a doubt, it's Kevin Spacey's charismatic villain that steals the show, dominating the CGI screen with every scaly scary moment. The story unrolls with inevitably hilarious consequences, and by this point you've come to love the characters so much that every little twist and turn in their lives has you cheering or laughing along with them. Okay, so at times the creators are a little over-indulgent with the syrup, especially when the little ant princess Dot comes on screen, but there's enough here to keep both kids and adults reaching for the popcorn till Doomsday. When *Toy Story*, the precursor to *A Bug's Life*, first exploded onto our screens, it may have seemed a hard act to follow, but this film definitely supersedes the adventure of Woody, Buzz and co (at least until *Toy Story 2* arrives on DVD). Just pay £19.99 for this £29 million movie and you'll discover that *A Bug's Life* really is an epic DVD of miniature proportions.

FINAL VERDICT

Picture ☆☆☆☆☆ Sound ☆☆☆☆☆
Entertainment ☆☆☆☆☆ Extras ☆☆☆☆☆
Value ☆☆☆☆☆
OVERALL ☆☆☆☆☆

BUGSY

Price: £19.99
Supplied by: DVD World (01705 796662)
Type of disc: Single layer, single-sided
No of chapters: 32
Film format(s)/length: 1.85:1 widescreen (enhanced for widescreen TVs) / 131mins
Audio format: Dolby Surround
Director: Barry Levinson

Starring: Warren Beatty, Annette Bening, Harvey Keitel
Year made: 1991
Extras: Multiple language subtitles; theatrical and DVD trailers; cast and director filmographies.

The real life story of how Benjamin 'Bugsy' Siegel romanced Hollywood actresses, created Las Vegas, but was ultimately undone by his own ego, must have seemed tailor-made for Warren Beatty. Upon its release, *Bugsy* received no less than 10 Academy Award nominations, including best film, best actor and best script. Although it won only in relatively minor categories such as best set, it did win the Los Angeles Film Critics' nod as best film. It's not difficult to see why, with an intelligent, interesting script which includes neat lines such as Bening to Beatty: "Why don't you go outside and jerk yourself a soda." It's clever and fun, although Beatty is perhaps a little too old and well-known to be entirely convincing as a psychopathic gangster. Such a high-class production is ideal for DVD format. The sharpness of the picture, the vividness of the colours, an immaculate sound-field; all these come across so much better than on VHS. Unfortunately, while the majority of the picture is a delight, there are the occasional scenes – such as a mist enshrouded train station – which is a challenge to DVD's resolution and the encoders don't appear to have tried overly hard to get around this. Further evidence of a somewhat lax approach to DVD conversions comes with the number of extras. There are filmographies for all the 6 principal actors, plus the director, but as these are simply film listings with no accompanying text it's hardly anything to rave about. The theatrical trailer is a welcome addition, as is a short DVD promo, but why no 'Making of' documentary, or promo interviews which almost certainly accompanied the film's launch? *Bugsy's* a lavish production which benefits from the high quality of DVD, but needs more extras. ~

FINAL VERDICT

Picture ☆☆☆☆ Sound ☆☆☆
Entertainment ☆☆☆ Extras ☆☆ Value ☆☆☆
OVERALL ☆☆☆

BULLITT

Price: £15.99
Supplied by: DVD Plus (0800 389 2875)
Type of disc: Single layer, single-sided
No of chapters: 22
Film format(s)/length: 16:9 widescreen / 109 mins
Audio Format: Dolby Surround
Director: Peter Yates
Starring: Steve McQueen, Jacqueline Bissett, Don

Gordon
Year made: 1968
Extras: Production notes; scene access; original 1968 trailer;15 minute featurette, *Steve McQueen's Commitment to Reality*.

These days the character of the bad-tempered, rebellious cop is an over-used cliché, however when *Bullitt* came out it wasn't. Detective Frank Bullitt (McQueen) is a hard-working detective assigned to protect a mob witness, only to have things go horribly wrong when the gangster is shot and killed. Bullitt sets out to find the men responsible, taking on his superiors along the way. *Bullitt* is a film people either worship as a classic or dismiss as boring. This is down to the attempt by director and cast to produce a 'realistic' film where instead of just repeated gun fights and car chases we get a picture of the lead's whole life, his family background and his deep-seated doubts as to the value of his occupation. *Bullitt* does, however, contain what is arguably one of the best car chases of any film then or since. The reason for this is explained in a 15-minute feature entitled *Steve McQueen's Commitment to Reality* in which we go behind-the-scenes on *Bullitt* and learn that all the driving sequences in the film and many of the other stunts were undertaken by McQueen himself, thus allowing some close-up detailed camera shots that wouldn't have been possible with a stunt double. In addition to this documentary feature the DVD also contains production notes and the theatrical trailer. While this isn't unusual for even UK DVDs, the interesting thing is that since its the original 1968 trailer, watching it shows just how much the cinema has changed since then. Rather than fast cuts and stirring music the trailer is basically just several long sequences taken direct from the movie with some really corny voice-over! As a package, *Bullitt* gives good value for money and Steve McQueen fans shouldn't miss it.

FINAL VERDICT

Picture ☆☆☆☆☆ Sound ☆☆☆☆
Entertainment ☆☆☆☆☆
Extras ☆☆☆☆☆ Value ☆☆☆☆☆
OVERALL ☆☆☆☆☆

THE CABLE GUY

Price: £19.99
Company: Columbia TriStar
Type of disc: Single layer, single-sided
No of chapters: 20
Film format(s)/length: 16:9 widescreen / 92 mins
Audio format: Dolby Digital 5.1
Director: Ben Stiller

Starring: Jim Carrey, Matthew Broderick, Leslie Mann
Year made: 1996
Extras: Scene selection; theatrical trailer; DVD trailer; filmographies.

Depending on who you believe, *The Cable Guy* is either the only blip in Jim Carrey's otherwise brilliant career or a severely underrated black comedy. The truth lies somewhere in the middle. Carrey plays a more sinister version of his trademark rubber-faced lunatic who forces his way into the life of a new cable customer (Broderick), only to turn nasty when his 'friendship' is rejected. Veering wildly between slapstick and dark satire, standout moments include a jousting contest at a medieval theme restaurant and a demented karaoke jam. Unfortunately the script tends to overstate its point about the potentially harmful effects of television, and this lessens the impact of the film as a whole. The DVD looks and sounds stunning, giving tremendous detail and colour to the picture, and making good use of surround sound. As far as extras go, you get the theatrical trailer, filmographies and standard scene selection but little of any real interest.

FINAL VERDICT

Picture ☆☆☆☆ Sound ☆☆☆☆ Entertainment ☆☆☆
Extras ☆ Value ☆☆☆
OVERALL ☆☆☆

CADDYSHACK

Price: £15.99
Supplied by: DVD World (01705 796662)
Type of disc: Single layer, single-sided
No of chapters: 28
Film format(s)/length: 1.85:1 widescreen / 94 mins
Audio format: Mono
Director: Harold Ramis
Starring: Chevy Chase, Rodney Dangerfield, Bill Murray
Year made: 1980
Extras: Scene access; mono soundtrack in English, French and Italian; multilingual subtitles; English and Italian subtitles for the hearing impaired.

Chevy Chase is renowned for clowning around in films where you find yourself either loving or loathing the him. This time, the action mostly takes place on the golf course and shows us the true meaning of crazy golf. While Chase, Dangerfield and Ted Knight concentrate on a battle between the snobs and slobs of golfing supremacy, the insane Bill Murray takes on the role of eradicating the gophers that seek to rule the golf course themselves. The humour is in the same vein as the *Police Academy* films, which is mainly down to Bill Murray as he goes totally overboard in his own personal war against the gophers. In true style of the comedy film genre, you would expect to find some outtakes and various extras on how the film was made, even perhaps including some credit for the gopher puppet makers, but sadly there's such inclusion in this weak DVD package. There's not even a trailer of the film to be seen, or still film clips for that matter, instead you simply get a scene access menu and language selection, which also offers a Warner Brothers website address if you are keen enough to explore further. The picture quality is standard DVD quality, but the sound is only available in mono, giving that annoying muffled sound to the dialogue and a tinny soundtrack. Although the extras fall short of what you expect, the film does provide good clean humour, and will appeal to many viewers, especially true Chase or Murray fans.

FINAL VERDICT

Picture ☆☆ Sound ☆ Entertainment ☆☆☆
Extras ☆ Value ☆☆
OVERALL ☆☆

THE CAINE MUTINY

Price: £19.99
Supplied by: Columbia TriStar Home Video
Type of disc: Dual layer, single-sided
No of chapters: 28
Film format(s)/length: 16:9 widescreen enhanced / 120 mins
Audio format: Mono
Director: Edward Dmytryk
Starring: Humphrey Bogart, Robert Francis, Fred MacMurray
Year made: 1954
Extras: Scene access; theatrical trailer; filmographies (brief); poster gallery; soundtrack in French, German, Italian and Spanish; subtitles in 20 languages.

Nominated for 7 Oscars, *The Caine Mutiny* tells the sea-worthy tale of a World War II minesweeper, *The Caine*, and its mentally unstable captain (Bogart). Having endured numerous paranoid outbursts from their Captain, one of which would have led them to a watery grave, the crew finally live up to the title and mutiny during a Pacific typhoon. The most impressive facet of the production is Stanley Roberts' sparkling and intelligent screenplay, which makes up for the questionable special effects. MacMurray is the unsung star as the dry humoured author/seaman who first diagnoses the Captain's condition. The picture has been impressively restored, but the movie shows tell-tale signs of its age as the image looks grainy – but it's still a huge step up from your VHS copy. The sound is also excellent, as there

have been no crude attempts to graft a DD5.1 mix onto it, and – thank goodness – we have the original soundtrack in pristine condition. There is a short theatrical trailer, a few still shots and some very brief filmographies. Given the high asking price, this would seem overpriced, but at least a good deal of attention has been paid to the print by the ever-impressive Sony Pictures. This is a classic war movie that has been much improved through the technology of DVD.

FINAL VERDICT

Picture ☆☆☆ Sound ☆☆☆ Entertainment ☆☆☆☆
Extras ☆☆ Value ☆☆☆
OVERALL ☆☆☆

CALFORNIA MAN

Price: £15.99
Supplied by: DVDplus (www.dvdplus.co.uk)
Type of disc: Single layer, single-sided
No of chapters: 13
Film format(s)/length: 1.85:1 widescreen / 85 mins
Audio format: Dolby Surround
Director: Les Mayfield
Starring: Sean Astin, Brendan Fraser, Pauly Shore
Year made: 1992
Extras: Scene access; soundtracks in French and Italian; subtitles in French and English; subtitles for the hearing impaired in English.

This is one movie that hopes you aren't going to be asking too many questions. Such as can you really find stone-age men in your back garden? Does being frozen really keep you a state of suspended animation, and how does Pauly Shore actually survive in the real world? Suspend your disbelief, however, and you're left with what is actually a very enjoyable film. At its heart it is just another high school, want to be cool, movie but Brendan Fraser's caveman antics carry off the twist with a smile. Disc-wise, things are not so good. The print is clear and the sound is what you would expect but where are the extras? This isn't the kind of film that will wow you with its crystal clear effects or deafen you with digital sound, so it's hard to justify the DVD price tag.

FINAL VERDICT

Picture ☆☆ Sound ☆☆ Entertainment ☆☆☆☆
Extras ☆ Value ☆
OVERALL ☆☆

CALIGULA

Price: £19.99
Supplied by: Metrodrome Video
Type of disc: Single layer, single-sided
No of chapters: 18

Film format(s)/length: 4:3 regular / 90 mins
Audio format: Stereo
Director: Tinto Brass
Starring: Malcolm McDowell, Peter O'Toole, Teresa Ann Savoy
Year made: 1980
Extras: Scene access

A full 20 years after its release, controversy still shrouds the Penthouse portrait of the astonishing excesses and perversions of Caligula Caesar, irrepressible and power-crazed Emperor of Rome. Peter O'Toole commands the all-star cast, turning in a deliciously vile performance. McDowell plays Caligula, but his Shakespearean efforts rapidly descend into amateur theatrics, unwittingly complementing the terrifically slapdash production. A steady stream of dramatic incidents (incest, childbirth, suicide, orgies, frenzied stabbings and the like), interlinked with what could be mistaken for lost amateur footage from a female nudist colony, loosely constitute the film's structure. The shenanigans reach Pythonesque proportions during the sensational mass execution, in which huge Flymo blades mow the heads off traitors buried in the garden. Watch out for the enormous phallic cakes too; they're a real eye popper. The most outrageous thing of all, however, is just how bad every aspect of the DVD itself is.

FINAL VERDICT
Picture ☆ Sound ☆ Entertainment ☆☆
Extras ☆ Value ☆
OVERALL ☆

CANDYMAN

Price: £19.99
Supplied by: Columbia TriStar
Type of disc: Single layer, single-sided
No of chapters: 20
Film format(s)/length: 1.85:1 anamorphic / 95 mins
Audio format: Stereo
Director: Bernard Rose
Starring: Virginia Madsen, Tony Todd, Xander Berkeley
Year made: 1992
Extras: Scene access; talent profiles; theatrical trailer; subtitles in 8 languages; soundtrack in English and German.

Say his name 5 times into the mirror and the Candyman will appear to bludgeon you to death with his bloody hook! It may sound like the stuff of tacky horror, but this tale of urban legends and myth is actually a highly enjoyable horror film based on a short story by the hellraising Clive Barker. It's just a shame that no attention has been paid to the disc.

The sound is bog-standard stereo and the extras appear to be added as an afterthought. What's even more amusing is that the back of the box boasts 'animated menus' which are nothing more than clips from the film playing in the background. This film is certainly well worth watching, but there is nothing to justify buying it again if you already own the video. In fact, this disc is almost as much of a tragedy as the existence of the sequels!

FINAL VERDICT
Picture ☆☆☆ Sound ☆ Entertainment ☆☆☆
Extras ☆ Value ☆☆
OVERALL ☆☆☆

CAN'T HARDLY WAIT

Price: £19.99
Supplied by: Columbia TriStar Home Video
Type of disc: Single layer, single sided
No of chapters: 28
Film format(s)/length: 16:9 widescreen enhanced / 96 mins
Audio format: Dolby Digital 5.1
Directors: Deborah Kaplan and Harry Elfont
Starring: Jennifer Love Hewitt, Ethan Embry, Seth Green
Year made: 1998
Extras: Scene access; film-maker's commentary; Smash Mouth music video 'I Can't Get Enough of You Baby'; theatrical trailer; DVD trailer; incomplete filmographies; tiny photo gallery; soundtrack in German (DD 5.1); subtitles in 15 languages.

There's a big party on graduation night and lovesick dolt Preston (Embry) plans to use the occasion to confess his love for the gravity defying Amanda Beckett (Hewitt). Oh, sorry – with hilarious consequences! For an unremarkable movie, *Can't Hardly Wait* does unusually well on the extra materials front, especially for a British disc. There's a full commentary, which, considering the artistic limitations of making a standard house party picture, miraculously avoids being pointless and dull. Smash Mouth's music video is of variable merit depending on your own taste, or lack thereof, but is basically podgy beach bums performing predictable MTV rock in a predictable manner. There are also a handful of filmographies, but a glaring oversight, betraying the indifferent way these things are produced, means the film's leading male, Ethan Embry, goes without an entry! Still, on the outside chance that this is really your kind of movie, the extras and admirable anamorphic picture will make it a worthwhile collector's edition.

FINAL VERDICT

Picture ☆☆☆☆☆ Sound ☆☆☆☆
Entertainment ☆☆ Extras ☆☆☆☆ Value ☆☆☆
OVERALL ☆☆☆

CARLITO'S WAY

Price: £19.99
Supplied by: Universal
Type of disc: Dual layer, single-sided
No of chapters: 16
Film format(s)/length: 2.35:1 letterbox / 138 mins
Audio format: Dolby Digital 5.1
Director: Brian De Palma
Starring: Al Pacino, Sean Penn, Penelope Ann Miller
Year made: 1993
Extras: Scene access; production notes; lead actors
and director bios and filmography; theatrical trailer;
soundtrack in English and French; subtitles in 8 lan-
guages.

The surviving directors of the New Hollywood
of the Seventies – Coppola, Scorsese, De Palma,
Bogdanovich *et al* – never seem to move their cameras
all that fast these days. Could be all that dead weight
baggage of history, peer expectations and the desire to
create conscientious films despite audiences' palates
being deadened by MTV-on-fast-forward style movie
making. Those directors have a weary integrity that
the hero of *Carlito's Way* knows all too well. When
former drug kingpin Carlito Brigante (Pacino) is
released after 5 years, he finds a lot has changed. He's
in the middle of the hedonistic, coked up Seventies
and old associates refuse to believe he wants to go
legitimate as he declares. Carlito wants to live his
dream away from crime and with old girlfriend Kate
(Miller), but his anachronistic sense of honour and
loyalty to his unstable lawyer (Penn) drags him forever downwards. De Palma, a man who averages about
two good films per decade, keeps his credibility intact
with this symphonically directed, impeccably acted
and compellingly told (if not overly original) movie.
Strange how those Seventies film-makers are also slow
to pick up on the benefits DVDs can have for their
films, considering how much it contributes to the
cult of the director. Where is De Palma's input? Audio
is all encompassing and suitably heavy as the bullets
start to fly, but the picture is merely letterbox when
we want and expect anamorphic. Special features are
a disappointment. Buy the DVD for the film, but not
for the extras.

FINAL VERDICT

Picture ☆☆☆ Sound ☆☆☆☆ Entertainment ☆☆☆☆
Extras ☆☆ Value ☆☆

OVERALL ☆☆☆☆

CARRIE

Price: £19.99
Supplied by: Warner Home Video
Type of disc: Dual layer, single-sided
No of chapters: 32
Film format(s)/length: 1.85:1 widescreen / 98 mins
Audio format: Dolby Digital 5.1
Director: Brian De.Palma
Starring: Sissy Spacek, John Travolta, Piper Laurie
Year made: 1976
Extras: Scene access; original theatrical trailer; 8-page
booklet ; German, Spanish, French and Italian mono
soundtracks; multilingual subtitles.

Though everything in the Seventies was terrifying – clothes, music and boys' haircuts spring immediately to mind – it was Hollywood's prolific output
of horror that best typifies the decade's scariness.
Those that grew up in the Betamax era will recall the
row upon row of huge videos that formed the horror
section down at the local video shop, all readily
dished out to obviously underage viewers keen to
have the living daylights scared out of them while
their parents were on their backs after swigging a bottle of Strongbow. The truth is that many of those
derivative slasher flicks were not scary at all. Let's face
it, at that age even the bloke off *Magpie* was enough
to send slippered feet scurrying behind the sofa.
Carrie's certainly not as terrifying as you'll remember,
but it remains a tense, stylish horror film that, with a
lick of paint here and there, would stand head and
shoulders above many contemporary aspiring knee-
tremblers. Those that think girl power started with 5
manufactured tarts are in for a shock. Relentlessly
bullied Carrie White – expertly played by the Oscar-
nominated Spacek – discovers shortly before her
prom night that she's telekinetic – that is, able to
move objects by the power of thought. Which is a
spot of bad luck for her tormentors, as she enacts savage revenge against those that ridicule her. Despite
the '18' certificate, the film's no gore-fest, preferring
instead to tease the viewer with minimal shocks en
route to the show-stopping finale. *Carrie's* no spring
chicken – indeed, since John Travolta was 'introduced' in this film, he's become a global megastar and
spent almost decade in the gutter before rising,
phoenix-like, back to his previous status, and all in
time for this DVD re-issue. For a film that collected
its key to the door two years ago, Carrie looks
remarkably fresh, with an extraordinarily sharp picture. The score, too, is as clean as a whistle, with the

Psycho-inspired shrills managing to shock, even though they're never unexpected. Enjoy laughing at the original theatrical trailer – mainly because it's the only on-disc extra, but also because it is so bad you can't imagine how anyone could have been convinced enough by it to trek to the cinema. The disc is accompanied by an 8-page booklet which reveals a little behind the film, but in truth it's a pretty lightweight affair. A disappointment considering the movie's heritage and stature among horror buffs. All in, though, *Carrie*'s a decent DVD. Despite offering little in the way of added value, it's a horror classic that deserves to be a part of anyone's collection. And it's almost worth the price alone to marvel at the unattractiveness of the supporting high school 'beauties'. Those, most certainly, weren't the days.

FINAL VERDICT

Picture ☆☆☆☆ Sound ☆☆☆☆
Entertainment ☆☆☆☆ Extras ☆☆ Value ☆☆☆
OVERALL ☆☆☆

CARRY ON AGAIN DOCTOR

Price: £9.99
Supplied by: Cinema Club
Type of disc: Single layer, single-sided
No of chapters: 16
Film format(s)/length: 4:3 regular / 85 mins
Audio format: Mono
Director: Gerald Thomas
Starring: Sid James, Kenneth Williams, Jim Dale
Year made: 1969
Extras: Scene access

There's one thing that can be said for all *Carry On* films – they're instantly watchable. No matter how many times they are shown on TV, or get re-released on video and now DVD, you just can't help but laugh at the endless double-entendres and crass jokes – *Carry On* films are part of our heritage! The latest *Carry On* DVD is a bit of a disappointment, though. Not because of the film, which is packed with all the trademark *Carry On* calamities and wisecracks, but because of the extras you'll find on the DVD – or won't find, as is the case with this disc! Go to the menu screen and all you'll get is the choice of 'play' or 'scene select', although there must be hours of behind-the-scenes *Carry On* footage and fascinating documentaries. We really should demand more for our money, but at £9.99 you just can't go wrong!

FINAL VERDICT

Picture ☆☆☆ Sound ☆☆☆ Entertainment ☆☆☆☆
Extras ☆ Value ☆☆
OVERALL ☆☆☆

CARRY ON CAMPING

Price: £19.99
Supplied by: Carlton Video
Type of disc: Dual layer, single-sided
No of chapters: 15
Film format(s)/length: 16:9 widescreen / 86 mins
Audio format: Mono
Director: Gerald Thomas
Starring: Sid James, Kenneth Williams, Barbara Windsor
Year made: 1969
Extras: Scene access; 50-minute *What's a Carry On?* documentary – a 40th Anniversary look at the series; biographies; subtitles in English.

Sid and Bernie struggle to get it up. Snigger. Barbara keeps popping out. Giggle. Kenneth Williams says "Oooh Matron" a lot. And Terry Scott takes a shot up the arse. Ahem. Yes, it's business as usual, in this celluloid seaside postcard which should list the double entendre among its principle cast, such is its reliance on thinly veiled sexism and risqué set-pieces. The advantage of the *Carry On* series is that you know exactly what you're getting. Once you've slid it in – the disc, mind – *Carry On Camping* delivers a fair dose of laughs, the odd tit and plenty of implied rudeness, though the family-friendly PG certificate gives some indication of the level of smut. By no means the best of the bunch it is, nonetheless, perfect Sunday evening viewing. You'll smile more than you should, thanks mainly to the inimitable Sid James and his infectious yak-yakking. There's little to complain about image-wise – after all, it's not as if the film relies on visual trickery to engage the viewer, with nary a special effect in sight, unless you count the obvious 'they're not really driving' driving bits. With its minimal demands on the hardware, *Carry On Camping*'s not the obvious choice for a DVD release. But Carlton has managed to bolster the original movie's meagre 88 minutes with the superficial documentary *What's a Carry On?* – a whimsical trip down memory lane, complete with clips from all of the *Carry On* movies and interviews with those behind-the-films. The censored scenes highlight the laughable censorship laws prevalent in the Seventies and go some way to justifying the documentary's self-indulgence. Comprehensive biographies complete the extras. As the other DVD trailers – thankfully not flagged as an extra – prove, Carlton doesn't have the best back-catalogue to play with, so the care and attention so obviously lavished on this first *Carry On* release is welcome. It'll be interesting to see what features on subsequent releases. But let's not unduly concern ourselves with that. *Carry On Camping* is a decent disc, with a healthy amount of supplementary material. Not a must by any means – but certainly miles better than a lot of Hollywood's dross.

FINAL VERDICT

Picture ☆☆☆ Sound ☆☆☆
Entertainment ☆☆☆ Extras ☆☆☆☆ Value ☆☆☆
OVERALL ☆☆☆

CASABLANCA

Price: £15.99
Supplied by: Warner Home Video
Type of disc: Dual layer, single-sided
No of chapters: 36
Film format(s)/length: 1.33:1 regular / 98 mins
Audio format: Mono
Director: Michael Curtiz
Starring: Humphrey Bogart, Ingrid Bergman, Paul Hendreid
Year made: 1942
Extras: Scene access; interactive menu; trailer; *You Must Remember This* featurette; soundtrack in English, French and Italian; subtitles in 10 languages.

Set against the backdrop of espionage in wartime Morocco, *Casablanca* is quite possibly the most perfect movie ever made. It encompasses every element that has made Hollywood the greatest movie factory in the world, and it even manages to include the contemporary ingredient of having a soundtrack that is almost as popular as the movie. Love, treachery, larger than life characters and a deadly setting; *Casablanca's* influences can be found in every movie from *Star Wars* to *Ferris Bueller's Day Off*, and it's packed with more memorable quotes than you can count. Telling the ultimate tale of lost love, Bogart plays Rick, the cynical owner of Rick's Café, meeting place for all European refugees during the German occupation of France. One of these refugees is Czech resistance leader Victor Laszlo (Henreid) who is married to Rick's old flame Ilsa (Bergman), and his only chance of escaping Casablanca alive is with Rick's help. Rick, however, sticks his head out for no one, but when the fate of the woman he still loves rests in his reluctant hands, he must begin to question his morals. Black and white, 4:3…but so what? With a film this good, the story is much more important than the format. Even the most stubborn colour elitist could not fail to be charmed. *Casablanca* is released by Warner with reluctant pride. It gets more extras than most of their DVD releases, but with just an updated trailer and 40-minute documentary, it's not

enough for one of the greatest movies of all time.

FINAL VERDICT

Picture ☆☆☆ Sound ☆☆ Entertainment ☆☆☆☆
Extras ☆☆☆ Value ☆☆☆☆
OVERALL ☆☆☆☆

CASINO

Price: £19.99
Supplied by: Columbia TriStar Home Video
Type of disc: Dual layer, single-sided
No of chapters: 16
Film format(s)/length: 2.35:1 letterbox / 171 mins
Audio format: Dolby Digital 5.1
Director: Martin Scorsese
Starring: Robert De Niro, Sharon Stone, Joe Pesci
Year made: 1995
Extras: Scene access; multiple languages ; multilingual subtitles; trailer; production notes; cast and director biographies (page after page of text screens).

Unfairly panned by some critics as being 'diet *Goodfellas*', *Casino* is a very different film to Scorsese's previous underworld epic. Where *Goodfellas* looked at the mob from the bottom, concentrating on low-level thugs and enforcers, *Casino* takes place in the high-rolling world of Seventies Las Vegas. De Niro is Sam 'Ace' Rothstein, a clinical gambling genius who is tasked by his mob bosses with running – ie, robbing – the Tangiers casino. Pesci tags along as Sam's buddy Nicky Santoro, another of his pocket-sized psychos, and Stone gives a career-best turn as Sam's hedonistic wife Ginger. The story follows the intertwined fortunes of the trio over the course of a decade, as they rise and, inevitably, fall. Scorsese films the mob-run Vegas of the Seventies as a glowing neon wonderland of gold-plated excess, backed by an almost continuous soundtrack of hits. Ranging between dazzling technical exercise (the scenes showing how the casino works are reminiscent of the Steadicam opening of *Goodfellas*) and near-documentary, *Casino* sweeps the viewer along in its complex narrative, so almost 3 hours flash past in no time. In among the glitz is Scorsese's trademark sudden, brutal violence that reminds you just who these people are. Pesci is the instigator of most of it, but the last few minutes will leave the unprepared squirming in their seats. It's not a good time to be eating, especially if ketchup is involved. Ultimately, *Casino* is a story about greed. Ginger's greed is for money, Nicky's for power, and it destroys them both. Even Sam, the most complex character in the film, is consumed by greed, though in his case it's a greed for perfection. Obsessed with turning 'his' casino into a perfectly functioning money-making machine – no detail is too small for him to care about, right down to the number of blueberries in a muffin – he gradually loses sight of why he was placed in charge, which eventually puts him in conflict with his mafia bosses. The rich visuals are perfectly captured on the DVD, with colours so vibrant you could almost be there rolling dice at the craps table or having your head squeezed in a vice. The extras are there too, but considering the sheer scope of the film they're a bit lightweight. It's about time that Scorsese himself, a world-renowned motormouth on the subject of films and film-making, was approached to do commentaries. Apart from the relative paucity of extras, *Casino* is everything you could want from a DVD, an enthralling story superbly presented. It may not be Scorsese's best film, but that still makes it better than 99 per cent of the other movies out there.

FINAL VERDICT

Picture ☆☆☆☆☆ Sound ☆☆☆☆

Entertainment ☆☆☆☆☆ Extras ☆☆☆ Value ☆☆☆

OVERALL ☆☆☆☆

CHAIN REACTION

Price: £19.99

Supplied by: 20th Century Fox Home Entertainment

Type of disc: Dual layer, single-sided

No of chapters: 24

Film format(s)/length: 16:9 widescreen enhanced / 102 min

Audio format: Dolby Digital 5.1

Director: Andrew Davis

Starring: Keanu Reeves, Morgan Freeman, Rachael Weisz

Year made: 1996

Extras: Scene access; *Making of Chain Reaction* featurette; subtitles in 11 languages; subtitles for the hearing impaired in Dutch.

Denise Richards may have been the world's most improbable nuclear scientist in *The World is Not Enough*, but Reeves (who plays Eddie Kasalivich) was the first to go against the grain of his previous roles. A present day setting sees a small group of scientists, privately funded by mysterious bureaucrat Paul Shannon (Freeman), develop a revolutionary new source of energy. But where the group wish to share their discovery with the world, an unknown organisation will stop at nothing to prevent them from divulging the information. Cover-ups, high-tech espionage and murders ensue shortly after the group's celebrations; resulting in wonderkid Kasalivich and fellow scientist Dr Lily Sinclair (Rachael Weisz) being

involved in the crime. Unlike the plot's proposed discovery, the script is far from exciting and the subsequent chase becomes laborious. *Chain Reaction* is best described as a stepping stone for the talents (well, so-called talents) of Reeves (*The Matrix*), Weisz (*The Mummy*) and Freeman (*Se7en*). The soundtrack is thankfully Dolby Digital, yet the picture quality is surprisingly not up to the standards of similar Fox titles; although the image is anamorphic, the colours are not displayed frivolously enough for a film only 5 years-old. Fortunately (or perhaps unfortunately) they try to make amends by including the 'Making of' featurette in place of the simpler – and no doubt less costly – theatrical trailer. But this is disappointing as it's nothing more than movie clips scattered around with overlaid monologue and interviews with the cast and crew; who themselves seem reluctant whilst wrapped in multiple layers of clothing and undergoing obvious frostbite from the icy locations. Even fans of Reeves will find it hard to justify shelling out £20 for this one.

FINAL VERDICT

Picture ☆☆☆ Sound ☆☆☆☆ Entertainment ☆☆

Extras ☆☆ Value ☆☆

OVERALL ☆☆

THE CHINA SYNDROME

Price: £17.99

Supplied by: Columbia TriStar Home Video

Type of disc: Single layer, single-sided

No of chapters: 20

Film format(s)/length: 16:9 widescreen enhanced / 117 mins

Audio format: Mono

Director: James Bridges

Starring: Jane Fonda, Jack Lemmon, Michael Douglas

Year made: 1979

Extras: Scene access; brief filmographies; trailer; soundtrack in English, French, German, Italian, Spanish; subtitles in 20 languages.

It's a classic movie and one everyone talked about when it was first screened 20 years ago. But is it worth buying on DVD? Well, no probably not unless you're a big fan of Jack Lemmon, Jane Fonda or a young and bearded Michael Douglas. Having said that, it's probably time we started thinking about DVD's in a different way. As this exciting format makes inroads on the old VHS empire, it'll not be long before we buy all our entertainment on disc, whether it be the *Teletubbies* or old classics like *The China Syndrome*. What is disappointing here is Columbia's distinct lack of effort in terms of extra features. It's widescreen which is some compensation, but let's see extra goodies – cast interviews about the film at the time or press coverage of the movie (which won 4 Oscars back in 1978) would have been appreciated. If you're tempted to upgrade your VHS copy, be warned, there's no noticeable picture improvement and even the sound comes in boring old mono!

FINAL VERDICT

Picture ☆☆☆☆ Sound ☆ Entertainment ☆☆☆☆
Extras ☆ Value ☆☆☆
OVERALL ☆☆☆

Chitty Chitty Bang Bang

Price: £19.99
Supplied by: MGM
Type of disc: Dual layer, single-sided
No of chapters: 40
Film format(s)/length: 4:3 regular / 145 mins
Audio format: Dolby Digital 5.0
Director: Ken Hughes
Starring: Dick van Dyke, Sally Ann Howes, Lionel Jeffries
Year made: 1968
Extras: 8-page glossy booklet; original trailer; French, Italian and Spanish soundtrack; multi-lingual subtitles.

Here's a quote from MGM's booklet that they include with the likes of *Carrie*, *Hackers* and *The Birdcage*: "Depending on how the film was shot, the widescreen format presents up to 50% more image to the left and right of the screen than the 'pan and scan' process, thus preserving the director's vision of each scene." The relevance? Because it's missing from *Chitty Chitty Bang Bang*, thanks to their decision to present the film in the same pan-and-scan format that – in their own words – leaves us without the full image. If DVD is to become a collector's format, then the lack of a widescreen version is a very poor decision – especially considering the price. Ironically, the company have given us a nice Dolby Digital 5.0 mix which quietly impresses, and the picture isn't the best we've seen, but isn't too bad for such an old film. And then the extras are okay – a passable 8-page booklet and the original trailer. But the overall feeling is of a disappointment that such a classic film hasn't fulfilled its DVD potential, with the similar Region 1 ruling out a better import version. At half the price, it'd be worth considering, but for this money? No thanks.

FINAL VERDICT

Picture ☆☆ Sound ☆☆☆ Entertainment ☆☆☆☆
Extras ☆☆ Value ☆
OVERALL ☆☆

Christine

Price: £19.99
Supplied by: Warner Home Video
Type of disc: Single layer, single-sided
No of chapters: 28
Film format(s)/length: 16.9 widescreen enhanced / 106 mins
Audio format: Dolby Surround
Director: John Carpenter
Starring: Keith Gordon, John Stockwell, Alexandra Paul
Year made: 1983
Extras: Scene access; audio set up; filmographies; soundtrack in German (stereo) and Spanish (mono); subtitles in 20 languages.

John Carpenter is the uncrowned king of shock-horror. Many of his films stand testament to what can be produced with latex skin and a gallon of fake blood. *Christine* is very much a departure from his usual standard of gore. The story is based on a Stephen King novel about a demonic car that seeks the all encompassing love of its owner and takes terrible revenge on anyone that stands in its way. The movie starts off, much the same as King's books, by slowly getting to know the characters before killing them off in a violent manner. This may work on paper, but unfortunately only bogs the story down on celluloid, making this a pretty dreary teen-horror flick. You'll soon want the characters to die painfully just for something to watch. The sterling rock 'n' roll soundtrack is well presented with laser quality. Picture is reasonably crisp, with very few glitches. But at the end of the day all you have is an average film, with a decent standard of sound and picture. What you get in this package is a substandard Carpenter film with no extras worth mentioning. There seems to be a common policy by DVD producers, who persist in cranking out back catalogue movies, to provide nothing whatsoever to interest buyers apart from the actual filmitself. Having seen the fantastic Region 1 version of Carpenter's *The Thing*, with all the extras it has on board, one can't help wondering why bland discs like this are still churned onto the shelves to take their place alongside other unwanted plastic.

FINAL VERDICT

Picture ☆☆☆ Sound ☆☆☆☆ Entertainment ☆☆
Extras ☆ Value ☆☆
OVERALL ☆☆

Citizen Kane

Price: £17.99
Supplied by: Universal
Type of disc: Single layer, single-sided

No of chapters: 18
Film format(s)/length: 4:3 regular / 120 mins
Audio format: Stereo
Director: Orson Welles
Starring: Orson Welles, Joseph Cotton, Agnes Moorehead
Year made: 1941
Extras: Scene access; original theatrical trailer; 8-page booklet describing history and making of the film; subtitles for the hearing impaired in English.

The word 'genius' is over-used by the media when describing artists today. It's become a shorthand description that celebrates the competent and disguises the mediocre. Yet to champion the genuinely great creative minds of the twentieth century as we settle into the next, there is no better word to apply to Orson Welles especially in the context of this, his masterpiece. *Citizen Kane* was Welles's cinematic debut, an autocratic *tour de force* that saw him direct, produce, co-screenwrite and star in the 1941 saga while still only 25 years-old. It charts the life of tycoon Charles Foster Kane and, in the process, 75 years of American history. The note perfect ensemble acting, naturalistic writing and innovative cinematography merged with Welles's past experiences in theatre and radio. The end result is routinely and universally hailed as the greatest American film of all time. The critics are right. The opportunity to have created the definitive version of the true classic on DVD though has, at least for the moment, been lost. Universal offers an unenhanced version of the film that threatens to let the flaws of the print distract from the drama and simple stereo when by now, 5.1 Dolby Surround should be industry standard. This DVD even lacks the *Reflections on Citizen Kane* documentary the VHS version carries, no doubt down to the usual transatlantic copyright nonsense. We do get a booklet and trailer though. For £17.99. Thanks. *Citizen Kane* is a social critique, a humanitarian comedy, a romantic soap, a media satire, a study of friendship and a cautionary tale. The tragedy is that the DVD is far from being an equal to the film.

FINAL VERDICT
Picture ☆ Sound ☆ Entertainment ☆☆☆☆☆
Extras ☆ Value ☆
OVERALL ☆☆

THE CLIENT

Price: £15.99
Supplied by: Warner Home Video
Type of disc: Single layer, single-sided
No of chapters: 47
Film length/format(s): 2.35:1 widescreen / 116 mins
Director: Joel Schumacher
Starring: Tommy Lee Jones, Susan Sarandon, Brad Renfro
Year made: 1996
Extras: Cast and crew biographies; production notes; theatrical trailer; scene access.

More thematically complex than it's given credit for, *The Client* is trademark Grisham with a few bolt-on extras for your money. Shot through the eyes of chief protagonist, 11 year-old Mark Sway, the film captures a child's perceived, if not actual, helplessness in a world of corrupt adults. Mark and his brother witnessed the suicide of Romy Clifford. This is no ordinary suicide though, Clifford is an attorney to a Mafia hitman, and knows one of the Mob's secrets. Unfortunately, Sway gets wind of this little secret, and there ensues a lengthy game of wits between the Feds, the Mob and plucky lawyer Susan Sarandon. Through strong performance and sensitive direction, Sway's impotence in the adult world is echoed throughout by legal wranglings between small-time Sarandon and big-shot Tommy Lee Jones. DVD extras run to production notes, the theatrical trailer and scene access, but nothing else. And while it's mildly interesting to read about the search for an actor to play 11 year-old Mark, the film is merely a switch-off blockbuster. For completists only.

FINAL VERDICT
Picture ☆☆☆ Sound ☆☆☆ Entertainment ☆☆☆
Extras ☆☆☆ Value ☆☆
OVERALL ☆☆

CLIVE BARKER'S LORD OF ILLUSIONS

Price: £19.99
Supplied by: MGM Home Video
Type of disc: Dual layer, single-sided
No of chapters: 30
Film format(s)/length: 1.78:1 anamorphic / 144 mins
Audio format: Dolby Digital 5.1
Director: Clive Barker
Starring: Scott Bakula, Kevin J O'Connor, Famke Janssen
Year made: 1995
Extras: Scene access; theatrical trailer; director's audio commentary; deleted scenes with audio commentary; subtitles in 8 languages.

This isn't just *Lord of Illusions*. This is *Clive Barker's Lord of Illusions*, and when a film-maker manages to get their name in the title of the movie, then it's usually the type of film-maker you can rely on to produce certain goods. Clive Barker, it would seem, is never one to disappoint. Virtuoso of the horror genre, master of the prosthetic head, and indeed his very own lord of illusion, Barker has made his name ring clearly in an overcrowded school of movie making. It was his 1987 runaway success, *Hellraiser*, that placed Barker at a level of creation in the horror genre only to be matched by the likes of Wes Craven, and with *Lord of Illusions* we see Barker treading a new path on similar ground. Hired by Dorothea (Janssen) to watch out for her husband Swann (O'Connor), a world-famous illusionist, New York private eye Harry D'Amour (Bakula) soon learns that there is more to performing illusions than merely stuffing a bunch of flowers up a jacket sleeve. This is *magic*. The real deal. Swann learnt his craft from a cult leader called Nix (a guy who got a little over-indulgent with his Paul Daniels magic set as a kid), who came to an abrupt end 13 years prior, in the opening scene of the movie. Unfortunately, there are some who didn't appreciate the demise of Nix, most notably his cult followers who conspire to resurrect Nix and let him carry on his rather too personal campaign of 'murdering the world'. Of course, murdering the world isn't the most popular outcome for a Hollywood movie, so it's up to D'Amour to rely on his wits and see to it that Nix's intended spree of mass genocide isn't quite the show-stopper it was intended to be. The whole thing plays out like a cross between the *noir* of *The Big Sleep* and the visceral horror of *Night of the Living Dead*, but is all packaged together in the reliable style that Barker has firmly made his own. Ultimately, it's nonsense, but it's enjoyable non-sense, and like most of the blockbusting page turners Barker puts out as an author, it's an absolute gore fest from start to finish. The disc itself is another slice of proof that MGM has really got its head screwed on properly when it comes to putting a decent disc together. The respectful treatment of the Bond series continues to prove its muscle in the DVD market, and now that respect is being extended to the individual director. Not only is this a full 2.35 anamorphic transfer, with the obligatory 5.1 Digital Dolby sound, but this is the definitive director's cut which means that we are treated to an additional 12 minutes previously unseen on any theatrical release. Highlights include the audio commentary that gives Barker a chance to demonstrate the real passion he has for his craft. Commentaries also grace the selection of deleted scenes which, unlike many other DVD outtakes, not only give you a reason for their exclusion, but also explain how they fitted into the original cut of the movie.

FINAL VERDICT

Picture ☆☆☆☆ Sound ☆☆☆☆
Entertainment ☆☆☆☆
Extras ☆☆☆☆ Value ☆☆☆☆
OVERALL ☆☆☆☆

COBRA

Price: £15.99
Supplied by: DVDplus (www.dvdplus.co.uk)
Type of disc: Single layer, single-sided
No of chapters: 27
Film format(s)/length: 1.85:1 widescreen / 83 mins
Audio format: Dolby Digital 5.1
Director: George P Cosmatos
Starring: Sylvester Stallone, Brigitte Nielsen, Reni Santoni
Year made: 1986
Extras: Scene access; multi-lingual subtitles; subtitles for the hearing impaired in English.

Well, it's all cuddly fun in this happy, heart-warming cop thriller – not! Sylvester Stallone plays disillusioned cop Marion (snigger) Cobretti, alias the Cobra. Assigned to the Zombie squad, Cobra gets all the lousy jobs. Taking out the bad dudes is his business and his laser sighted, high calibre machine pistol is his preferred method of justice. Things start to go wrong when Cobra discovers that a mass serial killer ring is operating inside the city. The one surviving witness is a pre-plastic Brigitte Nielsen. Cobra must protect her at all costs in order to bring the killers to justice, using as much firepower as he deems necessary. The film is formula stuff. Like many Eighties action movies, the bad guys are as interchangeable as the fight scenes. The plot did begin to show some promise, with a group of killers operating inside the city instead of the usual lone wolf maniac. Unfortunately, the director decided to beef up the plot by turning an interesting thriller into the shoot out at the OK Corral, albeit with automatic weapons. Despite the shortcomings of the film, it translates well to DVD. The picture quality is tiptop and the gunshots, explosions and bad Eighties music are all crystal clear in digital sound. It's a pity then, that like most early action films given the DVD treatment, there are no extras to speak of. Not even a measly biography or theatrical trailer managed to make it onto the disc. Let's hope this trend doesn't continue.

FINAL VERDICT

Picture ☆☆☆☆ Sound ☆☆☆☆
Entertainment ☆☆ Extras ☆ Value ☆
OVERALL ☆☆

THE COMMITMENTS

Price: £19.99
Supplied by: 20th Century Fox Home Entertainment
Type of disc: Dual layer, single-sided
No of chapters: 35
Film format(s)/length: 4:3 regular / 109 mins
Audio format: Dolby Surround
Director: Alan Parker
Starring: Robert Arkins, Michael Aherne, Angeline Ball
Year made: 1991
Extras: Scene access; behind-the-scenes featurette with director Alan Parker; theatrical trailer; music video; CD sampler.

Based in the working class area of Dublin, where your only way out is to be the next Sinead O'Connor or U2, *The Commitments* follows a group of youngsters trying to make it big as a soul band. Director Alan Parker plucked 7 people from virtual obscurity and cast them in this film in an effort to create a raw, back-to-roots type of movie – although it seems that once the hype died down, nearly all the stars vanished back into obscurity, never to be seen again. *The Commitments* is a cracking film, effortlessly moving from scene to scene, so much so that you don't really notice that it's two hours long. Great soul tunes are also rendered throughout; it's just a shame they aren't presented in 5.1. The 4:3 picture is a disappointment at this price, though, and it's not even all that good. As for extra features, this disc has fared better than some with a behind-the-scenes featurette by Parker and 4 songs from the film's much-loved soundtrack.

FINAL VERDICT
Picture ☆☆ Sound ☆☆☆☆ Entertainment ☆☆☆☆
Extras ☆☆☆ Value ☆☆
OVERALL ☆☆☆

COMPLICITY

Price: £19.99
Supplied by: Entertainment in Video
Type of disc: Dual layer, single-sided
No of chapters: 16
Film format(s)/length: 1.85:1 anamorphic / 100 mins
Audio format: Dolby Pro Logic
Director: Gavin Millar
Starring: Jonny Lee Miller, Brian Cox, Keeley Hawes
Year made: 1999
Extras: Scene access; *The Story of a Journalist* featurette (21 mins); trailer.

Thanks to a combination of Lottery money and general scrounging, the screen version of Iain Banks's novel makes for a fairly good British thriller, giving a rare leading turn for Jonny Lee Miller. He plays the journalist fighting wrongs (just like us), although when his championing of the underdog is taken up by a serial killer, the fit hits the shan and guess who becomes prime suspect? Sprinkle in a bonk or two, drugs, gore, childhood flashbacks and a couple of explosions, and you can't say you're not getting your money's worth. Mind you, the disc is once again subject to the oddities of the EiV DVD department. They've treated us to a sparkling picture, anamorphically enhanced and generally free of any blemishes. They've then coupled it with a mere Pro Logic soundtrack, which to be fair packs a bit of a wallop, but lacks the kind of subtlety that many other thrillers benefit from. Still, they've chucked in extra features, mainly a 21-minute behind-the-scenes film, which is little more than a straight promotional piece with the leading players trying to flog you the film you've already bought, plus the trailer. There aren't any subtitles at all though, so those who are hard of hearing presumably are best left to test their lip-reading skills. Still, it's encouraging to see a decent British thriller on DVD, even if the best quote they could find for the box came from that radical cultural oracle, the *Glasgow Sunday Herald*. Who reckon it's entertaining stuff, too…

FINAL VERDICT
Picture ☆☆☆☆ Sound ☆☆ Entertainment ☆☆☆
Extras ☆☆ Value ☆☆
OVERALL ☆☆

CON AIR

Price: £15.99
Supplied by: DVD World (01705 796662)
Type of disc: Single layer, single-sided
No of chapters: 18
Film format(s)/length: 16:9 widescreen / 111 mins
Director: Simon West
Starring: Nicolas Cage, John Cusack, John Malkovich
Year made: 1997
Extras: Interactive menus; scene access.

Without Jerry Bruckheimer, there'd be no need for DVDs. Think about it – which type of film benefits most from the superior imagery and digital sound? It's the big budget action flick – the type of film Bruckheimer's been producing his entire career. His finest moment has to be *The Rock*; his lowest point *Armageddon* – with *Con Air* sitting somewhere in between. Cyrus 'The Virus' Grissom, played with obvious glee by Malkovich, masterminds a mid-air hijacking of an aircraft carrying the worst scum of humanity you're likely to see this side of an Airtours holiday jet. Cage plays the good guy hitching a ride home to his family, having completed his jail sentence in the opening credits. All he wants to do is get home and see his daughter – so, obviously, it's up to him to slip on Willis' trademark white vest and save the day. Cage isn't your typical action hero. I'm sure Bruce, Sly or Arnie could have him if it came to it. But this is part of his appeal, and the demand for his talents has increased massively since he played the unlikely lead in *The Rock*. *Con Air* offers him the chance to flex his relatively new biceps every 15 minutes or so as the film builds to its inevitable conclusion (oh go on – guess who wins). It's an unashamed no-brainer, relying on a series of ever more outrageous set pieces to maintain interest. And that it does well, from the sombre opening moment to the contrived final sequence it's a visual feast and one that deserves to be shown with the lights down low and the sound full-on. For this reason, *Con Air* demands to be part of your collection, whether you like the film or not, especially if your screen is large and wide and your speakers many. Like *Face/Off* and, obviously, *The Rock*, *Con Air* should be nominated as an official DVD demonstration disc, such is its impact on all senses. With the exception of smell and touch – although I'm sure that future hardware will accommodate every sensory input. It's worth pointing out, however, that not even the high definition of the format can save one of the worst special effects you're likely to see. In this age of cinema, I fail to understand how we can bring dinosaurs convincingly to life, annihilate entire cities with meteors and create new scenes with long-dead actors – yet find it impossible to make model planes that don't look like posh Airfix kits. But if you can overlook these obvious blue-screen scenes then you'll find *Con Air* an adrenaline-pumping couple of hours, provided you don't demand too much in the way of plot from your action films. Where *Con Air* definitely doesn't excel, however – and how we're growing tired of this same old story — is in the extras department. Heck, there's not even a trailer on the disc. It's an absolute travesty that does nothing to further the development of the format. We can continue to forgive only for so long. This was so nearly a 5-star review.

FINAL VERDICT

Picture ☆☆☆☆☆ Sound ☆☆☆☆☆
Entertainment ☆☆☆☆ Extras ☆ Value ☆☆☆☆
OVERALL ☆☆☆☆

CONGO

Price: £19.99
Supplied by: Paramount
Type of disc: Dual layer, single-sided
No of chapters: 16
Film format(s)/length: 1.78:1 anamorphic / 104 mins
Audio format: Dolby Digital 5.1
Director: Frank Marshall
Starring: Dylan Walsh, Laura Linney, Ernie Hudson
Year made: 1995
Extras: Scene access; two trailers; soundtrack in English, German, Hungarian and Czech; subtitles in 8 languages; subtitles for the hearing impaired in English.

Can there be such a thing as too many films featuring both Tim Curry *and* Joe Don Baker? No – at least, not if you're a fan of the 'so bad they're good' genre. Despite being based on a novel from über-author Michael Crichton, *Congo* falls firmly into this category. The film has to be seen to be believed – and even then you still won't believe it. Walsh, Linney and former Ghostbuster Hudson lead an expedition into – duh – the Congo, to return Walsh's talking gorilla (yes, really) to the wild. Tagging along is a dodgily-accented Curry searching for the mythical lost city of Zinj, and Joe Don orchestrates the whole affair by satellite so that he can get his hands on some fabulous diamonds in order to make lasers. Still with us? The expedition encounters every possible rumble in the jungle cliché, with lost tribes, savage animals and erupting volcanoes – oh, and don't forget the attack of the killer hippos. By the time the beleaguered group reaches Zinj, the whole affair has become *Indiana Jones* on acid, big-budget insanity that nevertheless somehow managed to turn a profit. Presumably it appealed to the same crowd that made *Anaconda* a hit. Although the DVD can't scrape up any extras apart from two trailers, *Congo* has somehow managed to get outstanding audio and video presentation. The African vistas look superb, and atmospheric use is made of the surround sound. If only the film had actually been as good…

FINAL VERDICT

Picture ☆☆☆☆☆ Sound ☆☆☆☆
Entertainment ☆☆ Extras ☆☆ Value ☆☆
OVERALL ☆☆

CONSPIRACY THEORY

Price: £15.99
Supplied by: DVD World (01705 796662)
Type of disc: Single layer, single-sided
No of chapters: 33
Film format(s)/length: 2.35:1 widescreen anamorphic / 130 mins

Director: Richard Donner
Starring: Mel Gibson, Julia Roberts, Patrick Stewart
Year made: 1997
Extras: Chapter access; English/Arabic subtitles; production notes.

So, Brian Helgeland – talented scribe usually let down by poor movie making, or Hollywood hack who got lucky one time? Yes, he wrote *LA Confidential*, but he's also got *The Postman*, *Assassins* and *A Nightmare On Elm Street 4* on his CV. *Conspiracy Theory* doesn't do those who prefer the first description of Helgeland many favours. Big name cast, capable director…but silly and hackneyed story. New York cabby Jerry Fletcher (Gibson) is a paranoid conspiracy nut, padlocking his coffee jar to prevent tampering and delivering full-bore rants to anyone unlucky enough to get into his cab. In his spare time, he publishes his numerous conspiracy theories in a newsletter and all but stalks the object of his affections, attorney Alice Sutton (Roberts). All is 'normal' until the arrival of a goon squad suggests that one of Jerry's theories is true – the problem is, he doesn't know which one… The idea behind the story has promise, but it never really gets the chance to develop, the screenplay soon turning into a cross between *Marathon Man* and *The Manchurian Candidate*, with a couple of black helicopters thrown in to keep it up to date. Stewart shows up as a sinister intelligence agent whom you expect to ask, "Is it safe?" as he tortures Gibson, and Roberts actually namechecks the latter movie in order to explain the plot, which just exposes *Conspiracy Theory*'s lack of originality all the more. The only extra features on the disc are some thin production notes, but that's all. Iffy movie, nothing that takes advantage of DVD – it's all a conspiracy!

FINAL VERDICT

Picture ☆☆☆ Sound ☆☆☆ Entertainment ☆☆
Extras ☆☆ Value ☆☆
OVERALL ☆☆

CONTACT

Price: £15.99
Supplied by: DVD World (01705 796662)
Type of disc: Dual layer, single-sided
No of chapters: 43
Film format(s)/length: 16:9 widescreen / 144 mins
Director: Robert Zemeckis
Starring: Jodie Foster, Matthew McConaughey, James Woods
Year made: 1997
Extras: Interactive menus; production notes; scene access; trailer; 3 commentary soundtracks; music-only option; animation concepts and special effects tests; cast and crew biographies.

Intelligently adapted from Carl Sagan's Pulitzer Prize-winning novel, *Contact* is science fiction for grown-ups. The antitheses of no-brainers like *Independence Day* and *Mars Attacks*, the film highlights the obsession of those involved in the SETI (Search for Extra Terrestrial Intelligence) Project as they trawl the skies in search of conclusive proof that we are not alone. So far, so Hollywood – but *Contact* really comes into its own when that proof is discovered and a worldwide selection process is initiated to pick one representative of mankind to try to make…well, contact. Of course, it's easy to scoff at such theories when they are presented as fiction; but the truth is *Contact*'s premise seems more plausible than most. The weighty performances of the principal cast add a gravity and humility to the film without getting too bogged down in American sensibility – which would have been so easy to do in the hands of a less mature film-maker. By cleverly pitching science against religion, the audience is left to question whether Foster's motives are right or wrong – and a healthy debate is guaranteed as the credits roll. Robert Zemeckis has always demonstrated mastery of the subtle CGI, yet nowhere has it been as effective as in *Contact*. Whereas special effects are usually obvious, it is only by accessing one of the film's 3 commentary soundtracks that the care and attention put into the making of this extraordinary film are revealed. Little tricks, like cleaning up the real-life telescopes or changing the colour of the young Jodie Foster's eyes in order to ensure continuity, are invisible when watching the movie; yet these commentaries are of such interest that there is real reason to watch it 3 times back-to-back. Other, more ambitious special effects are obvious – no, Clinton did not appear in the film – but rest assured that they've never looked better. For such a long film told at such a slow pace, *Contact* surprisingly never becomes dull. Alan Silvestri's score is as powerful as they come and coming on Dolby Digital it's awesome. There's a soundtrack-only option, too, which will save you buying the separate audio CD if that's your thing. Additional features such as animation concepts, special effects tests and biographies complete this glorious DVD package. *Contact* is a lone finger to many higher-profile DVDs, demonstrating how effective the format can be if a little time and effort is applied to the disc. As it isn't an obvious choice for the die-hard DVD owner, it's clear this labour is necessary – but

Armageddon and its work-to-rule chums should hang their heads in shame.

FINAL VERDICT

Picture ☆☆☆☆☆ Sound ☆☆☆☆☆
Entertainment ☆☆☆☆☆ Extras ☆☆☆☆☆
Value ☆☆☆☆☆
OVERALL ☆☆☆☆☆

COP LAND

Price: £15.99
Supplied by: Buena Vista
Type of disc: Single layer, single-sided
No of chapters: 14
Film format(s)/length: 16:9 widescreen enhanced, anamorphic / 101 mins
Audio format: Dolby Digital
Director: James Mangold
Starring: Sly Stallone, Robert De Niro, Ray Liotta
Year made: 1997
Extras: English/French audio; English subtitles for hearing impaired; instant scene access; Dolby Digital.

Somewhat insensitively hyped as the film where Sly finally showed he could act, Stallone's performance is actually one of *Cop Land*'s principal strengths. Having put on weight to convincingly portray Sheriff Freddy Heflin, he provides the film with a highly effective central performance. Yet originally, he was seen as a weak link in a project featuring stars such as Robert De Niro, Harvey Kietel, Ray Liotta and script/direction by James Mangold. In the event, it's the script which is perhaps the weakest element with a somewhat muddled mid-section and a refusal to directly confront its principal themes. Still, one of the best lines of the film is Liotta's advice: "If you hit a red light, go diagonal, always go diagonal." This is a mature, rewarding film with some great performances, stylish direction, intelligent dialogue and a compelling story-arc as represented by Stallone's search for redemption. The script's intriguing conceit is that Cop Land – a suburb of New Jersey nicknamed for the high proportion of police living there – was set up as a peaceful refuge using some questionable financing deals. It's a familiar tale of a corrupt deal slowly bleeding poison into the surrounding community, good men turning bad under pressure from a history of past mistakes. Although not quite the masterpiece everyone wanted, on its cinema release it was widely passed over by the public and is now something of a lost gem perfect for rediscovery on DVD. If you haven't seen the movie and you fancy some serious entertainment, then *Cop Land* is really something of an essential purchase. That said, Buena Vista has pro-

vided the bare minimum in the way of DVD presentation. This fairly lengthy film is split into just 14 cryptically titled chapters and aside from this instant scene access, there's nothing other than the choice of swapping English dialogue for French. When so many tedious action pictures enjoy relatively extensive production notes, it's a real shame such a genuinely interesting movie gets nothing. Why no filmography for James Mangold and his stellar cast? How about some background material on the intriguing script? With *Cop Land* you sense the making of the movie was a real story in its own right, but sadly Buena Vista declined to share that with us. In terms of the DVD conversion of the movie itself, Buena Vista has done a decent job with a good, anamorphic widescreen production. It's an attractively lensed movie which is a pleasure to watch on DVD, even if there's nothing particularly spectacular to see other than a string of excellent performances. Similarly, the soundfield is never really called on for outrageous effects – although the movie's finale does make good use of Dolby Digital. Overall, *Cop Land* is a flawed masterpiece that comes highly recommended.

FINAL VERDICT

Picture ☆☆☆☆ Sound ☆☆☆☆
Entertainment ☆☆☆☆☆ Extras ☆ Value ☆☆☆☆
OVERALL ☆☆☆☆

COPYCAT

Price: £15.99
Supplied by: Warner Home Video
Type of disc: Single layer, single-sided
No of chapters: 39
Film format(s)/length: 2.35:1 widescreen / 118 mins
Audio format: Dolby Digital 5.1
Director: Jon Amiel
Starring: Sigourney Weaver, Harry Connick Jr, Holly Hunter
Year made: 1995
Extras: Production notes; scene access; audio commentary by director Jon Amiel; English, French, Italian soundtrack; subtitles in 7 languages.

If you're susceptible to the odd bout of paranoia, this is not a good film to watch late at night on your own. You may spend more time looking over your shoulder than watching the screen. Unfortunately, in-between the scary bits, *Copycat* isn't one of the greatest films, despite having all the elements present (quality actors, okay plot, okay script) but somehow the whole is less than the sum of its parts. Extras wise, there are a couple of bonuses, most notably a detailed audio commentary by director Jon Amiel. This does add an extra dimension, but is rather tedious as every single camera angle, sound effect and twitch of an actor's eyebrow is given a *raison d'être* that to be honest is rather excessive. These details may be important to him but would go completely unnoticed by the average viewer. Picture quality and sound are nothing special either, making *Copycat* a thoroughly mediocre package all round.

FINAL VERDICT

Picture ☆☆ Sound ☆☆ Entertainment ☆☆☆
Extras ☆☆ Value ☆☆
OVERALL ☆☆

THE CORRUPTOR

Price: £19.99
Supplied by: Entertainment in Video
Type of disc: Dual layer, single-sided
No of chapters: 23
Film format(s)/length: 2.35:1 widescreen enhanced / 110 mins
Audio format: Dolby Digital 5.1
Director: James Foley
Starring: Chow Yun-Fat, Mark Wahlberg, Ric Young
Year made: 1999
Extras: Scene access; 'Making of' documentary; theatrical trailer; music video; cast and crew details; audio commentary by director James Foley; English subtitles.

Okay, hands up if you've not heard of Chow Yun-Fat? If you're standing there with your arm in the air, then shame on you – Mr Fat is one of Hong Kong's most-loved exports, at least when it comes to movies. After starring in such John Woo classics as *Hard-Boiled* and *The Killer*, they shipped him out to Hollywood where he quickly jumped into the same league as Jackie Chan and Steven Seagal...though whether the latter is a good thing remains to be seen. Delving deep into the underworld of New York's Chinatown, *The Corruptor* is Fat's second major Hollywood flick and it makes for some compelling viewing. There are loads of spontaneous gunfights and explosive action for the people who like that sort of thing, but the story never fails to excite either. Mark Wahlberg, in particular, seems to have emerged into the acting world as someone with plenty of potential – at least he's started wearing his trousers around his waist again. Considering *The Corruptor* never really did anything major at the box office and stars a washed-up rapper and someone most British cinemagoers will never have heard of, it makes for one hell of a DVD. The picture and sound are absolutely brilliant, but where things really get a lot more interesting is in the extras. You might think that with such a low-profile film, you'd have done well to get a bog-standard mix of a trailer and a few subtitles – not so here. As well as the original trailer, you can check out the rather funky music video (although if you recognise the artists responsible, you'll be lucky) or just watch the interesting, if short, documentary concerning the making of the film. There are also plenty of details about the cast and crew, as well as a complete commentary by the director, James Foley – though why this isn't advertised on the back of the box, we couldn't tell you. If you fancy something with a bit more style than your average no-brain action movie, you'd be a fool not to check this one out. With more extras than some other 'quality' DVDs we could mention, *The Corruptor* certainly steals the award for surprising us by actually being good. Check it out – unless you detest this type of film with a vengeance, you won't be disappointed.

FINAL VERDICT

Picture ☆☆☆☆ Sound ☆☆☆
Entertainment ☆☆☆☆ Extras ☆☆☆☆ Value ☆☆☆☆
OVERALL ☆☆☆☆

COURAGE UNDER FIRE

Price: £19.99
Supplied by: 20th Century Fox Home Video
Type of disc: Dual layer, single-sided
No of chapters: 26
Film format(s)/length: 16:9 widescreen enhanced / 111 mins
Audio format: Dolby Digital 5.1
Director: Edward Zwick
Starring: Denzel Washington, Meg Ryan, Matt Damon
Year made: 1996
Extras: Scene access; theatrical trailer; subtitles in 9 languages; subtitles for the hearing impaired in English.

Whilst investigating the merits or otherwise of controversially awarding a medal to a female helicopter pilot (Meg Ryan) who was killed in the Gulf War, Lt Col Serling (Washington) finds some discrepancies in her crew members' accounts of the incident. Still wrestling with his own demons after making a tactical blunder whilst 'under fire' in Iraq, Washington's character has to decide whether or not 'courage' really was on display for either Ryan or himself. Told through many flashbacks which each paint a different picture, this is a slightly disjointed and thus uninvolving tale hampered principally by the scriptwriter's inability to portray the central conceit. On DVD, it looks pretty fabulous – falling short of perfection due to the lack of extras – and the war-torn sound will have your neighbours knocking your door before you can say 'Gulf War syndrome'. If you like your military dramas big and Hollywoodised, this might well be the disc for you.

FINAL VERDICT

Picture ☆☆☆☆ Sound ☆☆☆☆☆
Entertainment ☆☆☆ Extras ☆☆ Value ☆☆☆
OVERALL ☆☆☆

THE CRAFT

Price: £19.99
Supplied by: Columbia TriStar
Type of disc: Single layer, single-sided
No of chapters: 20
Film format(s)/length: 16:9 widescreen / 97 mins
Director: Andrew Fleming
Starring: Fairuza Balk, Robin Tunney, Neve Campbell
Year made: 1996
Extras: DVD promo trailer; instant scene access; multi-lingual subtitles; Dolby Digital.

A quartet of talented young actresses, a genuinely witchy plot and an MTV-soundtrack ensured a degree of cult success for this slick horror flick. Fairuza Balk is particularly effective as the trailer trash bitch, but the overall tone is uncertain as the script veers between celebrating the witches' early successes and then punishing them for it later on in an SFX overkill finale. The quality of the movie on DVD is excellent with great picture quality and highly effective Dolby Digital surround sound. However, as far as extras go this disc is a complete wash out. There's no production notes nor theatrical trailer, just a standard DVD/Columbia TriStar promotion. Instant scene selection is attractively and effectively designed, but that's about it. Ultimately, it all comes down to how much you liked the original movie. If you loved it, then this is highly recommended – just don't expect anything extra to impress your mates with.

FINAL VERDICT

Picture ☆☆☆☆☆ Sound ☆☆☆☆☆
Entertainment ☆☆☆ Extras ☆ Value ☆☆☆
OVERALL ☆☆☆

CRASH

Price: £19.99
Supplied by: Columbia TriStar Home Video
Type of disc: Single layer, single-sided
No of chapters: 21
Film format(s)/length: 1.85:1 widescreen enhanced / 96 mins
Audio format: Dolby Surround
Director: David Cronenberg

Starring: James Spader, Holly Hunter, Rosanna Arquette
Year made: 1996
Extras: Scene access; theatrical trailer; soundtrack in English and Spanish; subtitles in English and Spanish.

You must remember all the *Daily Mail*-led hype about this film and how it supposedly glamorises car wrecks by showing a group of people who quite literally get off on them! Quite how this film manages to glamorise sex 'n' wrecks, let alone sex on its own, is a mystery but the '18' rating is justified and if you're looking for some naked flesh then yes, you'll find no shortage of it here. A warning, though – almost every inch of that naked flesh is scarred to add to the effect of the film. It's with these close-ups of scars and the general weirdness in places that you can really see some classic Cronenberg touches. It's just a shame that this DVD doesn't do the film or its director any favours whatsoever. It would have been more than interesting to hear what the director had to say about this film. Instead, all you get is the usual fare of a theatrical trailer – yawn! The most annoying thing about this film is the sound. If you're fluent in Spanish then there's no problem as you get to watch the film in full 5.1 Dolby Digital. If not, you're stuck with normal Surround sound. Still, the Spanish does add some comedy elements to an otherwise fairly sobering film! Despite the fact this is full of sex and naked flesh there is little of any appeal here. Unless, of course, you're a devout Cronenberg fan, but even then there's better out there.

FINAL VERDICT

Picture ☆☆☆☆ Sound ☆☆☆
Entertainment ☆☆☆ Extras ☆ Value ☆☆☆
OVERALL ☆☆☆

CRAZY IN ALABAMA

Price: £19.99
Supplied by: Columbia TriStar Home Video
Type of disc: Dual layer, single-sided
No of chapters: 28
Film format(s)/length: 2.35:1 anamorphic / 108 mins
Audio format: Dolby Digital 5.1
Director: Antonio Banderas
Starring: Melanie Griffith, David Morse, Lucas Black
Year made: 1999
Extras: Scene access; 2 trailers; commentary by Antonio Banderas; commentary by Melanie Griffith; deleted scenes; filmographies; outtakes; photo gallery with commentary; soundtrack in English and German; subtitles in 16 languages.

Lucille is the sort of aunt that most kids would

want. Attractive, adventurous, destined for stardom, and running from the law across the country with her husband's head in a hatbox. Possibly this last element is a bit unnecessary, but it serves as the central plot drive for Banderas's 1965-set directorial debut. The plight of Lucille (an ideal showcase for Griffith's talent) is juxtaposed against that of her 13 year-old nephew Peejoe who, back in their home town of Industry, Alabama, has somehow managed to get himself involved in some black rights issues and a whole heap of legal trouble. The ultimate message from this movie about freedom and grabbing every possible chance in life is a noble one, but unfortunately it's not always worth hanging around to find it out. Stylish and well executed it may be, but *Crazy In Alabama* tends to wander in places, often unsure of its footing, and audience. Still, it does benefit from a great cast, and a competent first-time director. Again, this is a *tour de force* for Columbia TriStar. In addition to the 2.35:1 anamorphic transfer and the pleasingly clear 5.1 Dolby soundtrack, there are also two thoroughly intriguing commentaries, a small, but worthwhile selection of deleted scenes with a commentary by Banderas explaining their absence, and a photographic journal documenting the shooting process of the movie. Along with the film itself, these extras might not exactly go together to make this DVD an absolute must-have, but it's at least worth a look.

FINAL VERDICT

Picture ☆☆☆☆☆ Sound ☆☆☆☆☆
Entertainment ☆☆☆ Extras ☆☆☆☆
Value ☆☆☆☆
OVERALL ☆☆☆

CRIMSON TIDE

Price: £15.99
Supplied by: Buena Vista
Type of disc: Single layer, single-sided
No of chapters: 32
Film format(s)/length: 16:9 widescreen / 111 mins
Audio format: Dolby Digital 5.1 Surround
Director: Tony Scott
Starring: Denzel Washington, Gene Hackman, George Dzundza
Year made: 1995
Extras: Interactive menus/scene selection; multilingual subtitles.

On the brink of a nuclear holocaust, Captain Frank Ramsey (Hackman) and his newly appointed first officer Ron Hunter (Washington) receive an unverified message to launch their missiles against Russia. Ramsey and Hunter then clash over the valid-

ity of the orders and mutiny erupts as the entire crew are pitted against each other in a power struggle aboard the USS *Alabama*. Hugely entertaining, this confrontation, which every naval commander of a nuclear submarine could face, is brought to stark reality in gripping fashion. Hackman and Washington are outstanding in a film that portrays the post cold war in very much the same vein as *The Hunt for Red October*. Crammed beneath the tight, dark fittings of a nuclear submarine, it's hard to criticise the picture quality because of the nature of the film. Even so, the picture, although clear, is still only average compared to many DVDs being released – in particular the Touchstone titles. Fortunately the pin-dropping sound quality makes up for any imperfections of presentation with its drum shattering effects and claustrophobic settings. Just turn the lights down low and set the volume high, and you almost feel that World War III is in your living room. However, when the movie is finished, so is the entertainment as there are literally no extra features, just the standard scene selection function. This incredibly poor lack of special features rapidly nullifies what could have been a superb DVD.

FINAL VERDICT

Picture ☆☆☆ Sound ☆☆☆☆☆
Entertainment ☆☆☆☆☆ Extras ☆ Value ☆☆☆
OVERALL ☆☆☆

THE CROW

Price: £15.99
Supplied by: Entertainment in Video
Type of disc: Single layer, single-sided
No of chapters: 12
Film format(s)/length: 4:3 regular / 101 mins
Audio format: Dolby Surround
Director: Alex Proyas
Starring: Brandon Lee, Ernie Hudson, Michael Wincott
Year made: 1994
Extras: Scene access; on-set interview with Brandon Lee (6 minutes).

Alex Proyas' gothic masterpiece was released alongside *The Mask*, during the summer of 1994, and whilst their tones and styles are wildly different, both nonetheless remain the best examples of how to successfully translate a comic book onto the big screen. *The Crow* didn't win any awards, but it has had an impact rare among modern motion pictures, due to the fact that its star, Brandon Lee, died during production. A stunt scene went drastically wrong when Lee was accidentally shot by a live bullet when blanks were supposed to have been used. There is a disturbing irony to be found in the fact that, in his final film, Lee plays the part of a young man who also dies in tragic circumstances. Entertainment in Video is a keen supporter of the DVD format, and tends to release around 4 new titles per month, but it's a shame that the quality of its releases are not consistent. For every *Wag the Dog* and *Lost in Space* (which come replete with decent quality extras), there is an *Evita* or *Donnie Brasco*, which come across as slapdash packages, cynically pushed out with the apparent intention of raking in a quick buck. Unfortunately, *The Crow* belongs in the latter, as the only extra of note is the final ever interview conducted with Brandon Lee. There is plenty of scope for additional extras; the obvious inclusion of the cinematic trailer, music videos from the rock soundtrack, audio commentary from Proyas or even interviews with the other cast members. Even a number of deleted scenes that were on *The Crow* PC-CD-ROM from a couple of years back are absent. The reason for this lack of additional inventiveness on the DVD is inexplicable.

FINAL VERDICT

Picture ☆☆☆ Sound ☆☆☆

Entertainment ☆☆☆☆ Extras ☆☆ Value ☆☆☆

OVERALL ☆☆☆

THE CROW: CITY OF ANGELS

Price: £15.99

Supplied by: Warner Home Video

Type of disc: Dual layer, single-sided

No of chapters: 11

Film format(s)/length: 1.85:1 widescreen / 91 mins

Audio format: Dolby Digital 5.1

Director: Edward R Pressman

Starring: Vincent Perez, Mia Kirschner, Iggy Pop

Year made: 1996

Extras: Scene access; English closed captions.

Resurrecting a franchise after the first movie killed its star has a rancid taste about it, not least when the movie itself has such a bleak, Gothic obsession with death. However, *City of Angels* never even begins to take flight as a true sequel; this is more a remake, a tacky, blurry photostat of the original. In the first film, *The Crow* was born out of the death of Brandon Lee and his girlfriend in a random act of violence by drug fiends. In the sequel, it's Vincent Perez who dies with his son. As before, the quest for revenge involves ever more grotesque executions, goading the remaining killers into atrocity after atrocity upon the Crow's unfortunate associates. The original had a certain rock-opera grandeur despite its dubious ethics, but the sequel adds nothing new

except non-acting pop stars – such as Iggy Pop and Ian Dury – and subtracts everything of value from the original. A once dark vision has become simply murky and unclear. Leaving aside the dire plot, the most remarkable thing about '*Crow 2*' is the lack of memorable action sequences. The finale is particularly disappointing, as if the director himself simply couldn't be bothered trying anymore. About the only mildly worthwhile aspect of this sorry piece of bird droppings is all the murk and smoke points up how far DVD encoding has come – there are no blocky digital artifacts here.

FINAL VERDICT

Picture ☆☆☆☆ Sound ☆☆☆

Entertainment ☆ Extras ☆ Value ☆

OVERALL ☆☆

CRUEL INTENTIONS

Price: £19.99

Supplied by: Columbia TriStar Home Video

Type of disc: Dual layer, single-sided

No of chapters: 28

Film format(s)/length: 16:9 widescreen enhanced / 94 mins

Audio format: Dolby Digital 5.1

Director: Roger Kumble

Starring: Ryan Phillippe, Sarah Michelle Gellar, Reese Witherspoon

Year made: 1999

Extras: Scene access; commentary by Roger Kumble and the film-makers; 5 deleted scenes; behind-the-scenes featurette; 2 music videos: Placebo 'Every You, Every Me', Marcy Playground 'Coming Up From Behind'; US theatrical trailer; filmographies; soundtrack in French (DD 5.1); subtitles in 17 languages.

You have to admire the tenacity at work here. A first-time director takes pretty much the most unappealing collection of sophisticate characters ever written from *Choderlos de Laclos* to *Les Liaisons Dangereuses*, and casts a bunch of Hollywood's brightest and best paid young teenagers in their roles. But does this amount to a stroke of genius or stupidity? The big selling point was always straightforward – sex. Sex, sex and more sex, with a double side order of sex. And here the French 18th century tale of lust, corruption and betrayal unzips its way effortlessly into wealthy 1999 Manhattan's Upper East Side. The poisonous Valmont (Phillippe) and even more poisonous half-sister Kathryn (Gellar) have tortured, raging lust for each other. But rather than consummate their passion, they chose instead to engage in a bet. Valmont must bed the new headmistress's virtuous and vowed virginal daughter Annette (Witherspoon), but if he fails, Kathryn gets his Jaguar convertible. If on the other hand he succeeds, Kathryn says Phillippe can, er, park his other vehicle round the back. Well, no-one said it would be subtle. As the bet plays out among all sorts of intentional corruption (mainly involving the uncomfortably young Cecile, played by Selma Blair) there is an unforeseen hiccup. Against all the odds, Valmont falls in love with Annette, throwing something of a spanner in the works. With Kathryn all too ready to jeopardise the newfound domestic bliss by spilling the beans, does Valmont have to sacrifice the only person he has ever cared about for the sake of his reputation? On the page, it's dynamite drama, but on screen the *90210*-style set struggles. The cast is uneven – while Witherspoon impresses with some depth, Gellar mugs it like a pantomime dame and Phillippe is staggeringly bad in the pivotal central role. Combined with their inappropriately young age, the net result is that – at its worst – *Cruel Intentions* comes off like a school play. As time goes on though, Witherspoon has more to do and writer/director Kumble makes his only significant deviation from the original story. Although literary fans will abhor the changes, the film ends with a mix of bitterness, despair and, unlike the original, a smidgen of hope. Despite retaining more malevolence than you can shake a stick at – and it is damn sexy in places – Kumble has injected a glow of warmth into the cold heart of the story with some success. On DVD, we are treated to a glorious, grade A picture. In anamorphic widescreen, every bead of passionate sweat is tantalisingly rendered without a single blemish. Colours are crisp and vivid, compared to Warner's poor 1988 Stephen Frears' DVD, it's great. The sound is a bit of a disappointment. Although the last thing required in a film like this is a bevy of Apaches and F1-11s flying round your living room, some of the dialogue seems lacklustre and the hip-to-a-fault Brit soundtrack featuring Fat Boy Slim, Placebo, and The Verve amongst others, doesn't really impact as it should. But the really good news is in the extras department. First off are 5 deleted scenes introduced by the director: a nice touch, since he explains the original context and the reason for excising. There's also a full-length commentary, featuring an ever-increasingly inebriated but affable Kumble and his crew enthusiastically gibbering over their movie. The self-deprecating discourse on money, locations and censorship (only two consecutive thrusts are allowed by the US censors for an R rating) is a fun listen – unsurprisingly, they reveal that pretty

much all of Central Park ground to a halt for the kiss between Sarah Michelle Gellar and Selma Blair. When Kumble suggests the movie was better for having a lower budget, his Director of Photography hogs the mic. "I totally agree. For my next movie, I want $5". There are a couple of music videos (Placebo's, incidentally in 2.35:1 anamorphic widescreen), a trailer and a standard issue 6-minute promotional featurette (It's like nothing you've ever seen before, yadda yadda...) Overall, this disc inches Columbia ever nearer the role of Kings of Region 2.

FINAL VERDICT

Picture ☆☆☆☆☆ Sound ☆☆☆

Entertainment ☆☆☆☆ Extras ☆☆☆☆☆

Value ☆☆☆☆☆

OVERALL ☆☆☆☆

CUBE

Price: £19.99

Supplied by: Columbia TriStar Home Video

Type of disc: Single layer, single-sided

No of chapters: 20

Film format(s)/length: 16:9 widescreen enhanced / 87 mins

Audio format: Stereo

Director: Vincenzo Natali

Starring: Nicole de Boer, Nicky Guadagni, David Hewlett

Year made: 1997

Extras: Scene access; audio commentary by director; production sketches and storyboards; theatrical trailer.

A family man cop, a paranoid doctor, a pampered maths student, an autistic man, an escape artist and a man who has lost the will to live all wake up in a cube-shaped room with no recollection of how they got there or why. Only by working together can they hope to escape the never ending maze and beat the hideously lethal booby traps all around them. That's the fascinating premise behind *Cube*, the ultra-low budget film made by Canadian film school graduates that has quietly arrived on DVD. The plot itself is ingeniously simple and near flawlessly executed. Dialogue heavy, the suspense comes from watching how these 6 strangers deal with the rat maze they're trapped in and the intense emotions they all go through. The bonus commentary features director and writer Natali, co-writer Andre Bijelic and English actor Hewlett enthusiastically reminiscing how they created the film. There's also plenty of anecdotes and trivia, such as the 6 characters being named after prisons from around the world. The DVD's biggest failing is the poor audio. *Cube* uses ominous machine audio effects to heighten tension in quite a brilliant manner, so the effect would have been amazing if presented in Dolby Digital 5.1. Sadly, on flat stereo the impact is seriously diminished. For those looking for an intelligent, nail-biting thriller, your search is over with *Cube*. Sadly the DVD's content, while satisfactory, could have been more comprehensive.

FINAL VERDICT

Picture ☆☆☆☆ Sound ☆☆ Entertainment ☆☆☆☆
Extras ☆☆☆ Value ☆☆☆☆
OVERALL ☆☆☆

DANGEROUS LIAISONS

Price: £15.99
Supplied by: DVD Net (020 8890 2520)
Type of disc: Single layer, single sided
No of chapters: 34
Film length/format(s): 16:9 widescreen 115 mins
Director: Stephen Frears
Starring: Glenn Close, John Malkovich, Michelle Pfeiffer
Year made: 1988
Extras: Production notes; scene access; multilingual subtitles; interactive menus.

If period bonkbusters are your thing, you're well in here. Not to put too fine a point on it, they're all at it; John Malkovich, Michelle Pfeiffer, a pleasingly naked Uma Thurman, even Keanu Reeves (and if he's as wooden as his acting, you can guess why). There's more to the film than that though, with Glenn Close's deliciously nasty Marquise De Merteuil stealing the show as a wealthy widow manipulating those around her. The end result is a better than average, if cold, costume drama. Unfortunately, the disc itself has problems. The picture shows regular signs of grain, not helped by constant periods of darkness. The surround soundtrack is competent – there's not really a fat lot for it to do – but on several occasions throughout the movie there are lip-syncing problems. It's an irritant the DVD could really do without. Extras-wise, things are a little shy, although the standard biographies and notes are as interesting as always (if tricky to read). A fairly basic disc, really.

FINAL VERDICT

Picture ☆☆☆ Sound ☆☆ Entertainment ☆☆☆
Extras ☆ Value ☆☆
OVERALL ☆☆

DANGEROUS MINDS

Price: £15.99
Supplied by: Warner Home Video
Type of disc: Dual layer, single-sided
No of chapters: 14

Film format(s)/length: 16:9 widescreen enhanced / 95 mins
Audio format: Dolby Digital 5.1
Director: John N Smith
Starring: Michelle Pfeiffer, George Dzundza, Courtney B Vance
Year made: 1995
Extras: Scene access; soundtrack in French and Italian; subtitles in English or Dutch; subtitles for the hearing impaired in English.

The theory was fine. Robin Williams plays a teacher, gets some boys to stand on their desks and earns an Oscar nomination. Richard Dreyfuss plays a teacher, urges his student to 'play the sunset' and earns an Oscar nomination. And Michelle? She chose the wrong film. Patronising. Shallow. Clichéd. Bland. Take your pick, each fits *Dangerous Minds* like a glove. Based on a true story, it follows Pfeiffer as a former marine who teaches unruly kids and tries to make a difference to their lives. It just doesn't work very well on celluloid. The disc offers no incentive to reunite yourself with the film either, and there are no enticing extras to speak of. There is some decent anamorphically enhanced pictures and sound, but this just isn't enough for us to recommend you part with £16. It may sound like we're on a major downer and just doing a hatchet job (which we're not), but it frustrates the life out of us that for the same money you can get great packages such as *You've Got Mail* and *Lethal Weapon 4*, or great films such as *Contact* and *LA Confidential*. It's your choice, but you'll need to be a major fan of the film to shell out for this DVD.

FINAL VERDICT

Picture ☆☆☆☆ Sound ☆☆☆ Entertainment ☆
Extras ☆ Value ☆
OVERALL ☆

DANTE'S PEAK

Price: £19.99
Supplied by: Columbia TriStar
Type of disc: Dual layer, single-sided
No of chapters: 38
Film format(s)/length: 2.35:1 widescreen / 104 mins
Audio format: Dolby Digital 5.1
Director: Roger Donaldson
Starring: Pierce Brosnan, Linda Hamilton, Charles Hallahan
Year made: 1997
Extras: Production notes detailing volcano research; biographies of Pierce Brosnan, Linda Hamilton, Charles Hallahan and director Roger Donaldson; theatrical trailer.

Volcanoes are sly things. They erupt; spewing fire and ash onto the surrounding countryside; killing any living thing in their path. Then they go quiet – for 7,000 years! It's when they decide to come out of hiding again that you've got to worry – a great deal of pressure can build up over 7 millennia! *Dante's Peak* is the story of a small American town nestling at the foot of what they think is an extinct volcano. It has lakes, a forest and hot springs. But when the hot springs start boiling the bathers, there's definitely something to worry about. Enter Pierce Brosnan in another James Bond-style role. This time he's volcanologist Harry Dalton, who lost his fiancé to a volcano many years ago and is consequently hyper-sensitive. Dalton can sense that Dante's Peak is going to blow, but no-one will take him seriously. When he's proved right however, it's all too late and he must save the town's mayor, Linda Hamilton, and her children from being barbecued alive. On DVD, *Dante's Peak* comes with production notes, information on the cast and director and a cinema trailer to whet your appetite, but sadly no 'Making of' material, which could have easily been included. The notes explain that the movie is a mixture of live action, models and computer graphics, but you can tell without being told. The special effects shots that use models really stand out, letting the movie down dreadfully. One shot of a bridge about to be torn away by a rampaging torrent of ash-filled water is almost laughable as the actor is suddenly replaced with a *Thunderbirds* puppet... Add to this a script that will make you groan and a highly predictable storyline and you've got an unsatisfactory film. Pierce Brosnan goes some way to saving the day, but you have to wonder why he got involved in the movie in the first place. A few cheap thrills, but nothing outstanding – a humdrum DVD release that's just here to make up the numbers.

FINAL VERDICT

Picture ☆☆☆ Sound ☆☆☆ Entertainment ☆☆

Extras ☆☆ Value ☆☆

OVERALL ☆☆

DARK CITY

Price: £15.99

Supplied by: DVDplus (www.dvdplus.co.uk)

Type of disc: Single layer, single-sided

No of chapters: 16

Film format(s)/length: 2.35:1 widescreen / 97 mins

Audio format: Dolby Surround

Director: Alex Proyas

Starring: Rufus Sewell, Keifer Sutherland, Jennifer Connelly

Year made: 1998

Extras: Scene access; trailer; 'Making of' featurette of around 5 minutes.

There are plenty of equations that work. The circumference of a circle is its radius times Pi. There was something to do with the one side of an equilateral triangle equalling something else. And $e=mc^2$, as Einstein proved; though we're still not sure what he meant. Therefore, *Dark City* is a mathematical oddity. It looks fantastic – the set designs are spectacular and the special effects are on the whole impressive. The plot is as strange as they come – similar, sort of, to *The Matrix* – and the performances, especially from the rejuvenated Sutherland and creepy Richard O'Brien, top notch. Proyas's direction is even slicker than *The Crow*, his previous slice of MTV sci-fi, making the film a visual treat. But put those elements together and you're left with a film that's so unusual it's difficult to know whether you like it or not. The 'Making of' featurette – misleadingly flagged on the back of the box as 39 minutes long, only lasts just under 5 – offers as little back up as it is possible to do, content to pepper the already-included trailer with a series of press kit interviews. Little background, less insight, no substance – a huge letdown. Though the sound is only surround, there are few complaints in that department and the image clarity is superb, too – a triumph, considering the abundance of smoke, neon and darkness. Overall, then, *Dark City* remains less than the sum of its parts. The film obviously has its admirers, as the back of the box exclaims. But as we've proved with the inflated length of the disc's 'added value', you shouldn't believe everything you read.

FINAL VERDICT

Picture ☆☆☆☆ Sound ☆☆☆ Entertainment ☆☆☆

Extras ☆☆ Value ☆☆☆☆

OVERALL ☆☆☆

THE DARK CRYSTAL

Price: £19.99

Supplied by: Columbia TriStar Home Video

Type of disc: Dual layer, single-sided

No of chapters: 28

Film format(s)/length: 2.35:1 widescreen / 89 mins

Audio format: Dolby Digital 5.1

Directors: Jim Henson and Frank Oz

Starring the voices of: Stephen Garlick, Lisa Maxwell, Joseph O'Conor

Year made: 1982

Extras: Scene access; 60-minute featurette; deleted scenes; filmographies; teaser trailer; theatrical trailer; character profile; multi-lingual subtitles; soundtrack in

English, French, Spanish and German.

There's something instantly recognisable about the work of Jim Henson. Maybe it's the eyes. Maybe it's the flowing movements. Possibly it's the fact that every voice sounds like either him or Frank Oz, but whatever it is, there is an unmistakable magic to everything he laid his hands upon. Henson's puppetry skills are of legendary proportions in Hollywood and have been used in everything from *Star Wars* to *The Witches*. However, they are most notable for *The Muppet Show*. A family favourite for over 20 years, its light-hearted banter and enchanting antics set a precedent for the entire Henson ethos. Whether you agree with it or not, that ethos is well and truly broken with *The Dark Crystal*. Any light-hearted enchantment is thrown out of the window for a heavier, scarier type of puppetry. The premise of the movie revolves around the waif-like Gelfling named Jem recovering a shard from the 'Dark Crystal' that was shattered one thousand years ago. When the Crystal was divided, the world (one designed almost entirely by British fantasy artist Brian Froud) was split into two. The evil, bird-like race, the Skeksis, ended up bagging the Crystal, whereas the gentle Mystics got nowt. So it's up to Jem to find the shard on behalf of the dying Mystics and restore this wondrous world of fantasy to its former state of peace and tranquillity. The whole thing pans out like any other fantasy adventure with good versus evil, accompanied by extraordinary creatures and high adventure. But there's something that just doesn't sit right. This is a very dark film, a little slow moving, which requires a lot of exposition for everything to be made clear, which is where its intended audience also becomes a little hazy. *The Dark Crystal* looks like it could be aimed at kids, but one wonders if it would hold many children's interest until at least a third of the way in. It may be a superb feat of visual puppetry from the 'Master of Muppets', but it just doesn't seem to fit the ethos of Henson's other work. This aside, the DVD is assuredly one of the finest. The large selection of deleted scenes make you cringe at just how much effort went into the scenes that never even made the final cut. However, the *crème de la crème* is the 60-minute 'Making of' featurette that not only provides a rich history into the visual creation of this stunning movie, but also an insight into just how difficult the work of a puppeteer can be. Henson provides his own observations on what it takes to bring an inanimate object to life, but as this featurette clearly shows, working with stubborn film stars is a picnic compared to working with puppets on a movie set. Overall,

congratulations are due to Henson and Columbia for a vivid piece of film on an equally rich disc.

FINAL VERDICT

Picture ☆☆☆☆ Sound ☆☆☆☆

Entertainment ☆☆☆☆ Extras ☆☆☆☆

Value ☆☆☆☆

OVERALL ☆☆☆☆

DARKMAN

Price: £19.99
Supplied by: Columbia TriStar Home Video
Type of disc: Dual layer, single-sided
No of chapters: 16
Film format(s)/length: 1.85:1 widescreen / 91 mins
Audio format: Dolby Surround
Director: Sam Raimi
Starring: Liam Neeson, Frances McDormand, Colin Friels
Year made: 1990
Extras: Scene access; trailer; production notes; filmographies; soundtrack in German, French, Italian, Spanish (surround), Polish (mono) and Czech (stereo); subtitles in 9 languages.

Before he found respectability with *A Simple Plan*, Sam Raimi's *modus operandi* was gore, comic-book ultraviolence and demented camera trickery. The *Evil Dead* films were the high points of his 'anything goes' era, but *Darkman* comes a reasonable second. A pre-Schindler, pre-Jedi Neeson is the improbably named Dr Peyton Westlake, who falls foul of gangsters, is burned alive and becomes unable to feel pain. Using a synthetic skin he has developed, the horribly-scarred Westlake takes his revenge by making lifelike masks of his enemies and tricking them into destroying each other. A cross between *Batman* and *The Phantom of the Opera*, this is a marvellously demented horror thriller. The problem is that, if anything, Raimi had too much money to spend. The Gothic, high-energy action of the first half of the film suddenly turns into a parade of exploding helicopters. Not that there's anything wrong with exploding helicopters per se, but the whole sequence seems to have come from a different film. Still, *Darkman* is enjoyably silly (with a great over-the-top score by *Batman*'s Danny Elfman) and even spawned a pair of straight-to-video sequels, *The Return of Durant* and the fantastically-titled *Die, Darkman, Die*, both starring *The Mummy*'s Arnold Vosloo. Extras are not high on the agenda, though. For your money you get a trailer, a couple of pages of production notes and an out-of-date filmography that somehow forgets Neeson was in a little George Lucas project recently…

FINAL VERDICT

Picture ☆☆☆ Sound ☆☆☆

Entertainment ☆☆☆ Extras ☆☆ Value ☆☆☆

OVERALL ☆☆☆

DARK STAR

Price: £17.99

Supplied by: Fabulous Films Ltd

Type of disc: Single layer, single-sided

No of chapters: 18

Film format(s)/length: 1.85:1 widescreen / 81 mins

Audio format: Stereo

Director: John Carpenter

Starring: Brian Narelle, Dre Pahich, Dan O'Bannon

Year made: 1973

Extras: Scene access; theatrical trailer.

There's no doubt that John Carpenter has reached cult status as far as directors go. With his name attached to some of the best movies of all time, (*The Thing, Halloween* etc), you wouldn't think that the one-man movie machine would have ever put a foot wrong. Directing, writing and scoring most of his films, Carpenter knows pretty much everything there is to know about making movies. It's surprising then that he managed to turn out something like *Dark Star*. Okay, so it's a satire. 4 bored astronauts fly around the galaxy on a mission to blow up unstable planets in order for mankind to colonise outer space. However, due to the antics of the least convincing alien ever to be committed to camera, one of the bombs decides to carry out its mission to destroy an entire planet, even though it's still attached to the ship. The response of the bohemian team of spacemen is to reason with the bomb, give it a sense of self-awareness, and hope that it doesn't have suicidal tendencies. It's a nice try from Carpenter, but the movie fails to be a parody of *2001*, and ends up merely being a poorer copy of the Kubrick classic. Plus it has special effects that could make a *Dr Who* technician feel smug. No effort has been made to enhance the movie for DVD, as both the sound and picture quality are dire. In fact, returning to the menu screen (the fonts of which are just like those on *Star Trek: TNG*) is a pleasant ungrainy surprise. With just a trailer to pad out the extras, perhaps only hard-core Carpenter fans should venture this one. *The Thing* it is not!

FINAL VERDICT

Picture ☆☆ Sound ☆ Entertainment ☆☆

Extras ☆ Value ☆

OVERALL ☆☆

DAWN OF THE DEAD: DIRECTOR'S CUT

Price: £15.99

Supplied by: BMG Video

Type of disc: Single layer, single-sided

No of chapters: 25

Film format(s)/length: 4:3 regular / 139 mins

Audio format: Mono

Director: George A Romero

Starring: David Emge, Hen Foree, Scott H Reiniger

Year made: 1978

Extras: Scene access; stills gallery; audio commentary by special effects expert Tom Savini.

The cult classic *Night of the Living Dead* made its mark despite a minuscule budget and unknown actors. Hot on the heels of this horror tour de force (well…10 years later) came *Dawn of the Dead*. This sequel is a fairly average offering which takes the plot of the first film – a group of individuals stranded in a remote location besieged by zombies – and basically rehashes it, shifting location from the original graveyard to a modern(ish) shopping mall. It's not exactly Oscar-winning material, but a good gore-filled romp all the same. As far as extras go, this DVD isn't bad, with a stills gallery and an interesting and quite revealing commentary from special effects artist Tom Savini. Perhaps the best DVD-relevant bonus are the menu screens, which have really been created to tie in with the film. However, be warned. If you are of a nervous disposition, it's probably best to look away, as there's loads of blood pouring all over the place!

FINAL VERDICT

Picture ☆☆☆ Sound ☆☆☆ Entertainment ☆☆☆

Extras ☆☆☆ Value ☆☆☆

OVERALL ☆☆☆

DAYLIGHT

Price: £19.99

Supplied by: Columbia TriStar Home Video

Type of disc: Dual layer, single-sided

No of chapters: 43

Film format(s)/length: 1.85:1 widescreen (anamorphic) / 110 mins

Audio format: Dolby Digital 5.1

Director: Rob Cohen

Starring: Sylvester Stallone, Amy Brenneman, Viggo Mortensen

Year made: 1996

Extras: Soundtrack in 4 languages; multilingual subtitles; detailed production notes; cast and director biographies and filmographies; theatrical trailer.

Sylvester Stallone continues in his efforts to shake off his violent tough-guy image in this disaster thriller. He plays former Emergency Services

Chief Kit Latura, reduced to driving a taxi after a bad decision got one of his people killed. Fortunately for him, however, he just happens to be driving by when the New Jersey tunnel collapses, trapping a small group of commuters (and one dog) inside. The production notes describe this as an "Action picture without villains," in that the only enemy for Latura and the survivors to deal with is the tunnel itself. This isn't strictly true though, because the city officials – having waited about 10 minutes after sending Latura in on a rescue mission – decide to try and dig their way into the tunnel with heavy machinery, despite safety advisors telling them it will collapse as a result. In essence then the bad guys are – as usual – the people in authority and it's really them that Stallone's character is fighting against as he struggles to get his charges to safety. Although the plot is a little shaky to say the least, the special effects and action sequences are on the whole pretty impressive. As a DVD, *Daylight* offers some detailed production notes and fairly comprehensive biographies on the stars and the director Rob Cohen. You get 3 foreign language soundtracks in addition to the original English one, plus the theatrical trailer, but this is still an extremely lightweight DVD considering what could have been added. Picture quality is good, rather than great, but if you're after something which isn't too mentally taxing then you might give it a try.

FINAL VERDICT

Picture ☆☆☆ Sound ☆☆☆☆ Entertainment ☆☆
Extras ☆☆ Value ☆☆
OVERALL ☆☆

DAYS OF THUNDER

Price: £19.99
Supplied by: Paramount Pictures
Type of disc: Dual layer, single-sided
No of chapters: 23
Film format(s)/length: 2.35:1 letterbox / 102 mins
Audio format: Dolby Digital 5.1
Director: Tony Scott
Starring: Tom Cruise, Nicole Kidman, Robert Duvall
Year made: 1990
Extras: Scene access; theatrical trailer; soundtrack in English, German, Czech and Hungarian; subtitles in 9 languages.

Just because something is popular, that doesn't necessarily mean that it's always going to be good. Take boy bands, for example. Tom Cruise has sat merrily on the throne of Hollywood for well over a decade, and has yet to make a financial failure. However, he hasn't been so consistent with critical

success. *Days of Thunder* is a textbook case of how a movie can be, and is, built around as star's demands as opposed to placing a star in a pre-existing script. Based on an original idea by Cruise himself, the movie tells the well-worn story of the wannabe kid who comes from nothing, and goes on to win glory and fortune. Cruise plays Cole Trickle (ha!), an ambitious and talented stock car racer. Talent-spotted by businessman Randy Quaid, he's teamed with veteran car-builder Harry Hogge (Duvall), and, well, that's basically it. There are lots of impressive Tony Scott race sequences, a crash, and a romantic interlude with a doctor (Kidman), but if you're looking for character development, depth and something really engaging then you should look elsewhere. It's a movie that passes the time, but this is a disc that should itself be completely passed by. The video transfer is adequate (though disappointingly only in letterbox), and top sound is fast becoming a Paramount speciality. However, as regards to extras, all you have is a theatrical trailer, which probably will not be enough to convince you to part with £20 – especially when you consider how vacant the film is.

FINAL VERDICT

Picture ☆☆☆ Sound ☆☆☆☆ Entertainment ☆☆☆
Extras ☆☆ Value ☆☆
OVERALL ☆☆☆

DEAD CALM

Price: £15.99
Supplied by: Warner Home Video
Type of disc: Dual layer, single-sided
No of chapters: 37
Film format(s)/length: 2.35:1 widescreen / 93 mins
Audio format: Dolby Surround
Director: Philip Noyce
Starring: Nicole Kidman, Billy Zane, Sam Neill
Year made: 1988
Extras: Scene access; soundtrack in English, Italian and French; subtitles in 20 languages; subtitles for the hearing impaired in English and Italian.

This low-budget Aussie thriller opened to rave reviews and made director Philip Noyce into a major Hollywood player. A decade or so hasn't dulled its edge, and while Warner Bros has neglected the extras – there isn't even a theatrical trailer included – they haven't stinted on the quality of the DVD conversion. The picture definition is generally excellent, with only some minor anti-aliasing artifacting (along the yacht's waterline, for instance) on what's otherwise a first-class conversion with bright and sharply defined images. Sound is only Dolby Surround, but Noyce's use of audio is excellent – aside from a superbly unsettling score there's a full range of spooky creaking and lapping water effects to draw you into the movie's atmosphere. You've probably already seen this on TV, but most likely forgotten the unsettling opening – a car accident provides the impetus for Neill and Kidman to seek a sailing holiday. A drifting black schooner delivers Billy Zane onto the yacht and the voyage of terror begins. What the film lacks in budget, it more than compensates with a gritty realism which goes beyond Hollywood clichés, most notably in Kidman's sexual decoy games with Zane. Even if you've seen this film before, it's worth revisiting for the quality of the conversion. If you've somehow missed *Dead Calm*, then be in no doubt this is a great thriller.

FINAL VERDICT

Picture ☆☆☆☆ Sound ☆☆☆☆

Entertainment ☆☆☆☆☆ Extras ☆ Value ☆☆☆

OVERALL ☆☆☆

DEAD MAN WALKING

Price: £17.99
Supplied By: PolyGram
Type of disc: Single layer, double-sided
No of chapters: 17
Film format(s)/length: 4:3, 16:9 widescreen / 117 mins
Audio format: MPEG 2.0
Director: Tim Robbins
Starring: Susan Sarandon, Sean Penn, Robert Prosky
Year made: 1995
Extras: 4:3 or 16:9 widescreen included; English and German subtitles; 2 languages; biographies and production notes.

You can't help but be affected by *Dead Man Walking*. Based on the true story of Sister Helen Prejean (Sarandon) and her relationship with Death Row resident Matthew Poncelet (Penn), this is a powerful, non-judgemental tale of an extraordinary friendship. Sarandon won her Oscar for this, but the star of the show is the awesomely concentrated Penn, portraying a deeply flawed, fully rounded character as he encounters some form of redemption. This is powerful, intense movie-making, made all the more memorable by director Robbins' refusal to take sides. As one of the first DVDs on sale in the UK, the disk does have its problems. Top of the list has to be the most sluggish menu system you're ever likely to encounter, instantly taking the convenience out of the format. It's pretty basic on the sound and picture front too, although both a widescreen and fullscreen version is provided. Whether you'll actually want to

rewatch this harrowing film is up to you; what you need to know is that the DVD package is workmanlike more than outstanding, with with much better all-round packages on the market.

FINAL VERDICT

Picture ☆☆ Sound ☆☆

Entertainment ☆☆☆☆ Extras ☆ Value ☆☆

OVERALL ☆☆

DEAD RINGERS

Price: £9.99
Supplied by: Carlton
Type of disc: Dual layer, single-sided
No of chapters: 15
Film format(s)/length: 1.85:1 widescreen / 111 mins
Audio format: Stereo
Director: David Cronenberg
Starring: Jeremy Irons, Genevieve Bujold, Barbara Gordon
Year made: 1988
Extras: Scene access; subtitles for the hearing impaired in English.

Cronenberg is perhaps one of modern cinema's most respected directors, and it could be argued that *Dead Ringers* stakes claim to being perhaps his best film to date. It's a typically provocative and intelligent take on the true story of twin gynaecologists whose personalities are so interdependent as to be a single identity. Elliot provides the public face, glad-handing powerful clients, while Beverly is a brilliant clinician. It seems the perfect partnership, with the twins swapping identities at will when the other's skills are more appropriate to the task at hand. Elliot even provides his shy twin with lovers, but the entrance of Genevieve Bujold changes everything. A troubled actress with a bizarre fertility problem, her love affair with Beverly unravels the twin's relationship to disastrous effect. Cronenberg's intelligence makes the twins' plight not only fascinating, but also moving. As a DVD, picture quality through our grabbing system was unimpressive, but on a 29 inch television it seemed perfectly respectable, bar the odd imperfect fleck in the film stock. Sound quality is only stereo, but perfectly fine for this type of film. At any price, this is an excellent film, and at £9.99 it's an astonishing bargain.

FINAL VERDICT

Picture ☆☆☆☆ Sound ☆☆☆

Entertainment ☆☆☆☆☆ Extras ☆ Value ☆☆☆☆☆

OVERALL ☆☆☆☆☆

DEATH BECOMES HER

Price: £19.99
Supplied by: Columbia TriStar Home Video
Type of disc: Single layer, single-sided
No of chapters: 16
Film format(s)/length: 1.85:1 widescreen / 99 mins
Audio format: Dolby Surround
Director: Robert Zemeckis
Starring: Goldie Hawn, Meryl Streep, Bruce Willis
Year made: 1992
Extras: Scene access; behind-the-scenes featurette; theatrical trailer; production notes; cast and film-makers notes.

Starting as a black comedy about two women's quest for immortality, by the end this degenerates into a catfight between Streep and Hawn. An odd situation considering they're both immortal and there is no way a *Highlander*-style decapitation is going to end any life, as this film perfectly demonstrates! Despite all the death and violence, this is very much a Sunday afternoon family movie, a nice film which is pleasing to the eye and not too intellectually taxing to watch. As far as extras go there are enough to make you buy the disc if you're a devoted fan of the film, actors or Zemeckis, but there could have been so much more. The short featurette is the kind of thing you would expect to see on ITV as a filler between programmes! In fact, the notes are the only thing of interest here and then only if you can put up with reading through reams of text. This is all very interesting to plough through for a few minutes, but where are the deleted scenes? Tracey Ullman was completely cut out of the film after test screenings along with several other actors with speaking roles. And then there's the original super-happy ending – originally Bruce Willis and Tracey Ullman ran off to Europe together, until Zemeckis decided to film a slightly darker take! *Death Becomes Her* is a quite enjoyable film, presented well on DVD, but it's let down by far from enjoyable extras.

FINAL VERDICT

Picture ☆☆☆ Sound ☆☆☆☆ Entertainment ☆☆☆☆
Extras ☆☆☆ Value ☆☆☆
OVERALL ☆☆☆

THE DEBT COLLECTOR

Price: £19.99
Supplied by: VCI
Type of disc: Single layer, single-sided
No of chapters: 17
Film format(s)/length: 16:9 widescreen enhanced / 105 mins
Audio format: Dolby Digital 5.1

Director: Anthony Neilson
Starring: Billy Connolly, Ken Stott, Francesca Annis
Year made: 1999
Extras: Scene access; theatrical trailer; subtitles for the hearing impaired in English.

Can anyone really forgive and forget? Well, no-one in this superb film is willing to forget, but will anyone forgive? *The Debt Collector* is an intelligent, compelling and incredibly well-paced piece of film. The plot charts the attempts of Nickie Dryden (Connolly), a man who in his youth would collect others debts by way of the 'Policy' (don't hurt the ones who owe you money, hurt the ones closest to them.) Now, 18 years on Nickie is married and a successful sculptor. However, the officer who put him away is not willing to let him forget his past and certainly not willing to forgive him. Connolly is mesmerising in the role of Dryden; however, the show is defiantly stolen by the outstanding performance by Ken Stott as the obsessive policeman Keltie. He is forever pulling the audience between sympathy and resentment for his persistent hounding of a guilty man. Though the film comes at you like a harp blow to the head, the full force of the DVD would just about muster being tickled by a feather. With only a theatrical trailer posing as an extra, it's a crime that such a great British effort should be given such a weak forum.

FINAL VERDICT

Picture ☆☆☆☆ Sound ☆☆☆☆
Entertainment ☆☆☆☆☆ Extras ☆ Value ☆☆☆
OVERALL ☆☆☆

THE DEEP

Price: £19.99
Supplied by: Columbia TriStar Home Video
Type of disc: Single layer, single-sided
No of chapters: 28
Film format(s)/length: 16:9 widescreen enhanced / 119 mins
Audio format: Dolby Surround
Director: Peter Yates
Starring: Nick Nolte, Jacqueline Bisset, Robert Shaw
Year made: 1977
Extras: Scene access; filmographies; mono soundtrack in French, German, Italian and Spanish; subtitles in 20 languages.

A sex symbol of the Seventies, Jacqueline Bisset was the equivalent to our Nineties Kate Winslet – a posh English actress with unlimited sex appeal. Dressed in wet suits and bikinis, *The Deep* confirmed her status all the more. Gail Berke (Bisset) is on holiday in Bermuda with hubby David (Nolte) a couple who like to spend their time diving on shipwrecks to find lost treasure. When they find a ship full of morphine, Haitian drug dealer Cloche (Louis Gossett) becomes very interested in their discovery. In need of help, the two seek out professional salvager Romer Treece (Shaw – well-drilled at the 'sea dog' role after *Jaws*). There is a great deal of underwater filming which is visually gorgeous by Seventies standards, and the print has been cleaned up beautifully for DVD. The sound unfortunately offers only stereo or mono as you might expect. The extras are limited to cast filmographies, but the film offers some good home entertainment.

FINAL VERDICT

Picture ☆☆☆ Sound ☆ Entertainment ☆☆☆☆
Extras ☆☆ Value ☆
OVERALL ☆☆☆

Deep Blue Sea

Price: £19.99
Supplied by: Warner Home Video
Type of disc: Dual layer, single-sided
No of chapters: 33
Film format(s)/length: 2.35:1 anamorphic / 101 mins
Audio format: Dolby Digital 5.1
Director: Renny Harlin
Starring: Thomas Jane, LL Cool J, Samuel L Jackson
Year made: 1999

Extras: Scene access; audio commentary by director Renny Harlin and Samuel L Jackson; *When Sharks Attack: The Making of Deep Blue Sea* featurette; *The Sharks of Deep Blue Sea* featurette; deleted scenes with commentary by Harlin; stills gallery; cast and director filmographies; theatrical trailer; DVD-ROM links to original theatrical Web site; subtitles in English, Arabic, Romanian and Bulgarian; subtitles for the hearing impaired in English.

There's something about spying that single fin sticking out of the ocean that sparks a primal sense of fear in people – a fear that Hollywood capitalises on for the umpteenth time in *Deep Blue Sea*. A team of researchers, including minimalist shark wrangling hero Thomas Jane, sombre Ms Frankenstein Saffron Burrows, hip-hop chef LL Cool J and voice-of-reason millionaire Samuel L Jackson, genetically enhance mako sharks in a bid to cure Alzheimer's disease (yes, really). A tropical storm cuts off all communication and floods their undersea laboratory. As a result, the crew must fight and outwit these super-smart sharks or become fish food themselves. *Deep Blue Sea* is a knowingly derivative slice of hokum, best served with

lashings of popcorn, a large Coke and a sense of humour. It takes its '*Jaws* indoors' premise and attempts to splice the sub-aqua claustrophobia of *The Abyss* together with the disaster movie running and diving of *The Poseidon Adventure*. Unfortunately, the net result is a no-brainer that while entertaining for those who find *Commando* too subtle, will hold little long term fascination for anyone else. 50 years ago, these brutal creatures would have been seen going nuts thanks to a dose of radiation. Now society's bogeyman is genetic engineering. *Deep Blue Sea* can be seen as a ham-fisted morality tale, a classic case of man (or woman, in this case) tampering with big Mama Nature and paying the price. Bouquets for underwater director of photography Peter Romano, who captures some stunning footage of the sharks cruising menacingly below the waves, including several nifty point-of-view shots. Brickbats for composer Trevor Rabin, who apes John Williams' superior score too close for comfort. The 7 leads and director are given sparing filmographies but not biographies. The main event happens after accessing 'The Decompression Chamber,' which leads to a wealth of extras identical to the American version. In the commentary, android soundalike Harlin points out which sharks are real and which are not. Thank God for Jackson, who cheers things up with his cool-cat, piss-take delivery. It soon becomes clear that the main reason he agreed to appear in this movie was so he could play on Mexico's golf courses. *When Sharks Attack* is a well-rounded 15-minute featurette with interesting on-set footage and interviews with the exhausted cast. The 8-minute *The Sharks of Deep Blue Sea* focuses on the real, animatronic and CGI sharks that star in the movie and is an entertaining side order. An attractive set of 37 stills in the silent gallery and the familiar trailer complete this impressive package for an unchallenging, conservative but dumbly fun film.

FINAL VERDICT

Picture ☆☆☆☆ Sound ☆☆☆☆ Entertainment ☆☆☆
Extras ☆☆☆☆ Value ☆☆☆☆
OVERALL ☆☆☆☆

The Deep End of the Ocean

Price: £19.99
Supplied by: Entertainment in Video
Type of disc: Dual layer, single-sided
No of chapters: 12
Film format(s)/length: 1.78:1 anamorphic / 104 mins
Audio format: Dolby Surround
Director: Ulu Grosbard
Starring: Michelle Pfeiffer, Treat Williams, Whoopi

Goldberg
Year made: 1999
Extras: Scene access; featurette (4 mins); 'Making of' featurette (7 mins); 8 interviews; trailer.

From just a quick look at the synopsis, the story to *The Deep End of the Ocean* looks fairly banal: happy family has child kidnapped. Family begins to fall apart. Child eventually found. Family happy again. The end. This would make for fairly dull TV movie-type viewing, except there is a little more to it than that. While the story *does* concern the kidnap of the family's child and his return, the boy isn't found until 12 years later, by which time he's part of a family himself – a family who through a strange twist were never even aware that the boy had been kidnapped in the first place – and doesn't remember anything of his previous life. This makes for some fascinating watching as the two families unravel their conflicting emotions. *The Deep End of the Ocean* is essentially a chick-flick, but it's fairly intense viewing. As far as the DVD itself goes, there are some reasonable extras on offer which make this disc a pretty decent buy. 8 interviews are included and these are quite informative. The 4 minute featurette is a less-impressive affair – basically just an extended trailer – and it also repeats footage from the interviews. The most interesting thing is the 'Making of' footage which you'd expect to be a narrated short interspersed with more interviews, but in actual fact is simply uncut footage of the movie being filmed. This provides a rare opportunity to watch exactly how scenes appear from the point of view of a member of the crew and makes a change from the usual shorts that masquerade as 'behind-the-scenes' features.

FINAL VERDICT

Picture ☆☆☆☆ Sound ☆☆☆☆
Entertainment ☆☆☆☆ Extras ☆☆☆ Value ☆☆☆
OVERALL ☆☆☆☆

Deep Rising

Price: £15.99
Supplied by: Entertainment in Video
Type of disc: Single layer, single-sided
No of chapters: 12
Film format(s)/length: 2.35:1 widescreen enhanced / 106 mins
Audio format: Dolby Surround
Director: Stephen Sommers
Starring: Treat Williams, Famke Janssen, Anthony Heald
Year made: 1998
Extras: Scene access; 2-minute featurette; theatrical

trailer; subtitles in English.

Comprising of a B-list selection of actors, a fine array of special effects and a plausible story-line, *Deep Rising* is set aboard the luxurious ocean liner *Argonautica*. After an act of sabotage aboard the cruise liner, the ship is left floating adrift above the icy waters of the South China Sea. However, for those on board, the loss of radar and communications is the least of their worries, as from the bottomless depths beneath them something terrifying is rising at an exponential rate towards them. Finnegan (Williams) unwittingly boards the liner with the saboteur's accomplices – a small group of bad-ass mercenary soldiers. The delectable Trillian (Famke Jannsen) soon joins the group as the initial pre-contrived hijacking soon turns into a life and death struggle against a super-sized and incredibly intelligent sea creature. Within two shakes of a sea monster's tentacle, the remaining survivors are swiftly liquidated one-by-one. The advances in visual clarity thanks to DVD can often highlight poorly made special effects, but *Deep Rising*'s relatively small $45 million budget was not spent in vain. The picture quality remains constant and copes exceedingly well throughout – whether it's pitch black, blood red or explosive white. Coupled with a good audio quality, the DVD looks and sounds like most other discs to date – no better and no worse. Browsing through the blurb on the back of the box leads you to believe that the theatrical trailer and featurette are 'added value'. Unfortunately, the featurette is nothing more than a short trailer, fused with the odd spat of behind-the-scenes footage and crew/cast comments. The trailer is, well…a 'theatrical' trailer – just lacking any footage from the set. Nevertheless, *Deep Rising* is a fast-paced action ride that deserves more than the pitiful extras on offer here.

FINAL VERDICT

Picture ☆☆☆ Sound ☆☆☆ Entertainment ☆☆☆
Extras ☆☆ Value ☆☆☆
OVERALL ☆☆☆

Deep Throat

Price: £19.99
Supplied by: Cultporn
Type of disc: Single layer, single-sided
No of chapters: 16
Film format(s)/length: 4:3 regular / 51 mins
Audio format: Mono
Director: Gerard Damiano
Starring: Linda Lovelace, Harry Reems, Dolly Sharp
Year made: 1972

Extras: Scene access; commentary by UK producers; 'White rabbit' trivia screens; trailer; *Porno Chic* featurette; stills gallery.

We don't normally review porn here, because we're too high-class, and besides, it makes us giggle. In the case of *Deep Throat*, however, we're making an exception for a couple of reasons. Firstly, *Deep Throat* was the first – possibly only – hardcore movie to become a bona fide box office blockbuster, making (according to the FBI) around $500 million in its long lifetime. Forget *Blair Witch* – this is the most profitable film ever. Secondly, because this re-edited version adheres to BBFC guidelines on sexual content, it's not really porn any more. For those innocents who don't know what it's about, Linda Lovelace is a woman for whom sex is a bit of a bore – until her doctor (Reems) informs her that her clitoris is at the back of her throat. As a result, the only way she can reach climax is to…well, the title gives it away. But BBFC say, no BJ, no way. What Cultporn has done is to recut the film, using split-screens, zooms and video effects to ensure that anything dodgy is out of frame. The end result is about as explicit as *Postman Pat*. The commentary (by the UK producers) is interesting for both its cheery comments about the porn industry and the difficulty of cutting the film, and there's even a *Matrix*-style 'white rabbit' feature that reveals *Throat* trivia. But the lousy picture and sound, and lack of actual sex, make this one for fanatics only.

FINAL VERDICT

Picture ☆ Sound ☆ Entertainment ☆☆
Extras ☆☆☆ Value ☆☆
OVERALL ☆☆

DEFENCE OF THE REALM

Price: £9.99
Supplied by: Carlton
Type of disc: Single layer, single-sided
No of chapters: 15
Film format(s)/length: 4:3 regular / 92 mins
Audio format: Stereo
Director: David Drury
Starring: Greta Scacchi, Gabriel Byrne, Denholm Elliott
Year made: 1985
Extras: Scene access.

If ever there was a classic tale of government corruption, cover-ups and collusion, this is it. All the ingredients are here to make this an accomplished Cold War thriller: the London back drop filled with black cabs and red doubledeckers, the rogue Fleet Street newspaper reporter eager for a scoop, the disappearance of his trusty friend who's about to crack

the lid on a KGB plot… *Defence of the Realm* is worth seeing if only to remind you how grim the early Eighties actually looked. All this drabness is helped along splendidly by the washed out picture that's failed to get a fresh coat of paint in this new DVD version. Packaged under Carlton's budget Silver Collection, the credits read like a who's who of British cinema a decade ago. Produced by David Puttnam, the film stars Gabriel Byrne of *The Usual Suspects* fame supported by the likes of Denholm Elliott and Bill Paterson. The love interest comes courtesy of the fabulous Greta Scacchi. As for extra features, don't hold your breath, there's nothing other than the usual scene access, but hey, what more can you expect for £9.99? It's still a bargain, and a great film to boot!

FINAL VERDICT

Picture ☆☆ Sound ☆☆ Entertainment ☆☆☆☆
Extras ☆ Value ☆☆☆☆☆
OVERALL ☆☆☆

DELIVERANCE

Price: £15.99
Supplied by: Warner Home Video
Type of disc: Single layer, single-sided
No of chapters: 30
Film format(s)/length: 2.35:1 anamorphic / 105 mins
Audio format: Dolby Digital 5.1
Director: John Boorman
Starring: Jon Voight, Burt Reynolds, Ned Beatty
Year made: 1972
Extras: Scene access; soundtrack in English, French and Italian; subtitles in 10 languages; subtitles for the hearing impaired in English and Italian.

This is the film that should put anybody off canoes, camping trips and buggery for life. John Boorman's classic thriller benefits from a very simple plot – city boys on vacation are threatened by rednecks – given multiple layers by its stars. The aforementioned city boys (Reynolds, Voight, Beatty and Ronny Cox) are taking a last canoeing trip down a Georgia river before it's flooded to make a reservoir, when a run-in with two 'mountain men' both gives the film its most notorious scene and turns a holiday into a fight for survival. Each of the men responds in different ways; ironically, it's Reynolds (then at the height of his tough-guy popularity) whose macho decisions have the worst results, while family man Voight is forced into what in a conventional action movie would be the role of the hero, but here is pure desperation. The picture is remarkably good for a film of this age – at times it could have used a bit more contrast, and there are some ropey day-for-night shots that DVD makes look even more fake, but it captures the sweaty ambience of the forest settings very well. The 5.1 remix is generally serviceable rather than spectacular, but even so there are effective touches like chirping insects surrounding you on all sides. Bad news for those who like their movie classics to be accompanied by extras, though; *Deliverance* is yet another Warner DVD where multiple languages are considered more important than supplements. It's enough to make you squeal like a pig.

FINAL VERDICT

Picture ☆☆☆☆ Sound ☆☆☆☆ Entertainment ☆☆☆☆
Extras ☆ Value ☆☆☆
OVERALL ☆☆☆

DEMOLITION MAN

Price: £15.99
Supplied by: Warner Home Video
Type of disc: Single layer, single-sided
No of chapters: 30
Film format(s)/length: 2.35:1 widescreen / 110 mins
Audio format: Dolby Digital 5.1
Director: Marco Brambilla
Starring: Sylvester Stallone, Wesley Snipes, Sandra Bullock
Year made: 1993
Extras: Chapter Access; English/Arabic subtitles.

With a grunt of "Send a maniac to catch one!" Sylvester Stallone bungee-jumps from a helicopter and kicks off a Sly-ly (sorry) witty action romp. In the grim near-future of, er, 1996, Los Angeles is a warzone ruled by the demented Simon Phoenix (Snipes), and Stallone's John Spartan is the only cop tough – or indeed mad – enough to try to capture him. Capture him he does, though, only to find that in the resultant fireworks 30-odd innocent hostages were killed. Both Spartan and Phoenix are sentenced to long terms in a cryogenic deep-freeze prison, where they chill out until 2032. The world has become a peaceful, politically correct utopia of good manners and no crime, into which Phoenix escapes at a parole hearing and starts to wreak old-fashioned havoc. Since 21st century cops like Lenina Huxley (Bullock) aren't up to the task, Spartan is thawed to take Phoenix down, finding that the future isn't what it used to be… Being a Joel Silver (*Commando*, *Die Hard*, *Lethal Weapon 1* and *2* and more recently *The Matrix*) production, *Demolition Man* gets in more than its fair share of gun battles, car chases, snapping bones and ultra-large scale destruction. It's also got a decent sense of humour, especially with Stallone's culture shock and Bullock's sweet policewoman trying to

bring out the badass within herself. While *Demolition Man* is brutal fun (certainly miles better than Stallone's other sci-fi shoot-'em-up, the dismal *Judge Dredd*) it's only really a middling actioner, first-time director Brambilla going for fast cuts rather than creative choreography in his fights and chases. It's the humour that keeps things alive, with the cackling Snipes stealing the show and even Stallone displaying snappy comic timing. On the downside, Warner Home Video's usual policy of providing halfway decent extras has taken a downturn, *Demolition Man* lacking any features that could be described as special. You get the standard DVD picture and sound quality, but that's all. Hopefully this is a trend that will soon be reversed.

FINAL VERDICT

Picture ☆☆☆☆ Sound ☆☆☆☆
Entertainment ☆☆☆☆ Extras ☆ Value ☆☆☆
OVERALL ☆☆☆

DEMONS

Price: £15.99
Supplied by: Divid 2000
Type of disc: Single layer, single-sided
No of chapters: 12
Film format(s)/length: 4:3 regular / 88 minutes
Audio format: Dolby Digital
Director: Lamberto Bava
Starring: Urbano Berberini, Natasha Hovey, Karl Zenny
Year made: 1985
Extras: Audio commentary by Lamberto Bava, Sergio Stivaletti and journalist Loris Curci; theatrical trailer; behind-the-scenes segment.

This is a horror flick that wipes the smug smirk off the faces of more recent post-ironic teen scream movies. Two teenage girls are presented with free tickets to a movie premiere, and attend a screening along with a predictably balanced mix of the deserving and undeserving doomed. Only when events in the theatre begin to reflect the symbolism used in the film-within-in-a-film, does the gory fun start. *Demons* benefits from that rare commodity in Italian films – good dubbing, and will continue to horrify and repulse viewers well into the 21st century. The special effects are satisfyingly cringeworthy, with rivers of fake blood, open wounds by the score and more green pus than you could shake a sore-infested limb at. If the movie doesn't put you off with its Eighties fashions and dated flick haircuts, this DVD also offers some interesting extras. There are commentaries on the film from various involved parties, but the best add-on is an informative, if dated, documentary on the rudimentaries of the 'Making of' a horror flick. This little gem could become essential viewing for aspiring horror fiends or prank players! *Demons* is a brutal and gutsy horror cult classic which gains from its translation to DVD. Although it offers no more than the expected surprises, violence and unashamed gore, as well as the inventive use of a helicopter, this film should be welcomed to any collection with a gap for a horror flick. Just don't watch it on your own!

FINAL VERDICT

Picture ☆☆☆ Sound ☆☆☆☆

Entertainment ☆☆☆☆ Extras ☆☆☆ Value ☆☆☆☆

OVERALL ☆☆☆☆

DEMONS 2: DIRECTOR'S CUT

Price: £19.99
Supplied by: Divid 2000
Type of disc: Single layer, single-sided
No of chapters: 13
Film format(s)/length: 1.85:1 letterbox / 95 mins
Audio format: Dolby Digital AC3
Director: Lamberto Bava
Starring: David Edwin Knight, Asia Argento, Nanci Brilli
Year made: 1986
Extras: Director audio commentary; cinema trailer; special effects documentary; *Heavy Metal*, an original short film.

This follow-up to *Demons* brought Dario Argento back together with his long time collaborator Sergio Stivaletti. The film's plot, however, is as banal as ever. The Demons escape their captivity through the television sets of a new apartment block and soon hell is on the loose. The picture quality is, as you'd expect from a cheap horror flick, grainy and grim. However, the brilliantly creative effects of Sergio Stivaletti bring colour to the digital canvas, creating splashes of invention out of some lacklustre directing from Lamberto Bava. The DVD extras seem based around these effortless effects with 4 detailed mini-documentaries exhuming the secrets of how the creatures were created. Also worth noting is the short film by new director Bava, which, with a tight script and tense direction, is a vastly more engaging effort than the feature. Without the vigorous direction of Argento, *Demons 2* is a lacking horror that still delivers some excellent extras for the fans.

FINAL VERDICT

Picture ☆ Sound ☆☆

Entertainment ☆☆ Extras ☆☆☆ Value ☆☆☆

OVERALL ☆☆

DESPERADO

(on same disc as *El Mariachi*)
Price: £19.99
Supplied by: Columbia TriStar Home Video
Type of disc: Single layer, double-sided
No of chapters: 28
Film format(s)/length: 16:9 widescreen enhanced / 100 mins
Audio format: Dolby Digital 5.1
Director: Robert Rodriguez
Starring: Antonio Banderas, Joaquim De Almeida, Steve Buscemi
Year made: 1995
Extras: Scene access; audio commentary by director Robert Rodriguez; 2 music videos; theatrical trailer; 10-minute film – *Anatomy of a Shootout*; soundtrack in English and German; subtitles in 14 languages.

Gallardo made way for the more bankable Banderas, as the El Mariachi returns in a psuedo-follow-up-come-remake. The bigger budget allows Rodriguez to go all-out on action...and he does that in spades! Whilst the film languishes during the 'talky-bits', *Desperado* really shines in the outlandish, almost comic book-style violence – handguns roar and smoke like a Medieval dragon, whilst bad guys catapult into the air as if sampling the delights of an Alton Towers roller coaster ride. It's all nonsense, but extremely entertaining nonsense nonetheless. Extras-wise, Columbia has provided two music videos taken from the movie; another top quality audio commentary from Rodriguez; the theatrical trailer; and a 10-minute film school. You'll also be pleased to know that *Desperado* will put your home cinema set-up through its paces, with crisp quality visuals and an ear-shattering Dolby 5.1 soundtrack; you can almost smell the gunsmoke!

FINAL VERDICT

Picture ☆☆☆☆ Sound ☆☆☆☆☆

Entertainment ☆☆☆☆☆ Extras ☆☆☆☆☆

Value ☆☆☆☆☆

OVERALL ☆☆☆☆

DESPERATELY SEEKING SUSAN

Price: £19.99
Supplied by: MGM
Type of disc: Single layer, single-sided
No of chapters: 24
Film format(s)/length: 1.85:1 anamorphic / 97 mins
Audio format: Stereo
Director: Susan Seidelman
Starring: Rosanna Arquette, Madonna, Aidin Quinn
Year made: 1985
Extras: Scene access; audio commentary; original the-

atrical trailer; alternate ending; soundtrack in English, German and French; subtitles in 11 languages; subtitles for the hearing impaired in English and German.

Madonna made her big screen breakthrough in this story about a bored housewife (Arquette) who has a fixation on a girl called Susan. In her quest to be more like this mysterious character she manages to bang her head, lose her memory and think she actually *is* Susan! The film is essentially saying women *can* be individuals, which may seem a 'well, duh' message these days but still makes for an enjoyable movie. Surprisingly, Madonna isn't that bad – but then she doesn't really need to act, because her character, Susan, is exactly like Madonna in the Eighties! If you are a fan of Madonna, don't buy this expecting a musical triumph; she was only just hitting the big time so only a couple of her songs have been included. The picture and sound quality are what you might expect from a film this old but where this disc really shines is with the extras. The commentary comes from director Susan Seidelman, the vice president of production and the two producers. Despite the fact this is a large group it never degenerates into idle chat but instead remains informative and interesting. The alternate ending is the original closing scene shown to test audiences before the film opened in cinemas. Alas, there is no shocking change in plot; it merely adds an extra 5 minutes to the end and shows the girls going off together, *Thelma and Louise*-style across the Egyptian desert! If you're a Madonna fan you'll love this film; if not, it's still well worth a look.

FINAL VERDICT

Picture ☆☆ Sound ☆ Entertainment ☆☆☆
Extras ☆☆☆ Value ☆☆☆
OVERALL ☆☆☆

DETROIT ROCK CITY

Price: £16.99
Supplied by: Entertainment in Video
Type of disc: Dual layer, single-sided
No of chapters: 23
Film format(s)/length: 16:9 anamorphic / 94 mins
Audio format: Dolby Digital 5.1
Director: Adam Rifkin
Starring: Edward Furlong, Giuseppe Andrews, James Debello
Year made: 1999
Extras: Commentary; deleted scenes; behind-the-scenes featurette; music videos; original cinema trailer; cast and crew filmographies; multi-angle KISS concert; subtitles in English.

For 4 teenagers lodged in a basement in Seventies Detroit, there can be only one place to spend the weekend – at a KISS concert rocking and rolling with the kids. The hormonally-charged teens are about to dive face-first into a world of sex, drugs, and former playmates (Shannon Tweed). Filmed with a fine blend of sentimentality and gross-out gags that the Farrellys would bust a gut for, *Detroit Rock City* is a strange beast. You want to believe that director Adam Rifkin has bled his heart into crafting a homage to rock's most outrageous, excessive band and the heady time when drugs were still innocent and the only angst came from having loose flares. Then the crude jokes burst in; a cheerleader on the toilet, projectile vomiting and the 'serious' irony of sex in a confessional booth. And what more would you expect from the man behind straight-to-video classic *Bikini Squad*? This fast-paced whirl of fandom and fornication is a blessing all the more for the incredible DVD extras. Backing the now-standard behind-the-scenes featurette, commentary and deleted scenes are some bonuses that will place music fans on their personal stairway to heaven. The best is a full selection of the film's accompanying music videos and an interactive KISS concert; be the director and choose the camera angles! Managing to strike a fine balance between trouser-filling cheap laughs and poignant sentimentality, *Detroit Rock City* is a comedy in its purest sense; pathos and panty gags in one cool DVD package. Buy it and get ready to *rrrock*!

FINAL VERDICT

Picture ☆☆☆ Sound ☆☆☆☆☆
Entertainment ☆☆☆☆ Extras ☆☆☆☆
Value ☆☆☆☆
OVERALL ☆☆☆☆

DEVIL IN A BLUE DRESS

Price: £19.99
Supplied by: Columbia TriStar Home Video
Type of disc: Dual layer, single-sided
No of chapters: 28
Film format(s)/length: 1.85:1 / 97 min
Audio format: Dolby Digital 5.0
Director: Carl Franklin
Starring: Denzel Washington, Tom Sizemore, Jenifer Beals
Year made: 1995
Extras: Scene access; audio commentary by director Carl Franklin; Don Cheadle's screen test; filmographies; theatrical trailers for featured movie and *The Bone Collector*; soundtrack in English, French, Italian, Spanish and German; subtitles in 20 languages.

After making memorable low-budget thriller *One False Move*, director Franklin set about re-imagining classic *film noir* with a black protagonist in 1948 LA, a place of overt racism. Denzel Washington begins the film being fired by a white boss, so with house payments due, he's receptive to an offer by Tom Sizemore. And what could be easier than going down to his favourite bar and asking about some girl? The film's based on a novel by Walter Mosley and it shows, being long on character and plot, but short on cinematic pace. Don Cheadle adds much needed adrenalin as a usefully violent ally, but the movie never really catches fire. As a DVD, it enjoys reasonable picture quality and sound. The director's commentary is diverting enough, but including a screen test by Cheadle smacks of desperation. With Cheadle's performance so strong in the movie, why watch it again on grainy videotape?

FINAL VERDICT

Picture ☆☆☆ Sound ☆☆☆ Entertainment ☆☆☆
Extras ☆☆☆ Value ☆☆☆
OVERALL ☆☆☆

Devil's Advocate

Price: £15.99
Supplied by: Warner Home Video
Type of disc: Single layer, single-sided
No of chapters: 43
Film length/format(s): 2.35:1 widescreen / 138 mins
Director: Taylor Hackford
Starring: Keanu Reeves, Al Pacino, Charlize Theron
Year made: 1997
Extras: Director's commentary; scene access; theatrical trailers and TV spots; character biographies, production notes; 'About the Devil', about John Milton; subtitles.

What would you do if you found yourself working for Satan? That's just the predicament high-flying attorney Kevin Lomax (Reeves) finds himself in when he joins an elite New York law firm on the basis of his perfect case record. In many ways the opening moves in *Devil's Advocate* are similar to John Grisham's *The Firm*. Lomax and his spunky wife Mary Ann (Theron) are quickly seduced by the promise of a luxury apartment, sky high salary and instant friends, but all is not peachy in this heaven on earth and slowly the diabolical truth is uncovered. Once again, Reeves comes across as a mis-placed surfer dude (this time with a barely convincing Southern accent), but it is Al Pacino's excessive performance that steals the show as he tries to beat Jack Nicholson's Joker in the 'ludicrous grinning for most of the movie award.' Fortunately the film is well shot and there's a killer of

a twist in its tail, but it's Pacino's rabid finale which lingers in the mind long after the credits have rolled. As good a thriller as *Devil's Advocate* is, it is overshadowed by a DVD which packs in as much supporting material as the disc can handle – a truly excellent job on the part of Warner. The special features menu reveals biographies of 12 of the people involved in the film, including all principle actors – right down to the screenplay writers. You also get information on special effects, the locations, excellent and informative audio commentary by the director, a profile of the Devil (I'm not joking) plus various trailers. *Devil's Advocate* is a slick and erotic thriller which is well supported by one of the UK's best DVDs.

FINAL VERDICT

Picture ☆☆☆☆ Sound ☆☆☆☆
Entertainment ☆☆☆☆ Extras ☆☆☆☆☆
Value ☆☆☆☆
OVERALL ☆☆☆☆

The Devil's Own

Price: £19.99
Supplied by: DVD World (01705 796662)
Type of disc: Single layer, single-sided
No of chapters: 20
Film format(s)/length: 2.35:1 widescreen / 107 mins
Director: Alan J Pakula
Starring: Harrison Ford, Brad Pitt, Treat Williams
Year made: 1997
Extras: Multilingual subtitles; scene select; interactive menus.

Sentimentality is the order of the day in this fairly lacklusture offering from director Alan J Pakula. Harrison Ford stars as a grizzled Irish-American cop who unwittingly gives room and board to murderous IRA terrorist and fugitive Rory Devaney (Pitt). Described as a 'suspense drama' the story follows Rory as he travels to America to try and purchase Stinger missiles for the purpose of killing more soldiers. Rather than condemning him, the film takes an almost sympathetic approach as we witness him meeting old friends, arguing with his arms dealer and falling in love. The pace of the film is languid at best and the action sparse – it's like nothing so much as an extended version of one of the Murphy's 'Strong Words, Softly Spoken' adverts with a few gunfights thrown in to keep the audience awake. As far as DVD content goes it's fairly uninspiring too. Aside from multilingual subtitles and the obligatory scene selection all that's on offer is the theatre trailer – although that at least does have all the good bits of the film in it. Not one of Harrison Ford's best.

FINAL VERDICT

Picture ☆☆☆☆ Sound ☆☆

Entertainment ☆☆ Extras ☆ Value ☆

OVERALL ☆

DICK TRACY

Price: £15.99

Company: Touchstone Home Video

Type of disc: Single layer, single-sided

No of chapters: 16

Film format/length: 1.85:1 widescreen / 101 mins

Audio format : Dolby Digital 5.1

Director: Warren Beatty

Starring: Warren Beatty, Madonna, Al Pacino

Year made: 1990

Extras: Widescreen TV enhanced; multilingual subtitles; English/French/Italian soundtracks.

Dick Tracy really was the ultimate vanity project. Star/director/producer Beatty not only got to cast all his celebrity mates and his then-girlfriend (Madonna), he also made sure that he was the only male cast member not buried under pounds of hideous prosthetics. Nice work if you can get it. *Dick Tracy* was intended to be the next *Batman*, but it ended up as the first *Batman & Robin*. The luridly stylised 7-colour sets and costumes (meant to match those of the original newspaper comic strip) almost glow on DVD, and Danny Elfman's bombastic score fits the mood perfectly. However, sadly, the film itself is virtually plotless, as everyone bar Beatty hams it up shamelessly and the supposedly cute kid (called, imaginatively, 'The Kid') is downright annoying. This being a Touchstone disc there's the usual complete lack of any DVD-worthy extra features. Good old Disney strikes again!

FINAL VERDICT

Picture ☆☆☆☆☆ Sound ☆☆☆☆

Entertainment ☆☆ Extras ☆ Value ☆☆

OVERALL ☆☆

DIE HARD

Price: £19.99

Supplied by: 20th Century Fox Home Entertainment

Type of disc: Dual layer, single-sided

No of chapters: 30

Film format(s)/length: 16:9 widescreen enhanced / 127 mins

Audio format: Dolby Digital 5.1

Director: John McTiernan

Starring: Bruce Willis, Alan Rickman, Bonnie Bedelia

Year made: 1988

Extras: Scene access; behind-the-scenes documentary; theatrical trailer; cast biographies; soundtrack in Spanish; subtitles in 11 languages.

There are some films that any home cinema fanatic must have for their ultimate set-up. Movies such as *Terminator 2*, *Armageddon* and any of the *Lethal Weapon* series will give your subwoofer the work out it deserves. But for a truly dazzling display in a film that mixes all that wonderful noise and rumble with non-stop action entertainment, it could only be *Die Hard*. We first met John McClane (Willis) in the Region 1 version and were sufficiently impressed, leaving us impatient for a Region 2 release. But it also left us disappointed, along with numerous Americans, wondering why the film hadn't been anamorphically enhanced for widescreen televisions. So it's somewhat of a major scoop for the British market that 20th Century Fox have listened to us mere punters and given us what we want. Bursting with extra resolution and filling more of your widescreen TV than ever, the classic action flick has never looked better. Rarely has the fracas of gunfire sounded so ferocious with a Dolby Digital 5.1 soundtrack that's both wide in scope and ample in power. Your neighbours won't be complaining, they'll be wanting the prime seat on the sofa. 20th Century Fox have shown in the past, with such discs as the R1 *Alien* saga that they're right up there when it comes to piecing together a high quality Special Edition. It's therefore disappointing to report that the limit of the extra features here is a promotional behind-the-scenes feature (that doesn't even span 5 minutes) and the original theatrical trailer; for such a defining action movie you can't help wishing for more. Notwithstanding the poor extras, the film not only immortalised the white vest as an action accessory, it also made the big screen career of Bruce Willis and is far from disappointing in terms of visuals and sound. However, unlike the subsequent *Die Hard*s, there's more to this than a blood-stained Willis, repeated gun fights and massive explosions. Hans Gruber (Rickman) is the best villain of the series (so good that they wheeled out his brother for *Die Hard 3*) and the early tension and following action sequences leave its pretenders some way behind. Bottom line, *Die Hard* is a home cinema film, and whilst the absent array of extras is a little bereaving, it's hard to complain when the presentation of the film is so good. So let us salute a major release for the Region 2 market that incredibly outperforms its American cousin. You owe it to yourself to buy it.

FINAL VERDICT

Picture ☆☆☆☆☆ Sound ☆☆☆☆☆

Entertainment ☆☆☆☆☆ Extras ☆☆ Value ☆☆☆☆
OVERALL ☆☆☆☆

Die Hard 2

Price: £19.99
Supplied by: 20th Century Fox Home Entertainment
Type of disc: Dual layer, single-sided
No of chapters: 28
Film format(s)/length: 16:9 widescreen enhanced / 118 mins
Audio format: Dolby Digital 5.1
Director: Renny Harlin
Starring: Bruce Willis, Bonnie Bedelia, William Sadler
Year made: 1990
Extras: Scene access; behind-the-scenes documentary at just under 5 minutes; theatrical trailer; cast biographies; soundtrack in Spanish; subtitles in 11 languages including English, Czech, Swedish and Icelandic.

Director Renny Harlin is making something of a name for himself with DVDs in the States. *Cliffhanger* (featureless, but high quality) *Deep Blue Sea* (packed with extras) and *The Long Kiss Goodnight* have all sold well, with only the non-anamorphic *Die Hard 2* disappointing his legion of fans. However UK John McClane fans can rejoice, because unlike our friends from across the pond, we have been treated to the anamorphic transfer, instantly giving us a substantial smugness for once. We also get the '18' certified version of the film, as opposed to the theatrical and VHS rental release which was only granted a '15' certificate. However, the anamorphic transfer is the only addition of note, but it still feels satisfying to finally have the BBFC pass the US version uncut for once. The disc itself is another first rate piece of home cinema work from 20th Century Fox, not least because of the crisp widescreen picture (whoever invented anamorphic really does deserve a pat on the back). The star of the show once again is the Dolby Digital sound mix, which not only offers a wide and substantial sound stage, but plenty of bass to boost. Wall-shuddering stuff, and appropriate given the film in question. As far as the extras go, it's another pitiful performance that leaves us wondering whether there will be more substantial *Die Hard* DVDs unveiled in the near future. The familiar 5-minute behind-the-scenes promo is of little interest or entertainment. The rest of the disc is filled out with the theatrical trailer and the usual array of language and subtitle options. The film itself is a worthy sequel to *Die Hard*, if not coming close to eclipsing the original. Swapping a tower block for an airport, the film loses a lot of the tension and claustrophobia of the first film; substitut-ing instead, action by the bucket load and a wide selection of explosive speaker-testing moments. As a DVD package we'd have to be hard-hearted to argue that this is not an essential piece of digital home cinema – if only for the quality of the picture and sound.

FINAL VERDICT

Picture ☆☆☆☆ Sound ☆☆☆☆☆
Entertainment ☆☆☆☆ Extras ☆☆ Value ☆☆☆☆
OVERALL ☆☆☆☆

Die Hard With a Vengeance

Price: £15.99
Supplied by: Buena Vista Home Entertainment
Type of disc: Dual layer, single-sided
No of chapters: 27
Film format(s)/length: 2.35:1 anamorphic / 120 mins
Audio format: Dolby Digital 5.1
Director: John McTiernan
Starring: Bruce Willis, Samuel L Jackson, Jeremy Irons
Year made: 1995
Extras: Scene access; subtitles in English.

From the first big explosion we're safely back in McClane country, and this time Mr Willis has been given an entire city to destroy as an excuse for keeping the peace. Smoothly swerving the format towards the 'buddy' movie (*Lethal Weapon*, anyone?) McTiernan grabs hold of the *Die Hard* reins once again, and throws Willis, this time nicely paired up with Jackson, into a game of cat-and-mouse as the villainous Peter Gruber (hammed up a treat by Irons), brother of *Die Hard*'s Hans, has our heroes chasing around the Big Apple and solving riddles to prevent more explosive carnage. The whole reasoning behind this barmy plan has something vaguely to do with the typical revenge 'n' riches excuse that most big screen megalomaniacs prefer. But this really doesn't matter, as it's the adrenaline-fuelled rush from a relatively intelligent script that will keep you lapping up the action. Such praise is sadly unwarranted for the disc. Third outing this may be for the *Die Hard* franchise, but it's the second outing for this disc (originally recalled as they managed to use the heavily-cut TV edit for the master rather than the original source – d'oh!) and a real missed opportunity. The sound is pure class (it's worth having all those 'f' words back), but without even the inclusion of the theatrical trailer, there are more extras on the VHS version. This is another in a long line of DVD disappointments.

FINAL VERDICT

Picture ☆☆☆☆☆ Sound ☆☆☆☆☆
Entertainment ☆☆☆☆ Extras ☆ Value ☆☆☆
OVERALL ☆☆☆

DIRTY HARRY

Price: £15.99
Supplied by: DVDplus (www.dvdplus.co.uk)
Type of disc: Single layer, single-sided
No of chapters: 22
Film format(s)/length: 2.35:1 widescreen / 98 mins
Audio format: Dolby Digital 5.1
Director: Don Siegel
Starring: Clint Eastwood, Andy Robinson, Reni Santoni
Year made: 1971
Extras: Scene access; French and Italian mono soundtrack; multi-lingual subtitles; subtitles for the hearing impaired in English and Italian.

"You gotta ask yourself a question – 'do I feel lucky?' Well do ya, punk?" With these words, Clint Eastwood cemented his superstar status and created another iconic character to match The Man With No Name. We can only be talking about Inspector 'Dirty' Harry Callahan. Although later sequels would quickly turn Harry into a wisecracking cartoon of himself, to the point that by *The Dead Pool* he's as indestructible as The Mask, this first, and by far the best, of the series posed a serious question amongst the gunplay and chases – why do the rights of the criminal take precedence over those of their victims? Liberals in 1971 were appaled by what they saw as a glorification of police fascism, but by the standards of today's screen cops, Harry seems as reasonable as Dixon of Dock Green. *Dirty Harry* pits Eastwood's cynical and angry cop (a role originally written, bizarrely, for Frank Sinatra) against Robinson's hippie psycho in a cat-and-mouse game around San Francisco. Although it's a film that's been on TV often enough, the DVD has a few moments that tend to get cut out on the box. The '18' certificate is probably a bit harsh nowadays, since more violent new movies often get away with a '15'. The image is surprisingly good for a film of the era, when grainy film stock and washed-out lighting were fashionable, and Clint's booming .44 Magnum and Lalo Schifrin's distinctive score both come across well. Absolutely no extras, though so DVD owners won't feel lucky!

FINAL VERDICT

Picture ☆☆☆☆ Sound ☆☆☆
Entertainment ☆☆☆☆ Extras ☆ Value ☆☆
OVERALL ☆☆☆

DISCLOSURE

Price: £15.99
Supplied by: Warner Home Video
Type of disc: Single layer, single-sided
No of chapters: 44
Film format(s)/length: 16:9 widescreen / 123 mins
Director: Barry Levinson
Starring: Michael Douglas, Demi Moore, Donald Sutherland
Year made: 1994
Extras: Brief production notes; character biographies; scene access; 10 subtitle tracks.

Levinson's sexual discrimination role reversal film was meant for DVD. Not only does the entire movie have a glossy hi-tech sheen, completed by plenty of shots of pin-sharp computer screens and quite the most improbable email system ever devised, it also features Demi Moore at her most sizzling as the sexual predator who always gets what she wants. Crystal clear freeze-frames were made for the shapes Moore bends herself into during *Disclosure*'s pivotal coital act, and for the Kleenex brigade, the fact that you can watch this scene a million times without so much as a flicker is perfect. Based on the best seller by Michael Crichton, *Disclosure* is the story of sexual politics in the computer business. Family man Tom Sanders (a twitchy Douglas) has to forego his promotion to make way for old flame Meridith Johnson (Moore, tanned and taut). Unfortunately for Sanders, Johnson seems more interested in the contents of his slacks rather than the specification of his new Arcamax virtual corridor technology. The controversial question is who is harassing who? A standout feature of this DVD is the ultra-crisp soundtrack which ranges from VDU bleeps to grand orchestral arrangements. Certainly, anyone who has a 5-speaker sound system will not be disappointed although the picture is overly dark in places. The range of extra options is extremely limited though, and this is particularly galling when you consider the sumptuous computer graphics featured in the film itself. A bit of imagination and the presentation could have been stunning.

FINAL VERDICT

Picture ☆☆☆ Sound ☆☆☆☆
Entertainment ☆☆☆ Extras ☆☆ Value ☆☆
OVERALL ☆☆☆

DISTURBING BEHAVIOUR

Price: £19.99
Supplied by: Columbia TriStar Home Video
Type of disc: Single layer, single-sided
No of chapters: 36
Film format(s)/length: 16:9 widescreen enhanced / 80 mins
Audio format: Dolby Digital 5.1
Director: David Nutter

Starring: James Marsden, Katie Holmes, Nick Stahl
Year made: 1998
Extras: Scene access; music video by The Flys, 'Got You Where I Want You'; theatrical trailer; biographies; filmographies.

Arriving in idyllic Cradle Bay with his relocated family, James Marsden discovers that his new High School is apparently governed by the Blue Ribbons, aka the all-American beautiful people. With the help of a couple of fellow pupils outside the tribal system, Marsden reveals a Stepford Wives-style sinister underbelly to the Ribbons after he chances upon psychiatric hospitals full of freaks and gangs of club-wielding teenagers with laser eyes. Having skipped a UK theatrical release (unsurprisingly), the script by *Con Air*'s Scott Rosenberg and direction by *The X-Files* series' David Nutter does not exactly represent the high point in their respective careers. In fact, all it does is come over as one of the weaker episodes in the Duchovny/Anderson weirdfest (complete with the same music score), only without the imagination or self-deprecating humour. With a singular absence of suspense or shocks, all that is left is the gorgeous cast and a mercifully brief running time. At least the DVD does justice to Katie Holmes and co, with yet another top-notch, detailed image transfer from Columbia TriStar. Which really is the high point of the disc. The 5.1 sound generates as much suspense as the script and direction allows, although the dialogue seems a shade on the quiet side. Maybe the dubbing mixer was being kind… There's a hum-drum pop video, trailer and a few biogs to flick through, which does at least give lip service to the notion of added value. But with a film like this, the least disturbing behaviour of all is to avoid buying it completely.

FINAL VERDICT
Picture ☆☆☆☆ Sound ☆☆☆☆ Entertainment ☆
Extras ☆☆ Value ☆☆
OVERALL ☆☆

DOBERMANN

Price: £19.99
Supplied by: Metro Tartan
Type of disc: Single layer, single-sided
No of chapters: 16
Film format(s)/length: 16:9 anamorphic / 99 mins
Audio format: Dolby Pro Logic Surround
Director: Jan Kounen
Starring: Vincent Cassel, Monica Bellucci, Tcheky Karyo
Year made: 1999
Extras: Scene access; trailer; filmographies; review; stills gallery; subtitles in English.

For some, the 21st century is a nightmare, for Dobermann (Cassel) it's an opportunity. As the over-sexed leader of a gang of bank robbers he has one thing in his sights: the biggest heist the world's ever seen. Biting at his heels is maverick cop Christini (Karyo), whose sole intent is the painful destruction of Dobermann. The stark urban decay of Jan Kounen's *La Haine* has been transplanted cleverly into the high-tech thriller that is Dobermann, unfurling in a flirtatious ballet of destruction. With such a heady cocktail you'd be forgiven for forgetting the DVD extras. A smattering of filmographies, a cinema trailer and a dozen stills isn't enough to do the imaginative razzle-dazzle of the movie justice. The lack of extras aside, *Dobermann* is a classy splatter-house picture. Where *La Haine* was a masterful observation of inner-city claustrophobia, *Dobermann* is an explosively hip clash of humour and sadistic, stylish spectacle.

FINAL VERDICT
Picture ☆☆☆☆ Sound ☆☆☆☆
Entertainment ☆☆☆☆☆ Extras ☆☆ Value ☆☆
OVERALL ☆☆☆☆

DONNIE BRASCO

Price: £15.99
Supplied by: Entertainment in Video
Type of disc: Dual layer, single-sided
No of chapters: 12
Film format(s)/length: 2.35:1 widescreen / 120 mins
Audio format: Dolby Surround
Director: Mike Newell
Starring: Al Pacino, Johnny Depp Michael Madsen
Year made: 1997
Extras: Scene access; 7-minute 'Making of' (too brief); trailer; English subtitles.

Comparisons were made with Scorsese's epic *GoodFellas* when *Donnie Brasco* was released back in 1997. Though this belittles both movies, as apart from them both featuring mob families, and being based on true stories, they each took a different narrative view. Whilst *GoodFellas* revolved around a mob member who turned on his brethren, *Donnie Brasco*'s premise was that an undercover cop had to infiltrate an influential mob family. *Donnie Brasco* on DVD comes with a 'Making of' documentary which, due to its length (or lack thereof) does tend to make you wonder exactly why Entertainment in Video bothered sticking it on in the first place. It's only 7 minutes long (or should that be short?) and whilst you do get to see snippets of the film's production and brief interviews with Pacino, Depp and director, Newell, it really is a half-hearted effort. Oh, but you do get the trailer theatrical thrown in as well. Whilst Entertainment in Video should be given a pat on the back for producing *Donnie Brasco* as a dual layer DVD – avoiding the *faux pas* of releasing a dreaded flipper – it does seem a missed opportunity not to fill the extra space with some relevant *Brasco*-related goodies. Still, *Donnie Brasco* does remain an essential gangster movie, with or without the appropriate extras.

FINAL VERDICT

Picture ☆☆☆☆ Sound ☆☆☆☆
Entertainment ☆☆☆☆ Extras ☆☆ Value ☆☆☆
OVERALL ☆☆☆

DRAGONHEART

Price: £19.99
Supplied by: Columbia TriStar
Type of disc: Dual layer, single-sided
No of chapters: 33
Film format(s)/length: 2.35:1 widescreen / 99 mins
Audio format: Dolby Digital 5.1
Director: Rob Cohen
Starring: Dennis Quaid, Sean Connery, David Thewlis
Year made: 1995
Extras: Scene access; 'Making of' documentary (45 minutes); director's audio commentary; outtakes; cast and film-makers' notes; theatrical trailer; 5 TV adverts; Draco development archive; soundtrack in 5 languages, including English, German and French; subtitles in 9 languages.

It's a return to the Saturday matinee-style movie of old with *Dragonheart*, the kind of movie that, about 30 years ago, would probably have been animated by Ray Harryhausen. *Dragonheart* has no pretensions of being anything other than what it is, and that's a children's film. Whilst the likes of *Star Wars* can cater for both the young and the young at heart, *Dragonheart* has a certain child-like quality that may well alienate the more cynical adult. Set during a medieval time, Quaid plays Bowen, a knight of the old code, loyal to the cause set down by King Arthur and the Knights of the Round Table. Betrayed by his twisted prodigy and current King (camped up with relish by Thewlis) Bowen vents his rage at the dragons, vowing to slay them all. However, Bowen's misguided quest comes to an end when he teams up with Draco, the last of the dragons – stunningly realised by Industrial Light & Magic's computer effects, and aptly voiced by Connery. Columbia TriStar has really gone to town with this DVD package, which gives Region 2 users a genuine opportunity to hold their heads up high for once, rather than having to make

do with yet another shoddy Region 1 transfer. Extras are in abundance, including a 'Making of' documentary; audio commentary by the director; outtakes; production notes; cast and film-maker notes; two theatrical trailers; and, for completists, there are 5 TV advertisement spots. Okay, so the film may not be a classic, but fans of it should be royally pleased that Columbia has put together a top-notch DVD package. *Dragonheart* represents excellent value for money, and is an indicator of great things to come from the Columbia stable.

FINAL VERDICT

Picture ☆☆☆☆☆ Sound ☆☆☆☆☆
Entertainment ☆☆☆☆ Extras ☆☆☆☆☆
Value ☆☆☆☆☆
OVERALL ☆☆☆☆

DRAGON: THE BRUCE LEE STORY

Price: £19.99
Supplied by: Columbia TriStar Home Video
Type of disc: Dual layer, single-sided
No of chapters: 34
Film format(s)/length: 2.35:1 widescreen/ 114 mins
Audio format: Dolby Digital 5.1
Director: Rob Cohen
Starring: Jason Scott Lee, Lauren Holly, Robert Wagner
Year made: 1993
Extras: Scene access; 2 theatrical trailers; 'Making of' featurette; Bruce Lee interview; menu music; storyboards; Jason Scott Lee screen test; featurette outtakes; production photos; *Dragon* promo materials; Bruce Lee photos; feature commentary; production notes; cast and film-makers' notes; soundtrack in 6 languages including English, Czech, French, Italian and German; subtitles in 9 languages.

These things should always be taken with a pinch of salt. Well-crafted though *Dragon: The Bruce Lee Story* is, it's still a biography of a real celebrity who through cult status still has a lot of clout in Hollywood circles, despite being dead. As a result, and particularly due to his widow's huge involvement in the movie's production, there's a possibility that this could be a very one-sided account of the martial arts expert's life. Doubts aside, this is one hugely entertaining movie. From the opening sequence to the very last frame nearly two hours later, not one moment of this film is wasted, as the full and explosive life of Bruce Lee is lovingly crammed on screen. Starting at the moment when Lee is sent to America to forget a rebellious childhood and embrace his American heritage, the movie thankfully spends much of its time focusing on and chronicling his life prior to finding fame. For the most part, it concentrates on Lee's development as a family man and a philosophical apprentice. Elements such as starting his own martial arts school and eventually building his acting career seem to just happen, but much of this can be forgiven as it's always impossible to squeeze an entire lifetime into one movie. The movie seems content to depict Lee as a character rather than a social figure, and thanks to a stunning performance by Jason Scott Lee, this is pulled off fantastically, evoking genuine emotion as he spends his short 33-year life time struggling with his inner demons. Little is said of the man's demise, but then again the point of this movie is to examine how he lived his life, not how he finished it. Though a good movie, *Dragon* paints Lee to be whiter than white, concentrating on his plus points rather than the darker side of his psyche. Cohen spends an entire movie saying how great Bruce Lee was, and misses the opportunity to scratch below the surface. Once again, Columbia TriStar has outdone itself with this disc. There are an enormous number of extras, way more than you'd expect for what was in its cinema release a relatively low-profile film. There are actually more than you might at first think – on the menu screen, a continuation button leading to additional pages of extras is hidden at the bottom of Lee's tie, a bit of surprisingly poor design. The Jason Scott Lee screen test footage is fun, but it is the addition of an interview with the man himself, shot just after his rise to stardom, which is a superb counterbalance to everything that is presented in the movie.

FINAL VERDICT

Picture ☆☆☆ Sound ☆☆☆ Entertainment ☆☆☆
Extras ☆☆☆☆☆ Value ☆☆☆☆
OVERALL ☆☆☆☆

THE DRILLER KILLER

Price: £15.99
Supplied by: Visual Sales
Type of disc: Single layer, single-sided
No of chapters: 10
Film format(s)/length: 4:3 / 95 mins
Audio format: Dolby Digital Stereo
Director: Abel Ferrara
Starring: Abel Ferrara, Carolyn Marz, Baybi Day
Extras: None.

If there's one thing more painful than being killed by a powerdrill as it breaches your skull and sinks into your brain, it's watching *The Driller Killer*. The original 'video nasty' has either been the most consistently overrated film of its kind or it has aged worse than any other movie of the same period. Badly acted, poorly shot yet bound to sell through notoriety alone, this is cheap trash hailed as genius. If you want to feel like you're watching some sort of profound masterpiece, an exquisitely detailed and intelligent account of modern madness, you can put yourself through Xavier Mendik's introduction. Apparently a 'Cult Film Academic' from a university in Northampton, Mendik gushes sycophantic nonsense about *The Driller Killer*'s mile-deep message, its incredibly engineered impact upon the viewer and its astonishing relevance, while he himself gives off the impression of a sixth former delivering a forced class presentation. Though he and stylish cafés full of others like him will try to convince you that a few of Ferrara's clumsy directorial techniques qualify the film as 'more art house than atrocity,' it's impossible to be convinced upon watching the thing for yourself. Such 'experts' have gotten away with elevating *The Driller Killer* to the heights of greatness as a work of intense, poignant cinema while it has been out of the public's reach, but now that anybody can take home a copy the game's up. *The Driller Killer* is probably the most disappointing DVD you could buy, not least because the film's depiction of one man's descent into psychosis, fuelled by the repulsion of a diseased urban setting, was achieved so perfectly in *Taxi Driver*. As a tacky attempt to tell a similar story, *DK* is obsolete. Technically, this Visual Film pressing of the movie is an insult to the DVD platform. If you got a picture like this from a pirate video tape you'd take it back to the stall and demand vindication. The master was clearly appallingly dirty, clouding the screen in a hail of dust and scratches you'd expect from a strip of celluloid two or 3 times its age, and occasional massive corruptions look as though somebody took a big fat pen and scribbled mischievously over a couple of frames. Colour bleeding and image ghosting are horrendous, frequently stretching thickly out from their point of origin for one or two inches on an ordinary 30-inch RGB screen, especially where bright red often meets black. The picture jiggles around in a depressingly low-tech manner too, and then you've got the problems that were added at the encoding stage. Major pixellation or 'stepping' is evident wherever there are contrasting colours, showing how inadequate resolution was employed to immortalise this alleged classic, and the dark parts (most of every frame) are seething with an abhorrent mass of distracting compression artefacts. With only a Ferrara filmography that you could find on the Net in seconds and a disjointed collection of bizarre trailers left to bargain with, *The Driller Killer* DVD is a waste of vacuum-sealed aluminium.

FINAL VERDICT

Picture ☆ Sound ☆ Entertainment ☆ Extras ☆ Value ☆

OVERALL ☆

DRIVE

Price: £19.99
Supplied by: Medusa Pictures
Type of disc: Dual layer, single-sided
No of chapters: 30
Film format(s)/length: 2.35:1 anamorphic / 112 mins
Audio format: Dolby Digital 5.1
Director: Steve Wang
Starring: Mark Dacascos, Kadeem Hardison, John Pyper-Ferguson
Year made: 1995
Extras: Scene access; previously unseen footage (16 mins); audio commentary from director Steve Wang and actors Mark Dacascos and Kadeem Hardison; theatrical trailer; photo galleries (production, behind-the-scenes, candid camera); interviews with Mark Dacascos, Steve Wang, Wyatt Weed, Koichi Sakamoto, Kadeem Hardison; biographies and filmographies of the cast and crew; 4 deleted scenes and 2 extended scenes; *The Force Behind the Storm* documentary (47 mins); a selection of forthcoming Hong Kong movies (including trailers).

Filmed on a modest $3.5 million budget, *Drive* is one of those unknown films that, after a year or two in limbo, surfaces to claim its praise – and rightfully so. Marketing itself as high-impact action adventure that combines the ultra-slick fighting style of *The Matrix* and the comedic interplay of *Rush Hour*, it's not hard to see where their angle lies. Yet the team behind *Drive* explored these areas (however insignificant) before production even rolled on the aforementioned titles. Hong Kong action hero Mark Dacascos (*Crying Freeman, The Crow: Stairway to Heaven*) was drafted in to provide the necessary skills that fight-choreographer Koichi Sakamoto had envisioned. As the all-too-familiar story goes, Tony Wong (Dacascos) is a prototype cyborg assassin who has been enhanced both physically and mentally – sounds familiar! On the run from the Chinese mob that engineered him, Wong teams up with the reluctant Malik Brody (Hardison) as they try to evade their pursuers. The quick-witted banter between Dacascos and Hardison is often entertaining – although Chan and Tucker certainly did it better! But the action sequences are simply superb, as the versatile Dacascos displays his greatest assets to exemplary effect, cracking skulls,

breaking limbs and notching up kills. The Hong Kong formula combined with American action genre has never been more popular – or more used – than now, which is why *Drive* fails to win awards for originality. Due to its revival overseas and the ever-increasing popularity of this genre on British shores, the *Drive* team has spent a considerable amount of time in providing its small but loyal legion of fans something special. Boasting more features than you can shake a chainstick at (or at least a large remote control), *Drive* offers a better selection of extras than most blockbusting releases – which is why they feel the DVD is worthy of both 'Special' and 'Collector's' insignia. Efficiently organised in amongst the standard theatrical trailer, photo galleries and bi/filmographies are several interviews with the leading cast and crew members. The film's deleted scenes (which deserve to remain deleted) are well presented, with an introduction screen providing the reason behind their cutting room floor resting place. Naturally audio commentary is a must, and was recorded specially for the DVD release. But no extra-fest bonanza would be complete without a documentary, which is where the fabulously lengthy *Force Behind the Storm* documentary comes in – at a whopping 47 minutes! Although the picture and sound quality may not be as impressive as the extras on offer, they still put the VHS edition to shame – and so it damn well should! And, with an extra 16 minutes unseen by the VHS crowd, there can be no question which format to follow.

FINAL VERDICT

Picture ☆☆☆ Sound ☆☆☆☆ Entertainment ☆☆☆
Extras ☆☆☆☆☆ Value ☆☆☆☆

OVERALL ☆☆☆☆

DR NO

Price: £19.99
Supplied by: MGM Home Video
Type of disc: Dual layer, single-sided
No of chapters: 32
Film format(s)/length: 1.78:1 anamorphic / 110 mins
Audio format: Dolby Digital 5.1
Director: Terence Young
Starring: Sean Connery, Ursula Andress, Joseph Wiesman
Year made: 1962
Extras: Scene access; audio commentary by director, cast and crew; *Inside Dr No* documentary (40 mins); *Terence Young: Bond Vivant* (15 mins); 1963 *Dr No* featurette; stills gallery; original TV advert; radio spots; theatrical trailers; subtitles in English; subtitles in English for the hard of hearing.

It began on October 6, 1962 at the London Pavilion Theatre in Piccadilly Circus, when the world's paying audience first caught a glimpse of James Bond. One billion cinemagoers, 19 movies and 38 years later, *Dr No* reinvents itself once again, this time for the digital age. Introducing us to a world of espionage, glamorous girls, exotic locations, and a secret agent with the type of lifestyle most red-blooded men would kill for, *Dr No* was the first in a long line of films that led to the most successful movie franchise of all time. The period may scream 'retro' but the plot of *Dr No*, involving the mysterious sabotage of American rockets, provides enough dark cynicism, violence and black humour to put some of the more recent Bond efforts to shame. When Jamaica's British intelligence officer stumbles upon the doings of Dr No, he is mysteriously bumped off, and it is up to James Bond 007 to investigate. It might lack the traditional gadgets, but it's got the glamour, the style, the one-liners, and its fair share of girls with Honey Rider (Andress) yet to be outdone as the ultimate Bond babe. Ultimately what make this movie (and the legacy) so great is the shaken not stirred man himself. Connery wears the role like a perfectly tailored tux, and despite the chauvinism and the willingness to kill in cold blood at any given moment, James Bond is still without a doubt the coolest character in movie history. Never before has a film this old been treated with such respect on arrival to the digital format. Blessed with many of the same extras to be found in the Region 1 007 boxset, the mouthwatering animated menus are more than enough to ignite the excitement of *Dr No* before you've even seen one frame of the film itself. The *Inside Dr No* 40-minute documentary provides enough behind-the-scenes info to get even the mildest Bond fan salivating themselves to death. Missing, unfortunately, is the promised BBC *Omnibus* Special about Ian Fleming. In its place is an equally insightful 15-minute look at the life of Terence Young, which along with the countless trailers and TV/radio spots means that the James Bond Region 2 DVD adventure kicks off with a glorious bang.

FINAL VERDICT

Picture ☆☆☆☆ Sound ☆☆☆☆
Entertainment ☆☆☆☆ Extras ☆☆☆☆
Value ☆☆☆☆☆
OVERALL ☆☆☆☆

DRIVING MISS DAISY

Price: £14.99
Supplied by: Warner Home Video
Type of disc: Single layer, double-sided
No of chapters: 18
Film format(s)/length: 16:9 widescreen / 95 mins
Director: Bruce Beresford
Starring: Morgan Freeman, Jessica Tandy, Dan Aykroyd
Year made: 1989
Extras: Interactive menus; production notes; scene access; English subtitles.

Hoke Colburn (Freeman) chauffeurs aged, strong-willed Southern Matron Miss Daisy (Tandy) against her will. Hoke has been hired to drive Miss Daisy by her loving but exasperated son, (Aykroyd) after she spectacularly crashes her car. Freeman's character is equally stubborn and a great friendship forms through two people so different, they have a great deal in common. The widescreen format really shows off the absorbing, atmospheric photography, although the real beauty is the close up interaction between Freeman and Tandy. The director has applied a harsh, natural lighting and the attention to period detail can be appreciated in digital. Features include interactive menus, production notes (which are interesting and enlightening), scene access and with the trailer that seems to have been thrown in for no apparent reason. Adapted from Alfred Uhry's Pulitzer prize-winning play by Uhry himself, it is a compelling piece of acting and cinema.

FINAL VERDICT

Picture ☆☆☆ Sound ☆☆☆ Entertainment ☆☆☆☆
Extras ☆☆ Value ☆☆☆
OVERALL ☆☆☆

DROP DEAD GORGEOUS

Price: £15.99
Supplied by: Warner Home Video
Type of disc: Single layer, single-sided
No of chapters: 22
Film format(s)/length: 4:3 regular / 95 mins
Audio format: Dolby Digital 5.1
Director: Michael Patrick Jann
Starring: Kirsten Dunst, Kirstie Alley, Denise Richards
Year made: 1999
Extras: Scene access; filmographies; subtitles in English; subtitles available for the hearing impaired in English.

The cheesily grinning world of the American beauty pageant gets the *Spinal Tap* treatment in *Drop Dead Gorgeous*. In this mockumentary, a film crew records the run-up to the Mount Rose, Minnesota, Miss Teen America contest, along the way capturing the gradual whittling down of the field via various unfortunate 'accidents'. Gladys Leeman (Alley),

Mount Rose's richest woman and entirely uncoincidentally the contest organiser, is determined that her daughter Becky (Richards) should win, despite strong competition from trailer park resident Amber (Dunst). And Gladys always gets what she wants. Part satire and part black comedy, *Drop Dead Gorgeous* is clearly no fan of the small-town Americana it's mocking. The God-fearin' residents of Mount Rose (whether wealthy sleazeballs, trailer trash, corpulent rednecks or sweating perverts) all receive a roasting, and only tap-dancing mortuary beautician Amber gets any sympathy. The humour is sly rather than broad, almost to the point where some people might not even twig that it's a satire, but for them there are moments like Ellen Barkin's *Kingpin*-esque struggles with her artificial hook-hand or a parade of vomiting beauty queens to cackle at. The film doesn't really work as a mockumentary because it's too good. The camera doesn't do a *Blair Witch* shimmy, the lighting is always perfect and scenes are viewed from too many alternate angles. That said, it's an endearingly savage swipe at the distinctly American (naturally) attitude where for one person to win, everyone else involved has got to lose – utterly. Compared to the Region 1 disc, *DDG*, unfortunately, is more DOA. Widescreen version? Nope. DVD-ROM access to the screenplay? Uh-uh. A trailer? No sirree. All you get is a feeble filmography which even has the gall to admit that it's been cribbed straight from the Internet Movie Database. Pathetic!

FINAL VERDICT

Picture ☆☆ Sound ☆☆☆ Entertainment ☆☆☆☆
Extras ☆ Value ☆☆☆
OVERALL ☆☆☆

DR STRANGELOVE (OR, HOW I LEARNED TO STOP WORRYING AND LOVE THE BOMB)

Price: £19.99
Supplied by: Columbia TriStar Home Video
Type of disc: Single layer, single-sided
No of chapters: 28
Film format(s)/length: Widescreen (variable aspect ratios) / 90 mins
Audio format: Mono
Director: Stanley Kubrick
Starring: Peter Sellers, George C Scott, Sterling Hayden
Year made: 1963
Extras: Chapter access; English and German soundtracks; multilingual subtitles; trailer; filmographies; poster gallery; photo gallery; DVD trailer.

Some things never change. If you thought the recent moviemaking trend of having two films with identical storylines appearing at the same time was a new occurrence, think again. Back in 1963, shortly after the Cuban Missile Crisis and at the height of Cold War fear and paranoia, two films came out at the same time with the same plot – an accidental American attack on the Soviet Union. One was Sidney Lumet's *Fail-Safe*, which took the whole situation very seriously and was intended as 'A Very Important Movie With a Message'. The other was Kubrick's *Dr Strangelove*, which used thermonuclear war as a basis for the blackest of satire. *Fail-Safe* now looks dated, over-earnest and naive in its politics, while Kubrick's dark comedy is not only a modern classic, but is still just as effective as it was 36 years ago. Peter Sellers takes 3 roles; wimpish US President Merkin Muffley, stiff-of-lip RAF officer Lionel Mandrake and the eponymous ex-Nazi scientist with grandiose plans for every eventuality. When barking mad General Jack D Ripper (Hayden) flips and orders the bombers under his command to attack Russia, the story switches between 3 locations – the Pentagon War Room, where Muffley, Strangelove and gum-chewing General Turgidson (Scott) track the progress of the planes, Ripper's office (where Mandrake is locked in with the demented commander), and a nuke-laden B-52 bomber (commanded by Slim Pickens) on its way to really ruin some commie's day. The film turns into a nightmarish yet funny attempt to stop the bombers, where the very procedures that are intended to prevent an unplanned use of nuclear weapons end up impeding every attempt to recall the planes. Politicians, bureaucrats and the military – and the inflexible systems they create – all come in for scathing treatment by the script. Whether dealing with large or small targets, the film remains effective today because it attacks general human stupidity instead of specific policies. Enemies rise and fall, topical fears come and go, but politicians, generals and bureaucrats will always be with us. *Dr Strangelove* is a bit light on extras, particularly for a DVD that is targeted at collectors. The trailer is an interesting piece of near-experimental cinema, with images flicking past at almost subliminal speed, but the filmographies and picture galleries are very lightweight. It would have been interesting to see some deleted footage from the film, particularly the War Room custard pie fight that originally concluded the film (no kidding), but that didn't happen. Maybe it'll be on the 40th Anniversary Edition in 2003…

FINAL VERDICT

Picture ✩✩✩ Sound ✩ Entertainment ✩✩✩✩
Extras ✩✩✩ Value ✩✩✩
OVERALL ✩✩✩✩

DRUNKEN MASTER

Price: £17.99
Supplied by: Hong Kong Classics
Type of disc: Single layer, single-sided
No of chapters: 25
Film format(s)/length: 16.9 anamorphic / 106 mins
Audio format: Dolby Digital 5.0
Director: Yuen Woo Ping
Starring: Jackie Chan, Yuen Siu Tien, Hwang Jang Lee
Year made: 1978
Extras: Scene selection; trailer; music promo; photo gallery; biographies and filmographies of Jacki Chan and Yuen Woo Ping; interview with producer, Ng See Yuen; deleted footage; 'Kicking Showcase' featuring Jackie Chan, Yuen Siu Tien and Hwong Jang Lee; English or Mandarin soundtracks; subtitles in English.

The film that propelled Jackie Chan on his way to worldwide fame is was a groundbreaking one in the arena of martial arts films. Jackie plays Freddy, a young kung fu student with a skill for making trouble and not enough skill to fight his way out of it. Having displeased his father with his reckless ways and capacity for foolishness, he is banished to master the arts under Beggar Su (Yuen Siu Tien) – a notoriously harsh teacher. In one year, Beggar Su promises to teach Freddy how to become a kung fu master – but Freddy has to endure torturous training first. Only when he feels Freddy has suffered enough will Su reveal to him his secret fighting style, that of the Eight Drunken Gods. This film deserves its status as Jackie's best ever. The numerous fight sequences are enthralling; whipcrack fast and full of the warm, Carry On-esque humour that has allowed Chan to breach the difficult divide between martial arts and mainstream movies. Although it has done nothing to eliminate the Seventies haircuts, digital remastering for DVD means that the slick, quickfire moves of Drunken Master never looked better. The viewer also has the opportunity to choose between hilariously bad dubbing, and the original Mandarin vocals with subtitles. There are a plethora of special features including a fantastic 'Kicking Showcase' of moves from the lead actors. Drunken Master is not only a legendary and miraculous display of technical skill and Eastern humour, but the extra features make it a fantastic DVD to boot!

FINAL VERDICT

Picture ✩✩✩✩ Sound ✩✩✩✩

Entertainment ✩✩✩✩✩ Extras ✩✩✩✩
Value ✩✩✩✩
OVERALL ✩✩✩✩

DUMB AND DUMBER

Price: £19.99
Supplied by: Columbia TriStar Home Video
Type of disc: Dual layer, single-sided
No of chapters: 21
Film format(s)/length: 1.85:1 widescreen / 102 mins
Audio format: Stereo
Director: Peter Farrelly
Starring: Jim Carrey, Jeff Daniels, Lauren Holly
Year made: 1994
Extras: Scene access; cast filmographies/bibliographies; photo gallery; theatrical trailer; soundtrack in German; subtitles in English and German.

This is a road trip for those who are kids at heart. Dumb and Dumber is the Farrelly brothers at their best, it's their vintage film, and like all really good vintages, it matures with age. Harry and Lloyd are the intellectually vacant pair who take it upon themselves to travel across America to Aspen in order to return a briefcase that Lauren Holly left full of ransom money at an airport drop-off point. To be honest, that is the entire plot, but you get the feeling that the lack of narrative was intentional. In fact, the Farrelly brothers just emptied the stage and let their two leads take the spotlight. And it's a good job too. If there had been anyone else in these roles then there's a chance that this film would have fallen flat on its face at the first 'stupid' joke. As it stands the perfect casting of Jim Carrey and Jeff Daniels totally bring this film to life. From facial expressions to sharp line deliveries, everything about Carrey is achingly funny. There's one scene in the movie when Lloyd (Carrey) asks another character if he wants to hear "the most annoying sound in the world" and subsequently begins to make some loud but vague interpretations of a dying mule. There is a serious chance that Carrey could have played Lloyd this way throughout the entire movie. It would have been a lot easier to do so. Yet thankfully Carrey has managed to play Lloyd not only as a loving character, but also develop him as a showcase for the major talent that he is. Daniels however, clearly knows who he's up against as the other half of the idiot duo and so avoids all areas where Carrey excels. Instead of going for the facial and physical humour, Daniels plays the full notion of the film to the hilt. Of the pair of them, Daniels clearly plays 'Dumber'. And all credit to him. This is real virgin territory for Daniels and he manages to blend in seamlessly to the type of film that fits Carrey's capabilities like a glove. *Dumb and Dumber* was the film that really got the boat sailing for Peter and Bobby Farrelly, and to their credit, they produced possibly one of the best comedies of the Nineties. It's undeniable that the screenplay can't really hold a match to Oscar Wilde when it comes to intellectual humour, but thankfully this movie isn't trying to be anything more than a collection of schoolboy gags. It's just plain dumb and very simple humour; it's not big, it's not clever, but it is outrageously funny. The humour goes from regular witty one-liners to scenes that in any other film would be downright offensive. The idea of a little blind boy being duped into buying a dead, decapitated budgerigar whose head has been fixed back on with sticky tape on the understanding that it's just a quiet bird, doesn't actually sound funny, but on the big screen, it's priceless. It depends on your sense of humour as to whether you prefer this Farrelly brother movie to their other gross out romp, the ever popular *There's Something About Mary*. It all comes down to a matter of taste. What is clear is that Farrelly fans who buy the latter will get a much better deal on DVD. It's not that *Dumb and Dumber* is an empty disc. It's just that all it has going for it is a superb movie with superb picture quality. The rest of the disc is a decidedly half-hearted affair. The sound, though okay, is only in stereo rather than 5.1, which is an unbelievable decision by New Line for such a flagship product. Luckily most of the movie is made up of dialogue, so there's no huge explosions or special effects to be ruined by the stereo only transfer. There's a smattering of extras, but nothing outstanding: the photo gallery is worth a look, and the biographies are informative. That's it, apart from the standard trailer. The DVD is fine if you speak English or German, but beyond that you're a bit unlucky, which is quite harsh considering it's a European disc. A comedy classic, but the DVD offers little more than the VHS.

FINAL VERDICT

Picture ☆☆☆☆ Sound ☆☆☆
Entertainment ☆☆☆☆☆ Extras ☆☆ Value ☆☆
OVERALL ☆☆☆

Dumbo

Price: £15.99
Supplied by: DVD Net (0181 890 2520)
Type of disc: Single layer, single-sided
No of chapters: 12
Film format(s)/length: 16:9 widescreen / 62 mins
Director: Ben Sharpsteen

Starring the voices of: Sterling Holloway, Edward Brophy, Verna Felton
Year made: 1941
Extras: Illustrated scene selection; 5 different languages; subtitles in English and Dutch.

When a new format like DVD comes along, the executives at Disney must be rubbing their hands in glee. It means they can re-release every single animated movie the Walt Disney company has ever made – and that runs to an impressive number! Well, they do need the money to keep Walt's head encased in ice. Unfortunately for us DVD owners, Disney doesn't put much effort into its re-releases, so all you get is the bog-standard version of the movie with a few extra subtitles and a scene selector thrown in. A bit disappointing for Disney fans really, if Disney chose to embrace the DVD format, it could come up with some really special releases. Imagine preproduction sketches, documentaries, background information – it's all just sat in the Disney vaults. Of course, this doesn't detract from the fact that *Dumbo* is one of Walt Disney's all-time greats. First released in 1941, there are many generations of children who have grown up with the hilarious tale of the little elephant born with extra large ears. He causes nothing but trouble at his circus home, and so decides to pack his trunk (boom, boom) and head off to seek his fortune with his pal Timothy Mouse in tow. If you've managed to resist all the different versions of *Dumbo* on VHS, and you feel you need a good, wholesome family movie to enjoy on a Sunday afternoon (and remember you can watch it again and again without it losing quality) – *Dumbo* fits the bill perfectly.

FINAL VERDICT

Picture ☆☆ Sound ☆☆ Entertainment ☆☆☆☆
Extras ☆ Value ☆☆
OVERALL ☆☆☆

Dune

Price: £19.99
Supplied by: Castle Home Video
Type of disc: Dual layer, single-sided
No of chapters: 16
Film format(s)/length: 2.35:1 widescreen / 131 mins
Audio format: Dolby Digital 5.1
Director: David Lynch
Starring: Kyle MacLachlan, Sting, Max von Sydow
Year made: 1984
Extras: Scene access; theatrical trailer; slide show.

Planet Arrakis, known as 'Dune', is the sole source of the spice Melange. This valuable spice is used to enable navigators to travel enormous distances through space and time. Many factions wish to control Dune and retain the power of the spice. This film tells the tale of Paul Atreides, son of Duke Leto, and his ascension to power as the universe's super-being, amidst a backdrop of treachery and warfare. *Dune* is notorious for being the film that all but sunk Dino De Laurentiis' production company. The film cost $40 million to make and only managed to recoup half of that at the box office. The director is rumoured to have turned down *Return of the Jedi*, to make this film and the finished product has been no where near as successful. As you'd expect what we do have with Lynch at the helm, is a film interwoven with dream sequences and illusory visual effects. This, mixed with some outstanding costumes and spectacular scenery, helps create a vivid world in which all the characters appear larger than life. The story is told haphazardly and is sometimes confusing. It was a brave effort by Lynch to cram such an incredibly detailed book into a two hour film, but the cracks do show. You'll either have to read the book, or watch the film several times, to understand some of the nuances and secondary plot lines. As with most of Castle's DVD back catalogue, the extras are very sparse. Sure, there's a poorly-mastered theatrical trailer and well-presented scene access, but the introductory pamphlet that comes with the DVD is more interesting than both of these. The Dolby Digital soundtrack is spectacularly realised, particularly during the battle scenes, as the sonic weapons and giant sandworms roar into action. An enhanced digital picture brings out the richness of the costume and set design, both of which are very ambitious and without fault. The music score is also outstanding and richly deserves the laser quality of DVD. This is definitely a DVD that should be bought by fans of the book and those that love a good sci-fi yarn. Despite the lack of extras, the *Dune* DVD is a very worthy translation of a spectacular film.

FINAL VERDICT

Picture ☆☆☆ Sound ☆☆☆☆
Entertainment ☆☆☆☆ Extras ☆☆ Value ☆☆☆
OVERALL ☆☆☆

EAST IS EAST

Price: £19.99
Supplied by: FilmFour
Type of disc: Dual layer, single-sided
No of chapters: 17
Film format(s)/length: 1.85:1 anamorphic / 92 mins
Audio format: Dolby Digital 5.1
Director: Damien O'Donnell

Starring: Om Puri, Linda Bassett, Jimi Mistry
Year made: 1999
Extras: Scene access; theatrical trailer; director's commentary; deleted scenes with director's commentary; cast and crew interviews; behind-the-scenes footage; TV ads; audio description for the visually impaired; subtitles in English for the hearing impaired.

Avoiding the usual Britflick 'kitchen sink drama' label, *East is East* is a laugh out loud, yet all too frighteningly dramatic look at the trials and tribulations of the Khan family as they search for a variety of conflicting identities in an Anglo-Pakistani family as in Salford circa 1971. George Khan (Puri, giving a sincerely astounding performance) is the immigrant from Pakistan who has taken an English wife, Ella (Bassett), and has 7 children and a thriving chip shop to show for his time in England so far. Triggered by his elder son's refusal to have an arranged marriage, George's world begins to crumble around him and he seeks refuge deeper into the sanctuary of the tradition in which he was raised. His children each have their own response to the direction in which George is intent on taking their lives, and it is around this conflict of attitudes that the plot, humour and drama of the film happily entwine. O'Donnell has put together a movie full of oppositions that play against each other to resolve in a balanced equilibrium. Well paced, acted and shot, the true beauty here is that the audience is invited to float in their role of voyeur, rarely setting on one specific character as the protagonist of the piece, and never enforcing a single perspective. As a result the movie attempts to offer no real solutions to the problems it raises, a wise move considering how crass and messed up the outcome could have been in just the 92 minutes the film has to play out. It's not *East is East*'s job to suggest solutions, but to just show the eventual heartbreak. The set piece is charming and the family are immediately likable, realistic, and each flawed in their own tragic fashion, with the most memorable performance coming from the Khans' youngest son, Sajid, played with aplomb by the screen-stealing Jordan Routledge. This isn't a shallow DVD, but by no means is it inspirational. The picture quality is fine, yet oddly enough it is the 5.1 surround that proves to be the real treat. O'Donnell's commentary is interesting in terms of the film-making process, but reveals little about his thoughts for his characters. In fact it's the deleted scenes that O'Donnell's commentary really bring a shine to, and help make *East is East* a worthwhile DVD.

FINAL VERDICT

Picture ☆☆☆☆ Sound ☆☆☆☆☆
Entertainment ☆☆☆☆☆ Extras ☆☆☆☆
Value ☆☆☆☆
OVERALL ☆☆☆☆

EASY RIDER

Price: £19.99
Supplied by: Columbia TriStar Home Video
Type of disc: Dual layer, single-sided
No of chapters: 32
Film format(s)/length: 1.85:1 widescreen / 92 mins
Audio format: Dolby Digital 5.1
Director: Dennis Hopper
Starring: Peter Fonda, Dennis Hopper, Jack Nicholson
Year made: 1969
Extras: Scene access; 65-minute 'Making of' documentary; director's commentary; filmographies; soundtrack in French, German, Italian and Spanish (stereo); subtitles in 9 languages.

The name Fonda has a long history in Hollywood. 3 generations worth in fact. Henry, Jane, and now Bridget have all managed to attain star status for their sins, but there was one family member who failed to reach such dizzy heights. It was Peter, son of Henry, brother of Jane and father of Bridget who was the genuine enigma when it came to stardom. Having amounted very few major hits in his career, this cult classic is probably his most memorable work. And what a classic it is! Based on an idea by Fonda and co-scripted and directed by Hopper, *Easy Rider* tells the tale of two bikers named Wyatt (Fonda) and Billy (Hopper) who score some cocaine, sell it on and use the money to travel across America to New Orleans to see the Mardi Gras. On the way they smoke a lot of dope, pick up hitchhikers, and ride into the darker corner of America, the one filled with bigotry and ignorance. This is a seminal film, lovingly crafted by its maker that, though it may run along a slow track with a narrow script, has a very deep and broad message. Billy and Wyatt are two young drug-taking, easy-living men who are indigenous of the era that spawned them. 1969 was a landmark year in American history, and here are two men who chose to live the American dream the way their generation was supposed to. However, on their journey they find that the ethos of society has become twisted and to practice being a free man in the land of the free brings nothing but persecution and hate. The film has a mood that matches its era. There is a very mellow vibe to it, probably as a direct result of its infatuation with narcotics, but still underneath there is a dark impending unpleasantness which makes a rather slow-paced movie very compelling. Fortunately, this DVD is another release from Columbia TriStar, a distributor who are fast becoming the respectable market leaders when it comes to putting out decent DVD packages. There is a 65-minute, all new documentary featuring the principal cast and crew, though for the most part the cast was the crew. Fonda talks fondly about smoking marijuana in a tone of voice that could convince you that he still does and Hopper talks lovingly about his first experience as a director, and the cult road movie that he was forced to cut from 3 hours to 90 minutes. Hopper also provides one of the most engaging commentaries ever to appear on DVD. Considering that the two haven't spoken for the last 30 years, he has a great respect for the efforts made by Fonda in the movie. *Easy Rider* is one of those movies that Hollywood folklore states you must see and this DVD is definitely the most pleasurable way of doing it.

FINAL VERDICT

Picture ☆☆☆☆ Sound ☆☆☆☆
Entertainment ☆☆☆☆☆ Extras ☆☆☆☆
Value ☆☆☆☆
OVERALL ☆☆☆☆

EDTV: COLLECTOR'S EDITION

Price: £19.99
Supplied by: Columbia TriStar Home Video
Type of disc: Dual layer, single-sided
No of chapters: 18
Film format(s)/length: 1.85:1 anamorphic / 118 min
Audio format: Dolby Digital 5.1
Director: Ron Howard
Starring: Matthew McConaughey, Jenna Elfman, Woody Harrelson
Year made: 1999
Extras: Scene access; 'Making of' documentary *Caught in the Camera's Eye*; audio commentary by director Ron Howard; audio commentary by writers Lowell Ganz/Babaloo Mandel; deleted scenes; outtakes; soundtrack in English and German; subtitles in 20 languages.

At heart, *EDtv*'s a stereotypical romantic comedy with a 'voyeur-TV' twist. While it lacks *The Truman Show*'s intellectual aspirations, by way of compensation it's a much funnier film with a true star performance by good ol' boy Matthew McConaughey. It's also superbly packaged on DVD with plenty of extras. Most 'deleted scenes' rarely amount to much, but *EDtv* offers no less than 35 minutes of footage, ranging from minor transition scenes to major dramatic incidents. There's a lengthy cemetery confrontation between the two brothers, a few running jokes from an excised sub-plot featuring a black variation on *EDtv* called *Joma*, and numerous TV critic scenes – "I'd rather watch soccer," complains one commentator. Some of the character changes that seemed a little strange in the movie gain greater credence after watching the deleted scenes. On top of this, there's a generous, 7-minute plus portion of outtakes including numerous scenes of McConaughey and Harrelson cracking up, not to mention the Elizabeth Hurley-squashed feline scene. There's also a pair of audio commentaries, one by director Ron Howard and another by the writers, plus a 30-minute 'Making of' documentary. Admittedly, the latter is mostly an eulogy to how great a person Ron Howard is, but it all adds up to plenty of good value. The European version also has to squeeze in multiple languages, which means the loss of a pair of music videos – featuring Bon Jovi and Barenaked Ladies – plus some production notes, but nevertheless this is an excellent DVD.

FINAL VERDICT
Picture ☆☆☆☆ Sound ☆☆☆
Entertainment ☆☆☆☆ Extras ☆☆☆☆
Value ☆☆☆☆☆
OVERALL ☆☆☆☆

EDUCATING RITA

Price: £9.99
Supplied by: Carlton
Type of disc: Single layer, single-sided
No of chapters: 15
Film format(s)/length: 4:3 regular / 108 mins
Audio format: Mono
Director: Lewis Gilbert
Starring: Julie Walters, Michael Caine, Maureen Lipman
Year made: 1983
Extras: Scene access; Carlton Silver Collection trailer.

Of all the films Caine has made since the Sixties, the 4 that usually spring to mind are *Hannah and her Sisters*, *Dirty Rotten Scoundrels*, *Little Voice* and the stage play adaptation of *Educating Rita*. Caine is the self-loathing drunken English tutor teaching Open University students – enter Rita (Walters) stage left, a rough diamond Liverpudlian, desperate to escape her futureless existence and gain acceptance with the intellectual elite. While their relationship is handled well, both academia and working class life are depicted with the same stereotypical inaccuracy (the toffs laugh that a colleague cannot define 'assonance', while the proles have sing-songs to copyright-free music down the local boozer). The supporting cast are awful, much of the dialogue crass and direction

flat and uninspiring. The good news is it's part of Carlton's new budget Silver Collection series, all priced at £9.99. The bad news is the non-widescreen picture is dull and weaves hypnotically from side to side, while the scratchy mono sound (not stereo, as billed) merely drifts sync as it showcases the worst musical score in celluloid history. If you don't own the video and have a desperate urge to see it all again, this may be for you. Otherwise, it looks and sounds no better than VHS, so even the £9.99 asking price doesn't make for an educated purchase.

FINAL VERDICT
Picture ☆ Sound ☆ Entertainment ☆☆☆
Extras ☆ Value ☆☆☆☆
OVERALL ☆☆

8MM

Price: £19.99
Supplied by: Columbia TriStar Home Video
Type of disc: Dual layer, single-sided
No of chapters: 28
Film format(s)/length: 16:9 widescreen enhanced / 118 mins
Audio format: Dolby Digital 5.1
Director: Joel Schumacher
Starring: Nicolas Cage, Joaquin Phoenix, James Gandolfini
Year made: 1999
Extras: Scene access; behind-the-scenes featurette; theatrical trailer; cast filmographies; director's commentary; soundtrack in German; multi-lingual subtitles.

The only spark of intelligence in this dire movie is the title. Andrew Kevin Walker (who also wrote *Se7en*) vociferously distanced himself from Schumacher's gaudy, shallow take on his script, but it's hard to imagine even Fincher rescuing this trash. The core narrative has an intrinsic fascination; PI Nicholas Cage is called in to a rich widower's residence, where he's asked to investigate a snuff movie found amongst the deceased's belongings. Cage provides a brief glimpse of a more interesting movie in scenes with his wife; his abortive attempts at sex and chill conversations – he seems the sort of character ripe to be seduced. Sadly, the only subsequent development of Cage's character is the deterioration of his dress sense until he looks like a pimp. Compare Cage's blank performance to De Niro's masterful disintegration in *Taxi Driver*, and the banality of *8mm*'s script is most cruelly exposed. When *Taxi Driver* descended into its concluding bloodbath you were horrified, but had glimmerings of understanding. In *8mm*, you simply feel a sense of boredom at sitting through a weak *Silence of the Lambs* rip-off. The sharp, new print makes a finely defined DVD, although Schumacher's preference for muted colours and gloomy lighting makes for unexciting visuals. The featurette is the usual trailer with one-line snippets from the actors, leaving the most notable extra as Schumacher's droning commentary. It has its moments – "I come from the street, had some problems with drugs in my youth," – but is most soporific. Schumacher's observation that serial-killers tend to look normal on the outside speaks volumes about the level of insight of the whole production.

FINAL VERDICT

Picture ☆☆☆☆ Sound ☆☆☆☆
Entertainment ☆ Extras ☆☆☆ Value ☆☆
OVERALL ☆☆

ELIZABETH

Price: £17.99
Supplied by: PolyGram
Type of disc: Dual layer, double-sided
No of chapters: 21
Film format(s)/length: 4:3 regular / 121 mins
Audio format: Dolby Digital 5.1
Director: Shekhar Kapur
Starring: Cate Blanchett, Geoffrey Rush, Joseph Fiennes
Year made: 1998
Extras: Scene selection; cast and crew interviews; 'Making of' featurette; behind-the-scenes footage.

Being your average DVD owner – young(ish), male who who'd rather spend his hard-earned cash on essentials like the latest films on a silver disc than frivolous money-wasters like food – period dramas are not really my cup of tea. However, from the traumatic opening moments, to the powerful climax, *Elizabeth* is a gripping, harsh tale that is at home on DVD as *Face/Off* or *The Rock*. The story of England's 'Virgin' Queen has been told before, but never with as much style and guile as here. Rather than cramming her entire life into just under two hours, the film takes up just before her ascension to the throne and deals almost exclusively with the plot to have her overthrown. It's obvious the writers have taken dramatic liberties – but the result is a finely-woven thriller that could hold its own with almost all of its modern-day peers. This is due, mainly, to the very contemporary way in which this 400-year-old story is told. The direction is lively and slick, presenting history in a manner accessible to even the most fiction-hungry viewer. The picture quality isn't striking, but this is no fault of the transfer, rather the deliberate way in which

the film has been shot – muted and slightly grainy in places. Sonically, though, *Elizabeth* surprises, with excellent use of all available speakers. The arrow 'thwack', in particular, could be used as a surround sound showcase. Hit 'Menu' and there's all manner of extras – though it has to be said that they look more impressive on paper than the reality proves. The 'Interviews' are informative, if a little short and unspectacular, and the 'Making of' seems to bizarrely forget that the film's computer-generated sequences exist, preferring instead to provide additional interviews with those not interviewed in the, um, interviews. This is a shame, as an in-depth look at the subtlety of the CGI would have been fascinating. Finally, the behind-the-scenes section is nothing more than that – a few minutes' worth of footage. Worth a look, but probably only once. What's mildly disappointing is the lack of a widescreen version. PolyGram managed this with *Lock, Stock and Two Smoking Barrels*, so its exclusion comes as a little surprise. That said, the pan and scan is handled well, with no obvious cropping. *Elizabeth* is a cracking movie that most of you will no doubt overlook. Indeed, had this not been allocated as one of my reviews this issue, I would never have seen it. This comes highly recommended, even if it is not your usual kind of thing.

FINAL VERDICT

Picture ☆☆☆☆ Sound ☆☆☆☆☆
Entertainment ☆☆☆☆☆ Extras ☆☆☆☆
Value ☆☆☆☆
OVERALL ☆☆☆☆☆

EL MARIACHI

(on same disc as *Desperado*)
No of chapters: 28
Film format(s)/length: 16:9 widescreen enhanced/ 82 mins
Audio format: Stereo
Director: Robert Rodriguez
Starring: Carlos Gallardo, Consuelo Gómez, Peter Marquardt
Year made: 1992
Extras: Scene access; in-depth audio commentary by director Robert Rodriguez; cast filmographies; US theatrical trailer; 10-minute 'film school' by Rodriguez; Rodriguez's first short film, *Bedhead*; soundtrack in German; subtitles in 15 languages.

It is an impressive feat for a director to reach the major Hollywood directorial leagues after just one picture. But Robert Rodriguez ended up rubbing shoulders alongside the likes of Quentin Tarantino and Antonio Banderas after his first feature film, *El*

Mariachi. The tale of a naive guitar player (Gallardo) who ends up being mistaken for a gun-toting killer is an entertaining romp, given a unique touch due to its amateurish roots (it was originally designed to go direct to the Spanish-language video market) None of the cast were professional actors. Most of them being residents from the town the film was shot in who were roped in with the promise that their business would be promoted in the movie. *El Mariachi* is by no means a DVD filler for the bigger budget remake *Desperado*, as director Robert Rodriguez has provided one of the most in-depth audio commentaries ever put to DVD. He literally crams more information into 10 minutes than some audio commentaries manage in a full hour-and-a-half. There are some genuine nuggets of wisdom about film-making which make this essential listening for all aspiring movie directors. The extras are bolstered by the inclusion of Rodriguez's acclaimed short film *Bedhead*, a 10-minute film school documentary, the US theatrical trailer and cast filmographies. Not bad for a straight to video effort that ended up inspiring a remake.

FINAL VERDICT

Picture ☆☆☆☆ Sound ☆☆☆☆☆
Entertainment ☆☆☆☆☆ Extras ☆☆☆☆☆
Value ☆☆☆☆☆
OVERALL ☆☆☆☆☆

END OF DAYS

Price: £19.99
Supplied by: Warner Home Video
Type of disc: Dual layer, single-sided
No of chapters: 20
Film format(s)/length: 2.35:1 anamorphic / 123 mins
Audio format: Dolby Digital 5.1
Director: Peter Hyams
Starring: Arnold Schwarzenegger, Gabriel Byrne, Kevin Pollock
Year made: 1999
Extras: Scene access; *Spotlight on Location* featurette; *Special Effects* featurette; soundtrack presentation featuring Everlast and Rob Zombie music videos; theatrical trailer; soundtrack in English and German; subtitles in German and English for the hard of hearing.

Embrace the Christian faith, and you will have the strength to defeat Satan! That's the message that the Bible and every reverend, missionary, priest and vicar has been telling us for the last 2000 years. Well, in case it hasn't quite set in just yet, Arnold's back, after a little recovery from heart surgery, to hammer the message home with the full force of $80 million worth of special effects behind him. Schwarzenegger plays Jericho, a former New York cop who, after the murder of his wife and daughter, has sunk to the depths of suicidal self-despair. We find him living out his life as a security agent, who along with his partner is assigned to protect businessman Gabriel Byrne. Gabriel, however, is suffering from a bout of physical possession by the Devil himself. Beelzebub is back on Earth to claim a bride – young New York socialite called Christine (Robin Tunney) – in order to spawn his offspring. After a run-in with a tongueless old priest, our hero figures out what is amiss and goes about protecting Christine from the clutches of Satan until the stroke of midnight, New Year's Eve 1999. It's all fun stuff, but ultimately *End of Days* draws too heavily on other movies, the likes of *The Omen*, *The Exorcist* and even *Se7en* all too clearly showing their influence. What could have been a religious fright classic soon degenerates into another Arnie high-energy action feast. It was a brave move for Arn to take on one of the deepest roles of his career, but the moment Byrne hits the screen, he is totally outgunned. Still, it's by no means the worst movie Schwarzenegger has made, and if you're after a good piece of popcorn, then this is worth checking out. In fact, the extras alone are a decent reason to have a look. The *Spotlight on Location* is one of the best to be committed to DVD – it's insightful, revealing, and thankfully with hardly any clips from the movie itself to bulk up the running time. Even better than that are the 9 separate special effects featurettes covering different sequences. Ranging from minute subway carriages to computer-generated Lords of Hell, this kind of in-depth look has rarely been bettered on DVD.

FINAL VERDICT

Picture ☆☆☆☆☆ Sound ☆☆☆☆
Entertainment ☆☆☆ Extras ☆☆☆☆☆ Value ☆☆☆
OVERALL ☆☆☆☆

ENEMY OF THE STATE

Price: £15.99
Supplied by: Warner Home Video
Type of disc: Dual layer, single-sided
No of chapters: 29
Film format(s)/length: 2.35:1 widescreen / 127 mins
Audio format: Dolby Digital 5.1
Director: Tony Scott
Starring: Will Smith, Gene Hackman, Jon Voight
Year made: 1998
Extras: Scene access; multi-lingual subtitles.

After the US Navy (*Top Gun*), stock car racing (*Days of Thunder*) and contemporary dance

(*Flashdance*), the final co-production by Jerry Bruckheimer and the late Don Simpson deals with the hi-tech wizardry of the modern surveillance state. As Simpson's swan song it is a considerably better film than the inventor of the 'concept movie' deserved. Unlike the pallid *Wild, Wild West*, *Enemy of the State* is a smart, fast thriller which has the confidence to place Smith foursquare as the central character. Ex-*Crosby* star Bonet plays an ex-lover, and her metaphorically bruised beauty deepens the film's human dimensions, with Smith's troubled family life providing a solid core to the picture. Smith is eventually joined by a white co-star, but Hackman only plays up Smith's leading man role by providing a wonderfully introverted, misanthropic take on a rogue government agent. A scene wherein Hackman threatens Smith with a shotgun, but then backs off with a confession about a sugar deficiency prompting his bad mood, is representative of a witty gloss which lifts the whole film. However, while the look and feel of the film is very modern, its obsession with surveillance cameras seems very Seventies in the era of the Internet. *Enemy* is a film you've seen before: *The Conversation* and and *Blue Thunder* immediately spring to mind as very different takes on this government-paranoia sub-genre. As a DVD, *Enemy of the State* offers excellent picture quality – Scott excels at providing a sharp, colour-drenched 'look' to his films and anything less than first class would be immediately noticeable. This is easily one of Buena Vista's best DVD conversions. Sound is similarly impressive, with Dolby Digital 5.1 providing an all embracing soundscape which is dense with subtle – and not so subtle – effects: you really do need to play this DVD loud to get the full effect of the movie. Unfortunately, toward the end of the film the synching seems to slip a little, something which has been reported across a range of players so it's definitely the DVD, not the film. In terms of extras, the Region 1 version (reviewed last issue), offered no less than two featurettes…but neither was much more than a movie trailer with a few snippets of comment from the director and their absence isn't cause for concern. That said, being a little worse than a weakly presented US DVD is hardly cause for celebration.

FINAL VERDICT

Picture ☆☆☆☆☆ Sound ☆☆☆
Entertainment ☆☆☆☆ Extras ☆ Value ☆☆☆☆
OVERALL ☆☆☆

THE ENGLISH PATIENT

Price: £15.99
Supplied by: DVDplus (www.dvdplus.co.uk)
Type of disc: Dual layer, single-sided
No of chapters: 32
Film format(s)/length: 1.85:1 widescreen / 155 mins
Audio format: Dolby Digital 5.0
Director: Anthony Minghella
Starring: Ralph Fiennes, Juliette Binoche, Willem Dafoe
Year made: 1996
Extras: Scene access.

Winner of a squillion Academy Awards (well, 9, if truth be known), it should come as no surprise that *The English Patient* is an epic film. Like all big Oscar winners, it won't appeal to everyone but its DVD release is vindicated, despite the lack of extras, in order to appreciate the Oscar-winning cinematography. Fiennes puts in a sterling performance as an injured pilot forced to sit out the remainder of the Second World War in the care of an army nurse. As he remembers the events that lead to his predicament, a powerful and tragic love story is re-enacted. Yes, it's one of those films that will have you scrambling for the tissues. Set against the beautiful backdrops of North African and Italy, *The English Patient* is as close to a moving piece of art as you'll find. VHS just couldn't do it justice. Make the most of your new technology and see the film again, as it should have been.

FINAL VERDICT

Picture ☆☆☆☆☆ Sound ☆☆☆☆☆
Entertainment ☆☆☆☆ Extras ☆ Value ☆☆☆
OVERALL ☆☆☆

ENTER THE DRAGON

Price: £15.99
Supplied by: Warner Home Video
Type of disc: Single layer, single-sided
No of chapters: 28
Film format(s)/length: 2.35:1 widescreen enhanced / 95 mins
Audio format: Dolby Digital 2.0
Director: Robert Clouse
Starring: Bruce Lee, John Saxon, Ahna Capri
Year made: 1973
Extras: Subtitles for the hearing impaired.

Looking about as good as a 27 year-old martial arts movie can look, the epic that shot kung fu fighting legend Bruce Lee to stardom in America is back, on DVD. There is a sort of mild grainy static on most flesh tones, but for the most part increased resolution brings a weary old film back to life. Fanatics will be pleased to note that you can now see Bolo's bad dental work when he faces off against Roper towards the finale. Greater depth of colour also helps you out in the famously disorienting 'Reflection of Death' scene, when Lee pursues Han through a hall of mirrors. Spotting the difference between the actors and their reflections was hard work in the yellowed, cropped and stretched version of the movie that most TV stations like to broadcast; now it's all so clear. The fact remains, however, that the BBFC has not relaxed its strict rules about nunchaku being used on screen, so, as has always been the case with the British version of *Enter the Dragon*, a big chunk of Bruce's performance with the weapon is missing. What do we get as compensation? 3 newly-inserted minutes of extra strolling around that hall of mirrors. We're not expecting something to rival the $80 R1 anniversary edition (134 minutes, soundtrack CD, books, commentary, documentaries) but even the old 1993 videotape release had a good documentary on it! Oh, and the box's chapter list is out of step too – could Warner have cared any less?

FINAL VERDICT
Picture ☆☆☆☆ Sound ☆☆☆
Entertainment ☆☆☆☆ Extras ☆ Value ☆☆
OVERALL ☆☆☆

ENTRAPMENT

Price: £19.99
Supplied by: 20th Century Fox Home Entertainment
Type of disc: Dual layer, single-sided
No of chapters: 24
Film format(s)/length: 2.35:1 widescreen enhanced / 108 mins
Audio format: Dolby Digital 5.1
Director: Jon Amiel
Starring: Sean Connery, Ving Rhames, Catherine Zeta-Jones
Year made: 1999
Extras: Scene access; trailer; 'Making of' documentary (14 mins); Seal music video 'Lost My Faith'; soundtrack in English; subtitles for the hearing impaired in 10 languages.

A rich thief stealing art treasures; a female insurance investigator on his trail; carefully-planned robberies involving nifty gadgets and split-second timing. Sound familiar? It's not *The Thomas Crown Affair* but *Entrapment*, an altogether sillier affair than the Brosnan/Russo film. Connery, for once actually playing a Scotsman, is grizzled master thief 'Mac' MacDougal, at varying times opposed, partnered or bedded by Zeta-Jones's Gin, a woman whose true profession and loyalties change with every plot twist.

After test runs of the pair's tea-leafing talents, the true goal is revealed as the ultimate bank robbery, high inside the world's tallest building in Malaysia. Under the cover of the Millennium Bug (a gimmick that instantly dates the movie) Mac and Gin plan to break into the bank's systems and electronically swipe billions of dollars. If you predict that things will go wrong and the pair will end up dangling from said building, give yourself 10 points. Unlike the pairing of Pierce Brosnan and Rene Russo in *Thomas Crown*, where the two were of a similar age and had a genuine onscreen rapport, the combination of the bus pass-wielding Connery and lollipop-sucking Zeta-Jones happens for no better reason than the plot demanding it. Mind you, the experience apparently gave Zeta-Jones a taste for older men; a case of life imitating... well, not exactly 'art', but you know what we mean. Compared to *Thomas Crown*, *Entrapment* is, to paraphrase Dr Evil, the Diet Coke of heist movies. The whole film seems to exist solely to show off Catherine Zeta-Jones's leather-clad butt. Not that there's anything wrong with that, admittedly, but a plot that was remotely believable, or even just made sense, would have been nice. The so-called 'Special Edition' (though it's hardly on a par with *The Abyss*) boasts a few extras not found on the American disc. As well as a music video by Seal, there's a 14-minute 'Making of' documentary. Most of this is the usual PR waffle of the actors saying how brilliant the film is, backed up by numerous clips, but there's a section about filming a stunt in New York that edges toward actually being interesting. It's a pity there aren't more sequences like this. *Entrapment* is lightweight, harmless piffle that is at least watchable, though instantly forgettable. If you want to see the same story done properly, though, you should get *The Thomas Crown Affair* instead.

FINAL VERDICT
Picture ☆☆☆☆ Sound ☆☆☆☆ Entertainment ☆☆☆
Extras ☆☆☆ Value ☆☆☆
OVERALL ☆☆☆

ERASER

Price: £15.99
Company: Warner Home Video
Type of disc: Single layer, single-sided
No of chapters: 44
Film format(s)/length: 2.35:1 widescreen / 107 mins
Audio format: Dolby Digital 5.1
Director: Charles Russell
Starring: Arnold Schwarzenegger, Vanessa Williams, James Caan

Year made: 1996
Extras: Production notes; scene access; trailer; subtitles in English and Arabic.

Arnie's back, and true to form, he's going for the highly contested Most Special Effects per Minute award. Usually, if a film's promoted as a 'non-stop action-packed thriller' you can bet your salary that it's a rubbish script delivered by rubbish actors held together by the odd blindingly good special effect. Thankfully, *Eraser*'s different, and really is action-packed from the moment the opening credits fade to the moment the closing credits scroll into view. The acting is better than you'd expect, with Mr Muscle himself sticking wisely to short dialogue sequences and Vanessa Williams sticking equally wisely to the role of damsel in distress. It's up to James Caan and James Coburn to provide the not too obvious deception and betrayal that almost has you guessing who's good and who's not. In DVD terms, *Eraser* is the perfect way show off its superior sound and picture quality. The explosions are frequent and at full volume will probably cause vibrations big enough to send seismologists' needles a-twitching and the huge amount of chapters are perfect for skipping from one effect straight into the next. Sadly, Warner stopped there when it could have offered much more. The only added extras are production notes and a theatrical trailer which doesn't do the film justice. It's like offering wine with a meal instead of champagne. People will drink it but your party won't go with a bang.

FINAL VERDICT
Picture ☆☆☆☆ Sound ☆☆☆☆☆
Entertainment ☆☆☆☆ Extras ☆ Value ☆☆☆
OVERALL ☆☆☆

ESCAPE FROM NEW YORK

Price: £15.99
Supplied by: DVD World (01705 796662)
Type of disc: Single layer, single-sided
No of chapters: 27
Film format(s)/length: 2.35:1 widescreen / 99 mins
Audio format: Stereo
Director: John Carpenter
Starring: Kurt Russell, Lee Van Cleef, Ernest Borgnine
Year made: 1981
Extras: Scene access; 'Making the Film' (text pages); 'Special Effects', also displayed in text format; *The Edit*, details about the missing opening sequence from the original film.

This is a classic action sci-fi film where Kurt Russell plays the condemned convict Snake Plissken, a former war hero who is being sent to serve his term in New York, the futuristic equivalent of Alcatraz. The plot really starts to thicken when the escape pod carrying the President of the Unites States crash-lands in New York, leaving him stranded amongst the worlds worst criminals. This is where Snake is brought into the equation, as the officials offer him his freedom in return for rescuing the President. The DVD extras found within this title are very limited, with standard scene access and a special effects section that are almost as dated as the film itself. The most interesting extra is 'The Edit', which contains information about the 'missing' first reel in which Snake carries out a vicious bank robbery. This footage was cut from the film so has never been seen in the UK, and would have made a splendid extra. Sadly, the footage itself is not shown, but stills from the missing sequence are. It's an interesting section and does shed light on why Snake was imprisoned in the first place. Other features include 'Making the Film' and 'Special Effects', but both are just text documents supported by a couple of still clips. A classic like this deserves better.

FINAL VERDICT
Picture ☆☆☆ Sound ☆☆☆ Entertainment ☆☆☆☆
Extras ☆☆ Value ☆☆
OVERALL ☆☆☆

EVER AFTER

Price: £19.99
Supplied by: 20th Century Fox
Type of disc: Dual layer, single-sided
No of chapters: 14
Film format(s)/length: 2.35:1 widescreen enhanced / 116 mins
Audio format: Dolby Digital 5.1
Director: Andy Tennant
Starring: Drew Barrymoore, Anjelica Huston, Dougray Scott
Year made: 1998
Extras: Scene access; trailer; subtitles in 11 languages.

Between screaming for her life and for love in classics *Scream* and *The Wedding Singer*, Drew Barrymore stepped into the glass shoe of Cinderella. *Ever After* is a sassy reworking of the classic fairytale. Once-placid heroines are now feisty headstrong quoters of Thomas Moore, while headstrong princes are knotted balls of insecurity. As a modern woman of the 16th century, Danielle (Barrymore) is, as you'd expect downtrodden and penniless. As if that's not enough, she must share her late father's home and fortune with her elegantly vile stepmother, played with relish by Angelica Huston. In another part of the land a prince (Dougray Scott) must find a bride, so a masked ball is arranged, and scheming plans are hatched by the ugly sisters who arrive to steal the prince's heart. You know the story. Director Andy Tennant, better known for the recent epic gloss of *Anna and the King*, draws out the emotion and grandeur of this timeless tale. The scenery is breathtaking, as is the thunderously melancholic soundtrack. The remarkable Huston turns in a beautifully understated performance as the overly devious stepmother, gliding through scenes on a wave of curled lips and ravenous eyebrows. The cast throughout are perfect, in particular the whimsical Barrymore and Scott as the dazed and confused love-struck couple. Apart from a cinema trailer there are no outstanding DVD features, which is a shame. But *Ever After* does capture the innocence of the classic fable with enough modern twists and self-conscious verve to captivate and enthral to the final curtain.

FINAL VERDICT

Picture ☆☆☆☆ Sound ☆☆☆☆
Entertainment ☆☆☆☆ Extras ☆ Value ☆☆☆
OVERALL ☆☆☆☆

EVERYTHING YOU ALWAYS WANTED TO KNOW ABOUT SEX BUT WERE TOO AFRAID TO ASK

Price: £19.99
Supplied by: MGM Home Entertainment
Type of disc: Single layer, single-sided
No of chapters: 24
Film format(s)/length: 1.85:1 anamorphic / 87 mins
Audio format: Stereo
Director: Woody Allen
Starring: Gene Wilder, Anthony Quayle, Burt Reynolds
Year made: 1972
Extras: Scene access; theatrical trailer; subtitles in 12 languages.

It's odd how Woody Allen's very public split from Mia Farrow re-ignited his career. It's odd because far from being humiliated, Woody became an 'artist' and the patron saint of dull actors seeking credibility. In fact, it's now hard to even recall a time when we didn't have to take Woody's work 'seriously'. However, a little over 30 years ago, Allen was just a college dropout, scratching together a living by writing one-liners for sitcoms. His early pictures like *Everything...* make it obvious just how far Allen has come. In the film, Allen interprets various chapters of Dr Reuben's sex education manual (from which the film takes its name) as B-movies. So be prepared

for a giant tit on the rampage, a doctor having an illicit affair with a sheep called Daisy and a quiz show where contestants are interrogated about their perversions. Now that description may make the film sound better than it is. Let us put you straight. *Everything...* has an unsatisfying sketchy feel to it. Imagine watching one too many mediocre TV comedies in one stint. To make matters worse, it's dated badly too. The film's humour is old-fashioned to the point that it seems perverse to watch it on DVD – and that's without considering the distinct lack of extras! This, combined with poor picture and sound quality, makes *Everything...* a far from essential purchase. Of course, being a Woody Allen picture, it has its moments, but at best it can only be described as patchy. It's very much an 'early' Allen film – one for obsessive fans and completists only.

FINAL VERDICT

Picture ☆☆ Sound ☆☆ Entertainment ☆☆☆
Extras ☆ Value ☆☆
OVERALL ☆☆

EVIL DEAD II

Price: £15.99
Supplied by: BMG Video
Type of disc: Single layer, single-sided
No of chapters: 28
Film format(s)/length: 4:3 regular / 81 mins
Audio format: Mono
Director: Sam Raimi
Starring: Bruce Campbell, Sarah Berry, Dan Hicks
Year made: 1987
Extras: Scene access; production notes; background info on the *Evil Dead* trilogy.

This second installment in the *Evil Dead* trilogy was slightly more restrained than the original *Evil Dead*...but not much! This time, Ash finds himself in an isolated log cabin with his girlfriend Linda. Then it's only a matter of minutes before she's possessed by an evil force and has her head lopped off by Ash. Needless to say, this film has a blacker than black sense of humour! Considering how well revered this film is, it is quite deplorable that BMG has made no real effort in producing a worthy DVD package. The extras you get – brief production notes on *Evil Dead II* and info on the rest of the trilogy – could have been knocked up in 5 minutes. Where are the interviews with the cast and crew? How about a documentary on the film's production, or even an audio commentary from Sam Raimi? The likes of *Texas Chain Saw Massacre* and John Carpenter's *The Thing* are shining examples of how genre classics such as this should be represented on DVD. Back to the drawing board, BMG.

FINAL VERDICT

Picture ☆☆☆ Sound ☆☆☆ Entertainment ☆☆☆
Extras ☆ Value ☆

OVERALL ☆☆

EVITA

Price: £19.99
Supplied by: Entertainment in Video
Type of disc: Dual layer, single-sided
No of chapters: 30
Film format(s)/length: 2.35:1 widescreen / 129 mins
Audio format: Dolby Surround
Director: Alan Parker
Starring: Madonna, Antonio Banderas, Jonathan Pryce
Year made: 1996
Extras: Chapter access.

Perhaps the one thing that the motion picture rendition of the world-famous *Evita* musical is most famous for is Madonna actually succeeding at something she had always previously failed at: acting. Ironically, the most famous thing this version of *Evita* will be famous for is that it failed miserably at being what it should have been: a DVD. Whilst the quality of the picture and sound go to great lengths at creating the scope of the musical in your living room, *Evita* on DVD falls flat on its Argentinian arse when it comes to extras (ie, the distinct lack thereof). Even if you are a fan of the movie and musical, this DVD offers you no viable incentive apart from the improved picture and sound quality over the VHS version. Think long and hard before purchasing, but remember to ask yourself whether you, the consumer, deserve more from DVD.

FINAL VERDICT

Picture ☆☆☆☆ Sound ☆☆☆☆
Entertainment ☆☆☆ Extras ☆ Value ☆☆

OVERALL ☆☆

EXCALIBUR

Price: £17.99
Supplied by: Warner Home Video
Type of disc: Dual layer, single-sided
No of chapters: 45
Film format(s)/length: 1:85:1 anamorphic / 135 mins
Audio format: Dolby Digital
Director: John Boorman
Starring: Nigel Terry, Helen Mirren, Nicholas Clay
Year made: 1981
Extras: Scene access; soundtrack in English, French and Italian; subtitles in 10 languages; subtitles for the hearing impaired in English and Italian.

There have been some bizarre treatments of the legend of the Round Table. Monty Python parodied the many adaptations of the story, Richard Harris warbled through a lavish musical adaptation, and here the Arthurian myth is relived once again as *Excalibur*. Directed by John Boorman, and with early roles from Helen Mirren, Liam Neeson and a marvellously athletic and hearty performance from Patrick Stewart, Boorman's adaptation was to centre the famous story around the magical and spiritual. Nicol Williamson's portrayal of Merlin, sinister but compelling, and pivotal to the entire story, affects much of the events with hypnotic Pagan chanting. The film deals with the treacherous and violent early beginnings of English history, imbued with all the marvellous Arthurian legend, icons and imagery: Excalibur, the Sword in the Stone, the Lady of the Lake (who looks like she's been kitted out by Miss Selfridge), and the rather boastful but unbeatable knight, Lancelot. The battles are gloriously bloody and the romance rough and ready. It's a lush, no-expense-spared production and a visual treat, with Boorman's handy camera work allowing you to quickly become engrossed, even if the story is a well-trodden path. Every scene has an almost computer-generated clarity to it. But lush and lavish as the original production is, as a DVD programme it's a desert. The film is divided into 45 chapters, subtitles of just about every language and dubbed into French (mono), and that's your lot. A rather disappointing DVD.

FINAL VERDICT

Picture ☆☆☆☆ Sound ☆☆☆☆ Entertainment ☆☆☆
Extras ☆ Value ☆☆☆

OVERALL ☆☆☆

EXCESS BAGGAGE

Price: £19.99
Supplied by: DVD Net (020 8890 2520)
Type of disc: Single layer, single-sided
No of chapters: 36
Film format(s)/length: 1.85:1 widescreen / 97 mins
Audio format: Dolby Digital 5.1
Director: Marco Brambilla
Starring: Alicia Silverstone, Benicio Del Toro, Christopher Walken
Year made: 1997
Extras: German language option; scene selection; filmographies; theatrical trailer.

Professional car thief, Vincent Roche (Benicio Del Toro), chose the wrong car to steal in this middle-of-the-road romantic road comedy. In a bid for attention, Emily T Hope (Silverstone) fabricates her own kidnapping which leads her and Roche into a world of trouble. The visual design of the *Excess Baggage*'s interactive menu is of above average quality, and indicates that at least Columbia TriStar cares about giving the DVD punter that little bit extra. Unfortunately, that little bit, is just that. Little. Whilst the theatrical trailer is a welcome addition, the filmographies are not particularly exciting, and it would have been nice to have some interviews with the stars (What was the film like to make? Is Chris Walken as strange in real life as he appears on film? These are the things that enquiring DVD owners want to know, Columbia). In retrospect however, the film is pretty poor anyway, so Columbia's financial justification for going to town on the DVD is probably negligible.

FINAL VERDICT

Picture ☆☆☆☆ Sound ☆☆☆☆ Entertainment ☆☆☆
Extras ☆☆ Value ☆☆☆
OVERALL ☆☆☆

EXECUTIVE DECISION

Price: £15.99
Supplied by: Warner Home Video
Type of disc: Dual layer, single-sided
No of chapters: 37
Film format(s)/length: 2.35:1 widescreen / 127 mins
Audio format: Dolby Digital 5.1
Director: Stuart Baird
Starring: Kurt Russell, Halle Berry, Steven Seagal
Year made: 1996
Extras: Scene access; multilingual features.

5 miles above the earth, a hijacked 747 is heading towards the Eastern Seaboard of the United States. On board are 400 passengers whose lives are in danger, with a further 40 million below should the 747 reach United States soil. Enter an elite team of 6 men, commanded by Lieutenant Colonel Austin Travis (Seagal) and accompanied by intelligence agent David Grant (Russell). Together they must board the jumbo jet using a converted Stealth Bomber and defeat terrorist Nagi Hassan (David Suchet) from releasing dozens of nerve gas canisters upon millions of Americans. The most surprising element of the movie is the sudden – but not altogether sad – death of Seagal. If there is a fate worse than falling 5 miles to your death, we have yet to see it – although many would call it justice for all the terrible movies he's unleashed upon us in the past. Once onboard the jet, the remaining anti-terrorist team, aided by the beautiful Jean (Berry), face a race against the clock before an

Executive Decision is made to destroy the inbound aeroplane. There is very little you can say about the extra features on this DVD, as there are none. So it's not surprising to see that this is another Warner Bros title. You rarely see extra features on films more than a year old now unless they're re-released Special Editions or Director's Cuts. However, one thing you're assured of is the quality of the picture, the sharpness of sound and brilliance of colour.

FINAL VERDICT

Picture ☆☆☆☆ Sound ☆☆☆☆ Entertainment ☆☆☆
Extras ☆ Value ☆☆
OVERALL ☆☆

EXISTENZ

Price: £19.99
Supplied by: Alliance Atlantis
Type of disc: Dual layer, single-sided
No of chapters: 22
Film format(s)/length: 1.85:1 anamorphic / 93 mins
Audio format: Dolby Digital 5.1
Director: David Cronenberg
Starring: Jennifer Jason Leigh, Jude Law, Ian Holm
Year made: 1999
Extras: Scene access; director's commentary; visual effects supervisor's commentary; director of photography's commentary; *The Invisible Art of Carol Spier* 'Making of' documentary (53 mins); trailer; Sega Dreamcast section and web links; subtitles in English.

With its themes of untrustworthy reality, disease and paranoia – not to mention an obsession with yucky orifices – *eXistenZ* could really only have emerged from the mind of one man, David Cronenberg. The Canadian maestro of body horror turns his attentions to the world of videogames and virtual reality, but as with all his other films, it's far more weird and grotesque than the subject matter suggests. In an off-kilter, vaguely futuristic world, top game designer Allegra Geller (Leigh) is giving a demo of her latest title, *eXistenZ*. No joypads or goggles here – the game plugs directly into your body, via a hole in the spine that looks (quite deliberately, as Cronenberg's commentary points out) like a puckered arsehole. When pro-reality, anti-game terrorists try to assassinate Allegra, she goes on the run with only nerdy PR man Ted Pikul (Law) to protect her. Done by anyone but Cronenberg, *eXistenZ* would have been a high-tech action thriller – interesting enough, but nothing we haven't seen before. In his hands, however, it's a wilfully obtuse procession of disturbing organic imagery, strange sexual overtones, games within games within games and nasty, gory violence. Where it fails to live up to Cronenberg's best (*The Fly* and *Dead Ringers*) is with its limp storyline; virtual reality has been done to death. The final twist (and we're not talking about the one you'll guess 20 minutes in – the film's not *that* obvious) is hardly unexpected either, even though it is quite appropriate. What makes the DVD genuinely unusual for an R2 title is its inclusion of 3 commentary tracks. Cronenberg's is obviously the most interesting, as he mixes technical information about actually making the film with his own distinctive philosophical viewpoints. However, the other two commentaries – one by the effects supervisor, the other by the director of photography – are also detailed and worth a listen for those with an interest in the processes of film-making. The other main extra fits into the same category, being a 53-minute documentary on the making of the film and its production design. Though *eXistenZ* isn't Cronenberg's best film, oddly enough it's one of his most accessible to a general audience. In fact this well-presented DVD could introduce a whole new kind of audience to his uniquely mutated cinematic world.

FINAL VERDICT

Picture ☆☆☆ Sound ☆☆☆ Entertainment ☆☆☆
Extras ☆☆☆☆ Value ☆☆☆
OVERALL ☆☆☆

THE EXORCIST

Price: £15.99
Supplied by: Warner Home Video
Type of disc: Dual layer, double-sided
No of chapters: 47
Film format(s)/length: 1.85:1 widescreen / 117 mins
Audio format: Dolby Digital 5.1
Director: William Friedkin
Starring: Ellen Burstyn, Linda Blair, Max Von Sydow
Year made: 1973
Extras: Scene access; superb 52 minute documentary *The Fear of God: 25 Years of The Exorcist*, featuring new interviews with principal cast and crew members; introduction by director William Friedkin; original sketches and storyboards; 6 TV teaser trailers; 8 original theatrical trailers including one for *The Exorcist II: The Heretic*; audio commentary by William Friedkin; audio commentary by screenwriter/producer William Peter Blatty, plus sound effects tests; 3 interview clips of Friedkin and Blatty : 'The Original Cut', 'Stairway To Heaven' and 'The Final Reckoning'; the original ending, cut from the final version, remastered and in Dolby Digital 5.1; soundtrack in English, German and French; multi-lingual subtitles; subtitles in English for the hearing

impaired.

After the box office success of its theatrical re-release last year, *The Exorcist*, dubbed the scariest movie of all time, has finally been granted a home video certificate in this country a mere 26 years after it was made. On this 25th Anniversary DVD, the wait has been worth it. The film went straight to number one in both DVD and VHS charts, demonstrating what happens when a landmark motion picture is remastered, furnished with A grade extras and given movie-style exposure. This sets a standard as to how all classic films should be treated on DVD. Actress and single parent Chris MacNeil (Burstyn) has a good job, many friends and a comfortable house in New England's leafy Georgetown. Out of nowhere, Chris' 12 year-old daughter Regan (Blair) begins to behave violently and curse explicitly. Doctors and hypnotists cannot explain what's causing Regan's increasingly hideous transformation and, as a last resort, Fathers Karras and Merrin (Von Sydow) are approached for their help. *The Exorcist's* brand of horror emanates from the idea that good and evil are locked in an eternal battle that erupts into people's lives without warning. From the disarming start to the incredibly optimistic finish, its power to terrify remains undiminished even after this long. The remastering is a textbook success. Picture clarity is now close to perfection: the Northern Iraq prologue seems to radiate scorching heat before dissolving to autumn in Georgetown. For a film that uses sound so expertly to increase the tension, the addition of a 5.1 soundtrack means that the hospital examination scenes in particular become all the more harrowing. However, the real revelation has got to be the sheer time, effort, thought (and no doubt money) that has gone into the special features. Film journalist and associate producer Mark Kermode's in-depth documentary *The Fear of God* interviews all the key cast and crew members, going behind-the-scenes of the production in joyous detail. For instance, Jason Miller (Father Karras) recalls how director William Friedkin would fire off shotguns near actors' heads and film their shocked expressions to get the best possible facial reaction. The only flaw with this DVD is that the Region 1 disc has the 74-minute version of the *Fear of God* documentary, while we get only 52 minutes, but hey, that's a small niggle about an otherwise excellent overall package. Friedkin's closing audio commentary remarks acknowledge DVD's role in preserving motion pictures for posterity. "I feel it's most important to make this digital video the most definitive version of the picture, because this is the one that will last, this is the way the film will be remembered." Here's hoping more DVDs are approached like this.

FINAL VERDICT

Picture ☆☆☆☆☆ Sound ☆☆☆☆☆

Entertainment ☆☆☆☆☆ Extras ☆☆☆☆☆

Value ☆☆☆☆☆

OVERALL ☆☆☆☆☆

THE EXTERMINATOR

Price: £15.99

Supplied by: Synergy

Type of disc: Single layer, single-sided

No of chapters: 12

Film format(s)/length: 1.75:1 anamorphic / 97 mins

Audio format: Dolby Surround

Director: Jim Glickenhaus

Starring: Christopher George, Samantha Eggar, Bob Ginty

Year made: 1980

Extras: Scene access; theatrical trailer; Synergy showcase with trailers of *Maniac Cop*, *Frankenhooker*, *Red Scorpion* and *Basket Case 1*, *2* and *3*.

Here's a jolly story about a Vietnam veteran who turns vigilante after his friend is mugged. 'Story' is actually a fairly generous word; imagine the end of *Taxi Driver* being stretched out into a full-length film and you'll get the idea. This is an appallingly bad film and should not be watched without a psychiatrist to hand. There aren't even any extras to draw interest. The box may boast a director's cut with 'never seen before footage', but if you've seen this film before to know what has been left out then in all honesty you should know better than to buy it! In fact, the only possible reason to justify watching this is the comedy value of the *Littlest Hobo*-style music, which couldn't be more out of place. What's even more worrying is that a sequel was made. If you watch films and think you could do better, in this case you may just be right.

FINAL VERDICT

Picture ☆☆ Sound ☆ Entertainment ☆

Extras ☆ Value ☆

OVERALL ☆

EXTREME MEASURES

Price: £15.99

Supplied by: Warner Home Video

Type of disc: Single layer, double-sided

No of chapters: 39

Film format(s)/length: 4:3 regular and 2.35:1 anamorphic /114 mins

Audio format: Dolby Digital 5.1

Director: Michael Apted

Starring: Hugh Grant, Gene Hackman, Sarah Jessica Parker

Year made: 1996

Extras: Scene access; trailer; soundtrack in English, French and Italian; subtitles in 10 languages.

In the thick air of scandal after Hugh Grant's meeting with Miss Brown in the back seat of an LA car, *Extreme Measures* appeared, Hugh's first foray into US movies and the first hit for Grant and Liz Hurley's own Simian Films production company. Fresh from success as a floppy-fringed English fool in *Four Weddings...*, Grant takes the lead role again. Here, he plays Dr Guy Luthan, a do-gooder doctor who falls foul of the macabre plans of the untouchable Hackman. As disturbing conspiracies run riot beneath Michael Apted's tight direction, a nervous, jittering movie begins to unravel. There are patients dying at Grant's hospital and nobody seems to care. As Luthan digs deeper his life takes a downward turn, and the only common link is the disappearance of the city's poor and homeless. Grant plays the lost Englishman in New York with credibility and even allows the character to transform into a shambles of anxiety as the shadowy puppeteers tighten the strings that bind him. With all the Hitchcockian twists this movie thrusts your way, it's a shock to discover that the DVD extras aren't as thick on detail, with only a trailer to offer any bonus over the standard subtitles. Why Warner couldn't have included production notes, or even extracts from the taut original novel by Michael Palmer, is as much a mystery as the film's bloody conclusion. As is so often the case, *Extreme Measures* is an arresting movie that can't measure up to the potential of DVD.

FINAL VERDICT

Picture ☆☆☆☆ Sound ☆☆☆

Entertainment ☆☆☆☆ Extras ☆ Value ☆☆

OVERALL ☆☆☆

EYES WIDE SHUT

Price: £15.99

Supplied by: Warner Home Video

Type of disc: Dual layer, single-sided

No of chapters: 38

Film format(s)/length: 4:3 regular / 152 mins

Audio format: Dolby Digital 5.1

Director: Stanley Kubrick

Starring: Tom Cruise, Nicole Kidman, Sydney Pollack

Year made: 1999

Extras: Scene access; interviews with Tom Cruise, Nicole Kidman and Steven Spielberg (33 mins total); 2

TV trailers; cast and crew filmographies; multi-lingual subtitles; subtitles for the hearing impaired in English.

The last film of the late, legendary Stanley Kubrick proved to be just as controversial as any of his other works. Was it a deep, multi-layered piece of art exposing both the passions and the hypocrisies of human sexuality? Or was it just an excuse to get some shagging on screen? One thing that *Eyes Wide Shut* is definitely *not* is erotic. Despite the amount of flesh on display at various points in the film, the unblinking, clinical stare of Kubrick's camera makes the participants more like subjects in an experiment rather than a boost to sales of Kleenex. Anyone sitting down to watch the film with their hands in their pockets is going to be very disappointed. *Eyes Wide Shut* takes place over several days in New York. Wealthy married couple Dr William and Alice Harford (Cruise and Kidman) visit a party where William flirts with several young women. The following evening, during a dope-fuelled spat, Alice cuts the smug William down to size by brutally informing him that he's not the only one with an interest in the opposite sex. Stunned, William reels out into the cold winter streets of New York, to begin an odyssey of self-discovery in which sex lies at the centre of every experience. The most notorious part of the film is a prolonged masked orgy sequence, where Cruise (in disguise) drifts from room to room in a vast country mansion, witnessing all manner of sexual acts before eventually being unmasked as an intruder. For once, UK DVD owners get to gloat about the superiority of a Region 2 disc over its Region 1 counterpart – there are no ludicrous digitally-inserted onlookers covering up the naughty bits on our side of the pond. In fact, the BBFC didn't ask for *any* cuts for sexual content – although they did demand that the background recitation of a religious text during the orgy be replaced by music! Although the orgy is the visual centrepoint of the film, there's a lot more to it than just masked men and naked women going at it. In fact, Cruise's encounters with a broad range of New Yorkers – from a family friend who tries to seek physical comfort from Cruise practically on her just-deceased father's deathbed, through a friendly hooker whose story later takes a tragic turn, to Pollack's patriarchal and slightly menacing businessman – are what stick in the mind. These vignettes have an almost dream-like (or nightmarish) feel as William wanders from place to place, repeatedly finding himself unable to cope with the intensity of other peoples' desires or the strangeness of the world that exists below the surface of the one he knows. Cruise delivers a subtle,

understated performance that's light-years away from the brashness of Pete 'Maverick' Mitchell. Each new encounter drives him just a little further away from the security of his normal life, until he finally cracks with a tearful confession of his sins to Kidman. In addition to the film itself, there are 3 interviews taken from a Channel 4 documentary on Kubrick made shortly after his death. Cruise and Kidman talk about their relationship with the director and how it developed over the course of the lengthy shoot, but it is Steven Spielberg's memories of Kubrick that will be the prize draw for cineastes. It's possible that some people might feel short-changed by the lack of a widescreen option – this was done at Kubrick's behest, before his death, so there will never be another version. However, the film was shot full-frame and later letterboxed for cinema release, so theoretically you are actually seeing *more* of the picture! *Eyes Wide Shut* is as good a swansong as Kubrick could have hoped for – it's guaranteed to mesmerise some and infuriate others (the one-note piano score will set *everybody's* nerves jangling) and there's so much going on that repeat viewings are almost a prerequisite. As Spielberg says in his interview, "Kubrick's films grow on you – you have to see them more than once." He's absolutely right.

FINAL VERDICT

Picture ☆☆☆☆☆ Sound ☆☆☆☆

Entertainment ☆☆☆☆☆

Extras ☆☆☆☆ Value ☆☆☆☆☆

OVERALL ☆☆☆☆☆

THE FABULOUS BAKER BOYS

Price: £9.99
Supplied by: Cinema Club
Type of disc: Single layer, single-sided
No of chapters: 16
Film format(s)/length: 16:9 widescreen enhanced / 110 mins
Audio format: Dolby Surround
Director: Steven Kloves
Starring: Beau Bridges, Jeff Bridges, Michelle Pfeiffer
Year made: 1989
Extras: Scene access; theatrical trailer; featurette; interviews.

Because the Bridges brothers fit so perfectly into their roles as the titular *Baker Boys*, you'd be forgiven for thinking (aside from the novelty value) that the movie was conceived entirely to give them the chance to work together. Whether this is the case or not, what's certain about this tale of lounge lizard piano-playing brothers, who take on more than just the vocal talents of Michelle Pfeiffer when their career begins to flag, is that it is one of the most perfectly cast movies of its genre. First-time director Kloves managed to assemble a 3-piece cast who connect and disconnect to and from each other with such ease that you'd swear more than two of them were family. Beau plays Frank, the ever-straight, feet-on-the-ground husband and father who carries all the responsibilities of the trio; Jeff is Jack, full of talent and free of cares; and Michelle Pfeiffer makes every heterosexual male viewer break down on his knees and thank the Lord for his sight. The pacing of the movie may miss the beat every now and then, but sharper dialogue and deeper relations are rarely found. The disc doesn't fare too badly, either. Okay, so the sound might not be Dolby Digital 5.1, but for only £9.99 you're getting a nice picture transfer, and an array of fairly strong extras all for which other distribution companies would charge you nearly £20.

FINAL VERDICT

Picture ☆☆☆☆ Sound ☆☆☆☆

Entertainment ☆☆☆☆ Extras ☆☆☆

Value ☆☆☆☆☆

OVERALL ☆☆☆☆

FACE/OFF

Price: £15.99

Supplied by: DVD World (01705 796662)

Type of disc: Single layer, double-sided

No of chapters: 40 (23 Side A, 17 Side B)

Film format(s)/length: 1.85:1 widescreen / 133 mins

Director: John Woo

Starring: Nicholas Cage, John Travolta, Joan Allen

Year made: 1997

Extras: Scene access; subtitles.

You can spot a John Woo film a mile away. His trademarks are zillions of bullets fired from every conceivable automatic weapon (and some inconceivable ones too), sudden and inexplicable moments of slow motion to emphasise his character's coolness, and doves fluttering about the place before a big showdown. *Face/Off* is his most accomplished Western film yet and one of the all-time classic head-f*cks. Castor Troy (Cage – in his most OTT performance since *Wild at Heart*) is the world's most evil criminal; a grinning psychopath who likes nothing better than shooting cops with his twin gold-plated pistols, casual property damage and ruining the life of his nemesis, FBI hotshot Sean Archer (Travolta). The film's incredibly original premise occurs when Troy is captured alive but in a coma after a dazzling fiery shootout. Using revolutionary new surgery, Archer

agrees to have his face removed and replaced with Troy's to find the location of a bomb – made by Troy's brother Pollux – that's planted somewhere in LA. All goes well and Archer is sent to a high security jail to find out the information. Meanwhile, Troy wakes up and is, to say the least, a little annoyed to have his boat race missing, and forces the doctors to meld Archer's face onto his own; assuming his identity and condemning the real Archer to life imprisonment. Not surprisingly Woo relishes the chance to pit two of Hollywood's finest action stars against each other and the film rattles along from one slick set piece to the next. Cage in particular excels as both Troy and Archer, and you can see he's enjoying going off the rails. Travolta in contrast is as calm and collected as he was in *Broken Arrow* (also directed by Woo). *Face/Off* is a rollercoaster of an action movie that rarely puts a foot wrong and poses the sort of thought-provoking questions that rarely crop up in a traditionally brainless genre. The concept is a great one and the violence perfectly choreographed for maximum effect. At last John Woo finds a script worthy of his storytelling techniques and the resultant 133 minutes is a breathless cocktail of bullets and adrenaline. What a shame then that this is another deeply disappointing DVD. Not only are we given the most basic set of extras imaginable (scene access, subtitles – and that's it) but *Face/Off* is also one of the dreaded flippers, which means just after the tense prison break, the screen suddenly goes black and you are asked to change over the disc. Film companies, how many times do we have to say this – SORT IT OUT! With a format as advanced as DVD, we don't want to be getting up off the sofa and turning the disc over like a bloody LP! Just look at *Contact* to see how a long film can easily fit on a dual layer disc. Chopping films in half at crucial moments should simply never happen.

FINAL VERDICT

Picture ☆☆☆☆☆ Sound ☆☆☆☆☆

Entertainment ☆☆☆☆☆ Extras ☆ Value ☆☆☆

OVERALL ☆☆☆

THE FACULTY

Price: £15.99

Supplied by: Entertainment in Video

Type of disc: Single layer, single-sided

No of chapters: 31

Film format(s)/length: 1.85:1 widescreen enhanced / 100 mins

Audio format: Dolby Digital 5.1

Director: Robert Rodriguez

Starring: Elijah Wood, Josh Hartnett, Clea Duvall

Year made: 1998
Extras: Scene access; subtitles in English for the hearing impaired.

Most school kids probably felt at one time or another that their teachers were from another planet, but in *The Faculty*, they'd be right! *Scream* writer Kevin Williamson turns his patented brand of smartass irony into science fiction, and with zippy direction from Rodriguez (*From Dusk Till Dawn*) the end result delivers a subversive high school rewrite of *Invasion of the Body Snatchers*, where the geek gets the babe, the jock realises sports are stupid and winners definitely take drugs. When the teachers at a run-down Ohio school (played by Robert Patrick, Famke Janssen and Bebe Neuwirth) start inviting unruly pupils in for little one-to-one chats, after which they come out smiling and eager to learn, a group of misfits comes to the conclusion – they've been taken over by parasitic aliens! The only way to stop the invasion is to find and kill the alien queen – but who is the host? While it's pitifully devoid of extras (Hollywood Pictures is part of Disney, so that's no real surprise) *The Faculty* is still entertaining in the same way as *Scream* was – the characters have seen the same movies as us, and use them to help decide what to do next. There are also homages to rip-offs of *The Thing*, *Aliens* and the aforementioned *Body Snatchers*, so you end up with what is basically *Scream* with tentacles. There's even a cameo by tubby Internet movie critic Harry Knowles, as a character called, um, Harry Knowles. In all it's not as good as the films it references, but nevertheless *The Faculty* is still good, slimy fun.

FINAL VERDICT

Picture ☆☆☆☆ Sound ☆☆☆☆ Entertainment ☆☆☆☆
Extras ☆ Value ☆☆☆
OVERALL ☆☆☆

FALLEN

Price: £15.99
Supplied by: Warner Home Video
Type of disc: Single layer, single-sided
No of chapters: 32
Film format(s)/length: 16:9 widescreen / 119 mins
Director: Gregory Hoblit
Starring: Denzel Washington, John Goodman, Donald Sutherland
Year made: 1998
Extras: Interactive menus; production notes; scene access; trailer.

Serial killers pose a greater threat dead, it seems – so ugly people close to Cromwell Road need watch out, if the plot from this spookernatural thriller is anything to go by. Homicide detective John Hobbes (the pensive Washington, in a workmanlike performance) finally nails Azazel only to discover that he's no ordinary psycho – but an age-old demon, able to shift from body to body by touch alone. As the realisation dawns – conveniently explained by the subversive Sutherland and the surprisingly dour Goodman – Hobbes is engaged in a mildly chilling game of cat and mouse as the flick heads towards its refreshingly original conclusion. As one of Region 2's original releases, you'd expect *Fallen* to be a big-budget blockbuster. Yet it clearly didn't break the bank. Its style, so obviously in homage to David Fincher's visionary *Se7en*, is moody enough, but you can't help feeling that what may have worked so well on paper didn't quite translate so successfully onto film, hence its modest performance at the box office. Of course, us DVD owners are treated to all manner of extra treats which proudly display exactly why we've shelled out on our sexy new hardware? Well, no – *Fallen*'s special features are the bog-standard travesty us Brits are becoming increasingly used to: production notes, scene access and the trailer. Like, thanks. As with most Warner releases, the picture quality's decent enough. But overall, not exactly what the future of home entertainment is reportedly about.

FINAL VERDICT

Picture ☆☆☆☆ Sound ☆☆☆☆ Entertainment ☆☆☆
Extras ☆ Value ☆☆☆
OVERALL ☆☆☆

FALLING DOWN

Price: £15.99
Supplied by: Warner Home Video
Type of disc: Single layer, single-sided
No of chapters: 33
Film format(s)/length: 2.35:1 letterbox / 108 mins
Audio format: Dolby Surround
Director: Joel Schumacher
Starring: Michael Douglas, Robert Duvall, Barbara Hershey
Year made: 1992
Extras: Scene access; soundtrack in English, French and Italian; subtitles in 10 languages.

It's hard to believe that the man who completely ruined the *Batman* franchise could ever put out a movie this good. *Falling Down* is a compelling, tense and undeniably objective look at Nineties society. Set over the course of just one day, the movie follow the exploits of Douglas' character – a man known only as D-FENS after his car's licence plate – as a combination of heat, traffic jams and the depressing LA surroundings cause him to abandon his car during morning rush hour and walk home. On the way he encounters every problem of urban life and deals with them in his own 'ordinary guy, just trying to get home' way. Unfortunately, as the day goes on, D-FENS' responses to everyday hassles get increasingly more violent. *Falling Down* is a masterpiece for Schumacher. Not only provoking some stunning performances from his principal cast, he manages to turn in a movie that is shocking, entertaining, and thoroughly thought-provoking. As a case study of contemporary society it works like a charm; as far as essential movie viewing goes, it is a real must-see. Sadly, Warner has managed to completely miss the point of a DVD yet again. The non-anamorphic picture is little better than VHS, while the mere Dolby Surround sound, though doing the job, really should have been something more powerful. The notion of extras is a foreign concept to this disc, which is a shame, as *Falling Down* is truly a film worthy of the attention it now won't find among DVD fans.

FINAL VERDICT

Picture ☆☆ Sound ☆☆ Entertainment ☆☆☆☆
Extras ☆ Value ☆☆
OVERALL ☆☆☆

THE FAN

Price: £15.99
Supplied by: Entertainment in Video
Type of disc: Single layer, single-sided
No of chapters: 18
Film format(s)/length: 2.35:1 widescreen / 111 mins
Audio format: Dolby Surround
Director: Tony Scott
Starring: Robert De Niro, Wesley Snipes, Ellen Barkin
Year made: 1996
Extras: Scene access.

This was, to all intents and purposes, a showcase. An arena where two talented actors and one stylised director proved that they are as good as their fees suggest. It's just sad that they chose this film with which to do it. The film had potential. It nearly said something about the celebrity status of overpaid sportsman in the Nineties. It could have been a psychological drama focusing on a hero-worshipping obsessive who represents the bleaker side of fame. It came so close to being this bold, but instead went for the easy option of being just another big budget spoonful of Hollywood sugar. Instead of De Niro's unemployed knife salesman Gil Renard becoming an obsessive stalker, he simply turns into a murderous

nutcase. He kills the team rival of his baseball hero Bobby Rayburn (Snipes) and then kidnaps his hero's son, blackmailing him into dedicating his next home run to his "best friend Gil". Little reason is given for Renard's mental condition, but he was unsuccessful with both his job and his marriage, so he must be nuts, mustn't he? De Niro proves he can handle a role like this with ease, and indeed did a similar character to much better effect in *The King of Comedy*. Snipes is, as always, in good form, as Scott proves that his style is just too big for a script that is so flat. Sadly, the DVD is worse. Maybe one day studios will realise that scene access does not count as an extra, but until then, this DVD will continue to delude itself into thinking that it has some substance. In truth, it has nothing, so you'd be better off waiting for the television showing if you really feel that you have to see this film. It's not something to be avoided, but it's not worth buying on DVD either.

FINAL VERDICT

Picture ☆☆☆☆ Sound ☆☆☆ Entertainment ☆☆
Extras ☆ Value ☆☆
OVERALL ☆☆

FAR AND AWAY

Price: £19.99
Supplied by: Columbia TriStar Home Video
Type of disc: Dual layer, single-sided
No of chapters: 16
Film format(s)/length: 2.35:1 widescreen enhanced / 134 mins
Audio format: Dolby Digital 5.1
Director: Ron Howard
Starring: Tom Cruise, Nicole Kidman, Colm Meaney
Year made: 1992
Extras: Scene access; theatrical trailer; production notes; cast and film-makers' notes; soundtrack in 7 languages including English, German, French, Italian, Czech; subtitles in 9 languages.

You always know what you're going to get when you sit down to watch a Ron Howard movie: confrontation, sugary-sweet emotion, some light humour and a large helping of God Bless America. *Far and Away* is no exception to this formula, though it tries to throw the feel of an epic into the mix. Truth be told, the only Howard film that qualifies for that label is *Apollo 13*. Still, with its 65mm film, breathtaking landscapes and period setting it's not hard to see how this one attempts to fit into the category. This story of Joseph Donelly (Cruise), an Irish farmer's son who sets off in 1892 to claim revenge for his father's death and ultimately becomes one of the first land owners of Oklahoma, is a long and endearing one. Playing out at over two hours, 3 vivid locations, and including every dodgy variation of the Irish accent that you're every likely to hear, *Far and Away* is more of a Catherine Cookson novel than it is *Gone With the Wind*. The script is quite charming, Howard's direction exceeds anything he's done before (including his superb *Backdraft*) and the on-screen chemistry between Cruise and Kidman is more than enough to last the course. However, there is too much of a sugary coating for the whole movie to be believable. Playing out like a 130-minute promotional video for the American dream, Howard's view of Ireland does nothing but reinforce stereotypes, with every man over the age of 40 being both drunk and constantly singing an Irish shanty. For the record, Cruise's 'Oirish' accent is consistently on the ball, and he's one of the few lead Hollywood actors who could carry off a role like this for the full duration of the movie. Beautifully shot and quite compelling, the only thing that really lets this movie down is Howard's underwhelming original story, which leaves you with a feeling that this is not Hollywood retelling the past, but reinventing it. The disc is pretty bland, but the contents do at least amount to some fairly interesting revelations about the original concept of the movie, and you'll be hard pushed to find more thorough production notes.

FINAL VERDICT

Picture ☆☆☆ Sound ☆☆☆ Entertainment ☆☆☆
Extras ☆☆ Value ☆☆
OVERALL ☆☆☆

FARGO

Price: £17.99
Supplied by: PolyGram
Type of disc: Single layer, double-sided
No of chapters: 17
Film format(s)/length: 16:9 widescreen (side A), 4:3 (side B) / 94 mins
Director: Joel Coen
Starring: Frances McDormand, William H Macy, Steve Buscemi
Year made: 1996
Extras: Scene selection; multiple languages and subtitles; biographies; filmographies.

It's hard to take most of the characters in this film seriously owing to their strong accents, and yet *Fargo* is easily one of the best titles available on DVD at present. Jerry Lundegaard (Macy) needs money and comes up with an ingenious way to get hold of some; by having his wife kidnapped with the intention of

squeezing the ransom out of his bombastic but rich father-in-law. Sadly, Lundegaard's plans don't allow for his father-in-law's stubbornness and the fact that one of the kidnappers is a complete psychopath, with the result that events go a little awry. Enter Chief of the Brainerd Police Department, Marge Gunderson (McDormand), heavily pregnant and steadily plodding her way to the truth. McDormand's performance puts you very much in mind of a female version of Peter Falk's classic American TV detective Columbo, as she politely wanders around the snowy landscape of Brainerd like a whale with a badge, and as such she is eminently watchable. DVD-wise some attempt has obviously been made to give value for money. Both widescreen and regular televisions are catered for and in addition to scene selection and multiple languages and subtitles there are also biographies and filmographies on the cast.

FINAL VERDICT

Picture ☆☆☆☆ Sound ☆☆☆☆
Entertainment ☆☆☆☆ Extras ☆☆☆ Value ☆☆☆
OVERALL ☆☆☆☆

FEVER PITCH

Price: £15.99
Supplied by: VCI
Type of disc: Single layer, single-sided
No of chapters: 21
Film format(s)/length: 16:9 widescreen enhanced / 97 mins
Audio format: Dolby Surround
Director: David Evans
Starring: Colin Firth, Ruth Gemmell, Neil Pearson
Year made: 1998
Extras: Scene access; theatrical trailer; photo library; subtitles for the hard of hearing in English.

Ah, the trials and tribulations of a football supporter. Always the optimist, never satisfied, and despite probably never having kicked a ball in a professional capacity, in possession of seemingly more managerial knowledge than Ferguson, Wenger and Vialli put together! *Fever Pitch* – based on the Nick Hornby novel – is perhaps the finest film of its kind that homes in on the typical attitudes of the football supporter and uses them to great comic effect. The film revolves around Paul (Firth), an avid Arsenal supporter who juggles his love of the Gunners with his job as a teacher, whilst the whole time trying to woo new colleague, Sarah (Gemmell) The film raises many interesting points – most notably Paul's lifelong ambition to see his beloved 'Gooners' take the championship. The ironic thing is that when they do, he's left with a huge void in his life where the dreams and the expectancy once lay…so what will he fill it with? Sarah is totally uninterested in footie, so there are many elements featured here that everyday folk can relate to, not least any long-suffering woman who has to share her fella with 11 sweaty blokes twice a week! The film tackles this aspect tremendously well. Extras come in the form of the full theatrical trailer and a special photo library, but having watched the film, we certainly didn't want to spend yet more time staring at pictures of Faith's curly-haired, unkempt mug. *Fever Pitch* is a witty and charming film that is packed with sharp dialogue, acting and nostalgic tunes. Don't expect to watch it too often though.

FINAL VERDICT

Picture ☆☆☆ Sound ☆☆☆ Entertainment ☆☆☆
Extras ☆☆ Value ☆☆☆
OVERALL ☆☆☆

THE FIFTH ELEMENT

Price: £24.99
Supplied by: Pathé Distribution Ltd
Type of disc: Dual layer, single-sided
No of chapters: 22
Film format(s)/length: 2.35:1 widescreen / 121 mins
Audio format: Dolby Digital 5.1
Director: Luc Besson
Starring: Bruce Willis, Milla Jovovich, Gary Oldman
Year made: 1997
Extras: Scene access; theatrical trailer; 22 minute *Searching for the Fifth Element* documentary on the making of the film and interviews with the stars; cast and crew biographies and filmographies in written form; subtitles in English.

Provided you can stomach the high pitched and incomprehensible ravings of Chris Tucker as stellar DJ Ruby Rhod, *The Fifth Element* is a breath-taking piece of DVD entertainment that survives repeated viewings. Set in the year 2257, the film is about the age-old struggle of good against evil; the latter being personified in this case by a flaming ball of plasma 13,000 miles in diameter; racing towards a sloppy embrace with planet Earth. Only the ultimate weapon – mysterious Fifth Element Leeloo (Jovovich) – can defeat this evil 'death star', but there's a problem. She's disappeared with burnt-out cab driver Korben Dallas (Willis), while monstrous overlord Jean-Baptiste Emmanuel Zorg (Oldman) is tearing up the galaxy looking for the 4 remaining elemental stones so that evil can triumph and he can get paid. It's a confusing affair in places, with scant regard for character development, but you can for-

give all that thanks to Besson's eye for detail and the sheer energy of the 23rd century world he has created. Pop the DVD into the player and the improvements over the Region 1 disc are immediately obvious. The cool translucent menus overlaying animated scenes from the film give you access to a theatrical trailer, cast and crew biographies, and a never-before-seen 22-minute documentary about the making of the film. Not only does this present some fascinating insights into the way Besson works, complete with stacks of behind-the-scenes footage, you also get interviews with all the major players (it's strange seeing Milla Jovovich without orange hair!). It's just a shame that the wealth of outtakes that Besson boasts about in this short film are not included. Presented here in its original 2.35:1 widescreen format, few films are as good looking as *The Fifth Element* – it's most definitely a DVD showpiece. Thanks in no small part to the Technicolor set designs of Dan Weil and the sheer flamboyance of Jean-Paul Gaultier's stunning costumes, *The Fifth Element* jars the senses with its vivid colours and attention to detail – a futuristic vision that is the exact opposite of Ridley Scott's dark *Blade Runner*. The sound is also sharp and brutal, with a full dynamic range, from the delicate tones of the Diva's opera to the raucous gunfire of – well just about everybody. This 5.1 mix is quite superb, and it really makes you appreciate the effort put into the score by long time Besson collaborator, Eric Serra. This film will make the Dolby Digital buying decision for you, guaranteed. *The Fifth Element* was made for a format like DVD. With a picture that's sharper than one of Gaultier's suits, you can forgive its inevitable descent into comedy slapstick just so long as Miss Jovovich keeps jiggling about in those thermal bandages. For once, the Region 2 DVD is the best you can buy – what a shame Pathé has decided to charge £5 extra for it.

FINAL VERDICT

Picture ☆☆☆☆☆ Sound ☆☆☆☆☆
Entertainment ☆☆☆☆☆ Extras ☆☆☆ Value ☆☆
OVERALL ☆☆☆☆

FINAL ANALYSIS

Price: £15.99
Supplied by: Warner Home Video
Type of disc: Dual layer, single-sided
No of chapters: 37
Film format(s)/length: 1.85:1 widescreen / 120 mins
Audio format: Dolby Surround
Director: Phil Joanou

Starring: Richard Gere, Kim Basinger, Uma Thurman
Year made: 1992
Extras: Scene access; soundtrack in English, French and Italian; subtitles in 10 languages; subtitles for the hearing impaired in English and Italian.

There is a constant battle raging in Hollywood to reinvent the psychological thrillers of old. Phil Joanou of *Heaven's Prisoners* fame teamed up with the writer of *Cape Fear* to enter the fray with this rather successful candidate. It has all the prerequisites of a good thriller: gorgeous women, psychological tension and corkscrew twists. Richard Gere plays Isaac Barr, a psychiatrist trying to unravel the problems of the troubled Diana (Thurman) by pondering them with her sister Heather (Basinger). Unfortunately, in the course of his pondering, he falls for Heather, which doesn't make his life easy as she has enough problems of her own, not to mention a violent husband of whom she would rather be free. The surprises of the film are not harmed by a moderately soft picture and average sound. However, the film is all you're going to get on this disc as there are no extras to speak of whatsoever. A list of subtitles as long as your arm and scene access is what amounts to something 'extra' here…

FINAL VERDICT
Picture ☆☆☆ Sound ☆☆☆
Entertainment ☆☆☆ Extras ☆ Value ☆
OVERALL ☆☆

FINAL CUT

Price: £19.99
Supplied by: MGM Home Entertainment
Type of disc: Single layer, single-sided
No of chapters: 24
Film format(s)/length: 1.66:1 letterbox / 93 mins
Audio format: Dolby Digital 5.1
Directors: Dominic Anciano and Ray Burdis
Starring: Ray Winstone, Jude Law, Sadie Frost
Year made: 1998
Extras: Production notes; trailer; biographies; film credits; subtitles in English.

Jude is an obsessional film-maker and is secretly recording the foibles and betrayals of a group of friends. After his untimely death his widow insists on showing the film to them, thus revealing the dark secrets of their lifestyles and pre-empting some devastating consequences. Sterling performances from all 3 lead performers, as well as from the supporting actors, make this twisted, cruel and sometimes hilarious movie stand out as one of the most original to come out of the Brit Academy in recent years. The unusual, fly-on-the-wall style of filming and carefully

mounted levels of tension give *Final Cut* an immediacy and intensity which makes for compelling viewing. The shaky handheld cameras and often (intentionally) poorly-captured snippets of conversations can only be helped by the picture quality and ice-clear sound quality of DVD reproduction. The minimal add-ons are a disappointing detractor from an otherwise inspired DVD.

FINAL VERDICT
Picture ☆☆☆☆ Sound ☆☆☆☆
Entertainment ☆☆☆☆ Extras ☆☆ Value ☆☆☆
OVERALL ☆☆☆

FIRST KNIGHT

Price: £19.99
Supplied by: Columbia TriStar
Type of disc: Single layer, single-sided
No of chapters: 20
Film format(s)/length: 1.85:1 anamorphic / 128 mins
Director: Jerry Zucker
Starring: Sean Connery, Richard Gere, Julia Ormond
Year made: 1995
Extras: Widescreen TV enhanced; chapter select; multilingual subtitles.

When watching *First Knight*, it's hard to forget that its director brought you the *Airplane!* and *Naked Gun* movies. Certainly, the Disneyland version of Camelot, a ridiculous *It's a Knockout* obstacle course and knights' costumes left over from *Blake's 7* seem to be a joke on somebody's part. However, the film is entertaining enough. On the eve of her wedding to King Arthur (Connery), Guinevere (Ormond) is rescued from evil Prince Malagant by misplaced surfer dude Lancelot (Gere) and falls in love with him. Arthur, not knowing this, knights Lancelot as reward for saving the missus, and inevitably it all ends in tears. There are big battles – hardly *Braveheart*, as this is a 'PG', but well done – stunts and swordplay aplenty as is lush scenery, that come across well on DVD accompanied by Jerry Goldsmith's score. What's missing though are any exciting special features. Still, at least that means you don't have to listen to Gere drone on about Tibet.

FINAL VERDICT
Picture ☆☆☆☆ Sound ☆☆☆ Entertainment ☆☆☆
Extras ☆ Value ☆☆☆
OVERALL ☆☆

A FISH CALLED WANDA

Price: £19.99
Supplied by: DVDplus (www.dvdplus.co.uk)
Type of disc: Dual layer, single-sided

No of chapters: 32
Film format(s)/length: 1.85:1 widescreen / 108 mins
Audio format: Dolby Digital 5.
Director: Charles Crichton
Starring: John Cleese, Jamie Lee Curtis, Kevin Kline
Year made: 1988
Extras: Scene access; original theatrical trailer; English, French, German, Italian and Spanish soundtracks; multilingual subtitles.

What is it about British comedies? They seem to be the only films that can pull off storylines that come across as totally 'wacky' while avoiding the childish cheap shots of so many Hollywood attempts. *A Fish Called Wanda* is a fantastic example and the only thing that surpasses the writing is the exceptional casting. Although John Cleese is once again playing Basil Fawlty-type character, he does so brilliantly, and Jamie Lee Curtis pulls off another performance that will leave many male knees trembling. However, all the hats (including Oscar's) must be raised to Kevin Kline's pseudo-intellectual psychopath who easily steals the show. The hats can be quickly returned to heads when it comes to the disc however. The extras are sadly lacking. You get the trailer, multiple languages and an 8-page booklet about the creation of the film, but isn't that missing the whole point of DVD?

FINAL VERDICT

Picture ☆☆ Sound ☆☆ Entertainment ☆☆☆☆
Extras ☆ Value ☆☆
OVERALL ☆☆☆

A FISTFUL OF DOLLARS

Price: £19.99
Supplied by: MGM Home Video
Type of disc: Single layer, single-sided
No of chapters: 32
Film format(s)/length: 2.35:1 widescreen / 97 mins
Audio format: Mono
Director: Sergio Leone
Starring: Clint Eastwood, Johnny Wels, Marianne Koch
Year made: 1964
Extras: Scene access; 8-page colour booklet containing the history and trivia of the film; original theatrical trailer; subtitles in English; subtitles for the hearing impaired in English.

A stranger wearing a delightful poncho and sporting a permanent squint rides on a flea-bitten mule across endless prairies. He enters a deserted town called San Miguel, home to two families at war. A chirpy bell ringer warns that in this town, "People get rich or get killed." Our man opts for the latter and

expertly begins to work for and play one side off against the other. *A Fistful of Dollars* is the film that Eastwood owes his entire career to. His role as 'The Man With No Name' set up his screen persona for the next 30 years and established him first as a cult hero, then as an internationally renowned film-maker. As features go, the disc does seem bare, offering the same minimal extras as the Region 1 edition. Despite the well designed and animated menus, all that's present is the standard issue trailer. It's the 8-page booklet which attracts the greatest interest. Literate, informed and amiably written, it quotes the cast and crew including Leone who memorably compares Clint to a block of marble. Clearly this DVD's major selling point is the enhanced nature of the print and it's true – the Spanish outback, doubling for the Old West looks great. Audio lets the side down, being stuck in mono and even crackling at some points. It's a valiant effort by MGM to give this creaky classic a new lease of life but the definitive version of *A Fistful of Dollars* is not on this disc. In fact non-converts will probably wonder what all the fuss is about.

FINAL VERDICT

Picture ☆☆☆☆ Sound ☆ Entertainment ☆☆☆☆
Extras ☆☆ Value ☆☆☆
OVERALL ☆☆☆

FIVE EASY PIECES

Price: £19.99
Supplied by: Columbia TriStar Home Video
Type of disc: Single layer, single-sided
No of chapters: 28
Film format(s)/length: 16:9 widescreen enhanced / 94 mins
Audio format: Mono
Director: Bob Rafelson
Starring: Jack Nicholson, Karen Black, Susan Anspach
Year made: 1970
Extras: Scene access; filmographies for main stars; soundtrack in English, German, French, Italian and Spanish; subtitles in 20 languages.

Bob Rafelson's portrait of a man in contemporary America is anything but predictable. The audience is initially led to believe that Bob Dupea (Nicholson) is a simple oil worker with ideas above his station. Not content with his lot, which includes a dim white trash girlfriend (Black) Dupea finds himself at a crossroads between the working-class life he has chosen and the middle-class one he left behind. Both of these worlds collide when Dupea is drawn back to the home of his dying composer father, and embarks on a destructive affair with his brother's fiancé. This is one of Nicholson's finest performances, coming as it did so soon after *Easy Rider*, the film that introduced him to mainstream Hollywood. *Five Easy Pieces* opened in 1970 to rave reviews, and even earned Nicholson an Oscar nomination for Best Actor. In contrast to some of its previous DVD efforts, Columbia has provided little for Nicholson fans, and is content to offer nothing more than the movie itself and filmographies of the main stars. Audio commentaries from anyone involved in the production would have been a welcome addition, particularly in light of the film now celebrating its 30th anniversary. As it stands, it's a great film but a shoddy DVD.

FINAL VERDICT

Picture ☆☆☆ Sound ☆☆☆ Entertainment ☆☆☆☆
Extras ☆ Value ☆☆
OVERALL ☆☆☆

FLATLINERS

Price: £19.99
Supplied by: DVD Premier Direct (01923 226492)
Type of disc: Single layer, single-sided
No of chapters: 35
Film format(s)/length: 2.35:1 widescreen / 110 mins
Audio format: Dolby Digital Surround
Director: Joel Schumacher
Starring: Kiefer Sutherland, Julia Roberts, Kevin Bacon
Year made: 1990
Extras: Theatrical trailer; filmographies of all leading actors; DVD trailer of forthcoming titles.

What is death all about? Is there life on the other side? Some people have died and come back to life and tell of bright white lights and pearly gates – it's a question that we would all like answered. A group of medical students including Roberts, Sutherland and Bacon decide that they're going to find out for themselves by stopping their own hearts, dying, then relying on their friends to bring them back to life. *Flatliners* is a classic and has been shown on TV countless times, but now it's on DVD for the ultimate showing of the movie. It certainly is a gripping drama as the students dabble with death creating flatlines and experiencing the sensations for themselves. The out-of-body experiences in the movie are well put together – uncovering the hidden fears and sins of each 'death rider.' Obviously things don't go completely smoothly, and they soon begin to wish they hadn't messed around with immortality as each has recurring nightmares and they almost lose one of their friends. To be honest Columbia TriStar could have made a greater effort with the DVD extras

included – it seems that the bog standard theatrical trailer and some filmographies is all we can expect these days from our UK releases. DVD owners should start to demand more for their money – if US discs can have specially created extras then why not ours? Saying that, the movie is still a treat.

FINAL VERDICT

Picture ☆☆☆☆ Sound ☆☆☆ Entertainment ☆☆☆
Extras ☆☆ Value ☆☆☆
OVERALL ☆☆☆

THE FLINTSTONES

Price: £19.90
Supplied by: Columbia TriStar Home Video
Type of disc: Dual layer, single-sided
No of chapters: 47
Film format(s)/length: 1.85:1 widescreen / 87 mins
Audio format: Dolby Digital 5.1
Director: Brian Levant
Starring: John Goodman, Rick Moranis, Elizabeth Perkins
Year made: 1994
Extras: Scene access; *Discovering Bedrock* original documentary on the making of the film; feature commentary with director; teaser trailer; theatrical trailer; production photographs; art department concept sketches; opening sequence comparison; production notes; cast and film-makers notes; soundtrack in German, French, Italian and Spanish (5.1). Polish and Czech (stereo); subtitles in 9 languages.

Unfortunately, *The Flintstones* concept has become a franchise, especially in the eyes of Hollywood, and as with all franchises, a big budget movie is a must. What's apparent from the onset is that Levant is not the world's most inspiring director. As a result, *The Flintstones* movie practically bombed at the cinema when it was released back in the summer of 1994 against competition such as *The Lion King*. However, its poor performance was not down to a lack of enthusiasm, as Levant comes across in the bonus director's commentary as the biggest *Flintstones* fan in the world. The man knows *The Flintstones* inside out and so was able to bring an extremely loyal adaptation to the big screen; possibly the most loyal that Hollywood has ever seen. It may not have raked in millions at the box office, but it's exactly what it should be: an extended episode of *The Flintstones* television series. Levant was quick to recognise the roots of the franchise, and has stuck to them from the opening sequence right through to the final credits. Okay, so the original *Flintstones* concept was a little crazy; being not so much 'how we used to live', but more 'how we would live if there was a nuclear war and we were forced to rebuild everything out of rock and bones'. Still, it was a concept that became the most popular animated series of its time, only to be surpassed 20 years later by *The Simpsons*. Levant's attitude was: why fix something if it isn't broken? and this results in a perfect recreation of the original. Using the latest in puppetry and CGI the film brings the Bedrock everyone knows and loves to life. Both Goodman and Perkins were inspired choices for the title roles, with Goodman playing Fred Flintstone crossed with Oliver Hardy. Moranis and O'Donnell seem slightly lost, with the latter more brain-dead than her animated equivalent. Such flaws aside, this still amounts to the family fun that the TV show was always famous for. If the movie doesn't do it for you, then the disc definitely will. An abundance of extras that could take you the better half of an evening's entertainment to get through, the disc contains all the usual goodies that seem to be becoming the norm from Columbia TriStar. The 40-minute documentary compiled specifically for the DVD tells you everything that you need to know about recreating Bedrock, though director Levant does come across as being slightly obsessed. The production photographs and concept sketches show just how much hard work goes into a movie like this, and the split-screen comparison between the cartoon and movie opening sequences show just how loyal this film is. Overall it's a mediocre movie with interesting roots and extras.

FINAL VERDICT

Picture ☆☆☆☆ Sound ☆☆☆☆ Entertainment ☆☆☆
Extras ☆☆☆☆☆ Value ☆☆☆☆☆
OVERALL ☆☆☆☆

FLUBBER

Price: £15.99
Supplied by: DVD Net (020 8890 2520)
Type of disc: Single layer, single-sided
No of chapters: 18
Film format(s)/length: 4:3 regular / 90 mins
Director: Les Mayfield
Starring: Robin Williams, Marcia Gay Harden, Christopher McDonald
Year made: 1997
Extras: Scene access/interactive menus; Dolby Digital 5.1, Dolby Surround; multilingual subtitles.

Robin Williams and Walt Disney once more bring smiles and laughter to children everywhere in this latest DVD comedy. Williams plays Professor Philip Brainard – a well-meaning but absent-minded professor – who, on the wedding day to his colleague

Sara (Harden), stumbles across a revolutionary new compound. It's green. It dances. And it may just win back his bride to be and save his financially struck college. It's Flubber! Williams' visual humour is comical at best, as he tries to win back his girl (and the audience) from arch rival Wilson Croft (McDonald), who is also trying to steal the Flubber formula. Enter snooty millionaire Chester Hoenicker (Raymond Barry) and his two thugs to add more madcap mayhem – it's typical modern Disney. Intentionally aimed at a family audience, older children may enjoy its obvious *Home Alone* elements; in particular the slapstick bowling/golf ball incidents. As for the adult audience, that traditional Disney magic seems to have stayed firmly rooted in the animated genre. There is one memorable moment however that is sure to raise a giggle: in one final up yours to the bad guys, the Flubber enters the greedy Wilson Croft's mouth, only to exit via his back passage – ouch! The quality of the picture is as good as a regular full screen DVD can get, and the sound complements it nicely – although it's rarely put to the test. There are no extras to speak off – unless you count the standard scene selection, language and subtitles. The possibility for Flubber-esque jappery on this disc is immense, but no-one bothered to put in the effort.

FINAL VERDICT

Picture ☆☆☆ Sound ☆☆ Entertainment ☆☆
Extras ☆ Value ☆☆
OVERALL ☆☆

FOR A FEW DOLLARS MORE

Price: £19.99
Supplied by: MGM Home Entertainment
Type of disc: Dual layer, single-sided
No of chapters: 32
Film format(s)/length: 16:9 widescreen enhanced / 126 mins
Audio format: Stereo
Director: Sergio Leone
Starring: Clint Eastwood, Gian Maria Volonté, Lee Van Cleef
Year made: 1965
Extras: Scene access; theatrical trailer; soundtrack in French; multi-lingual subtitles; subtitles for the hearing impaired in English.

If you love Spaghetti Westerns, then you're no doubt already familiar with *For a Few Dollars More*. Set in the traditional wild wild west – bereft of giant spiders and Will Smith – it follows the exploits of two bounty hunters: Colonel Douglas Mortimer (Van Cleef) and Manko (Eastwood) who find themselves on the trail of the infamous bandit Indio (Volonté). The film itself is beautifully shot and the musical score is by Ennio Morricone; the master musician who scored Leone's *The Good, the Bad and the Ugly*. The performances are fine all round, though at some points you feel that Volonté or Van Cleef are stealing the show. Unfortunately, where the film is a classic, the DVD is disappointing. The picture quality is good considering the films age (an anamorphic treat) and is coupled well with a superb score. However, all the voices seem ever so slightly out of sync, but this may have always been the case rather than a specific fault with the DVD. There is only one extra of any interest is the theatrical trailer. And while an authentic slice of Seventies cheese, it can only amuse you for so long. Apart from that the disc is devoid of features, which is a shame because Leone's films are so masterfully made. An opportunity for some insight into this process has been wasted. If you are a fan then it's a must have, but if you want more than a film you'll be disappointed.

FINAL VERDICT

Picture ☆☆☆ Sound ☆☆ Entertainment ☆☆☆☆
Extras ☆ Value ☆☆
OVERALL ☆☆☆

FORTRESS

Price: £19.99
Supplied by: Columbia TriStar Home Video
Type of disc: Single layer, single-sided
No of chapters: 28
Film format(s)/length: 1.85:1 widescreen enhanced / 92 mins
Audio format: Dolby Surround
Director: Stuart Gordon
Starring: Christopher Lambert, Kurtwood Smith, Loryn Locklin
Year made: 1993
Extras: Scene access; English, French and Spanish soundtracks; multilingual subtitles; US theatrical trailer; DVD trailer; filmographies.

The time: somewhere in the not-too-distant future. The place: the United States. The problem: severe overpopulation and a lack of resources. The answer: breeding restrictions. Christopher 'The Highlander' Lambert is John Brennick, a Captain in the US Military's elite Black Beret unit. When his wife Karen becomes pregnant for a second time (their first baby having died) Brennick tries to get her to the safety of free Mexico but they get caught and sent to a high-tech maximum security prison. Harsh! Needless to say, Brennick isn't going to sit around and

accept his fate, particularly when he finds out that pregnant women in the prison have their babies removed during labour and turned into cyborg prison guards. Lucky that he's a highly trained special forces officer really! *Fortress* is a fairly cheesy but nonetheless relatively entertaining futuristic prison flick which contains a few original ideas coupled with a bunch of sci-fi and prison movie clichés. The gore factor is fairly high and money has obviously been spent on the special effects, although as this film is 6 years-old some of the aesthetics do look a little dated. Considering that *Fortress* is a UK DVD it's got a surprising number of extra features too, although in reality they're not actually as impressive as they seem at first glance. The US theatre trailer is supplied rather than the English version perhaps because *Fortress* didn't exactly receive a rapturous reception in the UK, getting as it did a limited cinema release in some areas and going straight to video just about everywhere else. A DVD trailer is included on the disc but this is just an advert for other DVD films and doesn't really show more than a few seconds of each, making it a pretty pointless watch not too worthy of the label 'special feature'. 3 different languages and a variety of subtitles are available, making this a title to suit not just the English-speaking amongst us, but one for minority groups as well. The filmographies are a welcome addition to the package but aren't really all that impressive, comprising as they do a few screens of text. Perhaps it should be made compulsory for all DVD filmographies to include clips from the actors' or director's previous work! Basically what you've got here is a DVD with all the fairly dull and mundane extra features that appear on UK discs. When looked at in summary the list is fairly impressive but when you actually sit down to watch them you realise there's not actually that much there. For a UK DVD this one does give you more than the majority, but it's still not much and for a film which has been out for years on video and has already been screened on TV you really need more.

FINAL VERDICT

Picture ☆☆☆ Sound ☆☆☆☆
Entertainment ☆☆☆ Extras ☆☆ Value ☆☆☆
OVERALL ☆☆☆

FOUR WEDDINGS AND A FUNERAL

Price: £17.99
Supplied by: PolyGram Filmed Entertainment
Type of disc: Single layer, single-sided
No of chapters: 21
Film format(s)/length: 4.3 only! / 112 mins

Director: Mike Newell
Starring: Hugh Grant, Andie MacDowell, Kristin Scott Thomas
Year made: 1994
Extras: Music video; theatrical trailer; multiple languages; multilingual subtitles.

Awkward but charming floppy-haired fop Charles (Grant) finds himself at 32 unable to make a commitment to any of his girlfriends. At one particular wedding he attends he sees Carrie (MacDowell). 3 weddings, one of which is Carrie's, and one funeral later and Charles finds himself at the altar, but not with Carrie. Never an awesome cinematic experience 'get that red bus, bobby and post box in shot'. But if the missus insists on a feel-good weepy in the collection, slotted betwixt *Evil Dead* and *Goodfellas*, it fits the bill. The DVD's not bad either with a decent amount of extra features for the discerning fan. For a start there's the original theatrical trailer and Wet Wet Wet's music video of 'Love is All Around' which is a good start. The film and biographies are a little light though, with just text and no images and it's a travesty that there is no widescreen version, but overall it's a strong British film backed by better than average DVD additions.

FINAL VERDICT

Picture ☆☆☆☆ Sound ☆☆☆☆ Entertainment ☆☆☆
Extras ☆ Value ☆☆☆
OVERALL ☆☆☆

FRANTIC

Price: £19.99
Supplied by: Warner Home Video
Type of disc: Dual layer, single-sided
No of chapters: 32
Film format(s)/length: 1.85:1 widescreen / 115 mins
Audio format: Dolby Surround
Director: Roman Polanski
Starring: Harrison Ford, Betty Buckley, John Mahoney
Year made: 1988
Extras: Scene access; soundtrack in French and Italian; subtitles in 10 languages; subtitles for the hearing impaired in English and Italian.

When an American doctor (Ford) returns to Paris for the first time since his honeymoon, the last thing he expects is to lose his wife! He gets into the shower – she's there, he gets out – she's gone. At first Ford's character just assumes she's popped out to buy something but it soon becomes clear that something has happened to her and so begins the 'frantic'. Polanski is known for quality films and *Frantic* is no exception. The cinematography is excellent and the pace of the movie perfectly judged as we follow the actions of Ford's doctor as he gets increasingly more worried, confused and frustrated by hotel staff, the police, shadowy gangsters and a mysterious young woman whose lost luggage holds the key to his wife's disappearance. Harrison Ford puts in a sterling and very un-Indiana Jones performance as the husband driven frantic with worry over his missing spouse and the supporting cast are all superb. While this movie now looks a little dated – one of the big mysteries in the film is what a small electronic device is for and any 10-year-old child would instantly know that it's the detonator for a nuclear weapon – it still manages to keep you gripped and puts most modern so-called thrillers to shame. Sadly, as far as the DVD itself goes, *Frantic* is totally devoid of special features with nothing that makes this a must-buy over the VHS version – particularly when you consider the quality of the picture – it's not very good at all. Nice film, shame about the disc.

FINAL VERDICT

Picture ☆☆☆ Sound ☆☆☆ Entertainment ☆☆☆☆
Extras ☆☆ Value ☆☆
OVERALL ☆☆

FRIDAY

Price: £15.99
Supplied by: Entertainment in Video
Type of disc: Single layer, single-sided
No of chapters: 12
Film format(s)/length: 1.85:1 widescreen enhanced / 88 mins
Audio format: Dolby Surround
Director: F Gary Gray
Starring: Ice Cube, Chris Tucker, Nia Long
Year made: 1995
Extras: Scene access; theatrical trailer; behind-the-scenes featurette (5 mins); interviews with the cast and crew members (13 mins).

Another day, another dollar. But in the case of Craig Jones (Cube) it's just another day without a job, smoking blunts and chillin' in the hood with a bottle of JD. Since his debut performance in the compelling *Boyz in the Hood*, Cube has appeared in a number of box office hits – most recently as Chief Elgin in *Three Kings*. In *Friday* he stars alongside Chris Tucker (Smokey) of *Rush Hour* fame, the two finding the funny side of life in the Los Angeles ghetto. Shot primarily from the porch of Craig's pad, the two experience the highs and lows as the script (written by Cube and fellow rapper DJ Pooh) provides a welcome breath of fresh air with every ghetto element featured: a jealous girlfriend, a drug dealer within a Seventies Kevin Keegan perm and Tom 'Tiny' Lister Jr as the neighbourhood bully. The picture quality is never in question, with not a flicker or glitch to be seen. Unfortunately the same can't be said about the soundtrack, as the mix is a poor Dolby Surround – however, the lack of explosions and loud dialogue contribute towards this less-than-impressive audio impact. Delightfully though, there is a reasonable number of extras included on the DVD, including the pre-ordained theatrical trailer, a 5-minute featurette and 13 minutes of interviews with the cast and crew. Considering Entertainment in Video is fortunately reluctant to be swayed by the increasingly popular (with companies, anyway) £19.99 price bracket, this moderately priced disc is a sound purchase for any ghetto genre fan.

FINAL VERDICT

Picture ☆☆☆☆ Sound ☆☆☆ Entertainment ☆☆☆
Extras ☆☆☆ Value ☆☆☆

OVERALL ☆☆☆

FRIED GREEN TOMATOES AT THE WHISTLE STOP CAFE

Price: £9.99
Supplied by: Cinema Club
Type of disc: Dual layer, single-sided
No of chapters: 24
Film format(s)/length: 16:9 widescreen / 125 mins
Audio format: Dolby Surround
Director: Jon Avnet
Starring: Kathy Bates, Jessica Tandy, Mary-Louise Parker
Year made: 1991
Extras: Scene access; featurette; theatrical trailer.

Frumpy Evelyn (Bates) feels her life is going nowhere. Her husband would rather watch the game than see her dressed only in clingfilm, but a sprightly 80 year-old (Tandy) tells her an inspirational story from her past. Flashback 50 years to spunky Idgie (Mary Stuart Masterson) and good natured Ruth (Parker) who open the eponymous restaurant. *Up Close & Personal*'s director Jon Avnet evokes the American South's rich heritage of whimsy, murderous intrigue behind decorum and racial intolerance, but not enough to distract too much attention from the two pairs of womens' warm and fuzzy journeys. The film's transfer is well done considering its asking price and includes some entertaining extras. The featurette, though, just splices superficial quotes from the cast and crew with footage you've already seen. It's a perfect Sunday afternoon film on an adequate disc.

There, and I managed to avoid using the term 'chick flick'. D'oh!

FINAL VERDICT

Picture ☆☆☆☆ Sound ☆☆☆ Entertainment ☆☆☆
Extras ☆☆☆ Value ☆☆☆☆

OVERALL ☆☆☆

THE FRIGHTENERS

Price: £19.99
Supplied by: Columbia TriStar Home Video
Type of disc: Dual layer, single-sided
No of chapters: 16
Film format(s)/length: 2.35:1 widescreen / 105 mins
Audio format: Dolby Digital 5.1
Director: Peter Jackson
Starring: Michael J Fox, Trini Alvarado, Jeffrey Combs
Year made: 1996
Extras: Scene access; cast and film-makers notes; production notes; trailer; soundtrack in 7 languages including French, Italian and German; subtitles in 9 languages.

This DVD is a surprisingly good package as the movie is great entertainment, and there are a whole host of extra features. With a name like *The Frighteners*, you might expect a pretty gory affair with a liberal splashing of tomato ketchup, what you get instead though is something a little more digestable. Fox plays Frank Bannister, a phoney ghost buster who uses spectacular special effects to create the illusion of dead people coming alive again. We're not talking gruesome zombie flesh-eaters here, as these ghosts can chat to our cutesy spook hunter and even help him when business gets a bit slow. A few suspicious deaths occur in the village of Fairwater and everyone thinks that the spooky conman is responsible, but there is a lot of history in this village, and only our hero can see who will be next! This thriller is not at all scary and has clearly been aimed at a fairly young audience. The plot has some unusual twists and plenty of comedy thrown in for good measure. It even retains a steady stream of suspense, keeping you guessing who's responsible for the unexpected deaths right up to the end. The special effects are excellent and really make the movie. The ghosts are magical and have plenty of character, and the effects seem to get better as the story progresses. The extra features are numerous and include a wide selection of language tracks, subtitles, cast filmographies and the standard trailer. An added extra to this list of features are the production notes, which contain loads of interesting information about how the film was made and what problems were encountered along the way. The picture quality is great, making the special effects seem even better and the Dolby Digital soundtrack performs exactly as it should. You don't need to be a Fox fan to enjoy this movie. It is light-hearted and humourous, with a touch of *Psycho*-style suspense. The special effects are dazzling throughout, but if you're looking for gore, you'll be sadly disappointed. In all, this is a thoroughly entertaining movie supported by a good range of extra features, making it a good value purchase and an excellent example of DVD.

FINAL VERDICT

Picture ☆☆☆☆☆ Sound ☆☆☆☆☆
Entertainment ☆☆☆☆ Extras ☆☆☆☆
Value ☆☆☆☆
OVERALL ☆☆☆☆

FROM DUSK TILL DAWN

Price: £15.99
Supplied By: DVD World (01705 796662)
Type of disc: Single-sided, single-layer
No of chapters: 26
Film format(s)/length: 16:9 widescreen /103 mins
Audio format: Dolby Digital
Director: Robert Rodriguez
Starring: George Clooney, Harvey Keitel, Juliette Lewis
Year made: 1996
Extras: Scene access.

While *Pulp Fiction* established Tarantino as one of Hollywood's most gifted scriptwriters, it shouldn't follow that it's worth filming his laundry list and sticking QT in as a lead player. *From Dusk Till Dawn* is one of Tarantino's earliest scripts and it shows, the central story arc being little more than anti-heroes Tarantino and Clooney taking an innocent family hostage, hitting the road and taking refuge in a sleazy bar with a dark secret. By the time the secret is uncovered, you need to care for the characters but sadly you don't. The film really is stolen by Salma Hayek's serpent dance, which while in itself something of an erotic masterpiece, proves an all too obvious divide between the film's preamble and the subsequent gore-fest. If you haven't seen the film before, then the outrageousness of the special effects and the big budget flair with which it's all filmed should make for an ideal post-pub diversion. If you have seen the film before – or haven't previously imbibed of alcohol – then the simplicity of the script and paucity of characterisation should make you pause before purchase. DVD serves to reveal the skills of the effects artists with consummate precision, but that aside it's a disappointing conversion with no 'Making of' documentary, production notes or even the theatrical trailer. All in all, *From Dust Till Dawn* is a conversion

as lazy as the script.

FINAL VERDICT

Picture ☆☆☆☆☆ Sound ☆☆☆☆
Entertainment ☆☆☆ Extras ☆ Value ☆☆☆
OVERALL ☆☆☆

FROM DUSK TILL DAWN 2: TEXAS BLOOD MONEY

Price: £15.99
Supplied by: DVDplus (www.dvdplus.co.uk)
Type of disc: Single layer, single-sided
No of chapters: 22
Film format(s)/length: 1.85:1 widescreen / 84 mins
Audio format: Dolby Surround
Director: Scott Spiegel
Starring: Robert Patrick, Bo Hopkins, Duane Whitaker
Year made: 1999
Extras: Scene access; subtitles in English; subtitles available for the hearing impaired in English.

When the biggest names on the box cover are the executive producers (those who got paid to say: "Yeah, make the movie, whatever") you know you're in the land of the quickie sequel. In this case, Quentin Tarantino and Robert Rodriguez probably didn't have to lift a finger to profit from a follow-up to their popular vampirefest *From Dusk Till Dawn*. No George Clooney or Harvey Keitel this time – the star of *Texas Blood Money* is *T2*'s Robert Patrick, trying to sound like a young Clint Eastwood. Patrick is a bank robber who, with his partners in crime, plans to blow a Mexican bank – the only drawback is that one of his crew made the mistake of stopping off for a swifty at the Titty Twister, the vampire-run bar from the first film. Now, not only is half the Mexican police force waiting outside the bank, but he's also stuck inside with a gang of newly undead criminals who see vampirism as the ideal route to big bucks! Director Spiegel is obviously a big fan of Sam Raimi, as he tries to outdo the director of *Evil Dead 2* by putting the camera in the most insane places imaginable. Just when you think a shot from inside a vampire's mouth has to be the limit, he goes one better and puts it inside somebody's neck! The whole film plays like a live-action *Itchy and Scratchy* cartoon, and while it's very cheesy, it's also quite entertaining. Unfortunately, it would appear that any extras were vanquished at dawn!

FINAL VERDICT

Picture ☆☆☆☆ Sound ☆☆☆ Entertainment ☆☆☆
Extras ☆ Value ☆☆☆
OVERALL ☆☆☆

FROM RUSSIA WITH LOVE

Price: £19.99
Supplied by: MGM
Type of disc: Dual layer, single-sided
No of chapters: 32
Film format(s)/length: 1.77:1 anamorphic / 115 mins
Audio format: Mono
Director: Terence Young
Starring: Sean Connery, Robert Shaw, Daniela Bianchi
Year made: 1963

Extras: Scene access; audio commentary by cast and crew; *Inside From Russia With Love* documentary; *Harry Saltzman: Showman* tribute documentary; 3 theatrical trailers; 6 radio and TV adverts; stills gallery; 'Making of' booklet; subtitles in English; subtitles for the hearing impaired in English.

It's the second chapter of the greatest movie franchise ever, but the first one that included Desmond Llewelyn as Q, the first one that 'killed' 007, the first one with a pre-credit sequence and tailor-made theme song, and it's this film more than any other that's parodied by *Austin Powers*. Bond, James Bond (Connery) is sent to Istanbul to accept a smuggled code decrypter from Soviet clerk Tatiana Romanova (the luminous Bianchi), even though it's obviously a trap for Britain's greatest secret agent. Set 6 months after *Dr No*, SPECTRE is determined to kill the man who thwarted their evil plans and despatches ice-cold assassin Donald 'Red' Grant (Shaw) after Bond, the girl and the code machine. With the principal baddies being an old woman with sapphic tendencies, a chess master or a faceless cat-stroker, it's down to Shaw to be the supervillain. And he does so brilliantly as Grant, a mirror-image nemesis to Connery's Bond just as Scaramanga would be to Moore's and Trevelyan would be to Brosnan's. All the surviving main players are brought in for the well-researched 34-minute documentary, which reveals there was almost as much crisis, tragedy and triumph behind the scenes as that which appears on screen. Elsewhere is an array of old-school publicity material, a text introduced (but sadly silent) picture gallery and the audio commentary. A Bond-literate American from the Ian Fleming Foundation fills in the gaps between archive interview clips from the late Young as well as key crew members and secondary cast. It's informative and concise, but lacking input from the major stars. In short, *From Russia With Love* is a top-notch Cold War thriller distinguished by a cast and crew who are firing on all cylinders. Though presented in an unenhanced state (the picture is specked with

dust and sound is mono), the volume of features will guarantee huge sales success, Bond fan approval, and that Region 1 producers will have a hard act to follow.

FINAL VERDICT

Picture ☆☆☆ Sound ☆ Entertainment ☆☆☆☆
Extras ☆☆☆☆☆ Value ☆☆☆☆
OVERALL ☆☆☆☆

THE FUGITIVE

Price: £13.99
Supplied by: DVD World (01705 796662)
Type of disc: Single layer, single-sided
No of chapters: 42
Film format(s)/length: 16:9 widescreen / 125 mins
Audio format: Dolby Digital 5.1, Dolby Surround
Director: Andrew Davis
Starring: Harrison Ford, Tommy Lee Jones, Sela Ward
Year made: 1993
Extras: Scene access/interactive menus; cast biographies; multilingual subtitles.

Things were going well for Dr Richard Kimble (Ford – bushy beard); a top surgeon at a Chicago hospital with a beautiful loving wife (Ward). However, things take a turn for the worst when on coming home late one evening, Kimble arrives to find his wife brutally murdered and a one-armed man legging it out the back window. The plot takes shape with the good doctor being questioned, then later wrongfully charged and sentenced to death for his wife's murder. An attempted break out on the transport ride to the prison results in the bus tumbling down a small hillside into the path of an oncoming train. In true traditional Hollywood style Ford leaps off the bus moments before the train hits in what is now a classic cinema moment. Now a fugitive, the tension builds as Kimble is determined to prove his innocence by finding the one-armed man. But hot on his heels is cunning US Marshal Sam Gerard (bloodhound Jones) whose relentless chase keeps the plot thick and furious in this excellent thriller. With a plunge down a waterfall and a cat-and-mouse pursuit through a Chicago Saint Patrick's Day Parade, you'll be glued to the edge of your seat. The quality of the sound seems to have a bigger presence in the film, as the picture only comes in a regular widescreen presentation, no enhancement. Yet the most surprising feature is that there are only 10 chapter locations (including end credits) within the scene index. This is unbelievable considering that there are actually 42 chapters on this DVD. The only redeeming inclusion is the cast biographies but these offer very little of worth. Still a gripping thriller, but this disc does it no favours.

FINAL VERDICT

Picture ☆☆ Sound ☆☆☆☆ Entertainment ☆☆☆☆

Extras ☆ Value ☆☆☆

OVERALL ☆☆☆

THE FULL MONTY

Price: £19.99

Supplied by: 20th Century Fox Home Entertainment

Type of disc: Dual layer, single-sided

No of chapters: 22

Film format(s)/length: 1.85:1 anamorphic / 87 mins

Audio format: Dolby Surround

Director: Peter Cattaneo

Starring: Robert Carlyle, Tom Wilkinson, Mark Addy

Year made: 1997

Extras: Scene access; theatrical trailer; soundtrack in English; subtitles in 10 languages; subtitles for the hearing impaired in English.

Although there are all sorts of bumps and grinds along the way, in essence stripping is about getting your kit off and The Full Monty keeps to the formula. It starts with a Chippendales poster getting a couple of Sheffield scallies thinking and ends with them dropping their pants. Despite the high concept structure, The Full Monty's still got more intelligence and snappy one-liners than any other half-dozen British movies. The opening footage of Sixties steelworks is heavy-handed, but the framing of character scenes with long shots of dreary Sheffield, of tower blocks and desolate factories, gives it a genuinely cinematic feel. The 6 strippers have varying amounts of screen time, but all are interesting and believable. Carlyle holds the movie together, pushing the idea forward as his ex-wife pursues him for maintenance and his beloved son cracks open the Post Office account for extra funds. Wilkinson is no less impressive, an ex-foreman who six months on from his sacking still hasn't told his wife – he's an unlikely Arlene Philips for the troupe. You can't help but feel a little cheated that the movie ends with the stripshow, rather than following the characters through, but it's an enjoyable enough ride while it lasts with an Oscar-winning soundtrack of old-time classics. It was also nominated for best director, picture and screenplay, none of which apparently counts for much with Fox which rolls out a threadbare package. Apart from a trailer and a neat animated zipper effect on the interactive menus, the DVD is entirely bereft of extras. No director's commentary, no 'Making of' documentary – nothing. Picture quality is only reasonable, but that's down to film stock, although at least the soundtrack

comes through well. Overall, a missed opportunity.

FINAL VERDICT

Picture ☆☆☆☆ Sound ☆☆☆☆

Entertainment ☆☆☆☆ Extras ☆ Value ☆☆☆

OVERALL ☆☆☆☆

THE GAME

Price: £17.99

Supplied by: PolyGram

Type of disc: Single layer, double-sided

No of chapters: 20

Film format(s)/length: Widescreen 2.35:1, 4:3 / 128 mins

Director: David Fincher

Starring: Michael Douglas, Sean Penn, Deborah Unger

Year made: 1997

Extras: Actor and film-maker biographies; scene access.

Fincher's creepy psycho thriller preys on the paranoia within all of us; the fear of losing everything we have and not being able to do a thing about it. Nicholas Van Orton (Douglas) is a successful commodities broker – cool, in control and seriously rich. He's also bored out of his mind which is why when slightly seedy brother Conrad (Penn) turns up on his birthday with an enrolment card for a mysterious organisation called CRS, Van Orton seizes the chance to participate in The Game. Dark and moody, you can see what attracted Fincher to the script following the morbid success of Se7en, and The Game is indeed a similar animal. You never know who's on the level and who's working for CRS, what's real and what's an elaborate stage show and it is this keep 'em guessing theme which helps to make The Game rivetting to the end. There's plenty of evidence too of Fincher's trademark rapid-fire editing during moments of stress and anxiety in an otherwise low-key film with understated performances from everyone except Douglas, who relishes the chance to go off the rails for the first time since Falling Down. Penn though, is wasted. As far as the extras go, The Game is a decent enough package which includes cast and film makers' biographies and a choice of 4:3 and 2.35:1 picture, but we expected more from such an exciting and innovative director as Fincher. This is after all the man who actually made us watch all the final credits of Se7en because they ran backwards and we all expected another twist before the lights came up.

FINAL VERDICT

Picture ☆☆☆☆ Sound ☆☆☆ Entertainment ☆☆☆☆

Extras ☆☆☆ Value ☆☆☆

OVERALL ☆☆☆☆

GATTACA

Price: £19.99
Supplied by: Columbia TriStar
Type of disc: Single layer, double-sided
No of chapters: 28
Film format(s)/length: 16:9 widescreen / 102mins
Audio format: Dolby Digital
Director: Andrew Niccol
Starring: Ethan Hawke, Uma Thurman, Alan Arkin
Year made: 1997
Extras: Mini-documentary; outtakes; photo gallery; instant scene access; theatrical trailer; filmographies; multi-lingual subtitles.

Tackling the topical subject of government-controlled genetic engineering – and the discrimination that can result – *Gattaca* is an unusually intelligent Hollywood sci-fi movie. Ethan Hawke plays an 'In-Valid' whose imperfect genes have doomed him to a life of drudgery – cleaning the toilets belonging to those who are 'Valid.' However, he refuses to accept his lot and successfully manages to 'swap' his DNA with a superior specimen (Jude Law) who has been disabled in a road accident. *Gattaca* feels like an arty French movie from the mid-Sixties, the emphasis is on style and cinematography, with the special effects almost always off screen. Of course, the problem with these 'Brave New World' films is that the pristine style of the fascist gene-police can seem superficially more alluring than the characters struggling against its dicta. The film tries so hard to be subtle, the characters never really engage our emotions and the flurry of twists comes much too late. It's a film which is more interesting and distracting than engaging. That said, *Gattaca*'s precise lighting, arty cinematography and haunting soundtrack make it particularly effective on DVD. With the added photo gallery, poster gallery, theatrical trailer and mini 'Making of' documentary, it is the veritable mountain of extras that make this movie a worthwhile buy. There's even a selection of out-takes, making you realise why it is always the directors who get the credits in the movies.

FINAL VERDICT

Picture ☆☆☆☆☆ Sound ☆☆☆☆☆
Entertainment ☆☆☆ Extras ☆☆☆☆
Value ☆☆☆☆
OVERALL ☆☆☆☆

THE GAUNTLET

Price: £15.99
Supplied by: DVDplus (www.dvdplus.co.uk)
Type of disc: Dual layer, single-sided
No of chapters: 34

Film format(s)/length: 2.35:1 widescreen enhanced (side A), 4:3 regular (Side B) / 105 mins
Audio format: Dolby Digital 5.1
Director: Clint Eastwood
Starring: Clint Eastwood, Sondra Locke, Pat Hingle
Year made: 1977
Extras: Production notes (text only); cast info; French and Italian mono soundtrack; multi-lingual subtitles; subtitles for the hearing impaired in English and Italian.

An alcoholic cop, an ageing schoolgirl looking like a Vegas hooker… Eastwood's character of Ben Shockley is an interesting move away from 'Dirty' Harry Callaghan. However it's not so much Eastwood as the thriller format itself which is in transition here – an A-list star toying with what would become a concept picture. Cop and hooker are hunted by both cops and mafia, leading Eastwood into running an awesome gauntlet of firepower to complete his mission. There are some big speeches, most notably about 'reasonable suspicion', and Eastwood's direction is as lean as the man himself with barely any incidental music prior to the bizarre ending, but ultimately it's not a about anything other than being an action movie. A Nineties movie would embroider its tale with all manner of CGI pyrotechnics, but *The Gauntlet* carries the legacy of serious Seventies movies with a 'realistic' take on hooker Locke. There's an obsession with her profession that verges on the pornographic, and as in Eastwood's *Pale Rider*, his spouse-to-be suffers a graphic attempted gang-rape. However, whenever the movie threatens to become at all serious, the dictates of a formula-action movie push it into something stupid. If you want a single word to sum up *The Gauntlet* it's the hitherto obscure word 'motherjumper' – it's a movie which doesn't know what it wants to be. It's got Clint and guns, but whatever's good about this picture is invariably overshadowed by the stupidity of its ending. DVD packaging and extras are absolutely minimalistic, while picture quality is impressive considering the age of the film, so it's not going to entirely embarrass your Clint film library.

FINAL VERDICT

Picture ☆☆☆ Sound ☆☆☆☆
Entertainment ☆☆☆☆ Extras ☆ Value ☆☆☆☆
OVERALL ☆☆

THE GENERAL

Price: £15.99
Supplied by: Eureka Video
Type of disc: Dual layer, single-sided
No of chapters: 12

Film format(s)/length: 4:3 regular / 75 mins
Audio format: Mono
Directors: Clyde Bruckman and Buster Keaton
Starring: Marion Mack, Charles Smith, Richard Allen
Year made: 1927
Extras: Scene access; bonus silent 18-minute short *Cops*; brief biography.

Releasing a silent movie on DVD may seem like commercial suicide, but as the saying goes "they don't make 'em like this anymore". *The General* may not have any speaker-shaking explosions and the love interest (Marion Mack) is best described as quaint and coy with a face like an undercooked pancake, but nevertheless, the film itself is a certified cinematic classic which has lost little of its ability to entertain. The story is based on a real incident during the American Civil War (remade by Disney as *The Great Locomotive Chase*) and follows the misadventures of hapless train driver Johnnie Grey (Keaton) who finds himself going behind enemy lines to retrieve his beloved locomotive, *The General*, and his sweetheart (Mack), both of whom have been whisked away and kidnapped by those dastardly Yankies. Not only is the film as fresh and button-burstingly funny as when it was first released over 70 years ago, but it also features one of the most impressive train wrecks in cinema history. This is all thanks to the tirelessly inventive Keaton insisting on sacrificing a real steam locomotive at the climax of the chase. DVD's greater depth of field and sharpness brings out an impressive degree of detail. This ensures that every frame looks like an authentic photograph from the period. Picture quality is first class, suggesting that it has been sourced from a restored print. It's just a shame that processing artifacts are so prevalent which constantly reminds you that you're viewing a disc, otherwise you could easily believe that you are watching history as it happened. There are minimal extras, but the 18-minute bonus short, *Cops*, is a gem which finds Keaton in a more conventional slapstick comedy with more laughs per minute than is good for the gut.

FINAL VERDICT

Picture ☆☆☆☆ Sound N/A

Entertainment ☆☆☆☆ Extras ☆☆☆ Value ☆☆☆

OVERALL ☆☆☆

GEORGE OF THE JUNGLE

Price: £15.99
Supplied by: Walt Disney Home Video
Type of disc: Single layer, double-sided
No of chapters: 19
Film length/format(s): 4:3 regular / 88 mins

Director: Sam Weisman
Starring: Brendan Fraser, Leslie Mann, John Cleese (voice of 'Ape')
Year made: 1997
Extras: Scene access; English subtitles.

George was raised by gorillas deep in the African jungle where he grew up to be a little more clumsy than that other famous jungle dweller. After falling in love with career city girl Ursula, who is on safari, he leaves his jungle friends for San Francisco, and the fun, as they say, starts. Jim Henson's Creature Shop breathed life into the animal special effects and the jungle sets are magnificent; the only problem is, the jaunt to the city seems like it might be an excuse to make a *Crocodile Dundee*-style sequel. As a package, it's not up to much: interactive menus, scene access, English subtitles, and the box inlay is a flimsy leaflet. I'm sure there must have been some great out-takes, and what about a documentary on how Creature Shop achieved the animal special effects? Come on Disney, how about giving DVD adopters a reason for moving up from VHS?

FINAL VERDICT

Picture ☆☆☆☆ Sound ☆☆☆ Entertainment ☆☆☆

Extras ☆ Value ☆☆

OVERALL ☆☆☆

GET SHORTY

Price: £19.99
Supplied by: DVDplus (www.dvdplus.co.uk)
Type of disc: Dual layer, single-sided
No of chapters: 36
Film format(s)/length: 16:9 widescreen enhanced / 105 mins
Audio format: Dolby Digital 5.1
Director: Barry Sonnenfeld
Starring: John Travolta, Gene Hackman, Rene Russo
Year made: 1995
Extras: Scene access; theatrical trailer; 8-page booklet with production info; multi-lingual subtitles; subtitles for the hearing impaired in English and German.

You'd think that being a genuine, full-time gangster would make the perfect CV for a career as a Hollywood producer. Chili Palmer (Travolta) certainly thinks so, as he sidelines from debt collector to Hollywood mover-and-shaker in this black comedy from Barry Sonnenfeld. This wry humoured, clever adaptation of Elmore Leonard's book, features some sparkling performances from Travolta, the ever-gorgeous Russo and the always entertaining DeVito. MGM has not really put the boat out on the extras department, as apart from the theatrical trailer and choice of language soundtracks/subtitles, there is only a rather skimpy booklet. This a mere 8 pages in length and contains production information and trivia snippets that should really have been incorporated into the DVD itself. It really is a shame that MGM didn't include a director's commentary, deleted scenes, or perhaps even an audio commentary from *Get Shorty*'s author Elmore Leonard. How did he feel the film measured up to his novel? What would he have liked to have seen in the final cut? Did he have much input into the production? It's obvious DVD additions like this that would have given *Get Shorty*'s score a boost. The film remains a quality piece of entertainment, but it is a pity that MGM didn't go that extra mile by providing some decent extras.

FINAL VERDICT

Picture ☆☆☆☆ Sound ☆☆☆☆ Entertainment ☆☆☆
Extras ☆☆ Value ☆☆☆
OVERALL ☆☆☆

GHOSTBUSTERS

Price: £19.99
Supplied by: Columbia TriStar Home Video
Type of disc: Dual layer, single-sided
No of chapters: 28
Film format(s)/length: 16:9 widescreen enhanced / 101 mins
Audio format: Dolby Digital 5.1
Director: Ivan Reitman
Starring: Bill Murray, Dan Aykroyd, Sigourney Weaver
Year made: 1984
Extras: Scene access; world premiere video commentary with Ivan Reitman, Harold Ramis and Joe Medjuck; storyboard split-screen comparison; still storyboards; 'Meet the SFX Team'; SFX before and after; Ghost Photo Gallery; behind-the-scenes featurette and interviews; concept drawings; deleted scenes; *Ghostbusters II* trailer; theatrical trailer; subtitles in 15 languages; stereo soundtrack in German.

If you were seeing 'things' that you knew didn't exist, you might want to do a little more than simply phone someone up and tell them about it. However, back in 1984 this was all just part of the blaze of mass hysteria and media hype that was the comedy blockbuster *Ghostbusters*. The names Aykroyd, Murray and Ramis might not fill seats like Cruise or Hanks, but for a long while the film that brought them into the public's eye did its tour of duty in the top 10 highest grossing films of all time. Its enormous success, spawning a generation of mid-Eighties iconography, and the fact that the film itself is 15 years-old, means that *Ghostbusters* is just settling into the role of being

a classic. Aykroyd's enthusiasm, along with the finely honed comedy developed through *Saturday Night Live* from the film's key players, brings both a cynical yet honest sense of Eighties humour to the film which is still cuttingly funny today. The film follows the exploits of 3 university Doctors, Peter Venkman (Murray), Ray Stantz (Aykroyd) and Egon Spengler (Harold Ramis). Convinced of a surge in the supernatural activity in New York city, they go into business as spectral policemen, chasing after and imprisoning any ghosts they can get their hands on. They picked the right time to do it too, as the building of their major client Dana Barrette (Weaver) is being used as a superconductor to draw together the ever-spiritual incarnation in the real world. Naturally, the good people of New York panic and so call on the 'Ghostbusters', now a foursome after being joined by the down-to-earth Winston Zeddmore (Ernie Hudson) to stop the world as we know it from coming to an unscheduled end. The entire film works superbly, and is a period marker of what Eighties film comedy was all about. However, nothing in this film works as well as Bill Murray. The character of Venkman was originally written with the late John Belushi in mind, yet when Murray was handed the part he did with Venkman what he manages to do to every other character he plays. He Murrayfied it. Murray is the Ying to the other Ghostbusters' Yang. Steeped in cynicism and only in on the whole ghost-busting venture to make money and meet women, most of the laughs in this film come straight from the mouth of Murray. Factually the whole thing works if only due to Aykroyd's genuine enthusiasm for all things ghostly. *Ghostbusters* saw the first major merging of comedy with a high volume of special effects to truly ground-breaking effect. Fresh from the success of *The Empire Strikes Back*, and long before the day of CGI trickery, the special effects department went all out to convince viewers that The Big Apple was rife with paranormal activity. *Ghostbusters* is a brilliant example of how older films work well on DVD. For a film that was made at a time when the most common notion of 'digital' was a wristwatch, the DVD is crammed full of extras that genuinely add to the enjoyment of the film. There are a couple of extras missing that were featured on the Region 1 disc, but then the UK version does have to compensate for having 15 language subtitles. Most of the best stuff is left in. There is a superb 15-minute meet-the-crew documentary reuniting the original special effect team so that they could reminisce about working on the movie. In fact, reminiscing is also a major part of the commentary by director Ivan Reitman, star and writer Harold Ramis, and associate producer Joe Medjuck. This is simply 3 men getting together and talking about how much fun they had making a movie, and is so funny that it can stand up to several viewings. This is where DVD is a blessing. It's a reason for people to get excited about films like this all over again, and if they get excited enough then decent extras are guaranteed. The production features are good enough, including over 70 creature stills, and concept drawing, a lot of which give hints to Aykroyd's original concept for the film, which was a far cry from the final outcome. It might not have the web links or screensavers that come with the Region 1 disc, but what you are getting is an innovative and at times extremely funny supernatural comedy you can keep forever.

FINAL VERDICT

Picture ☆☆☆☆ Sound ☆☆☆☆
Entertainment ☆☆☆☆☆ Extras ☆☆☆☆☆
Value ☆☆☆☆☆
OVERALL ☆☆☆☆☆

GHOSTBUSTERS II

Price: £19.99
Supplied by: Columbia TriStar Home Video
Type of disc: Dual layer, single-sided
No of chapters: 28
Film format(s)/length: 16:9 widescreen enhanced / 104 mins
Audio format: Dolby Digital 5.1
Director: Ivan Reitman
Starring: Bill Murray, Dan Aykroyd, Sigourney Weaver
Year made: 1989
Extras: Scene access; theatrical trailer; filmographies; production notes; subtitles in 20 languages.

It's 5 years since the Marshmallow Man trashed New York and time hasn't been kind to the Ghosbusters. Ray and Winston (Aykroyd and Ernie Hudson) are entertaining screaming brats at birthday parties, Egon (Harold Ramis) is performing pointless experiments on campus and Peter (Murray) presents a no-budget cable TV show. Luckily, when pink mood-slime starts oozing out of the sewers and spook-inspired craziness ensues, who does Sigourney Weaver call? The Ghosbusters! While *Ghostbusters II* is not as fresh as the first film, it's still a thrill to watch these 4 guys chasing spooks and trading hilariously sarcastic jibes. Much of the comedy stems from ghostbusting being treated like any other business. In fact, the gags are so good it makes you wish for another addition to the series! The special effects look a little transparent when compared to the Nineties'

blockbusting eye candy we're used to, but aren't too bad considering the age of the film. Watching the Statue of Liberty walk down Manhattan highways is still very, very cool. The picture is satisfactory, and the 5.1 Dolby sound is ace, especially when Ecto 1A zooms around with its sirens howling. Sadly, the DVD's special features are an anticlimax, especially when you compare them to the stellar treatment the original movie got on DVD. Here, 20 notes buys you the film, solid filmographies, the theatrical trailer and very brief production notes written on the sleeve. In essence, the film provides top quality entertainment, but the rather ordinary features mean the definitive version of this classic it is not.

FINAL VERDICT

Picture ☆☆☆☆ Sound ☆☆☆☆☆
Entertainment ☆☆☆☆ Extras ☆☆ Value ☆☆☆
OVERALL ☆☆☆

GHOST IN THE SHELL

Price: £19.99
Supplied by: Palm Pictures
Type of disc: Single layer, single-sided
No of chapters: 15
Film format(s)/length: 16:9 widescreen enhanced / 82 mins
Audio format: Dolby Digital 5.1
Director: Mamoru Oshii
Starring the voices of: Atsuko Tanaka, Mimi Woods, Akio Ōtsuka
Year made: 1995
Extras: Scene access; 30-minute 'Making of' documentary; trailer; DVD-ROM production and inclusive background notes; DVD-ROM music selection; DVD-ROM adverts for other products; soundtrack in English and Japanese; subtitles in English.

If you cast your mind back to the mid-Nineties, *anime* (Japanese animation) was one of the hottest things around, and for a while managed to push its way into the mainstream market. This was largely down to the efforts of Manga Entertainment, who despite a quite deliberate policy of concentrating on the sensationalist side of *anime* (brutal violence, demon rapes, gratuitous insertion of naughty words into the translated scripts) still managed to introduce British viewers to some high-quality animation that would otherwise have been relegated to minor cult status. *Akira* was the film that kicked off the *anime* boom, and a few years later Manga Entertainment had become a powerful enough force to become involved in the creation of brand new *anime* itself. *Ghost in the Shell* was the first major co-production between East and West, with a big budget that's evident in every frame. Based on a Manga series by Masamune Shirow, one of Japan's most influential comic creators, *Ghost in the Shell* is set in 2029 Hong Kong (an odd and unexplained switch by the director from the original Japanese setting) where a cybernetically-enhanced government 'dirty tricks' unit is involved in various operations. Into the equation falls the mysterious Puppet Master, supposedly a criminal who is able to brainwash people over the Internet, but who turns out to be something altogether more intriguing. *Ghost in the Shell* has its fair share of hard-hitting action sequences, enhanced by new technology gimmicks – holographic camouflage that makes the wearer invisible, near-superhuman feats made possible by cyborg bodies – but the main thrust of the film is actually a philosophical one. With the heroes all being cyborgs to varying extents, the question that keeps coming up is 'how do you define a human?' The heroine, Major Kusanagi, is almost completely robotic apart from a couple of pounds of brain matter, and it's her concerns over whether she has more of a right to be considered a person than the Puppet Master which forms the backbone of the story. Director Mamoru Oshii drops Shirow's unique mix of incredibly detailed hardware and stylised, almost cartoony characters in favour of an ultra-realistic look. A casualty of this approach is the Manga's humorous moments – the movie of *Ghost in the Shell* is played utterly stone-faced, with lots of sombre, moody sequences where characters silently regard each other and the city around them. There's nothing so vulgar as a joke to be found. To some extent, this works against the film, as it makes Kusanagi and her team rather unsympathetic. At just 82 minutes, *Ghost in the Shell* is also surprisingly short, and this makes some of the aforementioned moody moments feel rather like attempted padding. The DVD comes with both English and Japanese soundtracks, the latter obviously having the option of subtitles. This is probably the best way to watch *Ghost in the Shell* as the performances of the English-speaking voice actors are adequate at best, and as wooden as Epping Forest at worst. One curious 'feature', if it can be called that, is that the DVD offers only an anamorphically enhanced version of the film – fine if you've got a widescreen TV, but if you're limited to 4:3 there doesn't appear to be any way of forcing the disc to give either a cropped or letter box display without altering the settings on your player or on your television. *Ghost in the Shell* is one of the better examples of Japanese animation, but despite having Western money put into it, it remains

a product very much aimed at Japanese audiences. If you're not prepared for this, you might feel a bit disappointed. But if you get yourself in the correct mind-set, there's a lot of material to hold your interest.

FINAL VERDICT

Picture ☆☆☆☆ Sound ☆☆☆

Entertainment ☆☆☆☆ Extras ☆☆☆ Value ☆☆☆

OVERALL ☆☆☆☆

GLORIA

Price: £19.99
Supplied by: Entertainment in Video
Type of disc: Single layer, single-sided
No of chapters: 12
Film format(s)/length: 2.35:1 anamorphic / 103 mins
Audio format: Stereo
Director: Sidney Lumet
Starring: Sharon Stone, Jeremy Northam, Cathy Moriarty
Year made: 1999
Extras: Scene access; publicity featurette; behind-the-scenes feature; theatrical trailer.

Gloria (Stone) is released from chokey after a stretch for a crime she didn't commit. She heads straight for gangster ex-boyfriend Northam to demand payment as agreed. Elsewhere, in a brutal scene, little Nicky's family is gunned down over a disc containing the Mob's connections – which Nicky now holds. Together they go on the run, but can Gloria give up her new found 'son'? *Gloria* is a vehicle for Stone who gets to play the tough broad who sticks up hitmen and then adopt a maternal side with Nicky (Jean-Luke Figueroa). The DVD content focuses on the production. A promotional featurette soundbites the stars, but more interesting is the 9 minutes of narration-less behind-the-scenes footage. Biographies and filmographies are curiously absent. Disappointing plot holes aside, it's an enjoyable enough minor film for the talents involved, enhanced by the marginal understanding of its production thanks to the extras.

FINAL VERDICT

Picture ☆☆☆☆ Sound ☆☆

Entertainment ☆☆ Extras ☆☆☆ Value ☆☆☆

OVERALL ☆☆☆

GLORY

Price: £19.99
Supplied by: Columbia TriStar Home Video
Type of disc: Single layer, single-sided
No of chapters: 28

Film format(s)/length: 1.85:1 anamorphic / 117 mins
Audio format: Dolby Digital 5.1
Director: Edward Zwick
Starring: Matthew Broderick, Denzel Washington, Morgan Freeman
Year made: 1989
Extras: 3 documentaries: *Voices of Glory, Glory: The Making of History* and *The True Story of Glory Continues*; commentary by director Edward Zwick; deleted scenes; theatrical trailer; talent profiles; multi-lingual subtitles.

The DVD revolution and the increasing popularity of home cinema systems seems to be ushering in a new chapter of film history. From *The Matrix* to *Gladiator*, *Men in Black* to *Independence Day*, eye-candy cinema is calling all the shots. This is the era of the epic, effects-laden films that you experience more then you watch. You'd expect *Glory* to be at home in such company. It's a grand American Civil War story, full of gung-ho dialogue, ridiculous sentimentality, well-composed crowd scenes and silly but thrilling action. However, director Edward Zwick was clearly striving for something more, because *Glory* self-consciously twists the standard Civil War scenario. This picture follows the trials and tribulations of the North's segregated black regiments, putting an original and critical slant on the standard Hollywood depiction of the conflict. Potentially *Glory* deals with hypocrisy in race relations, the birth of a nation state and political struggle. Unfortunately, it's not as intelligent as it would like to be and not as exciting as it could have been. Not that we're faulting the ambition. It's just that in typical Hollywood stylee, the hard-hitting 'true story' very quickly becomes an exercise in mythologising. It's also disappointing that the extras on the disc play down the film's entertainment value and talk up its historical importance. Few will be able to stay awake through the pompous and self-congratulatory 'documentaries', especially since despite the pretentious guff, the film is little more than an old-fashioned epic – the Eighties' answer to *The Ten Commandments*.

FINAL VERDICT

Picture ☆☆☆ Sound ☆☆☆ Entertainment ☆☆☆
Extras ☆☆☆☆ Value ☆☆☆☆
OVERALL ☆☆☆

Go

Price: £19.99
Supplied by: Columbia TriStar Home Video
Type of disc: Dual layer, single-sided
No of chapters: 28

Film format(s)/length: 16:9 widescreen enhanced / 98 mins
Audio format: Dolby Digital 5.1
Director: Doug Liman
Starring: Katie Holmes, Scott Wolf, Sarah Polley
Year made: 1999
Extras: Scene access; behind-the-scenes featurette; deleted scenes; director's commentary; filmographies; international trailer; 3 music videos; soundtrack in German; subtitles in 15 languages.

These days, Hollywood seems to be full of television stars: George Clooney, Sarah Michelle Gellar and so on all built themselves a reputation on the small screen before transforming their talents to the more profitable silver screen. *Go* has slightly more than its fair share of ex-TV show regulars, calling on the likes of *Dawson's Creek*, *Party of Five* and even *Grange Hill* to supply the talent along with Jay Mohr and some other big screen players. The result is a thankfully refreshing and hip ensemble of gifted actors in a vivid and classy little number for Liman to follow his first hit, *Swingers*. Born from the Tarantino mould, *Go* consists of 3 interwoven narratives strung around the same plot line. With the typical insight into late Nineties' youth culture there's the obligatory centre around drugs. In this case the poverty-stricken Ronna (Polley) tries to avoid getting evicted on Christmas Eve by not only doing the supermarket shift of her stalker Simon (Desmond Askew) but also taking on his role as a small-time peddler. Nothing seems to go to plan for anyone in this movie, but it is this unpredictability that makes it such unique and essential viewing. This is the little brother of *Pulp Fiction*. It sticks to all of the rules of the Tarantino classic whilst managing to maintain some sort of realism. All be it improbable, the characters who inhabit this movie are not as flamboyant or egocentric as those found in its model, and so help to make the whole thing work both for laughs and originality. This is another superb disc from Columbia TriStar, which as well as supplying a near perfect picture and sound quality, comes with an array of extras that should be compulsory for any Nineties teen flick. To begin with there are 3 music videos, two from American favourites Len and No Doubt, plus a third starring cast members singing along to a remix of a Steppenwolf classic. The behind-the-scenes featurette is pretty lame at only 6 minutes and the director's commentary is a pretty uncompelling affair. However, the inclusion of 14 deleted scenes more than makes up for any slender efforts on the rest of the extras. In all, this is a better than expected film on a better than expected disc.

FINAL VERDICT

Picture ☆☆☆☆☆ Sound ☆☆☆☆☆

Entertainment ☆☆☆☆☆ Extras ☆☆☆☆☆

Value ☆☆☆☆☆

OVERALL ☆☆☆☆☆

GODS AND MONSTERS

Price: £19.99

Supplied by: MGM Home Entertainment

Type of disc: Dual layer, single-sided

No of chapters: 18

Film format(s)/length: 2.35:1 anamorphic / 101 mins

Audio format: Dolby Digital 5.1

Director: Bill Condon

Starring: Sir Ian McKellen, Brendan Fraser, Lynn Redgrave

Year made: 1998

Extras: Scene access; audio commentary by screenwriter/director Bill Condon; documentary entitled *The Making of Gods and Monsters: A Journey With James Whale*; stills gallery accompanied by film score; theatrical trailer; biographies of the cast and crew; subtitles in English.

On the surface, James Whale seems an unlikely candidate for biopic treatment. He was a flamboyant gay Englishman who directed horror movies in the Thirties. He's now perhaps best known as part of Hollywood's folklore, a man who drowned in his pool under 'mysterious circumstances' in 1957. Just before this unfortunate end, Whale (McKellen) convalesces at his home with only his cranky housekeeper (Redgrave) for company. He strikes up a friendship with handsome gardener Clayton Boone (Fraser) and life begins to be worth living. *Gods and Monsters* is a fictionalised speculation on what happened during Whale's last days. The 3 leads acquit themselves admirably throughout, although McKellen's role as a distinguished gay film-maker does not exactly test his extensive acting skills. It's more an example of perfect casting and his immaculate delivery, dramatic flourishes and comedic timing will make you want to return to this film again and again. The real beauty of this DVD is that it joins that elite collection of Region 2 discs that are better stocked with special features than their Region 1 counterparts. The extra that gives our version the edge is the gallery of 20 cast and behind-the-scenes photographs. In an innovation we want to see more of, Carter Burwell's beautifully lulling music accompanies each frame to heartwarming effect. Clive Barker narrates the 30-minute documentary, which

sheds light on the enigmatic director himself. The actors and film-makers offer their own thought-provoking insights into their characters, specifically *Titanic*'s Gloria Stuart who worked with Whale in his heyday. Condon himself goes into the recording studio well prepared and packs every second of his audio commentary with interesting facts and trivia. *Gods and Monsters* is both an expertly and wonderfully crafted motion picture and DVD. Together, it's something to be treasured.

FINAL VERDICT

Picture ☆☆☆☆☆ Sound ☆☆☆☆

Entertainment ☆☆☆☆ Extras ☆☆☆☆ Value ☆☆☆☆

OVERALL ☆☆☆☆

GODZILLA

Price: Price: £19.99

Supplied by: DVD Net (0181 890 2520)

Type of disc: Dual layer, single-sided

No of chapters: 28

Film format(s)/length: 2.35:1 widescreen anamorphic / 139 mins

Director: Roland Emmerich

Starring: Matthew Broderick, Jean Reno, Maria Pitillo

Year made: 1998

Extras: Widescreen TV enhanced; scene selection; subtitles; animated menus; 5 trailers (3 theatrical, 2 Japanese); 'Making of' featurette; full-length commentary by the special effects supervisor; SFX 'before and after' photos; publicity photos; director/producer biographies; cast filmographies; The Wallflowers music video 'Heroes'.

The plot of *Godzilla?* Big lizard tramples New York. There really is nothing more to it. And the big lizard doesn't get nearly enough screen time. Creators Emmerich and Dean Devlin seem convinced that their *Independence Day* was a huge hit because of its comedy, not action or spectacle or trivia like that. So now we get a bunch of whiny, annoying characters screeching at each other while Godzilla pops up occasionally to tread on things, a bit-player in his own movie. Popcorn movies demand spectacle, and *Godzilla* doesn't deliver. By setting the action on a rainy night Emmerich hides most of the effects' flaws, but also hides the action. Not enough landmarks get trashed, either. Fortunately, *Godzilla* does offer some decent special features. It's got an animated menu screen showing a huge eye opening with reflected scenes of the film, the theatrical trailer and those two much-talked about teasers (taking the piss out of *Jurassic Park*), plus a music video by The Wallflowers, filmographies, a photo gallery showing the special effects shots before and after, 'Making of' feature and commentary by the special effects wizards – you can't fault the disc itself and Columbia has done a magnificent job of giving the UK exactly the same DVD as the one you can buy in America. Nothing has been left out and the presentation throughout is excellent. Picture and sound quality are both also excellent – this is one for when you want to crank up the volume and give your neighbours headaches. Hell, you'll have one by the end of the film anyway, so why suffer alone? As a DVD package, *Godzilla* is superb. As a movie, it's like being locked in a cupboard with a fat man and shouted at for two hours. You'll wish for the subtlety of *Independence Day* but as a showpiece for your home cinema system you'd be hard to find fault.

FINAL VERDICT

Picture ☆☆☆☆ Sound ☆☆☆☆☆

Entertainment ☆☆ Extras ☆☆☆☆☆ Value ☆☆☆☆

OVERALL ☆☆☆

GOLDENEYE

Price: £19.99

Company: MGM Home Entertainment

Type of disc: Single layer, single-sided

No of chapters: 48

Film format(s)/length: 2.35:1 widescreen anamorphic / 125 mins

Director: Martin Campbell

Starring: Pierce Brosnan, Sean Bean, Izabella Scorupco

Year made: 1995

Extras: Widescreen TV enhanced; scene selection; subtitles; director/producer commentary; trailer.

Bond is back...what more need we say? As 007's introduction to DVD, *GoldenEye* does as good a job as the movie did in returning Bond to cinema screens after 7 years in the wilderness. Following a suitably OTT pre-credit sequence, which craftily obliterates Timothy Dalton from the Bond mythos by being set before *The Living Daylights*, Pierce Brosnan's James Bond is called into action to investigate the theft of a Russian satellite, the GoldenEye of the title. Naturally, his mission takes him to all manner of exotic locations, where babes are bedded, derring is done, expensive sets are blasted to atoms. It's the classic Bond formula, polished to perfection by *Mask of Zorro* director Campbell. While *GoldenEye* doesn't have many special features, the ones it does have are well done. Best of all is the commentary by Campbell and producer Michael G Wilson, who keep a (frequently witty) dialogue going on every single aspect of what happens on screen, as well as some revealing

behind-the-scenes information. There's also a trailer, but disappointingly it's not the superbly edited 'It's a new world…' version that reintroduced 007 to cinemas, but a longer one that gives away too much of the story. The 'Also on DVD' section is just a dodgy set of clips from other MGM movies. With pin-sharp pictures and a soundtrack to set speaker cones a-dancin', *GoldenEye* is a great package. The only annoyance is that it automatically sets subtitles to 'on', but apart from that it's a definite Region 2 highlight.

FINAL VERDICT

Picture ☆☆☆☆☆ Sound ☆☆☆☆☆

Entertainment ☆☆☆☆ Extras ☆☆☆ Value ☆☆☆☆

OVERALL ☆☆☆☆

GOLDFINGER

Price: £19.99

Supplied by: MGM Home Entertainment

Type of disc: Dual layer, single-sided

No of chapters: 32

Film format(s)/length: 1.85:1 anamorphic / 110 mins

Audio format: Mono

Director: Guy Hamilton

Starring: Sean Connery, Honor Blackman, Gert Fröbe

Year made: 1964

Extras: *The Making of Goldfinger* (25 mins); *The Goldfinger Phenomenon* (28 mins); audio commentary by director Guy Hamilton; audio commentary by members of the cast and crew; original theatrical trailer; original publicity featurette; TV spots; radio spots; original radio interviews with Sean Connery; The *Goldfinger* Gallery; subtitles in English.

Kissing and clobbering is what Bond is all about. The beautiful women, exotic locations, cool gadgets and dazzling stunts are a formula that made Connery a star and the series a legend. Arguably the best Bond film ever, *Goldfinger* has all the aforementioned traits. In the third tuxedo-ed outing for the suave secret agent, 007 finds himself pitting his wits against millionaire Auric Goldfinger (Fröbe) – who incidentally couldn't speak a word of English, so his voice was dubbed during the editing phase – who is plotting the daring heist of Fort Knox. A dangerous villain in his own right, Goldfinger enlists the heavy-handed help of Oddjob (played by 240lb Hawaiian wrestler, Harold Sakata). As Her Majesty's favourite spy draws ever closer to the truth, Goldfinger's beautiful, but deadly partner Pussy Galore (Honor Blackman) is given the pleasurable task of diverting 007's attention – and with a name like that, it's sure to work! Even with a film that is guaranteed to sell on

DVD (thanks partly to the remastered picture), those ever-so generous folks at MGM have supplied a wealth of special features that even Goldfinger would be overjoyed with. Two 25-minute documentaries cater for the fans and the ignorant; both are narrated by *The Avengers* star Patrick Macnee. Each documentary includes various interviews with the cast and crew that were conducted in the early Nineties, intertwined with the occasional screen test and radio/television interview. They each provide an excellent insight into the making of the film, as well as behind-the-scenes details and where the direction of James Bond was taking them. There are also two full audio commentaries provided. The first is by director Guy Hamilton who delves into the world of Bond – as any director would in his position – while the second features various members of the cast and crew. The obligatory trailers appear in TV spots, radio spots and the original theatrical trailer. There is even the original radio recording of Sean Connery's interview at the time of release. The special features are finally rounded off with 'The *Goldfinger* Gallery', a collection of black and white pictures taken during the filming. Although the picture and sound quality are superior to that of (spit!) VHS, the audio does leave something to be desired. Surely the mono recording could, no, *should* have been remixed into Dolby Digital 5.1 – it's the least they could have done for us die-hard fans! And so the high-octane cocktail of action, lust, greed and one of the world's greatest villains makes the third Bond extravaganza possibly the best to date. The digital formula of DVD makes this an essential purchase for any fan of action – James Bond or otherwise.

FINAL VERDICT

Picture ☆☆☆ Sound ☆☆ Entertainment ☆☆☆☆☆
Extras ☆☆☆☆ Value ☆☆☆☆
OVERALL ☆☆☆☆

GOODFELLAS

Price: £15.99
Supplied by: Warner Home Video
Type of disc: Single layer, double-sided
No of chapters: 34
Film format(s)/length: 1.85:1 widescreen / 139 mins
Director: Martin Scorsese
Starring: Ray Liotta, Robert De Niro, Joe Pesci
Year made: 1990
Extras: Production notes; scene access; subtitles in English, Arabic and English for the hearing impaired; production notes; scene access; theatrical trailer.

You can't help but be affected by Scorsese's definitive Mafia flick. Smoother than *Mean Streets*, harder hitting than *Casino*, this is his finest homage to Italian roots, family ties, and, ultimately, betrayal. Wonderfully scored and delicately handled despite the overt violence, no film comes closer to evoking the sanctuary afforded by the Mob's embrace – and, paradoxically, its cloying, poisoning elimination of outside contact. Liotta is Henry Hill, a wiseguy wannabe, gradually working his way into petty theft and violence. As the film pans out, so does Henry's involvement, sliding inexorably towards fully fledged underworld gangsterdom. Unfortunately, as Hill's crimes intertwine with those of De Niro and Pesci, his decline into murder, double-crossing and coke-fuelled paranoid psychosis is swift. Here we see Pesci at his most comically unstable – when he tells you to dance, you dance. Or you get a bullet in the brain. There are 3 types of people in this world: those who haven't seen *Goodfellas*, those who have, and those who own the film. The former need Pesci to come round and do a little persuading. The latter two will want this film on DVD. No ifs, no buts – this is one of the best films ever made. While only delivering a handful of unremarkable extra features – production notes, scene access, cast and crew biographies – the magic is woven into the film fabric itself. No more grainy, sepia-stained VHS disappointment and no more scratchy, through-a-flannel soundtrack. Don't buy this film on DVD because you can access any scene or for a biography of De Niro. Buy it because you must.

FINAL VERDICT

Picture ☆☆☆☆☆ Sound ☆☆☆☆☆
Entertainment ☆☆☆☆☆ Extras ☆☆☆
Value ☆☆☆☆
OVERALL ☆☆☆☆

GOOD MORNING VIETNAM

Price: £15.99
Supplied by: Touchstone
Type of disc: Dual layer, single-sided
No of chapters: 22
Film format(s)/length: 16:9 widescreen / 116 mins
Director: Barry Levinson
Starring: Robin Williams
Year made: 1987
Extras: None.

Younger readers could legitimately wonder what all the fuss is about when it comes to Robin Williams. Had I only seen him in such 'delights' as *Patch Adams*, *Flubber* and *What Dreams May Come*, I'd be firmly voting for him to be judged as having no worthwhile purpose and advise that he be put down, along with UB40 and Alisha's Attic. But the fact is, back in the 'good' old days, his box office output did his talents justice, and none demonstrates this more superbly than *Good Morning Vietnam*. Intertwining comedy and drama against one of man's darkest hours, *Good Morning Vietnam* is a powerful movie that hinted at Williams' sensitivity while allowing his comedic capability to shine without restraint. If you haven't seen it, you ought to – though whether that need be on DVD is your choice. Listing interactive menus and scene access under 'Special Features' should be punishable under the Trades Description Act. It's like listing 'heats food up' as an extra reason to buy a cooker – these should be considered a given rather than supplemental to the package. Indeed, had Touchstone done any less for the VHS-to-DVD transfer, we'd have ended up with sound only. That said, this is the one area that does benefit from the format, with the Sixties soundtrack in particular sounding superb. Picture-wise, there's little to grumble about, with hardly any noticeable artifacts or glitches. So, it's up to you really. A great film, that's for sure – but an essential DVD it is not.

FINAL VERDICT

Picture ☆☆☆☆ Sound ☆☆☆☆

Entertainment ☆☆☆☆☆ Extras ☆ Value ☆☆☆

OVERALL ☆☆☆

THE GOOD, THE BAD AND THE UGLY

Price: £19.99

Supplied by: MGM Home Entertainment

Type of disc: Dual layer, single-sided

No of chapters: 44

Film format(s)/length: 16:9 widescreen/154 mins

Audio format: Mono

Director: Sergio Leone

Starring: Clint Eastwood, Lee Van Cleef, Eli Wallach

Year made: 1966

Extras: Scene access; 14 extra minutes of never before seeing footage; original theatrical trailer; 8-page booklet detailing the history and making of the film; subtitles in English and Dutch; subtitles for the hearing impaired in English.

The Good, the Bad and the Ugly is the third, final and best instalment of Sergio Leone's 'Dollars Trilogy'. Clint Eastwood reprises the role that made his name, fulfilling the 'Good' quota in the movie, while Lee Van Cleef is the 'Bad' and Eli Wallach is just 'Ugly.' The Man With No Name (Eastwood) is, for all intents and purposes, back and just as inscrutable as ever. We catch up with him as he

works uneasily with Tuco Ramirez (Wallach) in a bounty hunting scam. Their paths cross with the sadistic assassin 'Angel Eyes' Sentenza (Van Cleef) when a dying Confederate tells Tuco about his hidden fortune buried in a graveyard. If there's one thing these 3 have in common, it's greed, and they go to any lengths to seize the fortune for themselves. The problem is, all 3 have a piece of the puzzle that is useless without the other two… *The Good, the Bad and the Ugly* is epic in scope and length, visiting ghost towns, POW camps, battlefields, custom made bridges, deserts and cemeteries, all this in a mere two-and-a-half hours. Sergio Leone's trademark flourishes are in full effect, starkly cutting between vista encompassing, deep-focused long shots and extreme close-ups of the actors' faces. This time he had a far bigger budget to work with and every penny is right up there on the plasma screen, even throwing in the American Civil War as an intriguing subplot. The film occupies the ground between John Ford's poetic melodramas and Sam Peckinpah's bloodbaths. Leone's characters are realistically amoral, but he's also aware he must spin a good yarn. *Il Buono, il brutto, il cattivo*'s special features include the ubiquitous trailer, a revealing 8-page booklet and most impressive of all, an extra 16 minutes of footage that MGM have dug up, dusted off and enhanced to the same excellent standard as the film. 7 scenes in total have been salvaged from the original 1966 print and it's a thrill to enjoy Leone's masterpiece the way he initially intended. This is Western action of the old school variety with its film-makers and cast at the top of their game. On DVD, it's the best looking – but not the best sounding– version yet, and well worth collecting.

FINAL VERDICT

Picture ☆☆☆☆☆ Sound ☆

Entertainment ☆☆☆☆☆ Extras ☆☆☆ Value ☆☆☆

OVERALL ☆☆☆☆

GOOD WILL HUNTING

Price: £15.99

Supplied by: DVDplus (www.dvdplus.co.uk)

Type of disc: Dual layer, single-sided

No of chapters: 21

Film format(s)/length: 1.85:1 widescreen / 121 mins

Audio format: Dolby Digital 5.0

Director: Gus Van Sant

Starring: Robin Williams, Matt Damon, Ben Affleck

Year made: 1997

Extras: Scene access; English subtitles; subtitles for the hearing impaired in English.

Considering that, at the time, Ben Affleck and Matt Damon were relative unknowns on the Hollywood scene, it's remarkable that their first collaborative effort became such a mainstream and critically-acclaimed hit. You would have thought that the success of *Good Will Hunting* would have seriously narked those independent film makers who have spent years striving to make a 'worthy' film that is accepted and embraced by the mainstream, without having to sacrifice any vital artistic integrity in the process. But considering that leading American indy director Kevin Smith (*Clerks, Chasing Amy*) receives a credit as co-executive producer, the chances are that Affleck and Damon have been lauded as vanguards of American independent film. So what made *Good Will Hunting* such a 'good' film? Without a doubt the main highlight would have to be the sterling performance by Robin Williams – after all, it did win him an Academy Award for Best Supporting Actor. Then there's the story itself, about roughneck university cleaner Will Hunting, who also happens to be a mathematical genius. Will's offered a post at a university helping solve mathematical theories that have long baffled the experts as long as he sees a shrink (Williams). Miramax has made a major *faux pas* by not giving such an outstanding movie the treatment it deserves for DVD. The lack of extras is completely unforgivable. There's not even a theatrical trailer, which seems to be a pre-requisite for the majority of DVD releases these days. On the flyer packed in with the DVD, there's a paragraph of text informing the purchaser that they can access its 'special features' by pressing the Menu key. Um, what extras would they be then, Miramax? It is only thanks to the overall quality of the movie, that *Good Will Hunting* on DVD just manages to scrape a two-star score. If we were judging it on the DVD alone, it would only have rated one star.

FINAL VERDICT

Picture ☆☆☆☆ Sound ☆☆☆☆
Entertainment ☆☆☆☆ Extras ☆ Value ☆☆
OVERALL ☆☆

THE GRADUATE

Price: £15.99
Supplied by: DVDplus (www.dvdplus.co.uk)
Type of disc: Single layer, single-sided
No of chapters: 25
Film format(s)/length: 2.35:1 widescreen / 101 mins
Audio format: Linear PCM Stereo
Director: Mike Nichols
Starring: Anne Bancroft, Dustin Hoffman, Katharine Ross
Year made: 1967
Extras: Scene access; original trailer of film; original film poster; stills gallery with both black and white and colour images.

Dustin Hoffman plays his first star role in this dated, but nonetheless superb film, that comes with a bona fide soundtrack performed by Simon and Garfunkel. The smooching begins when Hoffman's graduation party is abruptly ended by a middle-aged woman (Bancroft) whose passion for toy boys is made extremely apparent. After many a frolicking, the romance turns sour when Bancroft's daughter, played by Katharine Ross, makes an appearance and turns Hoffman into a lovesick puppy. Nothing like keeping it in the family! *The Graduate* is such a good film, it's a tough act to follow as far as special features are concerned, yet they're actually quite good. The picture quality has been re-mastered to leave out most of the original scratches that are common in dated productions, and the sound is now in Linear PCM stereo. There is the usual scene accessing to help find your favourite clips, as well as the original trailer of the film. Just comparing the film quality to the original trailer, with its scratches and warped sound, justifies all the efforts in upgrading the picture quality to DVD standard. Other features include the film poster used to advertise the film when originally released in the Sixties, and a stills gallery offering both colour and black and white images of film footage. Overall it deserves a welcomed slot into your DVD collection, especially if your vocal chords are just itching to warble along to the angelic sounds of Simon and Garfunkel.

FINAL VERDICT

Picture ☆☆☆ Sound ☆☆☆ Entertainment ☆☆☆☆
Extras ☆☆ Value ☆☆☆
OVERALL ☆☆☆

THE GREAT ESCAPE

Price: £19.99
Supplied by: DVDplus (www.dvdplus.co.uk)
Type of disc: Single layer, single sided
No of chapters: 32
Film format(s)/length: 2.35:1 letterbox / 165 mins
Audio format: Mono
Director: John Sturges
Starring: Steve McQueen, James Garner, Richard Attenborough
Year made: 1963
Extras: Scene access; soundtrack in 5 languages; *Return to The Great Escape* 24-minute documentary; 8-

page booklet containing trivia; subtitles in 7 languages.

Just like *The Sound of Music* and Bond films at Christmas, it's nothing but a myth that *The Great Escape* is constantly repeated on TV – which is why this excellently presented DVD is such a necessary treasure. From the disc packaging, you'd be forgiven for thinking that you've actually bought the 'Steve McQueen Show', but *The Great Escape* is one of the finest examples of ensemble casting in cinema. McQueen is joined by a breathtaking cast of classic actors – Attenborough, Garner, James Coburn, Donald Sutherland, David McCallum and Charles Brosnan all made their career or surpassed themselves as desperate men trapped in Stalag Luft North. Director John Sturges had wanted to create the film, working from Paul Brickhill's autobiographical novel for over a decade, but it wasn't until he'd had a major success with *The Magnificent Seven* that film companies began to take any notice. *The Great Escape* perhaps boasts the best action set-pieces of any film of its time: Hiltz, 'the cooler king', bouncing his baseball; Brosnan (with a particularly un-Irish accent) fleeing from the claustrophobia of the tunnel; the redistribution of tunnel soil; McQueen's motorcycle chase through the Austrian Alps. The excellent Region 2 disc not only gives you the remastered film, but an inspiring 24-minute documentary, *Return to The Great Escape*, covering the making of the movie itself with accounts of the screenplay nightmare, the difficulties of recreating a full-size camp in Germany and McQueen's prima donna behaviour. Not only this, but also the true story of the great escape from Stalag Luft III is documented, when 50 allied prisoners were killed by the Gestapo. There are also rare interviews with McCallum, Garner and Coburn. It's difficult to make a 36 year-old movie look or sound astounding, even on DVD, but this disc delivers the finest entertainment quality possible, with a crystal-clear picture, and composer Elmer Bernstein's legendary score sounding better than ever. Even if you taped it off the TV 10 years ago, watch it on a seriously good quality format and you can't fail to notice things you never saw before. (Such as the fact that Coburn and Brosnan were playing an Australian and an Irishman, without any attempts at accents.) This well-presented classic DVD really does deserve to be watched again and again. *Es ist wunderbar*.

FINAL VERDICT

Picture ☆☆☆☆ Sound ☆☆☆☆☆
Entertainment ☆☆☆☆☆ Extras ☆☆☆☆
Value ☆☆☆☆
OVERALL ☆☆☆☆

GREAT EXPECTATIONS

Price: £19.99
Supplied by: Carlton Video
Type of disc: Single layer, single-sided
No of chapters: 12
Film format(s)/length: 4:3 regular / 113 mins
Audio format: Dolby Digital 5.0
Director: David Lean
Starring: John Mills, Valerie Hobson, Alec Guinness
Year made: 1946
Extras: Scene selection; biographies on actors and even Charles Dickens.

The original and still the best, David Lean's Oscar-winning adaptation of Charles Dickens' classic novel *Great Expectations* is a true cinematic classic. You can keep the modern-day reworking with Gwyneth Paltrow, Ethan Hawke and Robert De Niro, as well as the recent BBC TV adaptation, because nothing has come close to this interpretation of the trials of a boy called Pip. There are some cracking performances from John Mills as the adult Pip and Valerie Hobson as the young and cruel-hearted Estella. However, it's Martita Hunt who steals the show in her genuinely insane portrayal of the barking-mad Miss Haversham. Since the film is over 50 years old, the likelihood of this DVD being stuffed with extras is understandably slim. However, Carlton has included biographies on *Great Expectations'* main stars, director David Lean, as well as the boy Dickens himself. And that's about it really. The quality of the sound and picture on offer does little to champion the benefits of the new format – whilst not bad, it doesn't really encourage viewers to jack in VHS and embrace DVD. Which leads us to wonder whether it is really worth forking out a hefty £19.99 for a DVD, when you could feasibly pick up the VHS version and still have a fair amount of change left over into the bargain?

FINAL VERDICT

Picture ☆☆☆ Sound ☆☆☆ Entertainment ☆☆☆☆
Extras ☆☆☆ Value ☆☆
OVERALL ☆☆☆

GREGORY'S TWO GIRLS

Price: £19.99
Supplied by: FilmFour
Type of disc: Single layer, single-sided
No of chapters: 21
Film format(s)/length: 16:9 widescreen enhanced / 111 mins
Audio format: Dolby Surround

Director: Bill Forsyth
Starring: John Gordon Sinclair, Carly McKinnon, Maria Doyle Kennedy
Year made: 1999
Extras: Scene access; subtitles in English for the hard of hearing.

The original *Gregory's Girl* was made the best part of 20 years ago, and was a delightful heart-warming comedy about schoolboy Gregory's adolescent crush on a footballing schoolgirl called Dorothy. Now, Gregory has grown up into a dull teacher (not a promising start) and there's hardly any football in it! The idea behind this movie was sound enough – take a popular story and give it the 'where are they now?' treatment. Unfortunately, what we get is a muddled and tedious plot revolving around Gregory's lust for a young schoolgirl (who happens to be pretty good at football) and his constant avoidance of fellow teacher Bell. The rest of the story involves some pointless and never quite explained waffle about human rights, while the ending is so anti-climactic it's just painful! As if things couldn't get any worse, FilmFour hasn't provided *Gregory's Two Girls* with any special features. Mind you, it has to be said that the only thing which could make this DVD a decent purchase would be if it came with a complete version of the original movie as part of the package! As it is, you're limited to scene access and one measly set of subtitles. Surely there must be something more that could have been added? Or did the publishers watch the movie and realise that it was beyond help? Save yourself a large amount of pain and boredom; dismiss the sequel from your mind and pick up a cheap second-hand VHS copy of the original movie instead!

FINAL VERDICT

Picture ☆☆☆☆ Sound ☆☆☆ Entertainment ☆☆
Extras ☆ Value ☆
OVERALL ☆☆

GREMLINS

Price: £15.99
Supplied by: Warner Home Video
Type of disc: Dual layer, single-sided
No of chapters: 27
Film format(s)/length: 1.85:1 anamorphic / 102 mins
Audio format: Dolby Digital 5.1
Director: Joe Dante
Starring: Zach Galligan, Phoebe Cates, Hoyt Axton
Year made: 1985
Extras: Scene access; soundtrack in English, French and Italian; subtitles in 10 languages; subtitles for the hearing impaired in English and Italian.

Despite many attempts, director Joe Dante has never really managed to break out of the 'cult filmmaker' box. *Gremlins* is one of his rare mainstream successes. Billy Peltzer (Galligan) gets an unusual Christmas present from his dad – Gizmo the mogwai, a cute and cuddly little creature who comes with some care and grooming rules that don't apply to the average household pet. Keep him out of the light, don't get him wet, and never, ever, feed him after midnight. Since films about people who follow the rules and live happy, normal lives generally don't do well at the box office, inevitably all 3 of these caveats are ignored and Gizmo spawns an army of gremlins, anarchistic lizard-like monsters hellbent on destruction and mayhem. The emphasis is more on wackiness than horror – people do get hurt, but on the whole it's the gremlins who take the punishment, undoubtedly acting as an inspiration for *Itchy and Scratchy* in the process. Besides, the gremlins are having so much fun being evil that it's hard not to get carried along. While it's still amusing, *Gremlins* definitely isn't as funny as you remember, and since we've all become so used to incredible special effects over the past few years, the titular creatures themselves now look a lot like...well, rubber puppets. There's still a lot of fun to be had, though, and any film that disposes of a baddie by exploding him in a microwave gets a big thumbs-up in our book. This being a back-catalogue title, Warner, as usual, hasn't really gone to town with either the transfer or the DVD package. The picture has a noticeable amount of grain and crawling effects, something that of late has become increasingly rare on DVDs, the sound mix – even in 5.1 surround – is adequate rather than outstanding, and the extras are distinctly absent. There were definitely 'Making of' programmes at the time the film came out, but you don't get them here. There isn't even a trailer. It's also one of those discs that can't even be bothered to include a full chapter listing. This part isn't hard, so what's the excuse?

FINAL VERDICT

Picture ☆☆ Sound ☆☆☆ Entertainment ☆☆☆☆
Extras ☆ Value ☆☆☆
OVERALL ☆☆

GROSSE POINT BLANK

Price: £15.99
Supplied by: Buena Vista
Type of disc: Single layer, single-sided
No of chapters: 17
Film format(s)/length: 1.85:1 widescreen / 103 mins
Director: George Armitage

Starring: John Cusack, Minnie Driver, Dan Ackroyd
Year made: 1997
Extras: Scene access; subtitles.

For reasons too complex to explain, supercool hitman Martin Q Blank (Cusack) has decided it's time he got out of the killing game. But he still has one last murder to perform, which just happens to coincide with his high school reunion in Grosse Point, Michigan. So while Blank tries to get back together with Debi (Driver), the school sweetheart he walked out on 10 years earlier, he also has to contend with a contract placed on him, two government agents and rival hitman Grocer (a fast and funny Ackroyd), who wants Blank to join his 'union' – or else. *Grosse Point Blank* is a sharp, witty and entertaining black comedy. Well worth a look, and it even shows you how to kill someone with a pen. As for special features…where are they? Scene access (which the producers couldn't even be arsed to put names on) and subtitles just don't cut it. Once again, Disney do a Mickey Mouse job!

FINAL VERDICT

Picture ☆☆☆☆ Sound ☆☆☆
Entertainment ☆☆☆☆ Extras ☆ Value ☆☆☆
OVERALL ☆☆☆

GROUNDHOG DAY

Price: £19.99
Supplied by: Columbia TriStar Home Video
Type of disc: Single layer, single-sided
No of chapters: 33
Film format(s)/length: 1.85:1 widescreen / 97 mins
Audio format: Dolby Surround
Director: Harold Ramis
Starring: Bill Murray, Andie MacDowell, Chris Elliott
Year made: 1993
Extras: Scene access; filmographies; theatrical trailer; soundtrack in English, French, German, Italian and Spanish; subtitles in 19 languages.

Forget anything Delia Smith might've told you. If you want to see what a perfect recipe is, simply buy this DVD. *Groundhog Day* has all the ingredients for making a movie masterpiece. A perfectly cast leading man, talented supporting cast, a director who is aware that he's not as important as his movie, a refreshing script and most importantly of all, a simple yet clever premise. There's only one bug in the mix, but we'll come to that later. Murray plays Phil Connors, a self-obsessed weatherman who reluctantly goes to the quaint little town of Punxsutawney, Pennsylvania to cover the annual Groundhog Day festival. Job done, Phil endeavours to leave the town he despises, only to

be forced back due to a blizzard he failed to predict. Cut to the next morning. Phil wakes up to find that locals are all set to celebrate Groundhog Day over again, and there is no trace of last night's storm. And so it goes – for a reason that is never explained (and doesn't need to be) – Phil is destined to live out February 2 over and over again, until he lives the perfect day. Neither concept nor star seem to be more important than the movie's delivery, which ultimately compliment one another superbly. Scenes where Murray (knowing everything will reset next morning) indulges himself and uses his predicament to get money, girls and a night in jail are downright laugh-out-loud funny, but there's something both sweet and intelligent lying beneath the surface of this movie. The subtlety with which Connors moves from heartless bastard to small-town hero harps back to the heartwarming feeling that you'd associate with the likes of *It's a Wonderful Life*. *Groundhog Day* sits in between the late-Eighties John Hughes humour and the Nineties Farrelly brothers fart jokes, and as a result stands out from everything else around it. In fact, it's got a very legitimate claim to being the best comedy of the Nineties. A definite classic. How sad it is then that Columbia TriStar, a real pioneer in the realm of Region 2 discs, saw fit to turn this classic into their first dud DVD. There's only a theatrical trailer to the extras' credit, and the sound isn't even of 5.1 standard. For such a great film to be treated with this little respect by a distribution house who've proved themselves time and time again as the market leaders is just plain criminal.

FINAL VERDICT

Picture ☆☆☆ Sound ☆☆ Entertainment ☆☆☆☆☆
Extras ☆☆ Value ☆☆☆
OVERALL ☆☆☆

HACKERS

Price: £19.99
Supplied by: Warner Home Video
Type of disc: Dual layer, single-sided
No of chapters: 32
Film format(s)/length: 16:9 widescreen enhanced / 108 mins
Audio format: Dolby Digital 5.1
Director: Iain Softley
Starring: Jonny Lee Miller, Angelina Jolie, Fisher Stevens
Year made: 1995
Extras: Scene access; theatrical trailer; 8-page booklet about the movie's production; English and German closed captions; English, French, German, Italian and

Spanish soundtracks; multiligual subtitles.

Back when the Internet was new, when it was Pentagon supercomputers at risk – rather than your credit card details – the Internet outlaw had a certain glamour. Director Iain Softley, fresh from his Beatles cult hit *Backbeat*, took a script by Rafael Moreau and made a very decent stab at capturing the hacker subculture. His movie even anticipated much of the PlayStation culture with Psygnosis' Wipeout making its first public appearance in a futuristic arcade. Cutting edge dance bands such as Leftfield, Orbital and Prodigy soundtrack the film, as later they did the game. Admittedly, Jonny Lee Miller is not Kevin Mitnick, but leaving aside the supermodel look of him (and would-be girlfriend Angelina Jolie) the spirit, attire and argot ring mostly true. This must be the only movie which uses RISC architecture as a chat-up line. Of course, Hackers aren't renowned for their love lives – the computer tends to be the obsession – but Miller's virginal enchantment with Jolie rings mostly true. When Jolie finally comes calling on Miller, the latter's mother makes for the perfect intro with: "So now I see what all the fuss is about…" Indeed. The movie's villain, a skateboarding, junk-food eating, super-egotist called Eugene (a Manic Miner reference?) may seem exaggerated, but from personal experience I'd beg to differ. There's so much that's good about *Hackers*, that perhaps that explains why the plot fails to grip. Sometimes it's perfectly contemporary, other times it's a mid-21st century lift from *Neuromancer*. There's too much content, too little focus. The central conspiracy takes too long to develop and, set against the high school realism of the hackers themselves, seems bizarrely lifted from a Bond movie. On DVD, the film looks as good as its low budget origins will allow. Definition is crisp, colours vivid. The Dolby Digital 5.1 soundtrack is never really pushed by outlandish effects, but that superb music selection comes through well. There are no extras, other than the trailer and an impressive, interesting 8-page booklet, but this is a film which belongs on DVD. Check it out while waiting for *The Matrix*.

FINAL VERDICT

Picture ☆☆☆☆ Sound ☆☆☆☆
Entertainment ☆☆☆ Extras ☆☆ Value ☆☆☆
OVERALL ☆☆☆

HALLOWEEN 4: THE RETURN OF MICHAEL MYERS

Price: £19.99
Supplied by: DVDplus (www.dvdplus.co.uk)

Distributor: Digital Entertainment
Type of disc: Single layer, single-sided
No of chapters: 8
Film format(s)/length: 1.85:1 widescreen / 85 mins
Audio format: Stereo
Director: Dwight H Little
Starring: Donald Pleasence, Ellie Cornell, Danielle Harris
Year made: 1988
Extras: Scene access; photo library.

He's been shot, stabbed and turned into a paraplegic, but still Michael Myers returns for another sequel. Set 10 years after the first two *Halloween* films, Mike is being moved to a secure mental facility, the day before Halloween, when he suddenly returns to full health, and vents his frustrations on the NHS. He then travels back to the town he ravaged 10 years earlier, to kill the last surviving member of his family. Pretty soon the quirky Doctor Loomis (Pleasence) is en-route to Haddonfield, in a bid to destroy his arch nemesis. At a mere 85 minutes, the film has barely enough time to get going before it's all over. Most of the violence takes place off screen, with the cops turning up too late and discovering a load of diced corpses. After the violence of Michael's initial escape, the film trundles along in tension-building mode, with Mike's young niece having disturbingly real flashbacks. The little kid factor gets a mite annoying after the fifth time she screams at a masked figure. You'll soon be wanting Mike to make a pretzel out of her just to shut her up and break the monotony. As you may have figured all hell breaks loose when Myers finally finds the child, and the ending is ultimately the film's saving grace. As a DVD the film is lacking in extras, and has a grainy picture to boot. The manufacturers haven't bothered with this disc, but given the lacklustre film, who'd blame them?

FINAL VERDICT

Picture ☆☆ Sound ☆☆ Entertainment ☆☆
Extras ☆ Value ☆☆
OVERALL ☆☆

HALLOWEEN II

Price: £15.99
Supplied by: DVDplus (www.dvdplus.co.uk)
Type of disc: Single layer, single-sided
No of chapters: 18
Film format(s)/length: 4:3 regular / 115 mins
Audio format: Stereo
Director: Rick Rosenthal
Starring: Jamie Lee Curtis, Donald Pleasence, Charles Cyphers

Year made: 1981
Extras: Scene access; laughably poor photo gallery.

Even though John Carpenter stepped down from the directorial post for the follow-up to his masterful 1978 bloodbath, he hung around to produce it. Rick Rosenthal closely mimicked Carpenter's style too, and thus *Halloween II* is the only one of 6 sequels to be taken as seriously as the original. It certainly deserves a great remastered pampering for DVD. It was with nothing less than disgust that we gazed upon the image of *Halloween II* as presented by Castle Home Video. The first sign of malice is the unforgivable use of the 4:3 pan and scan version of the movie, a fact that is suspiciously omitted from the back cover. Don't these people know what 'home cinema' means? As the standard in DVD is clearly widescreen, Castle could at least mention which version you are buying. Naturally, the US version features a full 2.35:1 transfer and typically costs under a tenner. The picture is also rather shaky and blurred, and suffers badly from washed-out colour definition in all normal lighting conditions. In darkness, which as you can imagine makes up much of the film, there's a blue grainy effect that gives the impression of old videotape rather than leading edge digital decompression. In fact, if you look at the edges of the frame, you'll notice little bands if image folding like those you'd find on (no, it can't be) video cassette playback. From the unpleasant bootleg appearance of the packaging you can tell this is a cut-all-corners production. The Region 1 pressing is infinitely preferable, so buy American or don't buy at all.

FINAL VERDICT

Picture ☆ Sound ☆☆ Entertainment ☆☆☆☆
Extras ☆ Value ☆
OVERALL ☆☆

HANG 'EM HIGH

Price: £19.99
Supplied by: MGM
Type of disc: Single layer, single-sided
No of chapters: 32
Film format(s)/length: 1.77:1 anamorphic / 109 mins
Audio format: Stereo
Director: Ted Post
Starring: Clint Eastwood, Ingar Stevens, Ed Begley
Year made: 1967
Extras: Scene access; original theatrical trailer; soundtrack in English, German, Spanish, Italian and French; subtitles in 9 languages.

This may not be a stunning DVD, but this film records an important moment in Clint Eastwood's lengthy film career. *Hang 'Em High* marks his very first appearance in an American-made movie Western. Filmed not long after *Rawhide* and the No Name trilogy, this movie tells the story of ex-lawman Jed Cooper (Eastwood), who is unjustly hung by a local gang that leaves him for dead. Of course, this being an Eastwood film he doesn't die, but instead turns back to his old trade of Marshal to hunt down the men who slipped a noose around his neck. It may not be up to the standards of his later films but it still makes for compelling viewing. In fact this Western has got 'classic' written all over it. The music, although not quite Ennio Morricone, is superb. It's just a shame this film is only in stereo, which pretty much sums up the rest of the extras – bog standard. There's only so many times you can watch the same trailer and unless you're studying for a language degree the plethora of soundtracks are pointless. On the plus side, the picture quality is surprisingly good for a film of its age. If you're a big Western or Clint Eastwood fan and can forgive the meagre extras, then *Hang 'Em High* is more than worth getting. If, on the other hand, you only dabble in Westerns it's still worth renting, if only for the brief appearance by Dennis Hopper as a prophet!

FINAL VERDICT

Picture ☆☆☆ Sound ☆☆ Entertainment ☆☆☆
Extras ☆ Value ☆☆
OVERALL ☆☆☆

HAPPINESS

Price: £19.99
Supplied by: Entertainment in Video
Type of disc: Dual layer, single-sided
No of chapters: 16
Film format(s)/length: 1.85:1 letterbox / 134 mins
Audio format: Stereo
Director: Todd Solondz
Starring: Jane Adams, Elizabeth Ashley, Dylan Baker
Year made: 1998
Extras: Scene access; theatrical trailer; 2 TV spots.

Happiness is…a film by Todd Solondz, the winner of the International Critics Prize at the 1998 Cannes Film Festival and a blackly comic drama which is an acquired taste to say the least. Taking such dinner party conversation staples as alienation, despair, masturbation and pederasty in its stride, it's as memorable as it is disquieting. A trio of middle-class sisters deal with each other, their separating parents and the human detritus that float in and out of their lives, including a Russian taxi driver thief and a telephone stalker (Philip Seymour Hoffman – brilliant). With an economical, low calorie filmmaking technique, Solondz lays bare contemporary self-obsession, noting that regardless of whether each character's nearest and dearest is emotionally falling apart, it's that person's own needs which come first (illustrated here with frequently disastrous consequences). *Happiness'* status as a critics' darling and box office non-event has sealed its lacklustre fate on DVD, which is the wrong way to go about it. It's these challenging and entertaining indie films which deserve lavish treatment just as much as multiplex fodder movies. Those looking for simple (and cheap to produce) information about this cast of unknowns are forced to look elsewhere. Even the production notes that most authoring houses consign to inner-case booklets are absent due to EIV consistently squandering the space by advertising its other titles. *Happiness* is a film you owe it to yourself to see, but DVD content is sadly not worth a first, let alone second, look.

FINAL VERDICT

Picture ☆☆☆☆ Sound ☆☆ Entertainment ☆☆☆☆
Extras ☆ Value ☆☆
OVERALL ☆☆

HAPPY GILMORE

Price: £19.99
Supplied by: Columbia TriStar Home Video
Type of disc: Single layer, single-sided
No of chapters: 16
Film format(s)/length: 1.85:1 widescreen / 88 mins
Audio format: Dolby Digital 5.1
Director: Dennis Dugan
Starring: Adam Sandler, Christopher McDonald, Julie Bowen
Year made: 1996
Extras: Scene access; trailer; production notes; cast and crew biographies; multilingual soundtracks; multilingual subtitles.

Depending on which of his films you see him in, Sandler portrays either an immature, bad-tempered jerk who comes out on top by shouting at people and getting a girlfriend who is blind to his bad points, or as an immature, mildly peeved jerk who also comes out on top. In *The Wedding Singer* it's the latter, while in *Happy Gilmore* it's very definitely the former. Sandler plays the title character, a wannabe ice hockey player hampered by a temper that's too seething even for hockey. The one talent he does possess is the ability to hit small objects with sticks very hard and very far, and when the taxman comes to take his grandmother's house away, Happy discovers

this skill is transferable to golf. All he needs to do is stop himself from punching out the other players during tournament matches, and granny could be saved… Teaming up with one-handed golf pro, Chubbs (Carl Weathers), Happy sets the staid world of golfing alight with his club-throwing, opponent-thumping and ball-cursing antics, snaring PR girl Virginia (Bowen) along the way. However, he attracts the instant enmity of snooty rival 'Shooter' McGavin (McDonald), who detests his blue-collar adversary and will stop at nothing – including hiring someone to run Happy over in a VW Beetle – to drive the uncouth newcomer out of the game for good. Although *Happy Gilmore* has some funny scenes – Happy screaming abuse at an uncooperative to name one – it can't quite seem to decide what kind of comedy to be. One minute it's trying to elicit sympathy for Happy and sticking firmly to the 'underdog wins out' Hollywood formula, the next it's off into Farrelly brothers territory with artificial hands being crushed under trucks and the ghost of Abraham Lincoln. Thankfully, the Region 2 release of *Happy Gilmore* is much better specced than its American counterpart, which has to be a first. It's goodbye to the Yanks' 4:3 aspect ratio and hello to a proper widescreen version, along with the addition of some production notes, cast and crew biographies and a trailer. *LA Confidential* or *Ronin* it may not be in terms of extras, but it shows that at least Columbia TriStar is willing to make an effort with its DVDs instead of just shovelling out discs that are no better featured than their VHS counterparts. If that doesn't make you happy, nothing will!

FINAL VERDICT

Picture ☆☆☆☆ Sound ☆☆☆☆ Entertainment ☆☆☆
Extras ☆☆☆ Value ☆☆☆
OVERALL ☆☆☆

HARD-BOILED

Price: £19.99
Supplied by: Tartan Video
Type of disc: Dual layer, single-sided
No of chapters: 16
Film format(s)/length: 1.85:1 letterbox / 122 mins
Audio format: Dolby Surround
Director: John Woo
Starring: Chow Yun-Fat, Tony Leung, Theresa Mo
Year made: 1992
Extras: Scene access; trailer; filmographies; stills gallery; interview with John Woo (30 mins); John Woo biography; text interview with Chow Yun-Fat.

If you're a fan of action films and you haven't

heard of *Hard-Boiled*, then frankly you're not a fan at all. This and *The Killer* (not currently down for a DVD release) are the films that got Hong Kong director John Woo (*Face/Off*, *M:I2*) noticed in Hollywood, and despite being made on budgets that wouldn't pay for a box for Tom Cruise to stand on during filming, they represent the pinnacle of gun-toting thrillers. Undercover cop Tony (Leung) and supercool, toothpick-chewing detective Tequila (Yun-Fat) enter an uneasy alliance to bring down a murderous mobster (Anthony Wong). The plot is nothing out of the ordinary, but what separates *Hard-Boiled* from the runny eggs of the action world is Woo's amazing direction. It's a bullet ballet, a storm of splattering squibs, and probably any number of other astounding alliterations. There are three main action sequences – in a restaurant, a warehouse and a hospital – and each is more jaw-dropping than the last. Who cares if nobody ever seems to reload their guns? By the end of the film you'll be raiding the kitchen for toothpicks to chew and looking for babies to hold while you bungee-jump out of windows. Sadly, a number of things conspire to reduce your viewing pleasure. Firstly, the sound. Admittedly it's dubbed, but even so there's no excuse for the sound effects being so grossly out of sync for the entire film. Secondly, there's the picture. There's a staggering amount of dirt, dust and who-knows-what on the film, and the actual DVD encoding is terrible. Shimmering artefacts abound, and in a true insult to Woo, there's often so much blocking visible on the muzzle flashes in gunfights that they look like they were drawn on afterwards with an Etch-A-Sketch. Extras-wise, *Hard-Boiled* includes an interesting (subtitled) 1994 interview with Woo which reveals that behind the gunfire he's quite the old softie, but that aside it's standard trailers and filmographies. The film deserved better than being scrambled by a duff disc.

FINAL VERDICT

Picture ☆☆ Sound ☆☆ Entertainment ☆☆☆☆☆
Extras ☆☆☆ Value ☆☆
OVERALL ☆☆

HARD RAIN

Price: £17.99
Supplied by: PolyGram
Type of disc: Dual layer, single-sided
No of chapters: 18
Film format(s)/length: 2.35:1 widescreen, 4:3 regular / 93 mins
Audio format: Dolby Digital 5.1
Director: Mikael Salomon
Starring: Morgan Freeman, Christian Slater, Minnie Driver
Year made: 1998
Extras: Chapter access; English and Spanish soundtracks; multilingual subtitles.

It did badly at the box office, but *Hard Rain* is one of those workmanlike action thrillers that might still get a second life on DVD. Written by Graham Yost (*Speed*, *Broken Arrow*) it sees security guard Slater and church restorer Driver as the only people who can stop Freeman and his gang of robbers from making off with $3 million from a flooded town. The waterlogged nature of the setting means there's not a great deal of room for fast-paced action, but there are a couple of reasonably thrilling scenes – a jetski chase inside a flooded school is one, along with Slater being trapped in a jail cell that's rapidly filling with water. There's even a surprising plot twist two-thirds of the way through, which is something of a rarity in this kind of film. *Hard Rain* obviously had quite a lot of money spent on it (apparently a huge town set was built in a tank so it could be flooded at will) but it's not in the league of other DVD actioners like *Face/Off* or *The Rock*. On the plus side, it's better than any Jean-Claude Van Damme disc currently available! The quality of the DVD transfer is pretty much irrelevant, since the entire film takes place at night, in a storm, so the picture is always murky. Soundwise it's 5.1 business as usual, with no really big noises until the *Thunderbirds*-style dam breaks and a flood wave sweeps through the town. As for extras, they appear to have drowned. Average movie, typical disc.

FINAL VERDICT

Picture ☆☆☆ Sound ☆☆☆ Entertainment ☆☆☆
Extras ☆ Value ☆☆
OVERALL ☆☆

HARD TARGET

Price: £19.99
Supplied by: Columbia TriStar Home Video
Type of disc: Dual layer, single-sided
No of chapters: 26
Film format(s)/length: 1.85:1 widescreen enhanced / 95 mins
Audio format: Dolby Digital 5.1
Director: John Woo
Starring: Jean-Claude Van Damme, Lance Henriksen, Yancy Butler
Year made: 1993
Extras: Scene access; soundtrack in English, French, Italian, German, Spanish and Czech; subtitles in 10 languages.

Despite being a legend in Hong Kong cinema, when John Woo came to Hollywood he was still forced to serve a kind of apprenticeship, where the very stylistic flourishes that made him popular in the first place had to be suppressed in order to knock out typical cookie-cutter 'product'. We shouldn't complain too much since it gave him the chance to make *Face/Off*, but you still wonder what an unfettered Woo could have done with *Hard Target*. Van Damme is a drifter in New Orleans who becomes the prey in evil Lance Henriksen's ultimate big-game hunt. For a Van Damme flick it's quite good, and Woo still manages to squeeze in a couple of his trademarks (standoffs! Doves!) but it falls short of *The Killer* or *Face/Off*. Extras are limited to the usual trailer and flimsy production notes – apart from the excellent sound, this is another disc that misses the target.

FINAL VERDICT

Picture ☆☆☆☆ Sound ☆☆☆☆☆
Entertainment ☆☆☆ Extras ☆☆ Value ☆☆☆
OVERALL ☆☆☆

HAVANA

Price: £19.99
Supplied by: Columbia TriStar
Type of disc: Dual layer, single-sided
No of chapters: 21
Film format(s)/length: 1.85:1 letterbox / 138 mins
Audio format: Dolby Digital 5.1
Director: Sydney Pollack
Starring: Robert Redford, Lena Olin, Alan Arkin
Year made: 1990
Extras: Scene access; behind-the-scenes featurette; production notes; cast and filmmakers' notes; theatrical trailer; Web links; soundtrack in English, German, French, Italian and Spanish; subtitles in 11 languages.

Every generation should have a *Casablanca* to call their own. That doesn't mean though that they should have a mere copy of that classic, and that's what *Havana* is. It's a study in Hollywood opulence and expensive ambition, but for all the attention to detail, the cast chemistry and air of magic of the original is missing from this movie. Redford plays another all-American hero, this time a gambler who travels to "the sexiest city in the world" for the game of his life. This is a time of revolutionary change however, set as it is in the last 8 hedonistic days of 1958 before the dictator Batista fled and Castro emerged. Redford (who normally wouldn't stick his neck out for nobody) gets mixed up with the wife of a revolutionary (Olin) and must decide whether to help fight her rebellion or keep on looking for

the big score. A Voice of God narrator, identical to the theatrical trailer, talks us through the 6 minute featurette, commendable for going behind-the-scenes of the production design. A massive undertaking, it involved building a replica Havana street from the ground up over 4 months at a Dominican air force base! Production notes are typically scant of any real depth while brief biographies and 'selected film highlights' (no, give us *all* the film highlights!) are provided for the three leads and director. Web links are DVD's most underdeveloped feature and don't improve here. A disc designed to wash over you, then be forgotten.

FINAL VERDICT

Picture ☆☆☆ Sound ☆☆☆☆ Entertainment ☆☆☆
Extras ☆☆ Value ☆☆
OVERALL ☆☆☆

HEAT AND DUST

Price: £19.99
Supplied by: Columbia TriStar Home Video
Type of disc: Dual layer, single-sided
No of chapters: 16
Film format(s)/length: 1.66:1 widescreen / 124 mins
Audio format: Dolby Surround 5.1
Director: James Ivory
Starring: Julie Christie, Shashi Kapoor, Greta Scacchi
Year made: 1982
Extras: Scene access; 30th Anniversary Merchant Ivory promo by Cinemax; original theatrical trailer; 8-page booklet containing production notes, synopsis, cast biographies and history of Merchant Ivory productions.; subtitles in English; subtitles for the hearing impaired in English.

The costume drama *Heat and Dust* is one of the first films in a wave of DVD releases from the multi-award winning team of James Ivory and Ismail Merchant. The 30-year-old Merchant Ivory formula of adapting classic texts, finding sumptuous locations and casting charming actors and actresses was in full effect by the time *Heat and Dust* rolled around, and it shows in this lavishly produced film. Swinging London icon Julie Christie stars as Anne, a modern woman researching the scandal her great aunt Olivia (Scacchi) caused in Twenties colonial India. Anne discovers how the young army bride's dormant passions were stirred by a dashing prince (Kapoor) while finding romance herself. DVD-wise, the well-written booklet forms the main highlight of a reasonable but not earth-shattering presentation. A more up-to-date assessment of the film from either cast or crew members would have made a distinguished film an equally distinguished disc.

FINAL VERDICT

Picture ☆☆☆☆ Sound ☆☆☆☆ Entertainment ☆☆☆
Extras ☆☆ Value ☆☆☆

OVERALL ☆☆☆

HEAVY METAL

Price: £19.99
Supplied by: Columbia TriStar Home Video
Type of disc: Single layer, single-sided
No of chapters: 24
Film format(s)/length: 16:9 widescreen enhanced / 87 mins
Audio format: Dolby Digital 5.1
Director: Gerald Potterton
Starring the voices of: Richard Romanus, John Candy, Joe Flaherty
Year made: 1981
Extras: Scene access; original 90-minute 'rough cut' version; *Imagining Heavy Metal* 35-minute documentary; deleted scenes; artwork of *Heavy Metal* gallery; *Heavy Metal* magazine cover gallery; soundtrack in French, German, Italian (Surround) and Spanish (Mono); subtitles in 20 languages.

Arguably, Disney, the home of Mickey Mouse, is the undisputed king of the mainstream animated movie...but that's not to say that Disney does not have its close rivals when it comes to producing great animated films. Little known on this side of the Atlantic, Columbia Pictures' *Heavy Metal* grossed over $20 million during its initial American theatrical run in 1981. Based upon the cult adult comic magazine of the same name, Columbia's brave stab at animated anthology fantasy proved to be a success both in terms of mainstream and cult audiences. *Heavy Metal* is comprised of 8 different animated short stories, with a ninth serving as a common thread that links them all. The latter, bizarrely enough, deals with a glowing green ball of pure evil...um, remember that this is fantasy, kids. Whilst the quality of the almost 20-year-old animation is dated, the originality of the stories – written and illustrated by some genuine comic book greats – means that *Heavy Metal* is still very much worth a watch. The DVD is yet another top quality package from Columbia TriStar who has wisely chosen not to just simply transfer the original print onto DVD. Fans of the movie have been rewarded with a remastered edition of the movie in two forms (the original feature-length 'rough cut' has been included), along with a host of worthwhile extras. The soundtrack, including the cheesy 'cock rock' antics of Black Sabbath, Nazareth and Blue

Oyster Cult, have also been represented in Dolby Digital 5.1...grrreat! Perhaps Columbia is re-releasing *Heavy Metal* now in anticipation of the forthcoming sequel – let's hope that the sequel will be as well presented on DVD as this is.

FINAL VERDICT

Picture ☆☆☆☆ Sound ☆☆☆☆☆
Entertainment ☆☆☆☆ Extras ☆☆☆☆ Value ☆☆☆☆

OVERALL ☆☆☆☆

HELLRAISER

Price: £19.99
Supplied by: DVD World (01705 796662)
Type of disc: Single layer, double-sided
No of chapters: 19
Film format(s)/length: 4.3, 16:9 widescreen / 90 mins
Director: Clive Barker
Starring: Andrew Robinson, Clare Higgins, Ashley Laurence
Year made: 1987
Extras: Scene access; sub-plots; theatrical trailers; photo library; two screen formats (16:9, 4:3); interviews/documentary.

Hellraiser makes compulsive viewing for anyone with a strong enough stomach to witness the horrors of Barker's most disturbing creations – the Cenobites, a group of sadistic demons so evil they make Freddy Krueger look like Andy Pandy! The twisted love triangle of Larry Cotton (Robinson), his wife Julia (Higgins – terrifyingly detached) and his eternally damned brother Frank are rendered all the more visceral when watched on crystal sharp DVD. Although this is ruined on side one (1.05) when you can clearly see the screen flicker severely due to a glitch on the original master. Sound on the whole though is good, and with Dolby Pro Logic on audio channel two you can delight in having the Cenobite's chattering teeth right behind your ear. VCI has done a terrific job in creating a real collectors' edition for horror fans, with this DVD dripping with extras such as a decent set of interviews, original trailers, sub-plots, a photo library and of course two different screen formats. A great value disc, but unfortunately the picture quality lets it down.

FINAL VERDICT

Picture ☆☆ Sound ☆☆☆ Entertainment ☆☆☆☆
Extras ☆☆☆☆☆ Value ☆☆☆

OVERALL ☆☆☆

HENRY & JUNE

Price: £19.99
Supplied by: Columbia TriStar Home Video

Type of disc: Dual layer, single-sided
No of chapters: 18
Film format(s)/length: 1.85:1 letterbox / 130 mins
Audio format: Dolby Surround
Director: Philip Kaufman
Starring: Uma Thurman, Fred Ward, Maria de Medeiros
Year made: 1990
Extras: Scene access; theatrical trailer; Web links; production notes; cast and crew bios; soundtrack in English, German, French, Italian, Spanish and Polish; subtitles in 9 languages.

Here's the pitch. *Henry & June* is a, quote, 'erotic period drama', charting the three-way relationship between American author Henry Miller, his wife June (that's where Uma comes in, Kleenex fans) and a young writer named Anais Nin. Set in 1930s Paris, for the most part this is a watchable, albeit unspectacular, period drama. Sure, there's a bucketload of humping going on, and there are the ingredients for an engrossing movie here, yet clichés and a drawn-out running time dilute the experience. Oh, and look out for Kevin Spacey in a minor supporting role. Discwise, the picture quality is problematic, with the print used in desperate need of some cleaning up. Filmed in 1.85:1, the packaging wrongly claims the disc is presented with a 1.66:1 picture, when it is in fact framed in the original ratio. It's not anamorphic either. The audio is in Dolby Surround only, but that's not too big a problem, given that this is a dialogue-driven film. Which just leaves extra features, best described as the usual suspects. To be fair, the production notes are lengthy and quite interesting, while cast bios and the trailer are okay. *Henry & June* turns out to be a middle-of-the-road piece of silver overall, but one that does raise a question over price bands. If this film were being released by Warner or Cinema Club, you'd expect a price tag in the region of £10-16. Isn't it time Columbia TriStar thus stopped charging us 20 notes for old films on ordinary production line discs?

FINAL VERDICT

Picture ☆☆ Sound ☆☆ Entertainment ☆☆☆
Extras ☆☆ Value ☆☆
OVERALL ☆☆

HERCULES

Price: £19.99
Supplied by: Warner Home Video
Type of disc: Dual layer, single-sided
No of chapters: 32
Film format(s)/length: 1.66:1 widescreen / 89 mins
Audio format: Dolby Digital 5.1

Directors: John Musker and Ron Clements
Starring the voices of: Tate Donovan, Danny DeVito, James Woods
Year made: 1997
Extras: Scene access; soundtrack in English, French Italian, Dutch and Greek; multiligual subtitles.

You'd think this far into the innings that Disney could churn these annual animations out in its sleep with out neither care nor thought. However, say what you will about the all-seeing mouse, these guys are still kings in the land of cinema cartoons; they take a classic story and animate the hell out of it! Like all Disney classics, the blatantly contemporary script works to desensitise the younger audience to a classic tale and to bring a bit of Hollywood life to every character. Hercules, new-born son of big cheese Greek God Zeus, is kidnapped by minions of villain-of-the-piece Hades (voiced by Woods) and 'mortalised' so that he won't be able to cock up Hades' plans for the future, as predicted by the Fates. Cut to 18 years later, and Hercules is a grown mortal with the strength of a God, and thus the only one in the world capable of foiling Hades' evil plans. It's a Disney movie, so expect the obligatory happy ending and soppy songs, but the visuals, chiefly designed by acid-penned British cartoonist Gerald Scarfe, are Disney's most inspired for years, and the action bounces along at such a lively rate that it's easy for the most cynical viewer to be charmed. The disc is pretty empty, but let's face it, this is a kid's movie, and they won't be enthralled by a director's commentary. By the way, keep an eye on James Woods as Hades, undoubtedly the coolest bad guy ever to be seen in a movie!

FINAL VERDICT

Picture ☆☆☆☆ Sound ☆☆☆☆
Entertainment ☆☆☆☆ Extras ☆ Value ☆☆☆
OVERALL ☆☆☆

HIDEAWAY

Price: £19.99
Supplied by: Columbia TriStar Home Video
Type of disc: Dual layer, single-sided
No of chapters: 28
Film format(s)/length: 2.35:1 widescreen enhanced / 102 mins
Audio format: Dolby Digital 5.1
Director: Brett Leonard
Starring: Jeff Goldblum, Christine Lahti, Alicia Silverstone
Year made: 1995
Extras: Scene access; theatrical trailer; filmographies; behind-the-scenes featurette; English, German, Italian,

Spanish and French soundtracks; subtitles in 20 languages.

So this is the pitch. We've got the rights to a psycho-horror best seller by Dean R Koontz. We've got Jeff Goldblum, of course, and we've got Alicia Silverstone just before she became too expensive after *Clueless* hit big. Trouble is, the budget's tight and there's no A-list directors who'll give us the time of day. So how about Brett Leonard? The guy who made *The Lawnmower Man* look big budget? As you'd expect, Leonard doesn't back away from any of the book's supernatural set pieces. Quite the reverse, with a light show finale that looks like a retread of former glories. Truth to tell, Leonard even manages to imbue some of the minor scenes with a spooky, supernatural feel. From start to end, there's a genuinely off-kilter feel to the movie and the violence has real impact. However, just as *The Lawnmower Man* was ultimately a bad idea made to look superficially impressive, so *Hideaway* suffers from an equally uninspiring plot. Goldblum has a near-death experience from a car crash, ends up being psychically linked to a psycho-killer who's been similarly resuscitated and the two spiral together for a cliched 'epic clash between good and evil'. Leonard brings little to the party except special effects and menace. DVD presentation is fine as far as the movie goes, but it's otherwise minimalistic. A 'Making of' featurette is really just a movie trailer in disguise, with Leonard wearing a 'Stunts Canada' baseball cap as he tiresomely hypes *Lawnmower*-style effects as an exploration of the afterlife. They're not, this is just a shock-horror, late night TV flick.

FINAL VERDICT

Picture ☆☆☆☆ Sound ☆☆☆☆ Entertainment ☆☆☆
Extras ☆☆☆ Value ☆☆☆
OVERALL ☆☆☆

HIDEOUS KINKY

Price: £19.99
Supplied by: VCI
Type of disc: Dual layer, single-sided
No of chapters: 16:9 widescreen / 95 mins
Film format(s)/length: Dolby Surround
Audio format: Dolby Surround
Director: Gillies MacKinnon
Starring: Kate Winslet, Saïd Taghmaoui, Bella Riza
Year made: 1998
Extras: Scene access; behind the scenes footage; interviews with cast and crew; theatrical trailer; booklet containing mini-biographies of the 2 leads.

The idea of discovering yourself by travelling the globe, meeting new people and sampling a copious variety of drugs always holds great appeal for Westerners. Kate Winslet's character in *Hideous Kinky* is no different. Marrakech, 1972: after her marriage falters, beautiful hippie Julia (Winslet) decides that her young daughters Bea and Lucy deserve more than their life in a South London bedsit has to offer, so sells up everything and moves to Morocco. *Hideous Kinky* follows the family as they encounter the vibrant people and culture of North Africa, specifically Julia's lover Bilal (played with verve by Taghmaoui). However, Julia's preoccupation with finding spiritual fulfilment in Sufism threatens to split the trio for good, just when they need to support each other the most. Everything about *Hideous Kinky* is beautifully done. Taking a leaf out of the original novel, the film often takes the perspective of the two girls by angling the camera up at the adults. The effect is to share in the girls' embarrassment for their mother's behaviour and desire for normalcy. VCI has made an effort to furnish the disc with a modicum of extras. The on-set interviews ask good questions for the most part and the interviewees (Winslet, Taghmaoui and McKinnon) talk enthusiastically. McKinnon recalls how he himself travelled around Africa for 6 months around the time the film is set, which explains the strong sense of authenticity from start to finish. More time could have been given to producer Ann Scott and screenwriter Billy MacKinnon, however. Fine performances from all concerned, the shimmering locations and an evocative soundtrack give *Hideous Kinky* a depth many films can only dream of. The DVD, while flawed (only Dolby Surround?), is better than the R1 equivalent and gives the film more warmth than ever before. You must watch this now.

FINAL VERDICT

Picture ☆☆☆☆☆ Sound ☆☆☆
Entertainment ☆☆☆☆ Extras ☆☆☆ Value ☆☆☆
OVERALL ☆☆☆☆

HOLY MAN

Price: £15.99
Supplied by: Warner Home Video
Type of disc: Dual layer, single-sided
No of chapters: 23
Film format(s)/length: 2.35:1 widescreen / 109 mins
Audio format: Dolby Digital 5.1
Director: Stephen Herek
Starring: Eddie Murphy, Jeff Goldblum, Kelly Preston
Year made: 1998
Extras: Scene access; soundtrack in German and Spanish; subtitles in 10 languages; subtitles for the hearing impaired in English.

Little of this film would ever happen in real life. What is presented is a well-meaning take on the consumer culture of the Nineties, and a critique of its seminal driving force, television. The film-makers attempt to squeeze a social observation into a comedy form, but the elements don't quite match, and so in order to fit them comfortably together, realism and the audience's intelligence are sacrificed. In trying to be both a comedy and an observation piece the movie loses integrity in the latter, and just plain loses the former altogether. The film has the stressed-out shopping network executive Ricky Hayman (Goldblum) using the spiritual guidance of the mysterious and blissfully naïve guru 'G' (Murphy) as a gimmick to boost the ratings on his flagging network. Predictably Hollywood wins out, and Hayman sees the error of his ways (which is sad because a realistic, nasty ending would have been much more exciting). For Murphy this is a wasted opportunity, as the character of 'G' is atrociously under-developed and far too quiet and hidden away to be a decent vehicle for him. In fact, it's Goldblum who has the much more interesting character (and more screen time than the supposed leading man), but this is really not developed until the third act of the film. By then most viewers would have lost patience! As for the DVD, there is nothing special to make a fuss about. Unless you count scene selection and subtitles, there are no extras at all. This really is a shame as it is basically a 'nice try', but fails to hit the mark, just at a time when Murphy was beginning to return to the roles his talent so deserves.

FINAL VERDICT

Picture ☆☆☆☆ Sound ☆☆☆ Entertainment ☆☆
Extras ☆ Value ☆
OVERALL ☆☆

Hook

Price: £19.99
Supplied by: Columbia TriStar
Type of disc: Dual layer, single-sided
No of chapters: 28
Film format(s)/length: 2.35:1 widescreen enhanced / 136 mins
Audio format: Dolby Digital 5.1
Director: Steven Spielberg
Starring: Dustin Hoffman, Robin Williams, Julia Roberts
Year made: 1991
Extras: Scene access; featurette; 4 theatrical trailers; 3 photo galleries; 'The Lost Treasure' set-top game; cast and crew biogs; soundtrack in English, French and German; subtitles in 17 languages.

Was this really necessary? Probably not! J M Barrie's classic tale of the boy who didn't grow up never really called for a sequel. Still, in the hands of Spielberg (and let's face it, no one else could get away with directing this) it becomes unclear as to whether *need* was the real burning motivation behind this movie. This movie was made because it had a big budget, big names and the world's most popular director, a man who was born for this genre. If one of these key factors were missing then this whole thing would have been a waste of time. As it is, it barely avoids being just that. Dialogue falls flat at an alarming rate, jokes are misfired and after 9 years the special effects now fail to convince. The notion of Peter Pan growing up and forgetting all about Never Never Land, until Captain Hook kidnaps Peter's children in order to fight a war with his life-long nemesis, sounds like an interesting idea. Perhaps it should have just stayed at that. There are many who will get some sort of enjoyment from *Hook*, but the whole thing plays like Spielberg-by-numbers, and it's only Hoffman who seems to be enjoying himself (and an admirable job he does of it too). Even Williams seems stifled at times. Never before has there been a movie which contained so many cute yet annoying kids. In all fairness it's not their fault. For a script that calls for so many children, it has so little for them to do. Their job is just to be as eye-catching as possible while it's left to Williams and Hoffman to act the immature parts. Though Spielberg's debut Region 2 disc may not be his best effort, it's by no means a poor DVD. Columbia TriStar have taken the movie's audience into consideration when deciding on the extras. The disc is clearly aimed at the young at heart, but avoids being patronising. The menu is charming and fun, the biogs are simple without being underwhelming, and the additional trailers are all kids' films that are worth knowing about.

FINAL VERDICT

Picture ☆☆☆☆ Sound ☆☆☆☆ Entertainment ☆☆
Extras ☆☆☆☆ Value ☆☆☆
OVERALL ☆☆☆

The Horse Whisperer

Price: £15.99
Supplied by: Buena Vista
Type of disc: Single layer, double-sided (flipper)
No of chapters: 10
Film format(s)/length: 2:35:1 widescreen / 163 mins
Audio format: Dolby Digital 5.1
Director: Robert Redford
Starring: Robert Redford, Kristin Scott Thomas, Sam

Neill
Year made: 1998
Extras: Scene access.

The Horse Whisperer, an epic saga of love, betrayal and horse healing set amid the sweeping vistas of Montana, is filmed in a honeyed glow of sentimentality. If you don't mind the permanent halo around Robert Redford, the DVD version will satisfy anyone who enjoyed the movie at the cinema, but you will need a widescreen TV to get the most from it. It's worth buying for the immortal line, from Kristin Scott Thomas to Redford: "Ooh, can we just have one more ride?" Sadly, *The Horse Whisperer* falls at the fence of DVD extras – there's nothing except for interactive menus and captions, which makes it a bit of an also-ran. A shame, really, as it would have been fun to see out-takes of Kristin falling off a horse or Robert f-ing and blind-ing as he tries to throw a lasso. Or what about a short film on real-life horse whisperer, Frank Bell? GP

FINAL VERDICT

Picture ☆☆ Sound ☆☆☆☆ Entertainment ☆☆
Extras ☆ Value ☆☆
OVERALL ☆☆

HOUSE

Price: £19.99
Supplied by: DVDplus (www.dvdplus.co.uk)
Type of disc: Single layer, single-sided
No of chapters: 7
Film format(s)/length: 16:9 widescreen / 99 mins
Audio format: Stereo
Director: Steven C Minor
Starring: William Katt, George Wendt, Richard Moll
Year made: 1986
Extras: Scene access; photo gallery.

Roger Cobb is a divorced, Vietnam veteran, currently writing a book on his experiences during the war. When Roger's Aunt hangs herself, he inherits an aged house, from which his son vanished two years ago. The house itself is, of course, not as it should be, with mysterious noises and spooky occurrences every midnight. The film opens, disturbingly, as a delivery boy chances upon the swinging corpse of Roger's Aunt. As she is buried, Roger decides to return to the house and confront the past, whilst continuing to write his book. As he spends more time in the house, Roger becomes aware of the spooky goings on, finally discovering a door to another world hidden inside a closet (memories of Narnia anyone?). This then prompts him to begin the search for his missing son. The story is told in an entertaining manner, with

tongue firmly in cheek. Some of the scenes are genuinely horrific, but there is always the comedy element in the shape of George Wendt (from *Cheers*) to raise a smile. The script is well written and the pace fast. Some of the comedy set pieces are among horror's finest. There is also enough slapstick comedy to raise an occasional hearty laugh. Unfortunately, as with many English DVDs, this title is let down by the lack of extras in the package. One lame gallery of shots from the film and a scene selector doesn't really cut it these days. A biography of the cast, or even the cinematic trailer would have brightened up the package. Sadly this DVD looks as low budget as the film itself.

FINAL VERDICT

Picture ☆☆☆ Sound ☆☆☆ Entertainment ☆☆
Extras ☆ Value ☆☆
OVERALL ☆☆

HOUSE ON HAUNTED HILL

Price: £19.99
Supplied by: Warner Home Video
Type of disc: Dual layer, single-sided
No of chapters: 30
Film format(s)/length: 2.35:1 anamorphic / 99 mins
Audio format: Dolby Digital 5.1
Director: William Malone
Starring: Geoffrey Rush, Famke Janssen, Taye Diggs
Year made: 1999
Extras: Scene access; audio commentary by director William Malone; *Tale of Two Houses* featurette; *Behind the Screams* mini-featurettes; innovative picture gallery; deleted scenes; extracts from *Creature*; cast, crew and William Castle biographies; theatrical trailers of the 1958 and 1999 versions; subtitles in English; subtitles for the hearing impaired in English.

Blame Gus Van Sant. When the success of *Good Will Hunting* gave him the clout to indulge his controversial dream of remaking Alfred Hitchcock's *Psycho*, updating established, beloved films turned from an act of creative desperation into a legitimate and lucrative business practice. Enter Dark Castle, a production company set up solely to update and remake the creaky horror pictures of William Castle for today's multiplexes, *House on Haunted Hill* being the first. In a performance not *quite* as moustache-twirlingly camp as his turn in *Mystery Men*, Rush plays a fairground impresario who throws a birthday party for his trampy wife Janssen in a haunted former mental institution. 6 strangers are invited. Their interest? They each get one million dollars, if they can survive the night. Trouble is, the house is out for revenge against these 6 descendants of the staff who tortured and murdered the asylum's inmates decades before… This DVD is a marvellous showcase for your system. Every mechanical clank, scream and eerie noise is perfectly rendered through the 5.1 Dolby audio. With the full setup you'll think the short-circuiting lights you hear in the film are in your room! *Behind the Screams* is a collection of two minute clips that sees Malone discuss 6 key special effects moments in the film. The director also includes a taster of his 1985 non-event movie *Creature* for our amusement. Warner still encodes DVD-ROM material and it still sends us nowhere we couldn't get to ourselves, namely www. warnervideo.com. There are, however, two official sites to promote the movie and undoubtedly no end of fansites dedicated to Castle's films. Why not use the disc to send us to these? The US disc contained a game, two genre essays and a link to the theatrical Web site (buries face in hands and weeps). *House on Haunted Hill* is cheery enough entertainment for those looking to throw popcorn at the plasma screen in laughter but there are no new or exciting thrills here to make you spill your cocoa in fright. Maybe Dark Castle needs to take a new direction.

FINAL VERDICT

Picture ☆☆☆☆☆ Sound ☆☆☆☆☆

Entertainment ☆☆☆ Extras ☆☆☆ Value ☆☆☆

OVERALL ☆☆☆

HOWARDS END

Price: £19.99

Supplied by: Columbia TriStar Home Video

Type of disc: Dual layer, single-sided

No of chapters: 16

Film format(s)/length: 2.35:1 widescreen enhanced / 136 mins

Audio format: Dolby Digital 5.1

Director: James Ivory

Starring: Anthony Hopkins, Emma Thompson, Helena Bonham Carter

Year made: 1992

Extras: Scene access; *Howards End* featurette; 30th Anniversary Merchant Ivory promo; interviews with cast and film-makers; behind-the-scenes featurette; theatrical trailer; subtitles in English; English subtitles for the hearing impaired.

The Americans may hold the monopoly as far as action, horror, and gross-out comedy go, but when it comes to period drama we Brits have the genre sewn up as tightly as Helena Bonham Carter's bodice. *Howards End* is one of the best examples of this: an excellent adaptation of the EM Forster novel, starring many of the usual suspects – Emma Thompson, Vanessa Redgrave, Anthony Hopkins – and maintaining the usual Merchant Ivory trademarks of lush cinematography and authentic costume and set design. The story traces the fortunes of two Edwardian families – the stuffy old Wilcoxes and the more liberal Schlegels – examining what happens when members of different social classes intermingle at the beginning of the century. Repressed feelings, big bay windows, picturesque locations and posh people taking afternoon tea; all the familiar elements are here, but the first-rate script and note-perfect performances raise *Howards End* well above standard period fare. With intelligently written dialogue and healthy doses of humour, there's even some dark irony; witness the bookish young man, who the Schlegel sisters take under their collective wing, getting crushed to death by an over-loaded bookcase. Refreshingly, on this occasion an exemplary film gets a Region 2 DVD to match, which surprisingly offers more in the way of extras than the Region 1 version. To begin with, the digital transfer is superb, with the gorgeous cinematography done full justice – colours are bright and vibrant, particularly in the numerous shots of the countryside, although even the duller colours of the interior scenes appear deep and grain-free. The picture is sharp and detailed throughout, with the anamorphic transfer ensuring that nothing is lost from director James Ivory's carefully framed shots. The audio is also good, but confined mainly to dialogue, background noise and the effective musical soundtrack. On reading the list of special features you could be forgiven for expecting a treat here, too, but unfortunately this is not quite the case. While there are certainly plenty to choose from – theatrical trailer, two featurettes, cast interviews and more – the total running time for all of these is less than half-an-hour. This wouldn't be so bad, but they all contain essentially the same material: the same clips from the film, the same interview snippets, the same cheesy American voiceover and even the same music. It's rather like buying the CD single for a song you like, only to be lumbered with a handful of decidedly similar-sounding remixes. The best thing about the extras – presented in their original 4:3 format – is that they demonstrate just how well the actual film has been digitally remastered. Unnecessary padding aside, the DVD for *Howards End* is a virtually faultless presentation of what is undoubtedly one of the best period dramas of the Nineties.

FINAL VERDICT

Picture ☆☆☆☆ Sound ☆☆☆ Entertainment ☆☆☆☆

Extras ☆☆☆ Value ☆☆☆
OVERALL ☆☆☆☆

HUDSON HAWK

Price: £19.99
Supplied by: Columbia TriStar Home Video
Type of disc: Dual layer, single-sided
No of chapters: 28
Film format(s)/length: 1.85:1 widescreen / 96 mins
Audio format: Dolby Surround
Director: Michael Lehmann
Starring: Bruce Willis, Danny Aiello, Andie MacDowell
Year made: 1991
Extras: Scene access; cast filmographies; DVD trailer; director's commentary.

Every big Hollywood star goes through a stage in their career when they suffer from 'tall poppy syndrome', where a film they're working on is selected for media vilification to stop them getting too big for their boots. Arnold Schwarzenegger had *The Last Action Hero*, Kevin Costner had, well, pretty much everything he's done lately (although *The Pozzzztman* clearly deserved it) and Willis had *Hudson Hawk*. The thing about *Hudson Hawk* is that it's actually not that bad a film. It's hardly a work of genius by any means – director Lehmann's other films are far more satisfying – but it's an entertaining caper comedy in which Willis sends up his tough guy image. The problem was, at the time it was released American audiences were expecting another *Die Hard*-style movie, and the only thing *Hudson Hawk* has in common with the overblown actioners apart from its star is the occasional explosion. Willis is the 'Hudson Hawk' of the title, an expert cat burglar blackmailed by the megalomaniacal Mayflowers (Richard E Grant and Sandra Bernhard, both in overblown scenery-chomping mode) into stealing various art treasures containing parts of a Leonardo da Vinci invention that can turn lead into gold. The Hawk's methods are a little different to the high-tech gadgetry seen in the likes of *Entrapment* – for a start, he performs his robberies while singing show tunes! Also thrown into the narrative, which even Lehmann admits makes little sense, are nun/secret agent Anna (MacDowell), James Coburn and his team of chocolate-codenamed CIA agents, and pretty much anyone else the makers could think of, including Sylvester Stallone's brother. The final result is a mish-mash of slapstick gags; some don't work, but most raise a smile – the scene where Willis and Aiello are hit by paralysis darts and then put into embarrassing poses stands out, and there's a dog-blown-through-window scene that predates

There's Something About Mary by the best part of a decade. The main extra is Lehmann's commentary; time has let him adopt a resigned, self-deprecating attitude to a film that was blasted by critics on release. As he repeatedly reminds us, "Did I tell you it was a big hit in Europe?" There's no real backstage dirt (he recommends you read Richard E Grant's books for that) but it's clear he's still annoyed by *Hudson Hawk*'s pasting. At the time, *Hudson Hawk* was slammed for its big-budget excesses – ironically, today it would qualify as a mid-budget movie, and its quirky humour could find a new life in the post-*Austin Powers* world. And where else can you see Andie MacDowell making a complete tit of herself by impersonating a dolphin?

FINAL VERDICT

Picture ☆☆☆ Sound ☆☆☆ Entertainment ☆☆☆☆
Extras ☆☆☆ Value ☆☆☆
OVERALL ☆☆☆

HUSH

Price: £19.99
Supplied by: DVD Net (0181 890 2520)
Type of disc: Single layer, single-sided
No of chapters: 28
Film format(s)/length: 1.85:1 widescreen / 92 mins
Audio format(s): Dolby Digital 5.1
Director: Jonathan Darby
Starring: Jessica Lange, Gwyneth Paltrow, Johnathon Schaech
Year made: 1998
Extras: Theatrical trailer; filmographies of all leading actors; German language.

A young bride, Helen (Paltrow) and Jackson her husband (Schaech) move from New York to live with his widowed mother and at first it seems like an idyllic existence. They have the run of a large farmhouse, stables full of the finest horses and the locals welcome them with open arms. The mother-in-law soon starts to show her true colours though, manipulating the newlyweds and turning her son against his new bride. Deep dark secrets are revealed, and living with the older woman becomes murder – almost literally! When a movie goes from a US cinema release direct onto video and DVD in the UK; bypassing our own cinemas, you'd be forgiven for thinking that it wasn't much good. Well you should trust that instinct where this is concerned. This isn't exactly Paltrow's finest film, and as for Jessica Lange as the mother-in-law – well, she's not often worth watching. To be fair, Gwyneth makes a performance on-par with all her other work, but the storyline is predictable, the characters completely unlikeable and you can tell why the UK cinemas passed up the opportunity to show it. Things do hot up towards the end of the film with suspense building to a dramatic climax, but most people won't watch long enough to get that far! By the end of the film you really do grow to hate the Jessica Lange character with a vengeance, but sadly the ending is a real let down. Not recommended, particularly since the extras are as poor as the film!

FINAL VERDICT

Picture ☆☆☆ Sound ☆☆☆ Entertainment ☆
Extras ☆ Value ☆☆
OVERALL ☆☆

THE ICE STORM

Price: £15.99
Supplied by: Buena Vista
Type of disc: Single layer, single-sided
No of chapters: 13
Film format(s)/length: 16:9 widescreen / 108 mins
Director: Ang Lee
Starring: Sigourney Weaver, Kevin Kline, Christina Ricci
Year made: 1997
Extras: Scene access; subtitles.

Set in the Seventies, *The Ice Storm* is a sorely underrated tale of sexual tension and undertones facing two neighbouring families. First off, you've got Kevin Kline having an affair with Sigourney Weaver, to the irritation of his wife, Joan Allen. Added to that, Kline's daughter, Christina Ricci is up to no good with Sigourney's son. It's all a bit of a mess. It's gripping stuff though, and enormously refreshing to find a good, grown up movie amongst the *Armageddons* and *Lethal Weapons* of the DVD world. Unfortunately, this genuinely superb movie is let down by the barest of discs. A two channel sound mix and non-anamorphic widescreen transfer are about as good as it gets (neither particularly impressing) and when you've got the special features list talking about menus and scene access, you know they're taking the piss. Ultimately, *The Ice Storm* has to stand as yet another example of how Buena Vista can make a cobblers of such a great film.

FINAL VERDICT

Picture ☆☆☆ Sound ☆☆ Entertainment ☆☆☆
Extras ☆ Value ☆☆
OVERALL ☆☆

AN IDEAL HUSBAND

Price: £19.99
Supplied by: Fox Home Entertainment
Type of disc: Single layer, single-sided

No of chapters: 16
Film format(s)/length: 1.85:1 letterbox / 93 mins
Audio format: Dolby Digital 5.1
Director: Oliver Parker
Starring: Cate Blanchett, Minnie Driver, Rupert Everett
Year made: 1999
Extras: Scene access; theatrical trailer; behind-the-scenes featurette; 2 deleted scenes; subtitles for the hearing impaired in English.

Given the proliferation of costume dramas on our screens, a filmmaker shackled with another 90-odd minutes of arch whispering about some limp woman's dowry behind open fans had better come up with something fresh if the audience is to pay it any attention. Oliver Parker's solution is to cast some of the hottest new actors around and it's just about enough. Lord Arthur Goring (Everett) is the layabout playboy of London society in 1895. When his old flame Mrs Chevely (Moore) attempts to blackmail hotshot politician Sir Robert (Northam) and ruin Robert's perfect marriage to Lady Chiltern, Arthur is drawn into a rather farcical web of deceit, romantic powerplays and sullied reputations. The featurette is the most entertaining special feature but clocking in at a mere 6 minutes it can't hope to explore the production very deeply. Actor input is also reduced to soundbites. In all, a charming film and cast with less than agreeable extras.

FINAL VERDICT

Picture ☆☆☆ Sound ☆☆☆☆ Entertainment ☆☆☆
Extras ☆☆☆ Value ☆☆☆
OVERALL ☆☆☆

IDLE HANDS

Price: £19.99
Supplied by: Columbia TriStar Home Video
Type of disc: Single layer, single-sided
No of chapters: 28
Film format(s)/length: 1.85:1 anamorphic / 88 mins
Audio format: Dolby Digital 5.1
Director: Rodman Flender
Starring: Devon Sawa, Seth Green, Jessica Alba
Year made: 1999
Extras: Behind-the-scenes featurette; director's commentary; alternate ending; storyboard comparison; trailer; filmographies; soundtrack in English and German; subtitles in 15 languages.

Wes Craven's *Scream* brought back the trend for stylish and sassy girls-in-pants-slashers. *Idle Hands* looks to bring back just the girls-in-pants-slasher part. Like *Scream*, *Idle Hands* is a torrent of over-sexed, under-educated teenage drop-outs fighting their hormones as much as the demonic presence that has taken over the hand of slacker Anton Tobias (Sawa). With his buddies in tow, Anton must prevent his hand from killing more innocent preppies before school hottie Molly (Alba) totally loses interest in him. With a script that is as slack as the characters it promotes, *Idle Hands* drifts too closely to the low budget, lowbrow videos that so inspired the formula in the first place. The DVD extras mirror the movie's mediocrity, with the director's commentary and trailers only being livened by a nice if unsurprising alternate ending. Even *Scooby Doo* did this with more wit and sophistication.

FINAL VERDICT

Picture ☆☆☆ Sound ☆☆☆

Entertainment ☆☆ Extras ☆☆☆ Value ☆☆

OVERALL ☆☆

I KNOW WHAT YOU DID LAST SUMMER

Price: £15.99

Supplied by: Entertainment in Video

Type of disc: Single layer, single-sided

No of chapters: 12

Film format(s)/length: 2.35:1 widescreen / 96 mins

Audio Format: Dolby Digital 5.1

Director: Jim Gillespie

Starring: Jennifer Love Hewitt, Sarah Michelle Gellar, Ryan Phillippe, Freddie Prinze Jr

Year made: 1997

Extras: Scene access.

The blockbuster success of *Scream* quickly resulted in writer Kevin Williamson being commissioned to knock out another slasher movie for the multiplex generation. Unfortunately, where *Scream* mocked the clichés of the slasher flick, *I Know What You Did Last Summer* is content just to rehash them. In *I Know...* 4 stereotypical American teens – beauty queen Helen (Gellar), jock Barry (Phillippe), brain Julie (Hewitt) and pauper Ray (Prinze) – are celebrating the end of the school year with booze and sex, when they run a man over on a remote coastal road. So they decide to dump the body off a pier. A year later, the guilt-wracked foursome reunite when Julie gets a letter saying, "I know what you did last summer!" The most frightening thing about *I Know...* is its predictability – it follows the pattern of the original slasher movies without a hint of irony. The quality of the DVD picture transfer is what you'd expect from a mid-budget Hollywood film – not too dark, clear if not especially vibrant colours – although only having 12 chapters in all seems a bit lazy. There are no extras on the UK disc (the American DVD, which is

thinner than Hewitt's top, still managed something) and the best that can be said about *I Know...* is that it's got surprisingly effective ominous sounds. Don't turn it up too loud, though – Hewitt's constant screaming will do irreparable damage to your crystal! As a DVD, *I Know...* is just shelf-filler, not offering any decent extras and being at best a mildly entertaining film. Admit it, if you're planning on buying this disc, it's because you want to ogle Jennifer Love Hewitt and her amazing disappearing clothes!

FINAL VERDICT

Picture ☆☆☆ Sound ☆☆☆☆

Entertainment ☆☆ Extras ☆ Value ☆☆

OVERALL ☆☆

IN LOVE AND WAR

Price: £15.99

Supplied by: Entertainment in Video

Type of disc: Single layer, single-sided

No of chapters: 12

Film format(s)/length: 2.35:1 widescreen enhanced / 108 mins

Audio format: Dolby Pro Logic

Director: Sir Richard Attenborough

Starring: Sandra Bullock, Chris O'Donnell, MacKenzie Astin

Year made: 1997

Extras: Scene access 'Making of' documentary.

In Italy during the First World War, we see 18-year-old journalist Ernest Hemingway (O'Donnell) become injured on the front line. He is taken to a nearby hospital where American nurse Agnes von Kurowsky (Sandra Bullock) helps him recover. Whether it be due to the uncertainty of war, a romance blossoms between the pair; a romance that inspired Hemingway to pen his masterpiece *A Farewell To Arms*. After Hemingway is posted back to America, Agnes carries on with the war effort and gains the attentions of an Italian doctor. When she agrees to marry him, Hemingway is devastated and retreats to a cabin to write. Even though 8 months later Agnes comes back realising her mistake, the writer is so stubborn his pride stands in the way of his heart. The war story acts as more of a sideline to the relationship of the nurse and soldier, and Attenborough controls this well; he could have included more fighting scenes, but instead chose to keep them to a minimum preferring to concentrate more on the hospital setting. It's a shame more wasn't included on the DVD though, as so much more could have been told about the early lives of Hemingway and Agnes, especially her diaries (from which the script was written). Instead, there is just a behind-the-scenes documentary. The transfer of the movie is also not too good, becoming very grainy and dark during the war scenes, but this doesn't detract from the very moving story.

FINAL VERDICT

Picture ☆☆ Sound ☆☆☆ Entertainment ☆☆☆☆
Extras ☆☆ Value ☆☆☆
OVERALL ☆☆☆

INSPECTOR GADGET

Price: £19.99
Supplied by: Disney DVD / Warner Home Video
Type of disc: Single layer, single-sided
No of chapters: 13
Film format(s)/length: 1.85:1 anamorphic / 75 mins
Audio format: Dolby Digital 5.1
Director: David Kellogg
Starring: Matthew Broderick, Rupert Everett, Joely Fisher
Year made: 1999
Extras: Scene access; soundtrack in 8 languages including English, French, Italian, Dutch and Polish; subtitles in 6 languages; subtitles for the hearing impaired in English.

If you ever wondered if a headache could take on physical form, let us confirm that it can: it's a shiny disc about 5 inches across with the words 'Inspector Gadget' printed on one side. At 75 minutes, *Inspector Gadget* is one of the shortest films we've ever reviewed. That works out at 26p per minute, and not even Sky's pay-per-view channels charge that much. Even so, it's not nearly short enough for our liking. In this witless live-action remake of the cartoon series, Broderick (in another of his great career choices after *Godzilla*) plays a dorky security guard who gets blown up by the evil Claw (Everett) and is rebuilt by Fisher as Inspector Gadget, the kid-friendly RoboCop. After that, the film kind of stumbles around aimlessly for a while before giving up and ending with the horrible threat of a sequel. *Inspector Gadget* is apparently aimed at two-year-olds, since these days three-year-olds are far too media-savvy to be amused by simple shouting and people running into things. This makes the few parent-friendly 'jokes' that have been crowbarred into the script at inappropriate moments seem even more out of place. Most nauseating is the blatant product placement; Coke, Sprite and Skittles are plugged remorselessly, making you wonder which will rot first – the kids' teeth or their brains. For no good reason, an evil Gadget clone is introduced, which gives Broderick the chance to do a really bad rip-off of Jim Carrey as The Mask for far too long. Not that this is the worst performance in the film; Everett's mugging is so embarrassing, it seems like he has to be doing it that way as a dare. As a DVD, *Inspector Gadget* is reasonable if not spectacular – a couple of scenes take full advantage of 5.1 surround, and for the most part the picture is good (though there's one FX scene, on a bridge, that looks truly awful, but this is probably down to the film rather than the disc). However, the Disney brand should immediately warn regular DVD buyers how many extras to expect – the same number as how many minutes of enjoyment you'll get from the film. A hint – it's not 75.

FINAL VERDICT

Picture ☆☆☆☆ Sound ☆☆☆☆ Entertainment ☆
Extras ☆ Value ☆
OVERALL ☆☆

INSTINCT

Price: £15.99
Supplied by: Buena Vista Home Entertainment
Type of disc: Dual layer, single-sided
No of chapters: 21
Film format(s)/length: 2.35:1 widescreen enhanced / 118 mins
Audio format: Dolby Digital 5.1
Director: John Turtletaub
Starring: Anthony Hopkins, Cuba Gooding Jr, Donald Sutherland
Year made: 1999
Extras: Scene access; sound track in English, German, French, Italian and Czech; multiligual subtitles; subtitles for the hearing impaired in English.

This tepid pairing of Oscar winners Hopkins and Gooding Jr isn't as bad as you may have heard, but still isn't exactly great. It's a bit of mystery, some prison drama thrown in and a hint of *Gorillas in the Mist*, yet fails to live up to the sum of its parts, opting for clichés throughout instead of exploring the potential of the premise. It's appropriate that our old friends Buena Vista are behind the disc, because if you want an empty disc to go with an empty film, they're the folks to call. Not even a trailer in the extras department just leaves you with the movie, which is actually presented well. The anamorphically enhanced picture is cleanly presented, while the sound mix thumps in all the right places. There may be enough here to warrant a curious rental, but unless you're a sucker for below-average films, there's no reason to buy it.

FINAL VERDICT

Picture ☆☆☆☆ Sound ☆☆☆☆ Entertainment ☆☆
Extras ☆ Value ☆☆
OVERALL ☆☆

IN THE LINE OF FIRE

Price: £19.99
Supplied by: DVD Net (0181 890 2520)
Type of disc: Single layer, single-sided
No of chapters: 21
Film format(s)/length: 2.35:1 widescreen anamorphic / 123 mins
Director: Wolfgang Petersen
Starring: Clint Eastwood, John Malkovich, Rene Russo
Year made: 1993
Extras: Scene selection; Dolby Surround or Dolby Digital sound options; subtitles; general trailer.

Frank Horrigan (Eastwood) is an embittered secret service agent plagued by memories of his inaction at JFK's side on that fateful day in Dallas, 1963. Thirty years later when called to a routine search Horrigan uncovers a sinister plot masterminded by ex-government assassin and 'Wet Boy', Mich Leary (Malkovich). A master of disguise and ruthless killer, Leary is intent on killing the President of the United States and the only thing between him and his ultimate goal is Horrigan, who's desperate to banish the demons of the past. Wolfgang Peterson once again shows his mastery of the lens and *In the Line of Fire* is surely his best film and one of the most accomplished thrillers this decade. Eastwood's gives his finest performance since *Unforgiven* and is ably supported by a sizzling Russo. Malkovich too is mesmerising as Leary, whose impassioned betrayal speeches and chilling moments of brutality make this film so exciting to watch. The picture quality of this DVD is high and complements Petersen's long tracking shots and dynamic composition (the rooftop chase is a perfect example of this). Run this DVD through a proper Dolby Digital sound system and you're in for a treat, with crystal clear gun shots, Leary's gravely tones, and of course Morricone's up-tempo soundtrack. *In the Line of Fire* is by any measurement a superb movie and all the better for being on DVD although Columbia TriStar has done nothing to enhance this disc for fans of the film. Apart from a choice of Dolby Surround or Dolby Digital, the only other option is a general DVD trailer. A dreadful shame given the potential – how the effects shots were done, profiles of the actors, perhaps something on the assassination of JFK?

FINAL VERDICT

Picture ☆☆☆☆ Sound ☆☆☆☆

Entertainment ☆☆☆☆☆ Extras ☆ Value ☆☆☆
OVERALL ☆☆☆☆

THE IRON GIANT

Price: £15.99
Supplied by: Warner Home Video
Type of disc: Dual layer, single-sided
No of chapters: 30
Film format(s)/length: 2.35:1 widescreen enhanced / 87 mins
Audio format: Dolby Digital 5.1
Director: Brad Bird
Starring the voices of: Jennifer Aniston, Harry Connick Jr, Eli Marienthal
Year made: 1999
Extras: Scene access; 'Making of' documentary; trailer; biographies; 'Cha-hua-hua' music video; soundtrack and subtitles in English; DVD-ROM Internet links and Web Chat access.

Once in a while, a film comes along that works so well on every level that it genuinely captures the heart of anyone who watches it, thereby deserving to be rightly considered a modern classic. That film is, of course, Steven Seagal's *Out for Justice*. Just kidding. It's actually *The Iron Giant*, the cinema debut of former *Simpsons* director Brad Bird, and it instantly establishes him as a name to watch out for in the future. *The Iron Giant* is as near to faultless as films can get, an utterly delightful fable that's genuine family entertainment while still having enough of an edge behind it to make it equally watchable for the sprogless. Based on the late Poet Laureate Ted Hughes's book *The Iron Man*, and 'Hollywoodised' with more fidelity than you might think, *The Iron Giant* is set in 1957, with Sputnik orbiting the Earth and America at its most paranoid about evil foreign invaders. Misfit schoolboy Hogarth Hughes (Marienthal, given dialogue that lets him talk and act like a real kid instead of Hollywood's usual miniaturised adults) hears a wild story about a giant metal man crashing to Earth outside his small town. Thrilled at the prospect of meeting a creature from outer space, he sets out into the woods that night and finds that the story is true. There's a 50 foot high, metal-eating robot wandering around, and after Hogarth rescues it from electrocution the two become secret friends. Unfortunately, Hogarth isn't the only one who's heard about the robot. Smarmy government agent Kent Mansley (Christopher McDonald), a kind of evil Fox Mulder, perceives the Iron Giant as a threat to national security, and will do anything first to find the Giant, and then to destroy it. Meanwhile, Hogarth and beatnik scrapyard owner

Dean McCoppin (Connick Jr) discover that the amnesiac Giant has a dark secret. The question is, will the robot's new-found friendship prove stronger than its original programming? The cynical will doubtless carp that the story is really just a variation on *ET*, but only the truly joyless could fail to be entertained by *The Iron Giant*. It's at once child-like wish fulfilment (what kid *wouldn't* want a friendly giant robot at their beck and call?), a simple but enormously enjoyable story expertly told, a very strong anti-war parable and a mildly subversive reminder that family and friends are more important than Big Brother. The animation – seamlessly mixing traditional hand-drawn characters with the computer-generated Giant – is as good as anything Disney has produced recently, and for the first time in decades brings Warner Bros on a level pegging with its long-time cartoon rival. This Region 2 DVD for once has all the extras of its Region 1 counterpart, right down to the DVD-ROM Internet links. While the list of extras isn't exactly massive, it does show that Warner is at the forefront of the UK's DVD companies when it comes to providing viewers with more bang for their buck. The 'Making of' is actually a TV special commissioned for Warner's US television channel The WB and comes complete with advert breaks, but even so it's quite insightful. Director Bird talks about the genesis of the film as well as the process of how it was made, and you also get to see a great deal of behind-the-scenes detail about the creation of the animation. *The Iron Giant* is one of the small number of DVDs that should be in absolutely everybody's collection. It works equally well for both kids and adults in the same way as *Toy Story*, and it's arguably a better story than *ET* because it manages to engage the emotions without using any of Spielberg's more manipulative tricks. In short, it's flawless entertainment.

FINAL VERDICT

Picture ☆☆☆☆☆ Sound ☆☆☆☆
Entertainment ☆☆☆☆☆ Extras ☆☆☆☆
Value ☆☆☆☆☆
OVERALL ☆☆☆☆☆

THE ISLAND OF DR MOREAU

Price: £15.99
Supplied by: Entertainment in Video
Type of disc: Single layer, single-sided
No of chapters: 12
Film format(s)/length: 2.35:1 anamorphic / 91 mins
Audio format: Dolby Surround
Director: John Frankenheimer

Starring: Marlon Brando, Val Kilmer, David Thewlis
Year made: 1996
Extras: Scene access.

Val Kilmer's acting career took a dive when this dire production staggered out in 1996. Loosely based on the H G Wells novel, the silver screen resurrects isolated genetic scientist Dr Moreau (Brando) and his human/animal experiments. Subject to much ridicule, and rightly so, *The Island of Dr Moreau* relies heavily on its acting talent to steer it in the right direction, and as such the one-time Godfather perhaps should call this acting lark a day. Never once is his character perceived as a genetic genius, and the result is a plot that's less convincing then the acting. Thewlis (replacing Rob Morrow during filming) and *The Craft's* Fairuza Balk (Moreau's daughter Aissa) provide the only stability for the viewer as, surprise surprise, the human-like beasts Moreau has created begin to instigate an uprising. The only positive point to be gained from this DVD is the good picture quality and excellent vibrancy of the colours throughout the movie – if only the actors were as such. Still, if it wasn't for this cheesy flick *South Park's* scientist Mephesto would be without his freaky assistant Kevin, and the inspiration for Mini-Me in *Austin Powers* would have only been a passing thought. Like the film's enjoyment factor the special features are completely absent – and distributors take note, scene access is not a 'special' feature, it's a requirement of the format. When all is said and done, this fickle flick will usurp 91 minutes of life that you will never get back.

FINAL VERDICT

Picture ☆☆☆☆ Sound ☆☆☆ Entertainment ☆
Extras ☆ Value ☆
OVERALL ☆

I STILL KNOW WHAT YOU DID LAST SUMMER

Price: £19.99
Supplied by: Columbia TriStar Home Video
Type of disc: Single layer, single-sided
No of chapters: 28
Film format(s)/length: 16:9 widescreen enhanced / 97 mins
Audio format: Dolby Digital 5.1
Director: Danny Cannon
Starring: Jennifer Love Hewitt, Freddie Prinze Jr, Brandy Norwood
Year made: 1998
Extras: Scene access; filmographies; 2 trailers; 'Making of' featurette; Jennifer Love Hewitt music video; sound-

track in German; subtitles in 15 languages.

He might have lost a hand and been dumped into the ocean, but that wacky Fisherman just won't give up. The very silly *I Know What You Did Last Summer* now gets an even sillier sequel with more gore and even fewer brains. Julie (Hewitt) and her replacement best mates – most of the original bunch were slaughtered in the last film – win a trip to a remote Caribbean island. When they get there, though, they find that their hotel is shut down for the hurricane season – it's a trap! It doesn't take long before a hook-handed guy in a raincoat is stalking Julie once again, and the bodies start piling up. There is only one good moment in the whole film: a cannon-fodder hunk is complaining about the turn of events, finishing his moan with, "And I haven't seen one god-damn psycho killer." Moments later, a goddamn psycho killer makes his on cue appearance. The rest of *I Still Know…* is utter tosh, with plot holes you could sail a trawler through and a gifted killer who can teleport between locations – as the script demands – and as for the 'surprise' ending. Guess what – he's not really dead! The behind-the-scenes feature is mostly made up of clips from the trailer (which is also on the DVD) and the less said about Hewitt's music video, the better. Not even the amazing number of cleavage shots make *I Still Know…* worth buying.

FINAL VERDICT

Picture ☆☆☆☆ Sound ☆☆☆ Entertainment ☆☆ Extras ☆☆ Value ☆☆☆

OVERALL ☆☆

It Could Happen to You

Price: £19.99
Supplied by: Columbia TriStar Home Video
Type of disc: Single layer, single-sided
No of chapters: 28
Film format(s)/length: 16:9 widescreen enhanced / 98 mins
Audio format: Dolby Digital 5.1
Director: Andrew Bergman
Starring: Nicolas Cage, Bridget Fonda, Rosie Perez
Year made: 1994
Extras: Scene access; theatrical trailer; filmographies; multilingual subtitles.

No, it won't be happening to you, despite this charming film trying to convince you otherwise. The chances of winning the lottery are slim enough, but finding a generous policeman to split his winnings with you are practically non-existent. Still, this is the scenario we are asked to believe, and this movie manages to bend realism rather effortlessly. Cage plays Charlie Lang, a policeman who offers to split his following day's lottery winnings with the waitress (Fonda) he can't afford to tip. Charlie wins the 4 million dollar Jackpot and eventually the affections of Yvonne, whilst his wife Murial (Perez) heads off to climb the social ladder. It's the far-fetched type of love story that could have easily been a Jimmy Stewart film 40 years ago, and is so enjoyable to watch, you feel guilty saying bad things to say about it. Unfortunately, a couple of things need pointing out. Despite the unexpected closing act, the midsection of this film slows down so much, you'd be forgiven for thinking that you've sat on the pause button of your remote. Also, Cage has trouble understanding the concept of too nice, and at times you may feel compelled to slap him rather than sympathise with him. The DVD itself is so typical of a Region 2 disc, that it's hardly worth mentioning the extras. The sad fact is that the only reason this DVD shines above any other that Cage has put out, is that it isn't a flipper. Hardly the mark of a great DVD.

FINAL VERDICT

Picture ☆☆☆ Sound ☆☆☆☆ Entertainment ☆☆☆☆ Extras ☆☆ Value ☆☆

OVERALL ☆☆☆

It's a Wonderful Life

Price: £17.99
Supplied by: Universal
Type of disc: Dual layer, single-sided
No of chapters: 18
Film format(s)/length: 4:3 regular / 168 mins
Audio format: Stereo
Director: Frank Capra
Starring: James Stewart, Donna Reed, Lionel Barrymore
Year made: 1946
Extras: Scene access; *Making of It's a Wonderful Life* (23 mins); an introduction by and interview with Frank Capra Jr.

The name Frank Capra has now become a descriptive term when it comes to reviewing films. Anything which has that all-important saccharine feel-good factor – for which the acclaimed producer/director is famous for – is instantly labelled as being Capra-esque. This can be alienating for the unenlightened, so it is good timing on Universal's part that it has remastered Capra's masterpiece, *It's a Wonderful Life*, on the modern medium of DVD. Originally released in 1946, this classic stars James Stewart as happy-go-lucky George Bailey, who lives in happy-go-lucky Bedford Falls. This idyllic representation of American small town life tapped into the hopes and desires of a country counting the cost of the Second World War, but has since come to represent a reminder of how a person's worth is measured by the friends they have. It may be a stomach-churning sentiment for a more cynical 21st century audience, but that hasn't stopped TV companies dusting down the movie for Christmas audiences for the past 5 decades. Universal has gone to town with its remastering of *It's a Wonderful Life* on DVD. From the attractive silver-embossed cover, through to its short, but appropriately sweet, 16-page booklet. It's a pity Universal couldn't remaster the soundtrack above the provided stereo format, but given the age of the film, it may have had its hands tied on that score. *It's a Wonderful Life* has been a family favourite for over 50 years and is an essential addition to any discerning DVD movie collection.

FINAL VERDICT

Picture ☆☆☆ Sound ☆☆☆ Entertainment ☆☆☆☆
Extras ☆☆☆☆ Value ☆☆☆☆
OVERALL ☆☆☆☆

Jackie Brown

Price: £15.99
Supplied by: DVD World (01705 796662)
Type of disc: Single layer, double sided (flipper)
No of chapters: 22
Film format(s)/length: 1.85:1 widescreen / 148 mins
Audio format: Dolby Digital 5.1
Director: Quentin Tarantino
Starring: Pam Grier, Samuel L Jackson, Robert Forster
Year made: 1997
Extras: Scene access.

I'm not a big fan of Quentin Tarantino. I liked *Reservoir Dogs*, but *Pulp Fiction* really annoyed me. I'm not a prude – either of my ex-girlfriends will tell you that I've occasionally had sex with the lights on (though eyes closed, obviously) – but *Pulp Fiction*'s ridiculous gratuity, so adored by the nodding, clever-clever *Guardian* readers, struck me as being cheap and easy. Its widespread acclaim from closet cinema-goers really bothered me the most. Many crawled out of the woodwork like Manchester United supporters at the end of a season to champion a film and director without being able to explain why. Those that shouted, swore and taunted me when I dared to think differently seemed a little too eager to appear to *love* it rather than just love it. It was an average story told in a pretentious manner, wrapped up with over-the-top swearing – hey, it's not hard; I was talking like that at school (but don't tell my parents) – and irrelevant moments of graphic violence. Anyone can write that mind-numbing nonsense. It takes real genius to steer clear. So it was with immense trepidation that I extracted *Jackie Brown* from its moulded plastic home and slid it into the front-loading carrier of the DVD player. At 148 minutes, it demanded a commitment, and one that I wasn't entirely confident I'd be able to give – being tantamount to asking me to move in when I'd prefer, you know, a little more freedom to see other DVDs. Thankfully, my fears were misguided. It's almost as if Quentin's mum threatened to ground him until he grew up, such is the restrained direction of the film. Elmore Leonard's *Rum Punch* was the film's inspiration and although it has obviously been Tarantino-ised, featuring copious amounts of 'f'-words, those expecting a similar amount of blood-letting and gunfire will thankfully be disappointed. Pam Grier is the eponymous airline stewardess caught between a sophisticated police sting and the loyalty to her not-so-gainful employer, brilliantly played by the ultra-cool Samuel L Jackson. When asked to ensure the safe but police-observed transfer of half a million dollars in cash to ensnare a high-roller in LA's underworld, Jackie Brown is faced with a stark choice: go along as planned, or try to double-cross one or more of the film's other leads. It's gripping stuff – and told well, with Tarantino's trademark chronology-manipulation working most effectively. Though the ending is not entirely unpredictable, it's never telegraphed, with enough shocks and twists to maintain interest. Picture-wise, everything's in order and the soundtrack – the definition of cool – excels on DVD. But while the lack of extras is a frustration one can bear, having to flip the disc three-quarters of the way through is unnecessary bother. There's no need for it, and Warner should hang its head in shame for squeezing an extra few pence in profit at the inconvenience of its audience. That said, short of *LA Confidential*, this is a crime *noir* that is worth the price – though many may prefer to rent and view once than demand its inclusion in their collection.

FINAL VERDICT

Picture ☆☆☆☆ Sound ☆☆☆☆
Entertainment ☆☆☆☆☆ Extras ☆ Value ☆☆☆
OVERALL ☆☆☆

Jakob the Liar

Price: £19.99
Supplied by: Columbia TriStar Home Video
Type of disc: Single-layer, single-sided
No of chapters: 28
Film format(s)/length: 1.85:1 anamorphic / 115 mins
Audio format: Dolby Digital 5.1

Director: Peter Kassovitz
Starring: Robin Williams, Bob Balaban, Liev Schreiber
Year made: 1999
Extras: Scene access; behind-the-scenes featurette; director's commentary; filmographies; theatrical trailer; *Awakenings* trailer; isolated score; soundtrack in English and German; subtitles in 11 languages.

The holocaust has been the subject of some exceptional films. Sadly, *Jakob the Liar* falls disappointingly short compared to the likes of *Life is Beautiful*. Though not a bad film, it doesn't quite come up to scratch. It tells the story of Jakob (Williams), a Polish Jew who discovers that, by falsely telling his friends that he has a radio and is passing on 'good news', he can spread hope in an embittered community. An odd combination of bleak realism (the portrayal of day-to-day life is excellent), humour and over-emotional scenes, it is thoroughly watchable but veers towards sentimentality too frequently. A slightly murky picture also does little to help the movie's gloomier scenes. A substantial collection of extras, including a commentary from Kassovitz and a short 'Making of' featurette, do make this a decent package, but the film is too schmaltzy to rank alongside its peers.

FINAL VERDICT
Picture ☆☆☆ Sound ☆☆☆☆
Entertainment ☆☆☆ Extras ☆☆☆☆ Value ☆☆☆
OVERALL ☆☆☆

JAMES AND THE GIANT PEACH

Price: £21.99
Supplied by: 20th Century Fox Home Entertainment
Type of disc: Single layer, single-sided
No of chapters: 15
Film format(s)/length: 16:9 widescreen / 76 mins
Audio format: Dolby Digital 5.1
Director: Henry Selick
Starring the voices of: Simon Callow, Susan Sarandon Richard Dreyfuss
Year made: 1996
Extras: Scene access; original theatrical trailer; music video by Randy Newman; production featurette; subtitles for the hard of hearing in English.

There's something uniquely endearing about Roald Dahl stories. This tale of a lonely orphaned boy who escapes his evil aunts by floating away to New York city in a gigantic peach is as quirky and lovable as Dahl could get. Fortunately, this adaptation doesn't stray too far from the story's original charm. The script retains the feel of a Dahl book, whilst the stunningly gorgeous stop motion animation has the

unique seal of Tim Burton (a producer on this project) all over it. Everything about this film is sweet and lovely. The sets and production design of the animated models bring the characters beautifully to life. The look of this film is simply mesmerising. The star-studded cast, hidden well behind their Plasticine counterparts, allows the characters to carry the film rather than the famous voices behind them. The childish theme of the film is scripted with such a mature nature that it is easy for any adult who's watching to be just as compelled as the under-12 audience. In fact the only thing to let you down on this DVD is the DVD itself. It just doesn't fulfil its promise. The production featurette is little more than a trailer with a voiceover and one or two behind-the-scenes clips thrown in, and the music video is a reshowing of the trailer, mixed with footage of Randy Newman recording the song 'Good News' in a studio. This film can do nothing but charm. It's beautiful, inoffensive, and the best Dahl adaptation to date. Shame the DVD doesn't use a similar amount of imagination.

FINAL VERDICT
Picture ☆☆☆☆ Sound ☆☆☆☆
Entertainment ☆☆☆☆ Extras ☆☆ Value ☆☆☆
OVERALL ☆☆☆

JASON AND THE ARGONAUTS

Price: £19.99
Supplied by: Columbia TriStar Home Video
Type of disc: Single layer, single-sided
No of chapters: 28
Film format(s)/length: 1.85:1 widescreen enhanced / 100 mins
Audio format: Mono
Director: Don Chaffey
Starring: Todd Armstrong, Nancy Kovak, Honor Blackman
Year made: 1963
Extras: Scene access; *The Ray Harryhausen Chronicles*, documenting the man and his movies; original theatrical trailer; interview with Ray Harryhausen; soundtrack in French, German, Italian and Spanish; multilingual subtitles.

Along with *The Wizard of Oz* and *The Sound of Music*, *Jason and the Argonauts* has been a firm family favourite for decades. Based upon ancient Greek mythology, this showcase for the animated modelling talents of Ray Harryhausen has lost none of its charm in 37 years. The plot has the hero embark on a quest to track down the legendary Golden Fleece, which he believes will help him reclaim the throne of Thessaly.

There are some truly unforgettable moments along the way, particularly if you originally saw the movie as an impressionable child, like the living 100-foot bronze statue of Talos and the seven-headed Hydra. However, the stand-out moment of this classic piece of fantasy fiction has to be the 'children of the teeth', the walking skeletons created by black magic and the teeth of the Hydra. Columbia has gone to town in the subtitles department, with a whopping 20 languages accounted for, and the picture quality is more than admirable considering that the original film is over 30 years-old. There's also the original theatrical trailer, which since it originates from the early Sixties has a certain nostalgic appeal, but the best extras are *The Ray Harryhausen Chronicles* documentary (providing all the essential info on Harryhausen and his films) and an interview with the man himself. You can keep *Episode 1* and the Battle Droids, ol' Harryhausen knew where it was at!

FINAL VERDICT

Picture ☆☆☆☆ Sound ☆☆ Entertainment ☆☆☆
Extras ☆☆☆ Value ☆☆☆
OVERALL ☆☆☆

JAWBREAKER

Price: £19.99
Supplied by: Columbia TriStar Home Video
Type of disc: Single layer, single-sided
No of chapters: 28
Film format(s)/length: 16:9 widescreen enhanced / 83 mins
Audio format: Dolby Digital 5.1
Director: Darren Stein
Starring: Rose McGowan, Rebecca Gayheart, Julie Benz
Year made: 1998
Extras: Scene access; behind-the-scenes featurette (approximately 10 mins); audio commentary by director Darren Stein; theatrical trailer; filmographies on main cast and crew; music video from Imperial Teen: 'Yoo Hoo'; soundtrack in German (5.1); subtitles in 15 languages.

Somewhat of a status symbol for schoolkids, the seemingly impossible task of successfully eating a jawbreaker sweet without actually choking to death was sure to earn you respect on the playground. However, one rather lethal ball of candy violently upsets life at a typically 'Hollywoodised' high school in Darren Stein's blacker-than-black comedy. A kidnapping prank between a group of girlfriends ends up with the prom queen dying via a jawbreaker lodged in her throat. The cover-up that follows is grotesque, as the

ringleader of the girl gang – played with relish by Rose McGowan – turns friend against friend in a comedy that never lives up to its potential. Owing more than a nod and an eye-linered wink to the likes of *Heathers* and, *Clueless, Jawbreaker* limps lamely along, and can almost be heard whispering in vain for a script rewrite. The performances are passable, and beyond the flimsy leching quality provided by McGowan, Benz and Gayheart (cleavages and butts aplenty!) there's nothing here to warrant more than one very painful viewing. Stein's direction is definitely his strong point – believe us, his writing certainly isn't! – and there are some clever moments, like his cartoon-style scene changes and sound-effects in particular. The weakness of the source movie is made up somewhat by the attractive spread of extras laid on by Columbia. After checking off the expected theatrical trailer, audio commentary and filmographies, Columbia also throws in the bonuses of a music video and a 10-minute behind-the-scenes featurette. It's a pity these great extras couldn't have been attached to a better movie, but they will probably make the package more attractive to a first time audience unaware of the dire quality of the film.

FINAL VERDICT

Picture ☆☆☆☆ Sound ☆☆☆☆
Entertainment ☆☆ Extras ☆☆☆ Value ☆☆☆
OVERALL ☆☆☆

JAWS: 25TH ANNIVERSARY EDITION

Price: £19.99
Supplied by: Universal
Type of disc: Dual layer, single-sided
No of chapters: 20
Film format(s)/length: 2.35:1 anamorphic / 125 mins
Audio format: Dolby Digital 5.1
Director: Steven Spielberg
Starring: Roy Scheider, Richard Dreyfuss, Robert Shaw
Year made: 1975
Extras: *The Making of Jaws* documentary (50 mins); 10 deleted scenes (9 mins); outtakes; original cinematic trailer, plus re-release special trailer; artwork gallery including storyboards; production notes; 'Get Out of the Water' trivia game; 'Shark World' shark trivia screens; screensaver for PC DVD-ROM; talent profiles on the stars and director, including filmographies; soundtrack in English, French, German, Italian and Spanish; subtitles in 21 languages.

Just when you thought it was safe to assume that Steven Spielberg was never going to release his early masterpiece on DVD…*Jaws* arrives and we are pleased to announce that it's every bit as good as you remember. *Jaws* was originally released in the summer of 1975 and quickly became one of the biggest-grossing films of all time. It's a story about control, the lack of it, and the small matter of a 25-foot shark who gets an attack of the munchies and lays claim to the beaches off sleepy Amity island. What makes *Jaws* such an enjoyable film is that it's a collection of classic scenes – each one better than the last. The death of the girl at the start is a masterful piece of cinema, as is the chaotic first beach scene, Quint's blackboard scratching, Ben Gardner's head, "You're gonna need a bigger boat", and of course Quint's chilling USS Indianapolis monologue. The first thing that strikes you about this DVD, particularly if you have a sound system that makes an F-16 on combat power sound shy and retiring, is that the Oscar-winning score has been fully restored. Not only is that soundtrack by John Williams intact, it's positively thriving. The separate audio channels pick out conversations you've never noticed before, particularly on the beach and in the school room scene. The tortured screams of the naked swimmer at the beginning have never sounded so terrifying. *Jaws* in glorious 2.35:1 anamorphic widescreen is how it was meant to be viewed, and for those who have only seen the pan-and-scan TV version, it is a rare treat to own the definitive copy. Spielberg makes no secret of his hatred for the 4:3 aspect ratio and you can see why. Widescreen *Jaws* is an epic movie that fills every corner of the screen. Many scenes, such as Brody's touching moment with his son, or the sweeping shot of the shark pulling all four barrels under the *Orca*, lose all impact when forced into multiple cuts or mis-framed. Make no mistake about it, this is the ultimate version of the film that invented the summer blockbuster. For the majority of the movie the picture quality is of such a high standard you'd think it was only filmed this year. Despite the age of the original stock, colours remain rich, particularly during Quint's lonely vigil on the bow of the *Orca*, and during the frenetic 4th of July beach scene. It is here that Spielberg's precise use of the colour yellow to denote danger and confusion is heightened by the DVD's vivid hues. Curiously though, certain shots, particularly at dusk, are packed with scratches and imperfections that betray the lack of thorough remastering. It's almost as if the guys in charge of cleaning the negatives got so enthralled by the thrill of the shark chase that they forgot to finish up. In fact the biggest disappointment of the film today, especially on pin-sharp DVD, is the shark itself. We defy anyone to not laugh when, at the climax of the film, what looks like a large flabby grey

dildo slaps onto the back of the boat and starts snapping its jaws with all the raw power of a ventriloquist's dummy. Perhaps Spielberg should have 'done a Lucas' and recreated the shark for this Anniversary Edition? The DVD itself is a restrained, nay respectful affair, which eschews gaudy presentation in favour of cool blues, lapping waves, and the highly resonant tolling of a lonely marker buoy. A major omission of course is a full length audio commentary, which would have been a fascinating insight into one of the toughest shoots in movie history. To make up for this, the 50-minute documentary is genuinely fascinating, and includes interviews and anecdotes with almost every actor, extra and effects dweeb. A worthy extra, but you do actually get it on the VHS version, as well as the outtakes and deleted scenes which could have done with some kind of explanation. *Jaws* on DVD is as it was meant to be. Bigger, wider, louder, better. A must buy for fans of Spielberg's more adult work and a fitting tribute to one of the most talked about films of the last millennium.

FINAL VERDICT

Picture ☆☆☆☆ Sound ☆☆☆☆☆

Entertainment ☆☆☆☆☆ Extras ☆☆☆☆

Value ☆☆☆☆

OVERALL ☆☆☆☆☆

JEAN DE FLORETTE

Price: £19.99

Supplied by: Pathé Distribution Ltd

Type of disc: Single layer, single-sided

No of chapters: 29

Film format(s)/length: 2.35:1 letterbox / 116 mins

Audio format: Dolby Surround

Director: Claude Berri

Starring: Gerard Depardieu, Yves Montand, Daniel Auteil

Year made: 1986

Extras: Scene access; theatrical trailer; subtitles in English.

Bonjour la class! Yes, that film your French teacher showed you before you failed your O-levels is back out again. It's a welcome return too, because *Jean De Florette* features increasingly rare virtues like acting (*mon Dieu!*) and an understandable script (*zut alors!*) Perhaps more importantly though, Claude Berri's film inspired a certain Flemish beer advert (ooh la la). There are plenty of reasons to watch the film, but are there any bonuses to buying it on DVD? Sadly, the answer is a resounding '*non*'! If you buy this Pathé disc you get a murky picture, a very dull trailer and English subtitles which you can turn on and off. Educational it may be but as entertainment it's missing more than a certain *je ne sais quoi*. More seriously though, why couldn't the film have been bundled with *Manon Des Sources*? Now that would have been quite a package.

FINAL VERDICT

Picture ☆☆ Sound ☆☆☆ Entertainment ☆☆☆☆
Extras ☆☆ Value ☆☆
OVERALL ☆☆☆

JEREMIAH JOHNSON

Price: £15.99
Supplied by: Warner Bros
Type of disc: Single layer, single-sided
No of chapters: 29
Film format(s)/length: 16:9 widescreen / 111 mins
Director: Sydney Pollack
Starring: Robert Redford, Will Geer, Stefan Gierasch
Year made: 1972
Extras: Scene access; production notes; featurette: *The Saga of Jeremiah Johnson*; trailer.

Disenfranchised by the encroachment of civilisation, circa 1825, Jeremiah Johnson (Redford) sets out as a lone trapper in the Rocky Mountains, only to discover an idealistic vision of nature has its price; harsh elements, wolves and grizzly bears. He finds help in the shape of an old mountain man (Will Geer, best known as grandpa Walton), but pays the ultimate price, as the Crow tribe massacres his family after he escorts the US Cavalry through a sacred burial ground. Pollack received best director Oscar for Johnson, filmed entirely in Utah, it's a panoramic, widescreen feast, although 21 chapters shows it doesn't linger too long. The package features production notes and scene access, as well as a mini biopic about the man. Achieves as much as *Dances With Wolves* in half the time.

FINAL VERDICT

Picture ☆☆☆ Sound ☆☆ Entertainment ☆☆☆
Extras ☆☆☆ Value ☆☆☆
OVERALL ☆☆☆

JERRY MAGUIRE

Price: £19.99
Supplied by: DVD World (01705 796662)
Type of disc: Single layer, single-sided
No of chapters: 24
Film format(s)/length: 1.85:1 widescreen /133 mins
Director: Cameron Crowe
Starring: Tom Cruise, Renée Zellweger, Cuba Gooding Jnr
Year made: 1996
Extras: Scene access/subtitles; MPEG Multichannel (5.1); Dolby Digital (5.1) audio set-ups; general forthcoming movies trailer.

Jerry Maguire is one of those films where you realise that it's okay to watch something that doesn't have a helicopter crash in it (they do exist). It's a feel-good movie. Yes, tears will be shed, but because it's got sports in it, you can easily claim you were wincing at a groin injury. Maguire (Cruise) is a sports agent, one of the frequently unseen sharks who negotiate ludicrous zillion dollar endorsement deals for America's sporting heroes. During a conference Jerry has a sudden attack of morals and writes a mission statement outlining the need for a more caring industry – less clients, more personal attention. Unurprisingly this doesn't sit well with his employers and he is promptly sacked by the superbly smarmy Bob Sugar (Jay Mohr). Left with his most outrageous but unsigned client Rod Tidwell (Gooding Jnr – deserving of the Oscar), Jerry must start from scratch and practice what he preaches. Cameron Crowe's film is pure entertainment with a script so character-driven you don't have to be a sports fan to enjoy it. Zellweger as Dorothy Boyd, Maguire's accountant and love interest wobbles her bottom lip a lot, and both are totally upstaged by her cute son Ray (Jonathan Lipnicki), but it's difficult to find fault with a film that is almost guaranteed to leave you with a broad smile long after it's over. As a DVD, *Jerry Maguire* is characteristic of many of Columbia's discs and includes the bare minimum of sound options and subtitles, plus a general trailer for forthcoming releases – not even the theatrical trailer for this film! Tom can grin all he wants, but it doesn't take away the fact that this DVD's bad value for money.

FINAL VERDICT

Picture ☆☆☆☆ Sound ☆☆☆
Entertainment ☆☆☆☆☆ Extras ☆ Value ☆☆
OVERALL ☆☆☆

JFK

Price: £15.99
Supplied by: DVDplus (www.dvdplus.co.uk)
Type of disc: Dual layer, single-sided
No of chapters: 42
Film format(s)/length: 2.35:1 widescreen / 181 mins
Audio format: Dolby Surround
Director: Oliver Stone
Starring: Kevin Costner, Kevin Bacon, Tommy Lee Jones
Year made: 1991
Extras: Scene access; French and Italian soundtrack; subtitles in 8 languages; English and Italian subtitles for the hearing impaired.

If there's one thing more scary than the conspiracy behind the assassination of President John Kennedy, then it's the fact that Oliver Stone can make you believe his version of events so utterly. *JFK* is so gripping from start to finish, you scarcely notice that the film lasts for more than three hours, and Stone's genius is being able to convey so much information in such a digestible form without boredom setting in. The entire film is a thundering mish-mash of facts, re-enactments, whispered conversations and strong performances from the likes of Tommy Lee Jones, Joe Pesci and Donald Sutherland. On DVD you'd expect the hundreds of different film techniques and effects to be brought to life, but instead the picture quality is only slightly above VHS. You'll find there's noticeable grain and some annoying flicker on subtitles. The real shocking aspect of this DVD, however, is that with all the source material, docu-footage and interviews that Stone must have had at his disposal, not one iota has been offered as an extra. Worst of all, the commentary from Stone himself that would have made this an essential purchase, is missing without trace. As it is, *JFK* on DVD is no improvement over the tape version. Pray for a special edition soon.

FINAL VERDICT

Picture ☆☆ Sound ☆☆ Entertainment ☆☆☆☆

Extras ☆ Value ☆☆

OVERALL ☆☆

JUDGE DREDD

Price: £19.99
Supplied by: Pathé Distribution
Type of disc: Dual layer, single-sided
No of chapters: 14
Film format(s)/length: 2.35:1 widescreen / 92 mins
Audio format: Dolby Digital 5.1
Director: Danny Cannon
Starring: Sylvester Stallone, Diane Lane, Rob Schneider
Year made: 1995
Extras: Scene access; featurette, *The Making of Judge Dredd*; cast and crew biographies; original theatrical trailer; subtitles for the hearing impaired in English.

Those who know nothing about the *2000AD* comic book character Judge Dredd will thankfully not be completely sold short by this big budget movie adaptation. The background history, character development and even the costumes mostly remain faithful to the original illustrated series. But there is still something that doesn't quite gel. This is Judge Dredd, but it's not the Judge Dredd that it could have been. The unhealthy elements of violence and a sterile society have been played woefully down in order to appeal to the mass market. It's quite sad really. This had all the potential to be a unique screen experience, taking one visual form and enhancing it by showing it through another. Unfortunately, *Judge Dredd* merely uses the original comic format as a backdrop on which to join up the same old Hollywood dots. Stallone clearly just watched *RoboCop* before each take to gain his experience and Rob Schneider, as Fergie, the comic relief sidekick, quickly becomes annoying. It's left to some stunning visual effects and a screen-stealing evil performance from Armand Assante to ressurect the proceedings. The disc has its fair share of extras, but nothing to knock your socks off. The animated menu is fun for a while, but the cast and crew biographies are somewhat lacking in detail and the 'Making of' documentary is more of a behind-the-scenes promo than anything of any interest. This movie is definitely worth a look, just to see how closely it sticks to the original concept, but if you've already got it on VHS, don't bother.

FINAL VERDICT

Picture ☆☆☆ Sound ☆☆☆☆ Entertainment ☆☆

Extras ☆☆ Value ☆☆☆

OVERALL ☆☆☆

JUNIOR

Price: £19.99
Supplied by: Universal
Type of disc: Single layer, single-sided
No of chapters: 18
Film format(s)/length: 1.85:1 anamorphic / 105 mins
Audio format: Dolby Digital 5.1
Director: Ivan Reitman
Starring: Arnold Schwarzenegger, Danny DeVito, Emma Thompson
Year made: 1994
Extras: Chapter access; featurette; trailer; Web links; production notes; cast and crew notes; soundtrack in English, French, German, Italian and Spanish; subtitles in 11 languages.

The Arnie/DeVito partnership that made a massive hit of *Twins* is dredged up once again in this comedy where chemistry is all-important. Arnie plays a man who, through the miracles of medicine and some persuasion from the devious DeVito, agrees to become pregnant. And herein lies the joke. The one and only, single, lonely joke. Yet it's quite funny. Watching the former action hero blast his way through gags instead of heads is fresh and amusing. Co-stars DeVito and Thompson – as the dazed scientist – thankfully add the more subtle laughs to the pot. With such an old film it's little wonder that there are few purposeful extras. The featurette is interesting as director Reitman makes a rare interview appearance, while the insights of the production notes only serve to show how the film misses the wider comments it seeks to make on sexual equality. *Junior* isn't a demanding DVD, but it's sure to please the puritans.

FINAL VERDICT

Picture ☆☆☆ Sound ☆☆☆ Entertainment ☆☆
Extras ☆☆ Value ☆☆
OVERALL ☆☆

JURASSIC PARK

Price: £19.99
Supplied by: Universal
Type of disc: Dual layer, single-sided
No of chapters: 20
Film format(s)/length: 1.85:1 anamorphic / 121 mins
Audio format: Dolby Digital 5.1
Director: Steven Spielberg
Starring: Sam Neill, Laura Dern, Jeff Goldblum
Year made: 1993
Extras: *The Making of Jurassic Park* documentary (50 mins); pre-production meeting footage; storyboards; animatics; foley artist spotlight; location scouting; production photos, design sketches and concept paintings; dinosaur encyclopaedia; trailers; *The Lost World* trailer; *Jurassic Park 3* teaser trailer; production notes; cast and crew notes; DVD-ROM features (including *Jurassic Park III* link); soundtrack in English and German; subtitles in 17 languages

Dinosaurs. Everybody loves 'em, it seems – judging from the box office results, nearly as much as they love camp comedy robots and noodle-armed teen pin-ups drowning on big boats. When they come from the world's most acclaimed director, people like them even more. So the only question that can be asked about the arrival of *Jurassic Park* on DVD can be, why has it taken so long? The movie, based on the novel by Michael Crichton, uses one of Crichton's (in fact, science fiction in general) most over-used themes – He Who Tampers In God's Domain Will Be Destroyed! From *Frankenstein* onwards, this seems to be a popular choice of plot, which makes you wonder why the cloners of Dolly and Monsanto's executives aren't being torn to shreds by giant mutant sheep and murderous GM soya beans. In this case, the tamperer is Richard Attenborough's John Hammond, a jovial Santa of a man who has financed the recreation of dinosaurs from fossilised DNA, with plans to profit from his mighty menagerie by turning a tropical island into the world's coolest zoo. Called into this setting are dinosaur experts Alan Grant (Neill) and Ellie Sattler (Dern), backed up by rock 'n' roll mathematician Ian Malcolm (Goldblum), Hammond's grandchildren and a slimy lawyer who might as well have 'eat me' tattooed on his forehead. The odd group has been summoned by Hammond to give his new attraction their thumbs-up and assure his investors that the park is safe – unfortunately, sabotage causes the dinosaurs to break free, and the gawpers find themselves hunted by predators that haven't had a decent snack for 65 million years… While the story is uncannily close to Crichton's own *Westworld*, with dinosaurs replacing robots, having Spielberg at the helm turns *Jurassic Park* into a ride as exciting as any roller coaster and a lot longer-lasting. Things take a while to get going, but once they do Spielberg uses every trick in his very fat book to heighten the tension. It's arguably more successful at doing so than *Jaws*, with a succession of nerve-shredding scenes – "Where's the goat?", the tree, the fence, the kitchen – that show exactly why Spielberg earns the big bucks. There's also the none-too-minor fact that *Jurassic Park*'s killers *don't* resemble deflated sex toys. As you'd hope for a film that won Oscars for Best Sound and Best Visual Effects, the DVD of *Jurassic Park* boasts suitably excellent picture and audio. The vivid greens of the jungle setting come through exceptionally well, and the transfer allows you to see every scale and wart on the dinosaurs' digitally-created hides. It's the sound department where *Jurassic Park* truly stands out, however – having the T-rex bellowing away seemingly inches from your face is the stuff of nightmares. (It could be argued that the 'PG' rating is a tad generous for younger kids, but saying that the BBFC is being too *lenient* for once is getting into weird Mary Whitehousian territory, so we won't.) While the list of extras is suitably monstrous, there is one roaring omission – Steven, where are you? For whatever reason, Spielberg has been unwilling to lend his voice to commentary tracks for his movies on DVD, and sadly his biggest hit to date is devoid of his movie-making insights. Of all the directors in the world, Spielberg (closely followed by Lucas and Cameron) is surely the one fans most want to go through all the details of his projects. All the same, even without Spielberg's direct involvement, *Jurassic Park*'s special features offer plenty to interest those who like hot behind-the-scenes action to accompany their blockbuster movies. *The Making of Jurassic Park* documentary, narrated by Darth Vader himself, James Earl Jones, is a surprisingly in-depth look at the film's shooting, concentrating heavily on the special effects side of things. Previously unseen footage includes the early tests done of the CGI dinosaurs, along with the original puppet footage, proving (if there were ever any doubt) that Spielberg made the right decision to go with computer animation. This is also the place to find Spielberg's thoughts on his movie, recorded at the time of filming or soon after. Other features include some 'animatics' scenes, which combine storyboards, stop-motion puppets and basic CGI to create shooting plans for the T-rex breakout and kitchen scenes – it's amazing just how closely the final film matches them. There is also an extensive set of production designs and photos, as well as a 'dinosaur encyclopaedia' of dino-factoids. There's even a trio of trailers, including one for the forthcoming (non-Spielberg directed) *Jurassic Park 3*, though it doesn't really give a lot away. Regardless of any plot criticisms, *Jurassic Park* tramples the competition as a DVD. The list of extras might not be as massive as *Men in Black*, but the film is a lot more entertaining, and if you ever wanted sound and vision with which to impress your friends and family, this is the disc for you. If you want, you can pick up *Jurassic Park* with its sequel in a boxset, but for the best dinosaur action around, stick with the original and best!

FINAL VERDICT

Picture ☆☆☆☆☆ Sound ☆☆☆☆☆
Entertainment ☆☆☆☆☆
Extras ☆☆☆☆ Value ☆☆☆☆☆
OVERALL ☆☆☆☆☆

THE JUROR

Price: £19.99
Supplied by: Columbia TriStar
Type of disc: Single layer, single-sided
No of chapters: 28
Film length/format(s): 16:9 widescreen / 113 mins
Director: Brian Gibson
Starring: Demi Moore, Alec Baldwin, Anne Heche
Year made: 1996
Extras: Multilingual subtitles; scene selection; theatrical trailer.

Demi Moore is Annie, a hard-working single mother coping successfully with bringing up her son Oliver. Successfully that is until she's selected for jury duty on a Mob trial and comes to the attention of a hitman-cum-Mafia consultant known as 'The Teacher' (Baldwin). He gives Annie a choice: bring in a verdict of not guilty or her son dies. *The Juror* is unusual in that for the most part it's fairly subtle, relying on strong performances from its actors rather than flashy effects. It's only near the end of the movie

that things get back on the usual Hollywood track as the plot shifts suddenly to Guatemala for a gung-ho showdown. You've got to wonder whether director Brian Gibson didn't just realise he was running under-budget and decide to splash out on some nice scenery for the finale! As a DVD *The Juror* is – like most UK releases at present – fairly underwhelming. Aside from subtitles in various languages and the scene selection facility all we get for our money is the original theatrical trailer. Are film companies trying to make us get our DVD players chipped or what?

FINAL VERDICT

Picture ☆☆☆☆ Sound ☆☆☆☆ Entertainment ☆☆☆
Extras ☆ Value ☆☆
OVERALL ☆☆

JUST CAUSE

Price: £15.99
Supplied by: DVD Plus (www.dvdplus.co.uk)
Distributor: Warner Home Video
Type of disc: Single layer, single-sided
No of chapters: 30
Film format(s)/length: 2.35:1 widescreen / 98 mins
Audio format: Dolby Digital 5.1
Director: Arne Glimcher
Starring: Sean Connery, Laurence Fishburne, Ed Harris
Year made: 1995
Extras: Scene access; soundtrack in French and Italian; subtitles in 10 languages.

. If you see Connery, Fishburne and Harris in the credits, you'd probably expect a decent film. Afraid not. '*Jusht Caushe*' (sorry) was obviously a project Connery accepted to pay his golf fees. Law professor Paul Armstrong (Connery) is brought out of legal retirement by a young criminal (Blair Underwood) on Death Row, who claims his murder confession was beaten out of him by sweaty sheriff Tanny Brown (Fishburne). It looks like a clear-cut case of police brutality once eye-rolling serial killer Blair Sullivan (Harris) cops to the crime, but when the supposed killer is acquitted just an hour into the film you know there are plot twists on the way – and the pity is that you can predict every one of them. With no extras – not even a trailer – the DVD is a total flop. *Just Cause* is a cheesy shelf-filler of the worst kind. Who do they think will buy this kind of junk?

FINAL VERDICT

Picture ☆☆☆☆ Sound ☆☆☆ Entertainment ☆
Extras ☆ Value ☆☆
OVERALL ☆☆

KALIFORNIA

Price: £19.99
Supplied by: PolyGram Film Productions
Type of disk: Dual layer, single-sided
No of chapters: 20
Film format(s)/length: 1.85:1 anamorphic / 118 mins
Audio format: Dolby Surround
Director: Dominic Sena
Starring: Brad Pitt, Juliette Lewis, David Duchovny
Year made: 1993
Extras: Scene access; theatrical trailer; 'Making of' featurette; filmographies and biographies.

Take two urbane middle-class artists on a cross-country road trip to research America's serial killers, and throw in drifters Earley and Adele, the ultimate white trash. Toss into the mix the fact that Earley himself is a psycho killer, and you have a slightly subversive take on the 'outlaw killer couple' road movie. The claustrophobia, severe mutual incompatibility and sporadic outbursts of frenzied killing create a wonderfully stomach-knotting atmosphere, thick with danger, fear and dread. Lewis is massively irritating with another retarded little girl lost routine. On the other hand, it's a joy to find Duchovny in full monotone Mulder mode, and Pitt gleefully invokes utter repulsion, fascination and fear all at once. As for the extras, they're sparse enough to send you on a killing spree yourself. The 'Making of' featurette lasts a ridiculously feeble 5 minutes, and is nothing more than a crummy sentence from each actor cut into a re-run of the theatrical trailer. 'Trailer trash', you could say.

FINAL VERDICT
Picture ☆☆☆☆ Sound ☆☆☆☆ Entertainment ☆☆☆
Extras ☆☆ Value ☆☆☆
OVERALL ☆☆☆

THE KILLING ZONE

Price: £19.99
Supplied by: Planet DVD (01992 707414)
Type of disc: Single layer, single-sided
No of chapters: 20
Film format(s)/length: 4:3 letterbox / 90 mins
Audio format: Dolby Surround
Director: Ian David Diaz
Starring: Padraig Casey, Oliver Young, Mark Bowden
Year made: 1999
Extras: Scene access; Making of the Killing Zone, 30-minute in depth documentary of the film.

Many British gangster style thrillers have tried and failed to match the never emptying wallets of Hollywood productions. Notably, the release of Lock, Stock and Two Smoking Barrels set an echelon for all other British film-makers to try and reach. So how do a group of outsiders to the film industry ever hope to get marginally close to such an achievement without funding? Simple, stick an ad in the paper for actors and actresses and invite total strangers to help finance a worthy cause. This may sound like it's a recipe for disaster, but The Killing Zone lived by these tight-budget rules and still managed to produce a film that is actually quite good. The main character is Palmer, played by Padraig Casey, and brilliantly styled as a Michael Caine lookalike assassin. Palmer sets out to stitch up the crime monopoly in the area, but it's not all about shoot-ups and torturing captured opponents (though there are some great scenes) as the humour and sly comments throughout the whole film greatly contribute to the uniqueness of this package. Extras include the usual theatrical trailer, and under 'Additional Material', a 30-minute documentary about the making of the film, which includes all the ups and downs that went with it and on the spot filming of all the stars. In all it's a shame the film will be compared to Vinnie Jones's first hardman role, as the originality of The Killing Zone deserves recognition in its own right. Get this film or else!

FINAL VERDICT
Picture ☆☆☆☆ Sound ☆☆☆☆
Entertainment ☆☆☆☆ Extras ☆☆☆☆ Value ☆☆☆☆
OVERALL ☆☆☆☆

KINDERGARTEN COP

Price: £19.99
Supplied by: Columbia TriStar Home Video
Type of disc: Dual layer, single-sided
No of chapters: 16
Film format(s)/length: 1.33:1 widescreen / 107 mins
Audio format: Dolby Surround
Director: Ivan Reitman
Starring: Arnold Schwarzenegger, Penelope Ann Miller, Pamela Reed
Year made: 1990
Extras: Scene selection; cast and film-makers' notes; production notes; theatrical trailer; soundtrack in 7 languages; subtitles in 9 languages.

To take the biggest action star of all time, in the height of his fame, and then put him in a role that is totally the opposite of what his fans are used to seeing is an intriguing idea, that worked. Once! The film was Twins, and as a result of that, director Reitman and star Schwarzenegger teamed up once again to milk the format with a film about tough streetwise cop, John Kimble, who is forced to undercover as a kindergarten teacher. Do you see where the humour lies? No? Well you should, it's pretty bloody blatant. Although the humour isn't as subtle as that in *Twins*, this movie is more to Arnie's suiting. At least he gets to hold a gun, grit his teeth and not look uncomfortable for nearly two hours. This is an easy on the eyes DVD. A simple, but well played film, on a simple yet substantial disc with enough extras to give it substance.

FINAL VERDICT

Picture ☆☆☆☆ Sound ☆☆☆☆ Entertainment ☆☆
Extras ☆☆☆☆ Value ☆☆
OVERALL ☆☆

KING OF NEW YORK

Price: £9.99
Supplied by: Carlton
Type of disc: Single layer, single-sided
No of chapters: 14
Film format(s)/length: 4:3 regular / 99 mins
Audio format: Dolby Surround
Director: Abel Ferrara
Starring: Christopher Walken, David Caruso, Laurence Fishburne
Year made: 1990
Extras: Scene access; English subtitles; Silver Collection advert.

This is one of those films where you can just sit back and pick out all the young actors who have built themselves successful careers in the last ten years. Former *NYPD Blue* man Caruso (okay, maybe not *that* successful) unsurprisingly plays a cop, who with partner Wesley Snipes is on the trail of Frank White (Walken), a New York crime boss hot out of prison. Shunned by the mafia for having a multiracial gang, Walken's right-hand man is none other than Laurence 'Larry' Fishburne! Also in his posse is a very young Steve Buscemi, who has a quick cameo role as a professional drugs tester. As ever, the best performance comes from Walken, who, straight out of prison, immediately sets about his usual business of drug running and bribing councillors. Someone should've put some money into bribing whoever put this disc together, because despite the film's quality it's no different to what you might get on VHS. It may be an old film, but widescreen alone could have done it so much more justice, not to mention the addition of any extras. As might be expected from a Ferrara movie, the picture quality is grainy and the sound a little dulled, but if anything this helps to add a gritty edge to the film. It's just a shame that no attention has been paid to the extras. If you want this film, pop into town and get it on video – it'll be the same but cheaper.

FINAL VERDICT

Picture ☆☆☆ Sound ☆☆☆ Entertainment ☆☆☆☆
Extras ☆ Value ☆☆
OVERALL ☆☆☆

KINGPIN

Price: £15.99
Supplied by: DVD Premier Direct (www.dvd premier. co.uk)
Type of disc: Single layer, single-sided
No of chapters: 12
Film format(s)/length: 16:9 widescreen enhanced / 99 mins
Audio format: Dolby Surround
Directors: Peter and Bobby Farrelly
Starring: Woody Harrelson, Bill Murray, Randy Quaid
Year made: 1996
Extras: Scene access; theatrical trailer; 'Making of' featurette (4 minutes); soundtrack in English.

The Farrelly brothers had a dazzling debut with *Dumb and Dumber*, a run away success with *There's Something About Mary*, but in-between was this little gem of a movie. *Kingpin* may have been a box office low point for the sibling director team and critically speaking, their worst, but it's still good fun. The plot follows a one-handed ex-champion bowler who pulls himself out of his mid-life rut by exploiting the talent of an Amish boy in order to win the Reno bowling championships. Far more subtle then the Farrelly's first comedy and a hell of a lot more coherent than their last, *Kingpin* (which does have its fair share of toilet jokes) mainly uses character-driven humour to get the laughs. And they do come thick and fast thanks to some excellent casting in the form of comedy veteran (anyone remember *Cheers*?) Harrelson as ex-champ Roy Munson and Murray also shining as the devious Ernie McCracken – a ruthless champion of bowling who shows the more cutthroat side of the sport. Though only a cameo role for Murray, it's quite possibly his finest performance since *Groundhog Day*. Sadly, the DVD is nowhere near as much of a hidden treasure as the film. Another limp effort from Entertainment in Video, the 'Making of' documentary is barely 4 minutes worth of promotion material, and the inclusion of the trailer does absolutely nothing to enhance the disc. Entertainment wise, Murray's deteriorating coiffure and the 'milking the cow' joke are truly unmissable, but can this alone warrant the purchase of the DVD? You decide.

FINAL VERDICT

Picture ☆☆☆ Sound ☆☆☆
Entertainment ☆☆☆☆ Extras ☆☆ Value ☆☆
OVERALL ☆☆☆

KNOCK OFF

Price: £19.99
Supplied by: Columbia TriStar Home Video
Type of disc: Single layer, single-sided
No of chapters: 28
Film format(s)/length: 2.35:1 widescreen enhanced / 88 mins
Audio format: Dolby Digital 5.1
Director: Tsui Hark
Starring: Jean-Claude Van Damme, Rob Schneider, Paul Sorvino
Year made: 1998
Extras: 'Making of' feature (20 mins); photo gallery; filmographies; French soundtrack; multilingual subtitles.

Let's face it – Van Damme was never in the league of top action heroes. Sure, *Timecop* was a bit of a hoot, and his earlier stuff passed the time, but once you get to the stage of *Knock Off*, the only possible reason you'd consider buying it (as opposed to renting the VHS) is as a workout for your system. It sets its stall out within five minutes, with fast edits, explosions, and plenty of girls in underwear. The presentation of the DVD is commendable though. Whilst the picture isn't 100% perfect, it's still a cut above some we've seen, and the sound mix is – predictably for a recent action movie – very good. *Knock Off* is a movie full of explosions, gunfire and generally lots of noise, and Dolby Digital 5.1 does it proud. Hey, there's even a short 'Making of' feature, too (that runs to just over 20 minutes). The film ranks neither as the best or worst of Van Damme (although it's closer to the bottom of the scale), following some hokum about a Russian mafia plot, Hong Kong on changeover day and some micro-bombs. A big excuse for a scrap really. In short, passable fodder for a night in with a curry and a sixpack. But only if you like the Muscles from Brussels.

FINAL VERDICT
Picture ☆☆☆☆ Sound ☆☆☆☆ Entertainment ☆☆
Extras ☆☆☆ Value ☆☆
OVERALL ☆☆

THE KRAYS

Price: £17.99
Supplied by: DVDplus (www.dvdplus.co.uk)
Type of disc: Single layer, single-sided
No of chapters: 18
Film format(s)/length: 4:3 regular / 115 mins

Audio format: Stereo
Director: Peter Medak
Starring: Martin Kemp, Gary Kemp, Billie Whitelaw
Year made: 1990
Extras: Scene access; 54-minute documentary *Flesh and Blood: The Story of the Krays*; English subtitles for the hearing impaired.

The original and true-life story of possibly Britain's most notorious gangsters is poignantly portrayed in this gripping film directed by Peter Medak. This no-holds-barred depiction of the East End Kray brothers, who modelled themselves on the Mafia and gang leaders portrayed in American movies of the Fifties and Sixties, shows the more gory parts of the pair's minds as well as their strange relationships with their mother and each other. The film translates well to DVD, with no apparent blocking or distortion, although there was a slight blurring of edges during the wedding scene when the confetti was thrown. The format also handles the dark scenes and the nature of the film brilliantly, successfully conveying the mood of the brothers as they killed. As for special features, you are presented with the 54-minute documentary: *Flesh and Blood: The Story of the Krays* which gives an insight into the East End and its illegal dealings over the past century – somewhat excusing the brothers' behaviour as 'natural'. In interviews with cousins and former gang members, and analyses from crime experts and psychologists, the documentary fills in the gaps the film left – such as Ronald's stay in a psychiatric hospital, and the brothers' first visit to the Old Bailey. Although watching it straight after the film is a slight disappointment in that anomalies are highlighted – such as when Ronnie shot a rival point blank in the head at the Blind Beggar Bar. The film reported it as happening after the suicide of Reggie's wife, while the documentary suggests that it happened just after the marriage and may have contributed to her demise. Despite these minor inconsistencies, this is actually a very entertaining and enlightening film, which highlights a side of life that many of us will hopefully never encounter.

FINAL VERDICT
Picture ☆☆☆ Sound ☆☆☆ Entertainment ☆☆☆
Extras ☆☆☆ Value ☆☆
OVERALL ☆☆☆

LABYRINTH

Price: £19.99
Supplied by: DVDplus (www.dvdplus.co.uk)
Distributor: Columbia TriStar Home Video
Type of disc: Single layer, single-sided

No of chapters: 28
Film format(s)/length:16:9 widescreen enhanced / 98 mins
Audio format:: Dolby Surround
Director: Jim Henson
Starring: David Bowie, Jennifer Connelly and lots of puppets
Year made:1986
Extras: Scene access; *Inside the Labyrinth* documentary (56 minutes); talent profiles; trailer; soundtrack in French, German and Spanish; multilingual subtitles.

Master puppeteer Jim Henson has led the way creating several wonderful productions including The Muppets and *The Dark Crystal*. This DVD is another classic Henson movie, which moves the boundaries of puppetry to another dimension by adding actors into the mix and a soundtrack written by rock legend David Bowie. To help create this imaginative world Jim Henson approached Terry Jones of *Monty Python* fame to write the script and also enlisted the help of George Lucas. The story tells of a young girl (Jennifer Connelly) who must cross the Labyrinth to save her baby brother from the Goblin King (Bowie). The path through the Labyrinth is tough but she makes plenty of friends who aid her along the way. This DVD has plenty of extras, including 'Talent Profiles' of the film's many stars. There's also a brilliant 56-minute documentary called *Inside the Labyrinth*. This splendid bonus film goes behind the scenes and shows how the film was made, including interviews with the cast, and a totally mind-blowing look at the puppets, from design through to the guys who bring the characters to life. The picture quality is superb and although the film has aged, the puppetry is a delight to behold. Essentially, *Labyrinth* is aimed at a young audience but the puppetry will nevertheless be enjoyed by all. Overall, this disc provides exceptional entertainment and the extra features prove that DVD is the only choice for real film fans.

FINAL VERDICT

Picture ☆☆☆ Sound ☆☆☆ Entertainment ☆☆☆☆
Extras ☆☆☆☆ Value ☆☆☆☆
OVERALL ☆☆☆☆

LA CONFIDENTIAL

Price: £15.99
Supplied By: DVD World (01705 796662)
Type of disc: Dual layer, single-sided
No of chapters: 40
Film format(s)/length: 16:9 widescreen / 132 mins
Director: Curtis Hanson
Year made: Kevin Spacey, Russell Crowe, Kim Basinger
Year made: 1997
Extras: Scene access/interactive menus; production notes; theatrical and TV trailers; 3 behind the scenes documentary features: *Off the Record*, including cast/creator interviews; director Curtis Hanson's photo pitch; *LA Confidential* interactive map tour; cast and crew biographies; Dolby Digital 5.1, Dolby Surround; recommended similar movies on DVD; multilingual subtitles.

Los Angeles, the early Fifties, a city of corruption, crime and double-dealings. When a cop is murdered at a late night diner, a relentless and violent hunt ensues that will rock the foundations of the city of Angels. The story follows three cops who honour the badge in very different ways. Bud White (Crowe) – tough, direct and merciless – is out for pay-back after the death of his partner. Jack Vincennes (Spacey) – is a celebrity cop who sets up vice busts of show-business personalities with tabloid sleaze-monger Sid Hudgeons (Danny DeVito). While Ed Exley (Pearce) – is the golden boy of the new LAPD – whose own agenda directly affects the other two. Centred around the Nite Owl massacre, the story flicks back and forth as their investigations gradually draw them close to the truth. Enter Lynn Bracken (Basinger) – a Veronica Lake lookalike call girl for the mysterious entrepreneur Pierce Pratchett (Strathairn) – whose charms and secrecy keep White busy whilst Exley and Vincennes follow a trail that takes them directly to the DA and chief of Detectives, Dudley Smith (Cromwell). Crowe and Pearce's characters are established early on, and with veteran Cromwell asserting a small but constant screen presence, this labyrinthine plot, fuelled with mystery, will keep you guessing until the explosive finale. This ravishing, thrilling tale of police corruption and Hollywood glamour doesn't just stop at a great movie however. Also included on the DVD are many extras such as cast and crew biographies, and the many awards and accolades they received. Information relating to the LA mob scene, the classic police series *Dragnet* and the real life 'Bloody Christmas' – which occurred on Christmas Day, 1951. They have even gone as far as to include the 1953 prices of food, clothes, tobacco and other items from that era. TV spots and Theatrical trailers can be viewed, as well as the soundtrack promo and alternative 'Music Only' soundtrack version of the film. But the most impressive extras that are packed onto the disc include information and visuals on all the locations where *LA Confidential* was shot and three behind the scenes documentaries, including cast and creator interviews – plus original screen tests of Guy Pearce and Russell Crowe. One of the many interviews that feature heavily on this DVD is the author of *LA Confidential*, James Ellroy: "It was big, it was epic, it was huge, it was a book for the whole family, if the name of your f*cking family is the Charles Manson family." Even director Curtis Hanson chips in with the original photo pitch. A superb movie that does the Warner Bros logo justice with its excellent direction, story and cast. If there is one DVD you buy this year, make it *LA Confidential* – the special features alone are worth your hard-blackmailed money.

FINAL VERDICT

Picture ☆☆☆☆ Sound ☆☆☆☆

Entertainment ☆☆☆☆☆ Extras ☆☆☆☆☆

Value ☆☆☆☆☆

OVERALL ☆☆☆☆☆

LADY AND THE TRAMP

Price: £19.99
Supplied by: Walt Disney Home Video
Type of disc: Single layer, single-sided
No of chapters: 22
Film format(s)/length: 2.35:1 widescreen / 76 mins
Audio format: Dolby Digital 5.1
Directors: Clyde Geronimi, W Jackson
Directors: Barbara Luddy, Larry Roberts, Peggy Lee
Year made: 1955
Extras: Scene access; English, French and Spanish language tracks; English subtitles; film recommendations.

There can't be many people who don't know the story of *Lady and the Tramp*. However, for those few people who've somehow missed it, here you go: Walt Disney's 15th animated movie is a musical adventure following the romantic adventures of Lady, a pampered, well-to-do cocker spaniel, and Tramp, a mongrel from the wrong side of the tracks with a heart of gold. This is a timeless movie which is still delightful to watch more than 40 years after it was made and it's as entertaining as any modern Hollywood blockbuster. The sound and picture quality are superb – as you'd expect from DVD – but there the good things end. With its high price, a paltry 3 languages and one lonely set of English subtitles there is little to recommend buying the DVD of *Lady and the Tramp* over the video. The 'film recommendations' – 4 pictures of DVD covers – are a truly laughable 'extra' goodie. What a shame!

FINAL VERDICT

Picture ☆☆☆☆ Sound ☆☆☆☆ Entertainment ☆☆☆

Extras ☆ Value ☆☆

OVERALL ☆☆

THE LAND GIRLS

Price: £16.99
Supplied by: VCI
Type of disc: Dual layer, single-sided
No of chapters: 16
Film format(s)/length: 2.35:1 widescreen enhanced, 4:3 regular / 106 mins
Audio format: Dolby Surround
Director: David Leland
Starring: Catherine McCormack, Rachel Weisz, Anna Friel
Year made: 1998
Extras: Scene access; short documentary (just over 6 minutes); audio commentary by director David Leland; theatrical trailer; alternate ending and deleted scenes; behind the scenes footage (almost 10 minutes); cast and crew interviews; archive footage from 1941 (3 minutes); photo library.

David Leland's film about life in 1941 wartime England is one that disappeared from cinemas almost as soon as it appeared. Lacking a big budget and blockbuster cast, *The Land Girls* is another FilmFour effort that ends up being critically-acclaimed and/or nominated at numerous awards ceremonies. Leland has co-written and directed a fascinating story of three land girls – the women who farmed the land whilst the men went off to kick Hitler's arse – and their adventures together on a farm in southern England. As a DVD it includes the obvious extras like a theatrical trailer and interviews with the cast and crew, but also provides a number of additional goodies. For starters, there's an audio commentary option from Leland, giving you a sneak peak into the movie-making art. There's a short documentary that runs a little over 6 minutes, and around 10 deleted scenes. The DVD also includes some genuine footage from 1941/42, taken in Dulverton where the film was shot. The latter is narrated by David Leland, and he describes how they blatantly 'borrowed' the town's parade and reproduced it within the film. The final extra on this stuffed DVD is about 10 minutes of behind the scenes footage, which is a random collection of scenes, depicting the cast having a break between takes, camera men stuffing film into their equipment or the setting up of shots, and it's interesting fodder for anyone interested in the film-making process. FilmFour has made up for its recent DVD release of the disappointingly packaged *The Acid House*, which was slightly anaemic when it came to the extra features department, but *The Land Girls* is positively full to bursting, something that's made all the more remarkable when the DVD itself is a single-sided dual layer and a Region 2… Could this indicate a step in the right direction for this often mistreated DVD region? We'd like to think so.

FINAL VERDICT

Picture ☆☆☆☆ Sound ☆☆☆☆

Entertainment ☆☆☆☆ Extras ☆☆☆☆☆

Value ☆☆☆☆

OVERALL ☆☆☆☆

LAST ACTION HERO

Price: £19.99

Supplied by: Columbia TriStar Home Video

Type of disc: Single layer, single-sided

No of chapters: 28

Film format(s)/length: 16:9 widescreen enhanced / 125 mins

Audio format: Dolby Digital 5.1

Director: John McTiernan

Starring: Arnold Schwarzenegger, Charles Dance, Austin O'Brien

Year made: 1993

Extras: Scene access; filmographies forSchwarz-enegger and McTiernan; behind-the-scenes featurette; theatrical trailer; music video AC/DC – 'Big Gun'; sound-track in German, Italian, French and Spanish; subtitles in 20 languages.

A critical and commercial disaster on its theatrical release, *Last Action Hero* is a film that's practically begging to be re-released on DVD. Was it really all that bad? Well, yes and no. Working from an interesting if not entirely original premise – young boy gets blasted into an action movie alongside his hero (Schwarzenegger) – the film actually shows potential in the first half, but then proceeds to completely botch it up. The annoyingly smug kid doesn't help matters, but it's the confused script – which seems unsure whether it wants to satirise or celebrate the action genre – that really tops it off. Most of the gags and deliberately over-the-top set-pieces work well, but ultimately the only point *Last Action Hero* makes is that action films are formulaic and unrealistic, which everybody knows anyway. As a DVD though, it does have some redeeming features. For one the picture is of high quality, nicely bringing out the bright colours and artificiality of the cinematic world, whilst emphasising the relative doom and gloom of the real one. The sound is also very good, lending clarity and volume to the big explosions, gunfire, and wittily cheesy music of the soundtrack. Extras include

the AC/DC video for 'Big Gun', which sees Arnie cavorting around in a schoolboy uniform; pointlessly brief filmographies ('Talent Profiles') for Schwarzenegger and director McTiernan; and a behind the scenes featurette, which as usual reveals far too much of the story and hardly anything about the actual production. Not a terrible package overall, but the film itself is a definite hit-and-miss affair.

FINAL VERDICT

Picture ☆☆☆☆ Sound ☆☆☆☆ Entertainment ☆☆

Extras ☆☆☆ Value ☆☆

OVERALL ☆☆☆

THE LAST BOY SCOUT

Price: £15.99

Supplied by: Warner Home Video

Type of disc: Dual layer, single-sided

No of chapters: 29

Film format(s)/length: 2.35:1 widescreen (anamorphic) / 101 mins

Audio format: Dolby Digital 5.1

Director: Tony Scott

Starring: Bruce Willis, Damon Wayans, Chelsea Field

Year made: 1991

Extras: English/French/Italian Dolby Digital 5.1; widescreen anamorphic picture

Like calculator watches, The Thompson Twins, Scalextric, Sun-In, *The A-Team*, pogo sticks, Pamela Stephenson, cider and ever-lasting 'Frenchies', *The Last Boy Scout* is probably best remembered fondly than re-lived and rubbished. Tastes were different when Tony Scott's testosterone-fuelled Bruce Willis vehicle was just what audiences wanted. Repeating his highly successful *Lethal Weapon* buddy flick formula almost to the letter, writer Shane Black's black narrative and humour, coupled with regular explosive set pieces and easy-on-the-eye macho leads, was the perfect Saturday night movie. Boys liked the bangs, and girls liked the blokes. But a few years on, *The Last Boy Scout* is unmasked as the cynical action-film-by-numbers it always was. Sure, you'll disagree with me now, remembering the adolescent high with which you left the cinema – but put this up against modern-day examples like *The Rock* and *Face/Off* and you'll see how far the genre has come. Which makes Warner's decision not to beef up the package with extra goodies all the more peculiar. The transfer's fine and the sound's meaty – but with compression quality improving all the time, these should be taken for granted. In fact, take for granted is exactly what Warner appears to have done here – even to the extent of listing the bog-standard production notes as one of the disc's special features when there are none evidently present. We know no-one buys a DVD for the superficial info pages, but their inclusion on the back of the box is nothing short of scandalous. So as the Scout motto goes: Be prepared.

FINAL VERDICT

Picture ☆☆☆☆ Sound ☆☆☆☆
Entertainment ☆☆ Extras ☆ Value ☆
OVERALL ☆☆

THE LAST BROADCAST

Price: £19.99
Supplied by: Metrodome
Type of disc: Single layer, single-sided
No of chapters: 18
Film format(s)/length: 4:3 regular / 96 mins
Audio format: Dolby Digital 2.0
Directors: Stefan Avalos and Lance Weiler
Starring: David Beard, Jim Seward, Stefan Avalos
Year made: 1998
Extras: Scene access; 2 trailers; 3 behind the scenes featurettes; photo library; *The True Legend of the Jersey Devil* short film; film-makers' biographies; production notes.

In a perfect world, all things would be fair. Everyone would win the lottery, annual tax would be less than a daily pint of milk, and *The Last Broadcast* would have come firmly into the public's imagination one whole year before the keenest of cyber-geeks had downloaded the first teaser for *The Blair Witch Project*. Comparison is often very unflattering, but considering both movies used 'documentary' footage to tell the tale of a group of film-makers who venture in to the woods investigating local mythology, and never make it out again, it might just be worthwhile. Made for a meagre $900 by two film enthusiasts, *The Last Broadcast* proves to be the more intelligent of the two movies, taking a much more psychological route to freak out its audience rather than using the edge-of-the-seat factor. *Broadcast* also uses a broader spectrum of footage to tell its story, thankfully without overstretching the mark. As it stands, *The Last Broadcast* is a chilling mockumentary which pieces together footage and interviews that could hold the answers as to who or what really killed the *Facts or Fiction* film crew as they headed into the Pine Barons to investigate the legend of the Jersey Devil. At the movie's opening, blame rests firmly on the shoulder of the introverted Jim Suerd, the only surviving crewmember, but with each new interview and examination of found footage, the certainty of Suerd's guilt rapidly fades away. If the movie isn't enough to inspire

you, then the extra features will have you grabbing your DV camcorder and rushing out your challenge to the crown of Spielberg. With a budget of under $1000, consumer equipment, an Apple Mac and the help of friends and family the two film-makers, Stefan Avalos and Lance Weiler, single (okay, dual)-handedly wrote, produced, directed, edited, starred in, and distributed *The Last Broadcast*. The amazing amount of patience, effort and ingenuity is fully explained in three featurettes. The most intriguing of these is the story of how they did all of their postpro-duction on a home computer. Add to this a feature explaining the legend of the Jersey Devil and two the-atrical trailers, and it's nice to see major Hollywood blockbusters being totally outclassed by the little fish.

FINAL VERDICT

Picture ☆☆☆ Sound ☆☆ Entertainment ☆☆☆☆☆
Extras ☆☆☆☆☆ Value ☆☆☆☆
OVERALL ☆☆☆☆☆

THE LAST EMPEROR

Price: £15.99
Supplied by: Second Sight Films
Type of disc: Single layer, single-sided
No of chapters: 18
Film format(s)/length: 2.35:1 widescreen / 160 mins
Audio format: Stereo
Director: Bernardo Bertolucci
Starring: John Lone, Peter O'Toole, Joan Chen
Year made: 1987
Extras: Scene access; 2 trailers; brief filmographies of director and producer.

The appealing young lad who appears on the cover of this DVD is Pu Yi, the last Emperor of China, and this modern classic, which won 9 Oscars, depicts his life. Having been crowned at 3 years-old and reigning for only a very short time, the revolution in 1911 forced his 12-year confinement within the fabled Forbidden City. The film is seen in flashback as the adult Pu Yi (Lone) 'confesses' the story of his life to his jailers: being treated as a god by thousands of slaves, his curiosity about the outside world encouraged by his teacher (O"Toole) and his eventu-al expulsion from the City by a republican warlord and ten year imprisonment on charges of collabora-tion with Japan. The stately pace perfectly suits the ceremonial mood of the Forbidden City and the rich-ly creative photography reveals a truly distant and exotic world whilst contrasting with the ordinariness and innocence of the boy himself. Thankfully, the effect of the cinematography is enhanced by the great colour reproduction, but the overall picture quality is merely passable, with some noticeable artefacting. The sound is average (stereo only), and has no language options or subtitles. The one unforgivable oversight is the lack of a 'Making of' feature, particularly considering it took director Bertolucci two years just to negotiate a way into the Forbidden City for filming. Ultimately, the calibre of the film means that you could happily watch it on snowy old VHS, but you wish somebody had put some work into making it look and sound every bit as good as it deserves by using the full capabilities of DVD. This movie deserves more.

FINAL VERDICT

Picture ☆☆☆ Sound ☆ Entertainment ☆☆☆☆
Extras ☆ Value ☆☆☆
OVERALL ☆☆☆

LAST MAN STANDING

Price: £15.99
Supplied by: DVDplus (www.dvdplus.co.uk)
Type of disc: Single layer, single-sided
No of chapters: 6
Film format(s)/length: 2.35:1 widescreen / 96 mins
Audio format: Dolby Surround
Director: Walter Hill
Starring: Bruce Willis, Christopher Walken, Bruce Dern
Year made: 1996
Extras: Scene access (all 6 of them); 'Making of' featurette (4 minutes); trailer.

Those expecting another Willis action film are likely to be disappointed by *Last Man Standing*, a brutal tale of Thirties rivalry between two gangs of Texan bootleggers. A relative flop at the US box office, taking just under a third of its production fee, it's essentially a remake of *Fistful of Dollars*, which in turn was based on the little-known Japanese movie *Yojimbo*. Director Walter Hill has at least tried to update the tale, not just by modernising the setting but the flavour of the movie. It's all style, from the muted hues of the image to the slick violence throughout, all looking and sounding spot-on in terms of transfer. Willis took a risk by accepting the role, and while *Last Man Standing* failed to convince everyone to sit down and watch it, it's well worth a look. And if you're a girl, you do get to see his bum. Now that the girls have rushed off to buy it, let's talk about the real reason to, or not buy this DVD. Once again, New Line has demonstrated that it can't count, as the promised 34-minute 'Making of' featurette runs for just over 4 minutes. It's a disgrace – and surely can't escape the eagle eye of Anne Robinson and her *Watchdog* mates for much longer. The trailer - the

only other extra - offers almost as much insight. And for some reason, it's split into only 6 chapters, making it difficult to rewatch your favourite bits. Which is a shame, because the movie's pretty good. But, without anything to back it up, it's really not an essential DVD purchase.

FINAL VERDICT

Picture ☆☆☆☆ Sound ☆☆☆☆ Entertainment ☆☆☆
Extras ☆ Value ☆☆
OVERALL ☆☆☆

LAST TANGO IN PARIS

Price: £19.99
Supplied by: MGM Home Entertainment
Type of disc: Dual layer, single-sided
No of chapters: 32
Film format(s)/length: 16:9 anamorphic / 124 mins
Audio format: Dolby Digital 2.0
Director: Bernardo Bertolucci
Starring: Marlon Brando, Maria Schneider
Year made: 1972
Extras: Scene access; trailer; soundtrack in English, German, French and Spanish; subtitles in 12 languages; subtitles for the hearing impaired in English and German.

Brando smoulders as a 45-year-old widower coming to terms with his wife's death. When viewing an apartment, he meets by chance a young woman, Schneider, and they begin an anonymous, and at times brutal, affair. Most DVD owners won't remember the uproar *Last Tango* and its 'knob of butter' scene caused upon release, which in retrospect seems rather restrained. This has the pleasing effect of drawing your attention to the performances. Schneider stands her own against an Oscar-nominated Brando performance. There are no special features on the disk, only a booklet with production details and trivia, which is disappointing for a film which was a cinematic revolution (and in the UK was taken to court). The quality of the transfer to DVD is more than adequate enough to enjoy the film, but Bertolucci is a master film-maker, and his thoughts and methods deserve more attention.

FINAL VERDICT

Picture ☆☆☆ Sound ☆☆☆ Entertainment ☆☆☆☆
Extras ☆ Value ☆☆
OVERALL ☆☆☆

THE LAWNMOWER MAN

Price: £19.99
Supplied by: First Independent
Type of disc: Single layer, single-sided

No of chapters: 20
Film format(s)/length: 16:9 anamorphic / 104 mins
Audio format: Dolby 5.1
Director: Brett Leonard
Starring: Jeff Fahey, Pierce Brosnan, Jenny Wright
Year made: 1992
Extras: Scene access; 12 deleted scenes; animated montage set to a musical score; cast biographies and filmographies; 'Making of' featurette; theatrical trailer; virtual reality mini-game; storyboard to film comparison.

Remember when *The Lawnmower Man*'s computer graphics looked impressive? How times change! Of course, now it's looking hellishly dated but the film itself is as cornily watchable today as it was years ago, and the DVD has a handful of extras to make the experience even more enjoyable. What's more, it'll be a long time before you see Pierce Brosnan in a cheesy film like this again! A quick glance at the sleeve reveals that the disc features '12 deleted scenes', but don't get too excited. If you've ever seen the Director's Cut then you'll already have seen every single one of those scenes before! It would've been so much better if this had *been* the Director's Cut. The murder of Brosnan's wife and the escape of the monkey in particular don't contain the same kind of emotions as they did when in the actual film. However, a moderately interesting featurette on the film, info on the cast and a bizarre animated montage of all the virtual reality sequences do to some extent make up for this blatant cop-out. Perhaps the strangest thing on the disc is the virtual reality mini-game which must be played before you can access the trailer! This may sound fascinating, but sadly it isn't, as all it involves is simply tapping your controller as a *Tron*-style race scene from the film plays out before you. This is a good disc, but you can't help but feeling a little cheated.

FINAL VERDICT

Picture ☆☆☆ Sound ☆☆☆☆ Entertainment ☆☆☆☆
Extras ☆☆☆ Value ☆☆☆
OVERALL ☆☆☆

A LEAGUE OF THEIR OWN

Price: £19.99
Supplied by: Columbia TriStar Home Video
Type of disc: Dual layer, single-sided
No of chapters: 28
Film format(s)/length: 2.35:1 widescreen enhanced / 123 mins
Audio format: Dolby Digital 4.0
Director: Penny Marshall
Starring: Tom Hanks, Geena Davis, Madonna
Year made:1992

Extras: 3 theatrical trailers; behind the scenes featurette; Madonna music video: 'This Used To Be My Playground'; historical documentary (28 mins); filmographies; soundtrack in English, German, Spanish, Italian and French; subtitles in 20 languages.

A *League of Their Own* not only managed to knock *Batman Returns* off the top of the US box office, but also ultimately accrued over $100m in the States alone. Much of that can be put down to the presence of stars like Madonna and Tom Hanks, but don't let that blind you to the fact that this frothy sporting comedy is an enjoyable, if over-long, piece of entertainment. And don't think that the disc is standard back-catalogue fare either. Unlike the version our Stateside cousins were given, this Region 2 release is a bit of a Brucie bonus where special features are concerned. Key attraction? A feature documentary, running just shy of 30 minutes, which talks to some of the people the film is based on and digs into the history of the All-American Girls Baseball League of 1943, from where the movie draws its source. You'll need to be a bit of an historian to get the most out of it, but it's a step up from the usual 5-minute interview reel we're used to getting – although one of those is included as well. Add to the mix a very strong enhanced widescreen picture that holds the bright palette with considerable style, and an unusual quad surround sound mix which holds up surprisingly well, and you're left with a very attractive package. It just goes to show you don't have to go to the lengths of *Ghostbusters* in order to offer an older title with considerable style.

FINAL VERDICT

Picture ☆☆☆☆☆ Sound ☆☆☆ Entertainment ☆☆☆
Extras ☆☆☆☆ Value ☆☆☆☆
OVERALL ☆☆☆☆

LEAVING LAS VEGAS

Price: £15.99
Supplied by: Entertainment in Video
Type of disc: Dual layer, single-sided
No of chapters: 12
Film format(s)/length: 1.85:1 widescreen enhanced / 107 mins
Audio format: Dolby Surround
Director: Mike Figgis
Starring: Nicholas Cage, Elisabeth Shue, Julian Sands
Year made: 1995

Extras: Scene access; 6-minute mini-documentary on the film's making; theatrical trailer; subtitles in English.

One critic semi-approvingly described Mike Figgis's sole mainstream Hollywood hit, *Internal*

Affairs, as 'art house sleaze'. In that thriller, he retained much of the gritty realism another director might have airbrushed out. *Leaving Las Vegas* is pretty much all gritty realism, yet unlike Paul Verhoeven's *Showgirls*, Figgis's Vegas flick places the emphasis on language rather than flesh. Elisabeth Shue's opening dialogue is as direct as can be imagined – 'Just don't come on my hair' – but we don't see her body, we watch her eyes and see the emotions swirling under the hard-faced mask. Shue plays a hooker who is drawn into the morbidly fascinating descent of washed-up screenwriter Ben Sanderson (Cage), who's come to Las Vegas with the express purpose of drinking himself to death. He hires Shue for sex, but his fracturing personality meets some need in Shue and the two bond. The ensuing romance is doomed, but the two leads are never less than convincing. It's no surprise that Cage carried off the Academy Award for Best Actor in 1996. There are moments of genuine lyricism, most notably the swimming pool scene and there's a superb score, penned by the multitalented Figgis himself. As a DVD, *Leaving Las Vegas* is lacking in extras and is hardly the picture to show off your hardware. Figgis shot the film on the little-used Super 16 film format, partly to keep down costs but also to keep with the intimacy of the script. Blown up to 35mm for a cinema release, the imagery is flecked with a film grain which you'd expect to have caused massive artefacting a year or so ago. The fidelity with which the DVD recreates the film's distinctive look is is testament to advances in encoding. More significantly, this is a great film which deserves to do well however it's presented.

FINAL VERDICT

Picture ☆☆☆☆ Sound ☆☆☆☆
Entertainment ☆☆☆☆☆ Extras ☆ Value ☆☆☆☆
OVERALL ☆☆☆☆

Leon

Price: £19.99
Supplied by: Touchstone Home Video
Type of disc: Single layer, single-sided
No of chapters: 27
Film format(s)/length: 2.35:1 widescreen / 106 mins
Audio format: Dolby Digital 5.1
Director: Luc Besson
Starring: Jean Reno, Natalie Portman, Gary Oldman
Year made: 1994
Extras: Scene access; soundtrack in English and Spanish; multilingual subtitles; subtitles for the hearing impaired in English.

A milk-drinking hitman who loves his potted plant. With a lead character like that you'd expect a high degree of Frenchness about the film, and you'd be right. What's different about Luc Besson's *Leon* is that it's a French film made in English and filmed in New York, and is for all intents and purposes as 'Hollywood' as anything from LA. Reno plays Leon, a shabby mob-employed hitman. Leon's life when he's not rubbing out the opposition is fairly aimless and empty, but all that changes when 12-year-old neighbour Mathilda (Portman) comes knocking on his door. Mathilda's family has just been wiped out by corrupt drug-dealing cop Stansfield (Oldman) in the aftermath of a deal gone bad, and once she discovers Leon's true profession, she wants him to teach her the tricks of his trade so she can get revenge. Although the action sequences in which Leon plies his trade are superb (it's too bad Besson didn't manage to capture even a fraction of this excitement in the execrable *The Fifth Element*), the heart of the film is the odd-couple relationship between Leon and Mathilda. The reclusive, taciturn assassin starts to thaw out as a result of unexpectedly becoming a surrogate parent, and mixed-up Mathilda learns how to get her life in order, in addition to useful stuff like how to cap somebody at 500 yards with a sniper rifle. So, a good film. Unfortunately, the mere presence of the words 'Touchstone', 'Home' and 'Video' on the sleeve should give you a hint about how many extras you're going to get, given that Touchstone is part of Disney. That's right, absolutely nothing. Even the US version (under its alternate name, *The Professional*) managed to scrape up a trailer. Some people might argue that the extras are unimportant and it's only the film that matters, but really, how hard could it have been to make even the tiniest effort of putting a trailer on the disc? Hell, it's not even anamorphic!

FINAL VERDICT

Picture ☆☆☆ Sound ☆☆☆☆ Entertainment ☆☆☆☆
Extras ☆ Value ☆☆☆
OVERALL ☆☆☆

Lethal Weapon 4

Price: £15.99
Supplied by: Warner Home Video
Type of disc: Single layer, double-sided
No of chapters: 45
Film format(s)/length: 2.35:1 widescreen anamorphic / 121 mins
Director: Richard Donner
Starring: Mel Gibson, Danny Glover, Joe Pesci
Year made: 1998
Extras: Chapter access; multilingual subtitles; produc-

tion notes; cast and crew bios; 30-minute 'Pure Lethal' documentary; cast interviews; extra scenes from *Lethal Weapon* 1-3; behind the scenes film clips.

Want to hear a really terrible joke? *Lethal Weapon 4* is a Richard Donner kebab – full of old bits and goes down better when you've had a few. Yes, it was a lousy gag, but it sums up *Lethal Weapon 4* rather well. The movie was put together in one of the shortest production schedules ever for a big Hollywood film, when Warner Bros realised it had no summer blockbusters, and it shows. The perfunctory plot involves the Chinese Triads and counterfeit money, but it's just a) an excuse to bring in a Hong Kong superstar (Jet Li) to kick ass, and b) the only way the creators could squeeze in some action between the well-worn character 'schtick.' The sole difference is that it's now Gibson's Riggs who has to utter the series' catchphrase of "I'm too old for this shit," since he's now where Glover was in the first film, 12 years earlier. Ho ho! Despite this, the DVD itself is rather good with all manner of extras, from a blooper-filled documentary about the series, to a selection of scenes cut from the first three films. Most are only a few seconds long, but a couple from the first movie (Riggs' encounters with a sniper and a hooker) are worth watching in their own right – if only to remind you that Riggs was once genuinely on the edge and not just a wacky human punchbag. Still, the familiarity provides some fun, and there's the odd bit of excitement. But this really was a sequel too far.

FINAL VERDICT

Picture ☆☆☆☆ Sound ☆☆☆☆ Entertainment ☆☆☆
Extras ☆☆☆☆ Value ☆☆☆☆
OVERALL ☆☆☆☆

LETHAL WEAPON 3

Price: £15.99
Supplied by: DVD Net (020 8890 2520)
Type of disc: Dual layer, single-sided
No of chapters: 31
Film format(s)/length: 2.35:1 widescreen anamorphic / 113 mins
Director: Richard Donner
Starring: Mel Gibson, Danny Glover, Joe Pesci
Year made: 1992
Extras: Chapter access; multilingual subtitles;English/French/Italian soundtracks; filmographies; 2 trailers.

The mere fact that *Lethal Weapon 3* is a '15' certificate, instead of the '18' of its predecessors, says a lot. This was the point where the series went from action thrillers with buddy comedy to buddy comedies with action. Unfortunately, it was also the point where things stopped being as good. This time round, Riggs and Murtaugh are up against a corrupt ex-cop who's gone into the arms trade. Pesci's Leo Getz returns, but now he's annoying rather than funny, and there's also a less-than-interesting sub-plot about Murtaugh and a young gang member. The best thing about *Lethal Weapon 3* is the arrival of Rene Russo as kickboxing cop Lorna Cole, who gets into an amusing, competitive romance with Riggs. All that *Lethal Weapon 3* offers on the extras front is a pair of trailers and the standard filmographies, so nothing special. A bit like the film, really.

FINAL VERDICT

Picture ☆☆☆☆ Sound ☆☆☆☆
Entertainment ☆☆☆ Extras ☆☆ Value ☆☆☆
OVERALL ☆☆☆

LETHAL WEAPON 2

Price: £15.99
Supplied by: DVD Net (020 8890 2520)
Type of disc: Dual layer, single-sided
No of chapters: 39
Film format(s)/length: 2.35:1 widescreen anamorphic / 110 mins
Director: Richard Donner
Starring: Mel Gibson, Danny Glover, Joe Pesci
Year made: 1989
Extras: Chapter access; multilingual subtitles; production notes; stunts micro-documentary; trailer.

Second and best of the series, *Lethal Weapon 2* pits the double act of Riggs (Gibson) and Murtaugh (Glover) against a group of nasty pre-Nelson Mandela Seth Efrikan diplomats, who are using their diplomatic immunity to smuggle drugs. This, naturally, leads to chases, gunfights, mayhem and the destruction of more of Murtaugh's hard-earned property. *Lethal Weapon 2* is where the character dynamics established in the first film really took off, giving Gibson and Glover (joined for the first time by Pesci) plenty of opportunities to banter in amongst the action without making the comedy totally overwhelming. Unlike the later films, there's always enough danger present to keep things exciting. Compared to the DVD of *Lethal Weapon 4*, this disc is rather light on extras. There are some brief filmographies and a very, very short featurette on a couple of the film's action scenes, but nothing out of the ordinary beyond that.

FINAL VERDICT

Picture ☆☆☆☆ Sound ☆☆☆
Entertainment ☆☆☆☆☆ Extras ☆☆ Value ☆☆☆☆
OVERALL ☆☆☆☆

LIAR LIAR

Price: £19.99
Supplied by: Columbia TriStar
Type of disc: Single layer, single-sided
No of chapters: 16
Film format(s)/length: 1.85:1 widescreen / 83 mins
Audio format: Dolby Digital 5.1
Director: Tom Shadyac
Starring: Jim Carrey, Jennifer Tilly, Amanda Donohoe
Year made: 1997
Extras: Scene access; multilingual subtitles; production notes; theatrical trailer.

Lawyers and Jim Carrey – two things that many people either love or hate. If you're the type that dislikes any of these then look away now 'cause it ain't going to be pretty. Carrey's talent lies in the realm of physical comedy and *Liar Liar* demonstrates this to the full. It's the usual 'son puts a curse on his father' story as Carrey finds he is unable to lie – a key part of his job as a lawyer. Needless to say, the slapstick comedy is poured on thick and fast as he tries to make it through his big day in court. Considering how the film is actually quite decent, the shameful thing is the quality of the DVD here. Although the extras on the disc aren't exactly sparse, they're the kind of things that we've come to expect from all DVDs. The usual mix of cinema trailer, production notes and cast biographies is getting tired now and to be frank, we all want something a bit different. Then there's the picture and sound quality. While the soundtrack is clear and precise (as it should be), the visual quality is rather below par – grainy and rough at the best of times, blocky and unsightly at the worst. Admittedly this doesn't effect the film but when the quality of a DVD looks worse than its VHS counterpart, you've got to think there's something wrong. Sadly this is one case where we have to say that maybe you should think twice before getting this DVD. The advancement of technology is one thing but it's examples like this that put the cause back a long way.

FINAL VERDICT
Picture ☆☆ Sound ☆☆☆ Entertainment ☆☆☆
Extras ☆☆ Value ☆☆
OVERALL ☆☆

LIFE

Price: £19.99
Supplied by: Columbia TriStar
Type of disc: Dual layer, single-sided
No of chapters: 18
Film format(s)/length: 1.85:1 widescreen enhanced /
104 mins
Audio format: Dolby Digital 5.1
Director: Ted Demme
Starring: Eddie Murphy, Martin Lawrence, Ned Beatty
Year made: 1999
Extras: Scene access; spotlight on location; outtakes; deleted scenes; director's edit; director's commentary; trailer; music highlights; production notes; cast and filmmakers' notes; animated menu; menu music; DVD-ROM options; soundtrack in English and German; subtitles in 11 languages.

If you've never been to prison, then you've clearly missed a wonderful life-enhancing experience. This seems to be what Hollywood is telling us recently and with the release of *Life*, we're now aware that being banged up can also be funny. Well, we would be if *Life* were actually the hilarious, laugh-out-loud type of comedy that Eddie Murphy could cough up in his sleep back in the early Eighties. Don't take this the wrong way. What you're actually getting for your money is a witty, engaging, and thoroughly watchable chance for Eddie Murphy to prove that he is one of the most talented men to grace the silver screen, but he is more likely to make you smile at the gentle humour rather than bust your gut. In recent years, Murphy has appeared in a variety of movies where the sum of the parts never quite equalled his comic talent. However, *Life* is Murphy and Lawrence at their best. A cross-purposed 'odd couple', loud-mouthed Rayford Gibson (Murphy) and mild bank teller Claude Banks (Lawrence) are falsely accused of murder and sentenced to life in a Mississippi prison. The two stars work brilliantly to flesh out a 60-year friendship on the screen. Rather than meandering, the plot stays perfectly still and lets the characters develop around it. If you're expecting a prison comedy of the calibre of *Stir Crazy*, then you might be a little disappointed. *Life* is respectful of the notion that innocent men being banged up for the best part of their existence isn't always a guaranteed laugh, and so produces a more gentle subtle humour that may not please all. But when push comes to shove, this is a very well made film containing some wonderful characters, and courteously allows Murphy to shine. You may be resistant to trying the movie, but this is one DVD that has to be embraced. Columbia TriStar not only gave director Ted Demme the opportunity to provide one of the most care-driven directors' commentaries ever, but also included a novel feature called 'director's edit', allowing us to see key scenes edited the way Demme, rather than the studio, originally intended. You should also note that there is a stockpile of laughs in one of the funniest outtake collections you're likely to see!

FINAL VERDICT

Picture ☆☆☆☆☆ Sound ☆☆☆☆☆

Entertainment ☆☆☆ Extras ☆☆☆☆☆

Value ☆☆☆☆

OVERALL ☆☆☆☆

LIFE IS BEAUTIFUL

Price: £15.99

Supplied by: DVDplus (www.dvdplus.co.uk)

Distributor: Warner Home Video

Type of disc: Single layer, single-sided

No of chapters: 27

Film format(s)/length:16:9 widescreen enhanced / 111 mins

Audio format: Dolby Digital 5.1

Director: Roberto Benigni

Starring: Roberto Benigni, Nicoletta Braschi, Georgio Cantarini

Year made: 1998

Extras: Scene access; soundtrack in English and Italian; multilingual subtitles; subtitles for the hearing impaired in English

Connoisseurs of screen professionals Schwarzenegger, Willis and Stallone hadn't heard of *Life Is Beautiful* until they saw a beaming little Italian man repeatedly stealing the limelight at the Academy Awards. Benigni left the ceremony with three Oscars for a film that he'd written, directed and starred in, and deservedly so. Resistance is futile against Benigni's tirelessly innocent charm as he portrays Guido, a dedicated father who uses his imagination and storytelling skills to suspend his son in a world of fantasy while they endure the horrors of a concentration camp. This sweet film is presented in Italian with English subtitles by default, but should you be the sort who says things like, "I don't go to the cinema to read for two hours!" you can relax those eyes and opt for a passable dubbed English language job as an alternative. Sadly, there are quite literally no proper special features on the disc. The movie, though, does play in a lovely anamorphic format (not mentioned on the box) and seems to be free from the half-frame flashing errors that plagued earlier titles on various susceptible DVD players. A slightly softer image than you may be used to can be explained either by the constraints of Benigni's budget or a dedicated attempt to replicate a warm celluloid feel for the Forties storyline. In any case, it's far from blurry, and the award-winning musical score tugs the heartstrings with every high definition swelling of the cellos in the DD

5.1 soundtrack. In all honesty, don't be dissuaded from seeing the film because it lacks any extras, you'll be missing out.

FINAL VERDICT

Picture ☆☆☆☆ Sound ☆☆☆☆

Entertainment ☆☆☆☆ Extras ☆ Value ☆☆☆

OVERALL ☆☆☆

LIFE IS SWEET

Price: £9.99

Supplied by: Cinema Club

Type of disc: Dual layer, single-sided

No of chapters: 36

Film format(s)/length: 16:9 widescreen / 113mins

Audio format: Dolby Surround

Director: Mike Leigh

Starring: Allison Steadman, Jim Broadbent, Jane Horrocks

Year made: 1990

Extras: Scene access; soundtrack in English.

Mike Leigh films are something of a genre in themselves; built upon improvisional development with the actors, it's no surprise they stress character over plot. *Life Is Sweet* is one of Leigh's more mainstream films, with politics mostly confined to the sidelines as a family struggles with a life which is only intermittently sweet. Broadbent is notionally head of the family, close cousin to Homer Simpson in his aversion to household chores and propensity for ill-starred business ventures. Stephen Rea takes a break from Neil Jordan films, playing an unemployed chancer who offloads a fast food trailer on Broadbent. Steadman is the true focus of the family, the wife who holds things together, despite the best efforts of Horrocks's teenage daughter who provides the principal dramatic interest, her spectacular angst constantly boiling over and "Bollocks!" punctuating her every line. A bulimic given to chocolate-coated bondage sex with David Thewlis, her plight would provide the central 'message' of a Hollywood flick. In this film, there are no such easy solutions; we get insights into Horrocks's character, we get glimmers of hope, but there's no direct comment. Hollywood has all but branded cinema as escapism, so it requires something of a mental gearshift to cope with a film so resolutely realistic. However with a little patience, the film yields an involving and moving experience. That said, the bargain price is matched by similarly cheap video and audio quality and minimalist presentation; a ghastly cartoon adorns the menu screen and that's it!

FINAL VERDICT

Picture ☆☆☆ Sound ☆☆☆ Entertainment ☆☆☆☆
Extras ☆ Value ☆☆☆☆
OVERALL ☆☆☆

LIMBO

Price: 19.99
Supplied by: Columbia TriStar
Type of disc: Single layer, single sided
No of chapters: 28
Film format(s)/length: 1.85:1 anamorphic / 122 mins
Audio format: Dolby Digital 5.1
Director: John Sayles
Starring: Mary Elizabeth Mastrantonio, David Strathairn, Vanessa Martinez
Year made: 1999
Extras: Scene access; director's commentary; filmographies; music highlights; cinema trailer; soundtrack in English and German; subtitles in 15 languages.

The struggles with secret histories that have defined John Sayles' movies are unearthed again in this film of regrets and inner struggle. As with *Passion Fish* and *Lone Star*, *Limbo* focuses on the tensions that envelop our lives. The relationship between Mastrantonio's Donna de Angelo and her daughter, Noelle, are sent into freefall with the arrival of another man in their lives, Joe Gastineau (*LA Confidential*'s David Strathairn). And then they're shipwrecked. As with all of Sayles' films, *Limbo* drawls along seductively. The use of the calm Alaskan scenery shadows the tensions played out on the cold landscape, only to shock with its surprising twist and numbing ending. The DVD extras mirror the movie's detailed observations with an enthralling commentary from Sayles. *Limbo* isn't the best of his films, but backed by an inspirational commentary and thorough script notes it comes close to being a good starting point for the newcomer to this acclaimed director's work.

FINAL VERDICT
Picture ☆☆☆☆ Sound ☆☆☆ Entertainment ☆☆☆
Extras ☆☆ Value ☆☆
OVERALL ☆☆

THE LIMEY

Price: £19.99
Supplied by: FilmFour
Type of disc: Dual layer, single-sided
No of chapters: 17
Film format(s)/length: 1.85:1 anamorphic / 85 mins
Audio format: Dolby Digital 5.1
Director: Steven Soderbergh
Starring: Terence Stamp, Lesley Ann Warren, Peter Fonda

Year made: 1999
Extras: 2 audio commentaries; isolated music score; cast and crew interviews; behind the scenes footage; theatrical trailer; subtitles for the hearing impaired in English.

We should have seen this coming. After the critical success of *Out of Sight*, Soderbergh's follow-up should have had the type of cult anticipation that only Mr Tarantino can expect. But did anyone see this in the cinema? The plot is deep yet simple, the look is enchantingly stunning, and the performances cut sharper than a knife. There are several volumes-worth of other praises that can be sung about this sleek, unimposing, yet highly contagious 90-minute crime thriller, but for now we'll just concentrate on the basics. Wilson (Stamp) is a thief by trade who, during a brief spell at Her Majesty's pleasure, learns of the death of his daughter in LA while in the care of veteran music producer Valentine (Fonda). On his release from prison Wilson heads straight for Tinseltown determined to get answers and revenge, violently if necessary, but is dogged by the distraction of whether his motives are those of a loving parent or a guilt-ridden failed father. Much of Soderbergh's movie is steeped in the burnt-out fag end of Sixties culture. His two protagonists represent the extreme counterpoints of the '66 to '67 era, with Fonda now using the laid-back 'road trip of the soul' of his easy rider days to get girls half his age into bed, and Stamp bullishly refusing to let go of the London hard-man mentality that made the Krays such resonant British icons of the era. Crowding bus pass age his stars may be, but Soderbergh has managed to capture some truly fresh and riveting performances, especially from Stamp who has moments of pure brilliance when he can produce the goods without even uttering a word. Visually the film is the ultimate Soderbergh trademark. Under-exposed film, jump-cuts and flashbacks all blend together to make Soderbergh one of the most innovative directors working in Hollywood today. Thanks to FilmFour the many subtleties of the movie are echoed in the disc's swell of extras (a Region 2 bonus – there's actually more here than on the American disc) with the 'Making of' featurette surprisingly benefiting from the lack of a voiceover. However, the real treat comes in the form of two separate audio commentaries, the first with Soderbergh being on top 'will get you interested in the film-making process' form, while the second allows the cast to talk far too passionately about the Sixties. Bloody hippies!

FINAL VERDICT

Picture ☆☆☆☆☆ Sound ☆☆☆☆☆
Entertainment ☆☆☆☆☆ Extras ☆☆☆☆
Value ☆☆☆☆☆
OVERALL ☆☆☆☆☆

THE LION KING II – SIMBA'S PRIDE

Price: £19.99
Supplied By: DVD Net (020 8890 2520)
Type of disc: Single layer, single-sided
No of chapters: 26
Film format(s)/length: 1.33:1 widescreen / 78 mins
Director: Darrell Rooney
Starring the voices of: Matthew Broderick, Neve
Campbell, Andy Dick
Year made: 1999
Extras: Illustrated scene selection; 7 languages; subtitles in Dutch.

The original *Lion King* movie was a huge success for Disney with its enchanting storyline, big names for the voices, and songs by Elton John and Tim Rice. The fact that the sequel has gone straight to video and DVD – bypassing the cinema completely – should give you some idea of the quality of this follow-up. All the big names have gone, even down to a replacement for Rowan Atkinson as Zazu, Simba's parrot sidekick. It's Disney cash-in time again and there are no fancy extras at all in this DVD version, something the company is fond of doing on the DVD format. The story of *The Lion King II: Simba's Pride* follows a very similar path to the original movie. Simba's young daughter Kiara ventures off from the Pride Lands and into the dark and dingy Outlands, getting herself into all kinds of trouble with Timon and Pumbaa following closely behind. Then she meets up with another lion cub and falls head over heels in love. Sound familiar? It should, exactly the same thing happened in the original with Simba. Of course the movie has plenty of redeeming features. It's very well animated with luscious backdrops and fluid movement. The musical score is atmospheric too, setting the scene perfectly, it's just a shame you can't help feeling you've seen it all before. If you've got some little cubs who were fond of the original, then sit them down in front of this for an afternoon of entertainment. It's watchable, but was never going to live up to the original.

FINAL VERDICT
Picture ☆☆☆☆ Sound ☆☆☆ Entertainment ☆☆☆
Extras ☆ Value ☆☆☆
OVERALL ☆☆☆

THE LITTLE MERMAID

Price: £19.99
Supplied by: Disney DVD
Type of disc: Single layer, single-sided
No of chapters: 27
Film format(s)/length: 1.66:1 widescreen / 79 mins
Audio format: Dolby Digital 5.1
Directors: Ron Clements, John Musker
Starring: the voices of Jodi Benson, Christopher Daniel
Barnes, Samuel E Wright
Year made: 1989
Extras: Scene access; 'recommended viewing' (ie, other
Disney trailers); soundtrack available in English, French,
Italian, Dutch, Polish, Czech, Hebrew and Greek; multilingual subtitles; subtitles available for the hearing
impaired in English.

Disney animation became big again with *The Little Mermaid* – between the death and freezing of Walt Disney in 1966 and *Mermaid*'s US release in 1989, the company's animated projects had generally been… well, iffy, to say the least. Remember *Oliver and Company*? Thought not. A retelling of Hans Christian Anderson's fairy tale in typical Disney style (ie, songs and comic-relief animals), *The Little Mermaid* sees teenage flipperfoot Ariel (Benson) falling in love with landlubber Prince Eric (Barnes) after saving him from drowning. Since her father, King Triton, doesn't approve, she's tricked into striking a Faustian pact with evil sea-witch Ursula so she can take on human form, at the cost of her voice. The catch is that if she doesn't get Eric to fall in love with her within three days, she loses her soul to Ursula. The downside of *The Little Mermaid* is entirely technical – it's not that good a DVD. The picture is frighteningly grainy, there are no extras, and the bizarre non-amamorphic 1.66:1 aspect ratio will annoy both 4:3 and 16:9 owners alike. Maybe it's a plot to make you buy a Special Edition three years from now. The upside is that the film is enormously enjoyable. Some of the songs are corny, but most are genuinely hummable (especially the Oscar-winning 'Under The Sea') and there's a gleefully nasty villain in the octopoid form of Ursula, who's just menacing enough to scare younger kids. A DVD showcase it isn't, but *The Little Mermaid* is irresistible family entertainment.

FINAL VERDICT
Picture ☆☆ Sound ☆☆☆ Entertainment ☆☆☆☆
Extras ☆ Value ☆☆
OVERALL ☆☆☆

LITTLE VOICE

Price: £15.99
Supplied by: Miramax

Type of disc: Dual layer, single-sided
No of chapters: 24
Film format(s)/length: 1.85:1 widescreen / 93 mins
Audio format: Dolby Digital 5.1
Director: Mark Herman
Starring: Michael Caine, Ewan McGregor, Jane Horrocks
Year made: 1998
Extras: Scene access; English subtitles.

This small-scale provincial comedy-drama boasts big stars in some of their best performances to date. McGregor (of *Star Wars Episode 1* and *Trainspotting* notoriety) plays it down as the shy boyfriend of a timid, house-bound girl (Horrocks) who has a remarkable talent for mimicking the singing stars of the past. Caine gets under the skin of his shabby character, Ray Say (a sleazy talent scout with an eye on the main chance) and Oscar nominee Brenda Blethyn steals every scene that she's in as the girl's motormouth mother. However it is Horrocks who turns in a superior performance as the epony-mous entertainer who emerges from her self-spun cocoon to sing in the style of Judy Garland, Marilyn Monroe and Shirley Bassey with such accuracy that you would be forgiven for thinking that you were lis-tening to the real thing. You would think that such a story would be the ideal subject for the small screen and that it would be wasted on DVD, but the delights of digital are not exclusively reserved for showing off special effects or being a canvas for large scale spectaculars. This Olivier award-winning stage play comes vividly to life on DVD in a way that it would not do on TV. Realistic flesh tones bring the actors into your living room, greater depth enhances the seaside locations and sharpness ensures that lights do not blur or bleed as they would do on VHS. Don't be put off by the sad lack of extras on this DVD. This is an acting masterclass and an acidly funny film which deserves to be seen by everyone. Who needs ephemeral extras with a film of this quality anyway?

FINAL VERDICT

Picture ☆☆☆☆ Sound ☆☆☆☆ Entertainment ☆☆☆☆
Extras ☆ Value ☆☆
OVERALL ☆☆☆

LITTLE WOMEN

Price: £19.99
Supplied by: Columbia TriStar Home Video
Type of disc: Single layer, single-sided
No of chapters: 28
Film format(s)/length: 1.85:1 widescreen (enhanced for 16:9 widescreen) / 114 mins

Audio format: Dolby Digital 5.1
Director: Gillian Armstrong
Starring: Winona Ryder, Gabriel Byrne, Trini Alvarado
Year made: 1994
Extras: Language and subtitle selections; audio options; behind the scenes featurette; theatrical trailer, simply a storyline brief; DVD trailer, motion clips of other Columbia Pictures on offer; filmographies of some of the cast.

Set in the Civil War, *Little Women* is the all-American classic of our own Jane Austen-style period dramas, where four sisters find their fortunes in life, love and liberation. Although this may not be every-body's cup of tea, the film does offer good wholesome viewing for the entire family. As a DVD package, *Little Women* offers nothing outstanding and sadly follows in the footsteps of other weakened DVD titles, where only the enhanced picture and sound quality (as you would expect from a DVD) justify their existence. Unfortunately the Special Features section is limited in quantity and entertainment. It even offers two virtually identical clips of preview footage, one labelled as the featurette, while the other is the US theatrical trailer, the only difference being that the featurette offers subtitles if required. Other additional features include filmographies, which pro-vide basic background information on the previous roles played by some of the better known actors and actresses from the film. Disappointingly this informa-tion is displayed on stale pages of text that could have easily been animated to enhance this dull feature. Also contained within the Special Features is the DVD trail-er, which although only lasts under a minute, delivers toe-tapping music and displays quick bursts of random film clips categorised as classics. Apart from the usual language and subtitle selections, you'll not find much else on offer, so if you're not into good old family val-ues and character-building lessons, steer well clear.

FINAL VERDICT

Picture ☆☆☆ Sound ☆☆☆ Entertainment ☆☆☆
Extras ☆☆ Value ☆☆
OVERALL ☆☆☆

LIVING OUT LOUD

Price: £19.99
Supplied by: New Line Home Video
Type of disc: Single layer, single-sided
No of chapters: 29
Film format(s)/length: 16:9 widescreen / 96 mins
Audio format: Dolby Digital 5.1
Director: Richard LaGravenese
Starring: Holly Hunter, Danny DeVito, Queen Latifah

Year made: 1998
Extras: Scene access; deleted scenes; trailer; cast and crew biogs; subtitles in English.

It really depends on your age as to how much you can appreciate this plot, but you'd have to be retarded not to appreciate the finest screen performance from Danny DeVito that has ever been committed to film. Judith (Hunter) is a recent divorcee who lives a lonely life spiced up by the odd brief encounter (and the wondering of her over-imagination) who, by chance, begins talking to Pat (DeVito). He's the elevator operator and also suffers loneliness (in this case, brought about by his daughter's death). The two find comfort in each other, and see each other as perhaps the only chance at rebuilding their quickly dwindling lives. The movie follows the lives and fortunes of two middle-aged people, and for all its reflection, realization and aching poignancy, may relate best to an audience of the same age. Still, the standard of the performances is superb, in particular DeVito, who shines so brightly it's blinding. The DVD, although not overloaded with extras, still has appealing deleted scenes, trailer, and fairly full cast and crew bios. Pleasingly, the charm of the film is matched by the contents of the DVD.

FINAL VERDICT

Picture ☆☆☆☆ Sound ☆☆☆☆ Entertainment ☆☆☆
Extras ☆☆☆ Value ☆☆☆☆
OVERALL ☆☆☆

Lock, Stock and Two Smoking Barrels

Price: £17.99
Supplied by: DVD Net (020 8890 2520)
Type of disc: Single layer, double-sided
No of chapters: 26
Film format(s)/length: 4:3, 16:9 widescreen /107 mins
Director: Guy Ritchie
Starring: Jason Flemyng, Dexter Fletcher, Nick Moran, Jason Statham
Year made: 1998
Extras: Interactive menus; trailer; behind the scenes interviews; fullscreen and widescreen versions.

DVDs are sexy – that's why we've all spent hundreds of pounds on a good-looking piece of kit which, we're promised, offers unparalleled picture and sound quality and, more importantly, makes us more popular with the opposite sex. Oh, and it will make us funny too apparently. Yet our cinematic technology is often let down by the shoddy packaging in which our visual delights are usually presented. The nasty Warner cardboard/plastic combo (no fries) is particularly offensive on the eye and cheap to the touch. What we need is a standard – and that standard, gentlemen and gentlemen (oh come on, only men are anal enough about movies to have already bought a DVD player) should be *Lock, Stock and Two Smoking Barrels*. It's a small point, but for the technology to succeed it needs to look good on the shelf. And there's no doubting that this example of British film-making superiority does just that. Thankfully, it also looks good on the screen – which, considering it doubles as a 'Where Are They Now?' of ex-*Grange Hill* stars, genuine crims and QPR mercenary Vinnie Jones, comes as a surprise. Set in London's East End, it's the tale of 4 friends' need to raise half a million quid in order to settle a gambling debt. It's a heist movie at heart – but to describe it in such simple terms would be a massive injustice. So I won't. There are so many interwoven narratives and sub-plots that it needs to be seen more than once in order to fully appreciate how tightly-knitted the film is. It's a sleek visual treat – stylish, witty and gritty, usually at the same time. Writer and director Guy Ritchie's first feature employs so many slick editing tricks that his music promotions past is immediately evident; yet rather than irritating it has the opposite effect. There's such an air of coolness to every aspect of the film, emphasised throughout by the fantastic soundtrack and excellent use of surround. It once again makes you proud to be British. Along with the – yawn – chapter selection, trailer and interactive menus, the DVD offers widescreen and pan-and-scan versions on alternate sides of the disc, and is accompanied by an excellent 32-page brochure. The behind the scenes interviews are a little light on content, but welcome nonetheless. Oh, the menus do look good, though, with plenty of FMV running behind the text. And for once, it's worth putting the subtitles on even if you're not hard of hearing, just to appreciate the quality and quantity of the swearing Also available is the *Director's Cut*, with 9 minutes of extra footage and outtakes during the credits.

FINAL VERDICT

Picture ☆☆☆☆☆ Sound ☆☆☆☆☆
Entertainment ☆☆☆☆☆ Extras ☆☆☆☆
Value ☆☆☆☆
OVERALL ☆☆☆☆☆

Lolita

Price: £19.99
Supplied by: Pathé Distribution Limited
Type of disc: Dual layer, single-sided
No of chapters: 30

Film format(s)/length: 2.35:1 anamorphic / 132 mins
Audio format: Dolby Digital 5.1
Director: Adrian Lyne
Starring: Jeremy Irons, Melanie Griffith, Dominque Swain
Year made: 1997
Extras: Commentary by director Adrian Lyne; casting session with Jeremy Irons and Dominque Swain; featurette; deleted scenes; original theatrical trailer; cast and crew biographies; subtitles for the hearing impaired in English.

It's a moot point whether Vladimir Nabokov's novel *Lolita* is a poignant artistic triumph or the ramblings of a dirty old man. However, it is indisputably a difficult work to film. Striking a balance between child porn and grown-up tragedy has proved even more difficult in pictures than it has been in print. When a director of the calibre of Stanley Kubrick fails to bring a conversion to life, you realise that the book is as good as unfilmable. And when one of the most complex literary works of the twentieth century ends up in the hands of *9 1/2 Weeks'* Adrian Lyne, then you fear the worst. As it turns out though, you needn't have worried. There's nothing here to get the Gary Glitter inside of you excited and nothing you wouldn't normally see in a Britney Spears video. In fact, if there's a criticism to be made of Lyne's work, it's that he's made *Lolita* incredibly middlebrow. Dull even. Sorry to disappoint the marketing people, but there's little particularly 'controversial' about this picture. Lyne's *Lolita* would have been better if it had retained some of the playfulness that leaps off every page of the book. This version is overly stern. Similarly, the extras on the disc are numerous, interesting and, for the most part, deadly serious. A competent and intelligent piece of film-making, this version of *Lolita* is coming soon to a Channel 4 screen near you. It's worthwhile but it's not *American Beauty*.

FINAL VERDICT

Picture ☆☆☆ Sound ☆☆☆ Entertainment ☆☆☆
Extras ☆☆☆☆ Value ☆☆☆☆
OVERALL ☆☆☆

THE LONG KISS GOODNIGHT

Price: £17.99
Supplied by: DVDplus (www.dvdplus.co.uk)
Type of disc: Single layer, single-sided
No of chapters: 12
Film format(s)/length: 2.35:1 widescreen / 115 mins
Audio format: Dolby Surround
Director: Renny Harlin
Starring: Geena Davis, Samuel L Jackson, Patrick

Malahide
Year made: 1996
Extras: Scene access; 'Making of' featurette; stunt scenes (access to action sequences in the film); cinematic trailer.

It took a radical move from Shane Black to distinguish *The Long Kiss Goodnight* from the formulaic buddy flicks pumped out in homage to his very own *Lethal Weapon*. Casting Geena Davis as the lead was a shrewd move; the film's appeal was broadened and the way was paved for girl power. The Spice Girls and Lara Croft owe much to Davis's Charly Baltimore. The plot – small-town teacher discovers her amnesia hides a previous life as a highly-trained secret agent – is obviously far-fetched, but it's the action sequences that aim to please. The film's set-pieces become increasingly ambitious, and with the exception of a couple of dodgy moments, are handled supremely. A booming soundtrack complements the slick on-screen action – in terms of bangs-per-buck, *The Long Kiss Goodnight* is another DVD showcase. The same can't be said of the disc's 'added value'. Lasting a measly 6 minutes, half of which is taken up by scenes lifted from the trailer, the 'Making of' features superficial interviews with the three principles plus director and half a dozen quick clips of proper behind the scenes footage. The promised section on stunts is nothing more than a way of beefing up the ridiculously few chapters the movie features, by allowing you to jump straight to one of four action sequences. A right royal rip-off. It's almost as if the disc would be better off minus these extras, such is the bitter taste they leave. Do yourself a favour – cover up the menu button with some chewing gum, and enjoy the feature presentation.

FINAL VERDICT

Picture ☆☆☆☆ Sound ☆☆☆☆
Entertainment ☆☆☆☆ Extras ☆☆ Value ☆☆☆
OVERALL ☆☆☆

LOOK WHO'S TALKING

Price: £19.99
Supplied by: Columbia TriStar Home Video
Type of disc: Single layer, single-sided
No of chapters: 35
Film format(s)/length: 1.85:1 widescreen enhanced / 92 minutes
Audio format: Dolby Surround
Director: Amy Heckerling
Starring: John Travolta, Kirstie Alley, (the voice of) Bruce Willis
Year made: 1989

Extras: Scene access; filmographies; soundtrack in French, German, Italian and Spanish; subtitles in 19 languages.

The instigator of a decade of voice-overs, *Look Who's Talking* broke new ground cinematically with arguably its biggest star – Bruce Willis – lending his vocal talents in the role of the confused infant, Mikey. The result was an endearing, at times hilarious comedy with something for everyone. As a film to release on DVD, *Look Who's Talking* is a great choice, because despite its age it's still great to watch and outshines the numerous sequels that it spawned. However, due to the age of the movie you'd expect to get something for your money that perhaps you didn't when you bought the video. What you get instead though is poor picture quality with the audio impression not that much better. It's a shame, because this movie really is a joy to watch, but the fact is you'd be better off purchasing a copy of the original video cassette version from the bargain basket in Woolworth's.

FINAL VERDICT

Picture ☆☆☆ Sound ☆☆☆ Entertainment ☆☆☆☆
Extras ☆☆ Value ☆☆
OVERALL ☆☆

THE LOST BOYS

Price: £15.99
Starring: Warner Home Video
Type of disc: Single layer, single-sided
No of chapters: 32
Film format(s)/length: 2:35.1 widescreen / 93 mins
Director: Joel Schumacher
Starring: Jason Patric, Corey Haim, Kiefer Sutherland
Year made: 1987
Extras: Chapter select; cast and crew biographies; theatrical trailer.

Joel Schumacher's stylish vampires-for-the-Eighties offering sees brothers Michael and Sam settling in California dream town Santa Carla following their mother's divorce. Dream soon turns into nightmare, though, as Michael – played by Jason Patric – falls in with the wrong crowd. The wrong crowd of vampires, that is. Encapsulating the glossy Eighties revival in teen culture, *The Lost Boys* is a flawed masterpiece. Vamps are cool, but clichéd – they wear leather jackets, ride motorbikes, and get the best gals. Playing on emergent MTV culture, *The Lost Boys* runs like an extended MOR video. After all, who didn't want to stay out partying all night and sleep all the day among the fledgling slacker youth? On DVD, *The Lost Boys* is guaranteed to evoke blood-red summer memories in those over 25. Revelling in a beach-party

atmos, with a beguiling soundtrack, rites of passage were never so darkly seductive. While extras are limited to a few notable production details and cast and director biographies, those who harken back to a time of shallow hedonism and the promise of eternal youth will find the fang-sharp detail a treat.

FINAL VERDICT

Picture ☆☆☆☆ Sound ☆☆☆☆☆
Entertainment ☆☆☆☆ Extras ☆☆☆ Value ☆☆☆
OVERALL ☆☆☆

LOST IN SPACE

Price: £19.99
Supplied by: Entertainment in Video
Type of disc: Dual layer, single-sided
No of chapters: 24
Film format(s)/length: 16:9 widescreen / 130 mins
Audio format: Dolby Digital 5.1
Director: Stephen Hopkins
Starring: Gary Oldman, William Hurt, Matt LeBlanc
Year made: 1998
Extras: Cast and crew information with video clips; 2 music videos; deleted scenes with preproduction animation; US and International trailers; special effects documentary; production design stills; director's commentary.

It's not very often a low-budget American TV series from the mid-Sixties gets made into a multi-million dollar movie, but New Line Cinema decided to do just that with *Lost in Space* – and boy, is the result trashy! The movie can't quite decide whether it's a camp update of the original TV series, or a serious science fiction epic. It's made up of mainly CGI effects with bad acting and poor dubbing piled on thick. Many have raved about the movie, but this reviewer found the whole experience quite hilarious! Having said that, *Lost in Space* makes quite a decent DVD. They have really gone all out to give fans of the movie the full *Lost in Space* experience with a good selection of extras, all packaged into a clunky but cool interactive menu system. There's a behind the scenes documentary where the English computer graphics producers talk you through the stages involved in creating slick sci-fi effects, and music videos by Apollo 440 and Crystal Method. The disc includes teaser and theatrical trailers to whet your appetite and loads of information on the cast and crew, including short interviews with the stars talking about their roles. If you're a true fan of *Lost in Space* you'll be interested to know that there's a complete director's commentary that you can switch on and off as you watch the movie where each scene is explained and the stresses and strains of movie production laid bare. There's also a special option to view deleted scenes that show entire storylines that were cut from the finished movie – these are particularly fascinating and include a large animatronic creature that they didn't use! There's no doubting that *Lost in Space* on DVD offers much more than your average Region 2 release and that's a real plus point. It's good to see New Line Cinema offering their viewers value for money with so many extras, it's just a shame the movie behind it all is so dire! One for fans only.

FINAL VERDICT

Picture ☆☆☆☆ Sound ☆☆☆☆
Entertainment ☆☆ Extras ☆☆☆☆☆ Value ☆☆☆
OVERALL ☆☆☆

THE LOVE BUG

Price: £15.99
Supplied by: Warner Home Video
Type of disc: Single layer, single-sided
No of chapters:
Film format(s)/length: 4:3 regular / 103 mins
Audio format: Dolby Digital 5.0
Director: Robert Stevenson
Starring: Dean Jones, Michele Lee, David Tomlinson
Year made: 1969
Extras: Scene access; English and French soundtrack; Dutch subtitles.

God bless the tiny children, that's what I say – unless, that is, they are using the grown-ups' DVD players. While I'm a firm believer in giving kids the best that you possibly can, if they haven't contributed a year's worth of their pocket money to the DVD kitty they can stick to watching Tots TV on – shudder – video, for all I care. However, *The Love Bug* is perfect children's entertainment. You know the pitch – it's the VW Beetle with attitude in a wholesome Disney extravaganza, and will keep anyone under the age of puberty quiet for nearly two hours. Best of all, with no extras to speak of the young unshaven have no excuse to grubby your remote. Slip down the pub when it's on though – the speeded-up car chases and hideous blue screen 'special' effects look worse in digital format. And the waste of Dolby Digital is bordering on criminal.

FINAL VERDICT

Picture ☆☆☆ Sound ☆☆ Entertainment ☆☆
Extras ☆ Value ☆☆
OVERALL ☆☆

LOVERS OF THE ARCTIC CIRCLE

Price: £19.99
Supplied by: MetroTartan
Type of disc: Single layer, single-sided

No of chapters: 15
Film format(s)/length: 2.35:1 anamorphic / 104 mins
Audio format: Dolby Surround
Starring: Julio Medem
Year Made: Najwa Nimri, Fele Martinez, Nancho Novo
Year made: 1998
Extras: Scene access; interview with director Julio Medem; star and director filmographies; photo gallery; film review; theatrical trailer; soundtrack in Spanish; subtitles in English.

Just when Hollywood's box office-friendly idea of a romantic drama seemed ready to drown us in saccharine, along comes a fresh, mesmerising new film that plays as much with time and space as it does with our hearts. *Los Amantes Del Círculo Polar* (to give it its original Spanish name) follows Ana (Nimri) and Otto (Martinez) over 17 years as fate conspires to make them fall in and out of a complex love affair. It's filled with touching understated performances, thought provoking ruminations on life and love and dashes of ironic humour. The symmetry of the film is carried through the attractive but static menu screens and supplements. A mini-essay, cast biographies and a Q&A session with Medem is presented in scrolling text, but no live interviews, unfortunately. In short, it's a fantastic, unforgettable journey of a movie on an inventive DVD. Two things they said would never happen on a region-free disc…

FINAL VERDICT

Picture ☆☆☆☆ Sound ☆☆☆
Entertainment ☆☆☆☆☆ Extras ☆☆☆ Value ☆☆☆
OVERALL ☆☆☆☆

MACBETH

Price: £19.99
Supplied by: Second Sight
Type of disc: Single layer, single-sided
No of chapters: 16
Film format(s)/length: 4:3 regular / 103 mins
Audio format: Mono
Director: Orson Welles
Starring: Orson Welles, Jeanette Nolan, Dan O'Herlihy
Year made: 1948
Extras: Scene access; Orson Welles' *Ghost Story: Return to Glennascaul* mini-film; brief context-giving notes on back sleeve.

Baby-faced film deity Orson Welles presents The Scottish Play in his own distinctive style, abridging, directing and starring in this 1948 production. The plot, as any GCSE student will tell you, follows veteran warrior Macbeth's fall from grace due to supernatural forces and his own lust for glory. Pop psychologists may speculate why Welles chose Shakespeare's darkest play to film above all others. Honourable Macbeth (Welles) encounters three crones who foretell a series of promotions for him, leading to the crown of Scotland itself. Lady Macbeth (Nolan) seizes the moment and rallies her reluctant husband to assassinate the king, but triggers Big Mac's descent into paranoia, duplicity and murder. *Macbeth* is presented here in its original cut. Though the dust-specked picture betrays its age and the hissing mono sound won't tax your system, hats off to Second Sight for having the good grace and initiative to encode *Ghost Story: Return to Glennascaul* along with the main feature. In a precursor to the *Alfred Hitchcock Presents* TV show, Welles uses his celebrity to introduce, act in and narrate this 26-minute curiosity from 1951, the addition of which makes the disc even more attractive to Welles fans. Filmmaker Peter Bogdanovich, Welles' friend during the Seventies, does a piece to camera from his home in 1992. He provides a nice snapshot of Orson's early career in the theatre and radio. *Macbeth* is a fine addition to any Welles collection but technical and feature improvements could have been made.

FINAL VERDICT

Picture ☆☆ Sound ☆ Entertainment ☆☆☆
Extras ☆☆ Value ☆☆
OVERALL ☆☆

MAD COWS

Price: £19.99
Supplied by: Entertainment in Video
Type of disc: Single layer, single-sided
No of chapters: 6
Film format(s)/length: 1.75:1 anamorphic / 87 mins
Audio format: Dolby Digital 5.1
Director: Sara Sugarman
Starring: Anna Friel, Joanna Lumley, Anna Massey
Year made: 1999
Extras: Scene access; theatrical trailer; interviews with cast and crew (8 mins); featurette.

Based on the novel of the same name, *Mad Cows* is a story of a single Australian mother who gets put in jail after she's caught stealing a bag of frozen peas. Despite the rather dubious and highly implausible plot this is enjoyable and at times very funny to watch. Just don't buy this expecting a 'laugh-a-minute', as all the quotes on the box seem to think. It's certainly a very fast-paced film though, and at times feels a bit like a music video. This is apt considering it has a fairly strong, if charty, soundtrack with music from Robbie Williams, Groove Armada

and Space. The sound quality actually does them the justice they deserve, which is more than can be said for the extras. At a first glance the extras sound quite appealing. Unfortunately, the featurette merely consists of cut-down versions of the trailer and the interviews are mixed up, so a lot of information is repeated. It's nice to have the extended and more complete versions of the interviews on the disc, but they only add up to 8 minutes, which isn't really much when split between several members of cast and crew. *Mad Cows* is an amusing little film and the extras will distract your attention for a short while, but the humour on display here really is quite different to most British comedies. Worth renting perhaps, but far from a must buy.

FINAL VERDICT

Picture ☆☆☆ Sound ☆☆☆ Entertainment ☆☆☆
Extras ☆☆ Value ☆☆
OVERALL ☆☆☆

MAD MAX BEYOND THUNDERDOME

Price: £15.99
Supplied by: Warner Home Video
Type of disc: Single layer, single-sided
No of chapters: 30
Film format(s)/length: 2.35:1 widescreen / 102 mins
Audio format: Dolby Digital 5.1, Dolby Surround
Directors: George Miller and George Ogilvie
Starring: Mel Gibson, Tina Turner, Angelo Rossitto
Year made: 1985
Extras: Scene access; interactive menus; production notes; theatrical trailer.

Miller and Ogilvie's bleak look a post-apocalyptic Australia is certainly not as good as the two previous films, and often plays for laughs rather than gritty realism. Mel Gibson reprises his role as the titular embittered ex-cop righting wrongs in the outback. Max arrives at Bartertown to trade his skills for information and is introduced to Aunty Entity (Turner – looking worse for wear). Entity promises to reveal the location of Max's stolen truck in return for solving a power battle with underworld rival Master-Blaster – a mutant comprising a giant, Blaster, and the brains of the operation, Master (Rossitto). After picking a fight with the muscle, a gladiatorial battle ensues in the Thunderdome arena where there is only one rule: two men enter, one man leaves. *Beyond Thunderdome* is undoubtedly the weak link in the trilogy, with more of a family emphasis (hence an abundance of squeaky vagrant kids who get annoying only seconds after they are introduced) and violence which is considerably tamer than the first two films. God help us, Mad

Max has become politically correct! Turner is weak and mumbling as the central villain and even Gibson himself seems resigned to going through the motions. The quality of the picture is average compared to most DVDs to date and the monotonous sandy backdrops and lack of positive set colours do little to help. As for the features, unless you're a fan of production notes there is little to make you 'mad' for this purchase.

FINAL VERDICT

Picture ☆☆ Sound ☆☆ Entertainment ☆☆
Extras ☆☆ Value ☆☆
OVERALL ☆☆

MAD MAX 2

Price: £15.99
Supplied by: DVD World (01705 796662)
Type of disc: Single layer, single-sided
No of chapters: 32
Film format(s)/length: 2.35:1 widescreen / 91 mins
Audio Format: Dolby Digital 5.1
Director: George Miller
Starring: Mel Gibson, Bruce Spence, Michael Preston
Year made: 1981
Extras: Dolby Digital English and French soundtracks; Italian soundtrack in mono; multilingual subtitles; English and Italian captions for hearing impaired.

It has to be said this is perhaps the worst packaged DVD we've seen to date, a crude collage of grainy imagery that is precisely what we don't expect from DVD. On opening the box you almost expect to see a spool of Super8 film which, funnily enough, is exactly what the film begins with: a collection of old news reels spliced together to set the scene for what's to follow. It's a hackneyed cliché, yet also highly effective, particularly when the roar of the Road Warrior's engine cuts in to give your Dolby Digital a good work out. The story is as brutally stripped down as Max's cruiser, creature comforts such as dialogue are pared back to the barest minimum. Mad Max begins the movie as a complete loner, but his apparent coldness is worn away by encountering a community besieged by bizarre warriors led by the Humungus, an SM-styled freak who says even less than Max. It's a standard plot-line fondly exploited by numerous Westerns, but what sets *Mad Max 2* apart is the relentless brutality – there's absolutely no sentimentality to soften the carnage. The pace of the move is fast and unrelenting, while the action scenes are often extraordinary with the finale a classic of its kind. Widely regarded as the best of the series, some shoddy packaging can't spoil a fine film. What is disappointing is presentation within the DVD. Of the 32 chapters, only 9 are highlighted for direct access off the main menu. Worse, although the packaging promises production notes, there's no sign of them on the disc itself. Picture quality is generally impressive although as a 2.35:1 widescreen production it barely fills half the screen on a conventional TV. Moreover, the film stock is far from flawless with the occasional scratch or other flaw appearing on screen. Given the post-apocalyptic feel, this doesn't ruin the atmosphere, but overall this is a serious missed opportunity.

FINAL VERDICT

Picture ☆☆ Sound ☆☆☆ Entertainment ☆☆☆☆
Extras ☆ Value ☆☆☆
OVERALL ☆☆☆

MANHATTAN

Price: £19.99
Supplied by: MGM Home Entertainment
Type of disc: Dual layer, single-sided
No of chapters: 24
Film format(s)/length: 2.35:1 anamorphic / 96 mins
Audio format: Mono
Director: Woody Allen
Starring: Woody Allen, Diane Keaton, Michael Murphy
Year made: 1979
Extras: Scene access; theatrical trailer; soundtrack in English, German, Spanish, French and Italian; subtitles in 12 languages; subtitles for the hearing impaired in English and German.

"Chapter One. He was as tough and romantic as the city he loved. Beneath his black-rimmed glasses was the coiled sexual power of a jungle cat. I love this. New York was his town, and it always would be…" With this monologue, cut together with black and white shots of the Big Apple and the beautiful music of George Gershwin's 'Rhapsody in Blue', Woody Allen ushers in *Manhattan*, a complex romantic comedy that's pure movie magic. Woody All… sorry, Isaac Davies is a 42-year-old Manhattanite who hates his job of writing gags for comedy shows but enjoys intellectual discussions with his 17-year-old girlfriend (Mariel Hemingway), plus close friends Yale (Murphy) and his wife. His lesbian ex-wife (Meryl Streep), is about to publish a tell-all book about their marriage, which just adds to his handwringing anguish. But into Isaac's life comes Yale's mistress, a headstrong journalist called Mary (Keaton), and the two instantly strike up a beguiling friendship, then romance. The stage is set for more angst-ridden meditations by Allen the auteur: sex, death, religion, New York, jazz, analysts, Ingmar Bergman, plus his anti-television and pro-cinema bias. It's a mix that hasn't always worked in his films before or since, but here they all gel perfectly, laced with memorable and funny lines. Credit to MGM for presenting *Manhattan* in 2.35:1 anamorphic widescreen, just as the Region 1 disc. The picture is surprisingly clear given the print's age, with the blacks and whites well defined. Audio, on the other hand, is not good enough – flat mono is far from the best way to hear Allen's quips or Gershwin's music. Why was this classic not given the enhanced treatment it deserves? *Manhattan* and *Annie Hall* are the two best discs to buy for fans of Allen, or if you want to find out why just about every cineaste is a fan of his. Unfortunately, the disc won't win over any new people to DVD.

FINAL VERDICT

Picture ☆☆☆☆ Sound ☆ Entertainment ☆☆☆☆☆
Extras ☆☆ Value ☆☆
OVERALL ☆☆

Manhunter

Price: £15.99
Supplied by: BMG Video
Type of disc: Single layer, single-sided
No of chapters: 26
Film format(s)/length: 2.35:1 widescreen / 115 mins
Audio format: PCM Linear stereo
Director: Michael Mann
Starring: William L Petersen, Brian Cox, Dennis Farina
Year made: 1986
Extras: Scene access; the novels of Thomas Harris (brief promotion blurb about each one); film notes; *Red Dragon* notes.

Though *Silence of the Lambs* is rightly revered as one of cinema's greatest thrillers, it owes at least one of its Oscars to *Manhunter*. It's as if Jonathan Demme, director of its sequel, *Silence of the Lambs*, used Michael Mann as a feasibility study, so similar are the two in content. Yet don't let that put you off – as *Jurassic 'Westworld' Park* and *El Mariachi Desperado* proved, it's perfectly possible to get two films out of one good idea. Anyone who has seen *Silence of the Lambs* will be in familiar territory – replace Clarice Starling with Will Graham, Buffalo Bill with The Tooth Fairy and Hannibal Lecter with, well, Hannibal 'Lecktor' and you'll have Manhunter's plot in a nutshell. Where the two films do differ though, is in style – Demme's flick was finely polished; Mann's treatment is much more raw. Although *Manhunter* predated *Silence of the Lambs* by 6 years,

the synthesised Eighties soundtrack and minimalist direction make the gap seem much larger, resulting in a tense thriller that is different enough to its higher-profile sequel to justify a DVD release of its own. Forgive the treble-heavy sonics and very occasional artefact, and you'll find everything in order as far as the main feature goes. The film notes prove interesting yet brief and the section on Thomas Harris's books nothing more than an advert for *Hannibal*, the third Lecter novel, but both are welcome nonetheless. And that's it, as far as extras go, unless you count chapter selection. But overall, you're buying *Manhunter* for the Lecter history lesson. Think of it as *Definitely Maybe* to *What's The Story...* – essentially the same, yet a lot less commercial.

FINAL VERDICT

Picture ☆☆☆☆ Sound ☆☆☆ Entertainment ☆☆☆☆
Extras ☆☆ Value ☆☆☆
OVERALL ☆☆☆

Maniac Cop

Price: £15.99
Supplied by: Synergy
Type of disc: Single layer, single-sided
No of chapters: 31
Film format(s)/length: 4:3 regular / 81 mins
Audio format: Stereo
Director: William Lustig
Starring: Bruce Campbell, Tom Atkins, Laurene Landon
Year made: 1988
Extras: Scene access; trailer; trailers for *The Exterminator*, *Frankenhooker*, *Red Scorpion*, *Basket Case* 1, 2 and 3.

With a title like that, and one of the greatest ever tag lines – "You have the right to remain silent... forever" – you know you're going to get. *Maniac Cop* is a good old-fashioned slasher flick from producer Larry Cohen, the man who brought you, er, *Q: The Winged Serpent* and *It's Alive!* When a New York cop starts murdering innocent citizens, suspicion falls on Jack Forrest (Campbell) – not least because shortly after she discovered he was having an affair, his wife's corpse was found in the same motel room used for his tryst. Jack and his lover (Landon) have to prove his innocence and stay one step ahead of the cops, while the real killer stabs and strangles his way through the police department on a trail of vengeance. *Maniac Cop* isn't nearly as exploitative as it could (and should) be, but as low-budget slashers go it's pacy, well-shot and has a suitably indestructable villain. Unfortunately, the DVD doesn't really do it justice. Offering only a 4:3 picture, the disc compounds this fault by using a dust-speckled, weaving print as the basis of its transfer, then rounds it off with encoding that hugely exaggerates the film grain and leaves intermittent ghost images wafting across the screen. The sound is basic stereo, but since that's how the film was made it would be unreasonable to expect anything more. As for it being a 'collectors [sic] edition', one trailer and adverts for its sister discs hardly justifies the term!

FINAL VERDICT

Picture ☆☆ Sound ☆☆ Entertainment ☆☆☆
Extras ☆☆ Value ☆☆☆
OVERALL ☆☆☆

THE MAN IN THE IRON MASK

Price: £19.99
Supplied by: MGM
Type of disc: Single layer, single-sided
No of chapters: 36
Film format(s)/length: 1.85:1 widescreen / 132 minutes
Director: Randall Wallace
Starring: Leonardo DiCaprio, Jeremy Irons, John Malkovich
Year made: 1997
Extras: Director's commentary; 8-page booklet; chapter search; original theatrical trailer.

With such incredible drama and a storyline of rare depth, it would only be fitting that *The Man in the Iron Mask* was done justice with a superb DVD version. While it still pales in comparison to many of the overwhelmingly comprehensive Region 1 discs, this is certainly a quality package for those who were captured by the gripping story of King Louis XIV. Most importantly, you get detailed commentary from the film's director, Randall Wallace. He speaks passionately about the project, scene-by-scene, giving an interesting explanation of the choice to incorporate certain shots or directorial techniques you probably didn't even notice the first time you watched. The 8-page booklet, only 5 pages of which contain written information about the film, would be disappointing if you hadn't come to expect so little from these read-once pamphlets. Text is clearly padded out to fill the space – and who wants to read something on old fashioned dead tree media that should have been part of the Special Features section on the disc itself? As consolation, the disc does contain the original trailer used to promote the movie in cinemas, which is again a once-only deal but you just like to know it's there. As an audio-visual experience, it's almost all good news. The orchestral score which is so vital to the grandiose, lump-in-the-throat proceedings is

extremely well reproduced, as are the crisp sound effects. The video track lets the film down a tiny bit with occasional speckles from the master. That ornate 17th century architecture plays havoc with the MPEG encoding at times too, although the colour and edge definition are excellent.

FINAL VERDICT

Picture ☆☆☆ Sound ☆☆☆☆
Entertainment ☆☆☆☆☆ Extras ☆☆ Value ☆☆☆☆
OVERALL ☆☆☆☆

THE MAN WHO KNEW TOO MUCH

Price: £9.99
Supplied by: Carlton
Type of disc: Single layer, single-sided
No of chapters: 15
Film format(s)/length: 4:3 regular / 72 mins
Audio format: Mono
Director: Alfred Hitchcock
Starring: Leslie Banks, Edna Best, Peter Lorre
Year made: 1934
Extras: Scene access; trailer for other Silver Collection DVDs.

This is one of Hitchcock's early British films, made before he went to Hollywood and never looked back. This relatively short work presents one of several favourite themes that the auteur would return to time and time again, that of the average man pursued and pushed to extremes by forces beyond his control. A family visiting a Swiss resort stumbles upon a plot to assassinate a politician. Their daughter is kidnapped to guarantee their silence, but the father (Banks) attempts to rescue her himself. Though lacking the expertise of Hitchcock's later films, this still stands as an interesting thriller all by itself. Granted, its copyrights may have changed many times, but Carlton has yet to realise that consumers are willing to pay more for a better presented and stocked DVD. The company should have spent extra time and money collecting assets for this film instead of throwing it out like this, half-baked.

FINAL VERDICT

Picture ☆ Sound ☆ Entertainment ☆☆☆
Extras ☆ Value ☆☆
OVERALL ☆☆

MARCH OF THE WOODEN SOLDIERS

Price: £15.99
Supplied by: Eureka Video
Type of disc: Single layer, single-sided
No of chapters: 12
Film format(s)/length: 4:3 regular / 77 mins

Audio format: Mono
Directors: Gus Meins and Charles Rogers
Starring: Stan Laurel, Oliver Hardy, Charlotte Henry
Year made: 1934
Extras: Scene access; Stan Laurel early silent *Hustling for Health* (1915); biographies of Stan Laurel and Oliver Hardy.

It's not really the sort of thing you'd expect. Admittedly, the content of most Laurel and Hardy films never seems that plausible, but this time, Hal Roach seemed to believe that their popular brand of comedy could shine out from the genre of children's fairy tales. But he wasn't completely wrong – the comedy duo still manage to reassure their audience they're not too out of their depth playing Stannie Dum and Ollie Dee, two brainless toy makers in Toyland. However, there is something that doesn't sit right about this. Their humour often seems out of place, and more often than not takes second place to the glorious sets and costumes. But at least the DVD format is refreshingly well respected. The possibility of getting a director's commentary was probably not on the cards, but the idea of using Stan Laurel's previous work as extra footage is a nice touch.

FINAL VERDICT
Picture ☆☆☆ Sound ☆
Entertainment ☆☆☆ Extras ☆☆ Value ☆☆
OVERALL ☆☆

MARS ATTACKS!

Price: £15.99
Company: Warner Home Video
Type of disc: Single layer, single-sided
No of chapters: 38
Film format(s)/length: 2.35:1 widescreen /102 mins
Director: Tim Burton
Starring: Jack Nicholson, Glenn Close, Pierce Brosnan
Year made: 1996
Extras: Production notes; scene access; theatrical trailer; multilingual subtitles; music only option.

Sod *Independence Day*, this is much more like it. Taking the basic premise of Martians invading the Earth, director Tim Burton assembles a cast of top names, and then proceeds to bump them off, one by one. There's Jack Nicholson's slimey President, trying to keep order whilst calming his stuck-up wife, Glenn Close. There's a beheaded Pierce Brosnan chatting up a similarly decapitated Sarah Jessica Parker. Danny DeVito and Michael J Fox interject for 5 minutes before being blown to bits, leaving none other than Tom Jones to save the world. It's a mighty cool film, done justice by a quality DVD. Top picks have to be

the cracking 5.1 sound mix and the option to cut the dialogue and just listen to Danny Elfman's excellent score. The picture is refreshingly bright and crisp too, competently reflecting the mayhem on screen. A few more extras would have been nice, but what you do get is damn fine stuff.

FINAL VERDICT
Picture ☆☆☆☆ Sound ☆☆☆☆☆
Entertainment ☆☆☆☆
Extras ☆☆ Value ☆☆☆☆
OVERALL ☆☆☆☆

MARY POPPINS

Price: £15.99
Supplied by: Buena Vista
Type of disc: Single layer, double-sided (flipper)
No of chapters: 25
Film format(s)/length: 1.85:1 widescreen / 139 mins
Audio format: Dolby Digital 5.1
Director: Robert Stevenson
Starring: Julie Andrews, Dick Van Dyke David Tomlinson
Year made: 1964
Extras: Subtitles in English, Dutch, and English close-captioned.

With a classic like *Mary Poppins*, you'd have thought Disney could supply at least a few additional treats. The option of skipping every scene featuring the execrable Dick Van Dyke would have been a start. Alas, this was not to be, and the Mouse House has scrimped on the extras once again. Julie Andrews stars as the magic nanny who's "practically perfect in every way", bringing an Edwardian family closer together by way of some brilliantly catchy songs and occasionally surreal set pieces (singing penguin waiters, anyone?). It all makes for top-notch family entertainment, carried out with wit, exuberance and charm. The DVD treatment has greatly enhanced the colour and contrast of the film, rendering the picture bright, crisp, and even perkier than before. Unfortunately, this also means that many of the effects shots and painted backgrounds are shown up for what they really are, which detracts from the overall magic slightly. Sound is generally very good if a little limited in scope by the nature of the music, although the chimney sweep 'Step in Time' number – culminating in fireworks – benefits greatly from the digital remaster. Shamefully, this is a flipper, and another letdown is the lack of extras. Apart from the scene selection, which is structured mainly around the score, there is nothing. In case you're wondering, the Region 1 doesn't have any either, so at least Disney's stinginess isn't selective. However, considering its status as one of the best film musicals ever made, *Mary Poppins* surely deserves better.

FINAL VERDICT

Picture ☆☆☆☆ Sound ☆☆☆

Entertainment ☆☆☆☆☆ Extras ☆ Value ☆☆

OVERALL ☆☆☆

MARY REILLY

Price: £19.99

Supplied by: Columbia TriStar Home Video

Type of disc: Dual layer, single-sided

No of chapters: 28

Film format(s)/length: 1.85:1 widescreen enhanced / 104 mins

Audio format: Dolby Digital 5.1

Director: Stephen Frears

Starring: Julia Roberts, John Malkovich, Michael Gambon

Year made: 1995

Extras: Theatrical trailer, Brief behind-the-scenes featurette; subtitles in 19 languages; soundtrack in English, French, German, Spanish and Italian; cast and crew biogs.

Oh dear. Presumably conceived just as *Bram Stoker's Dracula* was cleaning up at the box office, *Mary Reilly* is a film straight out of Julia Roberts' dodgy period, a flop that puts a none-too-impressive spin on the Dr Jekyll and Mr Hyde story. Poor but not a complete disaster, it's a film with some okayish moments, but a misjudged performance from John Malkovich and an underwhelming Roberts rob it of any drive. The disc is better though, with an above-average full Dolby Digital mix and a picture that shows the benefits of anamorphic enhancement. It's very dark in places though, which does highlight one or two flaws but generally it's a good piece of work. Extras include a 6-minute feature, standard cast and crew notes and not a lot else. A below par film, there's really little reason to spend your money on this. Not even in a sale.

FINAL VERDICT

Picture ☆☆☆☆ Sound ☆☆☆ Entertainment ☆☆

Extras ☆☆ Value ☆☆

OVERALL ☆☆

THE MASK

Price: £19.99

Supplied by: Entertainment in Video

Type of disc: Single-layer, single-sided

No of chapters: 30

Film format(s)/length: 16:9 widescreen / 97 mins

Audio format: Dolby Digital 5.1

Director: Charles Russell

Starring: Jim Carrey, Peter Riegert, Cameron Diaz

Year made: 1994

Extras: Theatrical trailer; interview bites; cast biographies; B-roll; the 'Making of' documentary; director's commentary.

One of the best cartoon-style special effects movies to be released in the last few years has to be *The Mask* and it has the added attraction of starring Jim Carrey – the king of rubber faces! The character originates from the Dark Horse comic books and has made a perfect conversion to film with brightly coloured costumes, exaggerated action sequences and great special effects. The movie also sees the big screen debut of the beautiful Cameron Diaz as the love interest for Carrey's character, and you really do get to see plenty of her! We all know it's a great film, many of us will already have it on video, but now it's out on DVD we can enjoy the full *Mask* experience with an enhanced picture and sound quality. Region 2 DVD owners have grown used to a disappointing experience when buying their movies. Over in the US, viewers have enjoyed documentaries, games, scripts and all kinds of wonderful extras, whereas in Blighty we've had to put up with a trailer and cast biogs – big deal! Well the tides seem to be turning. New Line Cinema seem to appreciate the custom of the Region 2 users and are including many more fun-packed features into their DVDs. *The Mask* has an excellent director's commentary where each wacky scene is explained as it plays so you can learn the thought processes behind creating such a visually fascinating movie. There's a 'Making of' documentary too with plenty of behind-the-scenes footage that will keep you glued to the screen. Add to this interviews with the cast, an interactive menu that keeps to the style of the movie and the run-of-the-mill trailers and cast biogs and you've got a really great package. If you've already got *The Mask* on video, it's worth buying again on DVD for an insight into the mad world of Jim Carrey, and a fascinating look at the movie production process.

FINAL VERDICT

Picture ☆☆☆☆ Sound ☆☆☆☆

Entertainment ☆☆☆☆☆

Extras ☆☆☆☆ Value ☆☆☆☆

OVERALL ☆☆☆☆

THE MASK OF ZORRO

Price: £19.99

Supplied by: Columbia TriStar Home Video

Type of disc: Dual layer, single-sided
No of chapters: 28
Film format(s)/length: 2.35:1 widescreen / 116 minutes
Audio format: Dolby Digital 5.1
Director: Martin Campbell
Starring: Antonio Banderas, Anthony Hopkins, Catherine Zeta-Jones
Year made: 1998
Extras: Scene access; 45-min documentary: *Unmasking Zorro*; deleted scene – 'The Wallet'; director's commentary; US theatrical trailer; music video by Tina Arena and Mark Anthony, 'I Want to Spend My Life Loving You'; publicity photos; filmographies; English and German soundtracks; subtitles in 15 languages.

There's a sense here that someone tried to jump on a band wagon, gave up and built their own. What *The Mask of Zorro* could have been, and what it is are two refreshingly different things. It could have been an opportunity for a studio to make some money and follow an unfortunately increasing trend to look to the past rather than it's own imagination for influence. The Robin Hood-style character of Zorro has been immortalised on screen nearly 40 times, so is one more outing really necessary? Well to be honest, it wasn't, but luckily the project fell into the talented lap of Campbell and so was blessed from the start. *The Mask of Zorro* isn't just another attempt at the Zorro genre. It's a respectful definition of it. What Campbell has done here is to take a classic screen icon from the past, and not try to reinvent it, but to enhance it into something greater than its previous incarnations have ever been. Campbell was also responsible for *GoldenEye*, so it's not surprising that certain Bond-esque elements are easy to spot. There might not be an in-depth plot, but there's plenty of action, an empire-driven villain, a bloodthirsty henchman, a gorgeous girl and loads of weapons. Even the opening sequence is Bond-like, as Zorro walks on in silhouette and carves a 'Z' into the screen in just the same way as Bond flashes his gunbarrel around in the title sequence of every 007 movie. Perhaps Campbell is paying homage to Bond. Perhaps not, but whatever the reason, he doesn't let these elements overplay the respect he pays to the original Zorro films. There's more than enough swashbuckling to keep any Douglas Fairbanks fan happy, and the action is choreographed with fresh beauty. Although the plot is fairly thin on the ground, it is thickened up by an above-average script, stunning action sequences, near visual perfection and a great cast. Hopkins plays the role of Don Diego De La Vega (the original Zorro), with a perfect balance of bitterness and wisdom. This is equally matched by the enthusiasm and excitement that Banderas pours out onto the screen as Alejandro Murrieta (Zorro in waiting). Catherine Zeta-Jones is rather exotic as the only central female character, and actually has a purpose in the movie, albeit not a very big one. In fact, every one of the cast does a superb job of turning this throwaway action movie into one you'd rather not throw away. It's also pleasing to note that of the principal cast, only one is a-non European. Zeta-Jones is convincingly Spanish, Hopkins is convincingly Welsh and Banderas is convincingly Spanish. Then he would be, as he very proudly points out in the documentary, he is the first Spanish actor to play this Spanish hero. This same documentary then goes on to point out that Zorro was invented by an American. The documentary is in fact of superb value considering the occasional 6-minute featurettes you find strung onto some DVDs these days. This is 45 minutes that can stand more than one viewing, it's factually interesting and packed with information about the legend of Zorro, his screen history and the secrets behind his latest incarnation. Just as interesting is the enthusiastic director's commentary from Campbell. Like listening to your Grandad getting lost in a war story, Campbell talks passionately about every aspect of the process of making the movie and leaves little room for questions. He also lets slip that many of the improvised moments came from the film's exclusive producer, Steven Spielberg, who you might not know had anything to do with this production before reading the extras on this disc. The only let-down that comes from otherwise flawless extra features is the fact that the documentary contains more deleted scenes than the deleted scenes section. Visually the animated menu page is just as gorgeous as the film and is an example of how Columbia are fully behind DVD and filling their discs with as many extras as possible. Fortunately they've done this on an entertaining and refreshing action film, making the overall package one of the finest DVDs Region 2 has to offer.

FINAL VERDICT

Picture ☆☆☆☆☆ Sound ☆☆☆☆☆
Entertainment ☆☆☆☆☆
Extras ☆☆☆☆☆ Value ☆☆☆☆☆
OVERALL ☆☆☆☆☆

THE MATRIX

Price: £19.99
Supplied by: Warner Home Video
Type of disc: Dual layer, single-sided
No of chapters: 38

Film format(s)/length: 2.35:1 widescreen enhanced / 136 mins
Audio format: Dolby Digital 5.1
Directors: The Wachowski Brothers
Starring: Keanu Reeves, Laurence Fishburne, Carrie-Anne Moss
Year made: 1999
Extras: Scene access; 'Follow the white rabbit' (special feature where behind-the-scenes special effects explanations can be accessed just before each scene when the white rabbit appears); 26-minute HBO First Look special documentary *Making The Matrix*; 6 minute *What is Bullet Time?* documentary; 11 minute *What Is The Concept?* documentary; PC DVD-ROM extras include 'Are you the one?' quiz, screenplay to print out, storyboards and essays, plus website samplers and hyperlinks.

We are not talking Merchant Ivory here, and therefore your enjoyment of the Wachowski Brothers' *The Matrix* will be directly related to the size of screen and level of volume your home entertainment system can muster. This movie requires your undivided attention, and shabby speakers or anything under 30 inches will definitely not do. By day, Thomas Anderson (Reeves) is a computer programmer for a large software company, by night he is Neo, a hacker who uses his home terminal for illegal activities whilst searching for the shadowy techno-anarchist, Morpheus (Fishburne). When Trinity (Moss – a goddess in PVC) introduces them, Morpheus reveals that life, civilisation itself, and even the shop where Neo goes for noodles, are in fact all part of an extraordinarily advanced computer simulation designed to keep human minds content while their bodies are used like batteries to power super-intelligent machines of the future. Morpheus is also convinced that Neo is 'The One' – a saviour who will bring an end to the reign of the machines and destroy the Matrix so that humanity can be freed, but the rest of his renegade crew are not so sure. Meanwhile, there's a traitor on board ready to sell out his friends in return for a cushy life in the blissful ignorance of the Matrix. Looking like a cross between *Blade Runner* and *Crash, The Matrix* is a 136-minute MTV video – a sensory bombardment of special effects set pieces, clever ideas, and pretty people wearing leather. The film's pioneering use of the special effect known as 'Bullet Time' (where hundreds of linked cameras shoot simultaneously from different angles allowing the director to freeze a scene and then pan around it) turns straightforward gun-blazing scenes into works of art. The violent ballet of Trinity dispatching a group of police; moving at twice the speed of sight and running up the walls, is a breathtaking piece of movie-making, but even that is surpassed as the Wachowski's become more adept with their new toys. Technology aside though, Neo's character is wafer-thin, Trinity gets far too few lines of any substance, and Laurence Fishburne is content merely to look cool in mirrored shades. That doesn't seem to matter however as the special effects and the ingenious premise of the Matrix itself steals the show. To be fair, the best performance goes to Aussie Hugo Weaving as Special Agent Smith – a bitter and unstoppable piece of computer code who makes every line he utters sound like Shakespeare. One thing that's never in doubt is the attraction of the film as pure gung-ho entertainment. Yes, you get a plot which will be the cause of many heated debates, but it's the sheer pace and exuberance of the action, coupled with a passion for weapons almost to the point of fetishism, and a sharp 5.1 soundtrack, that makes *The Matrix* a must have DVD. Without question this features some of the best images ever committed to DVD and as far as extras are concerned, you're definitely not short-changed. Like the region 1 DVD you get animated menus designed to tie in with the whole Matrix theme. The 26-minute HBO special is excellent and reveals many of the secret techniques used to create the dazzling array of super-human feats. Want to know how Morpheus hovers 25 feet in the area before delivering a floorboard-crunching knee thrust? Or how Keanu Reeves was able to dodge bullets? It's all here, including interviews and plenty of early production footage of Reeves in silly hats. In keeping with the film, you must take the red pill to find the remainder of the extras, and these consist of two more special effects spoilers and a host of cool items like the script and a quiz for PC DVD-ROM owners. Curiously we do not get the audio commentary by Carrie-Anne Moss nor the music only audio track found on the Region 1 US disc. But hey, Warner could have done a *Titanic* and stripped this DVD bare for maximum profit; instead we get one of the best action films of the decade on a DVD packed with everything the fan could want. It's a masterpiece. If you haven't already, buy it now!

FINAL VERDICT

Picture ☆☆☆☆ Sound ☆☆☆☆☆
Entertainment ☆☆☆☆☆
Extras ☆☆☆☆☆ Value ☆☆☆☆
OVERALL ☆☆☆☆☆

MAURICE

Price: £19.99

Supplied by: Columbia TriStar Home Video
Type of disc: Single layer, single-sided
No of chapters: 15
Film format(s)/length: 1.66:1 letterbox / 134 mins
Audio format: Dolby Digital 5.1
Director: James Ivory
Starring: Hugh Grant, James Wilby, Ben Kingsley
Year made: 1987
Extras: Scene access; 30th Anniversary promo from
Merchant Ivory; original theatrical trailer; subtitles in
English; subtitles for the hearing impaired in English.

When first published, EM Forster's novel
depicting a love affair between two male scholars at a
Cambridge college in Edwardian times caused a huge
public outcry. Given that at the beginning of the 20th
Century homosexuality was considered a crime, and
punishment included prison with severe flogging, it's
easy to understand why. This screen adaptation follows the life of Maurice Hall (Wilby) and Clive
Durham (Grant – in his first major role) through
their platonic friendship that turned into forbidden
love. Angst-ridden, they try to conceal and overcome
this terrible 'disease' (as it was considered then). This
DVD brings to light a forgotten tale and star-studded
cast (including Denholm Elliott, Simon Callow and
Billie Whitelaw) in scenery that shines with clarity.
Although the soundtrack does not tax the abilities of
Dolby 5.1, it certainly loses nothing due to its presence. As for extras, there's not much in the way of
soundtrack or subtitle options, but you are presented
with the original theatrical trailer There's also a 30th
Anniversary celebration of the film's creator,
Merchant Ivory which has already brought us the
classics such as of *A Room With a View* and *The
Remains of the Day*. The 8-page accompanying booklet contains a synopsis of the film, production notes
and cast biogs of the main stars. In all it's a quality
film on a low quality disc.

FINAL VERDICT

Picture ☆☆☆ Sound ☆☆☆
Entertainment ☆☆☆ Extras ☆ Value ☆☆☆
OVERALL ☆☆☆

MEET JOE BLACK

Price: £19.99
Supplied by: Columbia TriStar Home Video
Type of disc: Dual layer, single-sided
No of chapters: 18
Film format(s)/length: 1.85:1 widescreen / 173 mins
Audio format: Dolby Digital 5.1
Director: Martin Brest
Starring: Brad Pitt, Anthony Hopkins, Claire Forlani

Year made: 1998
Extras: Scene access; weak 10-minute documentary;
theatrical trailer; cast and film-maker biogs; production
notes.

Coming in at almost 3 hours, *Meet Joe Black* is
not the kind of film to be taken lightly. It needs to be
watched in a comfy chair, with plenty of munchies to
hand, as you will be in for a long haul. That's not to
say that watching *MJB* is a chore, far from it, as the
film is a thought-provoking piece of fantasy, laden
with genuine pearls of wisdom about life, love and –
obviously from Pitt's character – death. A remake of
1934's *Death Takes a Holiday*, it's the tale of how successful businessman Bill Parrish (Hopkins) discovers
his own mortality when Death pays him a visit.
Telling him that his time is almost upon him, Death
states that Bill will be his guide to humanity in the
days leading up to his eventual demise. Although the
subject matter may sound grim (apologies for the
pun), *Meet Joe Black* does have moments of genuine
humour, as the quirky Death takes pleasure in the
things that we all tend to take for granted… peanut
butter being one such example. The original theatrical trailer is included within the DVD package, but
since this has become a DVD standard, the real meat
comes from the documentary, production notes and
the cast and filmmaker biographies. The documentary, *Spotlight on Location* looks like it has been lifted
from an American TV programme and offers little in
the way of real behind-the-scenes information. The
production notes and cast biographies could be considered average fare, also – whilst the information
provided is interesting and relevant, it is the format
they are presented in that is uninspiring. Relying on
text listings is a remarkable waste of DVD's potential,
particularly as other DVD producers have provided
similar information in an engaging and exciting way.
Meet Joe Black is a very good and worthwhile motion
picture, but apart from the sterling quality of the both
picture and sound, there is not much that lifts this
DVD above the crowd.

FINAL VERDICT

Picture ☆☆☆☆ Sound ☆☆☆☆
Entertainment ☆☆☆☆ Extras ☆☆☆ Value ☆☆☆
OVERALL ☆☆☆

MENACE II SOCIETY

Price: £19.99
Supplied by: Columbia TriStar Home Video
Type of disc: Single layer, single-sided
No of chapters: 20
Film format(s)/length: 16:9 widescreen enhanced / 93

mins
Audio format: Dolby Digital 5.1
Directors: Allen Hughes and Albert Hughes
Starring: Tyrin Turner, Larenz Tate, Jada Pinkett
Year made: 1993
Extras: Scene access; featurette: *The Hughes brothers talk about Menace II Society*; filmographies; US theatrical trailer.

The debut film from the Hughes brothers caused a storm upon its release in 1993, with distributors New Line Cinema warned they would have 'blood on their hands' because of the fierce portrayal of the fight for survival among young blacks in American society. Although there are obvious parallels to *Boyz N the Hood* (John Singleton's movie, released two years earlier) *Menace II Society* eclipses it in terms of both style and script. There are no heavy monologues on the sociology of the ghetto, simply characters dealing with a world where the moral compass shattered 30 years ago. In the accompanying 10-minute featurette the Hughes brothers talk about how the film was received and the challenges of co-directing: with Albert handling visuals and Allen the actors. They also acknowledge their substantial debt to Brian De Palma and Martin Scorsese; citing in particular the stylistic resemblance with *Goodfellas*. *Menace II Society* is a very interesting film that is disappointingly short; whilst the filmographies and theatrical trailer (set to Marvin Gaye's 'What's Going On') are a fine example of enticing an audience. The Hughes brothers claim not to be making moral judgements – in fact in the featurette they reject the concept of moral artistic responsibility. But when *Menace II Society* finally slams into its heart-tearing finale, the caustic emotional impact of events ensures you're never less than certain that they set out to do the right thing.

FINAL VERDICT

Picture ☆☆☆☆ Sound ☆☆☆☆
Entertainment ☆☆☆☆☆ Extras ☆☆☆ Value ☆☆☆☆
OVERALL ☆☆☆☆

MEN IN BLACK

Price: £19.99 / £24.99
Supplied by: Columbia TriStar Home Video
Type of disc: Dual layer, single-sided / Dual layer, double-sided
No of chapters: 27
Film format(s)/length: 1.85:1 anamorphic / 94 mins
Audio format: Dolby Digital 5.1
Director: Barry Sonnenfeld
Starring: Will Smith, Tommy Lee Jones, Linda

Fiorentino
Year made: 1997

COLLECTOR'S EDITION
Extras: Scene access; visual commentary featuring Barry Sonnenfeld and Tommy Lee Jones with on-screen diagrams; character animation studies using angles; tunnel scene deconstruction using angles; extended and alternate scenes; conceptual art, storyboard and production photo galleries; storyboard comparisons; original featurette: *Metamorphosis of Men in Black*; music video; theatrical trailer; teaser for *MIB 2*; production notes; talent files; DVD-ROM and Web links; soundtrack in English, German and French; subtitles in 18 languages.

LIMITED EDITION
Extras: As above, plus: Widescreen and full screen presentation option; art gallery featuring over 1,000 images of conceptual art and production photographs; technical audio commentary with Barry Sonnenfeld, Rick Baker and Industrial Light & Magic team; 3 scene-editing workshops, plus commentary from Barry Sonnenfeld describing the editing process; Edgar Bug fight scene deconstruction using angles; creatures: concepts to completion.

The comic book adaptation is, quite simply, a hit and miss affair. There's a whole cavernous gulf of expanse between what counts as a fully bona fide 'hit' (*Batman, Superman, X-Men*) and a godawful 'miss'. Think of *Howard the Duck*, and then take a long, stiff drink. So, seeing as it's the 'biggest grossing Columbia TriStar release of all time', it's safe to assume that *Men in Black* proudly snuggles itself into the former category, and brings a whole new level of respect to the notion that using a comic book as source for a multi-million dollar movie can in fact be a good idea. Devoid of the usual superhero shenanigans, *Men in Black* safely runs wild in the realm of make-believe in which a highly secret government agency monitors the immigration of illegal aliens. Genuine illegal aliens. The type with 8 eyes, purple scales, and a UFO parked somewhere out in the Nevada desert. If you can trust a man who only has one set of clothing and would rather wipe your memory than smile at you, aliens have been regular visitors to our world since Roswell, and someone's got to keep that sort of thing quiet. Under the unique supervision of Sonnenfeld, *Men in Black* became the perfect buddy-buddy vehicle for Will Smith and Tommy Lee Jones. In amongst a haven of special effects is a tale of Jones's 'K' recruiting Smith's 'J' from the New York police department as his new partner, and then enlightening him in the ways of the universe as they attempt to hunt down a huge bug going by the name of 'Edgar' who has a plan that could mean the end of the world as we know it. With a background in cinematography, Sonnenfeld is the type of director who knows the definition of ocular style, and every one of his outings have been distinct since he first called 'action' on 1991's *The Addams Family*. Tight, sharp, and visually rich, it's this that helps to boost the humour that Sonnenfeld squeezes out of a top-rate script by Ed Solomon. Meanwhile, Smith and Jones obligingly fill their superstar status, and along with a talented supporting cast make this one of the most charming blockbusters of the latter half of the Nineties. All the right elements are in place. Sonnenfeld is the perfect choice to direct, and makeup maestro Rick Baker took the aliens' looks out of this world. But this is still one of those films that doesn't quite reach the sum of all its parts. Hindered by its own restrictions, there is far too much content here to fit comfortably into a 90-minute timeframe, and plot development is jettisoned so that special effects, Will Smith one-liners, and cool action sequences can all have their screen time. If you're one of the few who's yet to see *Men in Black*, don't be deterred. Despite any criticism the movie receives, its sheer energy, originality and tongue-in-cheek humour makes it one of the most fun blockbusters of the last decade. It's safe to say that Columbia TriStar loves its movies. Treated with tender loving care, they are wrapped up warm in a multitude of extras before being sent off into the big wide world. And *Men in Black* has been clothed in one of the greatest arrays of extras ever seen on DVD. Along with the help of an extremely enthusiastic Sonnenfeld, the studio has taken the DVD format right to its very limits. Let's simply forget about the fact that this disc has the best picture and sound quality you are ever likely to get from the format, and take a look instead at what made this release the biggest DVD had ever seen to that date. The extras. Each process of making this movie is stripped back to the bone, layer by layer, and then presented to you as a whole procession of character studies, scene deconstructions and conceptual art galleries. For your further enjoyment there is a collection of music videos, talent files and featurettes, all topped off with the most intriguing of commentaries where Sonnenfeld and Jones appear at the bottom of your screen with a pen for on-screen diagrams. And that's just the Collector's Edition. Yes, ladies and gentlemen, brace yourselves: there is also the special two-disc Limited Edition, packed with all the extras featured on the Collector's Edition, and a whole lot more besides. As

well as the option for widescreen or pan and scan, there is also a technical commentary by Sonnenfeld and Rick Baker plus over 1,000 images of conceptual art and production photos. However, the crème de la crème, the real reason why they invented DVD in the first place, is the chance to edit scenes from the movie yourself. It's mainly a gimmick, and you don't get to edit in the strictest sense; it's more of a 'choose some angles, and put them in the order you want' type of extra, but it really is great fun, and something for *Men in Black*, Columbia TriStar, and the DVD format to be proud of. You don't need us to tell you, it's sheer common sense – you *must* own this DVD!

FINAL VERDICT

Picture ☆☆☆☆☆ Sound ☆☆☆☆☆
Entertainment ☆☆☆☆ Extras ☆☆☆☆☆
Value ☆☆☆☆☆

OVERALL ☆☆☆☆☆

MERCURY RISING

Price: £19.99
Supplied by: Columbia TriStar Home Video
Type of disc: Dual layer, single-sided
No of chapters: 33
Film format(s)/length: 2.35:1 widescreen enhanced / 107 mins
Audio format: Dolby Digital 5.1
Director: Harold Becker
Starring: Bruce Willis, Alec Baldwin, Chi McBride
Year made: 1997
Extras: Scene access; *Watch the Mercury Rising* 30-minute documentary; audio commentary by director Harold Becker; theatrical trailer; deleted scenes; production notes; cast filmographies; production photographs; multilingual subtitles; English, German, French, Italian and Spanish soundtracks.

The NSA developed an uncrackable code, only for it to be cracked by a 9-year-old autistic boy. So, either the so-called National Security Agency is employing a bunch of chimps, or we have a savant on our hands. *Mercury Rising*'s premise deals with the latter, and it's up to a burnt-out FBI agent (Willis) to ensure that the boy isn't erased by NSA Chief Nick Kudrow (Baldwin). The idea floating *Mercury Rising* is an intriguing one, but it never really quite engages the viewer. Willis simply plays himself during the movie, and whilst Baldwin tries his best, he is never really quite as intimidating as he is supposed to be. That's not to say that this is a bad film, it is just that it never really gets started. So how does the DVD measure up? It's refreshing to find a Region 2 disc that can sit comfortably amongst its Region 1 contemporaries without fear of feeling inadequate. Region 2 *Mercury Rising* is stuffed full of delightful goodies, that will make fans of the movie giddy with delight… or something approaching that, anyway! Universal has supplied the bog-standard theatrical trailer, but has run the extra mile by also including an audio commentary from director Harold Becker. And the goodies don't stop there. The highlight of the package is the *Watch the Mercury Rising* documentary, which is supported by production notes, deleted scenes, cast filmographies, links to the Universal web site for PC DVD-ROM owners, and production photographs. Phew! Now that's some selection of extras, and the even better news is that *Mercury Rising* is a dual layer, single-sided DVD, so you don't even have to flip it over half-way through. Well done, Universal!

FINAL VERDICT

Picture ☆☆☆☆ Sound ☆☆☆☆☆

Entertainment ☆☆☆ Extras ☆☆☆☆ Value ☆☆☆☆

OVERALL ☆☆☆☆

MERRY CHRISTMAS MR LAWRENCE

Price: £19.99

Supplied by: Second Sight Films

Type of disc: Single layer, single-sided

No of chapters: 19

Film format(s)/length: 1.85:1 letterbox / 122 mins

Audio format: Stereo

Director: Nagisa Oshima

Starring: David Bowie, Ryuichi Sakamoto, Tom Conti

Year made: 1982

Extras: Scene access; picture gallery; theatrical trailer.

When pop stars declare their ambition to act in a film they're usually met with howls of derision. It's a stigma David Bowie knows all too well. The Star Man is probably best known in the thespian stakes for donning a mad Rod Stewart-esque wig and leather trousers in *Labyrinth*, but in this earlier POW camp drama he's on far more subdued form. Bowie is Major Jack Celliers, who's reprieved from a death sentence and sent to an internment camp in 1942 Java. Meanwhile, Colonel John Lawrence (Conti) speaks Japanese and maintains a volatile relationship with the camp commander. Celliers' anti-authority stance perplexes Captain Yonnoi (Sakamoto) and the two begin a battle of wits that can end in only one way. It's a strangely detached film that fails to let us really engage with the (stereotypical) characters and gives little reason to despise Japanese prison camp tyranny during WWII. It lacks the same emotional power and cultural clash that David Lean's *The Bridge on the River Kwai* has (sadly not out on DVD yet). The

transfer is crisp enough, with any apparent fuzziness due to the heat on location and the film stock used. The otherwise well-designed sleeve bizarrely neglects to say there is a 24-strong picture gallery here, as well as the usual trailer. This gallery contains two pictures which hint at a deleted scene where we see Lawrence with his sweetheart. *Merry Christmas Mr Lawrence* falls short of classic and Second Sight has once again made an average effort with the disc.

FINAL VERDICT

Picture ☆☆☆ Sound ☆☆

Entertainment ☆☆☆ Extras ☆☆ Value ☆☆

OVERALL ☆☆☆

MESSAGE IN A BOTTLE

Price: £15.99

Supplied by: Warner Home Video

Type of disc: Dual layer, single-sided

No of chapters: 35

Film format(s)/length: 2.35:1 widescreen / 126 mins

Audio format: Dolby Digital 5:1

Director: Luis Mandoki

Starring: Kevin Costner, Robin Wright Penn, Paul Newman

Year made: 1999

Extras: Scene access; 4 deleted scenes (with and without audio commentary); audio commentary by director Louis Mandoki and producer Denise Di Novi; original theatrical trailer; multilingual subtitles; subtitles for the hearing impaired in English.

As the opening credits fade away, it all comes flooding back – Costner's mullet-like hair in *Robin Hood: Prince of Thieves*, that inane southern drawl, the terrible wooden acting… It soon feels like a recurring nightmare. But hang on. Let's not get too carried away. *Message in a Bottle* isn't actually a bad DVD. The film itself is shockingly predictable – a veritable cliché-fest of epic Hollywood proportions – but nevertheless surprisingly watchable. It's got a simple plot: love struck, West coast boat-builder Garret Blake (Costner) struggles to come to terms with the untimely and shocking death of his painter wife. In an effort to get over her death, he writes a series of poignant messages in bottles. One of these is found by lonely researcher Theresa Osborne (Robin Wright Penn). She is intrigued by the deeply touching sentiment contained within. After much searching she finds the writer, and falls in love with his shy and retiring character. He too falls for her, but will not commit to the relationship. Yes, Costner is wooden as ever. Yes, Coltrane does a pretty ropey Yankee accent, and yes, even Wright Penn fails to liven up the proceedings. But Newman is a revelation as Costner's grouchy dad. Putting the film to one side, the main reason this DVD is a success is down to the extras. The audio commentary by director Louis Mandoki is excellent, and sheds light on many of the ambiguous moments throughout the film. There are even 4 deleted scenes, all with an audio commentary option. In all it's a pretty bad film, but it's presented on DVD so well you almost start liking it.

FINAL VERDICT

Picture ☆☆☆ Sound ☆☆☆☆

Entertainment ☆☆ Extras ☆☆☆☆ Value ☆☆☆☆

OVERALL ☆☆☆

METRO

Price: £15.99
Supplied by: DVD World (01705 796662)
Type of disc: Single layer, single-sided
No of chapters: 17
Film format(s)/length: 16:9 widescreen / 113 mins
Audio format: Dolby Digital 5.1
Director: Thomas Carter
Starring: Eddie Murphy, Michael Rapaport, Michael Wincott
Year made: 1997
Extras: Scene selection; English, French or Italian soundtrack.

Following a number of years languishing in the wilderness of faded Hollywood stars, motor-mouthed comedian Eddie Murphy returns to his wise-cracking action cop antic roots of *Beverley Hills Cop* in this above average thriller. The plot, as so often happens in this genre, is simple. Eddie plays the part of maverick San Francisco cop, Scott Roper, who finds his life under threat by the clean-cut diamond thief played by Michael 'gravel voiced' Wincott (previously seen hamming it up in *The Crow*). The action set pieces are entertaining, and the metro chase through the streets of San Francisco in particular looks and sounds fantastic when played on a decent set-up. However, the difference between *Metro* on DVD and VHS video is still noticeable even when played through a normal TV. Apart from the improved visual and audio aspects, there is really nothing in the *Metro* DVD that would actively encourage anyone picking it up over the video. Background information on how the metro chase was staged would have also been a welcome addition. Granted, *Metro* is not the greatest action movie ever made, but some scenes in particular make an adequate DVD showcase. *Metro* is an enjoyable thriller which sees Murphy in a more serious role for a change, but there's no real reason to pick it up on DVD because so little effort has been spent on it.

FINAL VERDICT

Picture ☆☆☆☆ Sound ☆☆☆☆☆

Entertainment ☆☆☆ Extras ☆☆ Value ☆☆

OVERALL ☆☆

METROPOLIS

Price: £19.99
Supplied by: Eureka! Video
Type of disc: Dual layer, single-sided
No of chapters: 27
Film format(s)/length: 4:3 regular / 139 mins
Audio format: Stereo
Director: Fritz Lang
Starring: Alfred Abel, Brigitte Helm, Gustav Fröhlich
Year made: 1927
Extras: Scene access; a brief history of the film.

In the 21st century, society has split into the rich Thinkers, 24-hour party people who live in gleaming skyscrapers, and the downtrodden Workers who toil in subterranean factories. While Freder, the pampered son of the city's dictatorial industrialist, joins the brewing revolution, his father plots with mad scientist Rotwang to create a replicant of the revolution's saintly leader Maria in a bid to destroy the movement from the inside. Filmed when the motion picture as we would recognise it was less than 10 years old, *Metropolis* still has the power to captivate. Irritatingly, though, no attempt has been made to remaster it for DVD. While Peter Osborne's new orchestral score is good, and certainly better than Giorgio Moroder's effort for the film's 1984 re-release, the 'film info' is an unnecessary reprint of the sleeve notes. Lang's masterpiece is worth watching by any cinephile's standards, but the disc could have made it a must-have collectable.

FINAL VERDICT

Picture ☆ Sound ☆

Entertainment ☆☆☆☆ Extras ☆ Value ☆☆

OVERALL ☆☆

MICKEY BLUE EYES

Price: £15.99
Supplied by: Warner Home Video
Type of disc: Single layer, single-sided
No of chapters: 33
Film format(s)/length: 1.85:1 anamorphic / 98 mins
Audio format: Dolby Digital 5.1
Director: Kelly Makin
Starring: Huge Grant, James Caan, Jeanne Tripplehorn
Year made: 1999

Extras: Scene access; theatrical trailer; audio commentary by director Kelly Malkin; multilingual subtitles.

So what have we learned about the Mafia? Well, if *Mickey Blue Eyes* is to be believed it's all about vengeance, good food and stereotypes. However, Hollywood clichés aside, this movie will still manage to keep you happy for 90 minutes. Once again Grant is simply playing himself, but this time he's called Michael Felgate and is a New York art auctioneer who falls for teacher Gina (Tripplehorn). Feeling that 3 months into a relationship is the perfect time to settle down and get married, Michael seeks out Gina's father Frank (a nicely cast Caan) to ask for his daughter's hand, only to find that he's getting into one of the biggest families in organised crime. Grant spends the rest of the movie farcing about trying to avoid the slippery slope into the Mafia world of 'a favour for a favour', and hiding his miserable failure to do so from his bride-to-be. Ultimately *Mickey Blue Eyes* doesn't fully hit the mark, but still manages to land pretty close to the target. Most of the highs come from the occasional laugh-out-loud gag, situation or performance (and there are a fair number to chose from) rather than the movie as a whole. Warner seems to have upgraded its special features content by adding commentaries to the list. Unfortunately, this is one of the few movies that doesn't really lend itself to that specific feature, and though Kelly Makin is enthusiastic to talk about his movie, there rarely is a lot to say.

FINAL VERDICT

Picture ☆☆☆☆ Sound ☆☆☆☆

Entertainment ☆☆☆ Extras ☆☆ Value ☆☆☆

OVERALL ☆☆☆

MIDNIGHT EXPRESS

Price: £19.99
Supplied by: Columbia TriStar
Type of disc: Single layer, double-sided
No of chapters: 28
Film format(s)/length: 1.85.1 widescreeen (Side A), 4:3 regular (Side B) / 116 mins
Audio format: Mono
Director: Alan Parker
Starring: Brad Davis, John Hurt, Randy Quaid
Year made: 1978
Extras: Scene selection; original theatrical trailer; full and widescreen versions; cast filmographies; 7-minute real-life Billy Hayes documentary.

This nightmarish tale of one man's time spent in a Turkish prison during the early Seventies is even more terrifying when you realise the events are based upon a true story. American student Billy Hayes (Davis) is caught smuggling a small quantity of hashish across the Turkish border. What begins as a 4-year sentence, spirals into a realm of sadistic torture and shattered hopes when Hayes discovers that his opportunity for parole is revoked. Facing the prospect of 30 years in prison, Hayes considers the only option left to him, and that's to catch the 'midnight express' – prison slang for escape. *Midnight Express* is a fascinating portrait of one man's descent into virtual insanity, in spite of some support from his fellow inmates, played by John Hurt and Randy Quaid. The torture scenes are never gratuitous, but serve to be no less disturbing in their sadistic and brutal nature. Interestingly enough, the movie's screenplay was written by none other than Oliver Stone. The good news is that Columbia TriStar has been generous on the DVD extras front. The first and most obvious bonus is the fact that it offers viewers the choice of both wide and full screen versions of the film on one DVD. Just imagine trying to get a similar bargain on VHS. Also included is an American documentary about the real-life Billy Hayes from 1978. It has the cringe-worthy title of *I'm Healthy, I'm Alive, and I'm Free!*, it is also pretty poor – both in the way it has been put together and also the grainy picture quality – and only runs for 7 minutes. However, regardless of the brief nature of the Hayes interview, it nonetheless still adds another fascinating layer of depth to this excellent movie. *Midnight Express* has been remastered for DVD, which is evident in the crystal-clear quality of the film stock, although the sound is still mono, which is a major disappointment. Whether this is intention or an attempt at being authentic is never explained.

FINAL VERDICT

Picture ☆☆☆☆ Sound ☆

Entertainment ☆☆☆ Extras ☆☆☆☆ Value ☆☆☆☆

OVERALL ☆☆☆☆

MIDNIGHT IN THE GARDEN OF GOOD AND EVIL

Price: £15.99
Supplied by: Warner Home Video
Type of disc: Dual layer, single-sided
No of chapters: 43
Film format(s)/length: 1.85:1 widescreen / 149 mins
Director: Clint Eastwood
Starring: Kevin Spacey, John Cusack, Irma P Hall
Year made: 1997
Extras: Interactive menus/scene selection; production and book adaptation notes.

The most significant party of the Savannah Christmas season ends with a bang when host Jim Williams (Spacey) shoots a man to death. The festive cheer stops and the mystery begins for freelance journalist John Kelso (Cusack). Based on true events, this adaptation of the best selling book by John Berendt fails to provide suspense or mystery of which this movie is based around. The picture quality, although still superior to VHS, is only average compared to most DVDs available. But most surprisingly, the sound (although Dolby Digital 5.1) is incredibly dull and rarely features surround sound. Unlike the story, the extras try to contribute to the overall presentation of this DVD. In addition to the standard scene access, there is a wealth of production notes covering many areas of the film and related subjects. Delving into the biographies you'll find background information on the actors and crew – including casting information about Kevin Spacey, ("I'm playing a person who was really a living human being") and other actors. There is also information about the location of the movie: Savannah. Even Johnny Mercer (big time musician) and Uga – the famous English Bulldog mascot of the University of Georgia – are profiled. Naturally the final feature is about the adaptation of the book. The film, although a condensed and spiced-up version of the original, is 149 minutes too long. There may well be a few extras, but if the movie is tedious there is little use for such bonuses.

FINAL VERDICT

Picture ☆☆☆ Sound ☆

Entertainment ☆ Extras ☆☆☆ Value ☆

OVERALL ☆

MIDNIGHT RUN

Price: £19.99
Supplied by: Columbia TriStar Home Video
Type of disc: Dual layer, single-sided
No of chapters: 16
Film format(s)/length:1.85:1 letterbox / 121 mins
Audio format: Dolby Surround
Director: Martin Brest
Starring: Robert De Niro, Charles Grodin, Yaphet Kotto
Year made: 1988
Extras: Scene access; multilingual subtitles; soundtrack in English, German, French, Italian and Spanish.

A welcome back-catalogue release for this entertaining and engaging action comedy, as De Niro's bounty hunter attempts to return an accountant who stole the Mob's money to LA. An obstacle-free journey it ain't, as the FBI, another bounty hunter and the Mob themselves all want a piece of the action, while Grodin the accountant certainly isn't going to come quietly. Perfect Friday night fodder, really. Save for subtitles and language options, the lack of extras is

disappointing though, as is the non-anamorphic picture, which is okay but leaves room for improvement. So does the sound, as the surround mix certainly has fun with the action but lacks some of the impact that modern action movie soundtracks pack. Yet while the disc is a disappointment – and the £20 price tag excessive – this is a fun film that's well worth rediscovering. Especially with a bag of popcorn and a six pack...

FINAL VERDICT

Picture ☆☆☆ Sound ☆☆☆

Entertainment ☆☆☆☆ Extras ☆ Value ☆☆

OVERALL ☆☆

MIGHTY JOE YOUNG

Price: £15.99
Supplied by: DVD Plus (www.dvdplus.co.uk
Type of disc: Dual layer, single-sided
No of chapters: 16
Film format(s)/length: 1.85:1 widescreen enhanced / 110 mins
Audio format: Dolby Digital 5.1
Director: Ron Underwood
Starring: Bill Paxton, Charlize Theron, David Paymer
Year made: 1998
Extras: Scene access; English subtitles.

If you're ever looking for a film that'll convince you to upgrade Pro Logic to full Dolby Digital 5.1, you may be surprised to hear that the early stages of *Mighty Joe Young* serve as a strong candidate. The thump of a 15-foot gorilla may not shake your brain, but it'll certainly rock the house if you've the sound system to enjoy it on. And what's this? A round of applause for Buena Vista? Sure, because the anamorphically enhanced image is both vibrant and strong, with the enhancement being something our American cousins weren't treated to. There are no extras though, but at least this was released on the same day as the VHS rental version. A basic summing up of the film would be to say that it was an adventure with a huge gorilla. It's an above average family movie, following the turmoils of Joe (that's the gorilla) and Jill (that's the thoroughly lovely Charlize Theron) as they relocate from the jungle to the city. It's a Disney film, so you can fill in the blanks yourself. Whilst Buena Vista's discs are predominantly disappointing, is it too much to forsake the extras in order to get a new film like this fast and intact? And if you don't agree? Vote with your pocket. It's your call.

FINAL VERDICT

Picture ☆☆☆☆ Sound ☆☆☆☆

Entertainment ☆☆☆ Extras ☆ Value ☆☆☆
OVERALL ☆☆☆

MISSION: IMPOSSIBLE

Price: £19.99
Supplied by: Paramount Pictures
Type of disc: Dual layer, single-sided
No of chapters: 13
Film format(s)/length: 2.35:1 anamorphic / 105 mins
Audio format: Dolby Digital 5.1
Director: Brian De Palma
Starring: Tom Cruise, Jon Voight, Emmanuelle Beart
Year made: 1996
Extras: Scene access; theatrical trailer; multilingual subtitles; subtitles for the hearing impaired in English.

Strike the match, light the fuse, and then run! The ultimate in TV spy caper kitsch, *Mission: Impossible* received the obligatory big budget Nineties update. Destined to be a summer blockbuster, *M:I* went on to make an international profit of $241 million at the cinema alone. Using the original television concept as a base for its source, *M:I* is an action-packed blockbuster which not only manages to find its own feet, but then uses them to go about giving the competition a firm kick up the backside. The focus is no longer on the team's leader Jim Phelps (Voight), and all eyes are on top agent Ethan Hunt (Cruise). Framed for the death of every other member of his IMF team, Hunt spends the rest of the movie tracking down the mysterious 'Job' (the code name used by the guy who set him up) by stealing a CIA 'NOC list' (a list of undercover agents) and then offering it to the highest bidder in an attempt to draw Job out into the open. The whole thing is pure fun from the word go to the very last second, which could, in a twist of irony, be the film's main downfall. The pace never slows down. Aiming to be a much more intelligent spy caper than the average Bond, the amount of concentration required to keep the audience in the plot loop can be exhausting, and if your mind drifts away for one moment then you'll struggle to claw your way back. But don't let this put you off. *M:I* is one of those rare films which gets better with each viewing. In other words, it's perfect for the DVD format. Unfortunately, the disc is far from perfect. Desperately lacking in extras, all you get is the original theatrical trailer, which is best to avoid before watching the film for the first time as it manages to show most of the climactic scene! Not all is lost as the 5.1 sound will really give your sound system something to chew on, and the combination of some ear-shattering explosions, the coolest theme tune known to man, and a highly riveting movie makes this a DVD not to be passed by.

FINAL VERDICT
Picture ☆☆☆☆ Sound ☆☆☆☆☆
Entertainment ☆☆☆☆ Extras ☆ Value ☆☆☆
OVERALL ☆☆☆

MONEY TRAIN

Price: £19.99
Supplied by: Columbia TriStar Home Video
Type of disc: Single layer, single sided
No of chapters: 28
Film format(s)/length: 16:9 widescreen / 106 mins
Director: Joseph Ruben
Starring: Wesley Snipes, Woody Harrelson, Jennifer Lopez
Year made: 1995
Extras: Multilingual subtitles; scene select; DVD trailer.

It's action all the way in this cops 'n' robbers film with a difference. The difference being that the cops *are* the robbers! Foster brothers John (Snipes) and Charlie (Harrelson) are two DC Transit Cops working the New York subway system. When Charlie's gambling habit gets him into trouble, he ropes his brother into helping him rob the armoured wages train which runs through New York every night – the 'money train.' Director Joseph Ruben doesn't offer any real surprises in this standard action-thriller that plays much like an elongated version of the train scene in *Speed* – just without Sandra Bullock. Snipes and Harrelson proved that they work well together in *White Men Can't Jump* however, and they liven up what is otherwise a fairly mundane plot. DVD special features though are sadly lacking. The only thing aside from subtitles and scene select is a trailer extolling the virtues of DVDs. Great idea, except that if you're watching it then chances are you've already bought one!

FINAL VERDICT
Picture ☆☆☆☆ Sound ☆☆☆
Entertainment ☆☆☆☆ Extras ☆ Value ☆☆
OVERALL ☆☆

MOONSTRUCK

Price: £19.99
Supplied by: MGM Home Entertainment
Type of disc: Dual layer, single-sided
No of chapters: 32
Film format(s)/length: 1.85:1 anamorphic / 98 mins
Audio format: Dolby Digital 5.1
Director: Norman Jewison
Starring: Cher, Nicolas Cage, Danny Aiello

Year made: 1987

Extras: Audio commentary with Norman Jewison, John Patrick Shankley and Cher; theatrical trailer; soundtrack in 5 languages, including English, French and German; subtitles in 11 languages.

MGM is a bit of a strange one to figure out. At the top end of its portfolio are discs like the James Bond DVDs and the recent *Thomas Crown Affair*, all of which offer unquestionable value for money. Then, both here and across the pond, they release some of their quality back catalogue titles on discs that are somewhat lacking. So who exactly waved the magic wand at *Moonstruck*? Hardly a video best seller, this 15-year-old romantic comedy has anamorphic transfer, full 5.1 sound and an audio commentary. We're not complaining, but it seems a curious choice. Perhaps it's because of the enduring nature of the film, which is still an entertaining, easy on the brain slice of fun, considerably strengthened by Cher's Oscar-winning turn in the lead role. An able supporting cast, led by Nicolas Cage and Danny Aiello, adds to the mix. Disc-wise, the image quality is quite good, suffering from occasional grain and artefacts but generally looking okay (the extra clarity offered by anamorphic enhancement helps). The sound mix too is a pleasant surprise, generally situating most of the work at the front, but broadening out to the surrounds for the frequent bouts of music. And finally, a nod too for writer John Patrick Shankley, director Jewison and his leading lady Cher for sitting down and recording a diverting commentary. Perhaps the pricing of the disc is a quibble, but generally this is more than we'd have expected, and thus due credit goes out to MGM.

FINAL VERDICT

Picture ☆☆☆ Sound ☆☆☆

Entertainment ☆☆☆☆ Extras ☆☆☆ Value ☆☆☆

OVERALL ☆☆☆

MORTAL KOMBAT

Price: £19.99

Supplied by: New Line Cinema

Type of disc: Single layer, single-sided

No of chapters: 20

Film format(s)/length: 1.85:1 widescreen enhanced / 97 mins

Audio format: Dolby Digital 5.0

Director: Paul Anderson

Starring: Christopher Lambert, Linden Ashby, Bridgette Wilson

Year made: 1995

Extras: Scene access; US theatrical trailer; Kombatants' filmographies.

After the *Street Fighter* videogame was made into a film, it wasn't long before its rival console fighting title also got transferred to celluloid. *Mortal Kombat* is better than *Street Fighter*, but that's not hard! After all, with Christopher Lambert in the lead role there's always going to be at least one cast member with *some* acting ability. The story revolves around a tournament in which humans with great fighting skills are plucked from obscurity to battle to the death; if they don't win, the demons of Outworld take over Earth. So, not too much pressure on our heroes, then. Full of dated CGI effects and with no worthwhile extras on the disc, this will mainly appeal to videogame purists, namely spotty 13-year-old oiks who spend hours in their rooms trying to perfect that special move. Let's hope Lara Croft's screen debut is a little more credible. Also available on DVD is *Mortal Kombat: Annihilation*, which is even worse than this!

FINAL VERDICT

Picture ☆☆☆ Sound ☆☆

Entertainment ☆☆ Extras ☆ Value ☆☆

OVERALL ☆☆

MR NICE GUY

Price: £15.99

Supplied by: Entertainment in Video

Type of disc: Dual layer, single-sided

No of chapters: 12

Film format(s)/length: 16:9 widescreen / 88 mins

Audio format: Dolby Digital 5.1

Director: Sammo Hung Kam-Bo

Starring: Jackie Chan, Richard Norton, Miki Lee

Year made: 1997

Extras: Scene access; theatrical trailer; stunt outtakes; subtitles in English.

Jackie Chan's physical action-comedy has made him a gigantic star in Asia. In fact, news of his marriage provoked a string of suicides among Japanese teenage girls! *Rush Hour*'s 1998 theatrical release served as his first big Western hit, but *Mr Nice Guy* was Chan's first film to be shot entirely in English. In fact, the makers hedge their bets by featuring a Hong Kong girlfriend who speaks only in Chinese, so as to not entirely alienate his core audience. English dialogue aside, the film seems little different to Chan's Hong Kong movies, with action sequences loosely linked by a simplistic action-thriller story line. A journalist has uncovered a drug ring, with a videotape serving as the catalyst for the plot. This drives the story from one set piece to another. Set in Australia, the budget is sufficiently low as to make you suspect overdubbing – and the Aussie accents are so grating you wish it was overdubbed! With that said, Chan's charm makes it all pretty entertaining. The obvious low budget only serves to emphasise the reality of his stunts. As usual, the movie concludes with outtakes that show stunts going wrong – and how nearly they could have gone fatally wrong! In a rather cheeky move, New Line has repackaged all of these outtakes in a (rather grainy) full screen version and listed them as a 4-minute extra! And, leaving aside a two-minute trailer, that's the only DVD extra you get. Picture and sound quality are only average. In fact, this is more a VHS rental product rather than a DVD collector's item. Scenes such as Chan clinging to an inflatable dinosaur at a Hell's Angel wedding, and some impressive destruction with a huge dumper truck, are fun but – as painful as it is to admit – Hollywood's *Rush Hour* is really a much superior film.

FINAL VERDICT

Picture ☆☆☆ Sound ☆☆

Entertainment ☆☆☆ Extras ☆ Value ☆☆☆

OVERALL ☆☆☆

MUCH ADO ABOUT NOTHING

Price: £15.99
Supplied by: Entertainment in Video
Type of disc: Single layer, single-sided
No of chapters: 6
Film format(s)/length: 16:9 widescreen / 104 mins
Audio Format: Dolby Surround
Director: Kenneth Branagh
Starring: Kenneth Branagh, Emma Thompson, Denzel Washington
Year made: 1993
Extras: Scene access.

On the face of it, this should have been a great DVD showcase. Big stars, lavish production values, lush landscapes and a much-loved script by that reliable old hack, William Shakespeare Esq. However, while the film is a success, the disc itself is less so. Kenneth Branagh adapted, directed and starred in the Bard's romantic comedy, along with then-wife Emma Thompson. Branagh is sarky bachelor Seigneur Benedick, Thompson is sharp-tongued singleton Beatrice, and Washington is matchmaking prince Don Pedro, who connives to get them together. Meanwhile, Don Pedro's bastard (in both senses) brother John (Keanu Reeves) skulks about in the background, trying to ruin things for everyone. Branagh makes everything accessible to modern audiences while keeping faithful to Shakespeare's text, producing a fast-paced and funny story set against some gorgeous Italian backdrops. The

only place he goes wrong is with Michael Keaton and Ben Elton, who ham it up hideously as a pair of thick-headed comic-relief constables. Apart from this minor miscalculation, *Much Ado About Nothing* is proof that Shakespeare is more fun than O-levels would have you believe. The downside is the DVD itself. Not only are there no extras, not even subtitles, but the picture quality is often stricken with probably the most obvious blocking artefacts ever seen. Some scenes, the masked ball for instance, look more like a dodgy cut-scene from a PlayStation game rather than a major film release. This lets down an otherwise enjoyable star-studded film.

FINAL VERDICT

Picture ☆☆ Sound ☆☆☆

Entertainment ☆☆☆☆ Extras ☆ Value ☆☆

OVERALL ☆☆

MULTIPLICITY

Price: £19.99
Supplied by: Columbia TriStar Home Video
Type of disc: Single layer, single-sided
No of chapters: 28
Film format(s)/length: 2.35:1 widescreen / 113 mins
Director: Harold Ramis
Starring: Michael Keaton (x4), Andie MacDowell, Harris Yulin
Year made: 1995
Extras: Widescreen TV enhanced; chapter select; multilingual subtitles; trailer.

Builder Doug Kinney (Keaton) just doesn't have enough time in the day to devote full attention to his work, his family and himself. So he does what any ordinary blue-collar regular guy would – he gets himself cloned. Doug 2 is a macho workaholic, giving Doug more time on the golf course, but wife Laura (MacDowell) and the kids still make plenty of demands on him. So he clones himself again, Doug 3 being a prissy homebody who handles the domestic chores. However, Dougs 2 and 3 decide they could use some help themselves, so one day Doug gets home to find the dimwitted Doug 4 – a copy of a copy – living above the garage as well as his other clones. Things get really complicated when Dougs 2, 3 and 4 decide they want some sack time with 'their' wife... *Multiplicity* was directed by Harold Ramis (the geeky Ghostbuster) who also directed *Groundhog Day*, but this clone comedy lacks the sharp edge of the Bill Murray time-twister. The greenscreen trickery used to get 4 Michael Keatons interacting with each other at once is impressive, but the jokes are fairly predictable – Doug's clones don't do what he wants, the various Dougs have to avoid being seen in the same place at the same time, and so on. *Multiplicity* is also yet another DVD release that can't really work up any enthusiasm for the concept of special features. A trailer, subtitles, and that's yer lot. All in all, a very average title.

FINAL VERDICT

Picture ☆☆☆ Sound ☆☆☆

Entertainment ☆☆☆ Extras ☆ Value ☆☆

OVERALL ☆☆

THE MUMMY

Price: £19.99

Supplied by: Columbia TriStar Home Video

Type of disc: Dual layer, single-sided

No of chapters: 18

Film format(s)/length: 2.35:1 widescreen / 120 mins

Audio format: Dolby Digital 5.1

Director: Stephen Sommers

Starring: Brendan Fraser, Rachel Weisz, Arnold Vosloo

Year made: 1999

Extras: Scene access; 'Making of' featurette: *Building a Better Mummy*; deleted scenes; visual and special effects formation featurette; theatrical trailer; feature commentary with director Stephen Sommers and editor Bob Ducsay; interactive DVD-ROM feature; Egyptology 101 (facts about Ancient Egypt); production notes; cast and film-makers' notes; soundtrack in German (5.1); subtitles in 11 languages.

More than 3,000 years ago, the high priest of Osiris, Imhotep (Vosloo), fell in love with Pharaoh Seti I's mistress: Anck-Su-Namum. In a fit of passion, the lovers murdered Seti and were consequently doomed for all eternity. Sentenced to perpetual suffering and cursed to live forever in the darkness of his tomb, Imhotep's diabolical secret remained buried for centuries. Stumbling across the ageless sands of the Sahara Desert in 1926, a small band of treasure hunters, lead by Rick O'Connell (Fraser) seek out the ancient Egyptian city of Hamunaptra. Believing a considerable fortune of gold was left by the second Pharaoh of the Nineteenth dynasty, Seti I, the group soon uncover a horror that was better left buried. Using the Book of the Dead, archaeologist Evie (Rachel Weisz) and her brother Jonathan (John Hannah) unwittingly release the vengeful reincarnation of Imhotep; now embodied as the most powerful of the living dead. Loosely based on Universal's 1932 original flick starring Boris Karloff as Imhotep, director Sommers (Deep Rising, The Jungle Book) was not looking to produce a simple remake. Instead, he opted for an action/adventure slant with a lead character who could pull off comic one liners and Indiana Jones-esque stunts. Filled with a dazzling array of visual effects (supplied by field leaders Industrial Light & Magic) The Mummy recreates a unique cinematic feeling not seen since the Indiana Jones trilogy. The DVD's picture and sound quality may not be the best we've seen so far, however, there can be no complaints as, like the special effects, there is not a glitch or lip synch to be found – and so there shouldn't be! Widescreen television owners will feel a little aggrieved by the non-inclusion of the anamorphic format, after all it appeared with great success on the Region 1 release. Fortunately though, few special features have been overlooked when producing the European version. Only the optional music-only audio track and Universal showcase extras have not made it onto the Region 2 disc. However, in their place lies the German Dolby Digital soundtrack and subtitles in 11 languages. The menu screen is almost identical to that of the Region 1 disc, but Columbia TriStar Home Video has once again included its coloured icons that have previously been the bane of many a DVD owner. The most impressive special features are undoubtedly the two featurettes. In the first, Industrial Light & Magic (ILM), reveals the secrets behind the sublime special effects on display. Focusing on 5 key special effects moments from within the film, ILM demonstrate and narrate within 4 stages how they went from drawing board to silver screen. The second featurette focuses on behind-the-scenes with interviews from the cast and crew responsible for this suspense-fuelled epic, opening, logically enough, with the black and white theatrical trailer for the original 1932 classic. The time and effort spent on this DVD is almost incredulous. Director Sommers was on hand from day one in the DVD's development to make sure it received all the care and attention afforded to the movie itself. A feature length commentary from Sommers and Editor Bob Ducsay provides a personal touch as the pair explain reasoning and motivation for many aspects of the story line and why this particular cast and crew got the jobs they did. A rare treat for Region 2 owners is the inclusion of a variety of deleted scenes that never made it to the theatrical release. In addition to this, the DVD boasts full uncut status, production notes, cast and filmmakers' notes and DVD-ROM features, bandaged together to make a formidable package. Time and care has obviously been taken with the variety of special features on offer. One example of this is the Egyptology 101 section, which contains all the facts about Ancient Egypt; their gods, immortals, plagues (10 of the buggers!) and even a map of Egypt. This attention to detail, information and feature entertainment is a refreshing change from the many stale releases around. If the UK DVD market is to step up another gear, then sensational releases such as The Mummy will need to be a regular occurrence – not every 3,000 years! Spectacular visuals, sensational sound, a thrilling movie and a momentous collection of extras make this a superb disc.

FINAL VERDICT

Picture ☆☆☆☆☆ Sound ☆☆☆☆☆
Entertainment ☆☆☆☆
Extras ☆☆☆☆☆ Value ☆☆☆☆☆
OVERALL ☆☆☆☆☆

MUPPETS FROM SPACE

Price: £19.99
Price: Columbia TriStar Home Video
Type of disc: Single layer, single-sided
No of chapters: 28
Film format(s)/length: 1.85:1 anamorphic & 4:3 regular / 85 mins
Audio format: Dolby Digital 5.1
Director: Tim Hill
Starring: The Muppets, Jeffrey Tambor, F Murray Abraham
Year made: 1999
Extras: Scene access; 4 trailers; live video commentary; deleted scenes; filmographies; music video: The Dust Brothers' 'Shining Star'; subtitles in 12 languages; soundtrack in English or German.

It's been a long time coming. Not *The Muppet Movie* – that was released way back in 1979. No, it's been a long time for avid Muppet fans to wait to finally discover who or what Gonzo is. And it's down to director Tim Hill, nephew of Roy Hill (*The Sting, Butch Cassidy*), to punch a heavyweight hole in the tale of a small freak lost in a big world. As Gonzo slips into deep depression (ie, he doesn't join in the songs) he begins to see weird lights and hear strange voices, and quickly becomes convinced – when his lunch talks to him – that he originates from deep space. Without a minute's notice Kermit, Miss Piggy, Fozzie and the gang launch into a sunshine singing number to try to cure their friend of his lunacy. A few screwball setpieces later the gang are off to save their furry pal's stomach from the government, and Miss Piggy's career as TV's first talk show pig. As with all the great Muppets moments it's the dumbfounded reactions of the live co-stars that make the films, and *Muppets From Space* is no exception. Andie MacDowell shines as a gloriously bitchy journalist while Tambor (Hank from *The Larry Sanders Show*) plays his government agent with a suitably paranoid eccentricity. It's a shame then that Hill's movie lacks the love affair with cinema that

so inspired previous capers such as *The Muppet Movie*'s grand bicycle number. The songs simply don't cut it any more, and the jokes lost their timing some 20 years ago. It's refreshing to find, then, that Columbia's DVD package comes with the saving grace of some excellently imaginative extras. The 4 cinema trailers are entertaining enough and the filmographies of Frank Oz and Dave Goelz are interesting, detailed insights. There's even a *Ghostbusters*/*MST3K*-style 'Live Video Commentary' by Tim Hill, Gonzo and Rizzo relating quirky tales of actors' strops during production. But what these funnily fascinating DVD extras hammer home is that, like all the showbiz greats, the Muppets' charms lie not in the film but in what surrounds it; in what wraps and huddles beneath and between its faults. For every flat gag there is an eye-watering outtake, and for every lacking song there is a brilliantly lavish music video. And yes, these good bits can only be seen on DVD.

FINAL VERDICT

Picture ☆☆☆ Sound ☆☆☆
Entertainment ☆☆ Extras ☆☆☆☆ Value ☆☆☆
OVERALL ☆☆☆

MURDER AT 1600

Price: £15.99
Supplied by: Warner Home Video
Type of disc: Single layer, double-sided
No of chapters: 37
Film length/format(s): 4:3 (side A), 16:9 widescreen (side B) / 102 mins
Director: Dwight H Little
Starring: Wesley Snipes, Diane Lane, Alan Alda
Year made: 1997
Extras: Production notes; scene access; multilingual subtitles.

Action junkie Wesley Snipes plays DC cop Harlan Regis in this tale of murder and deception at the most prominent address in the United States, 1600 Pennsylvania Avenue: The White House. Regis is called in after a young woman is found dead just a few rooms away from the Oval Office, only to find his investigation hampered at every turn by uncooperative Special Agents led by the folically-challenged Spikings (Daniel Benzali – best known for his role as an incorruptible attorney in hit show Murder One). Whilst director Dwight Little does a sterling job with this pacy action-thriller, lending yet more weight to the popular conception that the those in power are all untrustworthy despots, the DVD itself is not so impressive. When the packaging lists 'screen access' and 'menus' as two of the special features, you know you're not going to get anything particularly outstanding, and aside from the very brief production notes – which only cover two stars and the director – there's little to recommend this over the video. Disappointing.

FINAL VERDICT

Picture ☆☆☆☆ Sound ☆☆☆

Entertainment ☆☆☆ Extras ☆ Value ☆☆

OVERALL ☆☆

MYSTERY MEN

Type of disc: £19.99
Supplied by: Columbia TriStar Home Video
Type of disc: Dual layer, single-sided
No of chapters: 18
Film format(s)/length:1.85:1 anamorphic / 116 mins
Film format(s)/length: Dolby Digital 5.1
Director: Kinka Usher
Starring: Ben Stiller, William H Macy, Paul Reubens
Year made: 1999
Extras: Scene access; 'Origins of the Mystery Men' comic; spotlight on location feature; cast and film-makers' biographies; director's commentary; deleted scenes; music highlights; music notes; production notes; theatrical trailer; DVD-ROM features; soundtrack in English and German; subtitles in 9 languages.

Know a lot about superheroes? No? Don't worry, neither do the *Mystery Men*. Fortunately, this is still one of those great movies that manages to have an appeal broader than its subject. Taking the superhero movie and twisting it thoroughly on its head, the Mystery Men are an outfit of fourth-rate wannabe heroes with dubious powers such as getting angry, farting, and being able to dig quite well. When the true champion of Champion City, Captain Amazing, gets kidnapped by his arch-enemy Casanova Frankenstein (Geoffrey Rush), a madman Amazing freed from the asylum because he was running out of villains to battle, then it's up to the no-hopers to rescue him. Knowing there's little hope of liberating Amazing by themselves, Mr Furious (Stiller, on brilliant form), The Shoveler (Macy) and The Blue Raja (Hank Azaria of *Simpsons* fame) set about recruiting a suitable crew to go up against Casanova. Unfortunately, flies are attracted to dung, and it doesn't take them long to realise that the pickings are slim when it comes to untapped talent in the world of do-gooding. Handled differently, *Mystery Men* could have gone the way of so many superhero movies before it and been laughed off of the screen. However, a great script, fine performances and sharp direction tightly bind this movie into 2 hours of enjoyable fun, worth more than a single viewing. It's ironic that a comic book franchise which pokes fun at the medium should

actually pull off the movie conversion so successfully where others (Joel Schumacher, will you please stand up?) have failed. Perhaps it's the notion of superheroes who are rubbish at their job that has allowed the concept to be flexible enough for celluloid and print to meld so well. Columbia TriStar more than lives up to the standard you expect when it comes to putting out a quality DVD. Deleted scenes will make you laugh as much as the movie, and the 5.1 sound is superb. The comic's origins are well documented, along with cast and crew bios and an ultimately very enjoyable audio commentary. This disc is sheer fun; even if you've never picked up a superhero comic in your life, *Mystery Men* is still worth checking out.

FINAL VERDICT

Picture ☆☆☆☆☆ Sound ☆☆☆☆☆

Entertainment ☆☆☆☆

Extras ☆☆☆☆☆ Value ☆☆☆☆☆

OVERALL ☆☆☆☆☆

NATIONAL LAMPOON'S VACATION

Price: £15.99
Supplied by: DVDplus (www.dvdplus.co.uk)
Type of disc: Single layer, single-sided
No of chapters: 33
Film format(s)/length: 1.85:1 widescreen / 94 mins
Audio format: Mono
Director: Harold Ramis
Starring: Chevy Chase, Beverly D' Angelo, Randy Quaid
Year made: 1983
Extras: Scene access; soundtrack in English, French and Italian; subtitles in 6 languages; English and Italian subtitles for the hearing impaired.

Chevy Chase takes the Griswold family for a vacation they will never forget as they drive over two thousand miles to visit a family theme park called Walley World. However, each State they cross has an awaiting misadventure, and the humour escalates when a beautiful blonde in a Ferrari makes it impossible for Chase to keep his eyes on the road. Too bad the road for this title ends here, as the rest of the package is equipped with the barest of extra features, or more descriptively none at all. Only a scene access and language selection with a subtitles option is available on the disc. Picture quality also suffers, in places giving a grainy appearance, whereas the sound output is only in mono. Unfortunately, it's only the shiny-silver disc that indicates this film has been put onto DVD, making it an unsuitable candidate to include in your DVD collection.

FINAL VERDICT

Picture ☆☆ Sound ☆
Entertainment ☆☆☆ Extras ☆ Value ☆
OVERALL ☆☆

THE NEGOTIATOR

Price: £15.99
Supplied by: Warner Home Video
Type of disc: Dual layer, single-sided
No of chapters: 39
Film format(s)/length: 2.35:1 widescreen / 134 mins
Audio format: Dolby Digital 5.1
Director: F Gary Gray
Starring: Samuel L Jackson, Kevin Spacey, J T Walsh
Year made: 1998
Extras: Scene access; multilingual subtitles; theatrical trailer; 16-min behind-the-scenes documentary.

Samuel L Jackson is on fine form in this action-thriller as Chicago Police hostage negotiator Danny Roman, a man with a talent for handling tricky situations. When his partner is killed after uncovering incriminating information on a bunch of crooked cops, Roman finds himself being framed for the murder. He responds by taking a group of people hostage in order to try and track down the real killers and clear his name. *The Negotiator* is a film which, while action-packed, relies heavily on the performance of its main actors to portray the tension and confusion experienced by everyone in the hostage situation. Spacey is inspired as the outside negotiator faced with a room full of people who all seem to want to end the siege as quickly and bloodily as possible, while Jackson gives a powerful performance as the hostage breaker turned hostage taker who always manages to stay just one step ahead of the bad guys. A great deal of the action in *The Negotiator* takes place at night, but fortunately the excellent picture quality means that it's always clear what is happening. The sound is also superb, almost too good in fact – after a period of listening to Jackson and Spacey negotiate in subtle tones the inevitable burst of gunfire in stonking Dolby Digital 5.1 comes as quite a shock! Rather surprisingly, although *The Negotiator* is a UK DVD, it doesn't just go for the usual trailer and brief notes we're more-or-less coming to expect as standard. Instead an informative behind-the-scenes documentary gives insights into the production and gets across more information than a multitude of production notes and film biographies ever could. Add this to the theatrical trailer and the multilingual subtitles and you've got a DVD worth owning.

FINAL VERDICT
Picture ☆☆☆☆ Sound ☆☆☆☆
Entertainment ☆☆☆☆☆

Extras ☆☆☆☆ Value ☆☆☆☆
OVERALL ☆☆☆☆

THE NET

Price: £19.99
Supplied by: Columbia TriStar Home Video
Type of disc: Dual layer, single-sided
No of chapters: 24
Film format(s)/length: 1.85:1 anamorphic / 110 mins
Director: Irwin Winkler
Starring: Sandra Bullock, Jeremy Northam, Dennis Miller
Year made: 1995
Extras: Chapter select; multilingual subtitles; DVD promotion.

Whenever any nifty new technology appears, you can guarantee that some Hollywood hack will be quick to knock out a screenplay for a generic thriller where said technology is the MacGuffin that gets the story rolling. In the case of *The Net*, it's the turn of the Internet to turn the life of a Cute Yet Determined Heroine™ upside down and put her on the run. Software analyst Angela Bennett (Bullock) is the CYDH of *The Net*. Discovering an odd little bug in a program she's testing, she makes the mistake of letting her Internet buddies know about it. Before Angela knows it, her friends are being killed off and she escapes from a painful holiday encounter with Nasty English Villain™ Northam to discover that her identity has been erased from every computer database in America and replaced by that of a wanted criminal. The idea that control of computers means control of someone's life is a good one, but it's buried under a stack of standard 'innocent man on the run' (well, woman in this case) clichés that date back to Hitchcock. There are no surprises – the villains are obvious, and unlucky victims practically have bullseyes on their heads. The big conspiracy isn't that shocking either. Special features are church mouse-poor; apart from a grotty DVD promo, there's nothing of note. Some of the films on the promo aren't even available on Region 2 yet. The picture also seems slightly softer than we've become used to with DVDs. Only Sandra Bullock fans need log on.

FINAL VERDICT
Picture ☆☆ Sound ☆☆☆
Entertainment ☆☆ Extras ☆ Value ☆☆
OVERALL ☆☆

NEVER BEEN KISSED

Price: £19.99
Supplied by: Fox Home Video

Type of disc: Dual layer, single-sided
No of chapters: 30
Film format(s)/length: 2.35:1 anamorphic / 103 mins
Audio format: Dolby Digital 5.1
Director: Raja Gosnell
Starring: Drew Barrymore, David Arquette, John C Reilly
Year made: 1999
Extras: Scene access; original theatrical trailer; subtitles in English for the hearing impaired.

Does anyone else wonder what the legal implications would be if this actually happened? Tabloid journalists have a reputation for shameful methods of digging up a story, but if one did enrol in school posing as a student and then cop off with a teacher, it's pretty certain the whole affair would end in some sort of legal turmoil, and not a girl standing in a baseball field waiting for the man of her dreams. We haven't given away the ending. Never Been Kissed opens with a girl standing in a baseball field waiting for the man of her dreams, so it's a case of start as you mean to go on. The plot sees newspaper copy editor Josie Geller (Barrymore) so desperate to become a fully-fledged reporter that she agrees to claim she's 17 and go back to high school to study Nineties youth culture. The trouble is that Josie was a nerd at school, so the level of her social interaction remains as being the butt of jokes and hanging around with the biology club. Predictably the movie is about Josie getting a second shot at the traditional teen flick rites of passage, but it's all done in good spirit, and there are the odd moments of delight that will keep you hooked. The disc is nothing special, and with the only extra being the trailer that was murdered by overplay at the cinema then the only reason you'll want this one is for the movie.

FINAL VERDICT

Picture ☆☆☆☆ Sound ☆☆☆☆
Entertainment ☆☆☆ Extras ☆☆ Value ☆☆
OVERALL ☆☆☆

NEW JACK CITY

Price: £15.99
Supplied by: DVD World (01705 796662)
Type of disc: Single layer, single-sided
No of chapters: 34
Film format(s)/length: 1.85:1 widescreen / 96 mins
Audio format: Dolby Digital 5.1
Director: Mario Van Peebles
Starring: Wesley Snipes, Ice-T, Alan Payne
Year made: 1991
Extras: Scene access; English, French and Italian soundtracks in Dolby Digital 5.1; multilingual subtitles;

English and Italian subtitles for the hearing impaired.

Considering that *New Jack City* is a Nineties movie, it is surprising how dated it now looks. The fashions and hairstyles are laughably distracting, and as for some of the dialogue… However, as a representative of the modern-day gangster movie, *New Jack City* has a great deal going for it. Including sterling performances by bad-guy Wesley Snipes and undercover cop Ice-T (particularly as this was the latter's big screen debut), as well as an involving plot of lies, betrayal and crack. Unfortunately, *New Jack City* on DVD is yet another in a long line of mass market released dross, churned out with little or no effort to make a quick and easy buck. The quality of the picture is shoddy, with the defects of the print becoming painfully apparent from the film's opening. However, the sound quality is above average, with Warner Home Video making the effort to provide a Dolby Digital 5.1 language soundtrack in Italian and French, as well as English – this could be handy if you fancy brushing up on your languages before travelling around Europe, but let's face it, an extra like that is hardly going to send this DVD flying off of the shelves. No, Warner Home Video, we would rather see director's commentaries, behind-the-scenes featurettes, deleted scenes and bloopers. It's shocking that Warner didn't even bother to include the DVD standard of the theatrical trailer, so likewise, don't bother with this release.

FINAL VERDICT

Picture ☆☆ Sound ☆☆☆
Entertainment ☆☆☆ Extras ☆ Value ☆
OVERALL ☆

NIGHT OF THE LIVING DEAD

Price: £19.99
Supplied by: DVD Direct (01646) 686418
Type of disc: Single layer, single-sided
No of chapters: 31
Film format(s)/length: 1:33:1 widescreen / 96 mins
Audio format: Mono
Director: George A Romero
Starring: Duane Jones, Judith O'Dea, Karl Hardman
Year made: 1968
Extras: Theatrical trailer & television spot; *Night of the Living Bread* – a short parody; original commercials by Image Ten; THX approved transfer from original negatives; 2 full running audio commentaries by cast and crew.

Despite some clumsy editing and laughably bad acting, George Romero's hugely influential 1968 zombie-fest remains a powerful and chilling experience. Awakened from their graves by radiation from a downed satellite, hordes of living dead terrorise a group of survivors taking refuge in a farmhouse. While it suffers slightly from a non-existent budget and useless zombies, the relentlessly creepy tone of the film, right up to its suitably sick ending is enough to give the hardiest of souls nightmares. Where else can you find a flesh-eating zombie girl butchering her mother to death with a gardening trowel? The DVD is unmistakably excellent: the sound and picture have been remastered almost to perfection and you get a whole host of extras, too. These include two fascinating audio commentaries (by the cast and crew), a very silly spoof film *Night of the Living Bread*, and the original theatrical trailer. This is the ultimate version of a horror classic.

FINAL VERDICT

Picture ☆☆☆☆ Sound ☆☆☆
Entertainment ☆☆☆☆
Extras ☆☆☆☆ Value ☆☆☆☆
OVERALL ☆☆☆☆

A NIGHT TO REMEMBER

Price: £19.99
Supplied by: Carlton Home Entertainment
Type of disc: Single layer, double-sided
No of chapters: 20 (9 side A, 11 side B)
Film format(s)/length: 4:3,16:9 widescreen (b/w)/ 118 mins
Director: Roy Ward Baker
Starring: Kenneth More, Honor Blackman, Michael Goodliffe
Year made: 1958
Extras: Main character biographies; 60-minute colour 'Making of' feature with behind-the-scenes footage and interviews with the author of the book, Walter Lord, and producer William MacQuitty; original theatrical trailers; scene access; 2 picture formats (16:9, 4:3).

Not many people will have seen Roy Baker's original (and some would say superior) take on the tragic tale of the sinking of the RMS *Titanic*, but for movie fans it is a genuine delight and this enhanced version for DVD is surely definitive. Not only do you get the original print in widescreen and normal aspect ratios, but on side B there lies an hour-long documentary charting the making of the film from preproduction to worldwide release. This is priceless material, especially for the *Titanic* fan and collector, and includes an insightful interview with the author of the original book, Walter Lord and producer William MacQuitty who was actually present when the real *Titanic* was launched. Also included on the flipside are the original theatrical trailers and text-only biographies of the two main stars, Kenneth More and Honor Blackman. In terms of additional material you would be hard pushed to ask for more, and this is what makes *A Night to Remember* on DVD such an essential purchase, especially if the recent action movie made you curious to learn more about the famous shipping disaster. The film itself is a serious and coldly factual account of RMS *Titanic*'s maiden voyage and the subsequent iceberg/ship's hull interface on 14 April 1912. We join Herbert Lightholler (More) rushing to meet the *Titanic* at Belfast by train, and the first 15 minutes see various passengers leaving for the mighty ship's maiden voyage, including Mrs Liz Lucas (Blackman). Where the modern day rendition concentrated on two young lovers and their antics before and during the sinking, *A Night to Remember* coasts over all the main players in the hope of capturing the horror of the disaster from as many different viewpoints as possible. In part it works because you meet so many characters, but even More, the star of the film, gets relatively little screen time as the director quickly pans over to the next scene in order to illustrate an important moment. With so many doomed souls vying for your attention, it is little wonder that you can barely keep track of who's who – let alone care about any of them. Obviously the effects are not even vaguely special, with obvious scale models for all the exterior shots, but if you can bear to watch a film that didn't cost $200 million then it is a real treat, particularly as the quality of acting throughout is significantly better than Messrs DiCaprio, Winslet and Zane. Baker also manages to convey the sense of panic a great deal more convincingly than Cameron without trying as hard. This is really what DVD is all about – giving you far more than videotape ever could – and the excellent collection of features complements the film perfectly. It will be very interesting to see if James Cameron's DVD of *Titanic* will contain priceless extras of this quality.

FINAL VERDICT

Picture ☆☆☆☆ Sound ☆☆ Entertainment ☆☆☆☆☆
Extras ☆☆☆☆☆ Value ☆☆☆☆
OVERALL ☆☆☆☆☆

NOSFERATU

Price: £15.99
Supplied by: Eureka Video
Type of disc: Single layer, single-sided
No of chapters: 12
Film format(s)/length: 4:3 regular / 81 mins
Audio format: Stereo
Director: Friedrich Wilhelm Murnau
Starring: Max Schreck, Gustav Von Wangenheim, Greta Schroeder
Year made: 1922

Extras: Scene access.

It's hard to appreciate what cinema must have been like in the Roaring Twenties, when films were silent affairs and special effects budgets were non-existent. In recent years, motion pictures have relied upon sound effects and music to create mood and atmosphere, with the horror genre being one of the leaders in audio suspense. So, it is truly fascinating to watch a genuine horror classic such as *Nosferatu*, which belongs to a cinematic era before sound. The plot will be more than familiar to anyone who has ever watched a Dracula movie or read the equivalent book. In fact, *Nosferatu* so closely follows the plot of Stoker's influential horror masterpiece that his estate sued the film's German producers. Extras? Afraid not. Eureka Video has only included the obligatory scene access menu. Considering that *Nosferatu* has influenced many of today's current film-makers, it wouldn't have been too difficult to produce a documentary for the DVD release. A lazy way to treat a true genre classic.

FINAL VERDICT

Picture ☆☆ Sound ☆☆

Entertainment ☆☆☆ Extras ☆ Value ☆

OVERALL ☆

Notting Hill

Price: £19.99

Supplied by: Universal

Type of disc: Dual layer, single-sided

No of chapters: 18

Film format(s)/length: 2.35:1 widescreen enhanced / 119 mins

Audio format: Dolby Digital 5.1

Director: Roger Michell

Starring: Julia Roberts, Hugh Grant, Rhys Ifans

Year made: 1999

Extras: Scene access; cast and film-makers on screen biographies; a travel guide to Notting Hill with detailed maps of Portobello Road; DVD-ROM links to Universal websites; theatrical trailer; animated, music accompanied menu; booklet containing stills and actor biographies in English and German; subtitles in Dutch; English subtitles for the hearing impaired.

Five years after *Four Weddings and a Funeral* made box office history, its star Hugh Grant, producer Duncan Kenworthy and writer Richard Curtis reunited to work on a film that has become Britain's most successful movie. Netting £31 million in this country alone, it's the first Britfilm to smash the $100 million barrier across the pond in the US. Although the template of *Notting Hill* is familiar, this is a more mature film than *Four Weddings*. The characters' relationships

evolve and even take stock of their situations as in European cinema, and West London has never looked so good. William Thacker (Grant) is a regular chap living 'a strange half-life' and working in a Notting Hill travel bookshop. Lovelorn after his divorce, his ennui is not well assisted by scene-stealing, scruffy housemate, Spike (Ifans) and his ensemble of old friends, played by the charismatic Hugh Bonneville, Gina Mckee, Tim McInnerny and Emma Chambers. Anna Scott (Roberts) is the most famous movie star in the world but feels equally alone especially with the tabloids tracking her every move. When a chance encounter with William on Portobello Road sparks a relationship between the two, it hilariously throws William's ordinary life into total chaos. This being a British film, irony is never far away; when William is astonished that Anna is embarrassed and hurt after being caught by the omnipresent paparazzi, it's not as if Grant himself needs any help appreciating how showbiz gossip peddlers work. It's a credit to their acting that five minutes into the film, we stop seeing Hugh and Julia and care for William and Anna instead. Extra features for *Notting Hill* exist – but not in this region! Universal UK does treat us to an excellent 2.35:1 anamorphic transfer and a great 5.1 Dolby Digital soundtrack, showcasing the film's score to a jaw-dropping extent. Production notes and biographies are comprehensive but the opportunity to enclose quotes from the cast and crew is missed. The DVD-ROM materials are, unfortunately, nothing to get excited about – just links to tied-in Web sites. The main menu features looped clips from the film and some lovely incidental music, but the true novelty is a travel guide to the real Notting Hill. It pinpoints which locations the crew filmed and their relation to the real shops and landmarks that tourists can find today. *Notting Hill* is a warm and wonderfully entertaining fairy tale, crafted from engaging performances, sensitive writing and subtle direction. The DVD is only blighted by inexplicable regional differences.

FINAL VERDICT

Picture ☆☆☆☆ Sound ☆☆☆☆☆

Entertainment ☆☆☆☆ Extras ☆☆ Value ☆☆☆

OVERALL ☆☆☆☆

The Nutty Professor

Price: £19.99

Supplied by: Columbia TriStar Home Video

Type of disc: Single layer, single sided

No of chapters: 16

Film format(s)/length: 16:9 widescreen / 91 mins

Audio format: Dolby Digital 5.1

Director: Larry Miller
Starring: Eddie Murphy, Jada Pinkett, Tom Shadyac
Year made: 1996
Extras: Scene access; production notes; theatrical trailer; soundtrack in English (5.1), French, German, Italian, Spanish and Czech (stereo) and Polish (mono); subtitles in 7 languages.

This one pulled Eddie Murphy's flagging career out of the doldrums – if people can't laugh at flatulence and fatness after all, what can they laugh at? Obese Professor Sherman Clump (Murphy) is in love with the gorgeous Pinkett. One day he – if you will – 'nutty' professor stumbles across a chemical solution that makes fat hamsters thin again, takes a swig himself, and before you know it, he's transformed into Buddy Love (Murphy). But Love is not only thin and gorgeous, his testosterone levels are through the roof… The CGI transformation sequences hit a bullseye, and have to be seen to be believed. Clump's family from hell (all played by Murphy) are similarly clever, gross and funny while Larry (*Pretty Woman*) Miller's trademark slimy boss is both effect-free and hysterical. Disappointingly, the film's supposed message of 'forget your weight, be happy' rings hollow due to a totally unconvincing ill-matched romance and 50 per cent of the screen time being devoted to verbal and visual fat gags. The DVD is standard-issue Universal – it looks superficially splendid, if lacking absolute pristine perfection (see *Twister*, *River Wild*, *Waterworld* and so on). The sound is a blast though, with the fantasy and action sequences really coming alive and delivering the sonic goods right round the soundstage – this is Hollywood dubbing as slick as it comes. Aside from the production notes, trailer and biogs, that's it. Although there's little wrong with this disc, there's little to get too excited about either – and with a movie this old, don't Universal and Columbia figure that £19.99 is a tad on the porky side?

FINAL VERDICT
Picture ☆☆☆☆ Sound ☆☆☆☆
Entertainment ☆☆☆ Extras ☆☆ Value ☆☆
OVERALL ☆☆☆

October Sky

Price: £19.99
Supplied by: Columbia TriStar Home Video
Type of disc: Dual layer, single-sided
No of chapters: 18
Film format(s)/length: 2.35:1 anamorphic / 103 mins
Audio format: Dolby Digital 5.1
Director: Joe Johnston
Starring: Jake Gyllenhaal, Chris Cooper, Laura Dern

Year made: 1999
Extras: Chapter access; cast and film-makers notes; production notes; *Spotlight on Location* documentary; theatrical trailer; web links; soundtrack in English and German; subtitles in 11 languages.

The name *October Sky* is likely to be an unfamiliar one to many as, despite an ever-popular 'triumph-in-the-face-of-adversity' theme, the film received relatively little media attention on its release. Set in 1957, the story begins as the Russians send Sputnik into orbit. A teenager named Homer Hickham (Gyllenhaal) gazes up at the satellite and is inspired. Trapped in a small town where the only career path for most leads down the mines, Homer starts building amateur rockets which, ultimately, are the key to his freedom. Based on a true story, *October Sky* tells a tale of young ambition which, while predictable, is surprisingly endearing. The informative extras on the DVD allow you to find out more about the cast and film – particularly enlightening because of the lack of hype surrounding the movie – and the impressive audio quality enhances a great soundtrack. This disc certainly does Homer and his friends justice and should be enough to satisfy 'feel-good' fans everywhere.

FINAL VERDICT
Picture ☆☆☆ Sound ☆☆☆☆
Entertainment ☆☆☆ Extras ☆☆☆ Value ☆☆☆
OVERALL ☆☆☆

Once Were Warriors

Price: £15.99
Supplied by: DVDplus (www.dvdplus.co.uk)
Type of disc: Single layer, single-sided
No of chapters: 12
Film format(s)/length: 4:3 regular / 98 mins
Audio format: Dolby Surround
Director: Lee Tamahori
Starring: Rena Owen, Temuera Morrison, Mamaengaroa Kerr-Bell
Year made: 1994
Extras: Scene Access.

Let's face it, a New Zealand film with a cast that is difficult to pronounce and impossible to spell, with no extras and presented only in full-frame isn't likely to hit the top of the DVD charts, is it? Even the bold superlatives plastered all over the packaging will fail to convince, especially as the cover itself is so awful. So if nothing will persuade you to buy this, then why are you reading on? Well, maybe there's hope for you yet. Set in New Zealand, *Once Were Warriors* is a gripping, brutal tale of a family torn apart by violence. Unflinching in its portrayal of domestic brutality, it's a movie that depresses, staying with you long after the credits have rolled. It offers nothing in the way of extras and hardly pushes the DVD player to the limit in either the audio or visual department. But despite all this, it's a movie you'll never forget. Trust me on this.

FINAL VERDICT

Picture ☆☆ Sound ☆☆

Entertainment ☆☆☆☆☆ Extras ☆ Value ☆☆☆

OVERALL ☆☆☆☆

ONEGIN

Price: £19.99
Supplied by: Entertainment in Video
Type of disc: Dual layer, single-sided,
No of chapters: 12
Film format(s)/length: 1.78:1 anamorphic / 102 mins
Audio format: Dolby Surround
Director: Martha Fiennes
Starring: Ralph Fiennes, Liv Tyler, Toby Stephens
Year made: 1999
Extras: Scene access; interviews with cast and crew (23 mins); 4 news reports (16 mins).

A Ralph Fiennes project, directed by his sister, with music written by his brother. Nepotism? What's that? However, the Fiennes clan has actually done an admirable job of bringing this classic romantic tragedy to life. Based on Alexander Pushkin's epic *Eugene Onegin*, the film is set in 19th Century Russia and tells of a wealthy young player in St Petersburg's high society whose life alters dramatically after he inherits a country estate. Beautifully shot, and with an excellent score to match, it boasts a typically impressive performance from Fiennes, and looks spectacular on DVD. The advertised '38 minutes' of extras are slightly disappointing, comprising interviews and 'Making-of' snippets which, though interesting, occasionally get repeated under different guises. The standard of the disc itself does, however, do justice to the film's stunning settings and imaginative sequences, and as a visual spectacle, this classic melodrama is well worth a look.

FINAL VERDICT

Picture ☆☆☆☆ Sound ☆☆☆

Entertainment ☆☆☆ Extras ☆☆ Value ☆☆☆

OVERALL ☆☆☆

101 DALMATIANS

Price: £19.99
Supplied by: Disney DVD
Type of disc: Single layer, single-sided
No of chapters: 17
Film format(s)/length: 4:3 regular / 76 minutes

Audio format: Dolby Surround
Directors: Clyde Geronimi and Hamilton Luske
Starring the voices of: Rod Taylor, Cate Bauer, Betty Lou Gerson
Year made: 1961
Extras: Scene access; soundtrack in English, French, Italian, Dutch, Polish, Czech, Hebrew and Greek; multilingual subtitles; subtitles for the hearing impaired in English; advert for other Disney DVDs.

Disney has been making films almost since the dawn of time, and years after its original release the animated classic *101 Dalmatians* has become available on DVD. Disney has already produced an updated live-action version of the film, and with a sequel on the way the film's popularity is still evident. *101 Dalmatians* is the tale of Pongo and Perdita, two Dalmatians who after 'arranging' for their owners to get together do the same for themselves, producing a litter of 15 cute little spotted puppies. Since this wouldn't make much of a story on its own, things start to heat up when villain Cruella De Vil decides that spots are most definitely 'in' for this year and attempts to buy the puppies so that she can make herself a unique fur coat. The dogs' owners naturally refuse this request, but being a villain Cruella simply kidnaps the puppies anyway. Pongo and Perdita have to take matters into their own hands – er, paws – and set out to recover their offspring, getting the welcome help of the rest of the animal kingdom in order to bring Cruella and her dim-witted henchmen to justice. Unlike the live-action version, in the cartoon the animals are able to talk, which makes it a more witty film than the 'Home Alone' with dogs' of the remake. Although it has its moments, it wouldn't be cruel to say that this is not the most spectacular of Disney movies. The style of the animation was somewhat experimental at the time, and quite radical for a Disney film, but compared to the glossy, CGI-enhanced panoramas and fast action of more recent Disney cartoons it now has a rather scratchy and dated look. The picture occasionally suffers from a slight flickering effect, but it's less grainy than some of the other Disney DVDs reviewed this issue. Disney has become almost a synonym for 'no extras', and the DVD of *101 Dalmatians* doesn't change this. All you get offered as a special feature is a weedy couple of pages that amount to nothing more than an advert for other Disney flicks on disc. There's no shortage of alternate-language soundtracks, but who cares? We've seen a number of Disney releases just recently and this one is beginning to look outdated. The modern live-action version is far more enjoyable to watch.

FINAL VERDICT

Picture ☆☆ Sound ☆☆☆
Entertainment ☆☆☆ Extras ☆ Value ☆☆☆
OVERALL ☆☆☆

ONE NIGHT STAND

Price: £15.99
Supplied by: Entertainment in Video
Type of disc: Single layer, single-sided
No of chapters: 12
Film format(s)/length: 1.85:1 widescreen enhanced / 97 mins
Audio format: Dolby Pro Logic
Director: Mike Figgis
Starring: Wesley Snipes, Nastassja Kinski, Ming Na Wen
Year made: 1999
Extras: Trailer.

Perhaps some fetish is at play, but it just doesn't sit right that Carlyle (Snipes) strays from his sizzling Asian wife (*ER*'s Ming Na Wen) for the sagging clutches of Nastassja Kinski. Nevertheless, that's what *One Night Stand* is all about. Well, that and a pointless subplot about Carlyle's friend Charlie (Bobbie DJ) dying of AIDS, a transparent afterthought intended to be harrowing for the sake of it. The image quality is of the pristine crispness found in the best DVDs, aided by that widescreen enhanced polish. We're talking pores in people's skin and countable chin stubble. This only falters with some odd ghosting that can occasionally be found trailing from outlines of hard contrast, but your enjoyment certainly won't be dampened. Sound may be in Pro Logic only, but nothing more exciting than conversation ever occurs, so it's no loss. One muggy trailer hardly counts as 'Added Value', though.

FINAL VERDICT

Picture ☆☆☆☆☆ Sound ☆☆☆
Entertainment ☆☆ Extras ☆ Value ☆☆
OVERALL ☆☆

ON GOLDEN POND

Price: £9.99
Supplied by: Carlton Silver Collection
Type of disc: Single layer, double-sided
No of chapters: 15
Film format(s)/length: 1.85:1 widescreen / 104 mins
Audio format: Mono
Director: Mark Rydell
Starring: Henry Fonda, Katherine Hepburn, Jane Fonda
Year made: 1981
Extras: Scene access; subtitles in English.

Hollywood veterans Fonda and Hepburn both bagged Oscars for their portrayal of golden oldies, as did screen writer Ernest Thompson. Fonda, in his last ever film, plays 80 year-old ex-professor Norman, who's let old age turn him into a stubborn, cruel, senile old git. It's a painful, and at times painfully contrived, dissection of the lifelong rift between Norman and his daughter (Jane Fonda). Things start to erupt when Norman continues to reject her but forms a meaningful relationship with the 13 year-old son of her fiancé. *On Golden Pond* managed to break American box office records, but its success was due in part to audiences finding it a welcome contrast to the sex and violence-driven films dominating the time. Unfortunately this DVD leaves its pond life stagnating in the Eighties by providing nothing more than scene access, but the sound and picture quality are reasonable – and it only costs a tenner.

FINAL VERDICT

Picture ☆☆ Sound ☆☆ Entertainment ☆☆☆
Extras ☆ Value ☆☆
OVERALL ☆☆

ON HER MAJESTY'S SECRET SERVICE

Price: £19.99
Supplied by: MGM Home Entertainment
Type of disc: Dual layer, single-sided
No of chapters: 32
Film format(s)/length: 2.35:1 anamorphic / 145 mins
Audio format: Mono
Director: Peter Hunt
Starring: George Lazenby, Diana Rigg, Telly Savalas
Year made: 1969
Extras: Scene access; *Inside On Her Majesty's Secret Service* featurette; television spots; radio spots; *Q's Workshop* featurette; theatrical trailer; photo gallery; audio commentary by director Peter Hunt, cast and crew; subtitles in 9 languages.

Daunting! That can be the only word for it. Not only is the James Bond franchise one of the most popular in the world, it was also one of the first. And when the main appeal of the franchise decides that he wants to avoid being typecast as the ultimate gentleman spy, and kisses goodbye to MI6, then making the decision to keep going at full throttle is throwing caution to a Force 10 gale. To replace Sean Connery you either had to be incredibly brave or incredibly arrogant. George Lazenby was both, as well as being one jammy bastard. Not only did he have to face up to stepping into the public domain and filling the shoes of the Sixties' greatest cinema icon, he also had to deal with being in Connery's shadow, a heavy Australian accent to cover up, no previous acting experience, plus having to breathe life into one of the most emotionally fuelled

Bond stories that Fleming ever published. The novel *On Her Majesty's Secret Service* was written by Ian Fleming in Jamaica during the filming of *Dr. No*, and was supposed to be the follow-up movie to *Goldfinger*, but for various reasons was delayed until Lazenby's introduction into the series. Sticking religiously to the source novel, first-time director Hunt sends Bond off on a mission to track down his arch-enemy Blofeld, leader of the terrorist organisation SPECTRE, whose hair-brained world domination scheme for today is to brainwash 12 attractive young ladies, whom he has lured to his mountain-top hideaway under the pretence of being an allergy research clinic, to spread disease across the world when he contacts them via their make-up kit. Bond encounters Blofeld's rival, crimelord Marc-Ange Draco (Gabriele Ferzetti), who offers Bond key information is exchange for, bizarrely enough, taking his daughter's hand in marriage. However, the feisty Tracy Draco (Rigg) isn't taken by the idea of being married off, so Bond is faced with not only saving mankind from the world's most famous bald cat lover, but also breaking the habits of a lifetime, and falling lock, stock in love with Tracy. The result is an incredibly slick and intelligent spy caper of blockbuster proportions. Hunt, the editor of the previous 5 Bond outings, proved himself to be a highly competent and visually driven director, turning in a tight, concise and exciting 007 movie. Arguably the best of the series. Hunt's reluctance to rely on gadgets and lavish sets and indulge the plot a little more than in previous efforts means that it is Bond's persona that dominates nearly every scene, managing to be more intoxicating than the magnificent Swiss Alpine backdrop to the movie's glorious finale. It's unwise to consider how Connery would have fitted in, or to compare Lazenby to his predecessor. This is Lazenby's movie, so give him a chance. When all's said and done he has enough physical presence, arrogance and charm to bring Bond alive on the screen, and let's face it, this is a Bond movie after all, and not just a vehicle for Sean Connery. This DVD is another fine example of just how much MGM cares for its franchise. The *Inside* featurette runs at 40 minutes, for much of which Hunt proves that he is possibly the most enthusiastic man to ever cry 'action' in 007's direction, and also allowing Lazenby to admit to many of the mistakes he made during the filming of the movie – the biggest of which was leaving the franchise. There are the obligatory radio spots, trailers, and documentaries, and the audio commentary is a must. It's a shame that the famed deleted 'rooftop chase' hasn't been included on the disc, but in every other aspect this is near perfection. A must-have for all 007 devotees!

FINAL VERDICT

Picture ☆☆☆☆ Sound ☆☆

Entertainment ☆☆☆☆☆

Extras ☆☆☆☆ Value ☆☆☆☆☆

OVERALL ☆☆☆☆

ONLY YOU

Price: £19.99
Supplied by: Columbia TriStar Home Video
Type of disc: Single-layer, single-sided
No of chapters: 28
Film format(s)/length: 16:9 widescreen enhanced / 104 mins
Audio format: Dolby Digital 5.1
Director: Norman Jewison
Starring: Marisa Tomei, Robert Downey Jr, Bonnie Hunt
Year made: 1994
Extras: Scene access; 'Making of' featurette; filmographies; soundtrack in German and Spanish; subtitles in 20 languages; subtitles for the hearing impaired in Dutch.

For a movie that embraces the subject of fate and whether or not there's a partner or soul mate with whom you're supposed live in ecstasy, Only You is ironically predictable. Spookily, however, it's a film you'll enjoy, thanks to the appeal of the three leads glossing over the genre clichés. Or maybe it's just fate. It's will-they-won't-they territory here as Faith (Marisa Tomei) discovers the existence of Damon Bradley, the name of her true love predicted many years before by a Ouija board and fortune-teller. The trouble is, she's due to be married. To someone else. Blimey. She trots off to Italy to find this enigma, only to bump into Peter (Robert Downey Jr) who loves her but, as those more eager among you will have realised, doesn't sport the correct moniker. Thus ensues a pretty funny tale of deceit and love, which ultimately ends...well. I expect you can imagine. Amazingly, it's the sound that excels, with the Italian orchestration proving a revelation. Sure, there are no bangs to have you thanking you installed the rear speakers, but the soundtrack here is surprisingly wholesome. Little else is memorable, though – with a lack of complicated CGI or effects there's no real advantage of DVD's clarity, but a chick flick such as this doesn't exist on eye candy. On paper, the extras look promising, but the reality is much less attractive. The five-and-a-half minute 'featurette' lacks info, recycling the separate US trailer with B-roll footage and interviews. Finally, the filmographies are interesting only to those they refer to. But overall, *Only You* proves to be greater than the sum of its parts, though it's not outstanding in any capacity.

FINAL VERDICT

Picture ☆☆☆☆ Sound ☆☆☆

Entertainment ☆☆☆ Extras ☆☆ Value ☆☆☆

OVERALL ☆☆☆

THE OPPOSITE OF SEX

Price: £19.99

Supplied by: Columbia TriStar Home Video

Type of disc: Single layer, single-sided

No of chapters: 28

Film format(s)/length: 1.85:1 widescreen enhanced / 97 mins

Audio format: Dolby Digital 5.1

Director: Don Roos

Starring: Christina Ricci, Martin Donovan, Lisa Kudrow

Year made: 1998

Extras: Scene access; deleted scenes; director's commentary; DVD trailer; theatrical trailer; filmographies; German and English soundtracks; subtitles in 15 languages.

Dedee (played by Ricci) is a complete bitch. That's clear from the start – in fact she explains it in the voice-over. She doesn't want a loving relationship, she doesn't want people to like her, she just wants to enjoy herself and that's exactly what she does. Along the way she seduces her gay half-brother's current boyfriend, steals his dead ex-boyfriend's ashes, shoots her red-neck one-balled lover (in self-defence) and repeatedly tries to blackmail just about everyone. And yet, even with all this, you can't help liking her! *The Opposite of Sex* is an outstandingly good movie and one which everyone should see. The script is extremely well written and deals with all manner of social issues in a clever and funny way without sinking to the level of stereotyping anybody (although Lisa Kudrow does basically play an older and more bitter version of her *Friends* character Phoebe). The voice-over narration from Dedee is inspired and works extremely well, giving insights into scenes which might otherwise seem a little dull and her asides to the audience are solid gold. When you see the list of extra features on this DVD you'd be forgiven for wondering whether we'd managed to get the Region 2 and 1 versions mixed up! But no, you're not hallucinating – this really is a Region 2 DVD with a director's commentary and more than ten minutes of deleted scenes! The amount of features on this disc is outstanding, particularly considering that it's only single-sided and single layer! If ever there was a UK DVD which was a must-buy then this movie is it. Buy it today, you won't regret it.

FINAL VERDICT

Picture ☆☆☆☆ Sound ☆☆☆☆

Entertainment ☆☆☆☆☆

Extras ☆☆☆☆☆ Value ☆☆☆☆☆

OVERALL ☆☆☆☆☆

OUT FOR JUSTICE

Price: £15.99

Supplied by: Warner Home Video

Type of disc: Single layer, single-sided

No of chapters: 26

Film format(s)/length: 2.35:1 widescreen / 88 mins

Audio format: Dolby Digital 5.1

Director: John Flynn

Starring: Steven Seagal, William Forsythe, Jerry Orbach

Year made: 1991

Extras: Scene access; soundtrack in French and Italian; subtitles in 10 languages; subtitles for the hearing impaired in English and Italian.

Brilliant martial arts, hilarious inaudible dialogue and top-notch action...can all be found in a Bruce Lee movie. All Steven Seagal shares with him is a similar struggle with English language. Thank those lovely people at Warner for releasing this oldie from the destitute man's Bruce Willis, the cement-faced avenger, dispensing rough justice with his fists. This time he's chasing down portly would-be gangster William Forsythe in a bizarre display of outright bullying. Forsythe is such a poor villain, wheezing like an asthmatic buffalo throughout, that it's hard to root for Seagal, particularly when he's sporting such a spectacularly ill-advised ponytail and ridiculous beret. Of course, you may want to see a thug beat up middle-aged men who swear a lot, but that's what the pub is for. As for extras, fawgetabawtit. Picture quality? You're having a laugh aren't you! The only section of any audience that this film is likely to entertain is if you're a 14 year-old, with no mates to speak of and a strange penchant for irritation.

FINAL VERDICT

Picture ☆☆ Sound ☆☆☆

Entertainment ☆ Extras ☆ Value ☆

OVERALL ☆

ORGAZMO

Price: £19.99

Supplied by: Columbia TriStar Home Video

Type of disc: Single layer, single-sided

No of chapters: 20

Film format(s)/length: 1.85:1 widescreen enhanced / 91 mins

Audio format: Dolby Digital 5.1

Director: Trey Parker
Starring: Trey Parker, Matt Stone, Dian Bachar
Year made: 1997
Extras: Scene access; production notes; trailer; link to *Orgazmo* website.

Fans of crass comedy duo Parker and Stone will find their pre-*South Park* film every bit as entertaining. Written and directed by Parker, the film follows the exploits of struggling Mormon Joe Young (Parker). Preaching from door to door, Joe ends up on an adult movie set and is soon propelled into the giddy heights of the lead role in Hollywood's latest action-suspense porno: Captain Orgazmo. Proving Parker and Stone are hilarious in front of the camera as well as behind, the script, scenes and content are just what you've come to expect in a Parker and Stone production. Armed with his 'orgazmerator' ray gun (a hero's answer to impotency!) and aided by his sidekick Choda Boy and his varied arsenal of sex tools, the pair set out to foil crime in front of the cameras. Unfortunately, when Joe's prissy fiancée discovers his new career, Captain Orgazmo must climax for the last time. Porno director Maxxx Orbison is infuriated by this news and kidnaps Young's wife-to-be. Now, Orgazmo and Choda Boy must become real-life heroes offscreen. Stone's cameo appearances as 'Dave the Lighting Guy' keep the comedy coming thick and fast (if you'll pardon the phrase) while Parker demonstrates his martial arts abilities to the surprise of many. The picture quality is excellent, although the soundtrack is only mixed in stereo. The production notes present an opportunity to learn more about the pairing, but the trailer does little to persuade the purse strings. However, *Orgazmo* more than makes up for any inadequacies by way of the DVD's extras.

FINAL VERDICT

Picture ☆☆☆☆☆ Sound ☆☆☆
Entertainment ☆☆☆☆ Extras ☆☆ Value ☆☆☆
OVERALL ☆☆☆

OUTBREAK

Price: £15.99
Supplied by: DVD World (01705 796662)
Type of disc: Single layer, single-sided
No of chapters: 45
Film format(s)/length: 16:9 widescreen / 123 mins
Director: Wolfgang Peterson
Starring: Dustin Hoffman, Rene Russo, Morgan Freeman
Year made: 1995
Extras: Scene access; subtitles; bare minimum production notes.

The most deadly threat to man is a virus, due to their ability to take over cells and spread rapidly, and after watching Wolfgang Peterson's chilling film, *Outbreak*, you'll be left in no doubt. After an explosive opening (the fuel air bomb detonation is a showpiece for anyone with a beefy sound system) we are introduced via a cleverly joined tracking shot to the United States Army Medical Research Institute of Infectious Diseases (USAMRID) and the extremely dangerous work of virologist Sam Daniels (Hoffman). *Outbreak* is supposedly based on the true story of an Ebola incident in America, but obviously the world's most lethal real life bug was a little tame for Hollywood and so what we get instead is Motaba – 100% deadly, kills in two days and even smiles for the camera. The film notches up a gear as the infection starts to spread throughout the leafy Californian town of Cedar Creek. You can tell that Peterson enjoys depicting the many moments of infection and he uses many convincing camera tricks to puts us in the shoes of the soon-to-snuff-it victim. The film's strengths come from the shocking visuals (bleeding eye sockets, thousands of body bags) and the way the virus-eye view illustrates perfectly how such epidemics spread so easily. It's an unbeatable cast which makes *Outbreak* so watchable. Hoffman is surprisingly good as the hot-headed lead – although at times coming across as a wrinkled child (43.00) – but how could the film fail with likes of Donald Sutherland (sinister), Morgan Freeman, Cuba Gooding Jr (pre-Oscar), Rene Russo and Kevin Spacey (can do no wrong as far as this reviewer is concerned)? Peterson's direction is impeccable, with tense character-driven scenes handled with the same aplomb as large scale military manoeuvres (at times resembling the latter stages of *Close Encounters*). This DVD features brief character and production notes but nothing truly revealing. No-one should underestimate the value of some juicy on-the-set gossip. But at least you get the cinematic widescreen and full orchestral soundtrack. Picture quality, too, is faultless, although some blockiness was experienced on cheaper players and this is also one of those irritating discs that starts with the subtitles on automatically. A tense biological thriller that paints a grim picture of man's ultimate frailty. *Outbreak* is a good solid DVD, but it could have done with some documentary material on various killer viruses. Perhaps that'll come with the Special Edition.

FINAL VERDICT

Picture ☆☆☆☆ Sound ☆☆☆☆☆
Entertainment ☆☆☆☆ Extras ☆☆☆ Value ☆☆☆
OVERALL ☆☆☆☆

OUTLAND

Price: £15.99

Supplied by: Warner Home Video

Type of disc: Single Layer, single-sided

No of chapters: 31

Film format(s)/length: 16:9 widescreen / 105 mins

Director: Peter Hyams

Starring: Sean Connery, Peter Boyle, Frances Sternhagen

Year made: 1981

Extras: Scene access; cast biographies and filmographies; detailed production notes; theatrical trailer; multilingual subtitles; reel recommendations.

Sean Connery is Marshal William T O'Niel, a law-enforcement officer sent to the Jupiter moon-based mining colony Con-Am 27. In this vision of a corporate future, miners have been dying mysteriously and it's up to O'Niel to figure things out. Not everyone at the colony seems keen on uncovering the truth however, and the Marshal soon finds himself on his own in one of the most dangerous environments man has ever faced. With *Outland*, writer/director Peter Hyams is basically producing a Western in space. In writing he says he "Thought of the Dodge cities of the past and the oil rigs of the present." Io, one of the moons of Jupiter represents the new frontier while Connery fills the traditional role of sheriff. As such, the plot doesn't rely too much on predicted future technology – there are no matter-transporters or robots for instance and because of this the whole story seems that much more believable, that much more real. Although a fairly old movie, due to an impressive effects department and first-rate acting *Outland* hasn't really dated at all and the DVD version is full of special features which means you get good value for money. If you're after huge million-dollar special effects extravaganzas then you're better off looking at a film like *Starship Troopers*, however if you want a tense thriller with strong plot and some first-rate acting then *Outland* is one to watch!

FINAL VERDICT

Picture ☆☆☆☆ Sound ☆☆☆☆

Entertainment ☆☆☆☆ Extras ☆☆☆☆ Value ☆☆☆

OVERALL ☆☆☆

THE OUTLAW JOSEY WALES

Price: £15.99

Supplied by: DVDplus (www.dvdplus.co.uk)

Type of disc: Dual layer, single-sided

No of chapters: 35

Film format(s)/length: 2.35:1 widescreen / 130 mins

Audio format: Dolby Digital 5.1

Director: Clint Eastwood

Starring: Clint Eastwood, Sondra Locke, Bill McKinney

Year made: 1976

Extras: Scene access; French and Italian Mono soundtrack; multilingual subtitles; subtitles for the hearing impaired in English.

Two images immediately spring to mind when discussing Clint Eastwood: 'Dirty' Harry Callahan and the Man With No Name. The latter is the enigmatic character that our Clint personified in a host of Western classics, including *Hang 'Em High*, *A Fistful of Dollars* and *The Outlaw Josey Wales*. Granted, in the latter, Clint does 'have a name', but the character and formula are essentially the same: ie, he rides into town, someone upsets him (or his horse), and a barnstormer of a gunfight ensues. Although this theme is repeated again and again, the likes of *Josey Wales* nonetheless remain solid entertainment. So, why has Warner skimped on the DVD side of things? The picture looks reasonably sharp, and the audio is Dolby Digital, so the film's gunfights sound mighty impressive. But there's no extra goodies to sink your teeth into. "This one's for hangin', boys!"

FINAL VERDICT

Picture ☆☆☆ Sound ☆☆☆

Entertainment ☆☆☆ Extras ☆ Value ☆☆

OVERALL ☆☆

OUT OF SIGHT

Price: £19.99

Supplied by: Columbia TriStar Home Video

Type of disc: Dual layer, single-sided

No of chapters: 52

Film format(s)/length: 1.85:1 widescreen / 118 mins

Audio format: Dolby Digital 5.1

Director: Steven Soderbergh

Starring: George Clooney, Jennifer Lopez, Ving Rhames

Year made: 1998

Extras: Scene access; multilingual subtitles; Dolby Surround soundtrack in German, French, Italian, Spanish, Czech; audio commentary by director Steven Soderbergh and screenwriter Scott Frank; 25 minute *Inside Out of Sight* documentary on the making of the film, featuring behind-the-scenes footage and interviews with cast and crew.; 12 deleted scenes (21 minutes); including original 6-minute trunk scene; theatrical trailer; 12 pages of production notes; soundtrack music highlights; cast and film-maker's notes; technical information about the film's transfer (film to DVD); Swelltone – 'In One Ear, Out the Other', explanation of the American sound system.

On the run from the law, Jack Foley (Clooney) –

the most successful bank robber in the US – unexpectedly falls for Federal Marshal Karen Sisko (Lopez). As the infatuation grows, both become willing to risk everything to discover if they could extend their cop/criminal relationship. There is no denying the chemistry between Clooney and Lopez, as their on-screen electricity is superb. Unfortunately, the entire film is based solely around this connection and it eventually becomes a tiresome, character-driven plot. But where the movie is disappointing, the extras are very pleasing indeed. Like any good DVD, the clips that never made it into the final cut of the film are not left on the editing floor, but make it into the 'Deleted Scenes' section. A total of 12 deleted scenes are featured, lasting 21 minutes; including the original 6-minute car trunk scene where Clooney and Lopez first meet. The familiar cast and film-maker's notes and theatrical trailer are also included, plus 12 pages of production notes. Hell, there is even technical information about the film's original transfer to DVD, plus an unusual Swelltone explanation about the 'In One Ear, Out the Other' American sound system that features a whopping seven channels of digital surround. Yet the best extra is an original documentary on the making of the film entitled *Inside Out of Sight*. This includes behind-the-scenes footage and a number of interviews with cast and crew. Much like Lopez, the quality of the picture and sound are a treat on the senses. Although an average movie, the extras are brilliant. Well done Universal.

FINAL VERDICT

Picture ☆☆☆☆ Sound ☆☆☆☆ Entertainment ☆☆☆

Extras ☆☆☆☆☆ Value ☆☆☆☆

OVERALL ☆☆☆☆

PALE RIDER

Price: £15.99

Supplied by: DVDplus (www.dvdplus.co.uk)

Type of disc: Single layer, single sided

No of chapters: 28

Film format(s)/length: 2.35:1 widescreen / 111 mins

Audio format: Dolby Digital 5.1

Director: Clint Eastwood

Starring: Clint Eastwood, Michael Moriarty, Carrie Snodgrass

Year made: 1985

Extras: Scene access; French and Italian mono soundtrack; multilingual subtitles; subtitles for the hearing impaired in English and Italian.

Since the on-screen Clint is, even now, bedding women a third of his age, it's no surprise that the 1985 *Pale Rider* has both a mother and her 14-year-

old daughter falling for him. When not otherwise engaged, he's to be found doing his best *Shane* impersonation, as his travelling preacher-cum-gunslinger saves a peace-loving gold-digging community. The Panavision image quality is below par, with whole forests disappearing into a mush of digital green. Once again, Warner has abandoned even humble production notes, sealing the fate of this shoddy disc.

FINAL VERDICT

Picture ☆☆ Sound ☆☆☆ Entertainment ☆☆

Extras ☆ Value ☆☆

OVERALL ☆☆

PARENTHOOD

Price: £19.99

Supplied by: Columbia TriStar Home Video

Type of disc: Dual layer, single-sided

No of chapters: 16

Film format(s)/length: 1.33:1 widescreen / 118 mins

Audio format: Dolby Surround

Director: Ron Howard

Starring: Steve Martin, Rick Moranis, Mary Steenburgen

Year made: 1989

Extras: Scene access; production notes; cast and film-maker's notes; soundtrack in 8 languages including German, French, Italian and Spanish (5.1); multilingual subtitles.

Watching *Parenthood* is like looking at the brightest constellation of stars through the dirtiest of telescope lenses. There's an incredible amount of talent crammed into this cast, and the subject matter is compelling, but there's just the sense that this film could have made a good point, if it hadn't been blurred by going for laughs. Steve Martin plays Gil, an over-stressed family man with three out of sorts children, and a wife who's got another one on the way. He's got one sister who's managed to raise and then break a family and another who's produced a child prodigy and is in a constant state of marital frustration. The film itself has no real plot structure to speak of, but just looks at how one family is totally dissatisfied with life, and how it goes about dealing with the blows life throws at them. This is all far too schmaltzy and very American with resolves just happening because it's the end of the film rather than any one working to any conclusions, plus this is not Martin at his best. There are a few moments when he gets to shine, and when he does he's blinding, but he's not given enough material to develop a serious side to his nature, and thus this falls short of being labelled as one of Martin's 'classics'. Howard just manages to steer this film into the territory of 'feel-good' and encourages some superb performances from most of the cast, in particular Dianne Wiest. The DVD is completely passable but has a pretty poor transfer and only production notes as extra features. Still, this film is watchable, if only for Martin's hilarious turn as 'Cowboy Gil'.

FINAL VERDICT

Picture ☆☆☆ Sound ☆☆☆ Entertainment ☆☆

Extras ☆ Value ☆☆

OVERALL ☆☆

PASSENGER 57

Price: £15.99

Supplied by: Warner Home Video

Type of disc: Dual layer, single-sided

No of chapters: 30

Film format(s)/length: 2.35:1 widescreen / 80 mins

Audio format: Dolby Digital 5.1

Director: Kevin Hooks

Starring: Wesley Snipes, Bruce Payne, Tom Sizemore

Year made: 1992

Extras: Chapter access; Dolby Digital 5.1; English/French/Italian soundtracks; multilingual subtitles (NB: You'll search in vain for the production notes promised on the box – they're not there...).

While we wait for the big-name likes of *True Lies* to wend their lazy way across the Atlantic, we British viewers have to make do with the likes of *Passenger 57* for our DVD thrills. Which isn't that much compensation, really. It's that old favourite plot, *Die Hard* on a...(insert situation here). In this case it's a plane, as barmy British terrorist Charles Rane (Payne) is rather foolishly transported to the electric chair by the very mode of transport he's an expert at hijacking. Cue the handy two-fisted hardman who escapes capture by chance (anti-terrorism expert Snipes, who's on the bog), an army of villainous cannon fodder (including a pre-dress Liz Hurley as a treacherous stewardess) and loads of blood-spurting squib explosions and cracked skulls. Snipes is watchable as the kung-fu kicking hero, and both he and Payne get some decent wisecracks between the fisticuffs. Aside from that, it's predictable, mid-octane stuff that's so short – at just 80 mins – you keep expecting one of the villains to make the traditional return from the dead even as the credits are rolling. As a DVD, there's really nothing special to report about *Passenger 57*. Picture and sound quality are what you'd expect, as are the extras – ie, devoid of even a single dickie bird, unless you absolutely must hear Snipes quip, "Always bet on black," in Italian. Which is "Punta sempre sul nero." Who says action films aren't educational?

FINAL VERDICT

Picture ☆☆☆ Sound ☆☆☆ Entertainment ☆☆☆

Extras ☆ Value ☆☆

OVERALL ☆☆

PATCH ADAMS

Price: £19.99

Supplied by: Columbia TriStar Home Video

Type of disc: Dual layer, single-sided

No of chapters: 28

Film format(s)/length: 2.35:1 widescreen / 111 mins

Audio format: Dolby Digital 5.0

Director: Tom Shadyac

Starring: Robin Williams, Monica Potter, Daniel London

Year made: 1998

Extras: Scene access; 'Making of' documentary: *The Medicinal Value of Laughter*; audio commentary with director Tom Shadyac; scene outtakes; production notes; cast and film-maker's notes; English and German soundtrack; subtitles in 11 languages; subtitles for the hearing impaired in English and Italian.

A compelling real-life story that is so truly fascinating it's an act of genius to turn it into such a dull movie. The movie begins with Patch Adams committed to a mental hospital, an experience which, perhaps unsurprisingly, inspires him to help people in a better way. Once released, Adams sets about achieving this goal by attending a teaching hospital to become a doctor. It is here that his disaffection grows with the medical profession. The main focus seems to be the dourness of the doctors, with Adams risking his career to act the clown for the children. His point that patients deserve to be treated with respect seems beyond contest, particularly as the head of medical school propounds the maxim that students are to become, "Something better than human: doctors." However, anyone who is hellbent on wrestling with their desire to be a surgeon over their more human commitments, will find this simple-minded stuff. The triumvirate of TV hospital dramas – *St Elsewhere*, *Chicago Hope* and *ER* – has created a rich expectation of medical fiction. Multiple story lines, moral dilemmas and rich characterisations developed over many episodes would provide tough competition for any movie. However, *Patch Adams* doesn't even try. This an old school Hollywood flick, a straightforward story of a good man surviving his troubles to triumph in the final reel. *Ace Ventura*, *The Nutty Professor* and *Liar, Liar* isn't, perhaps, the best grounding for taking on such an ambitious project. Although director Tom Shadyac constantly expresses admiration for Milos Forman, even to the extent of lifting the opening shot of *One Flew Over the Cuckoo's Nest*, it's clear he isn't in his league. His opening prologue on the 15-minute 'Making of' documentary is meaningless mush. When the real life Adams appears, looking like an American Salvador Dali, it becomes obvious Shadyac hasn't attempted to engage with him, instead softening and idealising him for the mass market. Adams is the most fascinating thing about the documentary, but it leaves you wanting to know more about Adams' real hospital. Sadly, it's Shadyac as opposed to Adams who provides the movie's voice-over commentary, and it's scattered with numerous "you knows" and lazy colloquialisms such as "freak out". Where it is revealing, however, is in exposing the director's mangling of the script, cutting away at background scenes and attempts at symbolism in favour of simplicity. Williams is perfect for Shadyac's purposes, making Adams little more than a common sense comedian cum physician, rather than the radical he truly is. The downplaying of Adams' critique of capitalist health care is predictable, but disappointing. The end result is an uplifting, but simple-minded tale. The DVD presentation is first class on this particular film, boasting crystal clear picture and pristine sound quality. The various menus are all stylishly animated, while the short documentary is a welcome bonus. Williams' riotous outtakes, constantly referred to in Shadyac's audio commentary, fail to live up to their billing, but then that's true for the whole flick.

FINAL VERDICT

Picture ☆☆☆☆☆ Sound ☆☆☆☆☆

Entertainment ☆☆☆ Extras ☆☆☆☆☆ Value ☆☆☆

OVERALL ☆☆☆

PAYBACK

Price: £15.99
Supplied by: DVD World (01705 796662)
Type of disk: Dual layer, double-sided
No of chapters: 32
Film format(s)/length: 1.33:1 regular (Side A) and 2.35:1 widescreen (Side B) / 97 mins
Audio format: Dolby Digital 5.1
Director: Brian Helgeland
Starring: Mel Gibson, Gregg Henry, Maria Bello
Year made: 1999
Extras: Scene access; mini interviews with 4 of the film's stars (under 10 minutes); multilingual subtitles; English subtitles for the hearing impaired.

Mel Gibson made a name for himself in Hollywood with his almost-bad cop routine in the *Lethal Weapon* series, but in *Payback* he plays a bad guy…pure and simple. In a black and white world it

is easy to define who is good and who is bad, but *Payback*'s world is coloured a darker shade of grey. Gibson plays Porter who, by his own warped set of morals, is the closest the film gets to a good guy. He was double-crossed over $70,000 and left for dead, now he wants revenge and his money back, and he'll let nothing stand in the way. *Payback* is gritty *film noir* at its best, with a wicked tongue-in-cheek sense of humour, and some showcase DVD set pieces. The picture quality is top notch, even though it was filmed using a bleached process, giving the print an almost black and white feel, and emphasising *Payback*'s *film noir* roots. The Dolby Digital soundtrack rocks through a decent set of speakers. Despite getting the thumbs up for supplying *Payback* in regular and widescreen formats on one flipper DVD, Warner definitely gets a thumbs down in terms of extras. The only extra feature provided is under 10 minutes of interview clips with 4 of *Payback*'s stars. Where are the audio commentary and behind the scenes documentary? Hell, Warner, we'd even settle for a bog-standard theatrical trailer! Here's hoping it pulls its finger out in future, or we'll have to send Porter round for our own little version of *Payback*.

FINAL VERDICT

Picture ☆☆☆☆ Sound ☆☆☆☆

Entertainment ☆☆☆☆ Extras ☆ Value ☆☆

OVERALL ☆☆☆

THE PELICAN BRIEF

Price: £15.99
Supplied by: Warner Home Video
Type of disc: Single layer, double-sided
No of chapters: 42
Film format(s)/length: 2.35:1 widescreen / 135 mins
Director: Alan J Pakula
Starring: Denzil Washington, Julia Roberts, Robert Culp
Year made: 1993
Extras: Cast and crew biographies; production notes; theatrical trailer; scene access.

Often slated by critics for falling into paranoid cliché, Grisham's *The Pelican Brief* has Julia Roberts stumbling on corruption on high. Before you can say Presidential impeachment, her boyfriend is blown up, and wham-bam-thank-you-Ma'am all around her meet sticky ends. Yes, the film lapses into predictable directorial stereotype, but the convolutions and stock suspense devices are sometimes effective. Washington plays it cool as the only person Roberts confides in who doesn't die, and Robert Culp cuts a fine President. Only Roberts herself lets the side down – while as exquisitely fragile as she can be, her startled-faun expressions of fear and persecution only serve to slightly irritate after a while. While many will overlook this as a DVD, purists will relish the claustrophobic who-can-you-trust paranoia (not bettered in *Conspiracy Theory*). The changes in pace, from dark and moody to loud and garish, while many a director's stock in trade, come across as surprisingly fresh on DVD. As far as extras are concerned, the inclusion of cast profiles and film credits are overshadowed by the insights into Grisham's celebrated lawyer's psyche.

FINAL VERDICT

Picture ☆☆☆ Sound ☆☆☆ Entertainment ☆☆☆☆
Extras ☆☆☆ Value ☆☆☆

OVERALL ☆☆☆

THE PEOPLE VS LARRY FLYNT

Price: £19.99
Supplied by: DVD World (01705 796662)
Type of disc: Single layer, single-sided
No of chapters: 20
Film format(s)/length: 2.35:1 widescreen / 124 mins
Audio format: Dolby Digital 5.1
Director: Milos Forman
Starring: Woody Harrelson, Courtney Love, Edward Norton
Year made: 1996
Extras: Multilingual subtitles; scene selection; DVD promo trailer.

Based on a true story, *The People vs Larry Flynt* traces the illustrious career of one of America's most infamous outspoken figures. Flynt rose to fame in the Seventies with his controversial porn magazine, *Hustler*, attracting widespread attention for, amongst other things, nude photos of Jackie O and lewd depictions of Santa Claus. Even after an assassination attempt that left him half-paralysed, Flynt continued to stir up trouble against the establishment, particularly the Reverend Jerry Falwell whose attempts to sue *Hustler* saw the case taken all the way to the Supreme Court. Flynt's story makes for a wonderfully entertaining film, defiantly promoting the message that everyone has the right to freedom of speech, no matter how much of a 'scumbag' they are. Woody Harrelson gives a powerhouse performance as the increasingly barmy Flynt, while Courtney Love is surprisingly, or should that be unsurprisingly, convincing as his drug-addict wife. The mixture of comedy and drama ensures that the broader issues never bog down the story, with Flynt's outrageous performances in court providing by far the most memorable moments. The picture is sharp and colourful, emphasising nicely the gaudy décor and abominable clothes in the Seventies scenes. Unfortunately, the DVD offers the viewer nothing in the way of extras, which is a shame when you consider the fascinating real life people and events that the film is based on. There must be hours of documentary footage out there concerning Flynt and *Hustler* magazine, so why are we lumbered merely with standard scene selection and the paltry Columbia TriStar DVD promo?

FINAL VERDICT

Picture ☆☆☆☆ Sound ☆☆☆ Entertainment ☆☆☆☆
Extras ☆ Value ☆☆

OVERALL ☆☆☆

PERFECT BLUE

Price: £17.99
Supplied by: Manga Video
Type of disc: Dual layer, single-sided
No of chapters: 14
Film format(s)/length: 1.85:1 letterbox / 75 mins
Audio format: Dolby Digital 5.1
Director: Satoshi Kon
Starring the voices of: Junko Iwao, Rica Matsumoto, Masaaki Okura
Year made: 1997
Extras: Scene access; interview with director Satoshi Kon; interviews with Japanese and American voice actors; theatrical trailer; behind-the-scenes performance videos; photo gallery; Manga Video trailers; Web links; soundtrack in English and Japanese; subtitles in English.

Before we start, it should be pointed out that if you're expecting the ultimate porno flick you're out of luck. What we call 'blue' movies, the Japanese call 'pink'. Don't blame us – it's a cultural thing. That's not so say that there isn't a fair amount of flesh on show, but Kon's anime psychological thriller is designed to disturb rather than titillate. Singer Mina Kirigoe leaves behind her life in a squeaky-clean 'idol' band to become an actress, and in order to make a clean break with her old career she chooses to 'do an *FHM*', as it would be called over here, doing a risqué photoshoot and taking a role in a dark and gritty TV series about a serial killer. But it seems that one of her fans objects strongly to this change in image from innocent girl to real woman. Mina discovers a Website that goes into disturbing amounts of detail about her private life, right down to what she bought at the supermarket just hours earlier. And then the murders start… *Perfect Blue* is a film that makes a determined effort to screw with your head, and it succeeds. As Mina becomes increasingly paranoid about her stalker, reality, illusion and television start to twist together until she becomes unsure as to exactly what is real – particularly when she begins to have hallucinations of her old idol self taunting her about her 'filthy' career change. As the story builds to its climax, it becomes almost *Total Recall* meets *Psycho*, where Mina's (and the viewer's) perception of what's happening keeps having the rug pulled from under it. It's a twisted (and graphic) look at the nature of obsession, voyeurism and celebrity, and makes for compulsive, if unsettling, viewing. The DVD serves the high-quality animation well – it's not up to the megabucks level of Disney, but it's far above the *anime* norm, capturing the chaotic, claustrophobic feel of Tokyo perfectly. The soundtrack comes in English and Japanese; the latter has by far the best acting, though some people may be deterred by the need for subtitles. The extras package is mainly interviews, with director Kon's being the most interesting. Had this been made live-action in Hollywood, it would have been a *Sixth Sense*-size hit. Since it wasn't, you can feel all smug by buying it and knowing you've added an unsung classic to your collection.

FINAL VERDICT

Picture ☆☆☆☆ Sound ☆☆☆
Entertainment ☆☆☆☆☆ Extras ☆☆☆ Value ☆☆☆☆
OVERALL ☆☆☆☆

A Perfect Murder

Price: £15.99
Supplied by: Warner Home Video
Type of disc: Dual layer, double-sided
No of chapters: 32
Film format(s)/length: 1.33:1 (Side A) 1.85:1(Side B) widescreen / 114 mins
Audio format: Dolby Digital 5.1
Director: Andrew Davis
Starring: Michael Douglas, Gwyneth Paltrow, Viggo Mortensen
Year made: 1998
Extras: Dolby Digital 5.1 English soundtrack; multilingual subtitles; audio commentary by Michael Douglas, Andrew Davis and screenwriter PS Kelly; audio commentary by the film's producer, director of photography, costume designer, set decorator and production designer; alternate ending with 2 separate audio tracks.

Michael Douglas has a reputation as a star who takes risks, frequently appearing in controversial films such as *Wall Street*, *Basic Instinct* and *Falling Down*. *A Perfect Murder*, however, pretty much vanished without trace in the controversy stakes despite the potentially heretical nature of its script. As screenwriter Pat Kelly makes it clear in one of the two DVD audio commentaries, the starting point was Hitchcock's classic *Dial M for Murder*. The essence of both stories is a love triangle between a rich man, his wife and an interloper, with illicit passion inevitably leading to classic Hitchcock-style murderous intent. The original had a clever enough plot, but the remake adds further layers of complexity by transforming the boyfriend hero into 'the most evil character you ever met.' Michael Douglas claims what brought him to the project was the plot's sophistication, yet ironically it's this very cleverness which is perhaps the film's main problem as it progressively removes empathy from what were very sympathetic characters. Douglas and Viggo Mortensen dance around each other in ever more elaborate games, while Gwyneth Paltrow bounces between them as pallid and uninteresting as ever. While beautifully shot – and superbly encoded for DVD – it's an uninvolving thriller for those who don't know about all the film-makers' cleverness. The beauty of this DVD, however, is that with the audio commentary you get taken through the entire film with the director, script writer and Douglas explaining what their intentions were. This makes for a much more interesting experience, the viewer becomes a voyeur of the creative process with the added frission of knowing all their decisions have conspired to produce something of a train wreck. From the original concept, through to the way Douglas provided multiple takes on a single scene with ever more finely graduated expressions of anger, it is a diverting insight into the film-makers' world. Moreover, if that's not enough information for you, there's a second audio commentary featuring (deep breath!) the film's producer, director of photography, costume designer, set decorator and (gasp!) production designer. Another intriguing aspect of DVD production is the provision of an alternate ending, which is thoughtfully provided both with and without a commentary by the director. Although the outcome is much the same, it's a much cleverer, much more morally ambiguous ending which again makes you appreciate how much effort has gone into such an ultimately dull movie. If you want an exciting thriller, look elsewhere, but for film nuts this has much to commend it and it's a great advert for what DVD can offer.

FINAL VERDICT

Picture ☆☆☆☆☆ Sound ☆☆☆☆ Entertainment ☆☆
Extras ☆☆☆☆ Value ☆☆☆
OVERALL ☆☆☆

Pete's Dragon

Price: £15.99
Supplied by: Buena Vista
Type of disc: Single layer, single-sided
No of chapters: 16
Film format(s)/length: 4:3 regular / 123 mins
Audio format: Stereo
Director: Don Chaffey
Starring: Jim Dale, Helen Reddy, Mickey Rooney
Year made: 1977
Extras: English closed captions.

When you think of Disney classics, *Pete's Dragon* is not a film that automatically springs to mind. Made before the glorious days of computer technology, the star of the film is a huge, green and mostly invisible cartoon dragon with a low IQ. He's best buddies with poor little Pete, who escapes from life as a slave to his redneck adoptive parents, whose sole purpose in life is to make him unhappy — nice! True to Disney form he makes friends with a lovely pair of people who take pity on him and good overcomes bad, the dragon saves the day and everyone sings a song! The question must be raised as to why Disney bothered to release this film on DVD. Sure children love it, but it's on Sky nearly every month and as the disc doesn't boast a single extra feature there seems absolutely no point in this release whatsoever. True to its format the sound is better than usual but to be realistic you're not really going to crank this up on your sound system. The same goes for the picture – nice and sharp but that's what you'd expect from a DVD. Disney's apathy with this thrown together release is heightened by the fact they couldn't even be bothered to check the spellings on the box – what on Earth is a 'quardian?' The disc's one saving grace is that it's not a flipper – that really would rub salt in the wounds. If your kids ask you to buy this disc, save your cash and buy them a burger instead.

FINAL VERDICT

Picture ☆☆☆ Sound ☆☆ Entertainment ☆☆
Extras ☆ Value ☆
OVERALL ☆☆

Pi

Price: £19.99
Supplied by: Pathé Distribution
Type of disc: Single layer, single-sided
No of chapters: 17
Film format(s)/length: 1.66:1 widescreen / 80 mins
Audio format: Dolby Surround
Director: Darren Aronofsky
Starring: Sean Gullette, Mark Margolis, Ben Shenkman

Year made: 1998
Extras: Scene access; deleted scenes; separate audio commentary by director Darren Aronofsky and leading actors; music video; behind the scenes montage; original theatrical trailer; cast and crew biographies; subtitles for hearing impaired in English.

There's a term in poetry – the pathetic fallacy – that describes the notion of overcast skies reflecting an individual's mood rather than local weather conditions. It's a mind-set that has unexpected echoes in quantum physics, the effect of an observer on particle experiments raising questions of meaning. *Pi* reflects and amplifies the freaking out of modern science, with a stereotypically driven genius striving to uncover the secret of that most charismatic of numbers: 3.14… Maximillian Cohen (Gullette) wants to find the world's meaning in numbers. His belief set is encapsulated in a three sentence mantra: 1) Maths is the language of nature. 2) Everything around us can be represented and understood through numbers. 3) If you graph these numbers, patterns emerge. Therefore patterns are everywhere in nature. *Pi* hammers home this mantra in similar fashion to a pop video refrain. Max's increasingly unhinged obsession rotates around his daily routine of taking medication. Video insertions of these obsessions give *Pi* a pop video look and feel, something that is emphasised by a soundtrack featuring groups such as Orbital, Aphex Twin and Massive Attack. This fractured narrative undoubtedly gives a more accurate account of most people's routine-driven lives than a classical, three act adventure. Moreover, the cutting, the techno music and grainy, monochromatic photography make a scientist's introverted inner life somehow intriguing. There are also moments of genuine surprise, particularly the beguiling explanation of the numerical basis of Hebrew…but there's also the unsettling fear – eloquently expressed by one character – that Max is gradually slipping from forms of science into mysticism and numerology. Indeed, as the movie progresses, the speeches lessen and the freak-outs increase, taking in a bizarre subplot wherein rabbi's interrogate Max for God's number. Watching an unshaven, sunken-eyed mathematician suffering particularly gruesome nosebleeds, and near-continuous delusions, ultimately has limitations as entertainment. The eclectic structure of the movie finally descends into a downward spiral of ever-increasingly gruesome cinematic sequences that culminate in a memorable if disturbing finale. All in all, it seems a movie designed more to impress than to explain. That said, there's no doubting this is an impressive DVD –

aside from a pop video and impressively detailed cast biographies, there's a production montage which succeeds in deconstructing the glamour of the movie business – numerous college kids standing around, eating junk food and mumbling. There's also director and leading actor narratives but, unusually, these are entirely separate. Aronofsky's commentary tends to be more illuminating to directorial technique than mathematical philosophy, but that's no surprise. However, after being more than a little influenced by David Lynch's *Eraserhead* debut, the pressure will be on Aronofsky to match Lynch's *Elephant Man* as a follow-up.

FINAL VERDICT

Picture ☆☆☆ Sound ☆☆☆☆ Entertainment ☆☆☆
Extras ☆☆☆☆ Value ☆☆☆☆
OVERALL ☆☆☆

THE PIANO

Price: £15.99
Supplied by: DVDplus (www.dvdplus.co.uk)
Type of disc: Single layer, single-sided
No of chapters: 12
Film format(s)/length: 1.85:1 widescreen / 115 mins
Audio format: Dolby Surround
Director: Jane Campion
Starring: Holly Hunter, Sam Neill, Harvey Keitel
Year made: 1992
Extras: Scene access; subtitles in English.

With three Oscars under its belt and acclaim from around the world, *The Piano* arrives on the UK DVD scene some 6 years after its theatrical release, and has aged very well. The soundtrack still sounds fantastic, sitting comfortably on a frill-less DVD that gamely goes up front on its lack of extras by leaving a large red space in the 'Added Value' box on the sleeve. Unfortunately, the marker to the right that indicates a Dolby Digital 5.1 soundtrack isn't quite as truthful – it's surround only, so don't be caught out in the hope for a meaty bass track. However, the lack of two extra channels is not a problem, but it does highlight another example of packaging inaccuracies which we could do without. The film? It's the one that boasts a superb central performance by Holly Hunter as Ada, a woman who doesn't speak but loves her piano and her music. Following an arranged marriage, Ada's husband sells her piano against her wishes, meaning she has to let Harvey Keitel get a little closer to her than she'd like in order to still gain access to her beloved instrument (ahem!) That's, admittedly, the heavily simplified version, as this is a strong movie with a few twists in the tale that means you're bound

to watch it again. With no extras to talk about (aside from the uncredited English subtitles), an ugly menu screen and not a production note in sight, this is a disc that sinks or swims purely on how well the film has been reproduced on DVD. The sound, other than the score, is perfectly functional throughout, peaking whenever Nyman's music hits your speakers. The image is no award winner, but holds the action reasonably enough whilst not grabbing your throat and showing off about it. So it's a better than usual performance from EiV as it continues to find its way in the Region 2 market, but surely Oscar winning movies like this deserve a few extras?

FINAL VERDICT

Picture ☆☆☆ Sound ☆☆☆ Entertainment ☆☆☆☆
Extras ☆ Value ☆☆
OVERALL ☆☆

THE PILLOW BOOK

Price: £19.99
Supplied by: VCI
Type of disc: Dual layer, single-sided
No of chapters: 16
Film format(s)/length: 4:3 regular / 122 mins
Audio format: Dolby Surround
Director: Peter Greenaway
Starring: Vivian Wu, Ken Ogata, Ewan McGregor
Year made: 1996
Extras: Scene access; theatrical trailer; sleeve notes giving basic context and back ground; subtitles in English.

More arty pictures make a welcome addition to DVD with the release of *The Pillow Book*, a compelling picture from VCI. Japanese calligrapher Nagiko (Wu) writes intricate stories on the bodies of her lovers thanks to her father's example (who used to write intricate stories on her own flesh). English translator Jerome (McGregor) encourages Nagiko to write her books about him so the whole world can appreciate her genius, but before long, their lives spiral into obsession, suicide and vengeance. You might expect a rip-roaring ride but instead, writer/director Greenaway focuses on the sensual art of calligraphy itself, casting it as the calm eye of the emotional storm that it provokes. Though extras are thin on the ground (an audio commentary by Greenaway would be fascinating but is sadly lacking) picture and sound are crisp and the graphic designs are as elegant as the writing itself. *The Pillow Book* is an intriguing but oddly dispassionate film that makes a singular DVD, and in terms of originality this is a film that demands to be watched.

FINAL VERDICT

Picture ☆☆☆☆ Sound ☆☆☆☆ Entertainment ☆☆☆☆
Extras ☆☆ Value ☆☆☆

OVERALL ☆☆☆

PINOCCHIO

Price: £19.99
Supplied by: Disney DVD
Type of disc: Single layer, single-sided
No of chapters: 24
Film format(s)/length: 4:3 regular / 84 mins
Audio format: Dolby Digital
Directors: Hamilton Luske and Ben Sharpsteen
Starring the voices of: Dickie Jones, Cliff Edwards, Christian Rub
Year made: 1940
Extras: Scene access; soundtrack in English, French, Italian Dutch and Hebrew; multilingual subtitles.

This classic animated movie was made in 1940, and is finally available to buy on DVD! The story of a small wooden puppet and his creator, the kindly woodcarver Geppetto, is back and it's not showing its age one bit. One starry night Geppetto makes a wish upon a star and the Blue Fairy decides to grant him his wish to thank him for his years of kindness. In a flash, Pinocchio springs to life, but must choose his path wisely in order to become a real boy. Top-hatted insect Jiminy Cricket is given the task of acting as the young puppet's conscience and preventing him from getting into trouble. Needless to say, the easily-led young puppet keeps getting into trouble, and the adventure that follows is a true classic. The story is wonderfully told and the characters are superbly animated, but then it is a golden era Disney film. The picture is sharp and clear and the sound is perfect, making this DVD probably even better than watching it in the cinema. There are a wide range of different European languages available and there is also subtitles for the hearing impaired. On the downside, the film is only presented in 4:3. How about catering to widescreen owners, Disney? However, it's still a great family flick, and the good news about the DVD is that it ends Disney's old 'limited release' policy – Pinocchio will be staying around for a long time yet!

FINAL VERDICT

Picture ☆☆☆ Sound ☆☆☆ Entertainment ☆☆☆☆
Extras ☆ Value ☆☆☆

OVERALL ☆☆☆

PLEASANTVILLE

Price: £19.99
Supplied by: Entertainment in Video
Type of disc: Dual layer, single-sided
No of chapters: 37
Film format(s)/length: 16:9 widescreen / 120 mins
Audio format: Dolby Digital 5.1
Director: Gary Ross
Starring: Tobey Maguire, Jeff Daniels, Reese Witherspoon
Year made: 1998
Extras: Scene access; Fiona Apple music video; behind the scenes 38-minute featurette; theatrical trailer; detailed cast filmographies; director's commentary; subtitles in English.

Capra-esque fantasies such as *Big* and *Dave* made Gary Ross's scripts something to watch out for. Now, as writer-director-producer, he's made a film which not only harks back to Frank Capra's genial world-view, but actually inhabits the same time frame thanks to its rather whimsical central premise. Despite the political satire which comes later, *Pleasantville*'s incept is as childish as *Gremlins'* gift-shop: a TV repairman comes calling and provides Toby Maguire with a magic remote which zaps him and Reese Witherspoon into a Fifties TV series. The nerdish Maguire is a *Pleasantville* addict, thanks to divorced parents and a host of other modern-day ills making him a nostalgia freak. When the Nineties teenagers arrive in Pleasantville, Reese is unsurprisingly annoyed, but then sets about teaching the joys of sex with admirable gusto before unexpectedly transforming into a bookworm. The defining visual conceit of *Pleasantville* is the interlacing of monochrome and colour photography. As Toby and Reese shake up the sterile sitcom, spots of colour flourish, making for some genuinely inspired visuals; from a ride in an open-top convertible through falling pink cherry blossoms, to a dazzling ransacking of an artist's bar by monochrome neo-Nazis. Despite its lyrical moments, *Pleasantville* lacks a clear focus. Ross seems so pleased with his idea that he can't settle on a single interpretation. Is *Pleasantville* a satire of the Fifties, or US sitcoms in general? A glance across the Net found reader reviews evenly split between five star raves and one star pastings. The former adored the movie for the way its initial whimsy expanded to deliver real political points. The latter loved the concept, but found the story a big yawn. For those used to action and big explosions, *Pleasantville* is likely to seem tepid: a neat collection of ideas, visuals and the odd joke but without any real narrative drive. The execution of the film on DVD is first class. The contrast between monochrome and colour imagery is sharply rendered in a way blurry old VHS could only dream of. Similarly, Ross's well judged use of Fifties' music, and a Randy Newman score, comes over with enjoyable precision. There's also a very nicely executed and detailed filmography section which is far superior to the usual spartan notes, plus a confident and consistently interesting commentary by Gary Ross. Even the included pop video is first class, as acclaimed singer-songwriter Fiona Apple resurrects a Beatles song with an enjoyable *Pleasantville*-themed backdrop. The only disappointment is the 38-minute 'Art of Pleasantville' feature, which you expect to be a dazzling insight into Hollywood wizardry, but is instead quite astonishingly dull. To sum up, this is a superbly packaged piece of fluff. It's charming and diverting, pretty enough to be fondly remembered even if at the time the odd yawn or two is difficult to fight off.

FINAL VERDICT

Picture ☆☆☆☆☆ Sound ☆☆☆☆
Entertainment ☆☆☆ Extras ☆☆☆☆ Value ☆☆☆☆
OVERALL ☆☆☆☆

PLUNKETT & MACLEANE

Price: £17.99
Supplied by: Universal
Type of disc: Single layer, single-sided
No of chapters: 18
Film format(s)/length: 16:9 widescreen enhanced / 101 mins
Audio format: Dolby Digital 5.1
Director: Jake Scott
Starring: Robert Carlyle, Liv Tyler, Jonny Lee Miller
Year made: 1999
Extras: Scene access; behind-the-scenes documentary (4 mins); interview with the cast and crew (6 mins); theatrical trailer; soundtrack in Spanish and Italian; subtitles in Spanish and Italian; subtitles for the hearing impaired in English.

With a swashbuckler here and a swashbuckler there, Carlyle as Plunkett and Miller playing his reluctant partner, Macleane, bring the eponymous highwaymen screaming onto our television screens and drag the Dick Turpin story into the 21st century. Forming an uneasy partnership, the upper class Macleane mingles with the rich in order to identify the best targets for the uncouth Plunkett to rob. However, Macleane didn't count on falling in love with the Lady Rebecca (Liv Tyler) along the way. The comedy relishes in the contrast of very modern language and music, with a fusty 18th century setting. It generally works in a 'nice one, my lady' kind of way. The soundtrack thumps an impressive quality of

sound, although the picture is sometimes surprisingly patchy. The extra features are comprehensive but they're more promotional shorts than informative pieces. Errol Flynn must be turning in his grave.

FINAL VERDICT

Picture ☆☆☆ Sound ☆☆☆☆ Entertainment ☆☆☆
Extras ☆☆ Value ☆☆
OVERALL ☆☆☆

POCAHONTAS II: JOURNEY TO A NEW WORLD

Price: £19.99
Supplied by: Walt Disney Home Video
Type of disc: Single layer, single-sided
No of chapters: 23
Film format(s)/length: 4:3 regular / 70 mins
Audio format: Dolby Digital 5.1
Directors: Bradley Raymond and Tom Ellery
Starring the voices of: Irene Bedard, Linda Hunt, Billy Zane
Year made: 1999
Extras: Scene access; soundtrack in English, Portuguese, Czech, Greek, Hungarian, Hebrew; subtitles in English for the hard of hearing.

Computer technology has obviously been a fantastic boon to the animation industry in general and Disney in particular, because lately the undisputed king of cartoons has been churning out movies by the bucketload! Pocahontas is the latest character to get the sequel treatment, and it's fun and frivolity all the way. The beautiful Native American is now on her way to England on an important mission of peace, joined by a host of new characters and her old friends Meeko, Percy and Flit. If you've seen the original *Pocahontas* then you can basically expect more of the same; if you haven't, then it doesn't matter because the plot's fairly self-explanatory. Unfortunately, like many other Disney DVD offerings this one has a large helping of naff-all to offer as far as extras go. While you do get choice of 6 languages and some English subtitles, unfortunately that's about it! Disappointing Disney!

FINAL VERDICT

Picture ☆☆☆☆ Sound ☆☆☆☆ Entertainment ☆☆☆
Extras ☆ Value ☆☆
OVERALL ☆☆

POINT BREAK

Price: £19.99
Supplied by: 20th Century Fox Home Entertainment
Type of disc: Dual layer, single-sided
No of chapters: 19

Film format(s)/length: 16:9 widescreen enhanced / 117 mins

Audio format: Dolby Surround

Director: Kathryn Bigelow

Starring: Keanu Reeves, Patrick Swayze, Gary Busey

Year made: 1991

Extras: Scene access; theatrical trailer; subtitles in 10 languages; subtitles for the hearing impaired in English.

Rookie FBI agent Johnny Utah (Reeves) and his seasoned partner Angelo Pappas (Busey) find themselves assigned to an unsolved case that spans three years and 27 banks in this rush hour of adrenaline. A group of bank robbers calling themselves the Ex-Presidents hit one bank after another. Believing the crime sprees are linked to a group of surfers, Utah and Pappas begin an operation along the Southern Californian coast to identify the villains. Whilst undercover, Utah stumbles across Bodhi (Swayze) a surfer with a do-or-die attitude towards life. Quickly drawn into the world of surfing by day and partying at night, the two federal agents begin to close in on Reagan, Carter, Nixon and Johnson. Whilst the criminal element don't reveal themselves until late on in the film, the involvement of Swayze is obvious from the start. Swayze fans who witnessed him don tight trousers for *Dirty Dancing* will notice a familiar approach to his character in *Point Break*, albeit a slightly more evil one. This film remains a classic action flick of the Nineties that certainly sparked a rise in skydiving and surfing fanatics. The tag-line for *Point Break* is: if you want the ultimate thrill, you have to pay the ultimate price. Unfortunately, this kind of enthusiasm wasn't exhibited when producing the special features or presentation of the DVD. The film is great and the picture is impressive in its anamorphic state. However, the sound mix remains unchanged from the original recording and struggles to impress as the Surround only soundtrack does little to take your breath away. The offer of the original theatrical trailer fails to draw praise and the numerous subtitles included will only appease the minority market. Vintage performances from Reeves and Swayze, combined with top-notch action, are the only reasons to consider this purchase.

FINAL VERDICT

Picture ☆☆☆☆ Sound ☆☆☆ Entertainment ☆☆☆☆

Extras ☆ Value ☆☆

OVERALL ☆☆☆

POLICE ACADEMY

Price: £15.99

Supplied by: Warner Home Video

Type of disc: Single layer, single-sided

No of chapters: 31

Film format(s)/length: 1.85:1 anamorphic / 92 mins

Audio format: Stereo

Director: Hugh Wilson

Starring: Steve Guttenberg, Kim Cattrall, Bubba Smith

Year made: 1984

Extras: Subtitles in 10 languages.

If you don't know the *Police Academy* series then you should be ashamed (or proud) of yourself. Despite being atrociously bad and cheesy, this film is still a pivotal moment in cinema history and, like they say, the first one is always the best. Unfortunately, if you do buy this film then you'll realise just how dated it has become. It's a wonder how they got away with making one sequel, let alone 6! The biggest travesty about this disc are the extras, or rather the complete lack of them. The Region 1 disc had theatrical trailers for all the films and production notes thrown in, but all you get here is the chance to brush up on a few foreign languages. Even if you thought this film was funny as a kid, it's still not worth buying. Avoid like you would a real police officer!

FINAL VERDICT

Picture ☆☆ Sound ☆☆ Entertainment ☆☆

Extras ☆ Value ☆☆

OVERALL ☆☆

POODLE SPRINGS

Price: £15.99

Supplied by: Mosaic Movies

Type of disc: Single layer, single-sided

No of chapters: 17

Film format(s)/length: 4:3 regular / 96 mins

Audio format: Stereo

Director: Bob Rafelson

Starring: James Caan, Dina Meyer, David Keith

Year made: 1998

Extras: Scene access; production notes; cast biographies; photo gallery; original trailer.

Philip Marlowe is back and walking the mean streets of the City of Angels. Cops still bust his balls, dames are still untrustworthy and everyone still has something to hide but it's now 1963 and the ageing, cynical private detective is adjusting to marital bliss with Laura (Meyer). Although his new wife elevates Marlowe into California's elite society, a missing persons case draws him into a complex web of deceit, drugs, pornography, blackmail and moider. Only the first three chapters of *Poodle Springs* were written by Raymond Chandler before his death. Now, a fine cast and crew complete his last manuscript with this entertaining HBO television movie. The disc couches the movie with satisfactory extras but a 'Making of' featurette would have been fascinating. Stereo sound and the TV-sized picture are the only giveaways that this isn't a theatrical movie, so convincing are the acting and production values. Worth investigating further.

FINAL VERDICT

Picture ☆☆☆ Sound ☆☆☆ Entertainment ☆☆☆
Extras ☆☆☆ Value ☆☆☆
OVERALL ☆☆☆

PORRIDGE

Price: £9.99
Supplied by: Carlton Video
Type of disc: Single layer, single-sided
No of chapters: 15
Film format(s)/length: 4:3 regular / 90 mins
Audio format: Mono
Director: Dick Clement
Starring: Ronnie Barker, Fulton Mackay, Richard Beckinsale,
Year made: 1979
Extras: Scene access; subtitles available in English.

One of the truly great Seventies sitcoms was *Porridge*. Funny, irreverent and not afraid of sly social comment, the prison-set vehicle for Ronnie Barker was half-an-hour of classic, laugh-a-minute television humour. Yes, television. It's a shame they bothered to produce the film. Not truly awful, but never as sharp as the TV series, it feels tired and looks rather pathetic as a piece of cinema. If you're not familiar with the characters then it's hard to feel a great deal of sympathy with them and if you are, then it's just plain upsetting to see them limping along trying to stretch the laughs out over 90 minutes. This release seems even more unnecessary when you consider how many fantastic episodes could have fitted on the disc. Coupled with the insultingly lame 'trailer', which is actually just a shoddy advert for other releases, it's the makers who should be doing time.

FINAL VERDICT

Picture ☆☆ Sound ☆☆☆ Entertainment ☆☆
Extras ☆ Value ☆
OVERALL ☆

THE POSTMAN

Price: £15.99
Supplied by: DVD World (01705 796662)
Type of disc: Dual layer, single-sided

No of chapters: 44
Film length/format(s): 2.35:1 anamorphic / 170 mins
Director: Kevin Costner
Starring: Kevin Costner, Will Patton, Olivia Williams
Year made: 1997
Extras: Widescreen TV enhanced; chapter select; English/Hindi subtitles; cast and crew filmographies; production notes; effects featurette; trailer; mini-essay on post-apocalyptic movies; notes by the novel's author

Oops. Mankind's gone and destroyed the world again. Costner plays a drifter in an *après*-Armageddon America where the nasty General Bethlehem (Patton) and his thugs hold sway. Appropriating a postman's uniform from its long-dead owner, Costner's nameless character wears it with the intention of scamming a free meal, but finds his tall tales of a restored government 'back east' inspiring revolution against Bethlehem. As post-apocalyptic storylines go, *The Postman* isn't bad, although people whose image of the US Postal Service includes Cliff Clavin and loons with sniper rifles might have trouble accepting deliverers of bills and junk mail as symbols of hope. Anyone not born under the star-spangled banner will also struggle to choke back the vomit when they witness a level of misty-eyed Yank patriotism that even Jerry Bruckheimer would consider excessive. The real problem is that Costner has taken what would have made a decent 90-minute action film and tried to turn it into a sweeping *Dances With Wolves*-type epic. Almost three hours of panoramic vistas, people riding horses and Costner's steely gaze is just too much for the slim story. The extras are reasonable but not enthralling. The 10-minute featurette about *The Postman's* effects is pretty pointless, since a couple of matte paintings and some greenscreen work barely count as 'special' effects. This ain't *The Phantom Menace*. Aside from that, it's the usual filmographies and production notes. *The Postman* will certainly send your bum to sleep, and you'll probably join it.

FINAL VERDICT

Picture ☆☆☆☆ Sound ☆☆☆ Entertainment ☆☆
Extras ☆☆☆ Value ☆☆
OVERALL ☆☆

PRACTICAL MAGIC

Price: £15.99
Supplied by: Warner Home Video
Type of disc: Single layer, double-sided
No of chapters: 31
Film format(s)/length: 2.35:1 widescreen / 100 mins
Audio format: Dolby Digital 5.1
Director: Griffin Dunne

Starring: Sandra Bullock, Nicole Kidman, Aidan Quinn

Year made: 1998

Extras: Scene access; commentary by production team, including Sandra Bullock; *Making Magic* – author Alice Hoffman tells how the film is based on her book; *Casting the Spell*, where cast members praise each other's acting capabilities to the hilt; TV spot – short preview of the film; subtitles in English and Arabic.

Take two babes, add some cunning and manipulating twists and turns, then season with mild humour and you've got the recipe for *Practical Magic*. The film is mistakenly labelled as a drama and should be considered as a romantic-comedy with a few spooky moments thrown in to keep the name of the film relevant to its content. It's directed by Griffin Dunne, who also brought us *Addicted to Love*, and offers a united cast which provides good entertainment for the whole family. Seeing Sandra Bullock and Nicole Kidman together in DVD format is also another good reason to add this title to your collection, but unfortunately that's about as far as the magic goes. Although the disc is a flipper, the film is on one side whilst the Special Features (*Making Magic*, *Casting the Spell* and the TV Spot) are on the other side. *Making Magic* simply harps on about how the film is based on a novel written by Alice Hoffman, who herself tells you what the story is about, followed by a few clips of the film and a profile of the Director's magical skills. *Casting the Spell* is another talk show clip where each member of the cast praises how wonderful every other member of the cast is, turning it into an Oscar contender in itself. Once they've finished patting each other on the back, the Director, (again) talks about his interpretation of the cast and how they portray the characters within the film. This is basically an extended version of *Making Magic*, showing more film footage and the concept of one big happy family that makes the *Little House on the Prairie* sound like it should have be shown after the watershed. The TV Spot feature allows you to see a quick preview of the film itself, which provides an extra but somewhat pointless additional feature to the DVD. Within the Special Features there is also the option of being able to listen to a running commentary as you watch the film, with voice-overs from the production team and Sandra Bullock herself. The picture and sound quality are superb with no apparent glitches. Otherwise the package as a whole is missing certain key elements that could have pushed *Practical Magic* high up into the realms of a great DVD. However, as it stands, there's nothing magical about it at all, indeed if it fell into the hands of a novice DVD collector, it could seriously misrepresent the real wonders of DVD.

FINAL VERDICT

Picture ☆☆☆☆ Sound ☆☆☆☆ Entertainment ☆☆

Extras ☆☆ Value ☆☆

OVERALL ☆☆

THE PREACHER'S WIFE

Price: £15.99

Supplied by: Warner Home Video

Type of disc: Dual layer, single-sided

No of chapters: 17

Film format(s)/length: 16:9 widescreen / 119 mins

Audio format: Dolby Digital 5.1

Director: Penny Marshall

Starring: Denzel Washington, Whitney Houston, Courtney B Vance

Year made: 1996

Extras: Scene access; soundtrack in Italian; surround soundtrack in French; multilingual subtitles; subtitles for the hearing impaired in English.

Why Denzel Washington agreed to star in this tedious bilge is a mystery that will puzzle mankind long after we have a cure for cancer. Washington plays Dudley, an angel sent to help a struggling minister (Vance) and reconcile him with his neglected wife (Houston). It's basically a remake of the slight 1947 Cary Grant comedy, *The Bishop's Wife*, with heavy echoes of *It's a Wonderful Life*, but without any of the necessary Christmas magic. Almost totally devoid of laughs, charm or romance and cursed with a whining child actor virtually begging to be throttled, the film also isn't helped by this DVD. The colours lack vibrancy and while the sound quality is good, the only challenge is capturing Houston's incessant warbling, both in character and on the intrusive soundtrack. In fact there's so much of Houston's singing that the whole affair comes across as more of a Whitney promotional vehicle than a decent film. The paltry 'extras' consist of chapter access and subtitles. Hardly miraculous or surprising really.

FINAL VERDICT

Picture ☆☆☆ Sound ☆☆☆☆ Entertainment ☆☆

Extras ☆ Value ☆

OVERALL ☆

PRESUMED INNOCENT

Price: £15.99

Supplied by: DVDplus (www.dvdplus.co.uk)

Type of disc: Single layer, single-sided

No of chapters: 35

Film format(s)/length: 1.85:1 widescreen / 122 mins

Audio format: Dolby Surround

Director: Alan J Pakula
Starring: Harrison Ford, Raul Julia, Brian Dennehy
Year made: 1990
Extras: Scene access; English and Arabic subtitles.

And so once again we're faced with the challenge of making another bog standard disc sound interesting. Presented in Dolby Surround and sporting nothing other than a few subtitle options in terms of extras, *Presumed Innocent* enters the DVD arena with a faint thud. Perhaps we're missing the point. For the UK to build up a sufficient library of titles, not every disc will end up a Collector's Edition. Clearly there's a need to release older, back catalogue titles at a reduced price. Unfortunately in this case *Presumed Innocent* – a watchable enough whodunnit – is priced at exactly the same level as classic Warner discs such as *Contact*, *LA Confidential* and *Lethal Weapon 4*. Anyway, even in its most basic form we welcome *Presumed Innocent* to DVD, complete with a dated image and little in the way of a sound workout. You just can't help feeling, though, that this is exactly the kind of title that would sit nicely in a £9.99 budget line. Ah well.

FINAL VERDICT

Picture ☆☆ Sound ☆☆ Entertainment ☆☆☆
Extras ☆ Value ☆☆
OVERALL ☆☆

PRET-A-PORTER

Price: £15.99
Supplied by: DVD World (01705 796662)
Type of disc: Single layer, double-sided (Flipper!)
No of chapters: 32
Film format(s)/length: 1.85:1 widescreen / 127 mins
Audio format: Dolby Digital 5.1
Director: Robert Altman
Starring: Julia Roberts, Tim Robbins, Kim Basinger
Year made: 1994
Extras: Scene access; English and French soundtracks; closed caption subtitles.

There's been a murder at the world's most prestigious fashion show and unfortunately it wasn't one of the designers! The police have no clues and which therefore means everyone's a suspect, but nevertheless – the show must go on! There's something very strange about Hollywood and Robert Altman. It seems that any film the *M*A*S*H* director makes has a list of stars a mile long who are falling over themselves to get a part in it. And yet his movies just lately have all been pretty poor! They all end up as overly-long, self-indulgent diatribes on one subject or another and *Pret-a-Porter* is no exception. Positively

swarming with stars including many famous designers and models, *Pret-a-Porter* sets out – presumably – to ridicule the fashion industry. You can only assume that all the fashion gurus appeared in this movie thinking that by poking fun at their profession they'd be seen as cool. All they succeed in doing is to look foolish. And pretentious. Unfortunately the movie itself also suffers from a lack of a decent storyline and any kind of point to the whole thing. At just over two hours this film is too long and frankly wastes the talents of the likes of Tim Robbins, Richard E Grant and Lauren Bacall to name but a few. The DVD is similarly lousy providing as it does just scene access, two languages and one stingy set of subtitles. And worse than that…it's a flipper! No-one deserves to be forced to sit through *Pret-a-Porter* on DVD – except maybe Robert Altman.

FINAL VERDICT

Picture ☆☆☆☆ Sound ☆☆☆☆ Entertainment ☆☆
Extras ☆ Value ☆
OVERALL ☆

PRETTY WOMAN

Price: £15.99
Supplied by: DVD World (01705 796662)
Type of disc: Single layer, double-sided
No of chapters: 20
Film format(s)/length: 1.85:1 letterbox / 115 mins
Director: Garry Marshall
Starring: Richard Gere, Julia Roberts, Jason Alexander
Year made: 1990
Extras: Chapter select; trilingual soundtrack; subtitles.

Hey, girls! Become a prostitute and you too can find true love with a millionaire! Well, you can if you're in a movie. Romantic smash *Pretty Woman* streetwalks onto DVD, thigh length boots and all. You know the story by now. Heartless corporate raider Gere has a chance encounter with squeaky-clean hooker Roberts, and they fall in love. She teaches him not to be a complete bastard, and he buys her nice clothes. Ah, bless. Gere squints his way through the film as though he's lost his contact lenses, displaying all the emotion of an Easter Island head. Roberts is better, putting on a lively, engaging performance that frankly she's never matched since. Calling *Pretty Woman*'s features 'special' is surely a breach of the Trades Descriptions Act. Sure, you get French and Italian soundtracks using up DVD space. But you pay for this, as the disc is another damnable Disney flipper. What is this, vinyl? The picture also suffers from surprisingly visible MPEG crawl on areas of flat colour. You half expect the walls to come to life like some horrible mescaline nightmare. Missing the point still further, Disney put out the DVD of *Pretty Woman* around the same time as the longer Director's Cut of the film on VHS. So, you can choose from either a decidedly below-par DVD of a film you've already seen for £15.99, or a newly-extended copy on video for just £12.99. Wow, that'll really encourage Joe Public to risk trying a brand-new format!

FINAL VERDICT

Picture ☆☆ Sound ☆☆☆ Entertainment ☆☆☆
Extras ☆ Value ☆☆
OVERALL ☆☆

PRIVATE PARTS

Price: £15.99
Supplied by: Entertainment in Video
Type of disc: Dual layer, single-sided
No of chapters: 12
Film format(s)/length: 16:9 widescreen enhanced / 105 mins
Audio format: Dolby Surround
Director: Betty Thomas
Starring: Howard Stern, Robin Quivers, Mary McCormack
Year made: 1997
Extras: Scene access; theatrical trailer; interviews with cast and crew.

Compared to Howard Stern, so-called controversial British DJs like Chris Evans are outright amateurs. The self-proclaimed King of All Media's influence on American culture is indelible, and his frank biopic *Private Parts* is an entertaining romp, charting his rise to fame. There are many great moments in the film, from Stern's show-stealing performance as Fartman at the MTV Awards, to his having sex with an avid listener over the radio. Who cares if it's crass and tasteless? As well as the original theatrical trailer, Entertainment in Video has supplied a host of interview clips with the cast and crew. These were obviously used to promote *Private Parts* internationally – where TV companies would take which bits they wanted to spice up their news features on the film – but are still a welcome addition to the DVD. At least they give the majority of the UK audience who've not heard of Howard Stern before the opportunity to see if he is as brash and forthright as he appears in the movie. Which, of course, he is. One major niggle is the fact that the 105-minute movie has only been broken down into a measly 12 chapters, which makes finding your favourite scene that much more difficult. Quite why Entertainment in Video chose to skimp on this DVD-specific feature is anyone's guess,

but the rest of the package scores well.

FINAL VERDICT

Picture ☆☆☆☆ Sound ☆☆☆ Entertainment ☆☆☆☆
Extras ☆☆☆ Value ☆☆☆
OVERALL ☆☆☆

PUSHER

Price: £15.99
Supplied by: Metrodome
Type of disc: Dual layer, single-sided
No of chapters: 30
Film format(s)/length: 16:9 anamorphic / 109 mins
Audio format: Dolby Surround
Director: Nicolas Winding Refn
Starring: Kim Bodina, Zlatko Buric, Mads Mikkelsen
Year made: 1996
Extras: Scene access; audio commentary by director and friend; 'Making of' documentary; cast and director filmographies; 4 theatrical trailers; soundtrack in Danish with English subtitles.

If docudrama producers get bored of airports, supermarkets and abattoirs, or whatever, and decide to follow small-time drug dealers around with cameras, *Pusher* would be close to what they'd end up with. When his dope deal falls through thanks to the police, Frank (an excellent Bodina) has 48 hours to come up with the money he owes to his supplier or face the deadly consequences. *Pusher* shadows him as he desperately shakes down his Copenhagen customers and contacts to get the cash, but the hours are slipping away… Good menus lead to the commentary which sees the director and pal enthusiastically recalling the genesis of the film from start to finish, but only occasionally discussing the action on screen. Filmographies of the 5 principals and Winding Refn are sadly thin on details. The disc rallies with a fine 30-minute documentary that interviews the vaguely eccentric cast and crew. It's undoubtedly well produced and directed, but a few captions identifying the participants would have been helpful. Tired of stylised *Lock Stock…* mockney and Tarantinoism? Demanding an visceral, compelling thriller that portrays street life in the raw? *Pusher* is the film for you.

FINAL VERDICT

Picture ☆☆☆ Sound ☆☆☆☆
Entertainment ☆☆☆☆ Extras ☆☆☆☆ Value ☆☆☆☆
OVERALL ☆☆☆☆

PSYCHO

Price: £19.99
Supplied by: Columbia TriStar Home Video
Type of disc: Single layer, single-sided

No of chapters: 18
Film format(s)/length: 1.85:1 widescreen / 104 mins
Audio format: Mono
Director: Alfred Hitchcock
Starring: Anthony Perkins, Janet Leigh, Vera Miles
Year made: 1960
Extras: Production notes; 6-minute theatrical trailer; cast and film-maker's notes; English, Dutch and Swedish subtitles; booklet with background facts and quotes.

The first slasher of all time, Hitchcock's *Psycho* was initially slated by the critics, but became a film school favourite, was made in black and white when it could have been colour. In the 40 years since it was released, this tightly choreographed study of the human psyche has influenced everyone from Brian De Palma to Busta Rhymes. From the urgent, stabbing score by Bernard Herrmann and Saul Bass's disorientating titles until the closing scene when Marion Crane's car is dragged out of the swamp, *Psycho* is a suspense thriller of exceptional quality, and Hitchcock's first film of the decade that would see him at the height of his directorial powers. Secretary Marion (Leigh) swipes £40,000 from her boss and drives to meet her boyfriend. En route she stops off at a motel and meets Norman Bates (Perkins), a charming young man apparently under his invalid mother's thumb. One iconic shower scene later, Marion's sister Lila (Miles), the boyfriend (John Gavin) and a private detective (Martin Balsam) begin their investigation that eventually leads to both Norman and Mrs Bates. From this straightforward plot, the director hung his own meditations on humanity (good and evil, sexual repression, voyeurism) and of course his notorious macabre wit. The brutal yet non-gratuitous shower scene still has the power to shock no matter how many times it's seen, the power coming from more than 90 fast cuts and screeching violins, not the buckets of blood thrown around the place as is all too common these days. The fact that everyone should see *Psycho* goes without saying and, with its release on DVD, this is the finest format yet to watch it on despite the mono sound (which is either good or bad depending on how much of a purist you are). What this R2 disc carries is the reasonable but now overly familiar package of production notes, cast and film-maker's notes and theatrical trailer. The trailer is easily the biggest delight, more a micro documentary than the two-minute plot spoilers we're used to. In this 6-minute home movie, the portly Master of Suspense (and Sultan of Marketing) shows us around the motel set like a cross between a bumbling English squire and a tour guide from Hell. "This young man,

you have to feel sorry for him," Hitchcock tempts the audience. "After all, being dominated by an almost maniacal woman was enough to drive anyone to the extremes of, er...well let's go in." Given the tragic lack of documentaries or interviews with the surviving cast members (who include Leigh) you've got to wonder: is there going to be a *Psycho: Special Edition* in 2000 to celebrate its 40th anniversary? Let's hope so as the lack of extras effort means this DVD is a must-see if not a must-buy.

FINAL VERDICT

Picture ☆☆☆☆ Sound ☆☆ Entertainment ☆☆☆☆
Extras ☆☆ Value ☆☆☆
OVERALL ☆☆☆☆

PSYCHO

Price: £19.99
Supplied by: Columbia TriStar Home Video
Type of disc: Dual layer, single-sided
No of chapters: 26
Film format(s)/length: 1.85:1 widescreen enhanced / 100 mins
Audio format: Dolby Digital 5.1
Director: Gus Van Sant
Starring: Vince Vaughn, Anne Heche, Julianne Moore
Year made: 1998
Extras: Documentary: *Psycho Path (The Making of Psycho)*; feature commentary with Gus Van Sant, Anne Heche and Vince Vaughn; production notes; cast and film-maker's notes; theatrical trailer; screensavers; booklet with quotes and photos; multilingual subtitles; soundtrack in French.

When news spread that Gus Van Sant was bent on remaking *Psycho* for the *Scream* generation, the knives were soon out. But as the *Good Will Hunting* director states in this DVD's documentary *Psycho Path*: if Shakespeare's masterpieces can be remade why not Hitchcock's? "I had never heard it done before and I was aware that a lot of people are adverse to watching back and white movies...and although *Psycho* is like the Coca-Cola of 1960 movies, very prominent and famous, even then people know it or seem to know it as the icon rather than the whole movie." That's a reasonable justification for a reinterpretation but why copy shot-for-shot (but not frame-for-frame) the note perfect original? By saying everyone under the age of thirty would rather watch colour films over black and white, Van Sant badly second guesses the audience – right? Anyway, nothing major has changed in terms of plot. Secretary Marion Crane (Anne Heche) now steals £400,000 and fatefully meets Vince Vaughn as Norman Bates. To its credit, this *Psycho* does give more depth to the 'B' characters. Hitchcock, always more interested in the mechanics of mysteries, almost reduced the supporting cast to ciphers so as to propel the narrative. Here though under Van Sant's humanitarian direction, Julianne Moore and Viggo Mortensen flesh out their characters into the forthright city girl and hardware cowboy respectively by subtle actions and inflections though still speaking the same lines. What has been added is the odd reference to the original here, and the perplexing and unnecessary use of CGI in one or two scenes there. What has been lost is the original's psychological edge and suspense. Flashy cuts of what's going through Norman's mind during the murders just spell out what was once inferred. Vaughn, towering over the petite Heche, nervously giggles at the end of sentences, sending signals to your mind in flashing neon lights the message: "Yes, I am a bit nuts aren't I?" Package-wise, *Psycho* '98 offers a great deal, in fact it's practically the same disc as the Region 1's Collector's Edition – Yes! Well done Universal! From the startling animated menus it's a close tie for best special feature honours between the fascinating behind the scenes *Psycho Path* documentary with cast and crew interviews and the insightful, frequently hilarious audio commentary by Vaughn, Heche and Van Sant. Danny Elfman's reworking of Bernard Herman's classic evocative score gets bumped up from the original film's mono to a new full blooded Dolby Digital 5.1 stereo while picture quality is something close to perfect, capturing the bright colours and red blood to retina scorching effect. In short, Van Sant's *Psycho* is an interesting, entertaining experiment that on DVD is an excellent companion piece to the original but the original is, of course, still the best.

FINAL VERDICT

Picture ☆☆☆☆ Sound ☆☆☆☆☆
Entertainment ☆☆☆☆ Extras ☆☆☆☆☆
Value ☆☆☆☆
OVERALL ☆☆☆☆

QUADROPHENIA

Price: £17.99
Supplied by: Universal
Type of disc: Single layer, single–sided
No of chapters: 19
Film format(s)/length: 4:3 regular / 114 mins
Audio format: Stereo
Director: Franc Roddam
Starring: Phil Daniels, Leslie Ash, Sting
Year made: 1979
Extras: Scene access; 8-minute montage featurette,

including unseen photos with music by The Who; English subtitles.

It was 20 years ago when The Who financed a low-budget, big screen version of their classic 1969 mods versus rockers rock opera, *Quadrophenia*. Though it wasn't an enormous financial success on its initial release, it has become something of a cult classic amongst a new generation of cinemagoers. Its tale of sex, drugs, scooters and teenage disillusionment paved the way for such Nineties britflicks as *Trainspotting, Human Traffic* and *Shallow Grave*. In truth, *Quadrophenia* hasn't aged all that well. Although the film itself is a period classic (with an outstanding performance from Phil Daniels) it doesn't make an earth-shattering leap onto DVD. No effort has been made to digitally restore the film, resulting in a dull and grainy picture quality more suited to analogue VHS than Digital Versatile Disc. The extras too, are a disappointment. There's an 8-minute featurette included, though this is simply a montage of previously unseen photos set to the music of The Who. Frankly, such a good film deserves better.

FINAL VERDICT

Picture ☆☆ Sound ☆☆☆ Entertainment ☆☆☆☆☆
Extras ☆☆ Value ☆☆☆
OVERALL ☆☆☆

THE QUICK AND THE DEAD

Price: £19.99
Company: Columbia TriStar
Type of disc: Single layer, single-sided
No of chapters: 28
Film format(s)/length: 16:9 widescreen / 103 mins
Director: Sam Raimi
Starring: Sharon Stone, Gene Hackman, Russell Crowe
Year made: 1995
Extras: Scene selection; multilingual subtitles; theatrical trailer.

If you can believe the way Hollywood portrays the Old West, it's a wonder that America was ever colonised, what with everyone shooting each other all the time. This Western offers few surprises as we follow female gunfighter Ellen (Stone) to the town of Redemption. A ramshackle dump of a place, Redemption is about to host its annual gunfighting contest and thus fighters from all across America are gathering to try their luck. Gradually we learn through flashback sequences that Ellen is the daughter of Redemption's late Marshal who died at the hands of the current mayor/dictator, Herod (Hackman) who helpfully shows everyone just how evil he is by shooting his own son. Throw in reformed gunfighter Cort (Crowe), who's forced to take part in the competition and you've got the recipe for a fairly average Western. The majority of the action takes place on the main street as competitors line up and shoot each other, or in the saloon where stories, boasts and insults are swapped. The whole thing leads up to the inevitable showdown between Herod and Ellen for a fairly explosive finale. Aside from scene selection, subtitles and the trailer this DVD has nothing special to offer and the clarity of the picture does detract somewhat from many of the special effects – such as someone getting shot through an obviously fake head. There's nothing to really recommend this film unless you're a big Western fan, in which case you're probably better off going for something more classic.

FINAL VERDICT

Picture ☆☆☆☆ Sound ☆☆☆ Entertainment ☆☆
Extras ☆ Value ☆
OVERALL ☆☆

Quiz Show

Price: £15.99
Supplied by: DVD World (01705 796662)
Type of disc: Single layer, double-sided (flipper)
No of chapters: 30
Film format(s)/length: 1.85:1 / 131mins
Audio format: Dolby Surround
Director: Robert Redford
Starring: Ralph Fiennes, John Turturro, Rob Morrow
Year made: 1994
Extras: English, French and Italian language soundtracks; multilingual subtitles.

If asked to explain *Jerry Springer*, *21* is as good a place to start as any. *21* was a US Mastermind-type show which was enormously popular during the Fifties, before a Senate subcommittee exposed the show as rigged. Nowadays this would surprise no-one, but at the time, TV was a new phenomenon and Charles Van Doren, *21*'s star contestant, was a national hero. Under the shadow of Sputnik, America desperately needed a home-grown intellectual triumph and while NASA endured flop after flop, TV stepped into the breach by manufacturing its very own charismatic genius. The unravelling of the *21* conspiracy makes for a fascinating piece of entertainment. The bare outlines of the scandal can't begin to touch the real, very human depth of the true life events. All the principal characters are painted in well-judged shades of grey, making it easy for your sympathies to shift as the story develops. The script,

based on the memoirs of the Senate investigator who later became a speechwriter for Robert Kennedy, is a delight – resonant with all sort of historical detail. The middle section is a little prolonged, and some minor characters are sketchy – the only women are wives, and uniformly portrayed as harridans – but overall this is a startlingly intelligent movie. Just as Nixon's impeachment shattered the image of the presidency, so 21 smashed the reputation of the TV studios. Naturally, being such a startlingly intelligent piece of entertainment, the movie studio responsible has slapped *Quiz Show* onto a single-layer pressing – so you have to flip the disc half way through. There are no extras, not even a theatrical trailer, and sound is only Dolby Surround, not Digital 5.1. It's enough to make you believe there's a conspiracy going on…

FINAL VERDICT

Picture ☆☆☆☆ Sound ☆☆☆ Entertainment ☆☆☆☆
Extras ☆ Value ☆☆☆
OVERALL ☆☆☆

Raging Bull

Price: £19.99
Supplied by: MGM Home Entertainment
Type of disc: Dual layer, single-sided
No of chapters: 30
Film length/format(s): 1.85:1 widescreen / 123 mins
Director: Martin Scorsese
Starring: Robert De Niro, Cathy Moriarty, Joe Pesci
Year made: 1980
Extras: Chapter access; multilingual subtitles; soundtrack in 5 languages; trailer; other DVDs trailer.

Voted the best film of the Eighties by numerous critics, *Raging Bull* is the kind of movie that provokes endless pub arguments – is it Scorsese's best film, or should that title go to *Goodfellas*? Or *Taxi Driver*? Whatever your view, you'd have a job claiming that *Raging Bull* is anything less than great. *Raging Bull* tracks the real-life story of middleweight boxing world champion Jake La Motta (De Niro) from his early career in 1941, through his various fights and his taking of the title, to his inevitable defeat, retirement and attempts to reinvent himself as a comedian and raconteur. Parallel to the action in the ring is his private life, which definitely has more downs than ups as he struggles to hold things together with wife Vickie (Moriarty) and brother/manager Joey (Pesci). La Motta certainly isn't likeable – he's brutal in and out of the ring, suspicious to the point of paranoia and later, with De Niro almost unrecognisable under a nose as flat as a shovel and 60 pounds of genuine flab, it's painfully embarrassing as he tries to start a new career as a showman. Yet De Niro's Oscar-winning turn keeps you riveted to a flawed and often downright unpleasant man. *Raging Bull* also has the best boxing scenes ever filmed (forget *Rocky*) and the first Scorsese/De Niro/Pesci triple act. What it doesn't have are any extra features beyond a trailer. Scorsese can discuss films until he's used up all the air in the room, so it's a definite missed opportunity that he didn't comment on one of his career highlights.

FINAL VERDICT

Picture ☆☆☆ Sound ☆☆☆

Entertainment ☆☆☆☆☆ Extras ☆☆ Value ☆☆☆☆

OVERALL ☆☆☆☆

RAIN MAN

Price: £19.99
Supplied by: DVDplus (www.dvdplus.co.uk)
Type of disc: Single layer, single-sided
No of chapters: 40
Film format(s)/length: 16:9 widescreen / 128 mins
Audio format: Dolby Digital 5.1
Director: Barry Levinson
Starring: Dustin Hoffman, Tom Cruise, Valeria Golino
Year made: 1988
Extras: Chapter selection; multiple language soundtrack; subtitles in 11 languages; DVD footage of other titles; original theatrical trailer; 8-page booklet detailing the making of *Rain Man*.

The film that provided Dustin Hoffman with the Oscar for best actor in 1988, *Rain Man* is considered a classic that's guaranteed to entertain the whole family. Hoffman plays the roll of Tom Cruise's autistic brother, who meet each other for the first time after a death in the family. The film manages to cover both ends of the emotional scale by being humorous and heart-breaking. As far as the overall DVD package goes, it's above standard. Although no behind-the-scenes shots were made available for inclusion, at least there is a small booklet which gives a brief insight to the making of the film and a round-up of the story plot. The booklet even gets down to explaining the history of autism, which gives it that extra touch. Unfortunately, that's as far as the bonus material goes, except for the original trailer of the film preview and chapter selection. The language selection offers a wide range of spoken languages and plenty of subtitle languages. The section 'Also on DVD', is definitely a feature that all DVDs should include, as it offers actual DVD footage of other titles, instead of uninformative still pictures of the title covers. In addition, the film is displayed using 16:9 widescreen,

making it suitable for all televisions and it can be enhanced by using Dolby Digital sound to really thump out the soundtrack, which is available on CD. Overall it's a good film and a welcome title to the DVD family.

FINAL VERDICT

Picture ☆☆☆☆ Sound ☆☆☆☆

Entertainment ☆☆☆☆ Extras ☆☆☆ Value ☆☆☆

OVERALL ☆☆☆☆

RANDOM HEARTS

Price: £19.99
Supplied by: Columbia TriStar Home Video
Type of disc: Single layer, single-sided
No of chapters: 28
Film format(s)/length: 1.85:1 anamorphic / 127 mins
Audio format: Dolby Digital 5.0
Director: Sydney Pollack
Starring: Harrison Ford, Kristin Scott Thomas, Charles S Dutton
Year made: 1999
Extras: Scene access; 3 deleted scenes; audio commentary by director Sydney Pollack; 2 theatrical trailers; trailer for *The Devil's Own*; HBO First Look featurette (22 mins); filmographies; soundtrack in English and German; subtitles in 16 languages.

Random is probably the best word to describe this film, because it doesn't really seem able to make up its mind whether or not it's a thriller or a romance story. It starts out fairly promisingly after a Congresswoman (Thomas) and a police officer (Ford) are drawn together by the death of their respective partners, who have been cheating on them. The problem is the film sets you up with so much anticipation for a twist that you are left feeling a little cheated by the anticlimactic ending. You get exactly the same stuff here as on the Region 1 disc, apart from the lack of all the different versions of the theatrical trailer, but that's not exactly a major setback. The 3 deleted scenes are quite interesting to watch, providing a little more insight into the minor characters and some of the running subplots. What really does give an invaluable look into the main characters though is the well-edited featurette containing interviews with cast and crew. Sadly, this is very much a TV-style 'Making of' short and doesn't really go far enough beyond introducing the characters and the storyline. Fortunately, the commentary with director Sydney Pollack, who actually also stars in the film, makes up for all of that. Full of information on set construction, character development and the one or two anecdotes about the film, it's surprisingly interesting to listen to. Why is it that the bad films always get such good extras?

FINAL VERDICT

Picture ☆☆☆☆ Sound ☆☆☆☆☆

Entertainment ☆☆ Extras ☆☆☆☆ Value ☆☆☆

OVERALL ☆☆☆

RASPUTIN

Price: £15.99

Supplied by: Mosaic Movies

Type of disc: Single layer, single-sided,

No of chapters: 22

Film format(s)/length: 4:3 regular / 100 mins

Audio format: Dolby Digital 5.1

Director: Ulrich Edel

Starring: Alan Rickman, Greta Scacchi, Ian McKellen

Year made: 1996

Extras: Scene access; trailer; cast notes; production notes.

For those whose Russian history is a little ropey, Rasputin was the erratic mystic known as 'The Mad Monk'. He was also, despite his immoral ways, an advisor to the Tsar and Tsarina of Russia, having healed their haemophiliac son, and was heavily involved in events leading up to the fall of Imperial Russia. The powerful story of Rasputin is played out well in this TV movie, with some impressive performances from the lead characters, particularly Rickman, who earned himself a Golden Globe award for his portrayal of a wild-eyed Rasputin. Sadly, this dramatic tale and its elaborate settings are let down by a low-quality DVD. The picture quality is disappointing and the extras are minimal, with just the obligatory trailer, some very short cast notes and two sets of production notes on offer. A well-acted history lesson this may be, but the DVD itself does nothing to complement it.

FINAL VERDICT

Picture ☆☆ Sound ☆☆☆

Entertainment ☆☆☆ Extras ☆☆ Value ☆☆

OVERALL ☆☆

RAW DEAL

Price: £15.99

Supplied by: DVD World (01705 796662)

Type of disc: Single layer, single-sided

No of chapters: 29

Film format(s)/length: 4:3 regular / 100 mins

Audio format: Stereo

Director: John Irvin

Starring: Arnold Schwarzenegger, Kathryn Harrold, Sam Wanamaker

Year made: 1986

Extras: Scene access; Arnold Schwarzenegger biography; Schwarzenegger filmography; film awards won by Schwarzenegger; stills gallery featuring 5 black and white shots of Schwarzenegger in the film.

Schwarzenegger stars in this all-action film, where he pursues his favourite activity of destroying the bad guys with brute force. This time the unlucky opposition is a Chicago crime organisation headed by Sam Wanamaker. Unfortunately the excitement stops there as the DVD package simply sucks. The film format is in basic 4:3 and the sound dispensed in dated stereo. Only the die-hard Arnie enthusiast will be interested in reading a few text documents providing his biography and filmography. Equally disappointing are the few further pages on various film awards won by the great man, and to top it off, a section called the gallery provides 5 black and white stills of Arnie in the movie (5 hardly qualifies it as a gallery). The picture quality in all is okay but the audio is disastrous. Not having a digital remaster of the soundtrack is quite frankly lazy in this day and age, and gives the consumer another reason for not buying this already below average DVD.

FINAL VERDICT

Picture ☆☆ Sound ☆

Entertainment ☆☆☆ Extras ☆ Value ☆☆

OVERALL ☆☆

RED CORNER

Price: £19.99

Supplied by: DVD World (01705 796662)

Type of disc: Dual layer, single-sided

No of chapters: 32

Film format(s)/length: 1.85:1 widescreen enhanced / 122mins

Audio format: Dolby Digital 5.1

Director: Jon Avnet

Starring: Richard Gere, Ling Bai, Bradley Whitford

Year made: 1997

Extras: Scene access; commentary by director Jon Avnet; English subtitles and closed captions; 8-page glossy booklet including production notes.

Director Jon Avnet's audio commentary gets off to a nervous start, but he holds your attention nonetheless. That Chinese kite you barely noticed during the opening credits? Well, it's a CGI – cooked up at Digital Domain along with countless other 'invisible' effect shots which composited Richard Gere with Beijing – capital city of a country he's been so publically banned from visiting. The mannerisms of male Chinese officials, the authentic looking

Chinese villages actually are constructed in LA – for a while Avnet succeeds in making you look at the film anew. However, by the time the film reaches a scene where Gere is chased by the Chinese army – the director is reduced to enthusing: "Look, whoop, whoop! krrshhhh!!!" – it's doubly clear Avnet is not a natural storyteller. The included movie trailer creates the illusion of an exciting film, a tense legal drama that takes place in a foreign city where the death penalty is swift…and the family pay for the bullet! Sadly, it's entirely misleading. As a polemic against Chinese justice, *Red Corner* fails because the film-makers simply aren't interested in China, and Gere is improbably granted bail to conduct his own investigation. It's no surprise to learn the film was inspired by a wrongful arrest in Italy, and transposed to Russia by the wily scriptwriter, before moving to China at the behest of the producer! This is a dull mishmash of a film that tries to do a little of everything without being good at anything. Aside from the director's commentary, the only extra of note is a paper leaflet which actually includes some production notes – a much better presentation than simply slapping them on the DVD, to be honest.

FINAL VERDICT

Picture ☆☆☆ Sound ☆☆☆

Entertainment ☆☆ Extras ☆☆ Value ☆☆

OVERALL ☆☆

RED RIVER

Price: £19.99

Supplied by: MGM

Type of disc: Single layer, single-sided

No of chapters: 32

Film format(s)/length: 4:3 regular / 133 mins

Audio format: Mono

Director: Howard Hawks

Starring: John Wayne, Montgomery Clift, Walter Brennan

Year made: 1948

Extras: Scene access; subtitles in English, Spanish and French.

With its unrelenting detail and the soulful presence of John Wayne, *Red River* not only defined director Howard Hawks as a major Hollywood player, but also made Wayne *the* western hero. The story of a cattle drive from Texas to Kansas is one filled with western legend; betrayal, pitched rivalry between Wayne and Clift, and even Walter Brennan's classic 'old drunk' stumbles in. Great performances, sharp historical details and crisp direction define *Red River* as one of the classic westerns and one of Wayne's best.

It's a pity that the DVD package fails to measure up to the movie's status. With no worthy extras and only marginally sharper picture (in 4:3) and sound quality, this package offers little VHS wouldn't deliver. With such a rich genre cast and crew of Wayne, Clift, Brennan and Hawks this package should have been a nostalgic stampede. Instead, it was cut off at the pass.

FINAL VERDICT

Picture ☆☆ Sound ☆

Entertainment ☆☆☆☆ Extras ☆ Value ☆☆

OVERALL ☆☆

THE REPLACEMENT KILLERS

Price: £19.99

Supplied by: Columbia TriStar Home Video

Type of disc: Single layer, single-sided

No of chapters: 28

Film format(s)/length: 2.35:1 anamorphic / 84 mins

Director: Antione Fuqua

Starring: Chow Yun-Fat, Miro Sorvino, Michael Rooker

Year made: 1998

Extras: Widescreen TV enhanced; scene selection; subtitles in 14 languages; German dub soundtrack; trailer; filmographies.

After crimelord Terrence Wei's son is killed in a drugs bust by cop Stan Zedkov (Rooker), he demands revenge by sending hitman John Lee (Yun-Fat) to kill Zedkov's young son in return. When Lee develops a conscience and refuses to perform the hit, he finds himself the target of Wei's army of 'replacement killers', along with improbable forger Meg Coburn (Sorvino). John Woo is an executive producer, and debutante director Fuqua has obviously been studying his films hard. Two-handed gunplay, rapid cutting, Yun-Fat prowling around in slo-mo and mortal enemies with a gun at each others' head are all here. All that's missing are some flapping doves. Oh, and a story. Fuqua cuts everything so fast that you don't even have time to be thrilled. *The Replacement Killers* is pretty light on special features, too. While you get subtitles in 14 languages, incomplete filmographies of the stars and a trailer which suffers from some hideous blocking (thankfully the film is encoded just fine) there's nothing of interest beyond the movie itself, which is way below the standards of Yun-Fat's Hong Kong films. The sound is a bit of a let down, too – there's plenty of bass in the music, but the frequent gunfire seems oddly muffled. As Chow Yun-Fat's introduction to Hollywood, *The Replacement Killers* is tolerable – after all, long-time collaborator Woo had to make *Hard Target* before he could make *Face/Off*. But compared to something like *Face/Off*, it's pretty lightweight.

FINAL VERDICT

Picture ☆☆☆☆ Sound ☆☆☆

Entertainment ☆☆☆ Extras ☆☆ Value ☆☆

OVERALL ☆☆☆

RETURN TO A BETTER TOMORROW

Price: £19.99

Supplied by: MIA

Type of disc: Dual layer, single-sided

No of chapters: 17

Film format(s)/length: 16:9 widescreen / 103 mins

Audio format: Stereo

Director: Wong Jing

Starring: Ekin Cheng, Chingamy Yau, Ngal Shing

Year made: 1994

Extras: Scene access; trailer; English and Chinese captions composited with the film.

While *A Better Tomorrow* has obvious pretensions as a 'serious' film, the similar sounding but unconnected *Return* is purely a genre product. The plot has little function other than to connect the action sequences, with the soundtrack shifting gears as subtly as a steam engine. From blaring saxophones for romance to heavy metal for action, it's the direct approach that counts. That said, the lack of pretension means there's little to interrupt the stars looking cool. Ekin Cheng's gangster is as handsome as a computer-rendered Final Fantasy star, while girlfriend Chingamy Yau is, with reason, regarded as HK's hottest starlet. As you'd expect of the Heroic Bloodshed genre, there's a refreshing lack of Hollywood cod-morality. Shoot outs in a cinema and restaurant have scores of innocent bystanders blown to pieces, while women not only wield heavy firepower, they suffer the same as the men. This brutality goes hand-in-hand with some sentimentality, but as the plot twists tighten, you can't help but become involved. The initially laughable plot delivers at the close, while the final action sequence is a gory classic. As a DVD, presentation is minimalistic with English captions simply placed in the widescreen borders. However, film quality is radically superior to earlier films and looks (relatively) excellent on DVD. The soundtrack is crude, but similarly well presented.

FINAL VERDICT

Picture ☆☆☆☆ Sound ☆☆☆

Entertainment ☆☆☆ Extras ☆ Value ☆☆☆

OVERALL ☆☆☆

RHAPSODY IN AUGUST

Price: £19.99

Supplied by: Digital Entertainment

Type of disc: Single layer, single-sided

No of chapters: 9

Film format(s)/length: 4:3 regular / 98 mins

Audio format: Stereo

Director: Akira Kurosawa

Starring: Sachiko Murase, Hisashi Igawa, Richard Gere

Year made: 1990

Extras: Scene access; theatrical trailer; stills from the film.

Think Japan, and *manga*, *Chunking Express*, Pokémon and *Asian Babes* might pop into your head. Orientalism has rarely been so pronounced as it is today. With films like *Seven Samurai*, Kurosawa helped kickstart this wave of Western interest in Japan. Kurosawa is usually remembered for making the type of mythical, spectacular action films that have come to dominate today's tastes. However, *Rhapsody in August* is a very different kind of story about a different Japan. It's a quiet film that follows an old lady reliving her experience of the Nagasaki bombing. Visually subdued, the film has a totally unique slow, wry atmosphere. On the other hand, it's hard to imagine a film more out of time or a more unlikely DVD release. Kurosawa was 80 years old when he made *Rhapsody* and he was basking in the raptures of Spielberg and Lucas, so as you might expect, there's a heavy sighing tone to the film.

FINAL VERDICT

Picture ☆☆ Sound ☆☆

Entertainment ☆☆☆ Extras ☆☆ Value ☆☆

OVERALL ☆☆

RICHARD III

Price: £19.99

Supplied by: 20th Century Fox Home Entertainment

Type of disc: Single layer, single-sided

No of chapters: 18

Film format(s)/length: 1.77:1 anamorphic / 100 mins

Audio format: Dolby Surround 2.0

Director: Richard Loncraine

Starring: Ian McKellen, Annette Bening, Robert Downey Jr

Year made: 1995

Extras: Scene access; featurette; theatrical trailer; subtitles for the hearing impaired in English.

From the first shot, of tickertape relaying information about advancing forces, *Richard III* has an imaginative zest which raises expectations promptly trumped by a tank(!) motoring through a wall with gasmask-wearing assassins in tow. It's an opening more thrilling and breathless than many pop blockbusters. Thereafter the pace slackens with swelling big band Twenties music backtracking the hunched form of McKellen as Richard III, mingling with a parade of foreign diplomats at some diplomatic function. "Now is the winter of our discontent…" begins McKellen, perfectly enunciating the famous lines before the director cuts to him in the Men's, mumbling the more confessional sections of the text to himself. McKellen's performance is awesome, an utterly compelling picture of festering resentment fuelling the most heinous crimes. Compared to some portrayals, this Richard III is only mildly crippled with a withered left arm, but this only emphasises the psychological dimension as McKellen rants about being cursed by 'that witch' – his sister. There isn't much in the way of character development; Richard begins shooting an enemy in the head and ends despatching an ally in similar fashion. However, the way in which his Machiavellian ploys elevate him to power offers a fascinating glimpse of an alternate Thirties, one in which Britain goes Nazi. The surrounding cast is uniformly excellent, with Annette Bening as a fraught Elizabeth, the only person to see clearly what Richard plans. Kirsten Scott Thomas's Lady Anna is seduced by her husband's murderer, but Loncraine's version sees her turn to heroin for solace. Maggie Smith is a superbly venomous mother, while Nigel Hawthorne is unforgettable, believing his brother will rescue him even as Richard's paid assassins murder him. As a DVD, *Richard III* isn't really given the treatment it deserves, with the movie and extras comfortably squeezed into a single layer. Partly, this is due to the lack of Dolby Digital soundtrack (mere Pro Logic serves reasonably well), while picture quality is fine. Sadly, the accompanying 5-minute promo featurette hardly does the movie justice.

FINAL VERDICT

Picture ☆☆☆ Sound ☆☆☆

Entertainment ☆☆☆☆ Extras ☆☆ Value ☆☆☆

OVERALL ☆☆☆

RIDE WITH THE DEVIL

Price: £19.99
Supplied by: Entertainment in Video
Type of disc: Dual layer, single-sided
No of chapters: 12
Film format(s)/length: 2.35:1 anamorphic / 135 mins
Audio format: Dolby Digital 5.1
Director: Ang Lee
Starring: Tobey Maguire, Skeet Ulrich, Jewel
Year made: 1999
Extras: Scene access; 'Making of' featurette; behind-

the-scenes footage; theatrical trailer.

Ang Lee consolidates his position as one of the finest film-makers working today with the adept and humanistic approach he brings to a project that could easily have spiralled into merely a Boy's Own adventure. After deconstructing the American family in *The Ice Storm* and creating a landmark British film with *Sense and Sensibility* (both available on DVD), Lee casts his curious objective eye on the American Civil War in *Ride With the Devil*. Son of German immigrants Jake (Maguire) and best pal Jack (Ulrich) find their lives torn apart as the Yankees bring the war into their Missouri homes. Vowing revenge, the pair join the Confederate-supporting militia and start a bloody campaign of guerrilla attacks on Union soldiers and sympathisers. Jake encounters freed slave Jeffrey Wright and widowed Jewel on the road to a decisive showdown. Lee draws fine performances from a cast of newcomers. *Pleasantville*'s Maguire carries the film well as the young man forced to come of age before his time and *chanteuse* Jewel acquits herself soundly in this, her motion picture debut. The 5-minute feature is the standard issue affair of sound bites laced with film clips and the 5-minute location footage is interesting enough (but note that the length is roughly 5 minutes and not 14 as the sleeve claims). It's another triumph from Lee and American Civil War films have a new standard to aim for. The disc does its job competently enough with great sound and vision quality.

FINAL VERDICT

Picture ☆☆☆☆ Sound ☆☆☆☆

Entertainment ☆☆☆☆ Extras ☆☆☆ Value ☆☆☆

OVERALL ☆☆☆☆

RISING SUN

Price: £19.99
Supplied by: 20th Century Fox Home Entertainment
Type of disc: Dual layer, single-sided
No of chapters: 26
Film format(s)/length: 1.85:1 widescreen enhanced / 124 mins
Audio format: Dolby Surround
Director: Philip Kaufman
Starring: Sean Connery, Wesley Snipes, Harvey Keitel
Year made: 1993
Extras: Scene access; trailer; subtitles in 10 languages.

Everyone associates Michael Crichton with his successes, like *Jurassic Park*, *Westworld* or *ER*, conveniently overlooking the likes of *The 13th Warrior* or *Congo*. Or this. The original novel was a paranoid warning about Japanese corporations taking over

America. *Rising Sun*, the movie, is considerably toned down – in fact, the Japanese come off rather better than the Yanks. A hooker is murdered mid-coitus in the LA boardroom of a Japanese company; Snipes and Japanese expert Connery are called in to investigate, with Keitel's racist cop providing backup. As with most Crichton thrillers, there's a high-tech gimmick, but in this case – the digital doctoring of video footage – it's both implausible and silly, as Tia Carrera takes about 20 seconds to knock up an effect that would take Industrial Light & Magic a week. The soundtrack is only DD2.0, a trailer is the sole extra, and the whole thing is a waste of everyone's time.

FINAL VERDICT

Picture ☆☆☆ Sound ☆☆

Entertainment ☆☆ Extras ☆ Value ☆☆

OVERALL ☆☆

RISKY BUSINESS

Price: £15.99
Supplied by: Warner Home Video
Type of disc: Single layer, double-sided
No of chapters: 32
Film format(s)/length: 4:3, 16:9 widescreen / 95 mins
Director: Paul Brickman
Starring: Tom Cruise, Rebecca De Mornay, Curtis Armstrong
Year made: 1983
Extras: Interactive menus; scene access; subtitles in 9 languages; character biogs and production notes.

Like *Ferris Bueller's Day Off*, *Saint Elmo's Fire* and the *Breakfast Club*, *Risky Business* is one of those films you had to see in the Eighties whether it was to titter at a young Rebecca De Mornay in the buff or laugh out loud at an only-just-shaving Tom Cruise and his outrageous sweaters. Joel Goodsen (Cruise), aged 17, suddenly finds he has the family home and his dad's Porsche 928 to himself for the week – every student's dream, except Joel is torn between acting responsibly while his folks are away and being prompted by his over-imaginative buddy Miles (Armstrong), into having his cherry popped by a 'professional' (De Mornay – jail bait). The picture quality of this DVD is certainly not up to the standards of modern movies and curiously the sound is a little muted too, probably due to the production of the original. In terms of extras, all you get are some static character notes and two versions of the film in 4:3 and 16:9 picture formats. Decent enough movie, but not much else.

FINAL VERDICT

Picture ☆☆☆ Sound ☆☆☆

Entertainment ☆☆☆ Extras ☆☆ Value ☆☆

OVERALL ☆☆☆

THE RIVER WILD

Price: £15.99
Supplied by: Columbia TriStar Home Video
Type of disc: Dual layer, single-sided
No of chapters: 16
Film format(s)/length: 2.35:1 widescreen / 107 mins
Audio format: Dolby Digital 5.1
Director: Curtis Hanson
Starring: Meryl Streep, Kevin Bacon, David Strathairn
Year made: 1994
Extras: Scene access; production notes; cast and director biographies and filmographies; multi-lingual subtitles; stereo soundtracks in French, German, Italian, Spanish, Czech, Polish.

Around 22 years after *Deliverance*, the all-American river is once again a turbulent place to be. Trouble begins when a family decide to take some quality time. Streep plays an ex-ranger whose marriage is on the rocks, and decides that merrily swooshing down some rapids would be an ideal family vacation and provide a chance for them to bond. Things capsize with the arrival of Bacon and two other strangers, who turn out to be on the run from a murderous robbery. It may be stuffed with more formula than a Nestle baby in the Tropics, but that doesn't stop it from being pretty damn gripping. Streep is credible as mother and action girl, Strathairn, too, makes a believable transition from put-upon workaholic to resourceful hero, and Bacon turns in an insidiously creepy scumbag (impressively versatile thing that he is). Ignoring the ridiculous Hollywood Hero Labrador, director Curtis (*LA Confidential*) Hanson finds a good balance between character and action, eventually delivering some thunderous set-pieces. On DVD, the picture has a marginally processed feel to it and a minor blemish-cursed source print is used. This is nitpicking however as Dean Cundey's Panavision cinematography looks absolutely pin-sharp from the sofa. The sound, though, is a disappointment – there's some ropey dubbed dialogue near the start, and the soundstage otherwise is pretty uninvolving. Only the later action sequences provide much of a challenge for your subwoofer in the corner. Production notes are fairly interesting, but serve mainly to make you wish Universal included some behind-the-scenes footage. As so often, on that score it's wash out.

FINAL VERDICT

Picture ☆☆☆☆ Sound ☆☆☆

Entertainment ☆☆☆☆ Extras ☆☆ Value ☆☆
OVERALL ☆☆☆

ROBIN HOOD PRINCE OF THIEVES

Price: £15.99
Supplied by: Warner Home Video
Type of disc: Dual layer, single-sided
No of chapters: 34
Film format(s)/length: 1.85:1 widescreen / 137 mins
Audio format: Dolby Surround
Director: Kevin Reynolds
Starring: Kevin Costner, Morgan Freeman, Alan Rickman
Year made: 1991
Extras: Scene access; multi-lingual subtitles; subtitles in English for the hearing impaired.

There was a period when Costner could do no wrong, and *Robin Hood Prince of Thieves* was the pinnacle of his career. It has every ingredient of a Hollywood family entertainment epic: action, adventure, good versus evil, a damsel in distress, and of course, an Englishman with an American accent. Costner takes the 500 year-old, stocking-wearing legend, and puts him through his Nineties' paces with the enthusiasm and charm Errol Flynn put into the character 60 years before. Everything that makes the action adventure genre appealing is present in this movie. It's both throwaway and compelling at the same time. Okay, so there are a few potholes in the plot here and there, and the whole scenario is less likely than Costner having a decent comeback film, but so what? When a film's action sequences can keep you on the edge of your seat as often as this then who cares? Unfortunately, as the film harps back to the days of Errol Flynn, the disc harps back to the reign of VHS. The DVD, apart from having superior picture and sound, has nothing else which makes it better value than a cassette. It's certainly not worth buying if you already own it on tape.

FINAL VERDICT

Picture ☆☆☆☆ Sound ☆☆☆
Entertainment ☆☆☆☆ Extras ☆ Value ☆☆
OVERALL ☆☆☆

ROB ROY

Price: £19.99
Supplied by: MGM
Type of disc: Dual layer, single-sided
No of chapters: 32
Film format(s)/length: 2.35:1 widescreen / 133 mins
Audio format: Dolby Digital 5.1
Director: Michael Caton-Jones

Starring: Liam Neeson, John Hurt, Tim Roth
Year made: 1995
Extras: Scene access; booklet containing brief production notes and quotes; original theatrical trailer; soundtrack in German, French, Italian and Spanish; subtitles in 10 languages; subtitles for the hearing impaired in English and Dutch.

There's one thing that the Scots and Americans have in common, and it ain't McDonalds. It's that neither of them can stand the English, and Hollywood execs who'd struggle to find Scotland on a map will use almost any opportunity to remind the world how wickedly – and camply – Englanders used to live. This leads us neatly to *Rob Roy*, in which Michael Caton-Jones takes all the lessons he learned about how to make a Western from *Last of the Mohicans* and transplants them to 18th century Scotland. Neeson convincingly plays Robert Roy McGregor, a noble Scot swindled out of his village's loan from decadent aristocrat the Marquis of Montrose (Hurt) by his savage charge Archie Cunningham (Roth, snivellingly excellent). As the English murder and terrorise Rob's kith and kin, a showdown between warrior and fop becomes inevitable… The transfer to DVD is satisfactorily done. To see the stunning and beautiful panoramas of the Scottish Highlands on film is now, on disc, almost like viewing it through a window. Any insight into the film's production though is limited to fun-sized 'Making of' notes in the booklet. No historical context is provided nor is any background about the real Rob Roy included. Identical to the Region 1 equivalent, this disc gives more thought to the European market, packed as it is with multiple soundtracks (all 5.1 Dolby Digital), two tracks for the hearing impaired and 10 subtitle options. English credibility's loss, it would seem, is Scottish tourism's gain.

FINAL VERDICT

Picture ☆☆☆☆ Sound ☆☆☆☆
Entertainment ☆☆☆ Extras ☆☆ Value ☆☆☆☆
OVERALL ☆☆☆

THE ROCK

Price: £15.99
Supplied by: DVD World (01705 796662)
Type of disc: Single layer, double-sided
No of chapters: 22
Film length/format(s): 2.35:1 anamorphic / 131 mins
Director: Michael Bay
Starring: Sean Connery, Nicolas Cage, Ed Harris
Year made: 1996
Extras: Scene access; soundtrack in French and Italian,

multilingual subtitles.

The Rock is one of the best no-brainer action movies since the original *Die Hard*. It's got charismatic leads, a completely loopy plot, more gunfire than the Gulf War, sharp one-liners, explosions at regular intervals and enough thrilling action sequences to jumpstart the heart of any of the numerous corpses it leaves littered in its wake. So why the hell did Hollywood Pictures' parent company Disney make such a completely arse job of bringing it to DVD? First, the story. US Marines General Hummel (Harris), aggrieved that soldiers who die under his command on secret missions aren't being given any recognition, steals a bunch of nerve gas rockets and takes over Alcatraz Island. If the government doesn't pay the dead soldiers' families full reparations, he'll fire the missiles into San Francisco. FBI 'chemical superfreak' Stanley Goodspeed (Cage) and former SAS spy/Alcatraz resident John Mason (Connery) are sent with a platoon of commandos onto the island to disarm the rockets. Naturally it all goes pear-shaped, and the geeky Goodspeed and anxious-to-escape Mason have to face Hummel's forces alone. Yes, it's ludicrous, but director Bay (*Bad Boys*, *Armageddon*) keeps things moving at such a pace you don't have time to notice. The whole film is merely an excuse for a series of increasingly explosive set-pieces, from the opening scenes of Hummel's men silently taking over a military base to the final battle for control of the last rocket. There's even one of the most exhilarating car chases yet filmed, which is all the more enjoyable for being utterly gratuitous, as Connery flees through Frisco in a stolen Humvee and ends up completely obliterating a beautiful yellow Ferrari with a derailed tram. So *The Rock* is enormous, noisy fun as a movie – but how is it as a DVD? Well, the picture quality is good – streets ahead of even its laserdisc counterpart – but the sound seems to have suffered somewhere. Lower frequencies are muffled, as though someone's put a cushion over the speaker. In a film filled with booming explosions, this is particularly noticeable. No special features either. Then, of course, there's the ultimate humiliation. *The Rock* is a flipper. The moment you have to eject the DVD and turn it over isn't as ineptly positioned as in *Armageddon* (another Bay film, oddly) but it's nearly as bad. The commandos are just about to enter Alcatraz when pow! A big drawing of a Mickey Mouse hand, appropriately enough, appears and tells you to turn over the disc. Whatever Disney's excuse, it just isn't good enough, and really wrecks an otherwise hugely entertaining film. It's yet another example of Region 2 getting the thin end of the wedge.

FINAL VERDICT

Picture ☆☆☆☆☆ Sound ☆☆

Entertainment ☆☆☆☆ Extras ☆ Value ☆☆

OVERALL ☆☆☆

THE ROCKETEER

Price: £15.99

Supplied by: DVD World (01705 796662)

Type of disc: Single layer, single-sided

No of chapters: 15

Film format(s)/length: 2.35:1 widescreen / 104 mins

Audio format: Dolby Digital 5.0

Director: Joe Johnston

Starring: Bill Campbell, Jennifer Connelly, Timothy Dalton

Year made: 1991

Extras: Scene access; soundtrack in English, French and Italian; subtitles in Dutch and English.

When reckless stunt pilot Cliff Secord (Campbell) comes into possession of a top-secret jet-pack, it seems like the answer to all his money worries. Unfortunately, both the government and a sinister Nazi spy are keen to lay their hands on the invention and they'll stop at nothing to get it. The *Rocketeer* is a fun adventure movie with some nice action sequences and loads of tongue-in-cheek humour. It also stars the fabulously attractive Jennifer Connelly, which should in itself be more than enough reason to watch it. Unfortunately, in the DVD extras stakes, *The Rocketeer* doesn't so much reach for the sky as rather plummet to the ground like a fizzled-out firework. If your idea of value for money is behind-the-scenes documentaries, extra scenes and copious production notes, then look somewhere else because this disc doesn't deliver them. Instead we are left to mourn over the rather poor 15 chapter scene access (a feature which comes as standard), the multiple languages and captions. With not even a measly theatre trailer on offer, there's little to recommend this over the video.

FINAL VERDICT

Picture ☆☆☆☆ Sound ☆☆☆☆

Entertainment ☆☆☆ Extras ☆ Value ☆

OVERALL ☆☆

ROCKY

Price: £19.99

Supplied by: MGM Home Video

Type of disc: Single layer, single-sided

No of chapters: 24

Film format(s)/length: 1.85:1 widescreen / 119 mins

Audio format: Dolby Digital 5.1

Director: John G Avildsen
Starring: Sylvester Stallone, Talia Shire, Burt Young
Year made: 1976
Extras: Theatrical trailer; English/German/Spanish soundtracks; multilingual subtitles; 'Also on DVD' promo.

Sylvester Stallone once remarked, "I'll just go on playing Rambo and Rocky. Both are money-making machines that can't be switched off." Of course, this was before *Rocky V* and *Rambo III* rather spoiled his theory, but now that DVD has come along, you can see he might have a point. The inevitable DVD release of Stallone's first big film gives you the chance to see how the Italian Stallion became a star, before he began to believe his own press and the *Rocky* series imploded into flag-waving banality. It also made him a few extra quid into the bargain. Stallone wrote – well, dictated – the Oscar-nominated script, which deals with Rocky Balboa, a struggling, slow-witted Philadelphia boxer who makes a living breaking thumbs for the local loan shark. In one of those 'only in the movies' plot twists, world heavyweight champion Apollo Creed (Carl Weathers) is in town for the American Bicentennial. When his scheduled opponent pulls out and nobody is willing to replace him on short notice, Creed gets an idea for a great publicity stunt – find a local nobody and give him the once-in-a-lifetime chance to challenge the champion. Rocky, of course, is chosen, but nobody bothers to tell him that the big fight is just a show. To him, it's his one shot to prove to the world that he's not the loser everybody thinks he is... And so, the stage is set for what turned out to be one of Hollywood's definitive 'triumph of the underdog' feel-good movies. While Creed struts around in fancy suits and makes big-money deals, unworried by an opponent whom he thinks of as a joke, Rocky gets into shape with the help of best mate Paulie (Young) and crusty old coach Mickey (Burgess Meredith) by punching sides of beef and running around the docks. Will he go the distance against the undisputed heavyweight champion of the world? What do you think? DVD does a good job of showing both Rocky's run-down urban home and the glam and glitz of the big fight, with a scratch-free picture that's of much higher quality than many other older films that have been transferred to disc. However, the special features aren't very. Yet again, MGM has chosen to put all the supplementary information inside a flimsy pamphlet rather than on the disc, where it belongs. Hey, guys! Save a tree! Because of this, the only extra on the DVD itself is the trailer. Despite this, *Rocky* is still highly watchable, possessing a kind of innocence that was noticeably lacking in the sequels. It's also worth watching to see how many movies stole the formula – director Avildsen went on to make *The Karate Kid*...

FINAL VERDICT
Picture ☆☆☆☆ Sound ☆☆☆
Entertainment ☆☆☆☆ Extras ☆ Value ☆☆☆
OVERALL ☆☆☆☆

ROGUE TRADER

Price: £19.99
Supplied by: Pathé
Type of disc: Single layer, single-sided
No of chapters: 21
Film format(s)/length: 4:3 regular / 97 mins
Audio format: Stereo
Director: Jonathan Lynn
Starring: Ewan McGregor, Anna Friel
Year made: 1998
Extras: Scene access; theatrical trailer; subtitles for the hearing impaired in English.

When one man managed to bring down a 200 year-old financial institution, it was one of the biggest news stories of the Nineties, even if no one outside of London's Square Mile knew exactly what it meant. *Rogue Trader*'s fortunes are sure to drop thanks to this DVD though, one of the poorest discs on the shop floor. McGregor adopts a barrow boy accent to play the hotshot futures trader who finds himself spiralling into ridiculous debt after trying to cover up a young colleague's mistake, but keeps it all quiet from his unsuspecting wife Lisa (Friel). Meanwhile, Barings Bank rather unwisely decides to trust its entire future to its 'genius' investor... Knowledge of stocks and shares isn't required to enjoy *Rogue Trader*. It's a gambling movie with almost unimaginable amounts of money as the stakes. He may have expressed remorse to the media, but by the film's close, Leeson emerges as an chancer who didn't know when to quit. A great deal could have been done in the special features department – but wasn't. The hopeless disc doesn't come close to scratching the surface of this 'true' story. Where is the input from the writer, director and co-producer James Dearden? Did McGregor and Friel meet Nick and Lisa Leeson? Why not interview the man himself? What really annoys is the 4:3 presentation and low grade sound – how come the Americans get the movie in 1.85:1 widescreen? The film is an interesting example of British film-makers jumping on a headline-grabbing event like Hollywood constantly does, but *Rogue Trader* would have worked better on Channel 4 and the disc back on the drawing board.

FINAL VERDICT

Picture ☆☆☆ Sound ☆☆

Entertainment ☆☆ Extras ☆ Value ☆☆

OVERALL ☆☆

ROLLERBALL

Price: £19.99

Supplied by: MGM Home Entertainment

Type of disc: Dual layer, single-sided

No of chapters: 30

Film format(s)/length: 1.85:1 widescreen enhanced / 115 mins

Audio format: Dolby Digital 5.1

Director: Norman Jewison

Starring: James Caan, John Houseman, Maud Adams

Year made: 1975

Extras: Scene access; audio commentary provided by director Norman Jewison; theatrical trailer; trivia and production notes; soundtrack in French, German, Italian and Spanish; subtitles in 7 languages; subtitles for the hard of hearing in English and German.

Set in a society where large multinational corporations rule the world of tomorrow, the brutal sport of Rollerball is all that remains of the wars of yesteryear. Free speech and free will are things of the past, and no one knows who's really calling the shots. Jonathan E (Caan) is the captain and star for the Houston Rollerball team. But when he is ordered to retire against his wishes, he begins to question society itself. In a film that attacks the very core of violence it manages to provide some truly startling savage scenes of bloodshed while simultaneously evoking excitement for the viewer. Rollerball is a bloodsport to entertain (and subdue) the masses, so an existence without illness, poverty, crime and war relies on this bloody display heavily. The film doesn't explain how the deadly game came about, or why it was created, or indeed the world outside Rollerball, but it's this approach that gives *Rollerball* a different feeling than that of the usually stale action sport film. Caan's performance is both brilliantly brutal and collectively compelling, as he gradually becomes bigger than the sport itself – and a threat to the corporations that govern the world. The rules of Rollerball are gradually changed to make the game ever more lethal, with the intention of eliminating this dangerous individual and restoring corporate order to the world – the climax sees Cann in almost gladiatorial combat against his opponents, the game itself forgotten. Considering the vintage of the film the picture quality has stood the test of time well, and the anamorphic enhancement shows it off to good effect. The audio has been given a new Dolby Digital 5.1 soundtrack; unfortunately this is nothing to sing and dance about. Audio commentary is provided by director Norman Jewison and provides an interesting insight into the man's violent futuristic vision. The traditional theatrical trailer has also been included, but does little to boost its sales potential.

FINAL VERDICT

Picture ☆☆☆☆ Sound ☆☆☆

Entertainment ☆☆☆☆☆

Extras ☆☆☆ Value ☆☆☆☆

OVERALL ☆☆☆☆

ROMPER STOMPER

Price: £17.99

Supplied by: Medusa Pictures

Type of disc: Single layer, single-sided

No of chapters: 16

Film format(s)/length: 4:3 regular / 89 mins

Audio format: Stereo

Director: Geoffrey Wright

Starring: Russell Crowe, Daniel Pollock, Jacqueline McKenzie

Year made: 1992

Extras: Scene access; picture gallery; theatrical trailer.

Although he's more recently been on the silver screen as an honourable warrior righting an injustice, Russell Crowe's first outing as top-billed actor was as a fighter of a far more despicable nature. Crowe is Hando, the irredeemable leader of a gang of skinheads in modern-day Melbourne. Hando, his best friend Davey (Pollock) and fellow Neanderthals spend their time moshing to trite far-right music and assaulting Vietnamese locals. A spoilt junkie called Gabe (McKenzie) gradually comes between the pals and uses them for her own ends, but what ends are they? When the Vietnamese fight back, anarchy threatens to destroy the skinheads themselves. *Romper Stomper* caused a stir when first released and it's easy to see why. Disturbing, depressing and unforgettable all at the same time, this savage tale is almost Shakespearean in its violence, tragedy and betrayal. We have to form our own judgements on the vandals' actions – interesting because writer/director Geoffrey Wright creates a sexually charismatic and articulate leader in Hando. Film fans wanting to know more about the genesis of this movie and Wright's thoughts on the inflammatory subject matter will be disappointed, because no effort has been made to include even production notes. The trailer is present and correct but gives away too much of the ending. The picture gallery, always a good idea, is reasonably presented with 18 publicity shots mounted to good effect. *Romper Stomper* is a powerful, ambiguous film but the film-makers' input and thoughts are unfortunately lacking on the DVD.

FINAL VERDICT

Picture ✩✩✩ Sound ✩✩

Entertainment ✩✩✩ Extras ✩✩ Value ✩✩✩

OVERALL ✩✩✩

ROMY AND MICHELE'S HIGH SCHOOL REUNION

Price: £15.99
Supplied by: Warner Home Video
Type of disc: Single layer, single-sided
No of chapters: 16
Film format(s)/length: 1.85:1 widescreen / 88 mins
Director: David Mirkin
Starring: Mira Sorvino, Lisa Kudrow, Janeane Garofalo
Year made: 1997
Extras: Scene access; multiple languages; English and Dutch subtitles.

You have to feel sorry for Romy and Michele. These two lovely ladies bungle their way through an enjoyable but different comedy, clad in countless outfits that will make you blush if you watch with the family, giving suitably over-the-top performances – and what has Warner Home Video done for them? Stuck them on a low quality DVD without not a single trace of any special features. With the whole point of DVD video being the vastly superior quality compared to VHS cassette, it's positively disappointing to see all sorts of ugly bits and pieces flashing up on screen from the very beginning of the movie. Shocking as it may seem, the little black or white spots and curves are just like the little flecks you see when watching a reel at the cinema. Sure enough, catch one of the little blighters with that perfect freeze-frame and there's no mistaking: either the discs were erroneously pressed next door to a flour mill or something's badly wrong with the master. Backgrounds have a mysterious trailing effect, too. Zero extras and speckled video? No thanks!

FINAL VERDICT

Picture ✩✩ Sound ✩✩✩✩

Entertainment ✩✩✩ Extras ✩ Value ✩

OVERALL ✩

RONIN

Price: £19.99
Supplied by: MGM Home Entertainment
Type of disc: Dual layer, single-sided
No of chapters: 32

Film format(s)/length: 2.35:1 widescreen / 117 mins
Audio format: Dolby Digital 5.1
Director: John Frankenheimer
Starring: Robert De Niro, Jean Reno, Natascha McElhone
Year made: 1998
Extras: Scene selection; alternative ending; director's commentary; 'Making of' featurette; colour booklet with production information; original theatrical trailer.

Rather unfairly, *Ronin* received largely derogatory reviews when it received its cinematic release last year. Granted, the story itself was hardly ground-breaking, with its ragtag collection of killers-for-hire brought together to locate and retrieve a mysterious case. However, what makes *Ronin* so compelling is its understated performances from the likes of Robert De Niro, Jean Reno and Natascha McElhone, as well as the adrenaline-packed action set pieces. The best of the latter is without a doubt the climatic car chase through the Parisian streets, with the scenes where De Niro and co are speeding the wrong way down a one way street – it's guaranteed to leave your living room chair armrests with massive hand indents. De Niro plays Sam, an enigmatic ex-US Government employee who sells his specialist skills to the highest bidder. He and an international mix of like-minded individuals are gathered together by Deidre (McElhone), who gives them the task of taking the aforementioned case from its current owners. Understandably, the latter are not going to hand the case over, so what follows is the formation and execution of a strategic plan, which doesn't progress as hoped by the group. There are double-crosses and action aplenty before the film reaches its exciting finale. As a stand alone DVD, *Ronin* is up there with the very best. Any fan of the film will be more than pleased to shell out £20 on a product as good as this. As well as the obligatory interactive menus, scene selection and theatrical trailer, this DVD also comes equipped with a fascinating documentary on the film's production – replete with interviews with the cast and crew – as well as the option to watch the film with director John Frankenheimer's audio commentary, and best of all, you can also check out the film's alternative ending. The latter is something that should be the bread-and-butter of all DVD motion pictures, as the flexible, easy access format makes it an ideal platform to host such extras. It is also something that would have usually come as a separate 'director's cut' version on VHS video, meaning that punters would have probably felt obliged to buy the same film twice, just to see what they were missing. At least in *Ronin*'s case, you can see what happened to Deidre by simply pressing the alternative ending feature in the DVD extras menu, without having to buy another version of the film altogether. *Ronin* is an excellent movie, with some impressive acting, punchy dialogue and some breath-taking visuals. The DVD is of top notch quality as well, with some great extras and pristine audio/visual performance.

FINAL VERDICT

Picture ☆☆☆☆ Sound ☆☆☆☆

Entertainment ☆☆☆☆

Extras ☆☆☆☆ Value ☆☆☆☆

OVERALL ☆☆☆☆☆

ROXANNE

Price: £19.99

Supplied by: Columbia TriStar Home Video

Type of disc: Single layer, single-sided

No of chapters: 28

Film format(s)/length: 116:9 widescreen enhanced / 102 mins

Audio format: Dolby Surround

Director: Fred Schepisi

Starring: Steve Martin, Daryl Hannah, Shelley Duvall

Year made: 1987

Extras: Scene access; filmographies; theatrical trailer; soundtrack in French, German, Italian and Spanish; subtitles in 19 languages.

At the beginning of his screen writing career, Steve Martin couldn't put a foot wrong. With the likes of *The Jerk* and *Dead Men Don't Wear Plaid* he was churning out comedy classics like they were a means to breathe. Nice then that he was able to return to this form with his 1999 hit *Bowfinger*. So what happened in between? Well, apart from acting in other people's movies and churning out the more serious pieces of screenplays such as *LA Story* and *A Simple Twist of Fate*, there was this little number. Widely regarded as a Steve Martin classic, *Roxanne* is simply a reworking of the play *Cyrano de Bergerac* with Martin playing the role of CD, the small town fire chief who has a way with words and a heart for the new girl in town, astrologer Roxanne (Hannah). Sadly he's also afflicted with an extremely large nose (a work of prosthetic genius) and with this comes low self-esteem when dealing with the ladies. Thus he banishes himself to the emotional sidelines and allows Roxanne to court Chris (Rick Rossovich) the highly likeable fire fighter without enough happening between the ears. Thus, it's left to the enigmatic CD to be Chris's words and emotions by ghost writing all of his letters to Roxanne. It's all an emotional tragic romance of a movie with Martin taking the

classic tale under his wing and providing a comic overtone. Thankfully, it is only an overtone, with most of the laughs coming solely from Martin himself, with the occasional giggle added by the worst collection of volunteer fire-fighters ever to appear on screen. Unfortunately, in the hands of Schepisi, the pace of this movie is slowed down far below that of the average romantic comedy. There's often a dragging feeling to the proceedings which can't always be sped up by Martin throwing himself around the outside of a house like a gymnast. Indeed, like most of his movies Martin is the best thing on screen and puts forward an excellent portrayal of a man who refuses to put a physical difference ahead of his self esteem, except when it comes to love. Sadly this isn't one of Columbia TriStar's best efforts on DVD, but it's not completely barren. The filmographies and trailers are adequate, and the picture and sound quality are superior to VHS so it's worth buying if you're a Martin fan.

FINAL VERDICT

Picture ☆☆☆☆ Sound ☆☆☆

Entertainment ☆☆☆ Extras ☆☆ Value ☆☆☆

OVERALL ☆☆☆

THE RUGRATS MOVIE

Price: £19.99

Supplied by: Paramount DVD

Type of disc: Dual layer, single-sided

No of chapters: 19

Film format(s)/length: 1.85:1 anamorphic / 77 mins

Audio format: Dolby Digital 5.1

Directors: Norton Virgien and Igor Kovalyov

Starring the voices of: Elizabeth Daily, Christine Cavanaugh, Cheryl Chase

Year made: 1998

Extras: Scene access; theatrical trailer; *Catdog* bonus cartoon; soundtrack in English, Swedish, Norwegian, Finnish and Danish; subtitles in English; subtitles in English for the hard of hearing.

It's called a franchise. You start off with an inoffensive, unobtrusive, yet charming kids' cartoon about a bunch of babies, then soon you'll end up with books, videogames, CD-ROMs and soft toys, and then eventually you'll get this – the all-important movie release. Thankfully the Rugrats deserve all of their fortune and glory. Starting off as a Saturday morning cartoon, *The Rugrats* tells the tales of Tommy Pickles, his pals Chucky and Angelica, and his dog Spike. It follow the toddlers as they go through their days doing their baby things in their baby ways, and getting into enough trouble to give

Jimmy Saville a heart attack. The transfer onto the big screen thankfully keeps the pace, humour and attraction of its TV counterpart. This time, there is the addition of Tommy's new baby brother Dylan. Through all sorts of complications, the babies manage to get themselves lost in the woods and set off for high adventure that would frighten the life out of most, but with their over-active imaginations it seems like a walk in the park. Unlike the other animated series about a group of kids that made it to the big screen last year, *The Rugrats Movie* doesn't quite manage to sustain the full feature length treatment. At least *South Park* knew its audience, and knew what it wanted. Here the movie can't quite decide whether it wants to broaden its appeal to a more adult audience, and at times seems a bit lost and uncertain of itself. This is particularly true of the humour, which on television works a treat. Well, this is it. Paramount's first toe in the pool of the European DVD market, and to be honest the nicest thing that can be said is that the 'mount is playing it safe. *The Rugrats Movie* is a superb anamorphic transfer, and the 5.1 sound is terrific. Extras-wise it's the bare minimum, but still more than you find on most Region 2 discs (in fact, it's identical to the Region 1 version). But with a star-studded cast and some nice songs from the likes of Elvis Costello and No Doubt, this bit of celluloid fun is worth checking out for the young at heart.

FINAL VERDICT

Picture ☆☆☆☆☆ Sound ☆☆☆☆☆
Entertainment ☆☆☆ Extras ☆☆☆ Value ☆☆☆☆
OVERALL ☆☆☆☆

RUNAWAY BRIDE

Price: £15.99
Supplied by: Warner Home Video
Type of disc: Single layer, single-sided
No of chapters: 21
Film format(s)/length: 2.35:1 widescreen enhanced / 122 mins
Audio format: Dolby Digital 5.1
Director: Garry Marshall
Starring: Julia Roberts, Richard Gere, Joan Cusack
Year made: 1999
Extras: Scene access; soundtrack in English, German; Spanish and French; subtitles available in 11 languages.

It must have seemed like such a great idea at the time. Bring back the stars and the director of one of the most successful romantic comedies ever, put them all together in another romcom, and success is assured. Right? Wrong. *Pretty Woman*, the previous Roberts/Gere/Marshall collaboration, was a sleeper

hit and had an edge to it, thanks to the original (pre-Disneyfication) script's dark undercurrent. *Runaway Bride*, on the other hand, has an arrogant 'this is going to be a huge hit!' attitude and as much edge as a sneeze. So, what went wrong? For a start, putting the screenwriters of *Three Men and a Little Lady* in charge of the script is no way to avoid slushiness. Then there's the more serious problem that it's extremely hard to like the characters you're meant to be rooting for. Gere is newspaper columnist Ike Graham, a kind of American Jeremy Clarkson, only without the too-tight jeans. Stuck for an idea one day, he hacks out a misogynistic piece about Maggie Carpenter (Roberts), the 'runaway bride' – a woman who keeps deserting her grooms at the altar – he hears about from a man in a bar, only to end up being sacked when the aforementioned bride threatens to sue for libel. Rather than drown his sorrows like a real journalist, he decides to follow her around as she prepares for her next wedding in the hope that she'll bolt again and he'll be vindicated. Will Ike and Maggie fall in love? Duh. But who cares? Ike is smug and annoying, Maggie is kooky and annoying, and while they clearly deserve each other that's no reason to force their insipid romance on us for two hours. Also, *Runaway Bride* is set in a fantasy world where Gere's character can afford an apartment overlooking Central Park and a sports car despite having no apparent income beyond pecking out 500 words each day; the early Nineties were full of hippies; everybody in America reads the same newspaper; and Roberts's wedding videos are shot from 17 angles using a Steadicam. If the story were better it would be possible to overlook these dumb mistakes, but as it stands they just drag you even further out of the story. The disc is, if anything, even more tepid than the film itself. On the US disc, there was a certain amount of humour from director Marshall's commentary track, on which he sounded uncannily like Emo Philips, as well as a Dixie Chicks music video and the trailer. Hardly cutting edge stuff, to be sure, but the commentary at least provided a reason to sit through the film for a second time. The Region 2 disc of *Runaway Bride*, on the other hand, offers...subtitles. Golly gee. It does make you wonder if some companies, when faced with the DVD release of a film that didn't do too well in cinemas, simply want to shove it out of the door and forget about it rather than spend the time and effort adding extras to it. Why? If they don't make the effort, why would anyone buy a borderline film like this?

FINAL VERDICT

Picture ☆☆☆☆ Sound ☆☆☆
Entertainment ☆☆ Extras ☆ Value ☆☆
OVERALL ☆☆

Run Lola Run

Price: £19.99
Supplied by: Columbia TriStar Home Video
Type of disc: Single layer, single-sided
No of chapters: 28
Film format(s)/length: 1.85:1 anamorphic / 77 mins
Audio format: Dolby Digital 5.1
Director: Tom Twyker
Starring: Franka Potente, Moritz Bliebtrey, Herbert Knaup
Year made: 1999
Extras: Scene access; director and star commentary; trailer; music video, 'Believe'; filmographies; soundtrack in English (dubbed) and German; subtitles in English.

This is a European film that you can bet will be remade by Hollywood. You can also bet that the remake won't be nearly as good. The plot is simple: Lola (Potente) has 20 minutes to find 100,000 marks that her boyfriend Manni (Bliebtreu) owes to the Mob, otherwise he's going to rob a store to get it. The twist is that Lola's race against time is told in 3 ways, events unfolding differently depending on how long it takes her to get down the stairs of her apartment building. It might sound a lot like *Sliding Doors*, and it's true that the basic concept is the same. The difference is that instead of Gwyneth Paltrow simpering away and getting her hair cut, *Run Lola Run* is a whirlwind race as Lola pounds the pavements of Berlin, periodically causing traffic accidents, robbing banks, uncovering family secrets and changing the lives of the people she encounters. Or not, as the case may be. Camera tricks, split screens and even cartoon sequences make it clear that director Twyker's primary aim is to grab you by the eyeballs and drag you screaming into the chase, aided by an almost non-stop techno soundtrack. He succeeds – *Run Lola Run* is a rush from start to finish. Despite the low-budget nature of the film, picture and audio are both superb. The latter is particularly good if you have a nice big subwoofer – even in the few quiet moments, the bassline gradually starts to build up in the background, until it suddenly kicks in at full blast and Lola's off again. The extras package is actually quite decent. Twyker and Potente provide an entertaining commentary, backed up by standard material like a trailer and filmographies, and Potente also has a music video. In all, a highly watchable film on a well-made DVD – run to the shops and buy it.

FINAL VERDICT
Picture ☆☆☆☆ Sound ☆☆☆☆☆
Entertainment ☆☆☆☆ Extras ☆☆☆ Value ☆☆☆☆
OVERALL ☆☆☆☆

Rush Hour

Price: £19.99
Supplied by: DVDplus (www.dvdplus.co.uk)
Type of disc: Dual layer, single-sided
No of chapters: 37
Film format(s)/length: 16:9 widescreen / 98 mins
Audio format: Dolby Digital 5.1
Director: Brett Ratner
Starring: Jackie Chan, Chris Tucker, Tom Wilkinson
Year made: 1998
Extras: Trailer; cast and crew notes (text only); deleted scenes; behind-the-scenes feature (40 mins); 2 music videos; *Whatever Happened to Mason Rees* film (10 mins); English subtitles.

During the long summer movie drought of 1998, *Rush Hour* managed to collect an impressive roster of rave reviews. Not bad for a tired retread of the mismatched cop routine, but then this isn't so much a movie as a collection of routines – Chris Tucker's comedy riffs and Jackie Chan's spectacular comedy-action stunts. In fact, probably the best part of the movie is the outtakes, generously rolling alongside the credits. The kidnapping of a Chinese diplomat's daughter brings Chan to LA, where he's partnered with LAPD cop Tucker – the idea being to divert them both from the real case. Inevitably, it's the two rejects who end up saving the day. It's not a plot to get the brain cells tingling, but if your brain's in neutral thanks to beer and pizza, *Rush Hour* really can live up to the film reviews. Chan has a genuine demeanour and you're always entertained when he's on screen, while Tucker's 'unique' personality can grow on you over time. What's beyond doubt is *Rush Hour*'s quality as a DVD – you get loads of extras. There are two full-length pop videos, a 12 minute student film by the director, the usual cast notes, a dozen or so deleted scenes, plus a fun 'Making of' feature. This generous 40-minute special contains all of the usual promo-spiel, but the openness of the stars makes it highly watchable. In particular, there's a genuinely fascinating scene where we see Chan developing a fight sequence, in reality directing it, while Ratner struggles to keep up. The picture and audio quality of the film is first class, while the extras make this quirky film into an essential purchase on DVD.

FINAL VERDICT
Picture ☆☆☆☆☆ Sound ☆☆☆☆☆

Entertainment ☆☆☆☆
Extras ☆☆☆☆☆ Value ☆☆☆☆
OVERALL ☆☆☆☆

RUSHMORE

Price: £15.99
Supplied by: Warner Home Video
Type of disc: Single layer, single-sided
No of chapters: 20
Film format(s)/length: 2.35:1 widescreen / 89 mins
Audio format: Dolby Digital 5.1
Director: Wes Anderson
Starring: Jason Schwartzman, Olivia Williams, Bill Murray
Year made: 1999
Extras: Scene access; soundtrack in English and Czech; subtitles in 8 languages.

Exactly what were you up to at school? The gifted Max Fischer (the superbly talented Jason Schwartzman) is doing everything other than the work on the academic curriculum. Having written a play at the age of 11, the only child of a widowed barber won a scholarship to the private school of Rushmore, and devoid of any academic interest he goes about making a life for himself via extracurricular activity. Ignoring the traditional notion of education, he buries his head in a place where he'd like life to be comfortably nestled waiting for him. Think Woody Allen as an overly keen Boy Scout, and that's pretty much Max. Still, on every ideal lifestyle a little rain must fall, and in Max's world the puddles arrive in the form of first grade teacher Rosemary Cross. He falls instantly in love with her, and goes about trying to gain her affection in his own unique way. The problem is Herman Blume (Murray), a local businessman who finds reflection in Max's loneliness and love in the company of Cross. *Rushmore* is an absolute must for anyone who enjoys good humour yet still has the sour taste of adolescence in their mouths. Schwartzman is well cast, showing the right aptitude to be flirtatious, rebellious, and smug all at once. Many of his scenes are truly classic moments of cinematic immaturity, and all praise should go to Owen Wilson and Wes Anderson for penning such a likeably conniving 15 year-old. However, it is Murray who solidly steals the show. This is undoubtedly his best work since *Quick Change*. Played with charm, Murray is completely toned down, yet still effortlessly manages to toss out the odd hilarious moment as if it were as easy as blinking. It's criminal that *Rushmore* went mostly unnoticed, as it's possibly one of the best movies of 1999. Cast, script, and particularly director make this one of the richest treats of recent years. It's

sad that such a rich film comes on such a shallow disc. With the only extra being scene access, the only satisfaction comes in knowing that they are scenes worth accessing.

FINAL VERDICT
Picture ☆☆☆☆ Sound ☆☆☆☆
Entertainment ☆☆☆☆☆ Extras ☆ Value ☆☆☆☆
OVERALL ☆☆☆

SATURN 3

Price: £9.99
Supplied by: Carlton Silver Collection
Type of disc: Single layer, single-sided
No of chapters: 15
Film format(s)/length: 1.85:1 letterbox / 84 mins
Audio format: Mono
Director: Stanley Donen
Starring: Kirk Douglas, Farrah Fawcett, Harvey Keitel
Year made: 1980
Extras: Scene access; subtitles for the hearing impaired in English.

If you like your sci-fi lame and derivative, this is the DVD for you. Douglas and Fawcett are scientists and lovers on Saturn's third moon (duh), doing, you know, science and love stuff. Their happy life is ruined when bonkers spaceman Keitel (for some reason overdubbed by somebody else) shows up with an experimental robot, to which he has a telepathic link. Because Keitel is a loon, the robot soon goes mental too and starts clomping around killing dogs and lusting after the ex-Mrs Lee Majors. It's essentially *Alien* with a sex-crazed robot, and while some of the sets are interesting, the effects, and more importantly the script, are cheesy and unconvincing. Although the DVD beats most of the other Silver Collection discs by being widescreen, it's non-anamorphic and you only get mono sound. Those Farrah Fawcett fans trapped in a Seventies timewarp may be tempted; others should avoid.

FINAL VERDICT
Picture ☆☆☆ Sound ☆ Entertainment ☆☆
Extras ☆ Value ☆☆☆
OVERALL ☆☆

SAVIOR

Price: £19.99
Supplied by: Columbia TriStar Home Video
Type of disc: Dual layer, single-sided
No of chapters: 28
Film format(s)/length: 2.35:1 anamorphic / 99 mins
Audio format: Dolby Digital 5.1
Director: Peter Antonijevic

Starring: Dennis Quaid, Nastassja Kinski, Stellan Skarsgard
Year made: 1997
Extras: Scene access; audio commentary by director; filmographies; theatrical trailer; subtitles in English and Hebrew; subtitles for the hearing impaired in English.

Despite Kinski's top billing, she's soon despatched in a terrorist bombing which kicks off a genuinely shocking spiral of violence. Quaid plays her American husband, a familiar icon whose civilised veneer takes only a short while to shatter with appalling consequences. His descent from bland family man to deep-chilled mercenary, fighting alongside Serbian mercenaries and hunting down Muslims, is unnerving, but effectively explained with some deft flashbacks. Production notes reveal a real mercenary inspired the movie; however, this can't entirely rescue Quaid's redemption via an orphaned child seeming a little contrived. The movie's mid-section is a little sluggish as a consequence, but director Antonijevic ensures a harrowingly realistic tone throughout. A political prisoner during the war, he relentlessly piles grim detail upon detail; a Serbian soldier blithely chats about *Beverly Hills 90120*, mere minutes after he casually cut off a granny's finger to steal a gold ring. It's a scene with added resonance given the resemblance between the burning city centre and Belfast during the Troubles. The war crime scenes are more horrific than any slasher pic, entirely unbelievable in their cruelty but for the way they bring to mind contemporary newspaper reports. Despite a budget of just $10 million, the cinematography is impressive and encoding for DVD is excellent. A Dolby Digital soundscape is effective, but DVD extras are thin. A documentary about the war would've been useful, as the director's commentary is more about filmmaking than historical fact, but there's little else 'Hollywood' about *Savior*.

FINAL VERDICT

Picture ☆☆☆☆ Sound ☆☆☆☆
Entertainment ☆☆☆ Extras ☆☆☆☆ Value ☆☆☆☆
OVERALL ☆☆☆☆

SCENT OF A WOMAN

Price: £19.99
Supplied by: Columbia TriStar Home Video
Type of disc: Dual layer, single-sided
No of chapters: 16
Film format(s)/length: 1.85:1 widescreen / 150 mins
Audio format: Dolby Surround
Director: Martin Brest
Starring: Al Pacino, Chris O'Donnell, Gabrielle Anwar
Year made: 1992

Extras: Theatrical trailer; production notes; cast and crew biographies; soundtrack in English, German, French and Spanish; subtitles in 9 languages.

Think Pacino, you think *Scarface, Carlito's Way, Heat* and the *Godfather* movies. Yet it was this curiously lightweight drama that finally won him a Best Actor gong, in a role just made for luvvie-duvvie Academy voters. Pacino portrays Lieutenant Colonel Frank Field, a blind veteran who employs Chris O'Donnell to accompany him on a wild weekend. The resultant relationship between the two takes the majority of the over-stretched running time to develop, before arriving at its inevitable sappy ending. Still, there's some fun to be had along the way, and Pacino eats up his role. The length of the movie obviously limits the space on the disc for extras, with priority given to the numerous subtitle options. It certainly wasn't given to the picture, which not only lacks widescreen enhancement, but also comes across as quite soft. It's no disaster, but little effort has been made to hide the age of the film. Same again on the limited Dolby Surround mix, although the nature of the film means it's mainly dealing with dialogue anyway, so it's not such a big deal. The rest of the disc is filled out with the usual suspects – trailer, production notes and cast and film-maker biogs, which are as take-it-or-leave-it as ever. In short, what you're getting here is your standard back catalogue movie, neatly padding out the market but hardly justifying a 20 quid price tag. Buy it if you must, but this ain't the disc you'll be pulling out to impress your mates.

FINAL VERDICT

Picture ☆☆☆ Sound ☆☆☆ Entertainment ☆☆☆
Extras ☆☆ Value ☆
OVERALL ☆☆

SCREAM

Price: £15.99
Supplied by: DVD World (01705 796662)
Type of disc: Single layer, single-sided
No of chapters: 16
Film format(s)/length: 2.35:1 widescreen / 111 mins
Audio format: Dolby Digital 5.1
Director: Wes Craven
Starring: Neve Campbell, Courteney Cox, Skeet Ulrich
Year made: 1996
Extras: English subtitles; scene access.

In the tradition of Region 2 movies, this UK disc is without a single extra feature. Two versions are available from the US, both of which are better than this one. The US special edition is extremely well-featured, but even their bog standard version comes with director commentary and a theatrical trailer. If Wes Craven's self-mocking comical-horror is what gets you going, you will already own *Scream* on VHS as it's been available since before DVD was launched. Only a real devotee would want the same film, which is hardly a cinematic triumph, in this unfurnished state. Some consolation can be found in the very high image quality, save a few instances of colour banding in shots with out-of-focus backgrounds, but you should expect no less from this wonder-format. Being so reliant on a plot twist in its final minutes, *Scream* suffers from low replay value too. Basically, save your cash.

FINAL VERDICT

Picture ☆☆☆☆ Sound ☆☆☆☆ Entertainment ☆☆☆
Extras ☆ Value ☆☆
OVERALL ☆☆

SCREAMERS

Price: £19.99
Supplied by: Columbia TriStar
Type of disc: Dual layer, single-sided
No of chapters: 28
Film format(s)/length: 1.85:1 widescreen / 104 mins
Audio format: 2 Channel or Dolby Digital 5.1
Director: Christian Duguay
Starring: Peter Weller, Roy Dupuis, Jennifer Rubin
Year made: 1996.
Extras: Multilingual subtitles; theatrical trailer; filmographies; DVD trailer.

Peter Weller headlines in this sci-fi thriller which owes more than a little to the post-apocalyptic scenes in both *Terminator* movies. Weller plays Joseph Hendricksson, commander of an outpost on an alien planet involved in a war that's been waging so long nobody really remembers how it started. The plot centres around the 'screamers', tiny robots created to defend Hendricksson's outpost. The only problem is that the screamers are evolving and they've forgotten which side they're on. Although it's obviously fairly low-budget (don't expect *Starship Troopers*-style effects) *Screamers* does have its moments, largely due to a strong performance from Weller and some rather disturbing scenes from the animatronic screamers. As a DVD, *Screamers* is fairly average. The picture and sound quality are good but the extras – while not the worst – are not particularly impressive, encompassing as they do brief filmographies, some extra language subtitles and a theatrical trailer. There's also a DVD trailer, but this just extols the virtues of buying a DVD – which you presumably must have done already to be watching it!

FINAL VERDICT

Picture ☆☆☆☆ Sound ☆☆☆☆ Entertainment ☆☆
Extras ☆☆☆ Value ☆☆☆
OVERALL ☆☆

SCREAM 2

Price: £15.99
Supplied by: Warner Home Video
Type of disc: Dual layer, single-sided
No of chapters: 21
Film format(s)/length: 2.35:1 widescreen / 115 mins
Audio Format: Dolby Digital 5.1
Director: Wes Craven
Starring: Neve Campbell, Courteney Cox, David Arquette
Year made: 1998
Extras: Scene access; English subtitles.

Barely has Sidney Prescott (Campbell) got over being the target of a serial killer tag-team in *Scream*, than the gory murders start again at her new university. As a cheesy horror movie (*Stab*, which in the first of many in-jokes is filmed like a hack director's rip-off of the fantastic opening of *Scream* itself) based on the first wave of killings opens in town, somebody is recreating them in real life, with Sidney once again on the killer's list. But who's wielding the knives? Suspects abound. Could it be Sidney's too-perfect all-American boyfriend? Her ultra-friendly and helpful roommate? The wannabe film-maker who never goes anywhere without his camcorder? David Warner – he's English, dammit, so he's obviously suspicious – the drama professor? Or could it be one of the survivors from the first film – Randy, the movie geek, who is still obsessed with Sidney? Ex-deputy Dewey (Arquette), who's now got a bad temper and a limp, even though he was stabbed in the shoulder? Reporter Gail Weathers (Cox), who profited enormously from the events last time? Or even Cotton Weary, whom Sidney wrongly sent to prison and is now understandably annoyed with her? All the suspects are cleverly given moments of dodginess, whether by word, deed or something as simple as an ominous camera angle, therefore filling *Scream 2* with more red herrings than a communist trawler. If you haven't seen the film before, you really will be kept guessing until the villain is unmasked – or at least until the literal elimination of suspects means you run out of choices. (Just don't look at the chapter listing.) Although *Scream 2* is littered with movie references and in-jokes almost to the point of annoyance, Craven knows full well that, despite all the post-modernism, the film is all about shocks and scares. Which it delivers. The Münch-masked murderer pops up at unpredictable intervals to keep the body count rising, and there are some classic nail-biting moments – one involving a crashed car, another a pane of soundproof glass – to wind up the tension like a Swiss watch. *Scream 2* isn't quite as good as its predecessor, because the 'ironic horror' gimmick has lost its freshness. It's still very watchable though, with an appealing cast, lots of gory thrills and some sharp observations on the nature of sequels themselves. Disappointingly, *Scream 2* is entirely devoid of extras beyond subtitles, which is, well, a bit crap really. Surely Craven or writer Kevin Williamson could have been coaxed into providing a commentary? At the very least, how hard could it have been to stick a trailer on the disc? Come on, Miramax, at least pretend to make an effort!

FINAL VERDICT

Picture ☆☆☆☆ Sound ☆☆☆☆
Entertainment ☆☆☆☆ Extras ☆ Value ☆☆☆
OVERALL ☆☆☆

SCUM

Price: £19.99
Supplied by: DVDplus (www.dvdplus.co.uk)
Type of disc: Single layer, single-sided
No of chapters: 15
Film format(s)/length: 4:3 regular / 89 mins
Audio format: Mono
Director: Alan Clarke
Starring: Ray Winstone, Mick Ford, Phil Daniels
Year made: 1979 (original TV version 1977)
Extras: Scene access; 16-minute interview featuring producer Clive Parsons and writer Roy Minton; theatrical trailer; English subtitles.

There's only one thing harsher than the picture quality of this DVD, and that's borstal bovver-boy Carlin himself (Winstone, who is outstanding). However, numerous small flecks, slight discoloura-tion and the occasional hiccup with the soundtrack do nothing to spoil what is regarded by many as the most raw and powerful British film ever made. Even by today's standards, *Scum* is a shocking film. Set wholly in a young offenders institution (only the hang-glider collars of the warders date the film), it shamelessly lifts the lid on the wholesale violence and brutality of the Borstal regime – cons and screws – with Carlin, billiard ball-laden sock in hand, bludg-eoning his way to become the eponymous 'daddy'. What makes *Scum* so enjoyable 20 years after it was made, is the way Alan Clarke's shaky hand-held cam-era takes us beyond the senseless beatings and into the minds of the boys. There's so many powerful moments – Toyne callously being told of his wife's

burial, the boy's suicide right next door to an under-caring guard, the graphic male rape in the greenhouse ("get up son, this ain't Kew Gardens"), the blatantly racist sports session, and not least, the final epic riot and its bloody conclusion. As a DVD, the exclusive interview and trailer are a good start to the extras, but the former is way too short and lacks the recollections of any of the actors. This really is a glaring omission in such a character-driven film. Picture quality and the mono sound do this disc no favours, but the missed opportunity of including the original banned TV play, so fans can see what was omitted or expand-ed, is a crime as heinous as anything perpetrated by the boys of *Scum*.

FINAL VERDICT

Picture ☆☆ Sound ☆ Entertainment ☆☆☆☆☆
Extras ☆☆☆ Value ☆☆☆
OVERALL ☆☆☆

SEA OF LOVE

Price: £19.99
Supplied by: DVD Premier Direct (01923 226456)
Type of disc: Single layer, single-sided
No of chapters: 16
Film format(s)/length: 4:3 regular / 108 mins
Audio format: Dolby Surround
Director: Harold Becker
Starring: Al Pacino, Ellen Barkin, John Goodman
Year made: 1989
Extras: Production notes; text biographies of the cast and crew; theatrical trailer; English, German, Polish, Hungarian and Czech soundtracks; multilingual subtitles.

Okay, imagine you're in charge of Universal Studios' first foray into the UK DVD market, and you need to pick some titles to get things going. So you choose a 10-year-old thriller that's available on VHS at around a fiver, don't bother to put it in widescreen, choose a Surround only soundtrack and add sparse extras. And then you slap a £20 price tag on it. Frankly, it doesn't matter what you think of the film *Sea of Love* – a mildly effective, sex-charged mur-der thriller if you're interested – you'd be mad to hand over £20 for this. It's a great shame, as at the very least this offered a chance to get a decently priced back cat-alogue title onto the market. As it stands, whilst the picture and sound provided are of passable quality, there is simply little incentive to buy the disc. Pacino, and DVD fans, deserve better.

FINAL VERDICT

Picture ☆☆ Sound ☆☆ Entertainment ☆☆☆
Extras ☆ Value ☆
OVERALL ☆☆

SECRETS & LIES

Price: £9.99
Supplied by: Cinema Club
Type of disc: Dual layer, single-sided
No of chapters: 21
Film format(s)/length: 16:9 widescreen / 136 mins
Audio format: Dolby Surround
Director: Mike Leigh
Starring: Timothy Spall, Brenda Blethyn, Phyllis Logan
Year made: 1996
Extras: Scene access; theatrical trailer; subtitles for the hearing impaired in English.

When both her foster parents pass on, Hortense (Marianne Jean-Baptiste – brilliant) seeks out her birth mother Cynthia (Blethyn) only to discover her mum is white and a tragic hand-wringer living with her shrill daughter (Claire Rushbrook) in a shabby terrace. Meanwhile, Cynthia's cuddly brother Maurice (Spall) and nest-building wife (Logan) wear brave faces for the world despite their own painful circumstances. Everything inexorably winds to a climax at the family barbecue when the truth, finally, wins out. Written and directed by Mike Leigh, *Secrets & Lies* is an A-grade family drama, energised by sharp writing and an impeccable cast. It's not often that the Oscars reward the right people, but they did when Brenda Blethyn won Best Actress for this film in 1997. Her café scene in particular is unforgettable. In one take, Brenda goes through the emotional wringer, from confusion, to shame, to pride and then acceptance – it's a real acting masterclass. The film is crisply rendered on a welcome 16:9 widescreen transfer; however, the sound is trapped by (admittedly above average) Dolby Surround. While a commentary by Leigh or cast interviews would have made the disc as wonderful as the film, a trailer is all we get. For the price, though, the disc is a true bargain buy. There are no grand gestures or snap moments that exist to propel the narrative like in US melodramas. *Secrets & Lies* instead beautifully unravels over its lengthy running time to create a warm, funny and accurate picture of family life. Go buy.

FINAL VERDICT
Picture ☆☆☆☆ Sound ☆☆☆
Entertainment ☆☆☆☆☆ Extras ☆ Value ☆☆☆☆☆
OVERALL ☆☆☆☆

SET IT OFF

Price: £15.99
Supplied by: DVD World (01705 796662)
Type of disc: Single layer, single-sided
No of chapters: 12
Film format(s)/length: 2.35:1 letterbox / 117 mins
Audio format: Dolby Surround
Director: F Gary Gray
Starring: Jada Pinkett, Queen Latifah, Vivica A Fox
Year made: 1996
Extras: Scene access; 'Making of' featurette (4 mins approx); Andrea Martin and Queen Latifah: 'Set it Off' music video; English subtitles.

The idea of *Boyz 'n the Hood* meets *Thelma and Louise* promises far more than the contrived and derivative *Set it Off* eventually delivers. Four South Central LA girls each have their reasons to start a bank robbing spree – one penniless babe has to bring her son to work and is declared an unfit mother, another is sacked for just knowing a bank robber, yadda yadda. But will crime pay? Director F Gary Gray (*The Negotiator*) makes it all look good, and the DVD transfer does justice to his efforts (one gripe – shame the disc isn't anamorphic). The sound is perfectly serviceable, but lacks the extra 5.1 oomph that action movies cry out for these days. In keeping with Entertainment in Video's unique talent for underselling itself, the disc contains a featurette not listed on the box, and a music video. Though nothing is actually bad, nothing excels either. Ho hum.

FINAL VERDICT
Picture ☆☆☆ Sound ☆☆☆ Entertainment ☆☆☆
Extras ☆☆☆ Value ☆☆☆
OVERALL ☆☆☆

SE7EN

Price: £17.99
Supplied by: DVD World (01705 796662)
Type of disc: Dual layer, single-sided
No of chapters: 8
Film format(s)/length: 16:9 widescreen / 122 mins
Audio format: Dolby Surround
Director: David Fincher
Starring: Brad Pitt, Morgan Freeman, Kevin Spacey
Year made: 1995
Extras: Scene access; behind the scenes *Making of Se7en* documentary; cinema trailer; subtitles in English.

Two New York detectives called to a weird death find themselves on the trail of a ritualistic serial killer who's using the Seven Deadly Sins as a basis for his murder. Each kill graphically portrays one of the sins and events take a strange turn when the killer walks into a police station and apparently gives himself up… Pin-up Brad Pitt and Academy Award-nominee Morgan Freeman are perfectly cast as the eager young rookie and experienced old-timer in this darkly sinister movie from director David Fincher. A thriller which is more than a little disturbing thanks to a bizarre plot and some first-rate cinematography, Se7en is definitely not one for the squeamish. Nevertheless, it is a must-see movie that's perfect for watching in the dark with a partner – just don't expect a happy ending! In terms of extras, Se7en is fairly generous. Although it doesn't offer any extra languages, the disc comes complete with the cinema trailer and a rather cool featurette on the making of the movie. The only annoying thing about it is the number of chapters – 8. Although presumably an attempt to give the film a symbolic 7 chapters (the final one being the credits) this really only serves to make finding specific scenes a pain. Still, it's a good package nonetheless.

FINAL VERDICT

Picture ☆☆☆☆ Sound ☆☆☆☆
Entertainment ☆☆☆☆ Extras ☆☆☆☆ Value ☆☆☆☆
OVERALL ☆☆☆☆

THE SEVENTH SIGN

Price: £19.99
Supplied by: Columbia TriStar Home Video
Type of disc: Dual layer, single-sided
No of chapters: 28
Film format(s)/length: 1.85:1 anamorphic / 93 mins
Audio format: Dolby Digital 5.1
Director: Carl Schultz
Starring: Demi Moore, Michael Biehn, Peter Friedman
Year made: 1988
Extras: Scene access; filmographies; trailers for About Last Night and Mortal Thoughts; soundtrack in English, French, German, Italian and Spanish; subtitles in 20 languages.

It's a crazy, mixed up world – we all know that – but when the the rivers turn to blood, the sea dies, the desert is shrouded in ice and the moon becomes crimson you know there's something serious going down on the planet! The Seventh Sign tells the story of the Apocalypse – the Earth is destined to come to an end because God has run out of human souls. That is, unless the pregnant Abby Quinn (Moore) can do something to change it, but first she has to work out that the man staying in her spare room is Jesus Christ himself. If you enjoyed the film Stigmata, with its religious motif and priests running about trying to help save damsels in distress, then you'll also take to The Seventh Sign. Although obviously a 12-year-old film (the haircuts and music give it away), the storyline still packs a punch, and you'll be gripped to the end. As generally happens with second-division titles,

there are no real special touches for DVD besides two completely unconnected trailers and a bunch of language options – but then we're coming to expect that in this country, aren't we? Even the widescreen looks slightly dodgy, but you soon learn to forget that when the action in the film starts to hot up. Whether you like your horror films with a religious flavour, or you're just a fan of Moore, The Seventh Sign will deliver what you're looking for.

FINAL VERDICT

Picture ☆☆☆ Sound ☆☆☆ Entertainment ☆☆☆☆
Extras ☆ Value ☆☆☆
OVERALL ☆☆☆

THE 7TH VOYAGE OF SINBAD

Price: £19.99
Supplied by: Columbia TriStar Home Video
Type of disc: Dual layer, single-sided
No of chapters: 28
Film format(s)/length: 1.85:1 widescreen enhanced / 84 mins
Audio format: Mono
Director: Nathan Juran
Starring: Kerwin Mathews, Kathryn Grant, Torin Thatcher
Year made: 1958
Extras: The Harryhausen Chronicles documentary; The 7th Voyage of Sinbad featurette; Jason and the Argonauts featurette; This is Dynamation SFX featurette; filmographies; theatrical trailer; Jason and the Argonauts and Golden Voyage of Sinbad trailers; soundtrack in English, German, Italian, Spanish and French; subtitles in 20 languages.

The Fifties and Sixties bore witness to some of the greatest and most spectacular mythical adventures of old. Gargantuan giants and other creatures filled wondrous magic-wielding stories that entranced global audiences. Forget your Luke Skywalkers, your superheroes and do away with Bond, for the greatest hero of all was Sinbad – he sailed the 7 seas, you know! Igniting the era of Dynamation (think Phantom Menace special effects of the Fifties) The 7th Voyage of Sinbad created a new generation of movie-goers. Following the exploits of Captain Sinbad (Mathews), the story takes our manly hero to the Cyclops-infested island of Colossus in search of a cure for his betrothed, Princess Parisa (Grant), who has been shrunk to the size of a figurine. Shot in 1958, the film was the first to utilise Harryhausen's widely-applauded special effects technique known as Dynamation. Amazingly, the initial outing for Sinbad has stood the harsh test of time rather well and with the marvels of the digital age, it has actually never looked better. Yes, quite incredibly, Columbia TriStar has made the widescreen presentation anamorphically enhanced – will the wonders ever cease? Well not yet, because the selection of special features for this heroic DVD are impressive too. There are over 80 minutes of footage included, with featurettes and documentaries on the man who made it all possible, Ray Harryhausen, and his miraculous methods. The master of Fifties SFX also talks about *Jason and the Argonauts* – another classic that utilised Dynamation. Among the vast array of extras lie numerous theatrical trailers and filmographies. Although the soundtrack is only mixed in mono (c'mon, what else did you expect?) Columbia TriStar has included an incredible number of subtitled languages, plus 5 spoken ones. *The 7th Voyage of Sinbad* is a cinematic classic recreated wonderfully on DVD and thoroughly deserves the special treatment and recognition it has received.

FINAL VERDICT

Picture ☆☆☆ Sound ☆☆☆
Entertainment ☆☆☆☆☆ Extras ☆☆☆☆☆
Value ☆☆☆☆
OVERALL ☆☆☆☆

SEVEN YEARS IN TIBET

Price: £19.99
Supplied by: Entertainment in Video
Type of disc: Dual layer, single-sided
No of chapters: 12
Film format(s)/length: 2.35:1 widescreen / 129 mins
Audio format: Dolby Surround
Director: Jean-Jacques Annaud
Starring: Brad Pitt, David Thewlis, B D Wong
Year made: 1997
Extras: Scene access; informative but short 15-minute 'Making of' documentary; two different trailers; English subtitles.

This film received mixed reviews during its cinematic release, due to its apparently favourable portrayal of Brad Pitt's character, Austrian mountaineer Heinrich Harrer. To be honest, for the majority of the movie Harrer comes across as a self-absorbed git, and if that's being favourable... The picture quality and sound are top notch, particularly during the breathtaking mountaineering scenes – you get vertigo and short of breath as if you were there with Pitt himself. *Seven Years* has an interesting documentary concerned with the making of the movie, although it is unfortunately a little on the short side, coming in at approximately 15 minutes. However, there are some fasci-

nating nuggets of information on offer within, including the revelation that Pitt and Thewlis had to learn how to mountain climb in preparation for their roles. So, that should at least temporarily appease those of us who think Hollywood stars have an altogether easy life for the inflated salaries that they earn. As well as the documentary, there are two *Seven Years* theatrical trailers for cinema buffs to compare and contrast. The first runs just over a minute, and is commonly known as a teaser trailer – ie, there's no dialogue as such from the film, just a moody voiceover and some rousing music. The second trailer is longer and gives more of an idea what the film's story is actually about – both of the latter are ideal fodder for completists.

FINAL VERDICT

Picture ☆☆☆☆ Sound ☆☆☆☆
Entertainment ☆☆☆☆ Extras ☆☆☆ Value ☆☆☆
OVERALL ☆☆☆

SHAKESPEARE IN LOVE

Price: £19.99
Supplied by: Columbia TriStar Home Video
Type of disc: Dual layer, single-sided
No of chapters: 31
Film format(s)/length: 2.35: 1 letterbox / 119 mins
Audio format: Dolby Digital 5.1
Director: John Madden
Starring: Gwyneth Paltrow, Joseph Fiennes, Geoffrey Rush
Year made: 1998
Extras: Scene access; *Shakespeare in Love and on Film* 'Making of' documentary; director's commentary; cast and crew commentary; deleted scenes (including alternate ending); mini-documentary on costume design; trailer; 21 American TV adverts; English and German soundtracks; multilingual subtitles.

What's a young playwright to do when he's struck with writer's block? There are all sorts of possibilities, but finding the right one is of vital importance in this case, because the playwright in question is William Shakespeare (Fiennes), and the play he's having trouble with is currently called *Romeo and Ethel the Pirate's Daughter*. Luckily for English Literature teachers worldwide, Shakey's muse turns out to be Viola (Paltrow), a woman with a love of theatre – and its leading author – whose greatest wish is to be an actor. Two problems stand in the way: first is the fact that women aren't allowed to act on stage, and second is Viola's imminent marriage to the obnoxious Lord Wessex (Colin Firth). How William and Viola get around these difficulties, while transforming his unfinished comedy into the definitive tragedy, makes a funny and charming romantic comedy. Whether it's worth all the Oscars it was showered with is debatable (Dame Judi Dench received a gong for a role that probably amounts to less screen time than she gets as 'M' in the recent Bond films) but it's still clever, entertaining and visually rich – the Best Costume Oscar was certainly deserved. Best of all, *Shakespeare in Love* is positively brimming with DVD-worthy extras. As well as having not one, but two commentary tracks – the first from director Madden, the second featuring the writers, producers, designers and cast – it's also got a pair of 'Making of' documentaries, a trailer, 21 different American TV ads for the film and several deleted scenes, including one of a completely new ending. Coupled with top-notch picture and sound, the weight of additional material makes *Shakespeare in Love* one of the best-value Region 2 DVDs around. Obviously not every film will have, or even warrant, this amount of extras available for inclusion on a DVD, but it's discs like this that point the way forward for the format. Freeze-frame aficionados will also be delighted to learn that Gwyneth gets her kit off. Meaning that *Shakespeare in Love* has comedy, romance, action, satire, tons of extras and nudity – there's something for absolutely everybody!

FINAL VERDICT

Picture ☆☆☆☆ Sound ☆☆☆ Entertainment ☆☆☆☆
Extras ☆☆☆☆☆ Value ☆☆☆☆
OVERALL ☆☆☆☆

THE SHAWSHANK REDEMPTION

Price: £19.99
Supplied by: DVD World (01705 796662)
Type of disc: Single layer, double-sided
No of chapters: 18
Film format(s)/length: 4:3, 16:9 widescreen / 137 mins
Audio format: Dolby Surround 2.0
Director: Frank Darabont
Starring: Tim Robbins, Morgan Freeman
Year made: 1994
Extras: Interactive menus; scene index; sub-plots; theatrical trailer; interviews with cast; biographies.

I'll come straight to the point. You must watch this movie. Despite the title, the notion of a feelgood prison movie, the lack of Drew Barrymore (bummer) and the absence of action, *The Shawshank Redemption* is a killer movie. Hey, if Morgan Freeman's awesomely understated performance doesn't bring a tear to your eye, you're not human. As for the DVD though – bad news first. If you're after a reference title to

show off, this ain't it. Firstly, you've got sound that's only in Dolby Surround 2.0. Then there's the picture which, whilst not too bad, suffers from white specks and the occasional dodgy background. Fortunately neither matters that much. The film is more the quietly effective type than straight-in-your-face, and this is reflected in the audio. Thomas Newman's musical score is superb and 5 minutes into the film you'll be oblivious to the picture problems anyway. And extras? You'll find interviews with the key players (more promoting the film than offering insights), and an array of on-screen biographies. Then there's the sub-plots option, allowing you to skip directly to scenes that deal with specific segments of the story, although these add more of a novelty element. Oh, and there's an excellent animated menu, even if it gives away a little too much plot. We'd have killed for a director's commentary track, although that aside this is a strong all-round Region 2 DVD.

FINAL VERDICT

Picture ☆☆☆ Sound ☆☆☆ Entertainment ☆☆☆☆☆
Extras ☆☆☆ Value ☆☆☆☆
OVERALL ☆☆☆☆

SHE'S ALL THAT

Price: £19.99
Supplied by: VCI
Type of disc: Dual layer, single-sided
No of chapters: 17
Film format(s)/length: 6:9 widescreen enhanced / 92 mins
Audio format: Dolby Digital 5.1
Director: Robert Iscove
Starring: Freddie Prinze Jr, Rachael Leigh Cook, Matthew Lillard
Year made: 1999
Extras: Scene access; theatrical trailer; cast/director interviews; *Shooting the Movie* footage; yearbook photo library; subtitles for the hearing impaired in English.

At last, a film the vocal moral majority can really get their teeth into. Forget *Trainspotting*, this is a film that really could inspire you to start taking heroin. A lobotomised version of *Saved by the Bell*, this is another of those teen-angst 'comedies' where the hardest choice facing our hero Zack (Prinze Jr) is 'Dartmouth college or Harvard?'. A supposed twist in the tale is that ugly-as-sin unpopular chick Laney (Leigh Cook) actually turns out to be a real stunner hiding behind glasses. Zack bets he can transform her from inadequate social leper to prom queen, but how will he cope when he falls in love with her? Ultimately, you just won't care. The promised *Shooting the Movie* documentary is about 6 minutes of behind-the-scenes camcorder action, the trailer is suitably retarded, and the interviews are blink-and-you'll-miss-them slices of actors being insincere. Which is no more than this unhappy scrap of Pygmalionite deserves. A film for which the word 'risible' was invented. And the words 'banal', 'tedious' and 'hackneyed'. Don't buy it.

FINAL VERDICT

Picture ☆☆☆ Sound ☆☆☆ Entertainment ☆

Extras ☆☆ Value ☆

OVERALL ☆

SHOWGIRLS

Price: £19.99

Supplied by: Pathé Distribution

Type of disc: Dual layer, single-sided

No of chapters: 20

Film format(s)/length: 16:9 widescreen enhanced / 126 mins

Audio format: Dolby Digital 5.1

Director: Paul Verhoeven

Starring: Gina Gershon, Kyle MacLachlan, Elizabeth Berkley

Year made: 1995

Extras: Scene access; teaser theatrical trailer; standard theatrical trailer; production featurette; subtitles for the hearing impaired in English.

The movie that all but terminated Joe Eszterhas's screenwriting career has very little to its credit, so it's hard finding much to praise about a film where one character accurately dismisses the lead as getting her lines off T-shirts. Previously Eszterhas's success had been built on reviving hackneyed thriller plots, such as *Jagged Edge*, from a cynical perspective and with increasingly modern sexualities. *Showgirls* however has no such plot, although he does find room to insert a few unnecessary twists in an attempt to liven up a dull script. Unfortunately the lead character Nomi (Elizabeth Berkley) is so laughably stereotypical that it's impossible to feel empathy. The strait-laced *Saved by the Bell* star takes her role further than any mainstream actress to date in pursuit of her character, but is ultimately as arousing as a blind date with all 4 Teletubbies! There just isn't anything going on as the plot constantly mistakes cleverness for insight, with practically every line of dialogue anticipating some later plot twist. As a DVD, *Showgirls* benefits from a slick menu screen with layered scenes from the film, two trailers and a brief 5-minute featurette where cast and crew contribute snippets of dialogue. Any chance of director Verhoeven (*Total Recall*, *Starship Troopers*) providing an audio commentary is

about zero – then again what could he say, "Sorry" for two hours! Picture is excellent, and the David A Stewart soundtrack comes across well, it's just a shame there's nothing happening elsewhere on the disc.

FINAL VERDICT

Picture ☆☆☆☆☆ Sound ☆☆☆☆

Entertainment ☆☆ Extras ☆☆ Value ☆☆

OVERALL ☆☆

THE SIEGE

Price: £19.99

Supplied by: 20th Century Fox Home Video

Type of disc: Dual layer, single-sided

No of chapters: 30

Film format(s)/length: 2.35:1 widescreen / 111 mins

Audio format: Dolby Digital 5.1

Director: Edward Zwick

Starring: Denzel Washington, Annette Bening, Bruce Willis

Year made: 1998

Extras: Scene access; 'Making of' featurette; original theatrical trailer; subtitles in 11 languages.

Since the end of the Cold War, America has needed a new 'bad guy'. Middle Eastern terrorists have fitted the bill nicely, especially after the World Trade Centre bombing. While terrorist actions have been far more prevalent in Hollywood movies than real life, the next time one occurs, the US could do worse than let Denzel Washington go in and sort the whole thing out. Fantasy though it is, *The Siege* is nothing but first class Hollywood entertainment. Washington plays Anthony 'Hub' Hubbard, the FBI agent called in to investigate a bus that was blown up by…blue paint. Once a second bus, along with a group of pensioners, is blasted for real, the FBI know that they have a terrorist situation on their hands. Add to the plot General Devereaux (Willis), who has kidnapped a terrorist leader and has some extreme plans for New York's Middle Eastern population, and a mysterious CIA agent (Bening) who knows a little too much about the Palestinian community, and the whole thing becomes extremely compelling. The holier-than-thou attitude to the American Constitution is a little cheesy, and it's a shame that more of the place didn't get blown up before the finale. But this is a genuine movie to munch popcorn to, and is gripping enough, especially Washington's performance, to keep you firmly on the edge of your armchair until the very end. The disc isn't buzzing with extras, but the featurette is enough to sustain interest for its 20-plus minutes, at least once.

FINAL VERDICT

Picture ☆☆☆☆☆ Sound ☆☆☆☆☆

Entertainment ☆☆☆☆ Extras ☆☆☆ Value ☆☆☆

OVERALL ☆☆☆☆

SILVERADO

Price: £19.99

Supplied by: Columbia TriStar Home Video

Type of disc: Dual layer, single-sided

No of chapters: 28

Film format(s)/length: 2.35:1 widescreen enhanced / 128 mins

Audio format: Dolby Digital 5.1

Director: Laurence Kasdan

Starring: Kevin Kline, Scott Glenn, Kevin Costner

Year made: 1985

Extras: Theatrical trailer; cast info; *The Making of Silverado* documentary; Digital 5.1 soundtrack in English and French; Surround soundtrack in German, Spanish and Italian; multilingual subtitles; subtitles for the hearing impaired in English and Italian.

Digitally remastered for DVD with the bonus of a never-before-seen documentary on the film's making, this star-studded Western is a tempting package. Director Lawrence Kasdan made his name with *Body Heat* and *The Big Chill*, but *Silverado* is a lighter, more quirky cinematic adventure. DVD presentation is functional – no animated menu screens here – but picture quality is beyond criticism, while the Oscar winning soundtrack is perfectly recreated with Dolby Digital 5.1. Kasdan wrote *Silverado*'s script with his brother Mark, and their love of their genre is evident in a rich mix of familiar tropes. The central conflict is, of course, between evil ranchers and peaceful settlers with some grizzled cowboys coming to the latter's rescue. However, this lengthy two hour movie takes plenty of time getting to its final shootout. There are jail breaks, cattle stampedes and even a bar girl. Undoubtedly the most fun contribution comes from Kevin Costner. His hyper-active gunfighter, literally climbing the walls of his prison cell, lights up the screen whenever he appears. The principal lead, Kevin Kline, makes a memorable entrance in his long johns, after which he becomes slightly lost in an ensemble piece with a little too much plot. In fact, after watching the movie, another 40 minutes of *Silverado* is somewhat daunting, but the 'Making of' documentary is a real bargain. Unlike modern day films with their trailer-featurettes, this is the real thing, and watching Scott Glenn square off with his gunfighting tutor is good fun. There's plenty of interesting information to be gleaned, not least outtakes from a minor romance plot which was axed to bring down the film's length. The resulting film is a classy, if not classic Western, perfectly presented for DVD.

FINAL VERDICT

Picture ☆☆☆☆ Sound ☆☆☆☆

Entertainment ☆☆☆☆ Extras ☆☆☆☆ Value ☆☆☆☆

OVERALL ☆☆☆☆

SIMPATICO

Price: £17.99

Supplied by: Alliance Atlantis

Type of disc: Dual layer, single-sided

No of chapters: 16

Film format(s)/length: 1.85:1 letterbox / 102 mins

Audio format: Dolby Surround

Director: Matthew Warchus

Starring: Nick Nolte, Jeff Bridges, Sharon Stone

Year made: 1999

Extras: Scene access; behind the scenes featurette; theatrical trailer.

They say youth is wasted on the young. The characters in *Simpatico* would probably agree with you, for in this effort from first-timer Warchus, the sins of their teens have haunted this trio for more than 20 years. A great principal cast, Oscar nominees all, wrestle admirably with the piece but Sam Shepherd's play fails to catch fire on the big screen. When Bridges, as Carter, at first playing a confident self-made man as he did in *The Muse*, answers the desperate call of his old friend Vinnie (Nolte), he abandons the sale of his prize race horse Simpatico to help the recluse. Vinnie double-crosses Carter and flies to Kentucky, heart of the horse racing industry, with a shoebox containing the pornographic photographs they took of a racing commissioner (Albert Finney). Flashbacks explain just what event is weighing heavy on everyone's consciences. Their blackmail fixed the race and made Carter rich, Vinnie somehow destitute and Vinnie's former sweetheart and Carter's present wife Rose (Stone) miserable. The 6-minute featurette is slightly better than anticipated with most of the cast taking the opportunity to talk intelligently about their characters. Stone is particularly impressed with Kimberly Williams' performance of Rose as a teen, considering what the script asks her to do. What emerges before Petula Clark belts out 'Games People Play' as the credits roll is a mediocre thriller that convulses *this* way towards a MacGuffin then jerks *that* way to another undeveloped twist. Disappointing, both movie and disc.

FINAL VERDICT

Picture ☆☆☆ Sound ☆☆ Entertainment ☆☆☆

Extras ☆☆ Value ☆☆☆

OVERALL ☆☆☆

SINGLE WHITE FEMALE

Price: £19.99

Supplied by: DVD World (01705 796662)

Type of disc: Single layer, single-sided

No of chapters: 35

Film format(s)/length: 1.85:1 widescreen / 103 mins

Director: Barbet Schroeder

Starring: Bridget Fonda, Jennifer Jason Leigh, Steven Weber

Year made: 1992

Extras: Scene access; theatrical trailer; multiple languages/subtitles.

Allie Jones (Fonda) kicks out unfaithful lover Sam (Weber) and decides to rent a room in her cavernous New York apartment. Along comes obviously unhinged Hedra Carlson (Jason Leigh). Though fortunately for the plot development, Jones completely fails to notice that her new roomie is intent on stealing her looks, lifestyle and eventually her life. Schroeder's rudimentary thriller is stylish and at times brutal, but offers little that is new, and you soon get tired of Jason Leigh's constant whining and temper tantrums. The ending is signposted and it's one of those films where many of the events seem contrived to fill in the gaps between Hedra's next nutty act. A brief sexual harassment sub-plot is instantly dismissed with the line "All men are pigs," and Jones' fashion business seems to have been included purely to add a hi-tech computer angle which admittedly looks good in the trailer. Schroeder tries his best, but he's no Hitchcock. However, the picture quality is excellent and the DVD benefits from being in widescreen and makes the most of all those grand interior shots which are otherwise lost on a regular TV. As a DVD showpiece *SWF* fails dismally, with very little in the way of bonus material. The theatrical trailer is a lesson in how to make an unremarkable film look exciting, and you can always try to learn Hebrew using the subtitles, but that's about it. The menus look great, but it's a shame there's nothing worth using them for.

FINAL VERDICT

Picture ☆☆☆☆ Sound ☆☆☆☆

Entertainment ☆☆☆ Extras ☆☆ Value ☆☆

OVERALL ☆☆☆

SIX DAYS SEVEN NIGHTS

Price: £15.99

Supplied by: Buena Vista

Type of disc: Single layer, single sided

No of chapters: 23

Film format(s)/length: 16:9 widescreen/ 129 mins

Audio format: Dolby Digital 5.1

Director: Ivan Reitman

Starring: Harrison Ford, Anne Heche, David Schwimmer

Year made: 1998

Extras: Scene selection.

Stranded together on a deserted island, gruff, rough-hewn cargo pilot Quinn Harris (Ford) and New York magazine editor Robin Munroe (Heche) are forced down in a storm. Forced to confront their already-uneasy relationship, they must work together if they're to get off the island. After a series of box office hits, Harrison Ford's good fortune has finally taken a nosedive. Under the direction of Ivan Reitman you would have expected more, but somehow Ford's acting has taken a step back, allowing Heche to steal the limelight. The addition of *Friends'* David Schwimmer – playing Heche's fiancé, Frank Martin – certainly doesn't help. By far the best aspect of this DVD is the fantastic picture and sound quality – it's right up there with *Armageddon*. The scenic backdrops and beautiful tropical forests amplify the incredible sharpness and colour this title offers. Unfortunately that's where the fun stops. Apart from the standard DVD scene access there are no special features. The picture quality maybe exemplary, but the opposite is true of the extras.

FINAL VERDICT

Picture ☆☆☆☆☆ Sound ☆☆☆☆

Entertainment ☆☆ Extras ☆ Value ☆☆

OVERALL ☆☆

THE SIXTH SENSE

Price: £19.99

Supplied by: Buena Vista Home Entertainment

Type of disc: Dual layer, single-sided

No of chapters: 19

Film format(s)/length: 1.85:1 widescreen enhanced / 105 mins

Audio format: Dolby Digital 5.1

Director: M Night Shyamalan

Starring: Bruce Willis, Haley Joel Osment, Toni Collette

Year made: 1999

Extras: Scene access; *Storyboard to Film* featurette; *The Cast* featurette; *Music and Sound Design* featurette; *Reaching the Audience* featurette; *Rules and Clues* featurette; 4 deleted scenes; interview with director M Night Shyamalan; publicity material (including trailer); multilingual subtitles; subtitles for the hearing impaired in English.

The unexpected hit of last year, *The Sixth Sense* proved two things: a film doesn't need millions of dollars of CGI effects to be scary (take note, Jan De Bont) and that Bruce Willis doesn't need to wear a filthy vest and brandish a Beretta to have a success on his hands. Willis plays child psychologist Malcolm Crowe, a happily married man whose celebrations on receiving a prestigious award are rudely interrupted by a disturbed former patient with a gun. One shooting, one suicide, one marriage on the rocks and several months later, the despondent Crowe sees a chance to make up for his 'failure' by helping young Cole Sear (Osment), a boy with apparent psychological problems that turn out to be something far more chilling. As Cole tells Crowe, "I see dead people…" See dead people he does – they're all over the place, unaware that they've actually shuffled off this mortal coil yet still compelled to harrass Cole (the only person aware of their existence) in the hope that he can somehow help them. At first Crowe is sceptical, suspecting that the injuries Cole keeps receiving have somewhat more earthly causes, but before long the psychologist starts to believe Cole's story and becomes all the more determined to help him. Of course, Hollywood films with child stars often err on the side of sentiment (a surefire danger sign is any film featuring both a child and Robin Williams) but *The Sixth Sense* sticks firmly to its guns, delivering the kind of Kubrickian horror that sends chills shuddering down the spine as the ghosts manifest themselves to a terrified Cole. The Oscar-nominated Osment is a real standout performer, but Willis acquits himself well as the self-confident professional who finds his life spiralling out of control around him. Of course, it's the twist in the tail for which *The Sixth Sense* became noted. Without giving anything away, the clues are all there, but if you're watching the film for the first time even knowing that *something* is coming still can't quite prepare you for exactly *what*. You might think it's big and clever to say you spotted it a mile off, but admit it – you didn't. The Region 2 disc isn't quite as well-stocked with features as the US DVD, but it still has an impressive collection. Although there's no director's commentary (the US version was similarly lacking) there is a selection of interviews with Shyamalan and others involved in the production that are insightful, even if they do hurriedly gloss over some of the plot holes. The section where the composer claims that watching the film was a 'religious experience' for many is a bit much, though! The deleted scenes (including a longer, sadder ending) are also interesting to watch. A great chiller, ideal for rewatching to spot all the hints you missed the first time, and a decent DVD package. *The Sixth Sense* also

arrives remarkably soon after its cinema release, a trend that can only be welcomed.

FINAL VERDICT

Picture ☆☆☆☆ Sound ☆☆☆☆

Entertainment ☆☆☆☆☆ Extras ☆☆☆☆

Value ☆☆☆☆

OVERALL ☆☆☆☆

SLEEPERS

Price: £17.99
Supplied by: PolyGram
Type of disc: Single layer, double-sided
No of chapters: 23
Film format(s)/length: 4:3, 16:9 widescreen / 148mins
Director: Barry Levinson
Starring: Kevin Bacon, Brad Pitt, Jason Patric
Year made: 1996
Extras: Scene access; English/German languages.

A gang of tearaway boys steal a hot dog vendor's cart, but things get out of hand – the cart runs down a subway stairwell, killing a passer-by. The kids are charged and sentenced to a grim upstate reform school, where they are tortured and repeatedly raped by twisted guards led by an uncompromising Kevin Bacon. Then 14 years later, the boys are back and set on cold revenge. An emotionally charged revenge tale subtly mixing Catholic guilt with hefty side-swipes at prison reform, *Sleepers* leaves you exhausted but confused. At times distressing, the movie ultimately lacks cohesion, with plot threads spiralling out of control. No fault of the actors, though, the brat-pack performances of Bacon, Jason Patric and Brad Pitt – ably supported by Robert De Niro and Dustin Hoffman – are intense and captivating. It's fair to say, though, that the story is pea-soup thick, and the closing court scenes demand repeated viewing to aid plot penetration. While the DVD is bereft of any special features beyond two picture formats and scene access, being able to return easily to any of the plot twists is something of a relief.

FINAL VERDICT

Picture ☆☆☆☆ Sound ☆☆☆☆

Entertainment ☆☆☆☆ Extras ☆☆ Value ☆☆☆

OVERALL ☆☆☆

SLEEPLESS IN SEATTLE

Price: £13.99
Supplied by: Columbia TriStar
Type of disc: Single layer, single-sided
No of chapters: 20
Film format(s)/length: 16:9 widescreen enhanced / 101 mins

Director: Nora Ephron
Starring: Tom Hanks, Meg Ryan, Bill Pullman
Year made: 1993
Extras: Scene access; multilingual subtitles.

Down-to-earth newspaper reporter Annie Reed (Ryan) is driving to her fiancé's (Pullman) house for the Christmas holidays when she hears a late night phone-in on the radio that will change her life forever. Urged onto the phone by his eager son Jonah, widowed Sam Baldwin (Hanks) pours out his heart to the on-air agony aunt and so touched is Reed by his words that she is determined to meet him. So begins a touching long distance love story between two lonely people separated by thousands of miles (Reed's in Baltimore, Baldwin's in Seattle) and the story switches between the two until their meeting at the climax of the film. Meg Ryan's performance will warm even the cold-hearted to her character – after all, she's had enough practice playing the same role in nearly all of her films. The picture quality of this DVD is matched by its crisp, sharp colours and excellent sound quality. Unfortunately, as far as the extras go, they are not so easy to warm too. The only so called features that appear on this DVD are the standard scene selections and multiple choices of language subtitles. This is a problem becoming all too common in many Region 2 titles, compared to their Region 1 counterparts. However, the sheer quality of picture and sound will justify this purchase to many old and new romantics out there and it's still a great example of a fairy-tale comedy.

FINAL VERDICT

Picture ☆☆☆☆ Sound ☆☆☆☆ Entertainment ☆☆☆
Extras ☆ Value ☆☆☆
OVERALL ☆☆☆

Sleepy Hollow

Price: £19.99
Supplied by: Pathé Distribution Ltd
Type of disc: Dual layer, single-sided
No of chapters: 18
Film format(s)/length: 1.85:1 anamorphic / 105 mins
Audio format: Dolby Digital 5.1
Director: Tim Burton
Starring: Johnny Depp, Christina Ricci, Michael Gough
Year made: 1999
Extras: Scene access; *Behind the Legend* featurette (30 mins); *Reflections on Sleepy Hollow* featurette (12 mins); two trailers; audio commentary by director Tim Burton; cast and crew biographies; photo gallery; subtitles for the hearing impaired in English.

One of America's few pre-movie folk tales, Washington Irving's *The Legend of Sleepy Hollow* has been put onto film several times, most notably by Disney. Now, Tim Burton gives his own interpretation of the tale of the Headless Horseman. As retooled by the screenwriter of *Se7en*, hero Ichabod Crane (Depp) is no longer an ugly schoolteacher, but is instead a cross between Edward Scissorhands and Agent Scully, an ahead-of-his-time New York police constable keen to advance justice through deduction and science rather than good old-fashioned beatings. To get him out of their hair, Crane's bosses (including Christopher Lee in an amusing cameo) despatch him to the small town of Sleepy Hollow, where the locals have been losing their heads – quite literally. Something that comes as a surprise when viewing *Sleepy Hollow* for the first time is the amount of gore, especially considering it's only a '15' certificate. The film lives up to its tag-line promise that 'Heads Will Roll' - at times it's like some grisly bowling alley – and Burton misses no opportunity to have the prissy Crane sprayed, squirted or splattered with blood. However, despite all the carnage, Burton's off-the-wall humour can't help but poke through, even when a good fright would be more appropriate. And there's something inherently amusing about bouncing heads anyway. The end result is a curious halfway house – it's not funny enough to make you laugh, and it's not scary enough to make you jump. Like all of Burton's big-budget outings (the first two *Batman* movies, *Mars Attacks!*), *Sleepy Hollow* is all style and no content. There's so little spark between Depp and Ricci it's as if they were filmed on different days and put into the same scene with computer graphics. What meagre plot there is dances about at random, sometimes making you wonder if you've accidentally hit the chapter skip, and it's a relief whenever the Horseman appears because this means you at least get some quality beheadings to break up the story. One technical disappointment is that *Sleepy Hollow* was set to be the UK's first DVD movie with a DTS soundtrack. Pathé has now decided that it doesn't want to be the first to put its head over the parapet, presumably in case it gets lopped off. It's a shame, because DTS really needs a kickstart by somebody releasing a high-profile title in that format. As a result, *Sleepy Hollow* is presented in standard Dolby Digital 5.1. Not that that's any kind of criticism, because *Sleepy Hollow*'s audio is very strong indeed. Danny Elfman's music is used to the fullest. The picture is equally strong – *Sleepy Hollow* is filmed in colours so desaturated it's almost monochrome (only the blood stands out from the greys). This gives everything an unreal sharpness which comes across perfectly on the DVD, letting you see fantastic amounts of detail. Say what you will about Burton, but his films always give you plenty to look at. Burton's commentary is actually a major letdown. You'd expect him to have some fascinating things to say about moviemaking, but what you get are long periods of silence punctuated by remarks about wigs. Judging from the featurettes Burton had a ball making the film – too bad this isn't reflected in his narration. The other extras are quite decent – not awesome, but certainly worth investigation. In what should always be the norm, the R2 *Sleepy Hollow* gets as many extras as its US counterpart. Warner, Disney, are you taking notes? *Sleepy Hollow* is ultimately a top-quality DVD housing a beautiful-looking but empty movie – it fully lives up to the second half of its title.

FINAL VERDICT

Picture ☆☆☆☆☆ Sound ☆☆☆☆
Entertainment ☆☆☆ Extras ☆☆☆☆ Value ☆☆☆
OVERALL ☆☆☆

SNAKE EYES

Price: £15.99
Supplied by: Buena Vista
Type of disc: Dual layer, single-sided
No of chapters: 12
Film format(s)/length: 2.35:1 widescreen / 94 mins
Audio format: Dolby Digital 5.1
Director: Brian De Palma
Starring: Nicolas Cage, Gary Sinise, John Heard
Year made: 1998
Extras: English subtitles; closed captioned only.

Viewers used to (and expecting) Nicolas Cage's typically OTT action performances of late (*The Rock, Con Air, Face/Off*) won't be very happy to find more talk than gunfire in Brian De Palma's *Snake Eyes*. The fact is, Sinise and even the highly charged and charismatic Cage both play second fiddle to an incredibly gripping plot. The story is told with all the tension and intrigue required to make a 'thriller' truly thrilling and the direction is so frenetic that you stay glued even though the whole movie revolves around a single assassination. Flashback sequences piece together the event for you from three different perspectives (Cage's, Sinise's and damsel in distress Carla Gugino's versions) so if *Reservoir Dogs* gave you a headache and *The Usual Suspects* kept you awake at nights, *Snake Eyes* will send you to the loony bin. A very clever movie then. Pity Warner Home Video isn't as smart. The only mentionable 'feature' which the company has provided on the DVD is English subti-

tles. But they don't even use the extensive capabilities of DVD subtitling – they're of the closed caption kind, the sort you need a closed caption box to read, just like you get on scummy old VHS cassettes. Please. However, if *Snake Eyes* is your bag, don't despair. Somebody did a beautiful mastering job with this pressing of the movie, giving the picture a pixel-sharp sheen you can only get with DVD. Colours are very intense, bringing to life the distinctive stylised palette carefully created for the movie by De Palma and director of photography, Stephen H Burum.

FINAL VERDICT

Picture ☆☆☆☆☆ Sound ☆☆☆☆
Entertainment ☆☆☆☆ Extras ☆ Value ☆☆
OVERALL ☆☆

SNAKE IN THE EAGLE'S SHADOW

Price: £19.99
Supplied by: Hong Kong Legends
Type of disc: Single layer, single-sided
No of chapters: 25
Film format(s)/length: 1.77:1 anamorphic and 1.85:1 letterbox / 94 mins
Audio format: Dolby Surround
Director: Yuen Woo Ping
Starring: Jackie Chan, Yuen Siu Tien, Hwang Jang Lee
Year made: 1978
Extras: Scene access; photo library; Jackie Chan biography; Jackie Chan filmography; theatrical trailer; UK music promo; interview with producer Ng See Yuen; Hwang Jang Lee movie clips and biography; soundtracks in English and Cantonese; English subtitles.

Yet another classic Jackie Chan film out on DVD, and while it might not be up to the standards of *Drunken Master* this has some superbly choreographed fight scenes and some top extras to go with them. A quick glance through the filmography on this disc will show you that Jackie Chan has appeared in more than the odd one or two martial arts films. As any decent fan will tell you, some of his earlier stuff is in fact his best work and this film is no exception. As far as extras go this DVD isn't half bad; unfortunately on the other hand it isn't half good either! As well as the usual yet moderately interesting biography and filmography you get a photo gallery, comical music promo and an interview with producer Ng See Yuen. The supposedly 'rare' interview is an amateur affair made with a home video camera. Amusingly, the cameraman is obviously really excited to see the man, because he can't keep the camera still! The music promo is simply bizarre as it consists of some rather odd dance music set to clips from the fight scenes of the film. The best of the extras on this disc though remain hidden away inside the biography, not even mentioned on the back of the box. Seek and you shall find loads of clips of Hwang Jang Lee in action! The film on its own makes this DVD worth buying but some above-average special features gives it an extra edge.

FINAL VERDICT

Picture ☆☆ Sound ☆☆ Entertainment ☆☆☆☆☆
Extras ☆☆☆ Value ☆☆☆
OVERALL ☆☆☆☆

SNEAKERS

Price: £19.99
Supplied by: Columbia TriStar Home Video
Type of disc: Dual layer, single-sided
No of chapters: 16
Film format(s)/length: 1.85:1 anamorphic / 120 mins
Audio format: Dolby Surround
Director: Phil Alden Robinson
Starring: Robert Redford, Dan Aykroyd, Sidney Poitier
Year made: 1992
Extras: Scene access; theatrical trailer; production notes; cast and film-maker's notes; subtitles in 11 languages; audio soundtrack in English, French, German, Italian and Spanish.

If you haven't seen *Sneakers* by now, you've missed a quality feelgood movie which manages to set the perfect balance between comedy and drama. Soaked in high-tech gadgetry, this film is about a group of criminal type characters who set up a company which 'tests' the security levels of banks and other such high profile places. Of course, testing the security involves breaking into the place, but what better way to make a living than to be paid to do it? Everything goes a little pear-shaped when they're asked to recover a box for the government, a box which can apparently break any code known to man, and our heroes become the hunted. Extremely funny in places, this is the perfect heist movie; it's such a shame that the disc has been robbed of any extras. With the movie you get some production notes, the obligatory trailer and cast and film-maker notes. Interesting as all this is, it's not exactly going to keep you coming back for another read again and again! The cast and film-maker's section does contain a pretty comprehensive filmography for each of the main characters, but the production notes aren't really that informative. In fact the most interesting thing from the notes is that the town square set from *Back to the Future* was used as a college campus in *Sneakers*! This is a highly entertaining film, but it's a shame the

extras don't do it the justice it deserves.

FINAL VERDICT

Picture ☆☆☆ Sound ☆☆☆ Entertainment ☆☆☆☆
Extras ☆☆ Value ☆☆☆
OVERALL ☆☆☆

SOLDIER

Price: £15.99
Supplied by: Buena Vista Home Entertainment
Type of disc: Single layer, single-sided
No of chapters: 31
Film format(s)/length: 1.33:1 regular, 2.35:1 widescreen / 95 mins
Audio format: Dolby Digital 5.1
Director: Paul Anderson
Starring: Kurt Russell, Jason Scott Lee, Jason Isaacs
Year made: 1998
Extras: Scene access; English and Arabic subtitles.

The future is a world where soldiers are genetically conditioned to become merciless, obedient warriors without emotion. Now a new wave of bio-engineered combatants has been created to replace veterans such as Sergeant Todd (Russell). Tossed on the scrap heap of a distant world, an obsolete Todd finds refuge with a group of planetary outcasts and proceeds to adjust to his new surroundings. But when the soldiers that replaced him threaten this peaceful colony, he must fight one more war. Not many big-budget US films go straight to video (or in this case DVD) unless it flopped big time at the box office and *Soldier* is no exception. Although the script leaves much to be desired, the picture and sound quality once again prove why DVD is the entertainment format of the future. However, the continuing oceanic crossover from the US to UK once again begs the question: 'Why is the UK public getting screwed with extras?' The R1 version clearly has more features and an extra 4 minutes of running time. *Soldier* may have a 6 month retail head-start on VHS and feature both regular and widescreen formats, but there is little to prevent this DVD ending up on the scrap heap itself.

FINAL VERDICT

Picture ☆☆☆☆ Sound ☆☆☆☆ Entertainment ☆
Extras ☆ Value ☆
OVERALL ☆

SOMMERSBY

Price: £15.99
Supplied by: Warner Brothers
Type of disc: Single layer, single-sided
No of chapters: 30
Film format(s)/length: 2.35:1 widescreen / 109 mins

Audio format: Dolby Digital
Director: Jon Amiel
Starring: Richard Gere, Jodie Foster, James Earl Jones
Year made: 1993
Extras: Scene access; subtitles in 10 languages; soundtrack in English, Italian and French; subtitles for the hearing impaired in English and Italian.

Husbands, eh? Can't live with them, can't kill them...but what about if a whole new one walks into your life passing himself off as your man? It's a long shot we know, but that's the pitch here. The classic French film *Le Retour de Martin Guerre* has been translated into English and brought forward a few hundred years to the American Civil War. Jack Sommersby (Gere) returns from battle to his village and wife Laurel (Foster), but will anybody realise that 'Jack' is not the same man? His little eccentricities could easily be explained by the ravages of war, and who could find him suspicious when he knows so many details about all of the townsfolk? A few have their doubts, Laurel included – but he is a better man than her husband ever was and is making a success out of their farm, so she's willing to take him into her life and also her bed. In line with the time frame and change of country there are many references to the Civil war, slavery and the Ku Klux Klan. These elements move the viewer towards a heart-wrenching finale, when the love between Jack and Laurel faces a final test as he is convicted of the murder of the man he is impersonating. Co-written by Daniel Vigne, who also was involved in the original's script, *Sommersby* still tells an emotional tale of deceit which turns into love, and for once Hollywood has not taken away too much of the original sheen. The film is now over 7 years old which has not helped the DVD; it suffers very badly from poor lighting effects and the darkness is such you'll be reaching for the brightness button. There is also evidence of blocking on background scenery and the sky. However, the absence of Dolby Digital 5.1 is not noticeable as there are no massive sound effects that would warrant it. With no extras – apart from language options – on the disc either, this DVD is only an essential purchase if your VHS collection has been sold in a car-boot sale.

FINAL VERDICT
Picture ☆☆ Sound ☆☆☆ Entertainment ☆☆☆☆
Extras ☆ Value ☆☆
OVERALL ☆☆☆

SOUTH PARK:
BIGGER, LONGER & UNCUT

Price: £19.99
Supplied by: Warner Home Video
Type of disc: Single layer, double-sided
No of chapters: 26
Film format(s)/length: 1.85:1 widescreen enhanced, 4:3 regular / 78 mins
Audio format: Dolby Digital 5.1
Director: Trey Parker
Starring the voices of: Trey Parker, Matt Stone, Isaac Hayes
Year made: 1999
Extras: Scene access; trailer; three teaser trailers; 'What Would Brian Boitano Do?' music video; soundtrack in English; multilingual subtitles; subtitles for the hearing impaired in English.

Sweet! For one of the few times in history, a Region 2 DVD gets more extras than its American counterpart. Not many more, admittedly, but it makes a pleasant change. *South Park: Bigger, Longer & Uncut* is the big-screen debut of television's loveably foul-mouthed quartet of cutouts, Stan, Kyle, Cartman and Kenny. It's also that rare thing today, a musical, but the lyrics are about as far as you can get from the insipid dronings of most Disney films. Deliberately intended to earn the ire of conservatives everywhere (the right-wing Childcare Action Project described it as being "Straight from the smoking pits of Hell," and "Extraordinarily vulgar, vile and repugnant," which must have pleased creators Parker and Stone no end), *South Park: Bigger, Longer & Uncut* is actually a sharp-edged satire on censorship. Freed from the bleepings imposed upon them on television, the South Park gang go to see the obscenity-filled Terrance and Phillip movie, *Asses of Fire*, emerging from the cinema swearing like their Canadian heroes. Naturally their parents object strongly to this, but rather than take responsibility for their children or demand changes in the ludicrous American rating system that allows kids to see movies clearly meant for adults, they decide there's only one action that can be taken – to eliminate foul language and smut, Canada must be destroyed! Although the TV series has faltered lately, losing viewers at an alarming rate and suffering from some weak scripts, *Bigger, Longer & Uncut* is possibly Parker and Stone's finest hour. Ignore all the naysayers insisting it's just a regular episode padded out with the addition of too many songs – the extra length, fatter budget and lack of television restrictions means that the film is, in its own twisted way, almost an epic. The animation of the characters is still as limited as on TV (the screenplay even makes a joke of this) but the expanded camera movements, special effects and CGI sequences (Kenny suffers a descent into Hell that's easily as disturbing as anything you'd find in movies that *try* to be scary – it's certainly better than *Spawn!*), particularly during the musical numbers, turn it into a *Yellow Submarine* for the new Millennium. Tasteful *Bigger, Longer & Uncut* isn't – there's one truly near-the-knuckle gag about abortion that leaves even the movie itself speechless for a moment – but funny it certainly is. As well as all the usual fart, vomit and exploding body parts jokes, everything from self-help books, chat shows, the Baldwin brothers and the location of a certain hard-to-find female body part are used to inspire some genuinely hilarious comedy. There's also a lot of freeze-frame humour to be found (look at the soldiers' name tags or the duty list in the hospital) as an extra bonus for sharp-eyed DVD owners. The disc contains excellent quality anamorphic and 4:3 versions of the film, and a trio of short 'teasers' in addition to the theatrical trailer. The main addition over the R1 release is the 'What Would Brian Boitano Do?' music video. In all *South Park: Bigger, Longer & Uncut* ranks with the very best the TV show has produced, and is even a decent DVD in its own right. In short, it kicks ass!

FINAL VERDICT

Picture ☆☆☆☆ Sound ☆☆☆☆

Entertainment ☆☆☆☆☆ Extras ☆☆☆ Value ☆☆☆

OVERALL ☆☆☆☆

SPAWN

Price: £19.99
Supplied by: Entertainment in Video
Type of disc: Single layer, double-sided
No of chapters: 24
Film format(s)/length: 1.85:1 widescreen / 95 mins
Audio format: Dolby Surround
Director: Mark Dippé
Starring: John Leguizamo, Michael Jai White, Martin Sheen
Year made: 1997
Extras: Scene access; director and creator audio commentary; 20 minute 'Making of' documentary; 15 minute creator interview; movie trailer; music video.

Another big-budget Hollywood film inspired by a cult comic book that's laden with special effects – *Spawn* is seldom out of the US top 5 each month. It follows in the footsteps of the *Batman* quartet, *The Mask* and *The Crow*, but unfortunately lacks the finesse and general entertainment value of its contemporaries. The basic plot has special operative Al Simmons forced to make a deal with the Devil himself after he is betrayed and burned to death by his boss, Jason Wynn (Martin Sheen). Returning to Earth years after his death, Simmons discovers that you should never trust the Devil, as he is now the Spawn: a supernatural warrior with bizarre superpowers destined to lead Hell's armies come Armageddon. Simmons has to wrestle with his desire for revenge whilst also trying to do the 'right thing'. The likes of the evil Clown, played with immense relish and from under a mountain of latex by John Leguizamo, attempt to turn Simmons into a force for evil, while the wise mentor-figure of Cogliostro, played by Nicol Williamson, shows Simmons how to use the Spawn powers for the greater good. So, the premise is acceptable, it is just a shame that the film is dogged by an appalling script and ropey acting from all and sundry…the special effects are nice, though! As a DVD, *Spawn* is up there with the very best – which is ironic, considering the all-round crapness of the lead feature. Of course you get the movie's trailer (an addition that has now become a DVD standard), but you also get such delights as a 20-minute 'Making of' documentary: a 15-minute interview with *Spawn's* creator Todd McFarlane; an audio commentary of the film from the director and McFarlane; and a music video, 'Trip Like I Do', by US industrial rock outfit Filter. This is taken from the movie's soundtrack (although it would have been nice to also have included the more popular video of the Marilyn Manson song from the same movie…but maybe that's us just being greedy). *Spawn* really is a naff movie of the highest order, however, it is also an excellent quality DVD package. Although this does not alter the quality of the film itself, if you are a fan of the movie, the DVD offers tremendous value for money.

FINAL VERDICT

Picture ☆☆☆☆ Sound ☆☆☆☆

Entertainment ☆☆ Extras ☆☆☆☆☆ Value ☆☆☆☆

OVERALL ☆☆☆☆

THE SPECIALIST

Price: £15.99
Supplied by: DVD World (01705 796662)
Type of disc: Single layer, single-sided,
No of chapters: 34
Film format(s)/length: 16:9 widescreen / 105 mins
Director: Luis Llosa
Starring: Sylvester Stallone, Sharon Stone, James Woods
Year made: 1994
Extras: Production notes; instant scene access; theatrical trailer; reel recommendations.

The pairing of two of Hollywood's biggest stars in a high concept action movie might have seemed a sure-fire box-office winner, but Stallone and Stone never really sizzle – there's no chemistry between them, not even in the intimate shower scene. The plot is a standard B-movie revenge thriller pumped up with big-budget SFX and those stars. Stallone is an ex-CIA explosives expert hired by Stone – 'a beauty with a fatal past' – to incinerate the mobsters who killed her parents. Cue lots of explosions which serve as a perfect demonstration of DVD's ability to handle red without the fuzziness so characteristic of VHS. Picture quality is generally very good; Sly's every bulging muscle is vividly depicted right down to every last vein, while Sharon Stone wears short skirts to maximum effect. While the movie is trashy good fun, the presentation is up to Warner Bros' usual standard. There's the theatrical trailer, which is brief and not particularly good, while the production notes break down into: cast & crew biographies, special effects and Miami shooting details. These all sound quite interesting, but as UK DVD fans have come to expect consist merely of text and static pictures. You also get Reel Recommendations which recommends other (Warner Bros) films in the same genre as well as other movies by the film's stars – sadly no clips though. Overall then, *The Specialist* is the main reason for buying this DVD and the level of encoding is such that watching the VHS version afterwards would be unbearable. Both the film and the disc itself are a bit cold though.

FINAL VERDICT

Picture ☆☆☆☆☆ Sound ☆☆☆☆
Entertainment ☆☆☆ Extras ☆☆ Value ☆☆☆
OVERALL ☆☆☆

SPECIES

Price: £19.99
Supplied by: DVD World (01705 796662)
Type of disc: Single layer, single-sided
No of chapters: 36
Film format(s)/length: 16:9 widescreen / 104 mins
Director: Roger Donaldson
Starring: Natasha Henstridge, Ben Kingsley, Michael Madsen
Year made: 1995
Extras: Scene access; 3 language options; subtitles; original trailer; teaser for *Species II*.

For a relatively low budget sci-fi movie, *Species* certainly attracted some big name stars, notably Ben Kingsley as scientist Xavier Fitch and Michael Madsen who plays the ruthless, but let's face it, cool

government assassin Press Lennox. *Species* doesn't mess around and within 5 minutes a young girl, Sil (Henstridge in her debut) smashes out of a top secret military installation demonstrating superhuman strength and escapes. It turns out that Sil is a human/alien hybrid created from blueprints sent back by intelligent life in outer space. What the specialist team drafted in to hunt and kill Sil doesn't know is that she is desperate to mate with another human and create a race of her own on Earth. No man is safe. From this point on, *Species* becomes a rudimentary chase movie, with the hunters (Madsen, Kingsley, a biologist, entomologist and an empath) only managing to find the mutilated bodies Sil leaves behind, and all the while Sil is sizing up brainless macho men in her pursuit of the ultimate shag. It's easy to see why *Species* was so popular and spawned a sequel. Henstridge is stunning as the frequently in-the-buff perfect woman and although the acting is generally functional rather than inspiring (Madsen mumbles his way through as usual), the top drawer special effects, especially during the explicit metamorphosis sequences (H R Giger take a bow) are worth the wait. As far as the DVD itself goes, MGM bizarrely includes an 8-page book with the disc (duh – isn't that what DVDs were invented for?) and the list of extras isn't very inspiring either, with just scene access, a theatrical trailer and a plug for *Species II*. Great picture quality, but the DVD certainly offers nothing special.

FINAL VERDICT

Picture ☆☆☆☆ Sound ☆☆☆ Entertainment ☆☆☆
Extras ☆☆ Value ☆☆
OVERALL ☆☆☆

SPECIES II

Price: £19.99
Supplied by: DVD Net (020 8890 2520)
Type of disc: Single layer, single-sided
No of chapters: 36
Film format(s)/length: 1.85:1 widescreen / 89 mins
Director: Peter Medak
Starring: Natasha Henstridge, Michael Madsen, Justin Lazard
Year made: 1995
Extras: Scene access; animated menu screen; director's commentary; forthcoming features; subtitles; US theatrical trailer; 4 unseen/deleted scenes.

At last a truly inspirational Region 2 disc; something to be proud of and show exactly what DVD can do. The front end menus of *Species II* are really quite superb. Crackling sound effects accompany a high resolution display which features an animated morphing effect of Eve transforming into her alien form on a continual loop. The good news continues with an impressive array of extras such as high quality forthcoming releases, subtitles and a special features menu revealing not only audio commentary by the director, but also the US theatrical trailer and 4 pieces of unseen footage – try getting that lot on VHS! *Species II* has essentially the same plot as the first film, except that instead of a female alien running round bonking her way through dumb humans, it's a male – space shuttle commander Patrick Ross (newcomer Lazard). After being infected by alien DNA during a mission to Mars, Ross begins impregnating as many women as possible to create a small army of alien/human hybrids. Hot on the trail once again is super-cool assassin Press Lennox (Madsen) and sultry scientist Laura Barker (Marg Helgenberger) but this time they have an ally – alien clone Eve (Henstridge – in wearing clothes shocker) who through a psychic link can see what Ross is doing and hopefully lead the hunters to him before it's too late. Despite Medak's best intentions *Species II* is a vacuous experience and never once manages to match the atmosphere of the original. The special effects are laughable in places, with plainly obvious computer graphics for many of the alien scenes, rubber tentacles covered in HP Sauce for the rest. There are some truly nasty shots, particularly the first birthing sequence which has the poor girl's stomach split open like a ripe piñata, but by the time the special effects-charged finale arrives it's laughter not nausea that triumphs. Medak's commentary, though dreary, contains some genuinely fascinating facts about making the film on a shoestring budget (they had to borrow the spacecraft set from another studio, for example) and it's very interesting to hear him talk about the scenes which he is still not happy with and how the studio executives kept asking him to change certain parts of the film. If you compare this commentary to *Contact* you can tell instantly why it is much better to have more than one person talking so that they can play off each other. Jodie Foster is as subdued as Medak, but at least you can tune in to motormouth Robert Zemeckis at any time. The commentary in *Species II* badly needs another perspective. *Species II* is a stunning and well presented DVD, it's a pity the film's about as entertaining as being force-fed razor blades!

FINAL VERDICT

Picture ☆☆☆☆☆ Sound ☆☆☆ Entertainment ☆☆
Extras ☆☆☆☆☆ Value ☆☆☆

OVERALL ☆☆☆

SPEED

Price: £19.99
Supplied by: 20th Century Fox
Type of disc: Dual layer, single-sided
No of chapters: 24
Film format(s)/length: 16:9 widescreen enhanced / 111 mins
Audio format: Dolby Digital 5.1
Director: Jan De Bont
Starring: Keanu Reeves, Sandra Bullock, Dennis Hopper
Year made: 1994
Extras: Scene access; trailer; subtitles in 10 languages; subtitles for the hearing impaired in English.

This is one of those movies with a plot that can be summed up in one sentence – 'there's a bomb on a bus that will explode if it slows down'. With a story like that you know you're in for a thrilling ride, and *Speed* doesn't disappoint. Reeves is heroic cop Jack Traven, Hopper is one-thumbed mad bomber Howard Payne and Sandra Bullock is unwilling bus driver Annie inadvertently caught up in Payne's surreptitious plot. If he doesn't get his money, the bus goes bang and it's up to Jack to get on the bus and make sure that it stays above 50mph, no matter what. De Bont was a cinematographer before *Speed* and controlled the camera on the likes of *Die Hard* and *Basic Instinct*. Thanks to this experience, he's put together one of the best action films of the Nineties. Too bad every film he's made since has got steadily worse, but at least he managed one genuine action classic. On the downside, Fox appears to be modelling itself on Disney as far as the UK DVD market is concerned – charge a premium price and skimp on extras. *Speed* gets a trailer, and that's all. Considering that the 1995 video release featured the trailer, a 'Making of' documentary and even a Billy Idol music video, this is very poor.

FINAL VERDICT

Picture ☆☆☆☆ Sound ☆☆☆☆
Entertainment ☆☆☆☆☆ Extras ☆☆ Value ☆☆☆
OVERALL ☆☆☆

SPHERE (SPECIAL EDITION)

Price: £15.99
Supplied by: DVD World (01705 796662)
Type of disc: Dual layer, double-sided
No of chapters: 43
Film format(s)/length: 16:9 widescreen / 129 mins
Director: Barry Levinson

Starring: Dustin Hoffman, Sharon Stone, Samuel L Jackson

Year made: 1998

Extras: Audio commentary; behind-the-scenes documentary; 3 TV spots; history of science fiction.

If you looked at *Sphere*'s curriculum vitae you'd have no hesitation in offering it a job. After all, its vast array of qualifications include Barry Levinson, Dustin Hoffman, Sharon Stone and Samuel L Jackson. Its enclosed photo looks great, too – overall, of great potential. But on its first day in the office you'd find that it had glossed over its obvious failings and is as suited to the job as Clinton is to managing a cigar shop staffed by fat, weeping women. Another example of Crichton's book-by-numbers, *Sphere* is part science fiction, part deep sea diving – yet all pretty tedious, despite the effort that has gone into disguising the fact. Sure, the special effects are competent enough – on DVD they look even better – and the cast puts in a universally mature performance that lends the plot credence. But it lacks Levinson's usual passion and drive, giving the impression that everyone involved put in the minimum effort required and no more. Quite why it fails to hold the attention is perhaps more mysterious than the film's alien life forms, but the wall behind my telly has been analysed no less than 5 times during parts of *Sphere*'s oft-tedious two hours. Hit 'Menu', though, and the disc contains a number of interesting diversions – almost as though Warner knew its audience would be left feeling unsatisfied by the time the credits rolled and the kettle put on. The commentary offers Hoffman and Jackson a chance to demonstrate the clear passion that they had for the project and contains a host of interesting anecdotes. The behind the scenes documentary on the film's effects proves interesting, if smacking of American sycophancy. And the TV spots – trailers to you and I – demonstrate the art of making two hours of tedium look appealing over 30 seconds. A lesson to us all, I fear.

FINAL VERDICT

Picture ☆☆☆☆ Sound ☆☆☆☆ Entertainment ☆☆
Extras ☆☆☆☆ Value ☆☆☆
OVERALL ☆☆☆

SPICE WORLD: THE MOVIE

Price: £17.99

Supplied by: PolyGram

Type of disc: Single layer, double-sided

No of chapters: 17

Film format(s)/length: 4:3/16:9 widescreen / 89 mins

Director: Bob Spiers

Starring: Spice Girls, Richard E Grant, Roger Moore

Year made: 1997

Extras: Biographies of The Spice Girls, the cast and the film crew; a 20 minute documentary on the making of the film; German soundtrack.

As if you hadn't had enough of the Spice Girls through their meteoric rise to fame in the mid-Nineties, now you can enjoy the pinnacle of their career again in glorious DVD quality. *Spice World: The Movie* is a comical look at the life of the 5-girl band, fictitious but undoubtedly closer to the truth than they would ever admit. In addition to the girls themselves, the movie has cameo appearances by a host of big names. Elton John gets accosted in a hallway, Bob Geldolf has his hair done by Scary Spice and Jennifer Saunders hams it up in a celebrity party. Then there are the leading roles of Spice Girls manager, played by Richard E Grant, and the chief, played by Roger Moore in true Bond-villain style. In addition to the crystal clear pictures and sound, there are biographies of the girls, the cast and the crew, a German audio track and a complete 'Making-of' documentary lasting 20 minutes. What more could a Spice Girls' fan want?

FINAL VERDICT

Picture ☆☆☆☆ Sound ☆☆☆☆ Entertainment ☆☆☆
Extras ☆☆ Value ☆☆
OVERALL ☆☆☆

SPLASH

Price: £15.99

Supplied by: Warner Home Video

Type of disc: Single layer, single-sided

No of chapters: 20

Film format(s)/length: 1.85:1 widescreen / 105 mins

Audio format: Dolby Surround

Director: Hon Howard

Starring: Tom Hanks, Daryl Hannah, John Candy

Year made: 1984

Extras: Dolby Surround English, French and Italian soundtracks; English & English close captioned subtitles.

There are absolutely no extra features for this DVD. The grainy film stock leads to some minor artifacting, and, worst of all, there are occasional snatches of Eighties pop…but this is still a very worthwhile release. Ron Howard's literal 'fish out of water' romantic comedy was a sizeable hit upon its release and it still retains much of its charm today. After her impressive psycho-gymnast in *Blade Runner*, Hannah turns in an equally otherworldly performance as the mermaid who comes to New York in pursuit of Hanks. Her athletic build and imposing good looks make her an intriguing romantic lead, while Hanks is an instantly likeable and rather gawky co-star. The charisma of the two leads provides the movie's real appeal – they're good people to be with. Although the film touches lightly on the problems of real romance, its main dramatic engine is a clunky and predictable 'mad scientist' riff with Eugene Levy to capture Hannah. Nevertheless, *Splash* is quirky and agreeable, never more so than when John Candy is on screen. As Hanks' brother he steals almost every scene he's in. When a DVD budget range turns up, *Splash* will be an attractive purchase.

FINAL VERDICT

Picture ☆☆☆ Sound ☆☆☆ Entertainment ☆☆☆☆

Extras ☆ Value ☆☆☆

OVERALL ☆☆☆

STARGATE

Price: £19.99
Supplied by: DVDplus (www.dvdplus.co.uk)
Type of disc: Dual layer, single-sided
No of chapters: 18
Film format(s)/length: 16:9 widescreen / 116 mins
Audio format: Dolby Digital 5.1
Director: Roland Emmerich
Starring: Kurt Russell, James Spader, Jaye Davidson
Year made: 1994
Extras: Scene access; soundtrack in 5 languages; subtitles in 9 languages.

A mysterious artefact thousands of years old holds the secret to another world. Now one man has unlocked that secret and mankind is about to reach for the stars – just not in a way that anybody imagined. *Stargate* is an intelligent science-fiction movie with loads of special effects that are still impressive now, 5 years after the film was made. Kurt Russell's discipline-obsessed soldier and James Spader's quirky archaeologist play off well against one another and the finale is explosive, to say the least. Unfortunately the DVD offers very little in the way of extras – not even the original cinema trailer – and so once again, Region 2 owners are offered nothing that justifies buying this format over video. In addition, this is one of those annoying discs which shows a number of lengthy logo animations that can't be skipped before it brings up the menu. By all means, take a trip through the Stargate, just don't expect to receive anything special from this DVD version.

FINAL VERDICT

Picture ☆☆☆☆☆ Sound ☆☆☆☆☆

Entertainment ☆☆☆☆ Extras ☆☆ Value ☆☆

OVERALL ☆☆☆

STARSHIP TROOPERS

Price: £15.99
Supplied by: DVD Premier Direct (01923) 226492
Type of disc: Single layer, double-sided (flipper)
No of chapters: 9 (Side A), 8 (Side B)
Film format(s)/length: 1.85:1 widescreen / 130 mins
Audio format: Dolby Digital 5.1
Director: Paul Verhoeven
Starring: Casper Van Dien, Dina Meyer, Denise Richards
Year made: 1997
Extras: Scene access (not as many scenes as the US version strangely); multilingual subtitles.

We begged, we pleaded, and right up until the UK release date we hoped that Buena Vista would see sense and use the delay time to remaster the disc, but alas, to no avail. *Starship Troopers* is a Region 2 flipper disc. Two sides; film split crudely at a crucial moment – just like an old LP. What BV has done is take the most DVD-worthy film of the Nineties and butchered the European version. Has *Armageddon* taught them nothing? That's not to say it isn't still a fantastic film and that the fact that it's on DVD in the first place is a reason to rejoice, but you only have to go on the Internet (or in my case look at my DVD collection) to see that the American version of *Starship Troopers* is a hundred times better than this sorry effort. The Region 1 disc is also double sided, but in this case side B features all the extras. You know, the ones we don't seem eligible for. More about that later. Picture-wise *Starship Troopers* is a breathtaking spectacle and one that constantly assaults the senses. Quality throughout is top notch and Verhoeven's eye for vivid colour (okay, mainly blood red and intestine purple) makes this film perfect for DVD. The special effects are incredible too, and thanks to the image clarity of DVD, you can see every slashing Bug limb during the *Zulu*-style fort attack on planet P (counter reading 30.00 Side 2), and in particular the sublime blue streaks of Bug plasma that scythe through the Navy fleet are never more defined than here. Verhoeven is a master when it comes to science fiction. *RoboCop*, *Total Recall* and now *Starship Troopers* – every one a visual showpiece packed with black humour and devastating scenes of violence. Never afraid to show severed limbs and gushing blood, Verhoeven's world's are savage, but always moralistic – you know who the good and bad guys are, and in many cases the line is drawn with a high velocity bullet. Many people didn't 'get' *Starship Troopers* when it was released in America, but once you realise that the entire film is a parody of fascism, adopting the same xenophobic stance of many American propaganda films of WWII and the Korean war, it becomes supremely enjoyable. Who cares that almost all the performances are as wooden as Ikea garden furniture, and that Denise Richards does not stop grinning inanely for the full 130 minutes – it's all part of the act, and the occasional computer displays pointing to "Do you want to know more?" merely serve to remind you that this is a spectator sport. You don't need to care about the characters, just sit back and enjoy the multi-million dollar ride. Or at least you would enjoy it, if halfway through it didn't stop abruptly and the obligatory little Mickey Mouse hand appears; urging you to get up off the sofa and change sides. And then you'll probably realise that the disc appears a little empty for a new and important UK release. Shouldn't there be some juicy extras on side B. Er, no actually, because they've been removed from the American version. And it costs more. And it's appeared 6 months later. Oh dear. Gone is the audio commentary, original screen tests of Van Dien and Richards, the behind the scenes footage, mini-documentary, deleted scenes and theatrical trailer. What do we have instead? A disappointing DVD of a film that deserves much better. If ever there was a case for us all getting chipped machines and buying American. This is it.

FINAL VERDICT

Picture ☆☆☆☆ Sound ☆☆☆☆
Entertainment ☆☆☆☆ Extras ☆ Value ☆☆
OVERALL ☆☆

Star Trek: First Contact

Price: £19.99
Supplied by: Paramount
Type of disc: Dual layer, single-sided
No of chapters: 31
Film format(s)/length: 2.35:1 anamorphic / 106 mins
Audio format: Dolby Digital 5.1
Director: Jonathan Frakes
Starring: Patrick Stewart, Jonathan Frakes, Brent Spiner
Year made: 1997
Extras: Scene access; two trailers; subtitles in 9 languages; subtitles for the hearing impaired in English.

The Borg are back! If you think that's some kind of tennis reference, then clearly you've been avoiding pop culture for the last decade. The Borg, *Star Trek*-stylee, are a race of malevolent cyborgs from outermost space, whose *modus operandi* is to forcibly 'assimilate' other beings into their collective con-

sciousness and turn them into more Borg. Kind of like Microsoft. *Star Trek: First Contact*, the second big screen outing for the *Next Generation* crew, pits Picard (Stewart) and co against their most deadly enemies once again. The Borg have devised a foolproof plan to assimilate Earth – they'll go back into time to the 21st Century, just after the Third World War (a date to avoid in your diary), to conqüer the planet at its weakest and prevent the founding of the Federation. Unluckily for the Borg, Picard is no fool, taking the *Enterprise* back through time in pursuit. Unluckily for Picard, the Borg manage to board the *Enterprise* and start assimilating his ship, one deck and one crew member at a time... *First Contact*, in the *Star Trek* scale of things, ends up as a close second to *Star Trek II: The Wrath of Khan* out of the 9 films. It's got action and thrills (ably handled by debut director Frakes), excellent effects, a hissable villain in the form of Alice Krige's slimily seductive Borg Queen, plus all the moments of character and comedy that *Trek* fans expect from their heroes. Like the other even-numbered films in the series, it's accessible enough for even non-fans to enjoy, while the actual moment of 'first contact', right at the end of the film, should be enough to make long-term fans go all misty-eyed. The presentation of the movie on disc is superb, better even than the top-quality laserdisc. The vivid electric blues and garish greens inside the Borgified sections of the *Enterprise* really stand out, and the amount of detail encoded into the picture lets you pick out the minuscule form of Picard well into the mile-long opening pullback. Sound is equally well served, with Jerry Goldsmith's brassy score coming across particularly well, along with the ominous rumblings and weird mechanical rattles of Borg machinery and the powerful launch roar of the *Enterprise*'s spanking new quantum torpedoes. What is a disappointment, and one that looks set to continue through the whole of the *Star Trek* series on DVD, is the lack of extras. A pair of trailers doesn't really cut it, particularly for *Star Trek* fans, who are noted for their intense, even fanatical interest in the processes of making the movies and the TV shows. Why aren't there special effects featurettes? Production art and storyboards? Behind the scenes material on the alien make-up? Commentaries from the stars? As Fox found to its delight with *Alien*, adding this sort of stuff to a film that fans will already own on video is a guaranteed way to get them to buy it again on a new format. By omitting them, Paramount runs the risk that while the hardcore fan base will buy the movies anyway, those who don't stick melted Mars bars on their foreheads might balk at spending £20 on a film with little added value over the one they own on VHS. For *First Contact*, one of the best of the series, this probably won't be much of a problem, but it will be a different story when lamers like *Generations* or *The Final Frontier* roll around.

FINAL VERDICT

Picture ☆☆☆☆☆ Sound ☆☆☆☆☆

Entertainment ☆☆☆☆☆ Extras ☆☆ Value ☆☆☆

OVERALL ☆☆☆☆

STAR TREK: INSURRECTION

Price: £19.99

Supplied by: Paramount Home Entertainment

Type of disc: Dual layer, single-sided

No of chapters: 24

Film format(s)/length: 2.35:1 anamorphic / 103 mins

Audio format: Dolby Digital 5.1

Director: Jonathan Frakes

Starring: Jonathon Frakes, Patrick Stewart, Brent Spiner

Year made: 1998

Extras: Scene access; 'Making of' featurette; 2 trailers; soundtrack in English, German and Hungarian; subtitles in 6 languages; subtitles for the hearing impaired in English and German.

Paramount's curious decision to release the *Star Trek* movies in reverse order means that the UK first gets to see one of the infamous odd-numbered ones. Oh, they may have dropped the Roman numerals when the *Next Generation* crew took over, but they can't fool us. *Insurrection* is by no means the worst of the films, but after the Borg-battling action of *First Contact* this hippy-dippy, New Age tale of a planet that acts as a Fountain of Youth came as something of an anti-climax. Even the title is a misnomer, but presumably *Star Trek: Insubordination* wouldn't have sounded as good. Picard and crew discover a plot between a Starfleet admiral and a race of nasty, plastic surgery-addicted aliens led by F Murray Abraham to forcibly relocate the planet's occupants, so they can harvest its rejuvenating properties for themselves. Our heroes naturally won't stand for this, so phaser fights, starship battles and annoying bouts of technobabble ensue. Though the film does have its entertaining moments, some of the juvenile humour is laid on a bit thick, supporting characters like Geordi, Troi and Dr Crusher don't get a lot to do, and Worf (at the time a regular on *Deep Space Nine*) appears on the *Enterprise* on a pretext that would struggle to qualify as 'feeble'. The main failing, though, is that the villains are completely forgettable; simply casting a

respected actor like Abraham doesn't make his stretchy-faced thugs a memorable threat. On the plus side, the DVD is at least well presented, director Frakes' mountainous backdrops opening up the story and getting away from the usual metal corridors and polystyrene caverns. The picture is always vibrant and sharp (maybe a bit *too* sharp, as it makes it obvious that the *Enterprise* is now CGI rather than a model), and the surround sound is used well, particularly in the scenes where the crew is attacked by flying robot drones. The extras package is rather weak, however, consisting of only a pair of trailers and short 'Making of' featurette, but the R1 disc got exactly the same. *Insurrection* could have been worse, but it could also have been a whole lot better.

FINAL VERDICT

Picture ☆☆☆☆ Sound ☆☆☆☆ Entertainment ☆☆☆

Extras ☆☆☆ Value ☆☆☆

OVERALL ☆☆☆

ST ELMO'S FIRE

Price: £19.99

Supplied by: Columbia TriStar Home Entertainment

Type of disc: Dual layer, single-sided

No of chapters: 28

Film format(s)/length: 2.35:1 anamorphic / 110 mins

Audio format: Dolby Surround

Director: Joel Schumacher

Starring: Emilio Estevez, Demi Moore, Rob Lowe

Year made: 1985

Extras: Scene selection; soundtrack in English, French, German, Italian and Spanish; trailers; director's audio commentary; talent profiles; subtitles in 10 languages.

The Hollywood 'Brat Pack' was a group of young stars in the mid- to late-Eighties that provided a string of high earners for movie studio moguls. It's little wonder then that *St Elmo's Fire* has appeared as a DVD offering, with the studios hoping to recreate some of the magic. *St Elmo's Fire* tells the story of the trials of a group of young friends and the way they struggle against life's adversities. It is an easy going, relatively entertaining Eighties classic that is definitely one for the girls. The transfer to DVD has vastly improved the quality of the picture, restoring the image from a grainy VHS standard to its former glory. Despite the improved picture and sound quality, the rest of the DVD has a lot to be desired. The extras are thin on the ground and those that are featured contained little in the way of substance or information. The director's commentary offers no real background info and with the quality of stars in the movie and the success of the film at the time, you feel a lot more could have been done with it. As a package it's a bit hastily put together and is a poor attempt to cash in on the DVD phenomena. Overall the film is good for a nostalgia trip and the chance to see a pre-Bruce Willis Demi Moore in some rather tragic Eighties garb. But that really is it.

FINAL VERDICT

Picture ☆☆☆☆☆ Sound ☆☆☆☆
Entertainment ☆☆☆ Extras ☆☆☆ Value ☆☆
OVERALL ☆☆☆

STEPMOM

Price: £19.99
Supplied by: DVDplus (www.dvdplus.co.uk)
Type of disc: Single layer, double-sided
No of chapters: 28
Film format(s)/length: 4:3 regular (Side A), 1.85:1 widescreen enhanced (Side B) / 120 mins
Audio format: Dolby Digital 5.1
Director: Chris Columbus
Starring: Susan Sarandon, Julia Roberts, Ed Harris
Year made: 1998
Extras: Scene access; theatrical trailer; filmographies; behind the scenes featurette (just over 5 minutes); German soundtrack; subtitles in 15 languages.

Whether or not you like *Stepmom* depends on where you fall in the 'chic flick' divide. That's because this isn't one of those crossover chick flicks-that-have-an-element-of-appeal-to-blokes, this is a 100 per cent undiluted weepie You can probably guess your own reaction just by looking at the box. We quite liked the disc though, especially since it commendably appeared on the same date as the VHS rental release. We've never really been a fan of Columbia's £19.99 price point (although you can't buy this particular film on any other format), but we do have difficulty faulting the DVDs themselves. Even on a slow moving drama like *Stepmom*, the picture is sharp throughout the film, whilst the sound is also of a professional standard, so no complaints there. In terms of extras, you get a passable (albeit brief) behind the scenes featurette on top of the usual suspects of trailer, subtitles and filmographies. But really you don't need us to tell you whether to buy it – it's a fairly safe bet that you know the answer to that already. Just know that if the film's your thing, you'll be perfectly happy with its digital presentation.

FINAL VERDICT

Picture ☆☆☆☆ Sound ☆☆☆☆ Entertainment ☆☆
Extras ☆☆ Value ☆☆☆
OVERALL ☆☆☆

STIGMATA

Price: £19.99
Supplied by: MGM Home Entertainment
Type of disc: Dual layer, single-sided
No of chapters: 28
Film format(s)/length: 2.35:1 anamorphic / 98 mins
Audio format: Dolby Digital 5.1
Director: Rupert Wainwright
Starring: Patricia Arquette, Gabriel Byrne, Jonathan Pryce
Year made: 1999
Extras: Scene access; alternate ending; exclusive Region 2 *Divine Rites* featurette; 5 deleted scenes; music video by Natalie Imbruglia; director's commentary; original theatrical trailer; 8-page 'Making of' booklet; soundtrack in English, French, German and Spanish; subtitles in 13 languages.

Hollywood is without a doubt the world capital of bandwagons. If one rolls slowly through LA, every studio and his dog will hop aboard faster than it takes 24 frames to pass through a projector. One of the most overladen bandwagons of recent years has been the supernatural horror genre, often with more than a little religion mixed in, with films like *Stir of Echoes*, *The Blair Witch Project*, *The Sixth Sense* and *End of Days*. Luckily, though, a film's presence on the wagon doesn't necessarily reduce its merits. Joining the above party is *Stigmata*, a kind of *Exorcist* for the *Buffy* generation that manages to cut much of the stylish mustard that the likes of the *Scream* trilogy slipped up on. In the type of vivaciously innocent role that she seems born to play, Arquette is Frankie Page, a 23-year-old hairdresser from Pittsburgh who begins to experience the least common of skin conditions on her hands and feet, in the form of bleeding wounds. Being an atheist makes the case for Jesus impressions a little hard for Frankie to swallow, so it takes the appearance of Father Andrew Kiernan (the ever-charismatic Byrne), a Mulder-style investigator for the Vatican, to convince her that her attacks are signs of stigmata – the wounds of the crucifixion. Religiously, you can take out of *Stigmata* what you find. The Catholic faith is respectfully portrayed, as a contemporary institution never lit by bad light yet realistically riven with disagreements over the interpretation of the Gospels. However, Wainright and co are always careful to use the religious background only as a setting for their story, and not to preach. *Stigmata*, despite opening itself up for some obvious comparisons to a certain religious horror classic involving spinning heads and projectile vomiting, manages to bounce along at a captivating rate and throw the occasional shock in to the mix. Performance-wise Arquette and Byrne have rarely been better, but it's the stunning visuals which give this movie its own sense of identity. Energetic, contrasting and sometimes surprisingly subtle, *Stigmata* looks like the Gothic movement once it's been through the MTV wash. Better films have been made, but it still does the job of keeping the Saturday night audiences on the edge of their seats. As for the DVD, MGM has managed to pull their fingers out a whole lot further than they did on the Region 1 release. The audio and video transfer are up to DVD's highest standards, and MGM can feel smug for including another overly-informative 8-page booklet. The real bonus, however, is Wainwright's original ending, which adds a whole new mood to the movie. In addition to this, there is the *Divine Rites* featurette, an incredibly in-depth look at not only the making of the movie, but also all the gruesome details behind the phenomenon that is stigmata. It's a holy sign that the Region 2 DVD market is finally getting its act together.

FINAL VERDICT

Picture ☆☆☆☆☆ Sound ☆☆☆☆
Entertainment ☆☆☆☆ Extras ☆☆☆☆☆
Value ☆☆☆☆
OVERALL ☆☆☆☆

STILL CRAZY

Price: £19.99
Supplied by: Columbia TriStar Home Video
Type of disc: Single layer, single-sided
No of chapters: 28
Film format(s)/length: 1.85:1 widescreen / 92 mins
Audio format: Dolby Digital 5.1
Director: Brian Gibson
Starring: Stephen Rea, Billy Connolly, Jimmy Nail
Year made: 1998
Extras: Scene access; theatrical trailer; filmographies; production featurette; German soundtrack; multilingual subtitles.

If you've ever wondered what old rock stars do when they don't rock any more, then *Still Crazy* offers a possible answer. This British comedy charts the efforts of fictional Seventies band Strange Fruit as they try to make a comeback after 20 years of 'ordinary life'. There are a few problems with the whole comeback, notably that half the band don't get on with one another and the lead guitarist has – rather inconsiderately – apparently gone and died in the intervening years since the break up of the band. A whole host of comedy and musical stars have come to together for this film and various TV and movie per-

sonalities pop up throughout in different cameo roles. The whole thing has a very British feel and the humour is mixed with a heavy dose of nostalgia and moral soul-searching as the ageing rockers take a look at the way their lives have gone since the demise of their pop careers. *Still Crazy* is a riveting watch and proves that Hollywood isn't the only place that decent movies get made. And even better – it's a British movie without Hugh Grant! The DVD itself isn't too bad for a UK offering, providing amongst other extras a theatrical trailer and a 6 minute documentary and all in all this is a fairly nice package. If you're a fan of British comedy then this movie is definitely worth a look.

FINAL VERDICT

Picture ☆☆☆☆ Sound ☆☆☆☆
Entertainment ☆☆☆☆ Extras ☆☆☆ Value ☆☆☆
OVERALL ☆☆☆

THE STING

Price: £19.99
Supplied by: Columbia TriStar Home Video
Type of disc: Dual layer, single-sided
No of chapters: 16
Film format(s)/length: 1.85:1 anamorphic / 124 mins
Audio format: Mono
Director: George Roy Hill
Starring: Robert Redford, Paul Newman, Robert Shaw
Year made: 1973
Extras: Scene access; production notes; cast and film-maker's notes; soundtrack in English, French, German Italian and Spanish; subtitles in 11 languages.

Intelligent, gripping, superbly performed and steeped in that "best movie of the Seventies" feeling, *The Sting* is almost the definitive crime caper film. Redford and Newman play Hooker and Gondorff, two small-time grifters who attempt to pull the perfect scam on a gangster (Shaw) in revenge for the murder of Hooker's old partner. Everything is near perfection about this movie, from the electrifying dialogue, mesmerising performances and sublime use of the 1936 setting to the razor-sharp pacing and staging by director Hill. It's little wonder the movie was the winner of 7 Oscars, including Best Picture – a fact that is plastered all over the box. It's strange, then, that Columbia TriStar seems less than keen to do something special with a movie they seem so proud of. This is possibly one of the least inspiring releases from their stable. The production notes are indeed full and creditable, but that's it as far as extras go, and bragging about how classic this movie is gave the studio real scope for some retrospective features.

Even a commentary would have been nice. However, the end result amounts to little more than a mono track classic that visibly doesn't stand anywhere near to the standard that DVD sets. The lack of digital enhancement for the picture is incredibly noticeable, especially if you have a system built to stand a whole lot more. All in all, a great film, but a disappointing DVD.

FINAL VERDICT

Picture ☆☆ Sound ☆ Entertainment ☆☆☆☆☆
Extras ☆☆ Value ☆
OVERALL ☆☆

THE STRAIGHT STORY

Price: £19.99
Supplied by: FilmFour
Type of disc: Dual layer, single-sided
No of chapters: 16
Film format(s)/length: 1.85:1 anamorphic / 111 mins
Audio format: Dolby Digital 5.1
Director: David Lynch
Starring: Richard Farnsworth, Sissy Spacek, Harry Dean Stanton
Year made: 1999
Extras: Scene access; theatrical trailer; subtitles in English.

For a plot so simple that it makes *Sesame Street* look like *Catch 22*, *The Straight Story* manages to reel the audience in with mouth-watering bait in nearly every single scene. Alvin Straight is a 77-year-old small town American, who on hearing of the stroke of his estranged brother decides to travel halfway across the country to visit him one last time before they both go to the great cornfield in the sky. Being bereft of not only a driving licence, but also a car, Alvin builds himself a trailer, stocks up, and heads off down the road pulling his whole life behind him on a motor mower. Along the way he preaches elderly wisdom to whomever he encounters, and learns a lesson or two about the impracticability of using a garden utensil as a vehicle. The movie travels along at the same pace as Alvin's mower, but slow doesn't always mean dull, and this gentle movie is simply captivating. Though beautifully shot, Lynch avoids all of his famed stylised directing (don't let *Lost Highway* put you off), and allows the story to tell itself. The disc sounds superb, and you'll be hard pushed to find a clearer picture on DVD (pause the disc at any point and you could be looking at a picture by Hopper). However, apart from a mildly charming musical menu screen, that's your sorry lot as far as DVD goes. A shame, as this movie deserves much better.

FINAL VERDICT

Picture ☆☆☆☆☆ Sound ☆☆☆☆☆
Entertainment ☆☆☆☆ Extras ☆ Value ☆☆☆
OVERALL ☆☆☆

THE STRANGER

Price: £12.99
Supplied by: Eureka Video
Type of disc: Single layer, single-sided
No of chapters: 12
Film format(s)/length: 4:3 regular / 95 mins
Audio format: Mono
Director: Orson Welles
Starring: Edward G Robinson, Orson Welles, Loretta Young
Year made: 1946
Extras: Scene access; Orson Welles biography.

What a shambles. You'd expect an Orson Welles film to have been given a bit of care and attention before being slapped on to all-singing-all-dancing DVD, but not 'ere mate. Having wowed the world with *Citizen Kane*, the young upstart Welles went straight on to lesser things. 1946 heralded a partial return to form with *The Stranger*, telling the audacious and contemporary tale of a Nazi war criminal donning a wholesome new identity in Connecticut. Can investigator Edward G Robinson prove and unmask his background before he adds his new wife (Young) to his murder list? The film is not entirely successful, which may be down to the fact that it was a victim of rushed production. Welles hams it up once or twice, and the film's earlier stages are terribly dreary. On the plus side, there is a pleasing amount of mounting tension as the story unfolds, and events violently conclude up the creepy old clock tower in a manner straight out of the modern day thriller. Sadly, the transfer is despicable. A soft, scratchy print has been used, with each dissolve shot looking doubly soft, and there's lots of smearing in the blacks. The sound is similarly unimpressive and slapped on exactly as Eureka Video found it, without any attempt to clean things up for the digital age and ear. The only advantage of this DVD over its VHS equivalent is instant access, which clearly isn't anywhere near enough to justify the asking price. If this were sold at half price and you really love the film then, alright, go buy. Otherwise you're safe leaving this title a stranger forever.

FINAL VERDICT

Picture ☆ Sound ☆ Entertainment ☆☆☆ Extras ☆
Value ☆
OVERALL ☆

STREET FIGHTER

Price: £19.99
Supplied by: Columbia TriStar
Type of disc: Single layer, single-sided
No of chapters: 28
Film format(s)/length: 2.35:1 anamorphic / 96 mins
Director: Steven E DeSouza
Starring: Jean-Claude Van Damme, Raul Julia, Kylie Minogue
Year made: 1994
Extras: Widescreen TV enhanced; chapter select.

This, sadly, was Raul Julia's last film – you could probably power a dynamo from his grave. *Street Fighter* is so appallingly bad it's a camp cult classic. Van Damme leads the goodies against evil General Bison (Julia), and unintentionally hilarious kickboxing ensues. Another sad fact: director DeSouza wrote *Die Hard*. The mighty have fallen.

FINAL VERDICT

Picture ☆☆☆ Sound ☆☆☆ Entertainment ☆☆
Extras ☆ Value ☆
OVERALL ☆

STRICTLY BALLROOM

Price: £19.99
Supplied by: Carlton Video
Type of disc: Single layer, single-sided
No of chapters: 12
Film format(s)/length: 4:3 regular / 113 mins
Audio Format: Mono
Director: Baz Luhrmann
Starring: Paul Mercurio, Tara Morice, Bill Hunter
Year made: 1992
Extras: Scene selection; original theatrical trailer; music promo video; biographies; 20 minute behind the scenes documentary.

This Australian romantic comedy by Baz Luhrmann proved to be the director's ticket to Hollywood, as he went on to update Shakespeare's *Romeo & Juliet*…with the help of Leonardo Di Caprio and Claire Danes, of course. His first mainstream film, *Strictly Ballroom* is the tale of one man's quest to dance to his own tune by flaunting the conventions of the dance elite, and throwing out the proverbial rule book. Scott Hastings (Mercurio) is determined to win the Australian State Dance Championship, and teams up with 'ugly duckling' Fran (Morice), who becomes his initially reluctant dance partner. It will come as no surprise that the duo go down a storm with the judges, but the fun comes from watching the apparently mis-matched pair getting to the competition in the first place. The film is a heart-warming comedy, with some terrific performances, particularly from Morice . There are quite a few extras thrown in on *Strictly Ballroom*'s DVD. As well as biographies on director Baz Luhrmann, Paul Mercurio and Tara Morice, there is a behind the scenes documentary on the film's production. The latter gives a heady flavour of how the film was put together, as well as providing interviews with the actors and crew. Becoming something of a DVD standard feature, *Strictly Ballroom* also includes the original theatrical trailer, plus the added bonus of the 'Love is in the Air' music promo video sung by John Paul Young. Whilst Carlton is to be commended for supplying some decent extras, the overall quality of the film itself is lacking. Basically, it is obvious that the print has not been remastered or optimised for DVD – the sharp quality of DVD shows up the imperfections of the film stock. *Strictly Ballroom* is a solid movie, and apart from the extras, there is very little here to persuade anyone from choosing this over the VHS version – particularly when you could probably pick up a video copy for half the price of the DVD.

FINAL VERDICT

Picture ☆☆ Sound ☆☆☆ Entertainment ☆☆☆☆
Extras ☆☆☆☆ Value ☆☆☆
OVERALL ☆☆☆

STRIKING DISTANCE

Price: £19.99
Supplied by: DVD World (01705 796662)
Type of disc: Single layer, single-sided
No of chapters: 28
Film format(s)/length: 2.35:1 widescreen, anamorphic / 97 mins
Director: Rowdy Herrington
Starring: Bruce Willis, Sarah Jessica Parker, Dennis Farina
Year made: 1993
Extras: theatrical trailer; chapter select; multilingual subtitles.

It's a funny thing about Bruce Willis. People will forgive him for any amount of old crap like *The Jackal, Color of Night* or *The Fifth Element*, so long as he dons a dirty vest and crows, "Yippee-kay-ay, muddy funster!" (or something) every few years. *Striking Distance* is definitely in Brucie's 'old crap' category, so we're owed *Die Hard 4* pretty soon. He plays Tom Hardy, a Pittsburgh homicide detective who gets busted to the river patrol after his dad (*Frasier*'s John Mahoney) is murdered and Hardy accuses a cop of being the serial killer. Two years later, Hardy is still messing around in boats with new partner Jo Christman (Parker) when the killings start again, and he has to overcome the enmity of the cops to catch the killer. As a movie, *Striking Distance* offers nothing special, and the same applies to it as a DVD. The whole package sinks without a trace.

FINAL VERDICT

Picture ☆☆☆ Sound ☆☆☆ Entertainment ☆
Extras ☆ Value ☆☆
OVERALL ☆

STRIPTEASE

Price: £15.99
Supplied by: Warner Home Video
Type of disc: Single layer, single-sided
No of chapters: 35
Film format(s)/length: 1.85:1 widescreen / 112 mins
Audio format: Dolby Surround
Director: Andrew Bergman
Starring: Demi Moore, Armand Assante, Burt Reynolds
Year made: 1996
Extras: Scene access; soundtrack available in English, French and Italian; subtitles in 10 languages; subtitles for the hearing impaired in English and Italian.

Telling the story of FBI secretary Erin Grant (Demi Moore) who loses her job and has to resort to working as an exotic dancer in the Eager Beaver Strip Club, *Striptease* is a movie that received mixed reviews when it was released back in 1996. Erin needs money so that she can retain custody of her 7-year-old daughter (played by Demi's real-life daughter), but the sleazy work takes a turn for the worse when she receives the unwanted attentions of a corrupt congressman. The politician is played by a very old and decrepit looking Burt Reynolds and the movie soon turns into a story of cash, blackmail and murder. Of course, the main appeal of *Striptease* is a chance to see Demi Moore without her top on, and there are three sequences in the film that certainly don't disappoint as Erin seductively dances around the seedy club, allowing the flesh-hungry punters to fill her knickers with dollar bills! It's just a shame they didn't think about putting a good script behind the action. The tale soon becomes quite unbelievable and you inevitably lose interest. There's not much you could call special about *Striptease* on Region 2 DVD – beside the two obvious things that Demi Moore brings to the equation! The movie itself has now filtered through to terrestrial UK television, so it's not like you need to rush out to buy it when you could have recorded it from TV. This makes it all the more unbelievable that once again the film company has given us nothing in the way of additional features on the DVD, making the release virtually worthless! In the way of extras all you get is a nicely presented menu system, scene access (woohoo) and the usual mix of subtitles and dubbing in a variety of languages you'll probably never access. When are UK film companies going to learn that the joy of owning a DVD player has more to do with the extra features like director commentary, behind the scenes documentaries, production sketches or different endings, than with just owning an old movie on a new digital format instead of VHS? It all smacks of a lack of effort, really!

FINAL VERDICT

Picture ☆☆☆☆ Sound ☆☆☆☆ Entertainment ☆☆
Extras ☆ Value ☆☆
OVERALL ☆☆☆

SUMMER OF SAM

Price: £19.99
Supplied by: Down Town Pictures/MGM
Type of disc: Dual layer, single-sided
No of chapters: 22
Film format(s)/length: 1.85:1 letterbox / 120 mins
Audio format: Dolby Digital 5.1
Director: Spike Lee
Starring: John Leguizamo, Adrien Brody, Mira Sorvino
Year made: 1999
Extras: Scene access; audio commentary by director Spike Lee; cast and director interviews; cast and director biographies; behind the scenes footage; production notes; original theatrical trailer; 3 TV spots; 8-page booklet; subtitles in English.

Summertime, and the living is murder. At least it is in the Bronx of 1977. Ten years after *Do the Right Thing*, Spike Lee refocuses on a tight-knit group of New Yorkers dealing with their fraught relationships and a heatwave while violence is all around them. *Summer of Sam* concentrates on the strained friendship between Vinnie (Leguizamo) and Ritchie (Brody), the former dating Dionna (Sorvino) yet sleeping around whilst the latter has become a punk to rebel against their insular Italian American neighbourhood. Their touching, funny and dramatic relationships unfold during one of New York's craziest times; a summer of heatwaves, lootings, blackouts, disco, punks and an indiscriminate serial killer calling himself the Son of Sam. Lee's virtuoso direction creates a hypnotically good film packed with perfect performances, moments of terror, sharp humour and an eye for authenticity. The soundtrack is a dizzying mixture of Terence Blanchard's brooding orchestration, Sixties rock songs, punk and disco which often make ironic comments on the action; for instance, 'Don't Leave Me This Way' plays as Vinnie and Dionna fight. The menu screens are well designed in the style of newspaper pages and police files with animated inserts and music played from the film. A polished electronic press kit provides interesting interview quotes from the cast and director, while the biographies and notes are engagingly written. The 8-page booklet contains Lee's introduction of the movie to the London Film Festival. Blanchard's score accompanies the 14 minutes of behind the scenes footage along with the excellent picture gallery, which contains 35 publicity, cast and crew shots. *Summer of Sam* is a *tour de force* from Spike Lee and, with this impressive disc as follow-up to its equally stunning *Gods and Monsters* release, Down Town Pictures are quickly emerging as one of the most exciting Region 2 DVD producers working today.

FINAL VERDICT

Picture ☆☆☆☆ Sound ☆☆☆☆

Entertainment ☆☆☆☆ Extras ☆☆☆☆ Value ☆☆☆☆
OVERALL ☆☆☆☆

SWINGERS

Price: £19.99
Supplied by: Pathé Distribution
Type of disc: Single layer, single-sided
No of chapters: 10
Film format(s)/length: 16:9 widescreen enhanced / 92 mins
Audio format: Dolby Surround
Director: Doug Liman
Starring: Jon Favreau, Vince Vaughn, Heather Graham
Year made: 1996
Extras: Scene access; original theatrical trailer; teaser advert; subtitles for the hearing impaired in English.

As soon as Dean Martin starts crooning 'You're Nobody Till Somebody Loves You' you instantly know this American independent movie is something special. *Swingers* follows the night lives of 5 struggling actors cruising LA's bars, swing clubs and Vegas casinos. Writer and co-producer Favreau is Mike, a comedian dumped by his girlfriend 6 months ago. Now his friends, including Trent (Vaughn), are determined to get him back in the singles game. This film is the most accurate portrayal of guys being guys ever made, bristling with hilariously memorable lines, wry movie homages and naturalistic acting. Region 2 features have a slight edge over the Region 1 version – that

edge being an extra teaser advert and better use of the cool soundtrack. It's puzzling though why the cast and crew didn't get more involved in the disc's production. A commentary by Favreau would be the icing on the cake. Small discrepancies aside, *Swingers* is the freshest, funniest and hippest comedy yet to hit Region 2 DVDs. You must add it to your collection now.

FINAL VERDICT

Picture ☆☆☆☆ Sound ☆☆☆

Entertainment ☆☆☆☆☆ Extras ☆☆ Value ☆☆☆☆
OVERALL ☆☆☆

THE SWORD IN THE STONE

Price: £13.99
Supplied by: Buena Vista
Type of disc: Single layer, single-sided
No of chapters: 17
Film format(s)/length: 4:3 regular / 76 mins
Audio format: Mono
Director: Wolfgang Reitherman
Starring the voices of: Rickie Sorenson, Karl Swenson, Sebastian Cabot
Year made: 1963
Extras: Scene access; English, German, French, Italian, Dutch and Hebrew soundtracks; English and Greek subtitles.

Put away those rose-tinted spectacles for 76 minutes, and you'll discover that plenty of 'classic' Disney, thoroughly deserves the inverted commas. Bookended by brief Excalibur sequences, the rest of this movie is one excruciatingly long second act, telling of a time-travelling Merlin's tutoring of 12-year-old Wart (King Arthur) by rehashing most of Disney's better flicks in general, and *Fantasia* in particular. The only decent sequence is Merlin and a Witch trying to out-spellcast each other. The *Scooby Doo*-quality animation on DVD is clean, detailed, rock solid and also colourful for its day (although for some reason every alternate still frame is blurred). Sound is tidy enough, but the dub itself is very lacklustre compared to what MGM and Warner were up to a full 20 years earlier. In short, with no extras, this is exclusively for parents of hyperactive insomniacs - put on infinite repeat and just watch your brood slumber.

FINAL VERDICT

Picture ☆☆☆☆ Sound ☆☆ Entertainment ☆☆

Extras ☆ Value ☆☆
OVERALL ☆☆

TARZAN

Price: £22.99 (standard)/£24.99 (CE)
Supplied by: Disney DVD
Type of disc: Dual layer, single-sided
No of chapters: 36
Film format(s)/length: 1.66:1 anamorphic / 85 mins
Audio format: Dolby Digital 5.0
Directors: Kevin Lima and Chris Buck
Starring the voices of: Tony Goldwyn, Minnie Driver, Brian Blessed
Year made: 1999
Extras: Scene access; trailer; *Dinosaur* trailer; *From Burroughs to Disney* featurette; *The Making of the Music* featurette; *Tarzan Goes International* featurette; 3 music videos: 'You'll Be in My Heart', 'Strangers Like Me', 'Trashin' the Camp'; *Building the Story* featurette; storyboard to film comparison; 3 deleted/alternate sequences; 2 'read-along' stories; trivia game; subtitles in English

COLLECTOR'S EDITION

Extras: As above, plus: additional trailer; early presentation reel; research trip to Africa; original Phil Collins demo; characters of *Tarzan*: 'Creating Tarzan', 'Animating Tarzan', 'Creating Jane and Porter', 'Creating Kala and Kerchek', 'Creating Terk and Tantor', 'Creating Clayton'; animation: 'Deep Canvas Process', 'Deep Canvas Demonstration', 'Production Progression Demo', 'Story Reel', 'Rough Animation', 'Cleaned-Up Animation', 'Final Film in Colour', 'Intercontinental Film Making'.

After two years of releasing its movies via Warner Bros, Disney has finally taken the plunge and started selling DVDs under its own name. *Tarzan* is the first film from the House of Mouse to appear under this new umbrella – how does it fare? As a film, it does very well indeed. Yes, it sticks firmly to the long-established Disney formula, but it's a formula that's been proven to work over and over again. Edgar Rice Burroughs' original story is the string from which all the usual Disney elements – songs by a major MOR star, wisecracking animal sidekicks, an understated politically correct moral and a simple but likeable love story – are hung, and while the weight may stretch it a little, it's more than strong enough to hold together. In Disney's version, baby Tarzan is adopted by a group of gorillas after his shipwrecked parents are killed by a leopard, grows up struggling to fit in because he's different (moral alert!) and has to choose between the animal and human worlds when a group of explorers enters the jungle. Goldwyn's surfer dude Lord of the Apes suffers slightly from the tendency of Disney heroes to be a touch on the bland side, but Driver's prim-yet-passionate Jane is one of the best animated heroines in years, and there's plenty of capable support from the likes of Nigel Hawthorne, Lance Henricksen and Glenn Close. Blessed has a good time as the Great White Hunter who acts as the villain of the piece, although Rosie O'Donnell's comic relief ape gets annoying very, very quickly. The picture is excellent – very clean and sharp, showing off the impressive animation and backgrounds to their best effect – but the use of a 1.66:1 widescreen format seems a bit strange. On some widescreen TVs, this will result in black bars running down the sides of the screen. It's a weird choice, but one that Disney seems perfectly happy with, as several of the company's other animated titles (*Hercules*, *The Little Mermaid*) also appeared on DVD in this non-standard ratio. Why they didn't go for either a standard 16:9 (1.77:1) aspect ratio or a full widescreen format – hell, even *A Goofy Movie* managed a cinematic 1.85:1 on DVD – is a mystery. The sound is also a little disappointing – it's Dolby 5.0 only, rather than full-on 5.1. It's certainly not a bad mix, but considering the jungle ambience that could be wrung from the setting, it all seems just slightly flat. Musically, Phil Collins and his many, many songs aren't nearly as intolerable as you might think, because he seems to be making a deliberate effort to sound like his old Genesis mucker Peter Gabriel, and for the most part succeeding. That said, there is one musical number ('Trashin' the Camp') which is completely gratuitous, stopping the story dead in its tracks for 3 minutes because some suit at Disney seemingly decided that we hadn't seen enough wacky animals yet. Heart attack time – Disney disc in decent extras shocker! Yes, after years of considering 'scene access' and 'interactive menus' to be 'special' features, the Mouse has finally woken up to the concept of added value. The standard disc gets nearly an hour of (lightweight) making-of material, music videos and some deleted/alternate scenes, while the Collector's Edition goes into the design and animation process in more depth. By any standards it's a decent collection; by previous Disney standards, it's stunning. But then, you should damn well hope there'd be some added value. £25 for the Collector's Edition is tolerable, considering the weight of extra material… but £23 for the standard disc is outrageous. Disney may present a happy smiling face to the public, but with these prices, and rental windows on the way, behind the mask is the cold, greedy face of an accountant.

FINAL VERDICT

Picture ☆☆☆☆☆ **Sound** ☆☆☆☆
Entertainment ☆☆☆☆ **Extras (standard)** ☆☆☆☆
Extras (CE) ☆☆☆☆☆ **Value** ☆☆☆

OVERALL ☆☆☆☆

TAXI

Price: £19.99
Supplied by: Metrodome
Type of disc: Single layer, single-sided
No of chapters: 22
Film format(s)/length: 2.35:1 widescreen / 85 mins
Audio format: Dolby Digital 5.1
Director: Gerard Piries
Starring: Samy Naceri, Marion Cotillard Frederic Diefenthal,
Year made: 1998
Extras: Scene access; trailer; cast and crew filmographies; soundtrack in French; subtitles in English.

Maybe it's a sign that people are fed up with CGI-laden special effects blockbusters, but good old-fashioned car chase movies seem to be back in vogue. We've had *Ronin* and Nicolas Cage in *Gone in 60 Seconds*, and Luc Besson's contribution to the genre is *Taxi*. Besson didn't direct, but he wrote and produced this thin tale of a Marseilles taxi driver and a cop teaming up to catch a gang of German bank robbers. The whole thing is an excuse for a series of shootouts and chases with some corny gags thrown in along the way. Although *Taxi* is utterly brainless, it's definitely fun, and some of the chases are on a par with those in *Ronin* (not surprising, as a lot of the same stunt drivers were used). As it's subtitled, you also get to learn a load of amusing French obscenities into the bargain!

FINAL VERDICT

Picture ☆☆☆ Sound ☆☆☆ Entertainment ☆☆☆
Extras ☆☆ Value ☆☆☆

OVERALL ☆☆☆

TAXI DRIVER

Price: £19.99
Supplied by: Columbia TriStar Home Video
Type of disc: Dual layer, single-sided
No of chapters: 28
Film format(s)/length: 16:9 widescreen enhanced / 109 mins
Audio format: Stereo
Director: Martin Scorsese
Starring: Robert De Niro, Jodie Foster, Harvey Keitel
Year made: 1976
Extras: Scene access; behind the scenes documentary (70 minutes); video photo gallery with commentary; original screenplay; storyboard sequence; advertising materials; US theatrical trailer; filmographies; subtitles in 16 languages.

It probably isn't his Oscar-winning performance in *The Godfather Part II* that will stand out as the greatest role of the young Robert De Niro's life, but more likely his portrayal of Travis Bickle, the taxi-driving title character of this screen classic. Fuelled by insomnia and loneliness, Bickle is a forsaken figure, cruising society in his cab, and building up his own internal defences against a world that disgusts and repels him. Played neither as a hero nor a villain, Travis is purely and simply an isolated man, cut off from society by his own perverse logic, and a repulsion from a world that he must redeem. As a result of this, the audience are invited to feel what they want for Travis, riding a rollercoaster of emotions from sympathy to disgust. Travis is the focus of insanity within society. Society has made him the figure he is, and he has channelled these feelings into a violent retaliation. From Bickle's obsessions, director Scorsese has crafted a cinematic masterpiece that has often been referred to as one of the greatest films of its decade, and deservedly so. Scorsese uses the taxi both for exploring society and allowing Bickle the physical isolation to develop his own jaded view of American culture. The film talks sense even 23 years on, and the visual perfection crafted by Scorsese, along with his very loose editing and the chillingly calm music score by composer Bernard Herrmann (sadly, his final screen work) gives a comfortable feel to an uncomfortable story. It is fitting then that one of the greatest films ever made, should reach us on one of the best Region 2 discs yet. The transfer to DVD may not be at its optical best, but the extras beat anything that a genuine film enthusiast could have seen before. If you're a fan of this movie, then this disc is an insight into what a film lover's heaven could look like. There's a specially made 70-minute documentary (featuring director, screenwriter, and every member of the cast, including De Niro), that covers everything from script development to method acting to special effects. Producer Laurent Bouzereau uses the commentary on the photo gallery as a forum to talk about aspects of the documentary that never made it into the final cut, and the storyboard section is a wonderful insight to the way that Scorsese works. However, it's the screenplay aspect that truly makes this DVD, allowing the watcher to constantly cut between the movie and the corresponding scene in the shooting script. *Taxi Driver* is a powerful film on an exciting disc. In fact, it's a blessing for not only DVD, but for Region 2 as well. Buy it now, it's brilliant.

FINAL VERDICT

Picture ☆☆☆☆☆ Sound ☆☆☆☆

Entertainment ☆☆☆☆☆ Extras ☆☆☆☆☆

Value ☆☆☆☆☆

OVERALL ☆☆☆☆☆

10 THINGS I HATE ABOUT YOU

Price: £15.99

Supplied by: Warner Home Video

Type of disc: Single layer, single-sided

No of chapters: 21

Film format(s)/length: 1.85:1 widescreen / 93 mins

Audio format: Dolby Digital 5.1

Director: Gil Junger

Starring: Julia Stiles, Heath Ledger, Joseph Gordon-Levitt

Year made: 1999

Extras: Scene access; subtitles for the hearing impaired in English.

Classic literature has been the influence on many recent teen movies of late: *Clueless* was a retelling of *Emma*; *Cruel Intentions* was a latter day *Dangerous Liaisons*; *She's All That* was quite blatantly *Pygmalion*; and DiCaprio's *Romeo + Juliet* had an essence of Shakespeare in it… *10 Things I Hate About You* falls nicely into this vein of film-making, based on the great Bard's classic play, *The Taming of the Shrew* – say the two titles fast enough and they almost sound similar! A refreshingly mellow-paced movie in the latest pubescent trend from Hollywood, this teen flick tells the tale about the lengths guys will go to get a date. New boy Cameron (Gordon-Levitt) falls instantly head over heels in love with the popular Bianca (Larisa Oleynik) on his first day of school, only to find any chance of dating the girl of his dreams thwarted by her over-protective father. Parental preaching rules soon reach new highs, especially when her single dad paediatrician – with an ongoing paranoia that both his little girls will wind up getting pregnant if a member of the opposite sex just looks at them – senses danger ahead. Knowing that Bianca's ill-tempered, man-hating older sister Kat (Julia Stiles) will have nothing to do with boys, he decrees that Bianca can only date when Kat does. This doesn't bode well for the popularity dependent Bianca, and in a gallant attempt to get her onto the market, Cameron singles out the only boy in school who could possibly be a match for Kat: the rumour-shrouded man from 'down under', Patrick (Ledger). *10 Things* is a thoroughly engaging tale, told by an attractive and talented cast. Being based on Shakespeare means nothing is simple, and it's perhaps the unpredictability of the plot that will keep you watching. However, this isn't a joke-a-minute comedy, and if you're looking for the likes of

American Pie, you may well be disappointed. But the humour is there, and when it comes you will laugh out loud. It's just a shame then that such a gorgeous little film comes on such a mediocre disc, meaning it will only appeal to those who favour the genre. Yet the box will try and convince you that 'scene access' is a special feature – surely no-one's fooled by that! The soundtrack and subtitles are limited to English only; hell, even the US version had French subtitles, and that disc isn't supposed to cater for the European market. There's only one thing to hate here, and it's not the film.

FINAL VERDICT

Picture ☆☆☆☆ Sound ☆☆☆☆

Entertainment ☆☆☆☆ Extras ☆ Value ☆☆☆

OVERALL ☆☆☆

TERMINAL VELOCITY

Price: £19.99

Supplied by: DVD World (01705 796662)

Type of disc: Single layer, single-sided

No of chapters: 20

Film format(s)/length: 16:9 widescreen / 98 mins

Director: Deran Sarafian

Starring: Charlie Sheen, Natassja Kinski

Year made: 1994

Extras: Instant scene access; Dolby Digital (English, French).

High octane international spy thriller starring a skydiving instructor whose job allows for some spectacular aerial stunts… This is a high concept (read B-movie) thriller with a vengeance. As you'd expect, Sheen's character is a stereotypical rebel constantly on the verge of having his business shut down for playing fast and loose with the rules. In the real world, he'd have been sued to oblivion and back by litigious US customers, but in the movies Americans love dodgy characters. However, it's Natassja Kinksi who turns out to be the first skydiving student that Sheen actually kills. Or maybe not… The first couple of twists suggest this is a movie that cares about plot, but the film soon descends into simply presenting one big dumb action scene after another. It's the kind of movie *Hot Shots* star Sheen and his trademark perma-smirk seem made for. Obviously, his female side-kick should be some busty starlet who points her boobs at the camera every 15 minutes. Instead, it's Natassja Kinski and her subtle acting gives the initial scenes some spark of human interest, but as the action scenes unfold she simply seems out of place. Then again, this isn't a film that much cares about such details. The plot is trashed early on, characterisation and believability following in swift succession. This is simply big, dumb fun, and not bad for all that. As a DVD, the picture and sound are sharper than the film deserves. Freeze-framing through action scenes is mildly interesting, but these aren't James Cameron-style state-of-the-art effects, just old-style stunts that win you over with their sheer outrageousness. The lack of production notes is probably a blessing for all involved – you somehow doubt Natassja will feature this movie high on her CV – but why no theatrical trailer?

FINAL VERDICT

Picture ☆☆☆☆☆ Sound ☆☆☆☆

Entertainment ☆☆☆ Extras ☆ Value ☆☆☆

OVERALL ☆☆☆

THE TEXAS CHAIN SAW MASSACRE

Price: £17.99
Supplied by: Blue Dolphin
Type of disc: Single layer, single-sided
No of chapters: 16
Film format(s)/length: 1:85:1 anamorphic / 80 mins
Audio format: Dolby Surround
Director: Tobe Hooper
Starring: Marilyn Burns, Gunnar Hansen
Year made: 1974
Extras: Chapter access; audio commentary by director Tobe Hooper and star Gunnar Hansen; remixed surround and original mono soundtracks; original TV ads; original theatrical trailers and sequel trailers; stills gallery; bloopers reel; alternate footage and deleted scenes; posters and lobby cards.

The seminal slasher movie, which didn't so much break the horror genre mould as cosh it to a blood-sodden pulp. *The Texas Chain Saw Massacre* redefined many parameters in horror films, brought dark and disturbing new dimensions to the macabre, and challenged the film-going public's constitution to the max. If Hitchcock kept the audience on the edge of its seat, Tobe Hooper's style has you chewing the seat with your buttocks. It's a frenzied assault on the senses, and is often a sadistic, shocking and disturbing ride. Filmed and edited with all the ferocity of a roaring chainsaw, with a tinnitus-inducing soundtrack of clattering mill blades and chainsaw gurgle, a bunch of kids in a Mystery Machine-style camper van embark on an innocent afternoon drive, pick up a demented hitchhiker, manage to lose him and end up at a remote home-cum-slaughterhouse. Then, before you can say knife, or indeed chainsaw, the likeable youngsters are in turn hammer-pummelled, hung up on a hook to tenderise or dumped in a catering-size chest freezer. Based on true occurrences involving grave robbing and cannibalism in Texas, Hooper hands the hapless youths on a splatter platter to a charming family of demented psychopathic hillbillies with a penchant for human flesh. The supper scene with ol' Grandpa limply but excitedly trying to dent the girl's cranium with a hammer is enough to set your fillings on edge, and, however jollied and boozed up your mates are when you invite them round for a 'chain-saw-fest night', this 26 year old horror still demands hushed respect from the audience when it gets to those infamous nitty-gritties. What's more, there's a chest freezer full of extras to accompany the film, including full-length commentary from the director, director of photography and comments from Leatherface himself, Gunnar Hansen; plus a bloopers reel, deleted scenes and rushes of alternate footage, original trailers, sequel trailers, stills, posters and lobby cards. It's a deservingly packed DVD. Hooper supervised both the soundtrack re-mastering and high-definition Superscan from the original negatives, which has resulted in a crispness and clarity never seen before in this film, inspiring Hooper to comment, "The last time the film looked this good… I was looking through the viewfinder." Shot on a shoestring with a couple of pails of blood and enough petrol to keep the saw ticking over, it's as intense and thrilling as it was over two and a half decades ago, with loads of extra features.

FINAL VERDICT

Picture ☆☆☆☆ Sound ☆☆☆☆

Entertainment ☆☆☆☆ Extras ☆☆☆☆☆

Value ☆☆☆☆

OVERALL ☆☆☆☆

THELMA & LOUISE

Price: £19.99
Supplied by: DVD World (01705 796662)
Type of disc: Dual layer, single-sided
No of chapters: 36
Film format(s)/length: 2.35:1 anamorphic / 124 mins
Director: Ridley Scott
Starring: Geena Davis, Susan Sarandon, Harvey Keitel
Year made: 1991
Extras: Chapter access; multilingual soundtrack/subtitles; trailer; director's commentary; alternate ending.

Getting the director of definitive 'boy films' like *Alien, Blade Runner* and *Black Rain* to step behind the camera for what looks, on the surface, like a feminist outing must have seemed an odd move at the time. But looks can be deceptive. Ridley Scott's done a great job of making the central characters believable and likeable, and Callie Khouri's script isn't so much anti-men as it is pro-individuality, although any leering lechers out there are probably best advised to keep their comments strictly to themselves. Thelma (Davis) a put-upon, scatty housewife with a husband who takes her for granted, and best friend Louise (Sarandon) a hassled waitress whose boyfriend (Michael Madsen) just won't commit, decide to take a fishing trip to get away from their problems. Things take a nasty turn when a seemingly friendly redneck they meet in a bar tries to rape the drunken Thelma in the car park, prompting Louise – in a moment of unthinking anger – to shoot him dead. Scared of the consequences, the two women go on the run, with dogged cop Keitel and an increasing number of law enforcement types on their trail. *Thelma & Louise* is basically a road movie, its heroines learning about each other and letting their real personalities emerge as they travel across America in an attempt to reach Mexico. Along the way, a series of vignettes provide comedy and character development as the women meet an assortment of men – a sexist trucker, a fascist cop, Brad Pitt's charming thief – and deal with them in their own distinctive way. Scott isn't generally known for his films' humour quotient, but once past the unpleasantness in the car park that kickstarts the plot, *Thelma & Louise* is cheery, life-affirming stuff. If there's any real criticism to be made about *Thelma & Louise*, it's that all the male characters – even the sympathetic ones – are stereotypes, but that's sort of the point. After so many films where women are presented as cardboard cutouts (supportive wife/girlfriend, victim or shag) it's refreshing to see the tables turned, and the two female stars do their stuff while the useless men are left blubbering in their wake. As far as special features go, *Thelma & Louise* delivers admirably. Not only is there an alternate ending, but Ridley Scott provides a full-length commentary. For Scott fans it's a godsend, as he doesn't just limit himself to just the movie at hand, but takes you through the rest of his film career, including quite a bit on *Alien* and *Blade Runner*. Let's face it, if you're the kind of person who wants to listen to the directors' commentaries, those are the ones that you really want to hear about anyway…

FINAL VERDICT

Picture ☆☆☆☆ Sound ☆☆☆☆

Entertainment ☆☆☆☆ Extras ☆☆☆ Value ☆☆☆☆

OVERALL ☆☆☆☆

THERE'S SOMETHING ABOUT MARY

Price: £19.99
Supplied by: 20th Century Fox

Type of disc: Dual layer, single-sided
No of chapters: 30
Film format(s)/length: 1.85:1 widescreen / 114 minutes
Audio format: Dolby Digital 5.1
Director: Bobby & Peter Farrelly
Starring: Cameron Diaz, Ben Stiller, Matt Dillon, Lee Evans
Year made: 1998
Extras: Scene access; original theatrical trailer; music video; karaoke; audio commentary from the directors; *Behind the Zipper* featurette; subtitles in 10 languages; subtitles for the hearing impaired in English.

There's something about this DVD. It could be the fact that it's one of the biggest blockbusting comedies of the Nineties. It could be the fact that it's disgusted some of the most annoying Mary Whitehouses in the Western hemisphere. It could be the outstanding talent of the transatlantic cast. It could be the perfect picture and sound, or even the jaw-dropping barrage of extras that accompany the film on Region 2. Whatever it is, it's without a doubt the top disc for anybody with a DVD player. The Farrelly brothers have been grossing out comedy consumers for years with smash hits like *Dumb and Dumber* and *Kingpin*, but they never really hit the nail right on the head until this outstandingly weird romantic comedy came along. Cameron Diaz, Best Looking Actress In Hollywood™ plays the eponymous Mary: she's beautiful, fun, compassionate and intelligent. Unfortunately, there's just something about her that sends all the men in her life absolutely potty about her, and for 'potty', read 'clinically insane'. Ben Stiller is excellent as the lovelorn loser Ted, who fell in love with Mary at the tender age of 17 before a very regrettable experience with his flies that makes the audience laugh or cry (depending, strangely enough, on their gender). 13 years on, however, Ted is still obsessed with his near-date, and is talked into hiring seedy private investigator Pat Healey (Dillon) to find out where she is today. Which is fine, except Healey falls in love with Mary himself, and concocts a string of lies to get himself into her good books. One of the best reasons to watch the film is the UK's Lee Evans, who plays the mysterious 'Brit' Tucker, who also has a thing for you know who, and then there's… You get the idea. Through no fault of her own, Mary is placed on a pedestal in the centre of a story of love, pain, franks, beans, shoes and extreme cruelty to dogs. And only a mouthless suicidal could fail to laugh themselves silly at it. You know when you're talking to your mates after watching a movie, "well, it was good, but wouldn't it have been even cooler if…"? That can't happen with *There's Something About Mary*. Everything that you want is in this film, and it will leave you feeling exhilarated. The movie has been an unprecedented success on VHS, but there are so many more reasons to get the DVD version. If you thought the Region 1 disc was amazing, the UK version's possibly even better, with the same interesting director's commentary, mainly consisting of Peter and Bob Farrelly pointing out friends that they gave extra parts to, and the original theatrical trailer, plus hilarious animated menus and, best of all, the fantastic music video and karaoke version of the end credits tune 'Build Me Up, Buttercup', which is worth the price of the disc alone. However, what really makes this a standout, or even standout-on-top-of-a-chair-shouting-through-a-megaphone Region 2 release is the fact that, unlike our American cousins, we are also treated to a special featurette with Mary's revolting flatmate Magda, instead of the US outtakes. This spectacularly entertaining film should be on every DVD owners shelf, and with these added extras, only the criminally insane or those too dazed with love will be able to resist a purchase.

FINAL VERDICT

Picture ☆☆☆☆☆ Sound ☆☆☆☆☆
Entertainment ☆☆☆☆☆ Extras ☆☆☆☆☆
Value ☆☆☆☆☆
OVERALL ☆☆☆☆☆

THE THING

Price: £19.99
Supplied by: Columbia TriStar Home Video
Type of disc: Dual layer, single-sided
No of chapters: 37
Film format(s)/length: 2.35:1 widescreen / 104 mins
Audio format: Dolby Digital 5.1
Director: John Carpenter
Starring: Kurt Russell, Richard Masur, David Clennon
Year made: 1982
Extras: Scene access; 80-minute behind-the-scenes feature *Terror Takes Shape*; outtakes; production notes; storyboards and conceptual art; location design; cast filmographies and photos; commentary by John Carpenter and Kurt Russell; trailer; soundtrack in French (Surround), Italian (stereo), Polish and Spanish (mono); subtitles in 9 languages.

Quite simply a master class in DVD production, *The Thing* is one of the finest Collector's Edition DVDs yet. Aside from a mass of interesting special features, the film itself is quite wonderfully presented. Although not enhanced for widescreen TVs, a pristine print has been perfectly reproduced on DVD.

From the polar wastelands to the frequent use of blue-red lighting, every frame of film looks wonderful, without the barest hint of artifacting. Ennio Morricone's soundtrack, developed from a typical Carpenter synthesiser motif, met with a mixed response, but its presentation on Dolby Digital is crystal clear. Sound effects are finely placed, heightening the uneasy impact of the visuals. Inspiration for the film came from a short story by John W Campbell, previously made into a celebrated movie by Howard Hawks in the Fifties. SFX limitations of the period meant the Thing's ability to shapeshift remained undeveloped, but it's unlikely even Campbell's darkest imaginings could approach Rob Bottin's terrifying creations. Released just two months after *ET*, *The Thing* received a mixed critical response and box office indifference, but it went on to become a cult film, popular with horror fans and academics alike. It's not difficult to see why. *The Thing* showcases a director at the peak of his powers, developing a sustained atmosphere of claustrophobic terror only *Alien* can match. For academics, the protean horror of *The Thing* makes for a wonderful metaphor for horror's roots in our deepest fear of unstoppable disease. It's nature in revolt, morphing and destroying with wanton disregard for human frailty. That said, the commentary by Carpenter and Kurt Russell notably stumbles when the pair attempt to claim *The Thing* was influenced by AIDS. Blood tests at the point of a flamethrower make for a less than subtle metaphor! Carpenter's rasping dissection of his movie is an impressive bonus (taken from the Laserdisc version), even if Russell's interjections rarely offer much insight. Production notes are somewhat crudely presented, with huge text flicking across the screen, one paragraph per page, but the content is good and the pictures interesting. The real draw, however, is an 80-minute 'Making of' documentary which reunites many of the main players over a decade on from the original production. These bonus documentaries can often be disappointing in terms of picture quality, but not here, the presentation is as razor-sharp as the main feature. The cast and crew have plenty of interesting anecdotes, plus there's footage from an unused stop-motion finale. Overall, this is a modern day horror classic that fully deserves its lavish presentation on DVD.

FINAL VERDICT

Picture ☆☆☆☆☆ Sound ☆☆☆☆☆
Entertainment ☆☆☆☆☆ Extras ☆☆☆☆☆
Value ☆☆☆☆☆
OVERALL ☆☆☆☆☆

THE THIN RED LINE

Price: £19.99
Supplied by: 20th Century Fox Home Entertainment
Type of disc: Dual layer, single-sided
No of chapters: 31
Film format(s)/length: 2.35:1 anamorphic / 170 mins
Audio format: Dolby Digital 5.1
Director: Terrence Malick
Starring: Sean Penn, Nick Nolte, Jim Caviezel
Year made: 1998
Extras: Scene access; theatrical trailer; 11 Melanesian Songs (audio only); subtitles in 20 languages; subtitles for the hearing impaired in English.

Terrence Malick's 1998 war flick was one of the Nineties' most anticipated films. Even though it split critics upon its release, it's a perfect film for DVD. The pristine widescreen images would blur into incoherence on VHS, while the sophisticated multi-layered soundtrack demands Dolby Digital 5.1. The presentation of the film really matters because, despite its literary source, Malick has crafted a piece of pure cinema, where conventional plot is secondary to imagery and sound. Over and over, there are abrupt cutaways to nature shots and extraordinary landscapes, contrasts which could only work with perfect reproduction. Fox is to be congratulated on an extraordinary piece of coding. The military framework is bluntly described by John Travolta – a Pacific island is playing host to a Japanese airfield, which must be destroyed. Upon this simplistic plan, however, is laid a mosaic of human experiences, thoughts and feelings, laid bare by extraordinary imagery and a fragmentary voiceover. The film opens with a crocodile slipping beneath the water, while the voiceover talks about opposing forces in nature. Sean Penn lectures a deserter bluntly: "In this world, a man by himself is nothing. And there ain't no other world but this one." It's a very brutal, very un-American pessimism. As in real life, incidents spring out of nothing, without build-up or logic. A snake slithering out of the undergrowth, a native wandering past a patrol, Woody Harrelson's tragic grenade mishap – "I blew my butt off!" – are just a handful of memorable episodes in Malick's difficult, stridently uncommercial epic. Whether it's pretentious twaddle or a majestic achievement is still uncertain, but its 3-hour running time includes moments of brilliance and tedium. Unsurprisingly, Malick certainly isn't the sort of director to provide a chatty voiceover. Aside from 11 audio-only Melanesian tracks and a theatrical trailer, this is a DVD stripped to basics. But then, the film that looks

and sounds so good no other advertisement for DVD is needed.

FINAL VERDICT
Picture ☆☆☆☆☆ Sound ☆☆☆☆☆
Entertainment ☆☆☆☆ Extras ☆☆ Value ☆☆☆
OVERALL ☆☆☆☆

THE THIRTEENTH FLOOR

Price: £19.99
Supplied by: Columbia TriStar Home Entertainment
Type of disc: Single layer, single-sided
No of chapters: 28
Film format(s)/length: 2.35:1 anamorphic / 96 mins
Audio format: Dolby Digital 5.1
Director: Josef Rusnak
Starring: Craig Bierko, Vincent D'Onofrio, Armin Mueller-Stahl
Year made: 1999
Extras: Audio commentary from Josef Rusnak and Kirk Petruccelli (production designer); before and after SFX comparison; conceptual art gallery; filmographies; music video: The Cardigans' 'Erase/Rewind'; original theatrical trailer.

This film was criminally overlooked on release in favour of the box office-friendly bluster of *The Matrix*. Both films posed the same essential questions. What is reality? Who is the creator? But thankfully, *The Thirteenth Floor* offers answers from more distinct sources than the pages of a comic. Producer Roland Emmerich's foray into the deeper side of sci-fi, following the stagnant puddles of *Independence Day* and *Godzilla*, is based on the Seventies novel *Simulacron 3* by acclaimed author Daniel Galouye. On the thirteenth floor of a $2 billion high rise in downtown Los Angeles, the boundaries of real and unreal are set to combust when the company's high-tech visionary, Hannon Fuller (Mueller-Stahl), is found slashed to death in a Skid Row alley. The bewildered Douglas Hall (Bierko) becomes prime suspect for the murder, yet he is convinced that the real murderer's identity lies waiting in the revolutionary virtual reality created by Fuller. Hall jacks into the computer and becomes a new person, John Ferguson, in an artificially generated 1937. But is this 'reality' any less valid than the one outside? While the speculations on man's humanity are not particularly original (even *Tron* managed a few sobering moments), the calculated script has been transplanted with reverence to film. A little too much reverence perhaps, as a few moments of flippancy occasionally creep through the otherwise contemplative mood. It's clear that production designer Kirk Petrucculli has had a great impact on the movie, which looks even better on DVD. The picture quality is sharp and distinct with seamless special effects. The extras here showcase the effects that go unnoticed; the SFX comparison featurette is a surprising glance at how 1937 LA was created in the present. Other extras, such as the commentary and conceptual art files, offer an eye-opening look at the creation of the glamorous set piece bars and hotel lobbies that draw you into the film's *noir* illusion. It's rare to find a DVD that's as complete as *The Thirteenth Floor*; the film is a lavish and intelligent blend of film *noir* thrills and soul-searching sci-fi, with extras that compound the themes of the feature. It's a quality package, and one sci-fi fans would be foolish to miss.

FINAL VERDICT

Picture ☆☆☆☆ Sound ☆☆☆☆
Entertainment ☆☆☆☆ Extras ☆☆☆☆☆
Value ☆☆☆☆☆
OVERALL ☆☆☆☆

THE 13TH WARRIOR

Price: £15.99
Supplied by: Touchstone Home Video
Type of disc: Dual layer, single-sided
No of chapters: 17
Film format(s)/length: 2.35:1 widescreen / 98 mins
Audio format: Dolby Digital 5.1
Director: John McTiernan
Starring: Antonio Banderas, Diane Venora, Omar Sharif
Year made: 1999
Extras: Scene access; soundtrack in English, Spanish and Italian; multilingual subtitles.

When a film is flagged as being written by the author of *Jurassic Park* and directed by the man behind *Die Hard*, you rather expect that you're going to be given something special. Unfortunately, *The 13th Warrior* simply doesn't manage to deliver. Antonio Banderas plays an exiled Arab called Ahmed who is sent as an ambassador far from his homeland to a place where the savage 'North Men' live. In a rather laboured plot development, there is a sudden need for 13 warriors to cross the sea on a quest and one of them must (apparently) be a foreigner. So before you can say, 'You lot are Vikings, right?' the quest is on and Ahmed finds himself fighting a savage band of cannibals called the Wendol. There's nothing really bad about this movie, it's just that there's nothing particularly special about it either. The plot is fairly clichéd and most of the action scenes rather annoyingly take place at night, making it rather difficult to see what's going on. The whole thing is just, well it's

just very… average. The DVD, though, is not at all average – it's totally rubbish. A couple of extra languages and a handful of subtitles are all that we get. If there was a brief documentary or something on the rather gory fight scenes, then that at least would have been a decent selling point, but as it is you're probably better off buying the video!

FINAL VERDICT

Picture ☆☆☆☆ Sound ☆☆☆ Entertainment ☆☆☆
Extras ☆ Value ☆☆
OVERALL ☆☆

THE 39 STEPS

Price: £19.99
Supplied by: DVD World (01705 796662)
Type of disc: Single layer, single-sided
No of chapters: 10
Film format(s)/length: 4:3 regular / 82 mins
Audio format: Mono
Director: Alfred Hitchcock
Starring: Robert Donat, Madeleine Carroll, Peggy Ashcroft
Year made: 1935
Extras: In-depth biographies of all actors plus Hitchcock; scene access.

For a black and white classic made over 60 years ago, *The 39 Steps* has outdone even Joan Collins when it comes to holding back the ravages of time. Okay, so some of the special effects are pretty basic compared to modern equivalents, but hey, the computer hadn't even been invented in 1935, so fancy morphing graphics weren't exactly an option. What's important is that the plot, direction and acting are all top quality, and it shows. Robert Donat plays Richard Hannay, the dashing lead who's inadvertently caught up in a net of murder, mystery and intrigue. He spends the majority of the film fleeing from spies who always seem to be on the verge of killing him, but never quite finish the job. Donat is far too slippery to be caught for long, so there's ample mileage for Hitchcock to include many an epic escape and dice with death. There's one classic moment when the youthful Fraser of *Dad's Army* shops Donat to the police for a bribe, then a cat and mouse chase across the moors ensues. The overall picture quality is astounding for such an old film, with virtually no visible grain or lack of definition. Shamefully though, the audio has been left as mono, and crackles and hisses incessantly throughout the entire film. Surely a quick clean up operation would have been worth the effort, Carlton? The extra 'in-depth' biographies aren't exactly lengthy, but do provide the odd morsel of interesting information that might come in handy at social functions, when it all goes quiet and you can't think of anything to say. For instance, this was Hitchcock's first experimentation with ice cool blondes, apparently, and it was only because Madeleine Carroll gave such a sterling performance that he became hooked on the idea and made it a trademark of most of his later films. Since *The 39 Steps* is a Hitchcock classic, you would expect a few juicy extras about the fantastic director himself, but Carlton has chosen to stick to a pretty basic package. If you've got the VHS copy already, you'd be better off saving your money, but if you haven't, buy it now, if only to see a master director in action.

FINAL VERDICT

Picture ☆☆☆☆☆ Sound ☆ Entertainment ☆☆☆☆
Extras ☆☆ Value ☆☆☆
OVERALL ☆☆☆☆

THIS IS SPINAL TAP

Price: £15.99
Supplied by: Abbey Road Interactive
Type of disc: Single layer, single-sided
No of chapters: 44
Film format(s)/length: 1.75:1 widescreen / 79 mins
Director: Rob Reiner
Starring: Christopher Guest, Michael McKean, Harry Shearer
Year made: 1984
Extras: Quotable lines from the film; film chapters divided into music venues; character biographies; song lyrics.

Reiner's razor sharp, satirical rockumentary was revolutionary back in 1982, and the good news is that it's still as fresh and funny today on its DVD debut. The trim 79-minute film follows the Tap on their American promotional tour, and is filmed in a *cinema verite* style which reveals the group, warts and all, as they plunge from obscurity to utter non-existence and the inevitable split. Packed with quotable lines and held together by understated performances from the main band members Nigel Tufnel (Guest) and David St Hubbins (McKean), and particularly their long suffering manager Ian Faith (Tony Hendra), this DVD is perfect for devoted fans and those who haven't yet seen the film (myself included). Special sections on the front menu include song lyrics – "My baby fits me like a flesh tuxedo, I love to sink her with my pink torpedo" – legendary quotes, the film divided into tour venues not chapters, and finally some extensive character biogs which further enhance Tap mythology. *This Is Spinal Tap* is a genuine classic and one that should be in the collection of anyone who

enjoyed the Comic Strip's Bad News Tour. Buy it if you like to laugh. (Book editor's note: or opt for the extras-packed Special Edition, which is due out just as this goes to print. It goes up to 11, apparently).

FINAL VERDICT

Picture ☆☆☆ Sound ☆☆☆☆
Entertainment ☆☆☆☆☆ Extras ☆☆☆☆
Value ☆☆☆☆
OVERALL ☆☆☆☆

THIS YEAR'S LOVE

Price: £19.99
Supplied by: Entertainment in Video
Type of disc: Dual layer, single-sided
No of chapters: 12
Film format(s)/length: 16:9 anamorphic widescreen / 104 mins
Audio format: Dolby Pro Logic
Director: David Kane
Starring: Douglas Henshall, Catherine McCormack, Ian Hart
Year made: 1999
Extras: Scene access; featurette; various interviews; 'Making of' footage; trailer.

No matter how powerful the medium, if a film is awful it doesn't matter if it's in perfect Technicolor and tiptop Dolby sound, watching it is still a wasting your life. *This Year's Love* is just such a waste all round. Part of an irritating trend in both British and US cinema towards drama and comedy which claims to be based on 'real relationships' and is producing overlong, poorly scripted and soul-destroying representations of love. If life was as sod-awful and grey as is presented here, we'd all spend our time trying to find spectacularly inventive ways to kill ourselves. The story is that of 3 couples who, over the course of 3 years, end up coincidentally swapping partners in hopeful bids for happiness. This unconvincing plot contrivance is the first problem, but there are many more. Writer/director Kane seems to believe that in order for characters to be believable they have to be flawed. This is true, but everyone here is devoid of any redeeming feature whatsoever. It is a pointlessly depressing and damning take on relationships. The extras aren't much cop either. The 'Making of' is a slice of behind-the-scenes camcorder footage, without any attempt to package it into a programme, and the interviews are roughly cut together and dumped on the disc. But at least they're there. Together with the featurette, they offer snatches of the ebullient Douglas Henshall and Ian Hart, good actors who should be wondering why they appeared in such a vile movie.

FINAL VERDICT

Picture ☆☆☆☆ Sound ☆☆☆☆ Entertainment ☆
Extras ☆☆☆ Value ☆
OVERALL ☆☆

THE THOMAS CROWN AFFAIR

Price: £19.99
Supplied by: Warner Home Video
Type of disc: Dual layer, single-sided
No of chapters: 32
Film format(s)/length:1.85:1 widescreen / 102 mins
Audio format: Mono
Director: Norman Jewison
Starring: Steve McQueen, Faye Dunaway, Paul Burke
Year made: 1968
Extras: Scene access; original (and highly amusing) theatrical trailer; audio commentary by director Norman Jewison; 8-page booklet on film's production; soundtrack in English, German, Spanish, French and Italian; multilingual subtitles; subtitles for the hearing impaired in English and Dutch.

It's a canny move on behalf of Warner to re-issue this 1968 classic in the wake of the international success of the current remake. Whilst it's a commonly held view that the original is still the best, this steadfast McQueen vehicle is beginning to show its age, especially in comparison with *Thomas Crown* a lá Brosnan and Russo. Steve McQueen plays the titular rogue, an already wealthy businessman planning a bank robbery just for kicks. Crown doesn't have much opportunity to feel smug, though, as wily insurance investigator Vicky Anderson (Dunaway), is hot on his tail. The cat-and-mouse game that ensues between the pair is the film's real magic, with the highlight being the strangely erotic game of chess between the duo. Whilst most DVDs that are worth their salt at the very least include the movie's theatrical trailer as standard, these on their own are seldom anything to rave about. However, the fact that the *Thomas Crown Affair* DVD has the original trailer from the late Sixties is something worth mentioning, as it shows how far this understated art has come. Today's cinema audiences expect to see MTV-style editing married with a modern techno soundtrack in their movie trailers… one look at the original *Thomas Crown* Affair trailer will make the more cynical amongst you wonder how on earth it would encourage anybody to want to go and see the movie. Still, it's highly entertaining nonetheless. The recent glut of older movies being re-issued on DVD has meant that the majority of them are ill-conceived attempts to raise a quick buck. Apart from the occasional efforts to upgrade the quality of the picture and soundtrack (with some companies not even bothering to do even that), there is very little reason why anyone should spend £15-20 on a DVD when they could pick up a VHS version with the same contents and save £5-10 into the bargain. However, Warner have apparently twigged that the average DVD punter expects that little bit more, as there is an audio commentary from *Thomas Crown*'s director, Norman Jewison (who was also responsible for *Moonstruck* and *In the Heat of the Night*). There's also an informative 8-page booklet giving background details on the film's production. Nice effort, Warner.

FINAL VERDICT

Picture ☆☆☆☆ Sound ☆☆☆☆ Entertainment ☆☆☆
Extras ☆☆☆ Value ☆☆☆☆
OVERALL ☆☆☆☆

THE THOMAS CROWN AFFAIR

Price: £19.99
Supplied by: MGM Home Entertainment
Type of disc: Dual layer, single-sided
No of chapters: 36
Film format(s)/length: 16:9 widescreen enhanced / 113 mins
Audio format: Dolby Digital 5.1
Director: John McTiernan
Starring: Pierce Brosnan, Rene Russo, Denis Leary
Year made: 1999
Extras: Scene access; *The Making of a Masterpiece* 23-minute documentary about both the remake and the original; audio commentary by director John McTiernan; Sting's music video for 'The Windmills of Your Mind'; soundtrack in German and French; subtitles in English and French; subtitles for the hearing impaired in Dutch.

From the opening scene you know you're in for a fun time. We get a glimpse of Brosnan's trademark smirk, then we're off tracking him from the museum to his sprawling offices with a soundtrack of rhythmic applause. Whether Bond or a billionaire playboy, Brosnan is every man's favourite alter ego and the first robbery is a romp we can't wait to follow. Cleverly, McTiernan plays on our eagerness for some action in order to create an understanding of Crown's own impatience with the world of business, and his underlying temptation to steal what he could just as easily buy. One of 1999's least hyped movies, *The Thomas Crown Affair* provided a welcome sense of humour and zest. MGM clearly recognise this, lavishing plenty of attention on the UK DVD release, which is actually superior to the US version. Whereas the latter only offers a choice of widescreen and fullscreen versions, plus a trailer, director's commentary and booklet, the UK version retains the latter 3 but ditches the aspect ratio choice. Instead, we get Sting's pop video take on the original movie's Oscar-winning track, 'The Windmills of Your Mind', plus an 23-minute documentary, which proves to be unusually generous toward the original 1968 version of the movie, including an interview with director Norman Jewison and plentiful clips recounting the story of the film with some style. McQueen and Dunaway's charisma clearly hasn't dimmed with time, and a box set of both movies would be a real treat. The genesis of the remake was actually with Pierce Brosnan, who picked up the rights for his film production company, Irish Dreamtime, and produced the whole venture. Next on board was McTiernan, whose troubles with gloomy swords and cannibalism in *The 13th Warrior* no doubt helped make him receptive to such light fare. Brosnan actually appeared in McTiernan's 1986 debut flick, *Nomads*, and the two genuinely praise each other. Rene Russo completed the leading trio, and it's her performance which steals the picture. In shades, thigh-high boots and leather jacket, she wields a flick-knife with utter conviction during one memorable break-in. Where Dunaway's was little more than a momentary diversion in the original film, Russo's romance with Brosnan's billionaire playboy thief is central to the remake. Playing an insurance investigator, she's soon running rings around weary police detective Denis Leary, all the time moving closer to Brosnan. The original movie revolved around the notion of crime as sport, with McQueen as the bored millionaire testing his mind against a bank's defences. Brosnan is more of a prankster. He plays chess with a diversionary force but strolls in himself to steal a $100m Monet painting. The hirelings are left to serve time, but Brosnan moves on and the film takes flight, literally, with a romantic glider excursion which leads to a private jet trip to Martinique and more sex and games. Rene Russo led the film's PR, with marketing focusing on the notion of a 40-something actress daring to bare nearly all. In fact, it's difficult to recall any mainstream thriller quite so horny as this Brosnan production. The first coupling makes rabbits look leisurely as it progresses up marble stairs, through various rooms and on and on. Later, on the beach Russo blithely goes topless again, with Brosnan courting fashion disaster in a sarong. It's a European-style maturity, but McTiernan's style lacks the lightness of touch of, say, Milos Forman's classic *Unbearable Lightness of Being*. You understand what he's aiming for, without actual-ly being pulled in. That said, it's all done with such cheek… (Brosnan's for the most part, but his arse aside) that you can't help having fun. It's a reasonably smart film, the dialogue is actually pretty good, there are some neat exchanges which recall movies even older than the original, and it's the romance rather than the crime which provides the real tension. Does he really love her? Or is it all just another game? Aside from the wealth of extras, the production quality of the DVD is first class, with a bright, clean print transfer. Sound quality is similarly impressive, particularly during the glider scene. Overall, this is a first class flagship which, while hardly a classic film, is highly entertaining and superbly presented on DVD.

FINAL VERDICT

Picture ☆☆☆☆☆ Sound ☆☆☆☆

Entertainment ☆☆☆☆ Extras ☆☆☆☆☆

Value ☆☆☆☆☆

OVERALL ☆☆☆☆☆

THREE KINGS

Price: £19.99

Supplied by: Warner Home Video

Type of disc: Dual layer, single-sided

No of chapters: 31

Film format(s)/length: 2.35:1 anamorphic / 115 mins

Audio format: Dolby Digital 5.1

Director: David O Russell

Starring: George Clooney, Mark Wahlberg, Ice Cube

Year made: 1999

Extras: Scene access; audio commentary by director David O Russell; audio commentary by producers Charles Roven and Ed McDonnell; *Under the Bunker* behind the scenes documentary; David O Russell's video diary; an interview with Director of Photography, Newton Thomas Sigel; *Tour of the Iraqi Village Set* featurette; *An Intimate Look Inside the Acting Process with Ice Cube* featurette; stills gallery; theatrical trailer; subtitles in English; subtitles for the hearing impaired in English.

Hollywood has shown uncharacteristic restraint in depicting the Gulf War on the silver screen. Perhaps it's too soon after the last Scud missile was misfired, or perhaps it's because Industrial Light & Magic has yet to think of a way to better the hi-tech drama and explosions we saw and took for granted on CNN. In his first big-budget studio picture, David O Russell took John Ridley's conventional wartime heist novel and filtered it through 18 months of his own research of the Gulf War. What emerges is *Three Kings*, a gripping, ludicrous, action-cum-heist-cum-Western-cum-road-cum-event movie. Throw in the new Cary Grant, Dirk Diggler and a rapper from

NWA, season with $50 million and stand well back. This film really shouldn't work, but it does, brilliantly. It's March 1991 and baffled US soldiers turn the desert into a Venice Beach frat party to celebrate the end of the Gulf War. Among them are family man Troy Barlow (Wahlberg) and trailer trash hick Conrad Vig (Spike Jonze). When a map leading to Saddam's stolen Kuwaiti gold is found up the arse of an Iraqi POW, the pair go AWOL with disillusioned career soldier Archie Gates (Clooney) and Detroit baggage handler Chief Elgin (Cube) to steal the bullion for themselves. Outside the shelter of base camp, the war's consequences become starkly clear and they must make a moral choice between saving the their enemy's citizens or a life on easy street. *Three Kings* is laced with moments of incredility, Russell portraying a confused, indiscriminate war fought over microwaves, food mixers, jeans and colour TVs. However, the comedic elements sit uneasily with scenes of torture and atrocities committed against civilians. The immortality DVDs give to films and film-makers means the real drama behind the scenes is airbrushed away. An on-location brawl ensued between Russell and 'Gorgeous George' and is this genre-blurring fact-based, satiric action comedy really what Warner Bros suits wanted? A harmonious, mutually-respectful creative unit is always presented to the world. No doubt when a Collector's Edition of *Apocalypse Now* is authored, Francis Ford Coppola will come on and say making it was a breeze! The DVD is a formidable package for the UK. Picture quality is the best it could be and the 3 signifying changes in film stock work excellently here. Sound is dynamite, particularly during the plaza sequence. The best supplements have to be Russell's 'video journal', which sees our hero cycling to meetings with money men and Clooney and bumping into Spike Jonze, along with Cube's self-deprecating turn. Sadly, this being a Region 2 DVD, there apparently have to be drawbacks. To make room for subtitles (presumably), the production notes and bios on the Region 1 disc are abandoned. Both commentaries are good: Russell concentrates on the genesis of the script, while the producers discuss practical and technical concerns. All 3 fondly recall screening *Three Kings* to Clinton in the White House. Just one of the 3 Easter Eggs (hidden features) survives the Atlantic. The DVD-ROM material is also deficient. Instead of links to CNN.com's Gulf War archives, all this disc does is advertise Warner Bros merchandise. *Three Kings* is a remarkable, inventive, satisfying and challenging film with good performances and a witty script. It's a mod-

ern classic, a film so much of its time that it hurts. However, it also shows that DVD producers continue to walk the tightrope between consumer demands for identical (or better) products to the Americans and the financial imperative to make one disc for as many international consumers as possible.

FINAL VERDICT

Picture ☆☆☆☆☆ Sound ☆☆☆☆

Entertainment ☆☆☆☆☆ Extras ☆☆☆☆

Value ☆☆☆☆

OVERALL ☆☆☆☆

THUNDERBALL

Price: £19.99
Supplied by: MGM Home Entertainment
Type of disc: Dual layer, single-sided
No of chapters: 32
Film format(s)/length: 2.35:1 anamorphic / 125 mins
Audio format: Stereo
Director: Terence Young
Starring: Sean Connery, Claudine Auger, Adolfo Celi
Year made: 1965
Extras: Scene access; *The Thunderball Phenomenon* documentary; *The Making of Thunderball* documentary; *Inside Thunderball* featurette; stills gallery featuring over 50 images; 3 theatrical trailers; 5 TV spots; 10 radio trailers; booklet containing production notes; subtitles in English; subtitles for the hearing impaired in English.

Welcome to the biggest Bond of the Sixties! After breakthrough hit *Dr No*, the Cold War antics of *From Russia With Love* and the legendary fantasy of *Goldfinger*, Connery reunited with the first two films' director to create *Thunderball*, a free-for-all action caper of the first order. SPECTRE's Emilio Largo (Celi) steals two atomic warheads and holds the West to ransom. All 9 00 agents from across Europe are recalled (including one female operative) to track down the missing arsenal and thwart Largo's plans. After a sluggish start at a health farm James Bond is back in full effect, from the rocket pack escape before the credits to the dramatic underwater sequences which make up 25 per cent of the script. All the ingredients are here: exotic locations, diabolical villain, beautiful girls, casual violence and even more casual sex. The film also introduces a smattering of new concepts, like Bond's predilection for female doctors and nurses as well as a female assassin who gives Mr Kiss Kiss Bang Bang a good run for his money, and even tells him a few home truths. This being the first 007 movie filmed in widescreen, the picture is almost perfect save for the occasional dust specks, but these are few and far between enough to not distract from your enjoyment, but it would have been a simple operation for MGM to clean them up. The audio has been upgraded to stereo, but is prone to moments of hissing. A full 5.1 audio remaster would have been appreciated. The 3-minute featurette reveals how different versions made their way to theatres and video and talks about the two deleted scenes, of which only photographs remain. *The Thunderball Phenomenon* spends half an hour exploring the impact the movie had when it was first released in December 1965, how singing duties changed hands between Shirley Bassey, Dionne Warwick and finally Tom Jones, and that David Niven was Ian Fleming's first choice for Bond until he became enamoured with Connery's portrayal. *The Making of Thunderball* uses its 30 minutes to discuss the legal wrangles which resulted in 1983's godawful *Never Say Never Again,* a pale remake of *Thunderball,* and how the 102 cast and crew plus 12 and a half tons of equipment mobilised in the Bahamas for location shooting. Two commentaries at this price? Can't be bad. John Cork of the Fleming Foundation links testimonies from the film-makers and cast during the first while, on the second he talks with jovial supervising editor Peter Hunt and ponderous co-writer John Hopkins. *Thunderball* bridges the gap between the tough Fleming espionage stories and the multi-million dollar excesses of the Roger Moore years. Apart from the meaningless title and sub-standard theme song, it's what we demand from 007 and the DVD represents what we expect from MGM.

FINAL VERDICT

Picture ☆☆☆☆ Sound ☆☆☆ Entertainment ☆☆☆☆
Extras ☆☆☆☆☆ Value ☆☆☆☆
OVERALL ☆☆☆☆

TIMECOP

Price: £19.99
Supplied by: DVDplus (www.dvdplus.co.uk)
Type of disc: Dual layer, single-sided
No of chapters: 16
Film format(s)/length: 2.35:1 widescreen / 94 mins
Audio format: Dolby Digital 5.1
Director: Peter Hyams
Starring: Jean-Claude Van Damme, Ron Silver, Mia Sara
Year made: 1994
Extras: Scene access; production notes; cast and crew biographies; trailer; soundtrack in English, French, German, Spanish (5.1) and Czech (Surround); subtitles in 10 languages.

If you have geekish tendencies and enjoy picking holes in the plots of films involving time travel, you'll love *Timecop*. Just when you think the film-makers have done something clever with time paradoxes, they immediately go and contradict themselves, then end the story with the most corny 'reset button' trick imaginable. Wouldn't Van Damme's onscreen wife be disturbed that her husband has been replaced by a haggard double with completely different memories of the last decade, who doesn't even know the name of their son? Still, the target audience for Van Damme movies probably couldn't care less about gaping plot holes, as long as there's a bad guy getting his head caved in every 5 minutes. Reliable hack Hyams orchestrates some decent fights (though even with the '18' certificate, they seem toned down – the BBFC, working to protect you from high-kicking Belgians!) and Van Damme even makes a valiant stab at acting in a couple of scenes. However, Ron Silver steals the film away from him as a slimy, two-timing (in a quite literal sense), US senator who talks like Doctor Evil. The picture quality is a letdown; and it has a grainy look in places. DVD's better colour definition makes it really obvious when somebody's been superimposed onto a scene so they can meet an earlier version of themself. There aren't many extras either, though the trailer – which begins with the 1920's version of the Universal logo – is quite amusing. Overall, it's a reasonable piece of DVD action fluff.

FINAL VERDICT

Picture ☆☆ Sound ☆☆☆ Entertainment ☆☆☆
Extras ☆☆ Value ☆☆☆
OVERALL ☆☆☆

A TIME TO KILL

Price: £15.99
Supplied by: DVD Net (0208 890 2520)
Type of disc: Single layer, double-sided
No of chapters: 46
Film length/format(s): 16:9 widescreen / 143 mins
Director: Joel Schumacher
Starring: Samuel L Jackson, Matthew McConaughey, Sandra Bullock
Year made: 1996
Extras: Scene select; theatrical trailer; production notes; film flash; multilingual subtitles.

From the pen of John Grisham (*The Client, The Pelican Brief*) comes this powerful tale of the pursuit of justice amid the racial tension of the Deep South. When two drunken rednecks assault and rape his young daughter, black construction worker Carl Lee (Jackson) takes the law into his own hands and guns them down in front of dozens of witnesses. Matthew McConaughey is Jake, the young white lawyer assigned to defend him. With the town divided on the issue and the Ku Klux Klan on the march for blood, Jake has his work cut out, even with the help of attractive law student Ellen (Bullock). The DVD content is fairly good for a UK release, with production notes, the theatrical trailer and suggestions for other films you might enjoy if you liked this one. However, you do have to flip the disc halfway through, which is annoying, and the scene selection, although it contains 46 chapters, only lets you jump to a total of 9 from the main menu.

FINAL VERDICT

Picture ☆☆☆☆ S ound ☆☆☆☆

Entertainment ☆☆☆☆ Extras ☆☆ Value ☆☆☆

OVERALL ☆☆☆

TINA: WHAT'S LOVE GOT TO DO WITH IT?

Price: £15.99
Supplied by: DVDplus (www.dvdplus.co.uk)
Type of disc: Dual layer, single-sided
No of chapters: 22
Film format(s)/length: 1.85:1 widescreen enhanced / 113 mins
Audio format: Dolby Digital 5.1
Director: Brian Gibson
Starring: Angela Bassett, Laurence Fishburne, Vanessa Bell Calloway
Year made: 1993
Extras: Scene access; English and Dutch subtitles; soundtrack in English, French and Italian.

The continuing lack of extras on Buena Vista discs continue to infuriate, but this is an excellent film that, rather unexpectedly, is also a reasonable DVD. Telling the life story of Tina Turner (Bassett) and Ike Turner (Fishburne), it's no coincidence that the two leads were each nominated for Oscars for their powerful portrayals of these extraordinary characters. The picture quality is okay, but nothing to sing about. For the most part, this also applies to the soundtrack – although that changes when Turner's tunes turn up. The DVD is a fairly good effort, but as is the case with the movie, it's aimed more at the fans of the resilient rock star. As usual, we'd love to see a special edition at a later date, but as it stands, this will do for the time being.

FINAL VERDICT

Picture ☆☆☆ Sound ☆☆☆☆

Entertainment ☆☆☆☆ Extras ☆ Value ☆☆☆

OVERALL ☆☆☆

TIN CUP

Price: £15.99
Supplied by: Warner Home Video
Type of disc: Single layer, single-sided
No of chapters: 36
Film format(s)/length: 16:9 widescreen / 129 mins
Director: Ron Shelton
Starring: Kevin Costner, Rene Russo, Cheech Marin
Year made: 1996
Extras: Interactive menus/scene selection; production notes; cast biographies; film recommendations; Dolby Digital 5.1; multilingual subtitles.

The impossible challenge is what defines driving-range pro Roy McAvoy (Costner). Never one to denounce the unreachable, McAvoy takes on more than he can handle in big city shrink Molly Griswold (Russo). Battle-of-the-sexes banter with Molly and slick rivalry with ex-golfing partner David Simms (Don Johnson) ensues, as McAvoy sets out to do the impossible: win the US Open. Costner is reunited with *Bull Durham* director Ron Shelton, but once more his acting is more wooden than the Cuprinol man. Fortunately, the picture and sound quality are sharper than the scriptwriter's wit – you can literally hear the golf ball whistling cleanly through the air. As for the extras, the first is the scene selection menu – unforgivably, out of a possible 36, Warner Bros felt that only 9 staggered chapters were needed. Also included are production notes, cast biographies and film recommendations – if you like pages of text. A decent film, but below par DVD.

FINAL VERDICT

Picture ☆☆☆ Sound ☆☆☆ Entertainment ☆☆

Extras ☆☆ Value ☆

OVERALL ☆☆

TITANIC

Price: £24.99
Supplied by: 20th Century Fox
Type of disc: Dual layer, single-sided
No of chapters: 30
Film format(s)/length: 2.30:1 widescreen / 189 mins
Audio format: Digital 5.1
Director: James Cameron
Starring: Kate Winslet, Leonardo DiCaprio, Billy Zane
Year made: 1997
Extras: Scene selection; Dolby Surround or Dolby Digital sound options; subtitles; general trailer.

Amazingly, *Titanic* is still the highest grossing movie of all time. It's the film that made women cry, men cheer and teenage boys cross their legs. It's also the winner of 11, count them, 11 Academy Awards: Costume, Film Editing, Visual Effects, Original Dramatic Score, Original Song, Sound, Sound Effects Editing, Cinematography, Art Direction, Director and, finally, Best Film all went to Cameron's offering in the 1998 Oscars Ceremony. Which makes this DVD release all the more stupifyingly pathetic. Some people might say that the fact that the movie itself is over 3 hours long is reason enough not to include any extras, and it has to be admitted that it's a boon to be able to watch this monster of a movie at your leisure, chapter by chapter even, instead of sitting in an uncomfortable cinema seat. But that's no excuse for releasing such a barren disc. Surprisingly, even the Region 1 version is no better. You get the film (with improved sound and picture quality), the trailer, a choice of subtitles, and that's your lot. After Cameron spent the national deficit of a small country bringing his script to the screen, you could at least expect a bit of extra information thrown in, some background facts and so on, but even this is denied. Even the most hardened Leo-bashers had to begrudgingly admit, possibly with a lump in their throat, that *Titanic* was a good depiction of a tragic event, with shockingly good effects and genuine passion. But although the movie is presented here in a superior format, it's got to be far more sensible to go and buy the VHS for a few quid rather than forking out an extra £10 for a virtually extra-less DVD. With this *Titanic* DVD, the creators have taken a mindlessly successful cinematic presentation, and jumped on it from an extreme height. Pride comes before a fall, Mr Cameron.

FINAL VERDICT

Picture ☆☆☆☆☆ Sound ☆☆☆☆☆
Entertainment ☆☆☆☆ Extras ☆ Value ☆☆
OVERALL ☆☆☆

TOMBSTONE

Price: £15.99
Supplied by: Entertainment in Video
Type of disc: Dual layer, single-sided
No of chapters: 12
Film format(s)/length: 2:35:1 widescreen / 120 mins
Audio format: Dolby Surround
Director: George P Cosmatos
Starring: Kurt Russell, Val Kilmer, Michael Biehn
Year made: 1993
Extras: Scene access; trailer; 'Making of' featurette.

Inspired in part by Kevin Costner's mega-budget *Wyatt Earp* production, *Tombstone* turned out to be a cheaper, more zestful take on a much filmed

American legend. Kilmer makes for a wonderfully wasted Doc Holliday, while Russell is perfectly respectable as Wyatt himself, and Biehn turns in another of his trademarked, but nonetheless highly effective 'crazed loon with a gun' performances as Johnny Ringo. The supporting cast is also as impressive, ranging from rising stars such as Bill Paxton and Billy Zane through to Charlton Heston in a cameo role. There's even narration by Robert Mitchum. It's a shame then, that the villains are such obvious caricatures, but this is a film that is desperate to entertain rather than enlighten. The DVD reproduction is generally respectable. A little grain from the film stock sometimes becomes evident, but nothing which is really distracting. It's a pity the film hasn't been enhanced for widescreen, but this was never going to be a showcase DVD. The original movie was presented in Dolby Surround, not Digital, and there's been no attempt to upgrade it for DVD. A 'Making of' documentary is actually nothing of the sort, being instead an extended (6 minutes) trailer which intersperses the usual action clips with the actors and director chatting about characters and plot. They all struggle manfully to make *Tombstone* seem relevant to a modern audience by playing up family – *Tombstone* as *The Godfather* in spurs, basically. An interesting notion, although the ambitious comparison ultimately does this fun, but lightweight, movie no favours.

FINAL VERDICT

Picture ☆☆☆☆ Sound ☆☆☆ Entertainment ☆☆☆☆
Extras ☆☆ Value ☆☆☆
OVERALL ☆☆☆

TOMORROW NEVER DIES

Price: £19.99
Supplied by: DVD Net (020 8890 2520)
Type of disc: Single layer, single-sided
No of chapters: 28
Film format(s)/length: 1.85:1 widescreen / 114 mins
Director: Roger Spottiswoode
Starring: Pierce Brosnan, Jonathan Pryce, Michelle Yeoh
Year made: 1997
Extras: Scene access; theatrical trailer; audio commentary; soundtrack only option; other DVD trailers.

Brosnan was made to play Bond – that much was obvious from the moment he donned the tuxedo, holstered the Walther PPK and sipped that vodka martini. *Tomorrow Never Dies* starts with a bang even the Bond series should be proud of, as the invincible secret agent steals a plane loaded with nuclear missiles from right under the noses of the world's most diabolical terrorists just before a cruise missile turns the entire site into a gigantic fireball. Top stuff, thanks to some of the best sound effects we have ever heard. From then on it's very much business as usual, with the world threatened by media mogul Elliot Carver, who's trying to start a war in China just to secure the TV rights. *Tomorrow Never Dies* is well directed, features some great set pieces (motorbike chase through Saigon, remote controlled BMW), and the DVD isn't bad either, for a change. Although not in the same league as the Region 1 disc (boasting interactive menus designed to mimic MI5 computers), we do still get audio commentary, original trailer and a soundtrack option. MGM should have gone straight to the Collectors' Edition for Region 2, then this would have been a 5 star review.

FINAL VERDICT

Picture ☆☆☆☆ Sound ☆☆☆☆☆
Entertainment ☆☆☆☆ Extras ☆☆☆
Value ☆☆☆
OVERALL ☆☆☆☆

TOP GUN

Price: £19.99
Supplied by: Paramount
Type of disc: Dual layer, single-sided
No of chapters: 30
Film format(s)/length: 2.00:1 anamorphic / 105 mins
Audio format: Dolby Digital 5.1
Director: Tony Scott
Starring: Tom Cruise, Kelly McGillis, Val Kilmer
Year made: 1986
Extras: Scene access; soundtrack in English, German, French, Italian and Spanish; subtitles for the hearing impaired in English; subtitles in 15 languages.

Don Simpson and Jerry Bruckheimer were the two producers who owned Hollywood during the Eighties and it was this loud, contrived, ridiculous and mildly entertaining movie that helped put them in that position of power. Ushering in the high concept story pitch that still curses Tinseltown today, the diabolical duo cast Tom Cruise, who turns up the intensity of his halogen-bright grin to play cocky aviator Pete 'Maverick' Mitchell. With wacky sidekick co-pilot Goose (Anthony Edwards), the two aim to be the very best at the US Navy's top flight academy. It's a pretty vacant movie cynically boasting macho posturing, zero cast chemistry, a woeful theme song from Berlin and dialogue so badly written even Joe Eszterhas would wince. Still, it's interesting to see homo-eroticism breaking into mainstream cinema in such a big way, as Quentin Tarantino once so memo-

rably pointed out. The disc's contents are alarmingly bad – it's like a relic from the dawn of DVDs 3 years ago – and not lavished with features as we now (post-*Jaws*) expect a major back-catalogue film with big stars and an even bigger budget to be. Granted, Paramount joined the global DVD party very, very late, but wasn't it paying attention to what other distributors were doing? Static, dull menus lead to an almost absurd number of language and soundtrack options. Even the most cash-strapped distributor manages to pack the theatrical trailer! One star for extras is being incredibly generous. Audio seems oddly muffled for the most part, the roar of the planes' afterburners notwithstanding. The picture is good enough for the non-discerning consumer but the anamorphic presentation is in a bizarre 2.00:1 widescreen. *Top Gun* is the perfect formulaic action movie. If you like your films obvious and predictable, and your stars tanned and grinning, you can't go far wrong with this.

FINAL VERDICT

Picture ☆☆☆ Sound ☆☆☆ Entertainment ☆☆
Extras ☆ Value ☆☆
OVERALL ☆☆

TRAINSPOTTING

Price: £17.99
Supplied by: PolyGram Filmed Entertainment
Type of disc: Single layer, double-sided
No of chapters: 20
Film format(s)/length: 4:3 (Side A), 16:9 widescreen (Side B) / 89 mins
Audio format: Dolby Digital 5.1
Director: Danny Boyle
Starring: Ewan McGregor, Robert Carlyle, Jonny Lee Miller
Year made: 1996
Extras: Scene access; soundtrack in English, French and German; multilingual subtitles; cast and crew biographies.

As *Trainspotting* finally arrives on DVD, the ironic incitement in the opening monologue, to "Choose a f*cking big television," seems strangely apt. Since its release 3 years ago, the film has become as much a part of the iconography of Nineties culture as the Spice Girls and The Simpsons, not to mention remaining the jewel in the crown of the British film industry. Not bad for a story about Scottish heroin addicts distilled from the sprawling yet brilliant novel by Irvine Welsh that gave new meaning to the word 'unfilmable.' Ewan McGregor completed his transition to pin-up and serious actor with the role of Renton, an anti-hero if ever there was one, trying to kick the habit whilst surrounded by a motley crew of losers, psychos and junkies. These include Bond fanatic Sick Boy (Lee Miller) and the supremely nasty Begbie (Carlyle), whose senseless attacks on strangers make for some of the most eye-wincing scenes in the film. Combining inventive visuals with a strategically used soundtrack, and alternating between the hilarious and the harrowing, *Trainspotting* is a shrewdly calculated piece of film-making, but consistently powerful nonetheless. Images such as the dead baby turned blue, the worst toilet in Scotland and the various shots of drug abuse are the sort that linger with you forever. But the comic relief, fast pace and cracking dialogue ensure that the tone is never grim for too long, and the script always steers clear of making a moral judgement. Despite a certain air of smugness, *Trainspotting* is undoubtedly one of the best films of the decade, and surely a must for any self-respecting DVD collection. The picture on the DVD is of top quality, maintaining the grainy look of the film while enhancing its colour and depth. Although confined mostly to dialogue and music, the 5.1 sound is also impressive, especially on the more 'banging' numbers on the soundtrack. The disc offers both the widescreen and pan-and-scan versions of the film, but unfortunately little else in the way of extras. Sure, there are biographies of the main members of the cast and crew, but these could have been written on the back of a postage stamp. And while the English subtitles on the Region 1 disc may have provided an invaluable service to Americans who couldn't understand the accents, they're hardly a special feature over here. The truly gutting point is that the Canadian Region 1 disc includes a 22-minute documentary, several deleted scenes (presumably those present on the Special Edition VHS) and the original theatrical trailer. Considering that *Trainspotting* runs for a mere hour-and-a-half, the Region 2 disc is something of a disappointment.

FINAL VERDICT

Picture ☆☆☆☆ Sound ☆☆☆☆
Entertainment ☆☆☆☆☆ Extras ☆☆ Value ☆☆☆
OVERALL ☆☆☆☆

TREASURE ISLAND

Price: £15.99
Supplied by: Warner Home Video
Type of disc: Single layer, single-sided
No of chapters: 11
Film format(s)/length: 1.33:1 regular / 92 mins
Audio format: Mono
Director: Byron Haskin

Starring: Bobby Driscoll, Robert Newton, Basil Sydney
Year made: 1950
Extras: Scene access; soundtrack in German and French; subtitles in Dutch and Greek; subtitles for the hearing impaired in English.

When there are so many top quality films just begging to be transformed into this wonderful digital form, why do companies assume that we want to be subjected to poor quality wet Saturday matinée movies? Sadly, that's what Disney have presented us with here. *Treasure Island* is the classic Robert Louis Stevenson tale of buried gold, pirates and swashbuckling action However, this offering from 1950 cannot convey the excitement it might have had on original release. Disney are priding themselves in the fact that this is the 'original and uncut' version, complete with artefacting, dodgy lighting and poorly painted scenery – which DVD picks up only too well. Consider this together with poor sound quality, no extras and the £15.99 price tag, and you're best leaving this DVD on the shelf. As part of a reasonably priced 'classic' box set this may work, but iIt certainly won't be on many children's Christmas lists this year.

FINAL VERDICT

Picture ☆ Sound ☆ Entertainment ☆ Extras ☆ Value ☆
OVERALL ☆

THE TRENCH

Price: £19.99
Supplied by: Entertainment in Video
Type of disc: Dual layer, single-sided
No of chapters: 12
Film format(s)/length: 1.85:1 letterbox / 95 mins
Audio format: Stereo
Director: William Boyd
Starring: Paul Nicholls, Daniel Craig, Julian Rhind-Tutt
Year made: 1999
Extras: Scene access; featurette; cast and crew interviews; behind the scenes footage.

Former *EastEnder* Paul Nicholls joins a brigade of accurately young actors in this thoughtful movie, set in the 38 hours before the Battle of the Somme during the First World War. Writer/director Boyd (probably best known for co-scribing *Chaplin*) creates an unsensational account of trench life and death. The film refuses to comment on the senseless slaughter it re-enacts, and instead focuses on the fraught relationships between a unit of men before the Big Push. We don't need to be told by film-makers that war is bad – we know already, thanks – so this change in angle is refreshing. EIV serves up its by now overly-familiar package of a reheated EPK (electronic press kit), though it's more polished than previous efforts. The well-designed menus are also due special credit. Recommended for all who enjoy watching quality human drama and not limbs flying through the air, but EIV needs to innovate.

FINAL VERDICT

Picture ☆☆☆ Sound ☆☆ Entertainment ☆☆☆
Extras ☆☆ Value ☆☆
OVERALL ☆☆☆

TRUE CRIME

Price: £15.99
Supplied by: Warner Brothers
Type of disc: Dual layer, single-sided
No of chapters: 39
Film format(s)/length: 1.85:1 widescreen / 122 mins
Audio format: Dolby Digital 5.1
Director: Clint Eastwood
Starring: Clint Eastwood, Isaiah Washington, Denis Leary
Year made: 1999
Extras: Scene access; *The Scene of the Crime* featurette, featuring interviews and behind the scenes footage; *True Crime: True Stories* featurette recounting a real-life journalist's experiences, mirroring the film; Diana Krall music video 'Why Should I Care?'; theatrical trailer; multilingual subtitles; subtitles for the hearing impaired in English.

Meet washed up reporter Steve Everett. He's back on the wagon (just) and sleeping with his boss's wife while neglecting his own wife and young daughter. The one thing stopping editor James Woods from firing Everett is his nose for a story – and that nose is telling him that death-sentenced murderer (Washington) is innocent. For a film that covers just 24 hours of a man's life, the plot unravels at a maddeningly pedestrian pace. Key performances are superb (Leary restrained, Woods always reliable) and there are flashes of Clint's old intensity, but this is sub-par from the former man with no name. The DVD, meanwhile, is a revelation, packed with two behind the scenes featurettes that shed light on the Eastwood's film-making process and a music video of the haunting torch song-esque theme 'Why Should I Care?'. *True Crime* is an average, beat-the-clock thriller, but the great extras are a gift at this low price.

FINAL VERDICT

Picture ☆☆☆☆ Sound ☆☆☆☆☆
Entertainment ☆☆☆ Extras ☆☆☆☆
Value ☆☆☆☆☆
OVERALL ☆☆☆☆

TRUE ROMANCE: DIRECTOR'S CUT

Price: £15.99
Supplied by: Warner Home Video
Type of disc: Single layer, single-sided
No of chapters: 34
Film format(s)/length: 2.35:1 widescreen / 116 mins
Audio format: Dolby Digital 5.1
Director: Tony Scott
Starring: Christian Slater, Patricia Arquette, Dennis Hopper
Year made: 1993
Extras: Scene access; soundtrack in English; subtitles in English; subtitles for the hearing impaired in English.

Quentin Tarantino writing a love story? You know straight off that flowers, chocolates and moonlit dinners will not be making an appearance! Tony Scott (*Top Gun, Crimson Tide*) directed the film, but this has Tarantino's signature writ large on it. *True Romance* was the script Hollywood's *enfant terrible* wrote and sold to finance his breakthrough movie *Reservoir Dogs*. Written when QT famously worked as a video store clerk, *True Romance* reads like a fantasy of how he wished his life was, and presumably had himself in mind to play the lead character of Clarence, so close are their personas and pop culture tastes. Instead of video hire, though, Clarence (Slater) is a comic store counter jockey who adores kung fu movies, comics and bad TV. Quentin conjures up his dream woman in Alabama (Arquette), a giggly, shapely blonde hooker who unconditionally loves Clarence and the things he's into. Accidentally stealing a big suitcase of charlie from white rasta Drexl (Gary Oldman), the two lovers head for LA to sell the white stuff to decadent movie producer Lee (Saul Rubinek) and start their lives over together, but hot on their trail is drug overlord Coccotti (Christopher Walken) and grizzled cops Tom Sizemore and Chris Penn. Unfortunately, like each and every Tarantino release in this country, the disc is so barren of features a tumbleweed should be given away free with every copy. Whereas the Region 1 *True Romance* carries production notes and theatrical trailers, the European version is not seen as worthy of even those mediocre extras. It's a mystery, akin to the Vengaboys' ongoing popularity, why this title was delayed for so long. It's strange that Tarantino is apparently unwilling (or hasn't been approached) to provide extras for his work, considering what a showman he is. As it stands, this level of attention by DVD producers shown to one of the most influential film-makers of our time is a travesty.

FINAL VERDICT

Picture ☆☆☆☆ Sound ☆☆☆

Entertainment ☆☆☆☆ Extras ☆ Value ☆☆

OVERALL ☆☆☆

THE TRUMAN SHOW

Price: £19.99

Supplied by: Paramount Pictures

Type of disc: Dual layer, single-sided

No of chapters: 24

Film format(s)/length: 1.85:1 anamorphic / 99 mins

Audio format: Dolby Digital 5.1

Director: Peter Weir

Starring: Jim Carrey, Ed Harris, Laura Linney

Year made: 1998

Extras: Scene access; teaser trailer; theatrical trailer; soundtrack in English, German, Czech, Hungarian and Polish; multilingual subtitles; subtitles for the hearing impaired in English.

Paramount's choice for its first blockbuster entry into the Region 2 market is a careful one. Let's face it, the studio has one hell of a catalogue to choose from (including the *Indiana Jones* and *Star Trek* series), so why would they pick this (along with kiddie flick *The Rugrats Movie*) to be the first horse out of the stable? It's anyone's guess, but as *The Truman Show* was Carrey's first attempt at 'serious acting' and took $31m in its opening US weekend, they could have made a much worse decision. *The Truman Show* is a real 'what if?' movie. It studies the life of one Truman Burbank (Carrey), a man who has lived his entire life inside a television show. Truman has no idea that the dream town of Seahaven is actually a set, all his friends and family are paid actors, and every third item in existence is a television camera. Watched by over one billion people worldwide, the show is a phenomenal success, the brainchild of big time producer Christof (Harris), who has broadcast the life of Truman to an engrossed public since the moment he was born. However, at the age of 30, the wanderlusting Truman is repeatedly thwarted in his attempts to leave Seahaven, and this, along with the strange reappearance of his father, causes him to grow suspicious of his ever-perfect surroundings. Carrey's performance is masterful, as he takes Truman from contentment to restlessness, and the unwitting star is played much more subtly than any of his previous incarnations. In fact, the entire movie is deserving of much praise, as it elegantly walks the fine line between drama and humour, while still living up to its ambitions. As far as the disc is concerned, this is an average, fairly limp Region 2 turnout. The picture quality is stunning (and anamorphic) and the 5.1 digital does its stuff if you have the right equipment. However, with just one teaser, and one trailer (both the US versions), this is an overly cautious start from Paramount.

FINAL VERDICT

Picture ☆☆☆☆ Sound ☆☆☆☆☆

Entertainment ☆☆☆☆ Extras ☆☆ Value ☆☆☆

OVERALL ☆☆☆

TURBULENCE

Price: £15.99

Supplied by: DVDplus (www.dvdplus.co.uk)

Type of disc: Single layer, single-sided

No of chapters: 12

Film format(s)/length: 2.35:1 widescreen / 97 mins

Audio format: Dolby Surround

Director: Robert Butler

Starring: Ray Liotta, Lauren Holly, Hector Elizondo

Year made: 1997

Extras: Scene access; theatrical trailer; 'Making of' feature.

When 4 Federal Marshals and two shackled convicted criminals board a 747 bound for LA on Christmas Eve, you just know there's going to be a chance the plane won't make it there in time for Christmas dinner. The charming Ryan Weaver (Liotta) and Teri Halloran (Holly) work well together in a predictable Hollywood thriller on a plane. The action kicks off early when an armed robber needs to take an airborne leak. As we all know, escorting a dangerous criminal to a toilet on a plane is always a recipe for disaster, but, unfortunately, with a Federal Marshal's busy lifestyle, he never got the chance to rent *Con Air*. The DVD is completely in step with the norm when it comes to the extras. They consist of nothing more than a trailer and a 'Making of' feature which is really just an extended advert for the movie. However, if there was anything else on this disc you might get the feeling that someone was overloading the boat. Wonderful as the format might be, some films just aren't big enough to fill it, and fortunately for us, this movie seems to know its DVD limits. Although there's nothing new here, there are still some great special effects, topped off with plenty of evil cackles from Liotta; but be ready for the American salute at the end.

FINAL VERDICT

Picture ☆☆☆☆ Sound ☆☆☆

Entertainment ☆☆☆ Extras ☆☆ Value ☆☆

OVERALL ☆☆☆

TWELVE MONKEYS

Price: £17.99
Supplied by: DVDplus (www.dvdplus.co.uk)
Type of disc: Dual layer, single-sided
No of chapters: 18
Film format(s)/length: 1.85:1 widescreen / 124 mins
Audio format: DTS
Director: Terry Gilliam
Starring: Bruce Willis, Madeleine Stowe, Brad Pitt
Year made: 1995
Extras: Scene access; 87-minute behind the scenes documentary *The Hamster Factor, and other tales of Twelve Monkeys*; subtitles in English for the hearing impaired.

In 1997, the world was apparently engulfed by plague and 99 per cent of the human population was wiped out. If that's the case... how come there's still long queues in ASDA on a Saturday? Er...anyway, in *Twelve Monkeys*, the survivors of the holocaust find themselves living deep beneath the Earth's surface because the exterior of the planet is uninhabitable. Rather than spending their time making nice decorations for their caves, the inhabitants of this post-apocalyptic future instead set about trying to prevent the whole catastrophe from ever happening by sending agents back through time – the meddling fools! Enter Bruce Willis, a convict who's given the chance to earn his freedom by working for the time travel division. His mission is to find the founder of a group calling itself the Twelve Monkeys, which the future bureaucracy have deduced is responsible for the plague. Unfortunately, like most middle-management, Willis's bosses haven't quite understood all the facts and so things go a little bit wrong... *Twelve Monkeys* is a dark, fairly twisted movie with some outstanding visuals courtesy of ex-Python director Gilliam and some nice plot twists throughout. The storyline jumps backwards and forwards in time to keep you guessing. To begin with, it seems clear that Willis' character is a time traveller, but as the movie progresses it seems that it might all just be a paranoid delusion so vivid that it seems real. Gilliam manages to keep everyone guessing right up until the shocking and slightly depressing ending. The special features on this DVD don't look all that extensive when you list them on paper, but that's because one of them is an 87-minute making of documentary, so basically you're getting two movies for the price of one, making this disc extremely good value and a definite must-buy for all fans of Terry Gilliam's work. If only all UK DVDs gave us extras like this.

FINAL VERDICT

Picture ☆☆☆ Sound ☆☆☆☆ Entertainment ☆☆☆☆
Extras ☆☆☆ Value ☆☆☆☆
OVERALL ☆☆☆☆

TWINS

Price: £19.99
Supplied by: Columbia TriStar
Type of disc: Single layer, single-sided
No of chapters: 16
Film format(s)/length: 4:3 regular only / 102 mins
Audio format: Dolby Surround
Director: Ivan Reitman
Starring: Arnold Schwarzenegger, Danny DeVito, Kelly Preston
Year made: 1988
Extras: Production notes; cast and film-makers biographies; theatrical trailer; English, German and Czech language options; multilingual subtitles.

Deep in the production notes contained on the *Twins* DVD, the over-ambitious writer claims that, "*Twins* is a hilarious and touching comedy filled with adventure, but with a heart of genuine feeling that says something poignant about family life everywhere." This is rubbish of course, but *Twins* is still an engagingly distracting one joke comedy that pairs Schwarzenegger and DeVito as unlikely siblings. With a storyline about genetically engineering the perfect child, a topic that's always in the forefront of the science world. Oh, and it's by far the best of Arnie's so-called comedies. DVD-wise, the film shows all the hallmarks of a film made in 1988, with picture quality barely above that of the video version, and an efficient if uninspired Dolby Surround mix. Bad news for widescreen collectors too, as you get the full frame version only. Extras? Just some standard production and cast notes, with the original trailer. VHS price? £5.99. DVD price? £19.99. If you think it's worth an extra £14 for what little extra you get, you go ahead. Whilst it's great to have Universal in on the UK DVD scene, they're not going to win many friends ripping us off like this. Just buy the video if you must have it, and put the change towards something better.

FINAL VERDICT

Picture ☆☆ Sound ☆☆ Entertainment ☆☆☆
Extras ☆ Value ☆
OVERALL ☆☆

TWISTER

Price: £19.99
Supplied by: Columbia TriStar Home Video
Type of disc: Single layer, single-sided

No of chapters: 34
Film format(s)/length: 2.35:1 widescreen / 108 mins
Audio format: Dolby Digital 5.1
Director: Jan de Bont
Starring: Bill Paxton, Helen Hunt, Jami Gertz
Year made: 1996
Extras: Chapter access; Dolby Digital 5.1; multilingual soundtracks; multilingual subtitles; trailer; cast mini-biographies; very annoying and unskippable DVD trailer intro. [NB: Production notes promised by the sleeve are absent.]

Twister is one of those movies that's great for showing off the power of your shiny new Dolby Digital audio setup, but kind of embarrassing to sit and watch, unless you're just zapping through chapters to see Industrial Light & Magic's CGI tornados destroy the landscape. The story would barely support a ride at the Universal Studios theme park, so even at a fairly slim 108 minutes it scarcely registers a '1' on the brain-o-meter. Former tornado-chaser Bill (Paxton) is on the way to get divorced from his still tornado-chasing wife Jo (Hunt) when, wouldn't you know it, he gets dragged into one last tornado hunt. With Bill's nervous fiancee Melissa (Gertz) and a bunch of wacky comic relief meteorologists in tow, Bill and Jo try to deploy their miracle tornado-scanning gadget 'Dorothy' (geddit?) into a twister before a rival group of slimy corporate tornado-chasers beat them to it. And gee, will their shared love of rushing into harm's way help them reconcile? Director De Bont flings the camera around to deliver thrills, but that's all he seems able to do. *Twister* was made solely as a showcase for ILM's digital effects – the 'plot' is basically a series of chases after tornados, the dialogue is as tin-eared as you'll find this side of *The Phantom Menace* and characterisation is thinner than a supermodel's wrist. Poor Melissa is the only person you actually feel any sympathy for, and in terms of the love story she's meant to be the antagonist! Throw out your hopes that this is a good film in any conventional critical sense, however, and instead concentrate on turning your volume up to 11. Buildings disintegrate, vehicles explode, fenceposts slam into buildings like giant darts and tornados roar and scream like an entire circus of furious tigers, all in bowel-loosening surround sound. You'll enjoy it, although the neighbours will be most upset. *Twister* is a great showcase for DVD's audio capabilities, even though it's something of a one-time-watch as a movie. The extras seem to have been swept away by the wind as well!

FINAL VERDICT

Picture ☆☆☆☆ **Sound** ☆☆☆☆☆
Entertainment ☆☆ **Extras** ☆☆ **Value** ☆☆☆
OVERALL ☆☆☆

UNDER SIEGE

Price: £15.99
Supplied by: DVDplus (www.dvdplus.co.uk)
Type of disc: Dual layer, single-sided
No of chapters: 29
Film format(s)/length: 1.85:1 widescreen / 98 mins
Audio format: Dolby Digital 5.1
Director: Andrew Davis
Starring: Steven Seagal, Tommy Lee Jones, Gary Busey
Year made: 1992
Extras: Scene access; multilingual subtitles.

The battleship *Missouri* is scheduled for decommissioning after a long and glorious service. However, midway through the crew's celebration party, terrorists seize control of the heavily armed warship and only the ship's cook (Seagal) can save the day. Only in America! Enjoyable hokum would be the best way to describe this competent action-thriller, which marked the commercial peak for Seagal's career, and the springboard for director Andrew Davis; who later followed up with The Fugitive, which also starred Tommy Lee Jones but this time in the role of the good guy. As we've come to expect from a Seagal movie, explosions, gunfire and an abundant supply of testosterone are the key features to the movie's success – and this is where DVD comes into its own. The picture and sound quality do justice to the movie genre, considering the many darkly lit scenes illuminated only by gunfire. As usual, it's the stunning sounds shooting from your speakers that take the honours, with a wide and plentiful digital mix providing Seagal with a potent souvenir of his finest movie to date. As for the extras, once again we're let down with barren features on this otherwise good DVD. However, it is a notable improvement over its VHS counterpart, and if you like your action movies, you won't be disappointed.

FINAL VERDICT

Picture ☆☆☆☆ **Sound** ☆☆☆☆
Entertainment ☆☆☆ **Extras** ☆ **Value** ☆☆
OVERALL ☆☆☆

UNDER SIEGE 2

Price: £19.99
Supplied by: Warner Home Video
Type of disc: Single layer, single-sided

No of chapters: 31

Film format(s)/length: 1.85:1 widescreen enhanced / 94 mins

Audio format: Dolby Digital 5.1

Director: Geoff Murphy

Starring: Steven Seagal, Eric Bogosian, Katherin Heigl

Year made: 1995

Extras: Chapter access; multilingual subtitles; subtitles for the hearing impaired in English.

There are no complaints with the sound on *Under Siege 2*, as it kicks off with a space shuttle launch in Dolby Digital 5.1 and pretty much never shuts up from then. The picture's perfectly decent as well. Shame about the story, but you can't have everything. Seagal reprises his role as the commando chef from *Under Siege*, and this time the *Die Hard* rip-off plot is set on a train. Nutty scientist Bogosian is using it as a mobile base to blow up Washington with his killer satellite, and wouldn't you know it, only Seagal can stop him. This was one of Seagal's bigger-budget films, but it's still full of Hornby trains and Airfix planes. Seagal is the usual black-clad and paunchy acting vacuum who bullies bad guys to death in heavily cut ways. It is only Bogosian's snide wisecracks that raise the tone. A brain-dead time-passer.

FINAL VERDICT

Picture ☆☆☆☆ Sound ☆☆☆☆ Entertainment ☆☆☆ Extras ☆ Value ☆☆☆

OVERALL ☆☆☆

Unforgiven

Price: £15.99

Supplied by: DVD World (01705 796662)

Type of disc: Single layer, single-sided

No of chapters: 33

Film format(s)/length: 16:9 widescreen / 125 mins

Director: Clint Eastwood

Starring: Clint Eastwood, Gene Hackman, Morgan Freeman

Year made: 1992

Extras: Interactive menus; production notes; scene access.

By the time Clint Eastwood directed this gritty Western, the genre had been reduced to nothing more than a trickle of spoofs. Without him, *Unforgiven* would have attracted little attention at the box office and been quickly relegated to that strange selection of £5 videos you notice in newsagents when stopping off for 20 snouts (alongside most of Jean-Claude Van Damme's cinematic CV). With him, however, it was awarded 4 Academy Awards and, while not exactly kick-starting a new era of Westerns, rejuvenated interest in one of the silver screen's most appealing types of movie. A dark tale of revenge played against a backdrop of stunning 19th Century locales, *Unforgiven* sees Eastwood and Freeman as retired outlaws persuaded by vengeful prostitutes to collect one last bounty. A darker, more intelligent Western than most, its tale is well told and its conclusion powerful – easily one of Clint's finest cinematic moments. The quality of sound and vision is, like the film, excellent. But the disc's special features aren't. DVD owners should have decided already whether owning a copy of *Unforgiven* is their thing – after all, it's been out on video for 6 years now. So if you are a fan of the film, chances are you own it on VHS. There must be stacks of additional footage, behind the scenes interviews and other stuff Warner could have used to add value to the package. So why, then, is its digital debut marred by a lack of extras that even the most law-abiding massage parlour would feel ashamed of?

FINAL VERDICT

Picture ☆☆☆☆ Sound ☆☆☆☆

Entertainment ☆☆☆☆ Extras ☆☆ Value ☆☆☆

OVERALL ☆☆☆

Universal Soldier: The Return

Price: £19.99

Supplied by: Columbia TriStar Home Video

Type of disc: Single layer, single-sided

No of chapters: 28

Film format(s)/length: 1.85:1 widescreen enhanced / 79 mins

Audio format: Dolby Digital 5.1

Director: Mic Rodgers

Starring: Jean-Claude Van Damme, Michael Jai White, Kiana Tom

Year made: 1999

Extras: Scene access; trailer; behind-the-scenes featurette (4:43); *Looking Back, Moving Forward* – Jean-Claude Van Damme interview (9:14); Michael Jai White on-set workout featurette (4:03); soundtrack in English; subtitles in multiple languages (according to sleeve – none accessible on disc).

It's a time of great rejoicing for 14-year-old boys everywhere – Jean-Claude Van Damme has made another action movie! With thrash metal music! And a superstar wrestler! And guns so oversized they'd make Sigmund Freud choke on his cocaine! For anyone who isn't a 14-year-old boy, however, *Universal Soldier: The Return* is 79 minutes of your life that could be spent more profitably – and enjoyably – pulling out your armpit hair with tweezers. Set several years after Roland Emmerich's mindless but moderately entertaining original, *Universal Soldier: The Return* sees Van Damme in charge of training a new brigade of bionic zombies under the control of supercomputer SETH, an acronym that is never satisfactorily explained. When the government decides to pull the plug, SETH reacts predictably badly, transplanting its consciousness into the body of Michael Jai White and sending out the UniSols to cause havoc. Van Damme is the only man who can stop the computer's rampage, and doing so will naturally involve more high kicks than the chorus line at the Moulin Rouge. 'If you can't be good, be loud' is a maxim obviously embraced by everybody involved, since *Universal Soldier: The Return* is *extremely* loud. If there's one good thing that can be said about the DVD (and, in fact, there *is* only one good thing that can be said about the DVD) it's that it'll give your 5.1 system a good workout. You can practically see director Rodgers headbanging as vehicles explode and people are karate-kicked through windows. When it's not shamelessly plagiarising better movies (SETH's final demise rips off both *T2* and *Demolition Man* in the space of about 3 seconds) the script is mind-numbingly moronic, culminating in one of the most weedy endings of all time. You don't even get to see the bad guys die! The film is abysmal, but surprisingly the extras aren't bad. They aren't good either, but at least they're there. There are 3 featurettes (of less than 20 minutes in total) to watch, as well as a trailer and the usual uninformative filmographies. Van Damme's wibblings are of little interest (he describes *US:TR* as "Like a rolahcoast," and claims *Double Team* had a great script), leaving White to talk viewers through his workout video. Jane Fonda has very little to worry about.

FINAL VERDICT

Picture ☆☆☆ Sound ☆☆☆ Entertainment ☆
Extras ☆☆ Value ☆
OVERALL ☆☆

UP CLOSE AND PERSONAL

Price: £15.99
Supplied by: DVDplus (www.dvdplus.co.uk)
Type of disc: Single layer, single-sided
No of chapters: 12
Film format(s)/length: 4:3 regular / 118 mins
Audio format: Dolby Surround
Director: Jon Avnet
Starring: Robert Redford, Michelle Pfeiffer, Stockard Channing
Year made: 1996

Extras: Scene access; trailer; 'Making of' featurette (5 minutes); English subtitles.

This must have been easy to pitch. Robert Redford, Michelle Pfeiffer, and an unlikely but true love story. Naturally the truthful elements seem to take second place to giving the audience a sugary but watchable romance. However, it's not a bad film, which is mainly held together by the talent of the lead actors. DVD-wise, it's an EiV release, and considering it's been in the UK market for a while now, surely we deserve something a little better than this. We don't mean in terms of extras – although we'll come to them in a sec. No, we're talking the very fundamentals of providing a good quality image, and a strong quality digital soundtrack. *Up Close and Personal* scores best with the latter, although once again it's not *Terminator*, *Titanic* or *Aliens*, so it's a fairly leisurely film for your home cinema set up (hence the Surround only mix). The picture is reasonable enough, but presented full frame instead of widescreen. Although given the type of film we're talking about, this is a bit of a waste. The 5-minute 'Making of' feature mixes the usual 'everyone was great' style of interview with a few entertaining outtakes, although it doesn't run long enough to offer anything of real substance. Close-up, this DVD isn't special enough for inclusion in your collection unless you're a personal fan of one of the main cast.

FINAL VERDICT

Picture ☆☆☆ Sound ☆☆ Entertainment ☆☆☆
Extras ☆☆ Value ☆☆
OVERALL ☆☆

URBAN LEGEND

Price: £19.99
Supplied by: DVDplus (www.dvdplus.co.uk)
Type of disc: Single layer, single-sided
No of chapters: 28
Film format(s)/length: 2.35:1 widescreen enhanced / 96 mins
Audio format: Dolby Digital 5.1
Director: Jamie Blanks
Starring: Jared Leto, Alicia Witt, Robert Englund
Year made: 1998
Extras: Fold out pamphlet with some production notes; behind-the-scenes feature (6:20); a fun audio commentary featuring director Jamie Blanks, cast member Michael Rosenbaum and screenwriter Silvio Horto. Be warned, it gives bits away before they happen!; filmographies; theatrical trailer; English and German soundtracks; subtitles in 15 languages.

Life, it seems, is just not fair. Take two films –

Scream and *Urban Legend*. The former is a hugely entertaining reinvention of the slasher genre for the Nineties, the latter just the latest cheap derivative. So which Region 2 DVD gets the behind the scenes feature, film-maker's commentary, production notes and such like, and which gives you just the film? It's an odd situation to be in really, because – aside from the crappy jewel case packaging – you can't fault Columbia's handling of the disc, which really is a premium effort. The film, though, is a *Scream*-wannabe. It offers a simple join the dots mystery and some nice camerawork, although basically it does absolutely nothing that others haven't done better. The presentation is excellent though, with the Dolby Digital mix used with care, more to place individual effects around the room than an exercise in crash bang wallop. The film is dark for the majority of its running time, and the picture holds the colour with ease. The extras are diverting, with an extremely entertaining commentary (that works extra well by having 3 different people interacting on the same track – it's better than the film!) complemented by a brief behind the scenes documentary that springs no surprises but certainly passes a few of minutes harmlessly enough. And – is this a record? There are no less than 15 subtitle options to be found. At least if you get bored with the film, the disc offers a nice chance to expand on your Icelandic…

FINAL VERDICT

Picture ☆☆☆☆ Sound ☆☆☆☆ Entertainment ☆☆
Extras ☆☆☆ Value ☆☆
OVERALL ☆☆

US MARSHALS

Price: £15.99
Supplied by: Warner Home Video
Type of disc: Single layer, double-sided
No of chapters: 40
Film format(s)/length: 1:1.85 anamorphic / 126 mins
Director: Stuart Baird
Starring: Tommy Lee Jones, Wesley Snipes, Robert Downey Jr
Year made: 1998
Extras: Widescreen TV enhanced; scene selection; subtitles; multiple languages; cast filmographies; production notes; plane crash FX featurette.

You've seen *The Fugitive*, right? Well, you've seen this as well. Ostensibly a sequel, *US Marshals* is really a remake, only with Wesley Snipes in the Harrison Ford role and a plane instead of a train crash. When apparent murderer Snipes gets loose after the aforementioned crash, US Marshal Sam

Gerard (Jones) and his team go in pursuit. While the Marshals track him to New York, Snipes hunts down the real killer. It could almost be passable entertainment if not for the fact that the true villain might as well have a neon sign saying 'It's me!' the moment he appears. There aren't many special features to make up for the lack of originality. Some crew biographies, vaguely informative behind the scenes pages and a mini-documentary on the plane crash FX (annoyingly on side B) are all you get. While the picture is good, the sound occasionally suffers from some distortion later in the film. Probably best to let this one escape.

FINAL VERDICT

Picture ☆☆☆☆ Sound ☆☆ Entertainment ☆☆
Extras ☆☆☆ Value ☆☆
OVERALL ☆☆

THE USUAL SUSPECTS

Price: £17.99
Supplied by: DVD World (01705 796662)
Type of disc: Single layer, single-sided
No of chapters: 19
Film format(s)/length: Only 4:3 / 101 mins
Director: Bryan Singer
Starring: Kevin Spacey, Gabriel Byrne, Chazz Palminteri
Year made: 1995
Extras: Scene access; paltry character and director biographies; trailer.

If you hate multiple storylines, complex character development and some of the slickest lines since *Reservoir Dogs*, then *The Usual Suspects* is not for you. But if you are a connoisseur of cool and appreciate one of the greatest movie endings of all time, then this DVD is what you've been waiting for. The film revolves around a police line-up where 5 criminals: Keaton (Byrne), Fenster, Verbal (Spacey), McManus and Hockney meet for the first time and plan a series of jobs to avenge their wrongful arrest. Events take a turn for the worst when all 5 suddenly find themselves working for the mysterious and deadly Keyser Soze and in return for their freedom must undertake a suicide mission on Soze's behalf. The entire film is shown in flashback while Verbal, the only survivor of the mission, recalls to embittered investigator Dave Kujan (Palminteri) what happened. Direction is tight and not a single frame is wasted in conveying the sinister machinations of Soze and his pawns. Right up until the last scene we are left guessing as to the identity of the overlord, although Singer offers plenty of red herrings throughout. *The Usual Suspects* is a dark film and sometimes difficult to follow, but with a script that Elmore Leonard would have been proud of and standout performances by the 5 principle performers (Spacey – a deserving Oscar) makes it one of the best crime films since *The Godfather*. The bad news for DVD owners is that this disc is woeful when it comes to extras (anorexic character biographies, a single trailer) but the bitterest pill to swallow is that there's no widescreen option – a crime for such a stylish film.

FINAL VERDICT

Picture ✩✩✩✩ Sound ✩✩✩✩

Entertainment ✩✩✩✩✩ Extras ✩ Value ✩✩

OVERALL ✩✩✩

U-Turn

Price: £19.99
Supplied by: DVD World (01705 796662)
Type of disc: Dual layer, single-sided
No of chapters: 28
Film format(s)/length: 16:9 widescreen / 119 mins
Director: Oliver Stone
Starring: Sean Penn, Jennifer Lopez, Nick Nolte
Year made: 1997
Extras: Scene selection; soundtrack in German and English; multilingual subtitles; theatrical trailer; production notes.

This is the kind of film that proves even the best director can make a mistake. Oliver Stone has made some absolutely stunning films during his lengthy career, but just lately he seems to have lost it. *U-Turn* is a film about nothing and it's about 119 minutes too long. Sean Penn plays Bobby, a gambler on his way to Vegas to pay off an outstanding debt when his car breaks down forcing him to stop in the town of Superior – which is anything but. What follows is a convoluted series of unlikely encounters with various stereotype American small-towners as Bobby attempts to get out of town. The whole movie is filmed from all sorts of strange experimental angles with flashes of seemingly random objects in between. In addition to the multiple-language subtitles and a choice of English or German audio, the DVD provides the theatrical trailer and filmographies for 4 of the actors and the director, making it far from the worst of Region 2 discs. Shame the film is so lousy really.

FINAL VERDICT

Picture ✩✩✩✩ Sound ✩✩ Entertainment ✩

Extras ✩✩ Value ✩

OVERALL ✩

Vampires

Price: £19.99
Supplied by: Columbia TriStar Home Video
Type of disc: Single layer, single-sided
No of chapters: 28
Film format(s)/length: 2.35:1 widescreen enhanced
Audio format: Dolby Digital 5.1
Director: John Carpenter
Starring: James Woods, Daniel Baldwin, Sheryl Lee
Year made: 1998
Extras: Scene access; filmographies; behind the scenes featurette including interviews with Carpenter and cast; audio commentary by the director; theatrical trailer; soundtrack in Spanish; subtitles in 9 languages.

Master of terror John Carpenter returns to old form in this twist on the tale of vampirism. But the release of the film in the UK wasn't an easy one as the nation's guardians at the BBFC refused to pass Carpenter's original vision. Some 14 months after the US disc was released, the gruesome confrontation between Good and Evil was finally invited into our British homes. In the world of the film, vampires have existed for many millennia, and the Vatican – all too aware of their existence – has formed a special branch of vampiric investigations. Lead by the relentless and violently obsessed Jack Crow (Woods) they have the singular task of exterminating all dirtnappers. The movie steals your attention from the off, and the methods that Jack and his merry band of men use to wipe out the unnatural menace are delightfully inventive. Although the usual arsenal of semi-automatics, shotguns and wooden stakes are there, the simplicity of the drag-and-stab method of extermination remains the most entertaining. The film as a whole seems a fresh approach to the congested highway of vampire movies, helped along nicely by the anamorphically enhanced picture transfer and digital sound mix. A surprise to many Region 1 fans is soon uncovered when the special features are revealed. Not a minute goes by when extras on UK editions are openly criticised when compared to the US release, and in many cases this is fully justified. However, with *Vampires* the UK audience is treated to a behind-the-scenes featurette that includes interviews with Carpenter himself, along with the lead cast. But just as quickly as the celebrations began, they come to an unfortunate end. The disc may contain the audio commentary, filmographies and theatrical trailer, but the additional full-screen film format is missing – presumed dead and buried! Comparisons aside, the film is enjoyable and the DVD is a worthy addition to any horror/vampire fan's collection.

FINAL VERDICT

Picture ☆☆☆☆ Sound ☆☆☆☆
Entertainment ☆☆☆☆ Extras ☆☆☆ Value ☆☆☆
OVERALL ☆☆☆

Velvet Goldmine

Price: £19.99
Supplied by: VCI
Type of disc: Dual layer, single-sided
No of chapters: 21
Film format(s)/length: 16:9 widescreen / 118 mins
Audio format: Dolby Digital 5.1
Director: Todd Haynes
Starring: Ewan McGregor, Jonathan Rhys Meyers, Toni Collette
Year made: 1998
Extras: Full motion menus; scene selection; theatrical trailer; teaser trailer; 20-minute documentary: *Behind the Glam & The Glitter*; picture show/photo library; printable photo library.

It would be interesting to know whether David Bowie and Iggy Pop feel flattered or insulted by this film. Although it's intended as an homage to the glam rock era, *Velvet Goldmine* is so bloated and full of itself, if you pricked it with a pin it would explode in a shower of cheap sequins! Christian Bale plays a journalist unravelling the myth behind his former idol Brian Slade (Rhys Meyers), a glam megastar who disappeared after faking his own assassination in 1974. Adopting a *Citizen Kane*-type narrative structure, the film tells the story of Slade in flashback via the accounts of those who were closest to him, including his ex-lover and shake-it-all-about rocker Curt Wild (Ewan McGregor). Unfortunately, so much effort seems to have been put into the visuals and soundtrack of the film (which are admittedly superb) that the plot seems to have been forgotten, aside from some nonsense linking the glam movement to Oscar Wilde and UFOs. The flamboyant costumes and make-up of the stage routines look fantastic, and are rendered more colourful than ever by the digital transfer, but the uninvolving story and one-dimensional characters drag proceedings down. However, the DVD is packed with so much good stuff that you're almost willing to forgive the lack of substance. Extras include a behind-the-scenes documentary, the teaser and theatrical trailers, a moving picture library and a very informative booklet detailing everything you need to know about the production and its origins. *Velvet Goldmine* is an ambitious failure of a film, but a resoundingly impressive DVD.

FINAL VERDICT

Picture ☆☆☆ Sound ☆☆☆ Entertainment ☆☆

Extras ☆☆☆☆☆ Value ☆☆☆☆
OVERALL ☆☆☆

Vertigo

Price: £19.99
Supplied by: Columbia TriStar Home Video
Type of disc: Dual layer, single-sided
No of chapters: 35
Film format(s)/length: 1.85:1 anamorphic / 124 mins
Audio format: Dolby Digital 5.1
Director: Alfred Hitchcock
Starring: James Stewart, Kim Novak, Barbara Bel Geddes
Year made: 1958
Extras: Scene access; *Obsessed With Vertigo* featurette (29 mins); audio commentary by restorers and original crewmembers; trailer; production notes; filmographies; soundtrack in English, French, Italian, Spanish and German; subtitles in 11 languages.

Murder, obsession and necrophilia – just another day at the movies with Alfred Hitchcock. *Vertigo* was slagged by the critics on its original release, but is now regarded as one of the most important of his films. Stewart is Scottie Ferguson, a police detective whose fear of heights causes the death of a fellow cop. Months later, having retired from the force, he's asked by an old friend if he can keep an eye on his wife Madeleine (Novak). Madeleine, it seems, has been possessed by the spirit of an 18th century woman who committed suicide. Scottie naturally thinks this is nonsense but agrees to help anyway – and has to come to the rescue when Madeleine throws herself into San Francisco Bay. After this, he finds himself falling in love with Madeleine…but his vertigo leaves him powerless to save her when she flings herself from a high belltower. And that's only half the story. *Vertigo* is a murder mystery where the mystery is explained to the audience long before the hero discovers the truth, for the simple reason that what happened isn't nearly as important as what happens next. Scottie's obsession leads him to a woman with an uncanny resemblance to Madeleine and he begins to transform her into the image of his dead love, with eventual tragic results. The DVD contains the 1996 restored version of *Vertigo*. Accompanying it are a documentary and a commentary featuring the restorers and various *Vertigo* crew members. Casual viewers will probably find there's far too much detail, but those people who are genuinely interested in the works of the tubby master of suspense will be fascinated. The commentary is annoyingly bitty, however, switching between different groups of participants just when you want them to expand on a point. Considering the poor shape of the original footage (examples appear on the documentary), the restoration of the film has been done very well – it can't compete against a brand-new film, but that's an inevitable result of 40 years of advances in equipment. The remixed 5.1 soundtrack is impressive, though, with Bernard Herrmann's unnerving score getting a new lease of life. For sheer Hitchcock entertainment it can't compete with *North by Northwest*, but as a disturbing psychological thriller it's still compelling even today.

FINAL VERDICT

Picture ☆☆☆☆ Sound ☆☆☆☆
Entertainment ☆☆☆☆ Extras ☆☆☆ Value ☆☆☆
OVERALL ☆☆☆☆

VIRTUAL SEXUALITY

Price: £19.99
Supplied by: Columbia TriStar Home Video
Type of disc: Single layer, single-sided
No of chapters: 28
Film format(s)/length: 16:9 widescreen enhanced / 89 mins
Audio format: Dolby Digital 5.1
Director: Nick Hurran
Starring: Laura Fraser, Rupert Penry-Jones, Luke De Lacey
Year made: 1999
Extras: Scene access; theatrical trailer; 5-minute featurette; very poor 3-minute *Cast Video Diary*; soundtrack in German and French; subtitles in English and French.

A lively and entertaining comedy, *Virtual Sexuality* was 'virtually' ignored during its cinematic release during the early summer of last year. Whilst not in the same league as, say Notting Hill, it does succeed in providing its target audience (ie, late-teen fans of *Dawson's Creek* and *Hollyoaks*) with a unique brand of English humour. The tongue-in-cheek plot revolves around a 17-year-old virgin's adjustment to a new gender, after 'she' becomes a 'he', following an accident at a computer expo. Whilst it does get a bit silly towards the end, there are some great gags to enjoy along the way, as long as you leave your 'mature' head at the door. As well as the bog-standard theatrical trailer, the DVD comes bundled with two equally uninspiring extras. The featurette is nothing more than an extended trailer, coming in at just under a stingy 5 minutes, and the intriguingly titled *Cast Video Diary* leaves a lot to be desired too. Instead of a day-by-day look behind the scenes of a film shoot, we get little more than a few minutes worth of wobbly camera footage. The teen audience this release is

aimed at deserve more than to be ripped off with such shoddy extras. If you're in any doubt, check out the American-produced teen flick *Go*, which comes replete with an impressive array of extras. Not least of which are 3 music videos. Surely you can do better than this, Columbia?

FINAL VERDICT

Picture ☆☆☆☆ Sound ☆☆☆☆ Entertainment ☆☆☆
Extras ☆ Value ☆☆
OVERALL ☆☆

VOLCANO

Price: £19.99
Supplied by: 20th Century Fox
Type of disc: Dual layer, single-sided
No of chapters: 23
Film format(s)/length: 16:9 widescreen enhanced / 100 mins
Audio format: Dolby Digital 5.1
Director: Mick Jackson
Starring: Tommy Lee Jones, Anne Heche, Gaby Hoffman
Year made: 1997
Extras: Scene access; theatrical trailer; subtitles in 9 languages.

Blessed with one of the best taglines in movie history ('The Coast is Toast'), *Volcano* follows the very similar *Dante's Peak* onto DVD, with neither film particularly impressive, but both capable of giving your speakers a workout. Boasting an aggressive 5.1 sound mix and liberal use of the full surround capabilities, *Volcano* may not be subtle, but it's certainly thumping stuff. Anamorphic enhancement has done the picture proud too, especially during the broad sweeping shots of Los Angeles ravaged by, er, a volcano. In short, high marks should be awarded to Fox for the presentation of the film. Unfortunately the DVD's good points end there, as no matter how much polish the picture and sound add to the disc, there's still a weak film at the heart of it. If your memory fails you, this is the one where a volcano suddenly springs up in the middle of Los Angeles. It runs through the standard ensemble cast disaster movie clichés one after another. The fly-on-the-wall approach works well, but if interest isn't waning as you enter the second hour, you're the sort of person who doesn't get out much. *Volcano*'s probably a little better than *Dante's Peak*, and Tommy Lee Jones is able enough in the leading role. But given the fact that extras are non-existent (unless you count a very brief trailer and the standard few language options) you'd probably do yourself justice by giving this one a wide birth.

FINAL VERDICT

Picture ☆☆☆☆ Sound ☆☆☆☆☆

Entertainment ☆☆ Extras ☆ Value ☆☆

OVERALL ☆☆

WAG THE DOG

Price: £19.99

Supplied by: Entertainment in Video

Type of disc: Dual layer, single-sided

No of chapters: 18

Film format(s)/length: 16:9 widescreen / 92 mins

Audio format: Digital 5.1

Director: Barry Levinson

Starring: Dustin Hoffman, Robert De Niro, Anne Heche

Year made: 1997

Extras: Scene access; theatrical trailer; cast biographies with insightful interviews; *Macy About Mamet* – actor's commentary on author Mamet; stylish interactive menus; *From Washington to Hollywood* - documentary on film's influences; B-Roll – collection of outtakes during the making of the film; subtitles in English.

In a true case of life imitating art, *Wag the Dog* takes a poke at the American political process with its plot involving a scandal with the President and a young girl in the Oval Office. A Hollywood spin doctor is brought in to concoct a diversionary story for the scandal, which ends up being a fictional war between the US and Albania. Sound familiar? Well, surprisingly, the film came out before the Clinton/Lewinsky cigar story broke – which makes *Wag the Dog* an astute observation on US politicians. In fact, it's so good, it can even rival Hunter S Thompson's visceral commentary on the 1972 Nixon Presidential campaign, *Fear & Loathing on the Campaign Trail '72*. The quality of Entertainment in Video's DVD releases is decidedly erratic. The likes of *Evita* and *Donnie Brasco* are half-baked attempts to utilise the DVD format. Although the picture and sound quality are high, the distinct lack of relevant extras available makes you wonder why anyone would bother buying DVD over the VHS version. However, at the same time, Entertainment has also released *Spawn* and *Lost in Space* – top quality DVDs with extras comparable with Region 1 releases. Thankfully, *Wag the Dog* belongs to the latter camp. The film is not only a wry and blackly funny commentary on the American political process, this DVD comes with a whole host of extras. Getting the obvious one out of the way first, there is a theatrical trailer – what more can you say about it? A mention should go to the menu screen, which does away with the traditional

static image from the movie. It is designed like a TV production and looks like a CNN news broadcast. The scene selection takes this image further, with 3 TV screens running beneath a static image of Hoffman's Hollywood producer character in a booth. These TV screens run footage from the relevant scene, giving you a visual reminder of what happens in that particular sequence – it's very stylish as well as being appropriate to the film. *Wag the Dog* on DVD also presents the cast biographies in an interesting way – each of the main stars has a career biog, along with a list of the films they have appeared in. But the absolute best extras have to be the mini-interviews of the stars where they talk about their particular character and the film itself. *Macy About Mamet* is a welcome addition on the extras front too, as it offers the viewers a rare insight into what one of the cast, William H Macy, thinks about *Wag the Dog*'s writer and personal friend, David Mamet. *From Washington to Hollywood* is a welcome change of pace to the usual 'Making of' documentaries, as it is more concerned with exploring the various influences on the film rather than the production. All in all this is a really interesting film that's a definite must-buy, if only because of the excellent extras that you get.

FINAL VERDICT

Picture ☆☆☆☆ Sound ☆☆☆☆

Entertainment ☆☆☆☆

Extras ☆☆☆☆ Value ☆☆☆☆

OVERALL ☆☆☆☆

WAKING NED

Price: £19.99

Supplied by: 20th Century Fox Home Entertainment

Type of disc: Single layer, single-sided

No of chapters: 24

Film format(s)/length: 2.35:1 anamorphic / 85 mins

Audio format: Dolby Surround

Director: Kirk Jones

Starring: Ian Bannen, David Kelly, Fionnula Flanagan

Year made: 1998

Extras: Scene access; theatrical trailer; cast and crew biogs; subtitles in English; subtitles for the hearing impaired in English.

After it's discovered by a couple of elderly village rascals (Bannen and Kelly) that a lottery winner is living in their midst, they set about trying to discover the identity of the secret millionaire in the hope of a share. After some pretty poor but entertaining detective work on the village of Tully Moor's 52 inhabitants, the pair discover that the winner – the movie's namesake, Ned Devine – died in front of his TV, probably as a result of the realisation of actually racking up those 6 winning figures. Bummer! So, the mischievous pair set about posing as the late Devine in order to take the money for themselves, but when they realise the enormity of the win – nearly 7 million Irish pounds – and the impending investigation to ensure that the claimant really is Ned, they get the whole village involved in their web of deceit with the promise of an equal share for all. Waking Ned Devine (our R2 test disc had oddly gained the surname of the American version, though we're assured the actual product will go under its UK release title) is a great window into the closeness and community spirit of village life and Kelly and Bannen as the loveable rogues are just perfect. However, the DVD is not quite as perfect; with only a trailer and cast biographies it's a little bare. The picture is good and captures the rugged Irish countryside well, and although only offering two-channel Dolby Surround, it does the Irish fiddle and tin whistle proud – you could almost be there supping Guinness with them.

FINAL VERDICT

Picture ☆☆☆☆ Sound ☆☆☆☆
Entertainment ☆☆☆☆ Extras ☆☆ Value ☆☆☆
OVERALL ☆☆☆

WARGAMES

Price: £19.99
Supplied by: MGM Home Video
Type of disc: Dual layer, single-sided
No of chapters: 16
Film format(s)/length: 1.85:1 letterbox / 108 mins
Audio format: Dolby Digital 5.1
Director: John Badham
Starring: Matthew Broderick, Ally Sheedy, John Wood
Year made: 1983
Extras: Scene access; feature-length commentary by director John Badham and writers Lawrence Lasker and Walter F Parkes; trivia and production notes; original theatrical trailer; soundtrack in English, French, German, Italian and Spanish; subtitles in 10 languages.

In this classic example of Eighties technofear, the US government has a secret war strategy computer known as WOPR that spends its days planning every possible cause and outcome of World War III. Unluckily, the US government never reckoned on the hacking powers of high school student David Lightman (Broderick), who starts playing a war game with WOPR. Since the computer can't tell games from reality, it begins planning retaliation, taking control of America's nuclear missiles and targeting Russia, and the military soon finds they can't stop it. Only David can

prevent global thermonuclear war, by convincing the computer that some games aren't worth playing. Wargames seems very dated by today's standards, and also borders on the implausible by suggesting that all you need is a telephone line and an ancient home computer to bring about the end of the world as we know it. Despite this, as a thriller the movie has more than admirably stood the test of time, and is still a watchable and exciting story. The disc has benefited from a whole new 5.1 soundtrack mix, and the enthusiasm from Badham in the director's commentary adds some new life into the 17-year-old film. The picture quality is nothing outstanding and the chapter dividing is so limited it's basically a pointless feature, but despite this Wargames is still worth getting hold of, if only to reminisce over the early Eighties.

FINAL VERDICT

Picture ☆☆☆ Sound ☆☆☆☆
Entertainment ☆☆☆☆ Extras ☆☆ Value ☆☆☆
OVERALL ☆☆☆

THE WAR ZONE

Price: £19.99
Supplied by: FilmFour
Type of disc: Dual layer, single-sided
No of chapters: 16
Film format(s)/length: 16:9 widescreen enhanced / 95 mins
Audio format: Dolby Digital 5.1
Director: Tim Roth
Starring: Ray Winstone, Lara Belmont, Freddie Cunliffe
Year made: 1999
Extras: Scene access; behind-the-scenes featurette; cast and crew interviews; shooting the film video footage; theatrical trailer; subtitles for the hard of hearing in English.

Tom is a 15-year-old Londoner whose family has just moved to a cottage in the middle of the Devonshire moors. Not only must he deal with all the typical perils of a teenage boy who has been uprooted from his beloved urban environment, but also confront the ugly, secretive appearance of incest between his father and sister. Not necessarily gripping, this film will certainly linger. This is a very stark film with some true hidden beauty. The cast is perfectly convincing as an everyday middle class family, which makes the subject matter all the more upsetting. Incidentally, this has possibly the most beautiful music score committed to a British film. In fact, this is a cracking DVD from FilmFour, and sports one of the best menu screens yet to grace a DVD. The interviews, behind-the-scenes and 'shooting the film' footage may not be woven elegantly, but they do act as a fine example of what can be done to support a film on DVD.

FINAL VERDICT

Picture ☆☆☆☆☆ Sound ☆☆☆☆☆
Entertainment ☆☆☆ Extras ☆☆☆☆ Value ☆☆☆
OVERALL ☆☆☆☆

THE WATERBOY

Price: £15.99
Supplied by: Warner Home Video
Type of disc: Dual layer, single-sided
No of chapters: 25
Film format(s)/length: 1.85:1 widescreen / 86 mins
Audio format: Dolby Digital 5.1
Director: Frank Coraci
Starring: Adam Sandler, Kathy Bates, Henry Winkler
Year made: 1998
Extras: Scene access; soundtrack in German and Hungarian; subtitles in 12 languages.

Adam Sandler is one lucky puppy. Is there anyone else in Hollywood who could earn the kind of money he does by repeatedly making very simple films that stick to a formulaic pattern? The plot is always simple: a down on his luck reject manages to overcome a crisis and then somehow bags a girlfriend whom at first he thought was far beyond his reach. The plausibility is always zero, but the jokes are brilliant, and that's what matters in a Sandler film. In this offering he plays Bobby Boucher, a simple-minded mummy's boy who lives solely to provide water to his local American football team. After getting fired for being an idiot, Bobby is taken on by Coach Klein (Winkler) and the Mud Dogs college football squad. Predictably, Bobby ends up being a marvellous player, venting all of his pent up aggression on the field and being hero-worshipped by all. The Waterboy was never going to win an Oscar for Best Screenplay, but it doesn't try to be anything more than a comedy film, and fortunately there are plenty of jokes to carry it through. Sandler manages to be both sweet and pitiful at once (not annoying as he could have been!) and so brings out a genuine charm in Bobby Boucher, but it is Kathy Bates as his overbearing mother who really steals the show. The DVD is pretty bleak though. It might have subtitles in 12 different languages but it has nothing more.

FINAL VERDICT

Picture ☆☆☆☆ Sound ☆☆☆☆
Entertainment ☆☆☆☆ Extras ☆ Value ☆☆☆
OVERALL ☆☆☆

WATERWORLD

Price: £19.99

Supplied by: Columbia TriStar
Type of disc: Dual layer, single-sided
No of chapters: 16
Film format(s)/length: 1.85:1 widescreen / 129 mins
Audio Format: Dolby Digital 5.1
Director: Kevin Reynolds
Starring: Kevin Costner, Jeanne Tripplehorn, Dennis Hopper
Year made: 1995
Extras: Dolby Digital 5.1 English and French soundtracks; German, Italian and Spanish Dolby Surround soundtracks; multilingual subtitles; theatrical trailer; production notes including filmographies for cast.

'Kevin's Gate' was the joke as *Waterworld*'s budget ballooned and production delays multiplied. In the event, *Waterworld* didn't turn out to be a complete disaster – that would come later with *The Postman* – and it actually turned in a decent profit. Like *Jaws*, the difficulties of shooting on a real ocean led to endless problems in keeping to schedule, but as a finished picture the gamble paid off. Scene after scene has the camera swooping over the ocean, pulling back and showing some dramatic seaborne battle. Watching Costner's wonderfully Heath Robinson yacht deploy its sails into the wind is almost worth the price of the DVD alone. There's no way *Waterworld* could've been shot on a tank and the blue sea around Hawaii is the real co-star in this spectacular film. The various sets, particularly the artificial island seen at the start, are generally imaginative and packed with detail. At 129 minutes, it's clear the filmmakers wanted to show the studio that all their money ended up on screen, and for the most part they've succeeded. It's a great movie to show off DVD's high resolution picture quality and, equally, your sound system. Dolby Digital 5.1 is well used with a competent, often eerie soundtrack. However, the plot is fairly awful and there's no real chemistry between Costner and Tripplehorn. Aside from being the perfect home medium to experience *Waterworld*, there's no effort to exploit DVD. All you get are the usual trailer and cast and film-maker bios, plus fairly copious production notes.

FINAL VERDICT

Picture ☆☆☆☆☆ Sound ☆☆☆☆☆
Entertainment ☆☆☆☆ Extras ☆☆ Value ☆☆☆
OVERALL ☆☆☆

THE WEDDING SINGER

Price: £19.99
Supplied by: Entertainment in Video
Type of disc: Single layer, single-sided

No of chapters: 24
Film format(s)/length: 16:9 widescreen / 97 mins
Audio format: Dolby Digital 5.1
Director: Frank Coraci
Starring: Adam Sandler, Drew Barrymore, Steve Buscemi
Year made: 1998
Extras: Thorough profiles of all main cast members; original theatrical trailer; English subtitles; scene access.

Digitally Versatile Discs are a great invention – state of the art multimedia that intensifies and multiplies the experience of home entertainment. However, sometimes there is a film that comes along that is so good you have to have it among your personal effects – no matter how good the picture or sound. This can certainly be said to be true of *The Wedding Singer* – the deservedly blockbusting hit romantic comedy that managed to keep its head above water in the meteorsmashing, Door-Sliding summer of 1998. And now, bang on time, you can own the perfect Eighties movie on the ultimate Nineties invention. Hot US comedy machine Adam Sandler stars alongside the distinctly hotter Drew Barrymore as Robbie Hart, the ultimately romantic, perky master of ceremonies, *The Wedding Singer*. Or at least he is until he's stood at the altar at his own wedding to the ambitious Linda (Angela Featherstone) and his life falls apart. The only hope offered to him is by waitress Julia, played by Barrymore in a role that has basically proved her to be one of the finest romantic comedy actresses of the Nineties. Rather predictably, there's another problem, in the shape of Glenn, her typically rich and nasty fiancé. As you may have already guessed, the outcome is perfectly obvious all the way through, but the point is, it doesn't really matter. You love all of the characters so much you keep on watching to see how Robbie and Julia inevitably get together at the end. Equally importantly, despite the fact that the entire script is a little toned down for Sandler, the plot is unimportant, because there are so many gags along the way. Having said this, *The Wedding Singer* could have been confined to the 'straight to VHS' bin if it hadn't been for the inspired 1985 setting, perfectly captured not only through the nostalgic soundtrack, but through the mullets, designer stubble and spangly clothes worn by the brilliant cast. The Region 2 disc inevitably lets itself down when compared to its American cousin, which offers 5 Eighties Karaoke songs, Eighties music mania and a Wedding Album photo gallery in addition to cast biographies and theatrical trailer available here. Even the biographies only stretch as far as 6 actors. This is, of course, a regrettable weakness, but it also has to be

acknowledged that the interactive menu is very funky, with side scrolling titles and moving clips for the scene access screens. And, as the main reason for getting any romantic comedy is just to watch with a loved one and a bottle of cheap wine, it's not as big a loss as, for example, the Region 2 *Starship Troopers* extras were. If you want huge explosions, random love scenes, mutated aliens, apocalyptic events and 101 extras – I really wouldn't look twice at this DVD. Bruce Willis isn't in it, and the extras could not be described as a major asset. But you have no excuse for *The Wedding Singer* not being on your shelf if you want trouser-dampening laughs, tear-jerking romance and a nostalgically kicking soundtrack, all presented with top visuals and sound quality – and extra marzipan.

FINAL VERDICT

Picture ☆☆☆☆☆ Sound ☆☆☆☆☆
Entertainment ☆☆☆☆☆
Extras ☆☆☆ Value ☆☆☆☆
OVERALL ☆☆☆☆

WHAT DREAMS MAY COME

Price: £17.99
Supplied by: DVDplus (www.dvdplus.co.uk)
Type of disc: Single layer, single-sided
No of chapters: 18
Film format(s)/length: 2.35:1 widescreen enhanced / 108 mins
Audio format: Dolby Digital 5.1
Director: Vincent Ward
Starring: Robin Williams, Annabella Sciorra, Cuba Gooding Jr
Year made: 1998
Extras: Scene access; 5-minute 'Making of' featurette; theatrical trailer; booklet with production notes; soundtrack in German (DD5.1); subtitles in German; subtitles for the hard of hearing in English.

It's no fun for Annabella Sciorra. Having already had her two kids die in a car crash, she has to face the death of her own husband, Dr Robin Williams, as he is killed trying to save the life of another accident victim. Williams is shown around his own imagination-inspired personal afterlife by Cuba Gooding Jr. Being an art fanatic, Williams inhabits a world of pastels and acrylics. But his happiness is shattered when he learns that Sciorra has committed suicide, leading her to the 'other place'. Sod eternity, thinks Williams, there's my girl to save! It's not possible to pick bigger themes than this, even if they're thrown away when you realise that here, mankind dictates the rules of the universe (oh what humility). Whilst it would seem that Williams and Gooding Jr are on autopilot, the impressive

Sciorra shines at every turn. The image quality is perfectly respectable (don't even think about watching this on pan and scan VHS), and the Dolby Digital 5.1 sound is excellent, making full use of the format during the film's more fantastical elements (and in the gut-wrenching accident that started the whole mess in the first place). But the extras – or lack of them – really disappoint. Fancy a 6-minute alternate ending, a commentary from director Ward, visual effects breakdowns and a 15-minute 'Making of'? Then you'd better import the US version, 'cos us UK Region 2 watchers only get a trailer and 5 minutes of promotional fluff. Universal UK can't whinge about regional coding when they show this much contempt for the European market. Sort yourselves out, people!

FINAL VERDICT

Picture ☆☆☆☆ Sound ☆☆☆☆

Entertainment ☆☆ Extras ☆☆ Value ☆☆

OVERALL ☆☆☆

THE WILD BUNCH

Price: £15.99

Supplied by: Warner Home Video

Type of disc: Single layer, double-sided

No of chapters: 28 (side A), 18 (side B)

Film format(s)/length: 2.35:1 widescreen / 138 mins

Audio format: Dolby Digital 5.1

Director: Sam Peckinpah

Starring: William Holden, Ernest Borgnine, Robert Ryan

Year made: 1969

Extras: Cast and crew biographies, documentary on the making of the film; scene access; remastered.

This is really brutal! *The Wild Bunch* is surely Peckinpah's finest moment and for those of you who want to watch a real bloody western, it's essential viewing. Even over 30 years after its original release, The Wild Bunch is still a shocking and violent tale of life on the Mexican-US frontier, and both William Holden as Pike and Ernest Borgnine as Dutch excel as the desperadoes with a strong ethical code facing extinction at the hands of government bounty hunters. What makes this DVD so special is that real care has been lavished on the original print so that both colour and sound have been faithfully renewed and presented in a widescreen format. This Director's Cut also includes a half hour black and white documentary called *The Wild Bunch: A Portrait in Montage* which garnered an Oscar nomination in 1996 and goes into some considerable depth about how the film was shot and what tricks were used by Peckinpah to achieve some of the most memorable moments. For fans of the film, this is an excellent bonus. The Wild Bunch is far grittier and

more realistic than anything that has come since and even Eastwood's *Unforgiven* can't match its atmosphere or cinematography. The only big problem with this UK DVD is that it's a flipper, and the film is split over the two sides – unforgivable really. Without that it would be a 5 star review no question.

FINAL VERDICT

Picture ☆☆☆☆ Sound ☆☆☆☆

Entertainment ☆☆☆☆☆

Extras ☆☆☆☆☆ Value ☆☆☆

OVERALL ☆☆☆☆

WILDE

Price: £17.99

Supplied by: Universal

Type of disc: Single layer, single-sided

No of chapters: 18

Film format(s)/length: 2.35:1 widescreen / 112 mins

Audio format: Dolby Surround

Director: Brian Gilbert

Starring: Stephen Fry, Vanessa Redgrave, Jude Law

Year made: 1997

Extras: Scene access; 24-minute documentary *Simply Wilde*; English subtitles for the hearing impaired.

As Oscar himself might have said, there is only one thing worse than having a film made about you, and that is not having a film made about you. While others may have gone before – see *Oscar Wilde* (1959) and *The Trials of Oscar Wilde* (1960) – this is the first to tackle the playwright's homosexuality in any detail, tracing his tempestuous relationship with spoilt brat Lord Alfred Douglas. Although slow to start, the film picks up once Douglas (Law) or Bosie as he preferred to be called, enters the scene as he and Wilde (Fry) embark on an illicit affair that soon becomes the focus of scandalous gossip around 1890's society. Eventually, and almost inevitably given the fact that they aren't exactly secretive about it, word reaches Bosie's father, whose immense hatred of Wilde leads the case to court and eventually a two-year prison sentence for the self-proclaimed genius. Fry's Wilde lacks the pompous swagger you might expect from the role, but his doe-eyed portrayal brings a vulnerability and tenderness to the film that serves to compensate for a somewhat flaccid script. The picture quality is fine, with impressively bright colours (compared to the dingy greys and browns of many period pieces) and sharp, clean definition. That said, towards the end of the film there are a couple of interior scenes that seem a little too green. Sound is also good, emphasising well the clatter of carriage wheels across cobblestones, and the flapping of birds' wings in the background. Extras amount solely to a 24-minute documentary, lazily titled *Simply Wilde*, which refreshingly serves less as a 'Making of' and more as a look at the great man himself, with valuable insights from Fry and director Gilbert. This does however include far too much footage from the film, and comparatively little original material, so should be avoided until you've seen the feature proper. As both a film and a DVD Wilde is good but not great, not really in keeping with the flamboyant style of its subject, but a pleasant evening's viewing nonetheless.

FINAL VERDICT

Picture ☆☆☆☆ Sound ☆☆☆
Entertainment ☆☆☆ Extras ☆☆ Value ☆☆
OVERALL ☆☆☆

THE WILD ONE

Price: £19.99
Supplied by: Columbia TriStar Home Video
Type of disc: Single layer, single-sided
No of chapters: 28
Film format(s)/length: 1:33.1 regular / 76 mins
Audio format: Mono
Director: Laslo Benedek
Starring: Marlon Brando, Lee Marvin, Mary Murphy
Year made: 1953
Extras: Scene access; US theatrical trailer; photo gallery; filmographies; French, Italian, Spanish and German mono soundtracks; subtitles in 20 languages.

In 1947, *Life* magazine published photographs of a small town in California which had been destroyed by a couple of biker gangs that hit the place by storm. This article was the inspiration for *The Wild One*, although it ended up being very diluted for public showing in the Fifties. Brando stars as Johnny, the biker good guy (well weren't all the heroes called Johnny at that time?) who battles against his rival Chino, played by Marvin. Murphy enters the equation as Kathie, a sweet and innocent girl who gets caught in the middle of it all. The picture quality has been wonderfully re-mastered to omit the good old black and white frays and scratches. The sound is also of good reproduction, even though it's only mono. Extras comprise of the usual language and audio options, as well as subtitles. Scene access is also included, although the last track can be missed if you blink. There are a few stills from the film on offer under the 'Photo Gallery' section, mainly of Brando, as well as filmographies of Marlon Brando, Lee Marvin and Mary Murphy. If you fancy a giggle, check out the 'US Theatrical Trailer' for the film, where the ancient extra large white text fills the screen, while sounds of dramatic Fifties-style Wizard of Oz music screams out at you. Finally if you

need even more stimulation, have a wander through the inside cover which explains how the film is based on a true story of biker mayhem in the late Forties.

FINAL VERDICT

Picture ☆☆☆ Sound ☆☆☆
Entertainment ☆☆ Extras ☆☆ Value ☆☆☆
OVERALL ☆☆

WILD THINGS

Price: £15.99
Supplied by: Entertainment in Video
Type of disc: Single layer, single-sided
No of chapters: 12
Film format(s)/length: 2.35:1 widescreen enhanced / 106 mins
Audio format: Dolby Surround
Director: John McNaughton
Starring: Kevin Bacon, Matt Dillon, Neve Campbell
Year made: 1998
Extras: Scene access; theatrical Trailer; 'Making of' featurette.

Sex, revenge and double-dealing amongst the idle rich and the social-climbing poor is familiar ground for a thriller, but *Wild Things* adds a new high school twist, lacquered with cool unemotional postmodern distance. A more traditional piece would sweat to make its characters believable and its twists involving, however *Wild Things* would never dream of taking itself that seriously. Based on a novel, the film starts a little slowly, then accelerates through a convoluted story. Taking such a plot realistically would burn up a lot of screen time, so McNaughton takes the opposite approach, paring the film back to concentrate on the thrill of the chase. The characters are reduced to ciphers, mere counters on the directorial chessboard. As new situations arise, credibility drops to zero and even the first plot twist doesn't make a whole lot of sense, let alone the ninth. It's a nice touch that McNaughton provides a handful of scenes to help explain why things happened, but a lot more help is needed to rescue credibility. Where the film scores is with its sheer zest; producer/star Kevin Bacon has assembled a pretty impressive cast, but the emphasis is on prettiness rather than acting. A champagne-drenched threesome, a nighttime swimming pool tryst: you can't imagine any porno parody being any less unbelievable. It's not just that McNaughton has Denise Richards getting naked, it's the schoolgirl outfit, the pleated skirt and white ankle socks she wears beforehand. It's a film aching to be a parody of itself. A nervy Neve Campbell, and a ferocious Robert Wagner steal what acting honours there are, but Denise Richards and sleazy lawyer Bill

Murray best catch the film's tongue-in-cheek tone. As a DVD, Entertainment in Video has taken the decision that little more is needed to sell the package than DVD's reputation for razor-sharp picture quality. When watching the film on a PC, a little graininess is evident, but on a 29-inch TV, picture quality seemed impressive, with high definition allowing the lurid Florida palette to come through fine. The soundtrack isn't something to stretch Dolby Surround, but the music is carefully chosen and the overall feel is impressive. The 'Making of' featurette is disappointingly average and is nothing more than a movie trailer spliced up with a few snippet interviews with cast and director. There are no insights revealed, and you wish the producers had instead included some outtakes to further the tongue-in-cheek atmosphere of the main piece. As it is, this will sell like hot cakes on main street, while *The Big Easy* – a far superior thriller in both plot and sexual heat – remains sadly unreleased on DVD.

FINAL VERDICT

Picture ☆☆☆☆ Sound ☆☆☆

Entertainment ☆☆☆ Extras ☆☆ Value ☆☆

OVERALL ☆☆☆

WILD WILD WEST

Price: £19.99
Supplied by: Warner Home Video
Type of disc: Dual layer, single-sided
No of chapters: 31
Film format(s)/length: 1.85:1 widescreen enhanced / 102 mins
Audio format: Dolby Digital 5.1
Director: Barry Sonnenfeld
Starring: Will Smith, Kevin Kline, Kenneth Branagh
Year made: 1999
Extras: Scene access; *It's a Whole New West* TV special; *Wardrobes of the West* featurette; *Good Guys' Gadgets* featurette; *Loveless' Ladies* featurette; *Evil Devices* featurette; trailer; stills gallery; 3 music videos, including Will Smith's 'Wild Wild West'; DVD-ROM features: *Artemus Gordon's Mind-Projection Theatre* behind-the-scenes clips; 2 genre essays; *Steel Assassin* game; Web and chat links; original Website; multilingual subtitles; subtitles for the hearing impaired in English.

The most interesting thing about *Wild Wild West* is that it's not actually as bad as you might have heard. Sure, the story is wafer-thin, the effects are given more prominence than the characters and the ending shows signs of last-minute rewriting, but the same can be said of almost any recent blockbuster you'd care to mention. While hardly a work of genius by any means,

Wild Wild West achieves its admittedly limited goals and delivers a fair amount of entertainment. Based on a Sixties television series that nobody bar those glued to the Sci-Fi Channel at unsociable hours of the morning has ever seen, *Wild Wild West* sees 19th Century US government agents Jim West (Smith) and Artemus Gordon (Kline, in a role originally planned for George Clooney) paired up in a mismatched-partners-who'll-soon-become-buddies kind of way to hunt down the megalomaniac Dr Arliss Loveless (Branagh, with an atrocious Deep South accent). The legless lunatic intends to destroy the United States with his arsenal of clunky steam-powered war machines, and West's sharpshooting skills and Gordon's ingenious inventions and disguises – along with the almost totally irrelevant help of Hayek, whose sole purpose in the film appears to be to flash her cleavage and bum (and why not?) – are all that can stop the US being carved up by Loveless and his nasty foreign (ie, British) cohorts. God bless America! With 6 different credited writers, it's hardly a surprise that the story is a bit of a mess, wandering from set-piece to set-piece for no other reason than the need to come up with some new bit of Jules Verne-esque gadgetry for Industrial Light & Magic to play around with. There are also more cheesy double entendres than you'd find in a Roger Moore Bond film or the collected works of Viz comic's Finbarr Saunders, usually revolving around Hayek's ample assets. However, if you're even considering watching *Wild Wild West* then you almost certainly know that this kind of film requires certain parts of the brain to be given a couple of hours off. Sonnenfeld's talent has always been more in impressive visuals than memorable characters or depth of plot, and there's plenty to keep the eyes interested in *Wild Wild West*, whether it's the bizarre background characters, the elaborate gadgets or the seemingly endless parade of beautiful women in very low-cut outfits. (Alternately, female viewers get to see Will Smith butt-naked in the first 5 minutes.) Even though the film is hardly the greatest thing in the world, as a DVD it's surprisingly good, with nearly all the extras of its Region 1 counterpart. The glaring omission is the commentary track by director Sonnenfeld – like the commentary in *The Matrix*, this fell victim to minor cuts for violence making the commentary run out of sync. Don't blame the BBFC this time, though – according to them, Warner Bros wielded the scissors before the film was even submitted for certification. The extras are fairly shallow, since they're either made-for-TV promotional specials or publicity materials for the film's cinema release, but they're still interesting enough to rate a second look. Will Smith's 'Wild Wild

West' music video is also definitely worth repeat viewing – supposedly one of the most expensive music videos ever (and it looks it) it's also got as much of a storyline as the film itself! PC owners with a DVD-ROM drive are also well catered for with more behind-the-scenes clips, the usual Web links and even a game! Despite pricing it higher than the rest of their discs (a worrying trend, as £19.99 seems to be turning into the new 'normal' DVD price) Warner Home Video deserves a pat on the back for the *Wild Wild West* DVD. Apart from the annoying absence of the commentary, it's got an excellent package of extras, and is probably better than the film deserves. Some day, all DVDs will have this much extra material on them!

FINAL VERDICT

Picture ☆☆☆☆☆ Sound ☆☆☆☆☆
Entertainment ☆☆☆ Extras ☆☆☆☆ Value ☆☆☆
OVERALL ☆☆☆

WILLIAM SHAKESPEARE'S ROMEO AND JULIET

Price: £19.99
Supplied by: 20th Century Fox Home Entertainment
Type of disc: Dual layer, single-sided
No of chapters: 29
Film format(s)/length: 2.35:1 widescreen / 115 mins
Audio format: Dolby Digital 5.1
Director: Baz Luhrmann
Starring: Leonardo DiCaprio, Claire Danes, Pete Postlethwaite
Year made: 1996
Extras: Interactive menus; scene access; trailer; multilingual subtitles.

Considering the age of this story and how many times that it's been told, Baz Luhrmanns's decision to shoot this classic love story yet again (filmed over 18 times since 1900) is a brave move. However, Luhrmann has come up with an approach to this tale that is both original and authentic. You probably know the tale from O-level English. Romeo and Juliet, "Star-crossed lovers of two households, both alike in dignity," meet one another at a masked ball held in the house of the Capulets, the family from which Juliet descends. When they meet, neither realises that they are courting across a long-running feud between the Capulets and the Montagues, Romeo's family. Despite not being able to see each other (in all senses of the word) they fall in love at first sight. Later that night they decide to marry. It's a bit sudden, but maybe that's just the way of star-crossed lovers. Without wanting to ruin the story for the few people across the globe who don't know it, the two feuding households are naturally not too happy about the

pairing. Bearing in mind that this is a tragedy, you can probably guess that the movie doesn't end with a honeymoon in Paris. Luhrmann has taken the couple from their original Italian location to modern-day Verona Beach USA. Guns replace swords, ecstasy replaces alcohol, and beach bums and Hispanics replace feuding aristocratic households. However, Luhrmann stops short of reinventing the entire drama. He mostly retains Shakespeare's dialogue, shaved a little here and there to incorporate the standard 2-hour running time. Basically this is the Bard updated. Nothing new about that, nearly every Shakespeare tale has been performed its intended timeline and location. Where Luhrmann has managed to find new tread on this well-worn path is by filming the 400-year-old play successfully for the MTV generation. His styles are mixed and varied: encounters between the Capulets and the Montagues are run at a speeded-up slapstick pace, whereas the gun duelling scenes could make any Eastwood western proud. And of course, the whole thing still plays out as one of the most romantic stories ever told. Casting the world's hottest movie property as Romeo was also a wise idea. Here, prior to his *Titanic* success, DiCaprio proved not only could he handle the Shakespearean dialogue without sounding as though he was just reading from a script, but also that he had the capability to carry an entire movie as a leading man. His romantic opposite doesn't fare too badly either. Danes lends a sympathetic tone to her Juliet, making our heroine a lot more likeable than Danes's hormonally distressed Angela Chase form the great TV series *My So-Called Life*. It's a real shame that such a lively movie is housed on such a dead disc. The sound and picture are both superb, but with the exception of one theatrical trailer that's it as far as extras go. Even the animated menu is completely lifeless. It's not strictly accurate to say that Luhrmann has made Shakespeare accessible to the TV generation. There are many productions that have done this in the past. But what he has managed to do is to create a more vibrant, colourful and original film version of the play than has ever been seen before.

FINAL VERDICT

Picture ☆☆☆☆ Sound ☆☆☆☆
Entertainment ☆☆☆☆
Extras ☆☆ Value ☆☆☆☆
OVERALL ☆☆☆☆

WILLY WONKA & THE CHOCOLATE FACTORY

Price: £15.99
Supplied by: Warner Home Video
Type of disc: Single layer, single-sided

No of chapters: 40
Film format(s)/length: 16:9 widescreen enhanced / 96 mins
Audio format: Dolby Digital 5.1
Director: Mel Stuart
Starring: Gene Wilder, Jack Albertson, Roy Kinnear
Year made: 1971
Extras: Scene access; soundtrack in English, French and Dutch; subtitles in 12 languages; subtitles for the hearing impaired in English.

Even amid all the cocoa waterfalls and enormous edible toadstools, there is still something subtly sinister and, well, Roald Dahl about all this film... Dark chocolate, if you will. It all starts amiably enough with Charlie (Peter Ostrum), who lives with his mother and 4 bed-ridden uncles and aunts in abject poverty without the Social Services raising an eyebrow. With his humble resources, he nevertheless joins the global race to find one of 5 golden tickets hidden in bars of Wonka chocolate, since finding one would mean a free lifetime's supply of the brown nectar and fulfilling his dream of visiting the top secret factory. With said ticket duly found, he and his uncle join 4 other objectionable tykes on the tour, and discover that the rather eccentric factory of Willy Wonka (Wilder) is bizarre at best, and lethal at worst. The sequence as their riverboat goes through the dark tunnel is surreal and – to sensitive young children even now – pretty darned disturbing. Made all the way back in 1971, the film has aged gracefully. Wilder – in a role that today would surely be played by Robin Williams – is a hoot, and there are some lovely touches as satirical now as back then (the Arizona brat asks for a real gun: "Not until you're 12," beams his proud father). On the other hand, the few musical interludes leave a little to be desired, and the screenplay – adapted by Dahl himself – makes a few unwise changes to characters' portrayal in the book. The DVD has clearly been restored, and while there are a few minor pops and scratches on the print near the start, the widescreen image is rock solid, and the garish colour schemes of the factory have had to wait 30 years to look this good on TV. Happily, the upgrade from dull old mono to Dolby Digital 5.1 has the emphasis on subtlety rather than aural pyrotechnics, and nothing leaps out as horribly tacked on from the original. The music and sound effects spread out nicely across the front speakers, while the surrounds and subwoofer pretty much take the night off. And let's face it, they probably deserve it, don't they? What is a crying shame it is that, despite the effort on the transfer, Warner Brothers have spent precisely no time at all kitting the disc out with extra features. This is getting

to be a worrying trend with the Bugs Bunny Bunch – apart from their big blockbuster releases, nothing contains as much as a single, humble production note. And that means that even something as sweet as Willy Wonka's Chocolate Factory leaves a slightly sour taste in the mouth.

FINAL VERDICT
Picture ☆☆☆☆ Sound ☆☆☆☆
Entertainment ☆☆☆ Extras ☆ Value ☆☆☆
OVERALL ☆☆☆

THE WINGS OF THE DOVE

Price: £15.99
Supplied by: Buena Vista
Type of disc: Single layer, single-sided
No of chapters: 15
Film format(s)/length: 2.35:1 widescreen / 102 mins
Audio format: Dolby Digital 5.1
Director: Ian Softley
Starring: Helena Bonham Carter, Alison Elliott, Linus Roache
Year made: 1998
Extras: Scene access.

The visual opulence of DVD is ideally suited to this beautifully filmed and acted version of the Henry James classic. Since it's a James story, the sumptuous settings only serve to amplify the failings, vanity and greed of the major characters. *The Wings of the Dove* is exquisitely filmed, and this really comes out on DVD. We're talking beautiful people here, with Helena Bonham Carter and Alison Elliott for the blokes – HBC lets it all hang out at the end – while there's cerebral crumpet for the laydeez in the shape of Linus Roache (son of William 'Ken Barlow' Roache). The costumes look great, as do the exotic Venetian locations. Sadly, the disc doesn't offer much in the way of extra features – just the usual chapter search, captions and play. There's nothing on the making of the movie, for example, or no discussions of the social or historical context of the novel. So all you're really getting is a sharper-looking video with better sound. Your call.

FINAL VERDICT
Picture ☆☆☆☆ Sound ☆☆☆☆
Entertainment ☆☆☆☆ Extras ☆ Value ☆☆
OVERALL ☆☆

THE WINSLOW BOY

Price: £19.99
Supplied by: Columbia TriStar Home Video
Type of disc: Single layer, single-sided
No of chapters: 28
Film format(s)/length: 1.85:1 anamorphic / 100 mins

Audio format: Dolby Surround
Director: David Mamet
Starring: Nigel Hawthorne, Jeremy Northam, Rebecca Pidgeon
Year made: 1999
Extras: Scene access; behind-the-scenes featurette; audio commentary by director and principal cast; soundtrack in English and German; multilingual subtitles; subtitles for the hearing impaired in Dutch.

Families risking everything they hold dear to right a wrong is, tragically, not a new concept. Terence Rattigan wrote The Winslow Boy for the stage in 1944 but based it on a real case that split public opinion just before the outbreak of World War One. Hawthorne stars as Arthur Winslow, a middle-class patriarch who determines to clear his son Ronnie's name when he is expelled from a naval academy for stealing a 5 shilling postal note. Northam's coldly resolute barrister steps into to defend, but as the case drags on, the financial and public pressure begins to affect each member of the family. The featurette merely takes the trailer and mixes sound bites from director David Mamet, producer Sarah Green and the cast into the stew. The package is unsatisfying and you come away not much the wiser. The commentary makes up for the documentary's shortfall, Mamet ad-libs hesitantly at first and relies on his wife Pidgeon to prompt him. Mercifully, the couple are joined by Northam and Hawthorne, who regale the listeners with their observations and dry wit. Sample banter – Mamet: "I'm going to be glib and stupid throughout and you guys are going to have to pick your own persona." Hawthorne: "Have we the option to be glib and stupid as well?" Northam: "But Nigel, do you really have that option?" The Winslow Boy avoids American melodrama in favour of inferred emotions, subtle comedy and quality performances. Not an equal disc to the film but recommended nonetheless.

FINAL VERDICT
Picture ☆☆☆☆ Sound ☆☆
Entertainment ☆☆☆ Extras ☆☆ Value ☆☆
OVERALL ☆☆☆

With or Without You

Price: £19.99
Supplied by: VCI
Type of disc: Dual layer, single-sided
No of chapters: 16
Film format(s)/length: 16:9 widescreen / 86 mins
Audio format: Dolby Digital 5.1
Director: Michael Winterbottom
Starring: Christopher Eccleston, Dervla Kirwan, Yvan

Attal
Year made: 1999
Extras: Scene access; theatrical trailer; featurette; cast and crew interviews; subtitles for the hearing impaired in English

This is the bittersweet tale of a husband and wife's attempts to conceive a baby in contemporary Belfast. Overlooked at the box office, Michael Winterbottom's (*Welcome to Sarajevo*) comedy drama arrives on disc accompanied by what looks on the surface to be strong special features. Christopher Eccleston, forever seared in the mind after his performances in *Our Friends in the North* and *Shallow Grave*, plays Vincent. He's an ex-RUC officer now trying to impregnate Rosie (Kirwan), his beautiful wife of 5 years, and failing, much to his annoyance. More problems arise when Benoit (Attal), Rosie's childhood pen pal from France shows up and moves in and Vincent's strumpet ex-girlfriend (Julie Graham) makes her intentions clear. Although John Forte's screenplay skips nicely from scene to scene and quip to quip (Rosie: "I've been lying back and thinking of Ulster") the ending is never really in any doubt. Genuine guffaws are few and far between but it's refreshing to see Eccleston widening his theatrical palette by doing this light comedy. But all is not as it seems with the extras. The key problem is that solid interviews were made with the 3 leads but then edited together with some behind-the-scenes footage and then called a featurette. Eccleston and Kirwan are paraphrased in the booklet. Ultimately it looks like you're getting a greater quantity of extras, just going by the sleeve alone. Director Winterbottom's input is sadly absent. The cast and director are up to spec but in the end, the script and disc are firing blanks.

FINAL VERDICT
Picture ☆☆☆☆ Sound ☆☆☆
Entertainment ☆☆☆
Extras ☆☆☆ Value ☆☆☆
OVERALL ☆☆☆

Wolf

Price: £19.99
Supplied by: DVD World (01705 796662)
Type of disc: Single layer, single-sided
No of chapters: 20
Film format(s)/length: 16:9 widescreen / 120mins
Director: Mike Nichols
Starring: Jack Nicholson, Michelle Pfeiffer, James Spader
Year made: 1994
Extras: Theatrical trailer, Dolby Digital; multilingual sub-

titles; scene access.

Any Jack Nicholson film is something of an event, but *Wolf* seems especially tantalising with its combination of a stellar cast and highbrow director with that horror staple: the werewolf movie. Perhaps unsurprisingly, Nicholson only comes alive with the emerging wolf – as a timid book editor he is less than convincing, most especially when mumbling about the pseudo-mystical justification for his werewolf transformations. Since at heart this is horror internalised within Nicholson's character and his office politics, it's a critical flaw. Moreover, Nichols' restrained use of SFX wizard Rick Baker undermines the werewolf scenes – watching the somewhat pudgy, certainly middle-aged Nicholson tracking down a deer while wearing prosthetic werewolf teeth and exaggerated sideburns seems more Sixties Hammer Horror than anything else. Perhaps as a consequence, despite the cast this is a less than lavish DVD presentation. Nichols makes good use of the big budget to ensure almost every frame of film is immaculately composed, a sharp sense of aesthetics which DVD brings to the fore. Nevertheless, the encoding is only adequate and there are no production notes, just the trailer and instant scene selection. The real crime, however, is that a film with so much potential ultimately turns out to be so dull.

FINAL VERDICT

Picture ☆☆☆ Sound ☆☆☆☆

Entertainment ☆☆ Extras ☆☆ Value ☆☆

OVERALL ☆☆

THE WORLD IS NOT ENOUGH

Price: £19.99
Supplied by: MGM Home Entertainment
Type of disc: Dual layer, single-sided
No of chapters: 32
Film format(s)/length: 2.35:1 anamorphic / 122 mins
Audio format: Dolby Digital 5.1
Director: Michael Apted
Starring: Pierce Brosnan, Sophie Marceau, Denise Richards
Year made: 1999
Extras: Scene access; commentary by director Michael Apted; commentary by producer, stunt coordinator and composer; *The Making of The World Is Not Enough* featurette (15 mins); *The Secrets of 007* clips; music video – 'The World Is Not Enough' by Garbage; *Bond Cocktail* featurette (22 mins); *Bond Down River* featurette (25 mins); *A Tribute to Desmond Llewelyn* (3 mins); trailer; trailer for PlayStation *TWINE* game; subtitles in English; subtitles for the hearing impaired in English.

When Q says "Fully loaded, I believe is the term," in *The World Is Not Enough*, he could just as easily be talking about the DVD of the latest James Bond adventure as his BMW Z8. *The World Is Not Enough* marked the launch of the *Special Edition* 007 series, each of which comes equipped with more gadgets than Bond himself. As for the film itself… well, it's Bond. You know what you're going to get – chases, stunts, corny double entendres, beautiful women, fast cars, casinos, gadgets and gunfights. The faces and locations are really the only things that change; even Brosnan admits this in the *Bond Cocktail* featurette. *The World Is Not Enough* features all of the above in the appropriate quantities, but seems to lack spark. The main failing of *TWINE* is that it takes itself all too seriously, as if afraid that the spirit of Dr Evil might invade the set at any moment. Deciding that you want your plot to take place in the real world – or as near to the real world as any Bond film can be – is one thing, but this then makes the more fantastic elements seem out of place. And let's face it, wanting to knock out competing oil pipelines is pretty mundane stuff by any Bond villain's standards. This side of the story isn't helped by surprisingly flat direction and – unforgivably for a Bond film – slack editing. Action sequences that should be thrilling, like the ski chase, end up plodding and hard to follow, and if anyone can figure out the final reactor room fight without multiple viewings and a scorecard they deserve a medal. Director Apted (best known for *Gorillas in the Mist*) admits in one of the featurettes that he'd never directed a major action film before, and, sad to say, it shows. That said, *The World Is Not Enough* is far from being the worst Bond film ever. There's none of the "I'm only here for the money" attitude of the later Connery films or smarmy acting-by-eyebrow in front of a dodgy back-projection found in Moore's lesser attempts. But then, nor is it anywhere near the best of the series (*Goldfinger*, *The Spy Who Loved Me*, *Goldeneye*) either. Let's hope that for *Bond 20*, we see some proper Bond villainy with lasers and monorails and vast secret bases. However, while the plot might not be enough, the disc definitely is. The picture is as clear and colourful as you'd expect from such a major title, backed by some suitably rumbling explosions and well-mixed surround sound. There's also over an hour of supplementary material to watch, ranging from the shallow (*The Making of The World Is Not Enough*', a 15-minute puff piece done for American TV) to the almost insanely over-detailed (the 25-minute *Bond Down River* describes more than you need to know about the opening chase down the Thames). The *Secrets of 007* section is also quite interesting, with 9 short pieces showing how different action and effects sequences were put together, from storyboards to final film. *The World Is*

Not Enough even boasts not one, but two commentary tracks. The first is by director Apted and is dry but detailed, while the second is a rather more chatty affair by production designer Peter Lamont, second unit director Vic Armstrong and composer David Arnold. Both commentaries are interesting, even if they do cover similar ground. All in all, *The World Is Not Enough* is an excellent, value-packed DVD surrounding a rather uninspired movie. But then, it's Bond. You know you're going to buy it anyway…

FINAL VERDICT

Picture ☆☆☆☆☆ Sound ☆☆☆☆
Entertainment ☆☆☆ Extras ☆☆☆☆☆ Value ☆☆☆☆
OVERALL ☆☆☆☆

THE X-FILES (SPECIAL EDITION)

Price: £19.99
Supplied by: 20th Century Fox
Type of disc: Dual layer, single-sided
No of chapters: 18
Film format(s)/length: 16:9 widescreen / 91 mins
Audio format: Dolby Digital 5.1
Director: Rob Bowman
Starring: David Duchovny, Gillian Anderson, Martin Landau
Year made: 1998
Extras: Scene access; behind-the-scenes documentary *Fight the Future* with on location footage and interviews; audio commentary by director Rob Bowman and creator Chris Carter; theatrical trailer; subtitles in 10 languages; subtitles for the hearing impaired in English.

Mobile phones, long raincoats, shafts of torch light in dark corridors, paranoia in excess, languid dialogue and tangible sexual chemistry: *The X-Files* is back! With its 'Trust No One' ethic and the conviction that everyone in authority is working for 'The Man', *The X-Files* tapped into what the media jubilantly called pre-Millennium tension and inspired no end of spin-offs and rip-offs in the Nineties. When it came to make the leap to the big screen, creator, writer and producer Chris Carter knew the stakes had to be raised for Mulder and Scully both professionally and personally. What *The X-Files* movie delivers is a smart, high production value film dovetailing an intelligent, stylised mystery thriller for non-converts with continuing themes for its fans. With the X files department shut down, Mulder and Scully work with other FBI agents to track down a bomb planted in a Federal building. The astonishing explosion starts the team on a new trail that brings them closer to the shadowy conspiracy they've investigated over the previous 5 seasons. Old questions are answered, new ones are posed, humanity

is under threat by aliens but more importantly, do M&S finally get to rub it smooth? The answer, if you don't know already, is in chapter 12…The bonus audio commentary is a slight disappointment in that the film-makers sound like they recorded it in separate rooms, so there's no banter or spontaneity. Nevertheless, director Bowman enthusiastically recalls giving Oscar-winner Martin Landau instructions after growing up watching him on *Mission: Impossible*. Carter discusses how the sequences where Mulder and Scully are pursued by 300,000 bees and later run through towering cornfields in the dark were born out of his own childhood fears. The documentary is solid enough. Filmed on location, it focuses in particular on the Dallas bomb explosion and the Bee Dome set pieces and reports illuminating behind-the-scenes trivia. For example, on-set paranoia almost matched that in the story, with the script printed on red paper that cannot be photocopied. Unfortunately, we learn little about Duchovny and Anderson or their thoughts on their characters. The DVD also contains hyperlinks to Fox's numerous Websites but like Universal they seem unwilling to download the official movie sites onto the discs. Other extras include the inevitable trailer and extensive number of European subtitles. The menus themselves deserve a mention, as the well executed moving elements recreate the cloak and dagger atmosphere synonymous with *The X-Files*. Who knows if there will be a film sequel, but the series shows no immediate signs of drying up. *The X-Files* movie on DVD is a fine addition in itself, but considering that the franchise is one of Fox's family jewels, the disc could have been far better stocked.

FINAL VERDICT

Picture ☆☆☆☆ Sound ☆☆☆☆
Entertainment ☆☆☆ Extras ☆☆☆ Value ☆☆☆
OVERALL ☆☆☆☆

YELLOW SUBMARINE

Price: £19.99
Supplied by: MGM Home Entertainment
Type of disc: Dual layer, single-sided
No of chapters: 36
Film format(s)/length: 1.66.1 letterbox / 90 mins
Audio format: Dolby Digital 5.1
Director: George Dunning
Starring the voices of: John Clive; Geoffrey Hughes, Lance Percival, plus an appearance by The Beatles
Year made: 1968
Extras: Scene access; *The Mod Odyssey* documentary; audio commentary by George Dunnin and Heinz Edelmann; music only track highlighting the score; 3 sto-

ryboarded sequences; unused sequences; original pencil drawings; exclusive behind-the-scenes photo gallery; interviews with the crew and vocal talents; collectible 8-page booklet.

'In the town where I was born, lived a man, with DVDs...' Absolutely love them or inexplicably hate them, John Lennon, James Paul McCartney, George Harrison and Richard Starkey (aka Ringo Starr), otherwise known as The Beatles, are the single most influential group in the history of 20th century music, and indeed, musical film. And finally, it's here. 30 years on from the day that John, Paul, George and Ringo reluctantly tripped along to the World Premiere of *Yellow Submarine*, fans have the chance to buy the fantastically renovated editions of the soundtrack, and the film on VHS and DVD. But it's this DVD that is the most amazing buy. The ground-breaking animation has a plot that most people wouldn't understand, even though it can be written on the back of a single tab of LSD. When the beautiful, peaceful people of Pepperland are set upon by the startlingly nasty Blue Meanies, Captain Fred is sent on a mission to find the only people who can save them. Setting off in the Yellow Submarine, he touches down in Liverpool, where a young scouser called Ringo introduces him to his pals John, Paul and George. The Fab Four then set off on a psychedelic journey through the seas of Tim, Science, Monsters and Holes until they reach the Meanied Pepperland, picking up Jeremy Hillary Boob PhD, (the Nowhere Man), along the way. Armed only with the costumes of the legendary Sergeant Pepper's Lonely Hearts Club Band, a whole lot of Love and, of course, their music, the boys save the world and bring an end to the blues. Fine and funky, but it's basically an excuse for some of the finest musical set-pieces and examples of experimental Sixties animation seen in cinema history. The film was put together by the same team that created the low-quality US TV Cartoon of *The Beatles*, but when teamed up with an extraordinary German designer, Heinz Edelmann, the silver screen animated debut of the Fab Four became a very different experience. The innovative animation techniques and unique use of film and 3D effects enraptured audiences when it was first show – and it still has exactly the same effect today. This is particularly true of the DVD. The way that the psychedelic colours have been brought out by digital restoration, coupled with the outstanding sound quality, means that the music and images shout out at you better than new. The picture is inescapably a little grainy after 30 years, but you'd have to be a real pedant to complain about that when you see the extras. The storyboards, exclusive photos and

pictures and mini-documentary are simply gold dust for Beatles fans, but the added bonuses of the commentary and music-only tracks are crucial bonuses for any film fan, as are the interviews. It all adds up to the definitive *Yellow Submarine* experience, and what's more, it's out first on Region 2! It just shows that there's nothing you can do that can't be done.

FINAL VERDICT

Picture ☆☆☆☆☆ Sound ☆☆☆☆☆

Entertainment ☆☆☆☆☆

Extras ☆☆☆☆☆ Value ☆☆☆☆☆

OVERALL ☆☆☆☆☆

You Only Live Twice

Price: £19.99

Supplied by: MGM Home Entertainment

Type of disc: Dual layer, single-sided

No of chapters: 32

Film format(s)/length: 2.35:1 anamorphic / 112 mins

Audio format: Stereo

Director: Lewis Gilbert

Starring: Sean Connery, Akiko Wakabayashi, Donald Pleasance

Year made: 1967

Extras: Scene access; *Inside You Only Live Twice* documentary (30 mins); *Silhouettes: The Titles of James Bond* documentary (23 mins); audio commentary by director Lewis Gilbert, production designer Ken Adam, and cast and crew members; plane crash storyboards; 4 trailers; 7 radio spots; subtitles in English; subtitles for the hearing impaired in English

This is it; the film that made Mike Myers a very rich man indeed. Without *You Only Live Twice*, there would have been no Dr Evil, no Mr Bigglesworth and no ill-tempered mutated sea bass. With each Bond film making more money than the last, *You Only Live Twice* took full advantage of the studio's willingness to hand blank cheques over to 007's producers, creating an adventure so over-the-top that it went beyond the term 'spy thriller' into full-on science fantasy. Somebody is hijacking spacecraft in orbit; the Americans blame the Russians, the Russians blame the Americans, and unless a certain British agent can uncover the real culprit, World War III beckons. Connery made a big show during filming that *YOLT* would be his last Bond film, and at times his weariness with the role shows through, most notably during the action scenes where he's clearly just going through the motions while things blow up around him. It's undeniably true that Bond is almost overshadowed here by the giant sets and insane plot, but this just set the pattern for the rest of the series, where spectacle outweighs substance. MGM has done its usual bang-up job with digitally restoring the picture, bringing Japan, both real and in the form of Ken Adam's outrageous sets, vividly to life. There are occasional specks of dirt on the print, but overall things look as fresh as they would have 33 years ago. The sound is only basic stereo, however; a 5.1 remix would have been appreciated, though considering the effort MGM has put into the Bond series on DVD it's a bit churlish to complain too loudly. The audio commentary is interesting, but it's also rather disjointed. Instead of having people comment specifically on what's happening onscreen, the voiceover track is made up of a series of interview snippets, tied together by a narrator from the Ian Fleming Foundation. Compared to some of the other Bond titles, *You Only Live Twice* is less packed with extras. That said, those that are included are definitely worth a watch. *Inside You Only Live Twice* is the now-traditional look behind-the-scenes, complete with interviews and archive footage. A lot of time is spent looking at the film's centrepiece, the amazing volcano set, but there's still plenty of time to learn about how Japanese actress Mie Hama (Kissy Suzuki) threatened to commit suicide when she learned that she was about to be fired, and Connery's increasing dislike of the pressures of superstardom. The second documentary, *Silhouettes*, looks mainly at the career of Maurice Binder, the man who designed the title sequences for most of the Bond films, though it also takes a look at the work of Daniel Kleinman, who took over the job of doing arty things with naked women for the Pierce Brosnan era. Rounding off the extras package is a sequence of storyboards for the plane crash sequence and a bundle of trailers, which go to show just how far the art of trailer-making has come since the Sixties. If you like your films to have fine acting, deep, believable characters and credible plots, then *You Only Live Twice* is not for you. But then, by those criteria, neither is the rest of the Bond series. If, on the other hand, you like enormous action sequences, even bigger sets, ninjas, mini-helicopters and the feeling that a lot of talented people have their tongues very firmly in their cheeks as they see just how much they can get away with, then James Bond's fifth adventure deserves to infiltrate your player.

FINAL VERDICT

Picture ☆☆☆☆ Sound ☆☆

Entertainment ☆☆☆☆

Extras ☆☆☆☆ Value ☆☆☆☆

OVERALL ☆☆☆☆

YOU'VE GOT MAIL

Price: £15.99
Supplied by: Warner Home Video
Type of disc: Dual layer, single-sided
No of chapters: 33
Film format(s)/length: 1.85:1 widescreen / 115 mins
Audio format: Dolby Digital 5.1
Director: Nora Ephron
Starring: Tom Hanks, Meg Ryan, Parker Posey
Year made: 1998
Extras: Scene access; trailer; full-length director and producer commentary; Nora Ephron interview; 'Discover New York's Upper West Side' location guide; music-only soundtrack; interview gallery (individual clips) and Nora Ephron soundbites accessible only by DVD-ROM.

You may think fluffy kittens are the ultimate in cute. You may think big-eyed, mop-topped kiddiewinks are the cutting edge of cute. You may even think that cuddly stuffed animals with tiny hands are the absolute final word in cute. But believe me, they're about as cute as a rabid, scab-faced pitbull owned by a skinhead when seen next to *You've Got Mail*. This film is so overwhelmingly keen to be adorable that it's practically inviting you to tickle it under the chin. DVD early-adopters should be warned that the exploding helicopter and gunfire quotient in *You've Got Mail* is actually a negative number. Reuniting the *Sleepless in Seattle* team (Hanks, Ryan, writer-director Ephron), *You've Got Mail* is another somewhat implausible romantic comedy. Joe Fox (Hanks) and Kathleen Kelly (Ryan) are online soulmates, sending heartfelt pseudonymous emails back and forth over the Internet. What neither realises, at least for a while, is that they actually know each other in real life – and hate each other. Both are bookstore owners – he of a huge, cost-cutting superstore, she of a quaint children's shop – and Joe's ruthless approach to competition is driving Kathleen out of business. Much of the film has the pair trading insults face-to-face, then going home to their computers to continue their e-romance and offer each other advice. It's entertaining in a warm, fuzzy, highly predictable way – even the picture on the DVD's sleeve makes it perfectly clear how the story will finish! *You've Got Mail* is surprisingly well-stocked with extras, particularly for a romantic comedy, where you're normally lucky if you even get a trailer. On this disc, there's not only a trailer, but a full-length commentary from Ephron and fellow producer Lauren Shuler Donner, a music-only soundtrack, a 14-minute interview – well, interview in the gushing, American, "You're so wonderful" PR-puffery sense – with Nora Ephron from cable movie channel HBO, and a mini travel guide to New York's Upper West Side, where the story takes place. This last is quite a clever idea, a map showing the filming locations which, when selected, go into clips of the place along with some commentary about it. The clips aren't lengthy, but it's good to see that somebody is actually making an effort to include added value for the much neglected Region 2 viewer – almost as much as on the American version. Nice one Warners! PC owners with a DVD-ROM drive also get some extra extras to call their own. Pop the disc into your PC and you can check out a bunch of additional interviews and more Nora Ephron soundbites, although the lack of Macintosh compatibility is a point against the disc. Since one of the many, many examples of product placement in the film has Meg Ryan pouring her heart out into her trusty Apple PowerBook (ruthless businessman Hanks naturally uses a PC) it's something of an oversight. It might be soppy and sentimental, but *You've Got Mail* will eventually wear down even the most committed Steven Seagal fan with its relentless niceness and force them to admit that yes, Hanks and Ryan do make a cute couple. Unfortunately, it's all been done before – and better – in *Sleepless in Seattle*, which despite its lack of DVD-worthy extras is probably a better choice for super-cute romance.

FINAL VERDICT

Picture ☆☆☆ Sound ☆☆☆☆

Entertainment ☆☆☆ Extras ☆☆☆☆ Value ☆☆☆☆

OVERALL ☆☆☆☆

Zombie Flesh Eaters

Price: £19.99

Supplied by: Fantasy Blue (0161 832 4923)

Type of disc: Double layer, single-sided

No of chapters: 16

Film format(s)/length: 2.35:1 widescreen / 90 mins

Audio format: Dolby Digital 5.1

Director: Lucio Fulci

Starring: Ian McCulloch, Richard Johnson, Tisa Farrow

Year made: 1979

Extras: Scene access; director's filmography; actor's filmography; trailer; film flash.

When the title of the movie you are watching appears in the director's filmography under a different name, you can't help but worry about what lies ahead. What does lie ahead is a rather lifeless film concerning the daughter of a scientist and a Robert Redford lookalike journalist (Ian McCulloch), who head off to the Island of Mutal intent on knowing the fate of her father. The answer was a zombie bit him. Not too difficult seeing as the island is overrun by them. The reason for this? God knows! The film offers no explanation for its plot (or lack of it) and the script is of such

little value that you find yourself not caring about why anything is happening at all. As for the DVD, it holds just above the basic of extras, but the filmography of director Fulci is quite revealing. The title page resembles a Commodore 64 screenshot, and the eerie music is more annoying than frightening. If you're a fan of this type of movie then the DVD may be okay, however, if you're slightly squeamish or have any sense at all then steer clear.

FINAL VERDICT

Picture ☆☆ Sound ☆☆

Entertainment ☆ Extras ☆☆ Value ☆

OVERALL ☆☆

The following reviews of non-film Region 2 discs can only hope to scratch the surface of the titles already released. In this short round-up, we have attempted to cover some of the more popular music, comedy, adult, sport, children's, anime, cult TV series and documentaries now available on DVD, and these will hopefully at least provide an indication of the breadth of material now available.

THE BEST OF MONTY PYTHON'S FLYING CIRCUS

Price: £19.99
Supplied by: BBC
Type of disc: Dual layer, single-sided
No of chapters: 30
Film format(s)/length: 4:3 regular / 96 mins
Audio format: Mono
Directors: John Howard Davies and Ian MacNaughton
Starring: John Cleese, Michael Palin, Eric Idle, Terry Gilliam, Terry Jones
Year made: 1969-70
Extras: Scene access; sing-a-long Lumberjack Song; biographies; photo gallery; 'Palindromes': An explanation of...; *Radio Times* – the original billing; subtitles in English.

British comedy. You just can't think of those words without the title of one show appearing on your lips like the flash from a bullet. *Monty Python's Flying Circus*, whether you love it or hate it, is the mother of latter day British humour, with its influences making themselves apparent in everything from *Big Train* to Eddie Izzard's stand up routine. As demonstrated by repeated television showings over the years, or the fact that the *Monty Python* team now crop up in every corner of the entertainment industry, this show has defined itself in the realm of cult status. A style of comedy that was in its day genuinely a new phenomenon, *Monty Python* set a precedent and changed the way of looking at sketch-based television humour. In 1969 *Monty Python's Flying Circus* was just another obscure comedy that aired at 10 o'clock every Saturday evening. The series ran for 12 episodes (surprising for its time) without a pilot episode. Although some time before its international success, classic sketches such as 'Upper-Class Twit of the Year' and 'The Man With Three Buttocks' helped lead the programme to 3 more series, 4 feature films and worldwide recognition for the shows talented stars. It was the footlights of Cambridge that pooled the writing and performing talents of John Cleese and Graham Chapman, a society synonymous for churning out members of the British television comedy constabu-

lary. Teaming up with Oxford's Michael Palin and Terry Jones, Eric Idle and popular American artist Terry Gilliam soon joined the team. They were now all set to rewrite the rules of comedy. Gone were any grounds in social reality – or any sort of reality for that matter! *Monty Python's Flying Circus* found its humour in the lunacy of the world. It wasn't social commentary, it wasn't clever satire, it was just hit-or-miss craziness. Men dressed as women, medieval knights slapping folk with chickens for no apparent reason and anything obscure that could raise a smile would belong to *Monty Python*. Perhaps it's with respect that the BBC have chosen to recognize the importance of *Monty Python* and use it as one of their flagship titles when sailing into the ocean of DVD. Fans might be a little disappointed that the entire first series has been condensed down to a 90-minute 'Best of' format. Thankfully this isn't a jumbled mess of random sketches, but more of a record of achievements, scraping off the cream of the crop and repackaging it for digital prosperity. And what inspirational packaging it is! To begin with the animated menus remain faithful to the *Monty Python* bravado. All the Gilliam artwork you could hope to find is literally barking at you to make a choice. The extras appear to be aimed towards the die-hard fans, as the sing-a-long to 'The Lumberjack Song' and the explanation of the word 'Palindrome' will mean little if you don't already have a previous knowledge of their extraordinary folklore. The Pythonites' biographies are up-to-date and as interesting as biographies can be. Unfortunately the original billing by the *Radio Times* (who first introduced *Monty Python's Flying Circus* to the world) is a little disappointing. If only a fan within the executive hierarchy at the BBC had taken the bold decision to release the entire series on one disc – this would surely have been amongst the best Region 2 releases to date. As it stands, this is the only factor that spoils an otherwise excellent DVD.

FINAL VERDICT

Picture ☆☆☆ Sound ☆☆
Entertainment ☆☆☆☆☆
Extras ☆☆☆☆ Value ☆☆☆☆☆
OVERALL ☆☆☆☆

THE BLACK ADDER: SERIES 1

Price: £19.99
Supplied by: BBC Worldwide
Type of disc: Dual layer, single-sided
No of chapters: 6 episodes
Film format(s)/length: 4:3 regular/ 190 mins
Audio format: Stereo

Director: Martin Shardlow

Starring: Rowan Atkinson, Tony Robinson, Brian Blessed

Year made: 1983

Extras: Access to every episode; individual episode chapter guidance; subtitles in 9 languages.

This is often badged as the lesser known one of the *Black Adder* series, the one that people are more willing to dismiss as inferior rather than realise it's really a little gem. This is where it all began, the first 6 episodes that led to be 4 series of what's widely regarded as the benchmark of British sitcom in the Eighties. Each series retells a different historical period through the bitter eyes of Edmund Black Adder (Atkinson), or one of his ancestors, as he struggles against an inane hierarchy that is so clearly beneath his level of cunning and wit. The first series sees Edmund as the bastard son of Richard IV (Blessed) in 15th Century England, who spends each episode following some scheme or other to ruthlessly ruin the establishment and take over the kingdom. The trouble is, Black Adder himself is a complete idiot, and far too shallow and cowardly to actually succeed. What makes this series stand out predominantly from the other 3 is the writing. Here, star Atkinson, rather than the usual Ben Elton, partnered Richard Curtis. As a result, the humour is less offensive, perhaps not as sharp, and the characters of Black Adder and Baldrick (Robinson) are very different from the incarnations we've grown to know and love. The DVD is pretty thin on the ground when it comes to extras, but it has to be remembered that this is a television series, and an early Eighties BBC one at that, so the likelihood of a director's commentary or gallery is pretty slim. *Black Adder* on DVD is just a logical progression. It's the BBC catching up with fans that have already taken the digital leap to DVD, so no matter how tentative it is, at least the BBC are stepping into new waters and embracing new technology with open arms.

FINAL VERDICT

Picture ☆☆☆ Sound ☆☆☆

Entertainment ☆☆☆☆ Extras ☆ Value ☆☆☆

OVERALL ☆☆☆

BUBBLEGUM CRISIS VOLUME 1

Price: £44.99 (for the boxset)

Supplied by: DVDplus (www.dvdplus.co.uk)

Type of disc: Single layer, single-sided

No of chapters: 34

Film format(s)/length: 4:3 regular / 113 mins

Audio format: Dolby Surround

Directors: Various

Starring the voices of: Sakakibara Yoshiko, Oomori Kinuko, Michie Tomizawa

Year made: 1987

Extras: Chapter access; English and Japanese sound-tracks; English and French subtitles; DVD-ROM features: hi-res image gallery; Internet links; partial liner notes; complete song lyrics; cast and crew lists.

In the year 2032, the monolithic and corrupt Genom corporation is in a position of worldwide economic dominance. Key to its power are its android 'boomers', but when these malfunction, they can be lethal. Since the police are both useless and in Genom's pocket, the only thing standing in Genom's way is a mercenary group called the Knight Sabers, 4 women in power armour with their own reasons for opposing the company. Bubblegum Crisis is a Japanese *anime* series (only the uninformed call it *manga*) that's a cross between *Batman* and *Blade Runner*, with more than a little *Terminator* mixed in. This first of 3 BGC DVDs features 3 episodes, which make up a complete story arc. 'Tinsel City' kicks off with the Knight Sabers hired to recover a kidnapped girl, who turns out to be the key to control of a super-weapon. 'Born to Kill' makes the mission personal when one of Linna's friends is murdered, and 'Blow Up' sees the Knight Sabers finally confronting the slimy Genom exec who has orchestrated the whole affair. Certain features are common to all 3 DVDs, so we'll cover them here. For a start, despite being available through Region 2 outlets, the 3 discs in this boxset are region free, so can be enjoyed by all. Then there's the matter of subtitles. Purists maintain that the best way to view *anime* is in the original Japanese with subtitles. There's a good reason for this; in Japan, voice-acting for animation is considered a perfectly legitimate part of the art. In the West, it tends to attract people who couldn't get a role in community theatre. *Bubblegum Crisis* was one of the first *anime* to appear in the West, and as a result the English voices are appalling. A quick switch of the audio setting brings up the original soundtrack, featuring actors who can act! Unfortunately, a flaw on all 3 volumes is an irritating pulsing background noise on the Japanese soundtrack, which was absent from both VHS and laserdisc and has no place on DVD. It's dodgy mastering, pure and simple. In a rare reversal of the norm, picture quality is actually lower than laserdisc, with a generally soft look and some artifacting and picture jitter. *Bubblegum Crisis* is one of the best and most accessible anime series around. M2K should at least be given credit for introducing *anime* to DVD, but it's a shame they didn't put more effort into it.

FINAL VERDICT

Picture ☆☆ Sound ☆☆

Entertainment ☆☆☆☆ Extras ☆☆☆ Value ☆☆☆

OVERALL ☆☆☆

DANGER MAN

Price: £9.99
Supplied by: Carlton
Type of disc: Single layer, single-sided
No of chapters: 4 x 4
Film format(s)/length: 4:3 regular / 100 mins
Audio format: Mono
Directors: Various
Starring: Patrick McGoohan
Year made: 1960
Extras: Scene acces; John Drake character profile; trailer for other ITC titles; subtitles in English.

Yikes! A TV show that's 40 years old is quite a scary thing to find on a new format like DVD. What's even more frightening is that while it's obviously dated in its details, the basic premise actually works better than any action-adventure show on the air today. McGoohan is John Drake, Danger Man, an international troubleshooter who travels around the world (or at least to anywhere that has stock footage available) cracking crimes and busting enemies of the state, a James Bond before there even was a James Bond as we know him. (McGoohan was actually offered the role, but turned it down because he thought 007 was too promiscuous!) These are the first 4 episodes of the series, and at only 25 minutes each there's not much that Drake can cram in, but apart from the stilted dialogue and black-and-white picture, the way it's shot is surprisingly contemporary, meaning either it was years ahead of its time or TV hasn't advanced much in 4 decades. The plots are straightforward (Drake catches bullion thieves, brings down slave traders and the like) but entertaining in a retro way, and you can always guarantee that there will be at least one fistfight per episode. Interestingly, the first episode on the disc ('View from the Villa') features the Welsh resort of Portmerion, which would go on to greater fame as the setting for McGoohan's follow-up to *Danger Man*, *The Prisoner*. It's not exactly everybody's cup of tea, but at only £9.99 it's worth a look for the curious.

FINAL VERDICT

Picture ☆☆ Sound ☆☆

Entertainment ☆☆☆ Extras ☆☆ Value ☆☆☆

OVERALL ☆☆☆

DOCTOR WHO: THE FIVE DOCTORS SPECIAL EDITION

Price: £19.99
Supplied by: BBC Worldwide
Type of disc: Dual layer, single-sided
No of chapters: 24
Film format(s)/length: 4:3 regular / 102 mins
Audio format: Dolby Digital 5.1
Director: Peter Moffatt
Starring: Peter Davison, John Pertwee, Patrick Troughton
Year made: 1983
Extras: Scene access; music selection; multilingual subtitles.

The Five Doctors is heralded as a 'special edition', with 'extended scenes, previously unseen sequences [and] new visual effects' (it's been available on video for a few years). If you're expecting something like the *Star Wars* Special Edition, forget it – some of the dodgier effects have been replaced by slightly better computer generated ones, and there are a couple of extra bits of dialogue, but the TARDIS computer is still a BBC Micro. *The Five Doctors* was a 20th anniversary special, bringing together all, er, 5 Doctors. That is, all 5 apart from William Hartnell, who was dead and had to make do with a lookalike. And what about Tom Baker, who didn't want to do it and was represented by unused footage from another episode. Basically, someone has hijacked the various Doctors out of their own times and dropped them in the Death Zone on their homeworld of Gallifrey, facing old enemies like the Daleks and the Cybermen. Davison's Doctor has to uncover a Time Lord plot while the others fight for their lives. Pretty flat stuff really. but hey this is *Doctor Who* were talking about. In the main though, *The Five Doctors* is an amusing celebration, but hardly the best story ever – the absence of Tom Baker sees to that. (How about a 'special edition' of *Terror of the Zygons* with a new *Walking With Dinosaurs*-style Loch Ness Monster, BBC?) It's still fun, though, and even includes a music selection (though it does sound a bit slowed-down). This is a good start from the BBC in terms of DVDs – let's hope there's more to come.

FINAL VERDICT

Picture ☆☆☆ Sound ☆☆☆

Entertainment ☆☆☆ Extras ☆☆ Value ☆☆☆

OVERALL ☆☆☆

THE DOORS LIVE IN EUROPE

Price: £19.99
Supplied by: ILC

Type of disc: Single-layer, single-sided
No of chapters: 10
Film format(s)/length: 4:3 regular / 58 mins
Audio format: Dolby Digital 5.1
Directors: Paul Justman, Ray Manzarek, and John Densmore
Starring: Jim Morrison, Rob Krieger John Densmore
Year made: 1968
Extras: Scene access.

It's 1968 and The Doors are on tour in Europe; fortunately, somebody had a cine camera with them to film the proceedings! There can be little doubt that The Doors made an important contribution to music, but upon watching this DVD you could easily be persuaded otherwise. This has to be one of the most unpleasant DVD experiences ever. Imagine the worst home video coupled with two musical has-beens warbling on in a more anecdotal, rather than factual fashion about their time with The Doors back in 1968 and you might get some idea of just how bad this is. Obviously there are always going to be limitations with such archived material, but no real attempt has been made to make up for that. Apart from the dire, and frankly diabolical, introduction, you get nothing but the raw footage of a number of European performances stitched together in a feeble attempt to produce a coherent whole. So while you get a fair smattering of The Doors' hits such as: 'Light My Fire', 'Hello I Love You' and 'When the Music's Over', the cut and paste job has resulted in some of the patchiest visuals and sounds that you are likely to find on DVD. There's no attempt to do justice to the band, and in this case, the 'rare' footage is really 'crap' footage. Even the raw power and intensity of Morrisons' voice cannot save this laughable sham of a DVD.

FINAL VERDICT
Picture ☆ Sound ☆
Entertainment ☆☆ Extras ☆ Value ☆
OVERALL ☆

FARSCAPE (BOX SET 1)

Price: £24.99
Supplied by: Kult TV
Type of disc: Single layer, single-sided
No of chapters: 16 (8 per disc)
Film format(s)/length: 4:3 regular / 250 mins
Audio format: Dolby Digital 5.1
Directors: Andrew Prowse, Pino Amenta and Rowan Woods
Starring: Ben Browder, Claudia Black, Virginia Hey
Year made: 1999
Extras: 'Making of' documentary; original Jim Henson Company trailer; on-set interviews with Ben Browder and Claudia Black; scene access; link to official *Farscape* web site.

Stop me if you've heard this before. A hotshot, all-American astronaut and scientist test pilots his new super-fast space craft (called *Farscape*), only for it to send him hurtling into a wormhole. Emerging into unknown space far from Earth, he finds himself caught between the sinister black clad Peacekeepers and a rag-tag group of fugitives on the run. Captured by the aliens, he must comprehend the situation he's in, attempt to trust his argumentative new comrades and return home in one piece. As science fiction goes, *Farscape* gets off to a sluggish start. The foundations of the show are far too familiar from other shows, such as *Buck Rogers* and *Blake's 7*, with non-too-subtle echoes of *Babylon 5*'s Psi-Cops in the Peacekeepers and *Star Trek*'s Worf in the proud, aggressive D'Argo. Strange, considering that science fiction gives writers more free rein for their imaginations than any other genre. The other 3 episodes also involve a lot of familiar elements – time travel, space pirates, English-speaking aliens with big foreheads – but *Farscape* does soon start to develop its own style, even if the stories have all been seen before. This Anglo-American and Australian venture is the first sci-fi series that really makes an effort with DVD. The strikingly-designed box set contains the uncut episodes 'Premiere', 'Throne for a Loss', 'I, ET' and 'Back and Back and Back to the Future' in better-than-TV audio, and also features exclusive interviews with the cast and crew. DVD-ROM is not forgotten, with the second disc taking you straight to www.farscape.com and its choice of desktop images. Hopefully, other companies releasing TV shows onto DVD will follow Kult TV's example and also make effective use of the format. *Farscape* sports an intriguing cast of characters and good use is made of CGI effects and puppets, courtesy of the Jim Henson Company. In fact *Farscape* has the potential to be very good indeed if it can build on both this excellent R2 box set and the episodes within.

FINAL VERDICT
Picture ☆☆☆☆ Sound ☆☆☆
Entertainment ☆☆☆ Extras ☆☆☆☆ Value ☆☆☆
OVERALL ☆☆☆☆

FRIENDS (SEASON 1 BOX SET)

Price: £69.99
Supplied by: DVD Plus
Type of disc: Single layer, double-sided
No of chapters: 8

Film format(s)/length: 4:3 regular / 528 mins
Audio format: Dolby Stereo
Director: Various
Starring: Jennifer Aniston, Courteney Cox, Lisa Kudrow
Year made: 1994-5
Extras: Episode access; music video: The Rembrandts' 'I'll Be There for You'; internet links; subtitles in 8 languages; subtitles for the hearing impaired in English.

Six years ago, an American sitcom started about the lives and loves of a group of 6 good-looking young New Yorkers; they're still going strong now, and in fact have been signed up to continue as far ahead as 2002. They are, of course, the Friends, and looking at these episodes from their very first series, the thought that springs to mind is, "Don't they look young?" Yes, you can now see the cast of *Friends* in the days before marriages, children, diets, drugs, liver transplants and all the usual might-not-be-entirely-true tabloid hoo-hah attached to celebrities. These early episodes show that, despite some of the cast barely looking out of their teens, the show's creators had done a good job setting things up. Although they've evolved over the last 6 years, the characters are all immediately identifiable, and more to the point, funny. Good episodes from this first season include 'The One with the Butt', where Joey gets an acting job as Al Pacino's 'butt double', and 'The One with the Boobies', where the gang inadvertently get to see each other naked. There's even a cliffhanger ending as Rachel discovers Ross loves her and realises she feels the same way, only to find him returning from abroad with another woman… Like the other *Friends* DVDs available, the episodes here are transfers of the American NTSC masters, so garish colours (or maybe that should be 'colors') and an overall fuzzy look are par for the course. As for flashy surround sound or widescreen – come on! It's a sitcom! Although you get 8 episodes per disc, the price has been bumped up accordingly, so if you're buying them individually rather than as a boxset you're still paying more than you would to get them on VHS. But it's not much more, and while the picture and sound are never going to be brilliant, they're better than video and there's no more winding through tapes. The boxset is definitely a better deal – it works out cheaper than buying them all on tape! If you want the shows to keep, you might as well get them on the best format possible.

FINAL VERDICT

Picture ☆☆ Sound ☆☆
Entertainment ☆☆☆☆☆ Extras ☆☆ Value ☆☆☆
OVERALL ☆☆☆☆

GORMENGHAST

Price: £29.99
Supplied by: BBC
Type of disc: 2x dual layer, single-sided
No of chapters: 4 episodes, 6 chapters per episode
Film format(s)/length: 1.77:1 anamorphic / 270 mins
Audio format: Dolby Surround
Director: Andy Wilson
Starring: Jonathan Rhys Meyers, Christopher Lee, Neve McIntosh
Year made: 1999
Extras: Scene access; 30-minute 'Making of' and 'Enhanced Making of' featurette with cast and crew interviews; set and costume design notes; 'The deaths in *Gormenghast*'; character/cast information; subtitles in English.

Breaking away from the typical catalogue of literary costume dramas and docusoaps, the BBC boldly ventured into uncharted territory by assembling some of Britain's finest acting talent for the epic fantasy *Gormenghast* – a screen adaptation of Mervyn Peake's classic trilogy. Within the decaying castle of Gormenghast, the birth of the 77th Earl of Groan – and heir to the throne – is a joyful occasion. However, the celebrations and tradition of this great realm are soon muted as a virus within the kingdom slowly threatens its very foundations. Steerpike (Rhys Meyers), a kitchen-boy from the gutter, has ambitions beyond his current stature, and sets out to terrorise the ancient dynasty of Groan – with a particular penchant for murder and skulduggery. As the Machiavellian upstart Steerpike charms his way through the ranks of the kingdom, the continuing array of acting talent throughout the episodes is truly astounding. Appearances from Stephen Fry, Warren Mitchell, Ian Richardson and the great Christopher Lee add a wonderful blend of acting styles from the leading and supporting talent. But it's the outstanding performances from Rhys Meyers and John Sessions that stand out the most. The Beeb's previous DVD release, *Walking with Dinosaurs*, was a magnificent step in the area of digital picture transfer, and *Gormenghast* is destined to impress consumers with its sharp images, crisp motion and splendid array of colours. Superior to its VHS counterpart in terms of picture and audio, the Dolby Surround soundtrack is the only disappointing aspect of the DVD. As one would hope from such an elaborate tale of fantasy and drama, the inclusion of the 'Making of' featurette can be found on the second disc – along with the fourth episode. Cast and crew interviews are foremost, but production secrets and special effects information are also contained within the 30-minute feature. In addition, original set and costume design/sketches can also be found within the bonus material, along with character/cast information and the more macabre extra of *Gormenghast*'s deaths – who, how and why? *Gormenghast* has taken years to come to fruition, but the excellent screen adaptation by director Andy Wilson proved enough to convince the Peake family that this inspired story should become a television reality. A wonderfully enjoyable story that, although tending to flail towards the end, is done some justice on the digital format.

FINAL VERDICT

Picture ☆☆☆☆☆ Sound ☆☆☆

Entertainment ☆☆☆☆

Extras ☆☆☆☆Value ☆☆☆☆☆

OVERALL ☆☆☆☆

INSPECTOR MORSE: THE DEAD OF JERICHO

Price: £19.99

Supplied by: Carlton Home Entertainment

Type of disc: Single layer, double-sided

No of chapters: 9 'The Dead of Jericho'/8 *The Mystery of Morse*

Film format(s)/length: 4:3 / 105 mins

Director: Ted Clisby

Starring: John Thaw, Kevin Whately, Gemma Jones

Year made: 1988

Extras: Interactive menus; scene access; behind-the-scenes footage; cast interviews; biographies.

The first episode in series one, in which Morse finds romance (Gemma Jones) only to find her hanging from a beam in suspicious circumstances. Nine chapters for the mystery and an extra 8 for *The Mystery of Morse*, a behind-the-scenes look including: interviews, biographies, the Jaguar and a tour of Morse's Oxford. You get more on the VHS version.

FINAL VERDICT

Picture ☆☆ Sound ☆☆☆

Entertainment ☆☆ Extras ☆☆☆ Value ☆☆

OVERALL ☆☆

JEFF BUCKLEY: LIVE IN CHICAGO

Price: £19.99

Supplied by: SMV Enterprises

Type of disc: Single layer, single-sided

No of chapters: 13

Film format(s)/length: 4:3 regular / 98 mins

Audio format: Dolby Digital 5.1

Director: Gary Fisher

Starring: Jeff Buckley, Michael Tighe, Mick Grondahl,

Matt Johnson

Year made: 1995

Extras: Song access; previously unreleased electronic press kit; 'So Real' and 'Last Goodbye' accoustic versions; Dolby Digital 5.1, PCM Stereo or Dolby Surround options; album discography.

When Jeff Buckley accidentally drowned in Memphis on 27 May 1997, he deprived the world of a major musical talent. He was blessed with rock god looks, the ability to play just about any instrument going and possessed a bruised, soulful voice that effortlessly ascended to the heavens, sounding like a corrupted angel. Nowhere is this more evident than with 'Mojo Pin', his sublime reading of Leonard Cohen's 'Hallelujah' and arguably his best fully realised composition, 'Last Goodbye'. Jeff's on top form in Chicago. Relaxed, charming, chatty and even making (ironically) jokey references to Hendrix and Morrison, he and his band run through 13 songs. Picture quality is almost faultless and the audio is truly brilliant. The exclusive 17 minute electronic press kit is more like a featurette and contains revealing interviews with the man himself. It's a vital purchase for Buckley's growing legion of fans and the closest we'll ever get to seeing him perform live again.

FINAL VERDICT

Picture ☆☆☆☆ Sound ☆☆☆☆☆

Entertainment ☆☆☆☆

Extras ☆☆☆ Value ☆☆☆☆

OVERALL ☆☆☆☆

JERRY SPRINGER: TOO HOT FOR TV!

Price: £15.99

Supplied by: DVD World (01705 796662)

Type of disc: Single layer, single-sided

No of chapters: 6 (!)

Film format(s)/length: 4:3 regular / 53 mins

Audio format: Dolby Surround

Director: Unknown

Starring: Jerry Springer, the US public

Year made: 1997

Extras: 12 minutes of bonus extra footage, but that forms part of the 53 minute running time.

The BBFC rating on the box of *Jerry Springer: Too Hot for TV* states that "It may have some strong scenes of sex or violence or bad language." Well let's remove the ambiguity – it's got them all in a sparse DVD that brings the circus that is *The Jerry Springer Show* to the most exciting video format of the Nineties. For starters, this is an uncensored selection, so all the bleeps are replaced by the original expletives, which are nowhere near as entertaining. Then there's no build up – you enter the action just as the fight is starting or as latest blonde is removing her underwear. This offers approximately 5 minutes worth of entertainment before you realise that's pretty much your lot. At 53 minutes though, there should be plenty of room on the disc to get the picture and sound up to speed, right?. Bad luck. It's got possibly the ropiest direct-from-videotape looking transfer yet, and little to test out the speakers. Add to that a lack of extras and the fact that the VHS version is hitting bargain bins across the country, and there is no incentive in the world to own this disc. If you must have your fix of Springer, just turn on your television.

FINAL VERDICT

Picture ☆ Sound ☆☆

Entertainment ☆ Extras ☆ Value ☆

OVERALL ☆

THE LARRY SANDERS SHOW

Price: £19.99

Supplied by: Columbia TriStar Home Video

Type of disc: Dual layer, single-sided

No of chapters: 7 episodes, 5 chapters per episode

Film format(s)/length: 4:3 regular / 167 mins

Audio format: Stereo

Directors: Various

Starring: Garry Shandling, Jeffrey Tambor, Rip Torn

Year made: 1992-98

Extras: Scene access; theatrical trailer: *What Planet Are You From?*

Bathed in satire, irony and often downright stupidity, *The Larry Sanders Show* is the point at which mainstream and cult meet, shake hands, exchange a few jokes, and go their separate ways. Running from 1992 to 1998 on America's HBO, and sporadically on BBC2 whenever the BBC felt like showing it, the show is a behind- (and occasionally in front of) the-scenes look at the sweat, tears and egos that go into producing a major nightly US talk show. Larry (Shandling) is the self-obsessed, paranoid host, Hank Kingsley (Tambor) is his oafish, bitter sidekick and Artie (Torn) is the fatherly-yet-ruthless producer who has to keep his spoilt child of a star happy, usually at the expense of his stooge and the show's overworked, resentful production staff. Where *Larry Sanders* differs from other sitcoms, apart from having big Hollywood names begging to appear as themselves and be quite ruthlessly sent up, is in its attitude. Larry is spineless, full of self-loathing and cruelly manipulative – and he's one of the more well-adjusted characters. The blissful lack of a laugh track, not being 'filmed before a live studio audience' (except for when Larry's on-air), and the consciously liberal HBO all allow

for sharper, edgier, more adult-orientated humour than you'd find anywhere else. All of this works towards one of the most consistent, original, self-aware and downright hilarious comedies to come out of America in the last decade. Don't believe it? Well, Columbia TriStar has 7 pieces of evidence to prove the point. Seven selected episodes make up the box cover's quota of 'the best episodes', though to be honest that could be said about any episode in the entire 6 seasons of the show's life. The fact that the disc doesn't reach the limits that DVD is renowned for is a little disappointing; plain stereo and near-VHS picture quality are what you're paying your money for. 'Extras' are just one movie trailer (for Shandling's flop *What Planet Are You From?*), and the menu proves a little troublesome to navigate. But let's face it, this isn't a multi-million dollar studio motion picture, it's the cream of television comedy from the last decade, and there's enough of it to keep you happy until the next decade is out.

FINAL VERDICT

Picture ☆☆ Sound ☆☆

Entertainment ☆☆☆☆☆ Extras ☆ Value ☆☆☆

OVERALL ☆☆☆

LED ZEPPELIN: THE SONG REMAINS THE SAME

Price: £15.99

Supplied by: Warner Home Video

Type of disc: Dual layer, single-sided

No of chapters: 26

Film format(s)/length: 1.85:1 anamorphic / 132 mins

Audio format: Dolby Digital

Directors: Peter Clifton and Joe Massot

Starring: Jimmy Page, Robert Plant et al

Year made: 1976

Extras: Scene access

The embodiment of every rock cliché, Led Zeppelin are still kind of hip. Dance acts sample their thunderous back beats, and Noel Gallagher sports Jimmy Page T-shirts. So it's timely that 'The Song Remains the Same', a movie of their 1973 concert at Madison Square Garden, has made it to DVD. As a widescreen DVD transfer of the movie, the disc's a right rocker, with Zeppelin's 200 horsepower brand of heavy blues and folk sounding as electrifying as it did 30 years ago. Page and Robert Plant may be old duffers now, but back then these guys could raise the roof. Sadly, though, the absence of any DVD extras strikes a bum note – there are no band interviews, no discography, no extra pics, nowt. You can't even mess around with the camera angles, though at least it's easier on DVD to avoid 'Bonzo' Bonham's interminable drum solo. There are other bits you'll want to fast-forward through as well, such as the notorious (and rather self indulgent) fantasy sequences involving each band member. Sadly these don't involve groupies and fish (if you don't know what we're talking about, read *Hammer of the Gods*). Guitarist Jimmy Page's section is suitably occult, while Plant makes a right knob of himself as King Arthur, poncing around the countryside shaking his locks and rescuing some Seventies 'Guinevere' from a bunch of roadies dressed in chain mail. It's all classic Spinal Tap stuff. The rest of the disc is a blast, but the lack of DVD extras remains a big let-down.

FINAL VERDICT

Picture ☆☆☆☆ Sound ☆☆☆☆
Entertainment ☆☆☆☆ Extras ☆ Value ☆☆☆
OVERALL ☆☆☆

MADONNA
THE VIDEO COLLECTION 93:99

Price: £19.99
Supplied by: DVD Premier Direct
(www.dvdpremier.co.uk)
Distributor: Warner Music Vision
Type of disc: Single layer, single-sided
No of chapters: 14
Film format(s)/length: 4:3 regular / 67 mins
Audio format: Linear PCM Stereo
Director: Various
Starring: Madonna
Year made: 1999
Extras: Song access.

Madonna addressed Cambridge University last December with a lecture entitled 'Image and Reality'. Appropriate when you think about it – there's no megastar alive who can appreciate those issues better than her. The first to harness music promos as a vehicle for fame and a platform for controversy, Madonna was so influential during the Eighties that Music TeleVision could have been more accurately called Madonna TeleVision. This disc documents the best music of Madonna's career – always provocative but now credible as well thanks to her 1998 collaboration with producer William Orbit. Each one of the 14 tracks is like a mini movie, and there's no mistaking who's the star. All chronologically ordered, the videos collected on the disc demonstrate Madonna's gift for constant reinvention: In 'Secret' she's a Harlem bar room floosie, 'Take a Bow' is her virtual screen test for Evita while 'Bedtime Story' is a trippy journey through her nihilistic mind. The world's most famous woman turns dominatrix to answer her critics in 'Human Nature' before evolving into the pure and natural look

she's adopted in the 'Ray of Light' era. The DVD offers nothing that the VHS doesn't give except marginally improved sound and vision, and that's why the disc gets such a low rating. This collection sees the material girl improving as an artist, the music darker in tone and heavier in beat than anything produced before. Here's looking forward to her new images in the 21st century. Hopefully, music DVDs will have reached their full potential by then.

FINAL VERDICT

Picture ☆☆☆ Sound ☆☆☆☆
Entertainment ☆☆☆ Extras ☆ Value ☆☆
OVERALL ☆☆☆

MEN BEHAVING BADLY

Price: £19.99
Supplied by: Pearson
Type of disc: Single layer, single-sided
No of chapters: 5 per episode
Film format(s)/length: 4:3 regular / 203 mins
Audio format: Stereo
Director: Martin Dennis
Starring: Martin Clunes, Neil Morrissey,
Caroline Quentin
Year made: 1995
Extras: Scene access; 4 pub quiz games with series outtakes.

As you must know by now, *Men Behaving Badly* is one of the best sitcoms to come from the BBC in years, and compared to the drivel you find today it's a work of genius! The extras may not be overflowing on this DVD, but you do get an entire series on one disc, one of the better ones to boot (all the other episodes from the various series are also available on DVD). This series focuses around the relationship between Dorothy and Gary and kicks off with 'Babies', in which Dorothy decides she wants a child. Needless to say Gary takes this far from seriously and Dorothy decides against the whole idea after finding some fizzy fish in Gary's briefcase. Put off by his immaturity Dorothy goes off after another man and in the next episode, 'Infidelity', she leaves Gary! All this time, Tony is practically hunting Deborah (it's the British version of Ross and Rachel) and you know that eventually something's got to happen. Not for now though, because in the next episode – 'Pornography' – Tony gets a new girl and has to face the age-old question of which to keep – the girl or his porn mags! Obviously the mags win, because in the next episode Tony has 3 completely new girlfriends – how does he do it? Eventually, Dorothy and Gary get back together again and everything's back to normal for 'Drunk' in which

Gary misses a romantic dinner. The reason? Free beer at the pub, of course! All of this is just leading up to the climactic episode, when Dorothy hops into bed with Tony while Gary's away for the weekend! If you're a fan of the series then you'll already know what you're getting, and this disc does have some classic moments, like the 'Tony gets glasses' episode. There is no anamorphic widescreen or DTS sound but then you wouldn't expect this from a TV series. The pub quiz feature is moderately amusing for the amount of time it takes to view all of the outtakes, but it's not something you'll come back to over and over again. Unless, of course, you like watching the cast making arses of themselves and lots of rude hand gestures; but then again, if you buy this disc isn't that what you're getting anyway?

FINAL VERDICT

Picture ☆☆ Sound ☆☆

Entertainment ☆☆☆ Extras ☆☆ Value ☆☆☆☆

OVERALL ☆☆☆

OASIS: THERE AND THEN

Price: £19.99
Supplied by: Sony Music Entertainment
Type of disc: Single layer, single–sided
No of chapters: 18
Film format(s)/length: 4:3 regular/ 85 mins
Audio format: Stereo
Directors: Mark Szaszy and Dick Carruthers
Starring: Oasis
Year made: 1996
Extras: Scene access (song selection).

Back in 1995, Oasis played a string of sell-out concerts in Manchester and London. *There and Then*, originally released on VHS a couple of years back, is a cut and paste compilation of all the best bits from these legendary gigs. It's basically 85 minutes of Oasis at their arrogant and electrifying best. The sound quality is excellent (but let down by a stereo only transfer) while the picture is above average. Unfortunately, there are no extras other than the standard song selection access and interactive menu. So while Oasis fans will lap it up, *There and Then* is nothing more than a badly repackaged version of an existing video title. Such a shame when DVD is capable of so much more. And we thought Liam and co were supposed to be up on new technology. Pah!

FINAL VERDICT

Picture ☆☆☆ Sound ☆☆☆

Entertainment ☆☆☆☆ Extras ☆ Value ☆

OVERALL ☆☆

OVER 250 PREMIERSHIP GOALS

Price: £17.99
Supplied by: Quantum Group Ltd (01480 450006)
Type of disc: Single layer, single–sided
No of chapters: 20
Film format(s)/length: 4:3 regular/ 120 mins
Audio format: Stereo
Year made: 1999
Extras: Scene access; a screen pointing you to a place that sells pictures.

Over 250 goals on one DVD, and not one for Birmingham City? Hmmm, but then what you are getting here is a collection of goals from the Premiership spanning 1992-1997. First impressions are poor, with the disc packaging looking like it was produced on a cheap-got-it-free-with-my-computer printer. However, slap the disc into the printer and it's quickly clear it's going to do exactly what it says on the box and not a jot more. You get goal after goal, each separated by a title card stating the scorer, the teams and the date. Hey, you even get commentary with some of them. As for the action, it's presented pretty much as you'd expect – broadcast television standard image (ie not very good) and a bog standard sound channel that varies in quality depending on the clip. But to be fair, this isn't a big surprise, and as the disc's aim is to give you over 250 goals (ranging from the spectacular to, er, penalty kicks) you can quite honestly say that it delivers on its promise with the minimum of frills. They even try and sell you some pictures as the DVD's extra features. They key problem here though is there's very little reason why this should be chosen above the umpteen VHS footy tapes on the shelves, which are both cheaper and often more specific to your team than this DVD. So whilst it's nice to have this title out there broadening the marketplace, and it's handy to have the clips broken up into 20 chapters, I couldn't honestly say that I'd go out and buy it myself. Ho hum

FINAL VERDICT

Picture ☆☆ Sound ☆

Entertainment ☆☆☆ Extras ☆☆ Value ☆☆

OVERALL ☆☆

A PERSONAL JOURNEY WITH MARTIN SCORSESE THROUGH AMERICAN MOVIES

Price: £19.99
Supplied by: BFI Video
Type of disc: Dual layer, single–sided
No of chapters: 11
Film format(s)/length: Various / 224 mins
Audio format: Dolby Digital
Directors: Martin Scorsese and Henry Wilson

Starring: Martin Scorsese, Clint Eastwood, Gregory Peck
Year made: 1995
Extras: Chapter access.

As a small child, Martin Scorsese satisfied his love of film at the New York Public Library, poring over the pages of his favourite book, *A Pictorial History of the Movies*. In the opening chapter of this documentary, the director, best known for the gangster movies *Goodfellas* and *Casino*, confesses to a crime of his own – tearing out pages to take home with him. The opening confessional sets a tone for this outstanding documentary – this is not just a well-researched and exhaustive documentary on the history of cinema, it is much more of a personal view of that history, as told by one of America's most accomplished directors. In the chapter on 'the Gangster Film' you learn that *Goodfellas* was influenced by films like the original *Scarface* and *The Roaring Twenties*; in 'Musicals' Scorsese reveals that the Doris Day vehicle *My Dream Is Yours* inspired his *New York, New York*. Scorsese talks you through 11 chapters of cinema history from D W Griffith's *Birth of a Nation* up to Clint Eastwood's *Unforgiven*, to show the development of storytelling, filmmaking technology, and the Hollywood studio system with the aid of interviews with the likes of Eastwood and Gregory Peck. There's plenty of archive footage here too; of note is a verbose Frank Capra talking about the role of the director, and a terse John Ford talking about his love of Westerns. This documentary has already been screened on Channel 4, and the DVD contains no more material than the VHS version. So why should you get this on DVD? For the outstanding collection of old movie clips. Taken from fresh transfers, all the colours and details spring out at you (a reminder to our generation that once upon a time they were in pristine condition), and not just dodgy video transfers from old prints. Scorsese's choice of films is eclectic, but by the end of the documentary you'll have a new list of movies you'll want to see in full. And you'll also want to get hold of Scorsese's own movies to watch them through fresh eyes.

FINAL VERDICT

Picture ☆☆☆☆ Sound ☆☆☆
Entertainment ☆☆☆☆☆ Extras ☆ Value ☆☆☆☆
OVERALL ☆☆☆☆

THE PLANETS

Price: £34.99
Supplied by: BBC Worldwide
Type of disc: 2 x dual layer, single-sided

No of chapters: 8 episodes
Film format(s)/length: 16:9 widescreen / 390 mins
Audio format: Dolby Surround
Director: David McNab
Year made: 1999
Extras: Scene access; subtitles in 7 languages; subtitles for the hearing impaired in English.

It might not have had all the media hoopla of *Walking with Dinosaurs*, but the BBC's science series *The Planets* was arguably more spectacular, and certainly included a lot more interesting scientific fact. That's not to say it's only for beardy boffins (though you certainly get to see quite a few of them during the series) as it continues the BBC's tradition of making science accessible without ever dumbing it down. Although it's quite expensive, you get a lot for your money – well over 6 hours of high-quality, widescreen-enhanced documentary spread over two discs. There's plenty of spectacular footage taken from telescopes, space missions and probes, and to give viewers a look at the big picture there's also plenty of spectacular CGI showing the various worlds of our solar system. *The Planets* certainly doesn't lack scope – starting from before the solar system was born and going through to its eventual and inevitable end, covering about 10 billion years in the process. Dinosaurs? Ha! Just a snap of the fingers in cosmic terms. The picture quality is excellent throughout, and though the sound is only Dolby Surround rather than 5.1, it doesn't skimp on sofa-shaking rocket launches or the occasional exploding planet. Even the menu interface is good, with a *Voyager* probe whipping past Mars and depositing the options in its wake. The only annoyance is the lack of timer or chapter information during play, which makes it hard to find a specific section. Considering *The Planets* is likely to be used by schools, it's a strange oversight. Nobody does this kind of documentary better than the BBC and *The Planets* is a fantastic package, designed to amaze even the most Earthbound of viewers.

FINAL VERDICT

Picture ☆☆☆☆☆ Sound ☆☆☆
Entertainment ☆☆☆☆☆ Extras ☆ Value ☆☆☆☆
OVERALL ☆☆☆☆

PLAYBOY: THE BEST OF PAMELA ANDERSON

Price: £15.99
Supplied by: Medusa Pictures
Type of disc: Single layer, single-sided
No of chapters: 24
Film format(s)/length: 4:3 regular / 54 mins

Audio format: Stereo
Director: Various
Starring: Pamela Anderson Lee
Year made: 1995
Extras: Not a chance!

DVD's never wear out, right? Therefore that means you can watch them again and again, or more specifically, certain bits over and over, right? So doesn't that make it…quite good for, ahem, films of a more adult nature. Damn straight! Hugh Hefner's global soft porn business knows no bounds it would seem, and it was only a matter of time before the wrinkled perennial pyjama poser saw the potential of his special brand of entertainment on perfect quality DVD. Well they're here, and what a disappointment this initial batch of Playboy DVDs are. Kicking off with *The Best of Pamela Anderson*, you'll immediately notice that the lacklustre menu screen offers no special features whatsoever. Buena Vista DVDs are positively brimming with goodies in comparison. Fans expecting to see a wealth of supporting 'Pamaterial' will be sorely disappointed and the chance to include some high resolution pictures of her 5 *Playboy* centre spreads is missed with almost embarrassing incompetence. You've also got to be the most dedicated 5 knuckle shufflist to get any kind of gratification from this kind of top shelf smut. Yes, Pammy is naked for the majority of the miserly 54 minutes, but it's so tame and untitilating that you're more likely to 'get wood' watching *Coronation Street*. Couple these sad pantomime performances with the frankly worthless interview snippets and you've got a DVD that neither delivers on the promise of the box, nor provides an insight into the career and inner thoughts of the *Baywatch* star. To make matters worse, the picture quality is barely above VHS quality, with frequent areas of unnecessary fuzziness, and the lack of anything extra for DVD betrays the fact that it has simply been ported over as a quick money spinner. Even the all-important freeze-frame suffers badly from blurring. Treat this cynical piece of tat with the respect it deserves, and give it a wide berth. Also in the Playboy range is the *Best of Anna Nicole Smith*, *Kathy Lloyd* and *Voluptuous Vixens*, a trio of similar quality DVDs which offer high production values, zero special features and the same degree of video transfer which spoils their appearance on DVD. The latter offers an insight by veteran film maker and bustmeister Russ Meyer, but this proves to be simple clips where Russ reads out the next cheesy tag line from an obvious autocue while surrounded by giggling girls with breasts like barrage balloons. Gorgeous sex objects or sad showbiz freaks? You decide. Someone obviously thought it would be a great idea to actually talk to the featured models in-between spontaneous strips – a big mistake, because from the first syllable you wish they would just shut up. Kathy Lloyd for example tells us, "I love high heeled shoes, they are really sexy." Who cares? Do you really think anyone is remotely interested in what you have to say Kathy? It is frankly hard to see why Playboy continues to be so successful when the material on offer here is so lame. If you are the sort of person who titters when the word vagina is mentioned then these DVDs are a must, but for the more balanced majority, they are a major waste of money and talent.

FINAL VERDICT

Picture ☆☆☆ Sound ☆☆
Entertainment ☆ Extras ☆ Value ☆
OVERALL ☆

THE PRISONER BOX SET

Price: £59.99
Supplied by: Carlton
Type of disc: 5x dual layer, single-sided
No of chapters: 8 per episode
Film format(s)/length: 4:3 regular / 950 mins
Audio format: Stereo
Directors: Various
Starring: Patrick McGoohan
Year made: 1967
Extras: Scene access; series trivia; alternate version of 'The Chimes of Big Ben'; *The Prisoner Companion* documentary; biography of Number 6; biography of The Butler; biography of The Supervisor; biographies of each of the actors playing Number 2; map of The Village; original *Prisoner* artwork; production stills; episode trailers; promotional series trailers; subtitles in English.

Cult television shows get made because their creator has gained a certain amount of influence from a previous success, and finally gets the chance to make his dream project. They always follow the same pattern – critics of the time dismiss the series as self-indulgent or nonsensical claptrap, the show builds up a small but fanatical following before being cancelled, then years later it's regarded as a classic. *Star Trek* and *Twin Peaks* exemplify the American side of things, while keeping the British end up is *The Prisoner*. Patrick McGoohan's dream project had a simple enough premise – a former secret agent is imprisoned by forces unknown and tries to escape – but turned out to be one of the most bizarre and allegorical shows ever made. The 5 DVDs in the set include all 17 episodes of *The Prisoner*, along with an alternate version of 'The Chimes of Big Ben' with different credits and some new scenes, and a documentary about the series. Also thrown in is an assortment of production notes, trivia and stills. The picture has been given a digital spring clean for the DVD release. Although it's not as good as some of the recent restorations of old shows we've seen (in particular, the Region 1 versions of the original *Star Trek*), it's a definite step up on the grainy, ancient VHS releases. The sound isn't especially amazing, being in basic stereo only, but does the job well enough to let you bop along to the theme music. Each of the discs in the set gets some extras, though they're a bit of a mixed bag. The last disc gets the most, but since it's only got one episode on it you should hope so! *The Prisoner Companion* is an American-made documentary (complete with 'have a nice day!'-style voiceover) that does delve into some of the unanswered questions about the series, though with rather too much emphasis on simply showing clips from the episodes. It's a pity that Carlton didn't take the opportunity to interview McGoohan himself. Somebody could have grilled him mercilessly and got him to tell the world what *The Prisoner* meant, once and for all!

FINAL VERDICT

Picture: ☆☆☆ Sound: ☆☆ Entertainment: ☆☆☆☆

Extras: ☆☆☆ Value: ☆☆☆☆

OVERALL ☆☆☆☆

QUEER AS FOLK

Price: £24.99
Supplied by: VCI
Type of disc: 2 x dual layer, single-sided
No of chapters: 16 (each disc)
Film format(s)/length: 1.85:1 widescreen / both discs 130 mins
Audio format: Dolby Surround
Directors: Charles McDougall and Sarah Harding
Starring: Aidan Gillen, Craig Kelly, Charlie Hunnam
Year made: 1999
Extras: Scene access; photo library; behind-the-scenes featurette (disc 1); cast and crew interviews (disc 2).

Both the discs in this critically acclaimed series from VCI are divided into chapters, so you can jump instantly to the start of your favourite episode, or simply skip ahead two or 3 scenes during a particular episode. One of the major talking points over the retailing of DVDs is the price tag. Although many people/consumers are reluctantly accepting the standardised £19.99 pricing, some titles (such as 20th Century's *Titanic*) have been slapped with a higher pricing. However, in this case you're actually getting a two-disc set for only £5 more than VCI's standard releases. Both discs are dual layered, bringing the entire 4 hours and 20 minutes of the series to your living room without unnecessary compromises in terms of quality. In case you missed the Channel 4 production: it's an 8 part mini-series based around Manchester's Canal Street, following the lives of gay men and the people they encounter. It is an amusing tale with some truly comical moments intertwined with tempered tragedy. Although the occasional graphic moment means that it's not a disc suitable for budding Mary Whitehouse's who worship the nuclear family structure, it is, however, a very funny and honest portrayal of contemporary love. The DVD itself is presented in widescreen with the standard two channel Dolby Surround soundtrack. The audio may sound quite limited from a purely technical standpoint, but it carries the mixture of music and sound effects convincingly. The picture itself is strong throughout, with no blindingly obvious blemishes to report. Normally with a DVD of this nature you wouldn't expect to see many, if in fact any, extras included, however VCI have been thoughtful enough to incorporate such extras as a photo gallery – which will briefly pass the time – and some decent, if not altogether brief, behind-the-scenes information. Fans of the series will be well served by this latest quality release from VCI, and it certainly bodes well for many other TV titles held under the same roof. *Queer As Folk* is a fine example of how to break into the mini-series DVD market, so now you too can enjoy watching this excellent gritty drama and benefit from the marvels of DVD quality visual and sounds.

FINAL VERDICT

Picture ☆☆☆☆ Sound ☆☆☆

Entertainment ☆☆☆☆ Extras ☆☆ Value ☆☆☆☆

OVERALL ☆☆☆☆

ROBBIE WILLIAMS ANGELS

Price: £12.99
Supplied by: EMI
Type of disc: Single layer, single-sided
No of chapters: 5 songs
Film format(s)/length: 4:3 regular / 60 mins
Audio format: Stereo
Director: N/A
Starring: Robbie Williams
Year made: 1999
Extras: Song access; poetry recitals of 'Hello Sir, Thank You for Letting Me Be' and 'Naked at an Awards Ceremony'; in-depth interview with Robbie Williams; 'Find the Lady' card game.

If the results of the Music of the Millennium fiasco were anything to go by, and remember, it's all a matter of opinion, then this young man is certainly a musical force to be reckoned with. Young, explosive and rarely out of the headlines, Robbie Williams has collected all of his energy and poured it onto a new format in the guise of this 'Angels' DVD. Despite only containing 5 of his previously released music videos, none of which are all that recent, this disc amounts to much more than just another artist jumping on the DVD bandwagon. As well as some classic Robbie videos, the disc also includes footage of Robbie bumming around in Jamaica trying to write a song, as well as first time 'on camera' recitals of some of his poetry. In addition to this there's a 'not as easy as you would like' card game, which if you win, will reward you with access to a secret programme. Though strictly for fans only, no Robbie follower is going to be disappointed by this effort. If only other artists would follow his example then music on DVD would be a far grander thing.

FINAL VERDICT

Picture ☆☆☆☆ Sound ☆☆☆☆

Entertainment ☆☆☆☆

Extras ☆☆☆☆ Value ☆☆☆☆☆

OVERALL ☆☆☆☆

THE ROCK: THE PEOPLE'S CHAMP

Price: £19.99
Supplied by: Silver Vision
Type of disc: Dual layer, single-sided
No of chapters: 6
Film format(s)/length: 4:3 regular/43 mins
Audio format: Dolby Digital 5.0
Director: n/a
Starring: The Rock, Mankind
Year made: 1999
Extras: Scene access; interviews and promos; slideshow of still photos.

You know things are getting desperate when they start converting wrestling videos to DVD. Fair enough, it's the format of the future and pretty soon everything will be on DVD, but for now it hardly seems worth it. So then, The Rock. What you've got here is essentially a direct transfer of the video release as well as a few 'extended' features – namely, a slideshow offering several action shots of the big man himself in all his sweaty, testosterone-driven glory and full versions of the interviews and in-ring promos shown as clips during the main feature. It's all quite interesting in an 'if you like this sort of thing' way, but there's really nothing here that hasn't already been aired on TV months ago. As DVDs go, this serves up the admittedly limited material on offer rather nicely. Of course, the number of people who'll buy it might be questionably low...but we liked it all the same.

FINAL VERDICT

Picture ☆☆ Sound ☆☆☆

Entertainment ☆☆☆ Extras ☆☆ Value ☆☆

OVERALL ☆☆☆

THE SECOND WORLD WAR IN COLOUR

Price: £19.99
Supplied by: Carlton Video Ltd
Type of disc: Dual layer, single-sided
No of chapters: 76
Film format(s)/length: 4:3 / 165 mins
Audio format: Stereo
Director: Various
Starring: Winston Churchill, Adolf Hitler and a cast of millions
Year made: 1999
Extras: Scene access; letters and diaries selection; extra footage not broadcasted on television; the Carlton Silver Collection trailer; booklet containing an extract from The Second World War in Colour companion book; subtitles for the hearing impaired in English.

Thought you knew everything about WWII? Well, you'll have to make sure you watch The Second World War in Colour before you make that assumption as this expertly crafted DVD uses newly unearthed colour footage that makes the saga even more powerful than before. The colours are rich and drawn together with stirring orchestration and narration by John Thaw, the documentary presents an eerie, humbling and sometimes unflinching account of the war we're still recovering from. Credit is due to Carlton for recognising that the best place to showcase and preserve their finest programmes is on DVD. British broadcasters though have yet to fully explore what the format can do for them: this is almost a straight transfer from the broadcast tapes, and unfortunately it remains in stereo and 4:3 ratio. However, The Second World War in Colour is a provocative and compelling documentary on a DVD that deserves to be seen by everyone.

FINAL VERDICT

Picture ☆☆☆ Sound ☆☆

Entertainment ☆☆☆☆ Extras ☆☆☆ Value ☆☆☆☆

OVERALL ☆☆☆

SEX PISTOLS: LIVE AT THE LONGHORN

Price: £19.99
Supplied by: Castle Music Ltd
Type of disc: Single layer, single-sided
No of chapters: 11
Film format(s)/length: 4:3 regular / 44 mins

Audio format: Stereo or Dolby multichannel
Director: Eric Gardner
Starring: Johnny Rotten, Sid Vicious, Steve Jones, Paul Cook
Year made: 1978
Extras: Song access; animated, music accompanied menus; narrated history of the band; discography.

Punk rockers are like dinosaurs. They were once fierce creatures who roamed the earth destroying everything in their wake, but time has neutered them of their danger and hindsight has distorted what they were really about. And they're extinct, too. *Sex Pistols: Live at The Longhorn* captures arguably the definitive punk band in the final chapter of their short career. It was recorded by amateurs having fun with cameras (very punk) on 28 January 1978 at the Longhorn Ballroom in Dallas. By the end of the month (very possibly hours after this concert) the Sex Pistols split up forever. During this shambolic gig, the Pistols play 9 of their forever awesome anthems including 'Pretty Vacant', 'Anarchy in the UK' and 'God Save the Queen' in front of a crowd of dumbstruck long-haired Americans who hilariously fail to get it. Promo quality videos for the latter two are also added. A male voice narrates their history instead of printing the notes in a booklet. It's a good idea that works, but something to look at while he talks, such as a picture gallery, would have been a very welcome addition to the proceedings. The discography is unfortunately a simple scrolling list, not nearly as developed as it could well have been. Nevertheless, this DVD is an important document for Sex Pistols completists and far more reliable than other period films based on them, such as *The Great Rock and Roll Swindle*. *Sex Pistols: Live at The Longhorn* is worth investigating by anyone fascinated by rock 'n' roll's often mythologised past.

FINAL VERDICT

Picture ☆☆ Sound ☆☆
Entertainment ☆☆☆ Extras ☆☆☆ Value ☆☆☆
OVERALL ☆☆☆

SOUTH PARK (VOLUME 1)

Price: £19.99
Supplied by: DVD Premier Direct (01923 226492)
Type of disc: Single layer, single-sided
No of chapters: 8
Film format(s)/length: 4:3 regular / 4 x 22 mins
Audio format: Dolby Digital 2.0 Stereo
Directors: Matt Stone and Trey Parker
Starring the voices of: Matt Stone, Trey Parker, Isaac Hayes
Year made: 1998

Extras: English/French soundtracks; multilingual subtitles; 'Fireside chats' with the creators; Series 1 trailer.

What else can anyone find to say about *South Park*, the animated series that came from nowhere, took the world by storm and now, in the manner of most brightly blazing candles, looks set to burn out and become a victim of its own success? Unlike *The Simpsons*, which for the past 10 years has been consistently the funniest and most subversive comedy around, *South Park* has already run out of boundaries to push. With a movie that finally allows the kids to swear for real instead of being bleeped, where else is there to go? That doesn't mean that *South Park* has lost what made it such a hit in the first place – even after repeated viewings, it's still damned funny. *South Park: Volume 1* has 4 stories, which are: 'Cartman Gets an Anal Probe': the first-ever episode, wherein Cartman is abducted by aliens and has an 80-foot satellite dish implanted in his rectum; 'Volcano': Stan's gun-crazy Uncle Jimbo takes the boys on a hunting trip, unluckily just as the local volcano blows its top; 'Weight Gain 4000': Cartman cheats on an essay and wins an award, resolving to 'buff' (ie bulk) up for his TV appearance; and 'Big Gay Al's Big Gay Boat Ride': Stan gets a dog ('voiced' by George Clooney) which turns out to be gay. As well as the episodes, the DVDs also include creators Matt Parker and Trey Stone's 'fireside chats', mock-earnest interviews where they gaze adoringly at each other in front of a roaring log fire. Although mildly amusing, the joke soon gets very repetitive. Fortunately, the fireside chats are chaptered at the beginning of each episode, so you can skip past them to reach *South Park* itself. While it's good to get 4 episodes to a disc, instead of the meagre two offered on VHS, there aren't any extra features on offer over what you'd get on tape. The 'fireside chats' were included on video as well, so if you're a *South Park* fanatic who's already bought the tapes, the DVD doesn't give you anything you haven't already seen. Some behind-the-scenes material (the show is now created with computer graphics designed to look like paper cutouts) would have been good, but none of the *South Park* DVDs have any new extras. Not even the menus are animated!

FINAL VERDICT

Picture ☆☆☆ Sound ☆☆☆
Entertainment ☆☆☆☆ Extras ☆☆ Value ☆☆☆
OVERALL ☆☆☆

STARGATE-SG1 (VOLUME 1)

Price: £19.99
Supplied by: MGM

Type of disc: Dual layer, single-sided
No of chapters: 48
Film format(s)/length: 16:9 widescreen / 99 mins
Audio format: Dolby Digital 5.1
Directors: David Warry-Smith and Martin Wood
Starring: Richard Dean Anderson, Michael Shanks, Amanda Tapping
Year made: 1997
Extras: Scene access; episode access; subtitles in English and German; subtitles for the hearing impaired in English, German and Dutch.

This good-looking double DVD is the first volume of episodes from *Stargate SG-1*, the increasingly popular television series that carries on from where the original 1994 Roland Emmerich movie left off. The US military has gained control of a 'Stargate', a piece of technology built by aliens thousands of years earlier that allows near-instantaneous travel to hundreds of alien worlds. A number of teams have been assembled to explore these (frequently bizarre) planets and guard against attack by the malevolent Egyptian-themed aliens, the Goa'uld, who control much of the stargate network – the lead team is the imaginatively-named SG-1. Saturday afternoon TV hero Richard Dean Anderson (*MacGyver*) leads SG-1 as the sarcastic but tough Colonel Jack O'Neill, previously played by Kurt Russell. His team includes James Spader's former character Dr Daniel Jackson (Shanks), an Egyptologist whose scientific enthusiasm often causes friction with his military companions; new character Samantha Carter, brought to life by Amanda Tapping, a dedicated captain – and later major – who's smarter than the other 3 put together; and finally, another new character completes SG-1 – Christopher Judge's noble alien freedom fighter Teal'c. This first volume contains the 'Best of Season 1' – the feature-length 'Children of the Gods', an action sequel to the movie, plus a 3-part adventure made up of 'There But for the Grace of God', 'Politics and Within' and 'The Serpent's Grasp'. This epic sees our heroes trying to stop slimy bureaucrat (is there any other kind?) Ronny Cox from closing the Stargate for good just when the evil Goa'uld forces are about to devastate Earth. Current episodes find the cast and crew more comfortable in their roles when compared to these very early outings. Though production values are inevitably lower than the movie version of *Stargate,* the stories are superior in acting, drama and pathos. Audio quality is good, with the Chulak energy weapon blasts sounding particularly heavy, but the picture is mystifingly grainy. Extras are non-existent and consequently make it hard to recommend the DVD version of *Stargate SG-1* over the cheaper VHS

edition.

FINAL VERDICT
Picture ☆☆☆ Sound ☆☆☆
Entertainment ☆☆☆ Extras ☆ Value ☆☆☆
OVERALL ☆☆☆

TALKING HEADS: STOP MAKING SENSE

Price: £17.99
Supplied by: Palm Pictures
Type of disc: Dual layer, single-sided
No of chapters: 16 songs
Film format(s)/length: 16:9 widescreen enhanced / 87 mins
Audio format: Dolby Digital 5.1
Director: Jonathan Demme
Starring: David Byrne, Bernie Warrell, Alex Weir
Year made: 1984
Extras: Song selection; 3 bonus tracks: 'Cities', 'Big Business' and 'I Zimbra'; audio commentary by all 4 band members and director Jonathan Demme; storyboard-to-film comparison; original US promotional trailer; *David Byrne Interviews... David Byrne*; 'Big Suit' concept; video montage; web link; discography; bibliographies.

You might wonder why an Oscar-winning director (of *Silence of the Lambs* fame) would want to direct what is ultimately just another taping of a live show from a million selling rock band. Actually, you might not put Talking Heads in the category of a 'rock' band. Maybe, 'soft rock', defiantly not 'pop', but still completely original. One of the greatest and most inventive bands to come out of America during the late Seventies/early Eighties period, it's the innovation and artistic resourcefulness of lead singer David Byrne that gave director Demme the opportunity to make one of the finest concert movies to date. Blessed with an enthusiastic, and talented band, Demme has managed to craft a stellar piece of work, despite only having footage shot over 3 live performances and a few small pieces of extra film to work with. Luckily for Demme, Byrne had a plan – to make the staging develop alongside the concert. To begin with, it is just Byrne, a guitar and an empty stage. As the show progresses, more musicians come out, joined by stagehands that build the setting as the concert carries on around them. *Stop Making Sense* is more than just a good video though, it's packed with an incredible amount of extras for a music disc. There is superb commentary from Demme, Byrne and other members of the band, an insightful *David Byrne Interviews... David Byrne* section, and a storyboard section which reveals ideas behind Byrne's original concept for the concert. You really don't have to be a full-blown fan to get some enjoyment out of this DVD. There's just too much on this disc to allow for disappointment, and all music fans should buy it.

FINAL VERDICT

Picture ☆☆☆ Sound ☆☆☆☆☆

Entertainment ☆☆☆☆☆

Extras ☆☆☆☆☆ Value ☆☆☆☆

OVERALL ☆☆☆☆

THE UNAUTHORISED STAR WARS STORY

Price: £15.99
Supplied by: Visual Entertainment
Type of disc: Single layer, single-sided
No of chapters: 10
Film format(s)/length: 4:3 regular / 63 mins
Audio format: Stereo
Director: None specified
Starring: Star Wars actors, fans and commentators
Year made: 1999
Extras: Scene access (and that's it!).

The problem with unauthorised documentaries like this one is that the makers are seldom granted access to legitimate and authoritative sources, meaning that the end result comes across as an amateurish effort resembling an end of term college piece. Whilst Visual Entertainment has certainly made a sterling effort in regards to compiling as much *Star Wars* info as possible with the restriction of not being able to use official LucasFilm footage, *The Unauthorised Star Wars Story* will still fail to satisfy even the most die-hard of *Star Wars* fanatics. Visual's documentary has a mixed bunch of sources, with the bulk of the footage consisting of clips from what looks suspiciously like a promo piece for the 1997 Special Edition re-release of the original trilogy. This is interspersed with panoramic shots of Hollywood (for the story of how George Lucas tried to sell the original movie) and Tunisia (the backdrop for Tatooine), as well as embarrassing shots of gurning fans, sometimes dressed as their *Star Wars* character of choice, queuing outside cinemas for the original movie as well as the recent *Episode 1*. Incidentally, whilst the actors from the original trilogy and the new film have equal billing on the – quite frankly – crap cover, the likes of Ewan McGregor and Samuel Jackson probably only say about 6 words a piece (and, to be honest, after watching it we didn't remember seeing Liam Neeson in this documentary at all). *The Unauthorised Star Wars Story* would by no means be an essential purchase on video, let alone on such a premium format as DVD – unless of course you are a *Star Wars* completist who simply has to have anything which vaguely has a Force connection. Regardless of some of the genuinely fasci-

nating nuggets of information strewn through the documentary – like Anthony (C3-PO) Daniel's recollection of the original vision that George Lucas had for C3-PO's voice – Visual's DVD package smacks of the quick buck mentality, and it's no doubt crossing its fingers that it will sell bucket-loads on the success of *The Phantom Menace* (particularly as George Lucas has yet to allow any of the *Star Wars* movies to be committed to DVD). Use the Force and resist the temptations of The Dark Side, *The Unauthorised Star Wars Story* is unauthorised for a reason, and that's because it isn't *Star Wars*!

FINAL VERDICT

Picture ☆☆☆ Sound ☆☆ Entertainment ☆☆

Extras ☆ Value ☆

OVERALL ☆

WALKING WITH DINOSAURS

Price: £24.99
Supplied by: BBC Worldwide
Type of disc: 1x dual layer, single-sided, 1x single layer, single-sided
No of chapters: 6 episodes
Film format(s)/length: 1.85:1 widescreen enhanced / 230 mins
Audio format: Stereo
Directors: Tim Haines and Jasper James
Starring: Dinosaurs!
Year made: 1999
Extras: Scene access; special 50-minute behind-the-scenes feature; subtitles in English; subtitles available for the hearing impaired in English.

The dawn of man has been studied for years, while the exploits of our ancestors have fascinated entire generations. Now, through the marvels of modern technology, the dinosaurs are next in the limelight with the latest documentary from the BBC. *Walking with Dinosaurs* covers an incredible 155 million years of dinosaur history, beginning in the mid-Triassic period and ending with the death of a dynasty in the late Cretaceous period. The task set before the BBC, and most notably animation team Framestore, was truly astonishing. Unless you were asleep throughout last autumn, you should have seen this incredible look into the lives of the most notorious creatures to ever have populated the Earth. The series is split into 6 episodes, covering the Triassic, Jurassic and Cretaceous periods. Although the portrayal of these stunning CGI dinosaurs living in real-life environments is impressive, what sets them apart is the way that the series team captured the essence of a documentary. Utilising well-positioned camera close-ups and a variety of other techniques, the feeling is that the camera crew were actually amongst the mammoth beasts. Each episode steals your attention as you're continually surprised, amused and awed at the lives of these astounding creatures. The telling of these prehistoric tales is wonderfully conveyed through the traditional wildlife documentary method of narration, provided in this case by the commanding tones of Kenneth Branagh. What makes this series even more incredible – for the DVD audience in particular – is the widescreen anamorphic digital transfer. Now standard practice for the BBC, DVD takes advantage of the already impressive visuals created by the animators and pushes the format one step ahead of its VHS counterpart. Unfortunately, while the viewer is spoiled by the incredible images on screen, the audible offerings fall somewhat short of monstrous. Dolby Digital 5.1 and Surround owners will have to make do with the stereo soundtrack, so forget about hearing deafening roars behind you. Pleasantly, the BBC had the vision to create a 50-minute behind-the-scenes special in tandem with the series. This focuses on the techniques used to create the series, while giving away some of the secrets. Amazingly, the special was also created in the widescreen anamorphic format, and again using a digital transfer – giant pat on the back to the BBC! Fans of dinosaurs, newcomers to their world and documentary lovers everywhere will find this an essential purchase, cultivated to the best it can be by DVD.

FINAL VERDICT

Picture ☆☆☆☆☆ Sound ☆☆☆

Entertainment ☆☆☆☆☆

Extras ☆☆☆☆ Value ☆☆☆☆☆

OVERALL ☆☆☆☆☆

XENA: WARRIOR PRINCESS

Price: £15.99

Supplied by: DVD Plus (www.dvdplus.co.uk)

Type of disc: Dual layer, single-sided

No of chapters: 3

Film format(s)/length: 4:3 regular / 126 mins

Audio format: Stereo

Directors: Charles Siebert, Anson Williams and Gary Jones

Starring: Lucy Lawless, Renee O'Connor, David Taylor

Year made: 1996

Extras: Scene access; star biographies; photo gallery.

Tall, dark and fitting snugly into her costume (just), Lucy Lawless stars as the leather-clad vixen Xena, along with her spunky sidekick Gabrielle (before the lesbian undertones of the third series) in 3 choice episodes from the second series. The warrior princess faces her past as she returns to the land of the Centaurs and the son she gave away in 'Orphan of War.' Immediately, you begin to notice the difference between terrestrial transmission and the digital quality of DVD; however, the same thing can be said of Sky Digital. In 'Remember Nothing' Xena defends the temple of the Three Fates against a band of unruly outlaws and is rewarded with one wish. Wishing that she never followed the ways of the sword, her perception of reality is accordingly altered. As with the previous episode, the image quality and colouring are fine when everyone remains calm. But the second the swords start flying, the picture loses some of its sharpness. Xena's loyalties conflict with her principles when an old friend teams up with the enemy in 'The Giant Killer'. This sees the shows producers work the classic story of David and Goliath to fit comfortably around the 5ft 10inch New Zealand beauty, leaving no stone unturned or heaving breast uncovered – well, one out of two at least! Xena comes armed with a standard stereo soundtrack, limited biographies and photo gallery. In fact it's only the finely tuned frame of Lucy Lawless herself and the reasonable price tag which would persuade you to part with your hard-earned drachma (that's Greek money, people).

FINAL VERDICT

Picture ☆☆☆ Sound ☆☆

Entertainment ☆☆ Extras ☆☆ Value ☆☆☆

OVERALL ☆☆

The following Region 1 film reviews can only hope to give a very small sampling from the wide range of titles now available, but they should provide some indication of the breadth of material already released. Nevertheless, space has prevented us from looking at the more specialist titles available on Region 1 disks, for example the films of Italian horror directors or American 1950s B movie film-makers, but we feel these reviews cover some of the main titles currently being imported.

It is also worth noting that in the two or three months following publication of *The Ultimate DVD Guide*, some of the films featured in this section will be available on Region 2 discs (for example, *Fight Club* or *The Nightmare on Elm Street* box set), often in a similar or identical form to the Region 1 release. In fact, Region 2 discs are rapidly approaching the standard of their American cousins in terms of extras, whilst further good news can be found in the decision of a number of companies to release their discs on the same date in both regions.

Finally, please note that not all machines in the UK will play Region 1 disks, so please check your DVD player before ordering any of the following films.

THE ABYSS: SPECIAL EDITION

Price: $25-35
Supplied by: Personal import
Type of disc: 2x dual layer, single-sided
No of chapters: 54/45 (2 cuts of movie), 18 (documentary)
Film format(s)/length: 2.35:1 widescreen / 171/140 mins (2 cuts; 59 mins (documentary)
Audio format: Dolby Digital 5.1
Director: James Cameron
Starring: Ed Harris, Michael Biehn, Mary Elizabeth Mastrantonio
Year made: 1989
Extras: Scene access; seamless branching between Theatrical and Special Edition versions; text-only commentary for both versions; 10-minute featurette; 59-minute documentary, *Under Pressure: Making The Abyss*; cast and crew biographies; production notes: 'About the Story', 'Filming Underwater', 'Recording Dialogue Underwater', 'Building Deepcore', 'The Diving Gear', 'The Submersibles'; 3 trailers; complete shooting script by director James Cameron; Cameron's original story treatment; all 773 storyboards, in order; photo and artwork gallery; multi-angle SFX footage of the pseudopod; time-lapse photography of Deepcore set construction (7 mins); videomatics footage; visual effects showreel for

Oscar nomination (20 mins); 'Crane crash' SFX filming; 'Surface unit montage' – filming of ocean footage; 'Engine room flooding' SFX filming; 'Montana bridge flooding' SFX filming; videomatics montage – video story-boards; 'Miniature rear-projection' SFX filming; Time-lapse photography of model filming; 'Mission Components' – individual design, construction and filming production notes on the tidal wave, Bethnic Explorer, Cab Three, Deepcore, Cab One, the pseudopod, Flatbed, Little Geek, the USS Montana, NTI Scout, NTI Manta, the Deep Suit, Big Geek, NTI Ark and the NTIs; 'Operations' – production notes on 'Writer/Director and Screenplay', 'Production Team', 'The Design Team', 'The Storyboarding Process' and 'Character Development and Casting'; Easter egg – *True Lies* trailer; 3 DVD-ROM games.

It was somehow inevitable that James Cameron would decide to do things bigger than everyone else. After the Special Editions and Director's Cuts of *RoboCop*, *Alien*, *Armageddon*, *Brazil* and *A Bug's Life* all progressively leapfrogged each other with ever-increasing amounts of extras, the Canadian 'King of the World' now stomps the lot with *The Abyss*. You only have to look at the size of the special features list to see that Cameron doesn't do things by halves. *The Abyss* is Cameron's 'forgotten' movie, unless you count *Piranha 2: The Spawning*, which is mysteriously absent from his on-disc filmography. A US nuclear sub takes a one-way trip to Davey Jones's Locker after encountering an alien underwater craft; the crew of Deepcore 2, an experimental underwater oil drilling rig, are press-ganged into a rescue operation. Deepcore boss Bud (Harris) is dismayed to learn that joining him aboard the rig is not only buggo SEAL commander Coffey (Biehn), but soon-to-be-ex-wife Lindsey (Mastrantonio). Naturally their love is rekindled over the course of the film, but in the meantime the couple have to deal with fires, floods, explosions, imploding submersibles, crazed commandos, nuclear bombs, the aforementioned aliens and the not-inconsiderable problem that one of them dies. Don't worry, it all makes sense in the end. In fact, it makes even more sense on this DVD. Thanks to the miracle of 'seamless branching', it's possible to choose either the original cinema version or the *Special Edition*. The latter is almost half an hour longer, and in addition to extending numerous scenes (mainly with more character material) adds an entirely new plot thread in which the aliens use their power to control water to convince the US and the USSR (well, the film was made in the Eighties) that nuclear war is something to be avoided. Guh. Actually, sarcasm aside, the *Special Edition* is the better of the two versions, but at a hair short of 3 hours long you'll need to set an evening aside to watch it. Once you've done that, you might as well set a whole day aside to view all the extras. Lumping together all the documentaries, SFX footage and behind-the-scenes material will add well over two more hours to your viewing time, and then there's a staggering amount of text and still photos covering every aspect of the film's production, as well as every single storyboard and the *entire* script. There are hundreds, possibly even thousands of pages (no, we didn't sit down and count them all) of material to view. *The Abyss* also boasts what are without doubt the best animated menus to date. Normally these are just fripperies, and can even be annoying, but in this case they're actually impressive in their own right as choosing options takes you on a whirlwind tour of the Deepcore drilling rig. There are only two disappointments about *The Abyss: Special Edition*, one minor and one major. The minor one is the lack of a Cameron commentary – while you get a chatty and informative text-based commentary telling you more than you needed to know, it's not the same as having the man himself. The major one is that despite what it says on the box, *The Abyss: Special Edition* is *not* anamorphically enhanced, but is only letterboxed. Even though the picture is superb throughout, it seems a definite missed opportunity to make it the perfect DVD.

FINAL VERDICT

Picture ☆☆☆☆☆ Sound ☆☆☆☆☆
Entertainment ☆☆☆☆☆
Extras ☆☆☆☆☆ Value ☆☆☆☆☆
OVERALL ☆☆☆☆☆

ANTZ

Price: $25-30
Supplied by: Personal import
Type of disc: Dual layer, single-sided
No of chapters: 26
Film format(s)/length: 1.85:1 widescreen / 83 mins
Audio format: Dolby Digital 5.1
Directors: Eric Darnell and Lawrence Guterman
Starring the voices of: Woody Allen, Sharon Stone, Gene Hackman
Year made: 1998
Extras: Audio director's commentary; production featurette; *Basics of Computer Animation* feature; *Antz Facial System* feature; production notes; TV spots; cast list and director biogs; theatrical trailer.

Dreamworks' CGI *tour de force* locked horns with Disney's own *A Bug's Life* last year and came away with an Oscar (for the lead song) and a whole heap of acclaim. For a new company, it was an incredible achievement to take on the creators of *Toy Story* and

take the lion's share of praise, and on DVD you can appreciate those sumptuous computer graphics as they were originally intended. Although *Antz* is not a direct digital transfer like *A Bug's Life*, the picture quality is still mightily impressive, even if some of the large scenes do resemble matt paintings. It's an overrated movie, with Disney's *A Bug's Life* covering similar ground better. Slightly adult in tone, *Antz* does possess its fair share of jaw-dropping moments and is worth watching for Woody Allen's terrific turn as the voice of Z – the paranoid underachiever. What *Antz* lacks is the vibrant colours of *A Bug's Life*, with the majority of the film taking place inside an ant hill or garbage dump (the so-called Insectopia). What makes the DVD essential though is the quality of extras. The director's commentary isn't the best, but it still provokes interest. The background info on the making of the film though is excellent, and you really wish there was more of it and it's a shame the trailer isn't in widescreen. You also get some excellent behind-the-scenes information, such as details about the facial system and how the characters were developed. Cracking menus, too.

FINAL VERDICT

Picture ☆☆☆☆☆ Sound ☆☆☆☆
Entertainment ☆☆☆ Extras ☆☆☆☆ Value ☆☆☆☆
OVERALL ☆☆☆☆

ARMAGEDDON: SPECIAL EDITION

Price: $35-55 (some charge $80!)
Supplied by: Personal Import
Type of disc: Dual layer, single-sided (Disc 1), single layer, single-sided (Disc 2)
No of chapters: 31
Film format(s)/length: 2.35:1 widescreen / 153 mins
Audio format: Dolby Digital 5.1 (Disc 1), stereo (Disc 2)
Director: Michael Bay
Starring: Bruce Willis, Liv Tyler, Ben Affleck
Year made: 1998
Extras: Commentary by director, producer, Bruce Willis and Ben Affleck; commentary by the cinematographer, NASA consultant and asteroid specialist; gag reel and bloopers; deleted scenes; storyboards and production designs; special effects documentary; behind-the-scenes footage; production designer interview; every theatrical trailer and teaser; Aerosmith video; interview with Aerosmith.

Okay, let's cut to the chase, this film should be in every DVD owner's collection. Last year's apocalyptic space thriller is destined to make more impact on the DVD world than an asteroid ever could. Re-released on two separate discs, one for the special edition film, the other for the plethora of extras, Criterion

Collection's *Armageddon: Special Edition* packs so many extra features, mouth watering footage and audio-visual quality it quite simply knocks you off your feet. Bay's cut of the film hasn't altered drastically from the cinematic release, only paying attention to the relationship between Willis and his father as well as elaborating slightly the sub-plot of prematurely exploding the nuclear device. The story itself remains firmly in the 'explosive' category as before. The extras are what make Criterion Collection's *Armageddon* such an earth-shattering package though. A mildly amusing blooper reel sees Willis spewing forth colourful language and Billy Bob Thornton camping it up and amusing the crew. Theatrical trailers polka-dot the second disc, cranking up the hype before viewing commences, special effects guys lovingly guide us through intensely informative design procedures and post production jiggery-pokery, whilst every aspect of asteroid animation is gushed over by the visual effects supervisor. Somehow they've even managed to get Bruce himself narrating with Bay and Bruckheimer (a reassuringly authoritative NASA official also lends himself to the party). If that wasn't enough, the picture and sound quality are pristine and sharp, allowing full appreciation of the Oscar nominated Aerosmith song and an interview. It's expensive, but more than worth it.

FINAL VERDICT

Picture ☆☆☆☆☆ Sound ☆☆☆☆☆
Entertainment ☆☆☆☆☆
Extras ☆☆☆☆☆ Value ☆☆☆☆
OVERALL ☆☆☆☆☆

ARMY OF DARKNESS: LIMITED EDITION

Price: $30-35
Supplied by: Personal import
Type of disc: Director's cut: Single layer, single-sided; Theatrical version: Dual layer, single-sided
No of chapters: 46
Film format(s)/length: Director's cut: 16:9 widescreen enhanced / 96 mins; Theatrical version: 16:9 widescreen enhanced and 4:3 regular / 81 mins
Audio format: Director's cut: Dolby Surround; Theatrical version: Dolby Digital 5.1
Director: Sam Raimi
Starring: Bruce Campbell, Embeth Davidtz, Richard Grove
Year made: 1993
Extras: Scene access; behind-the-scenes documentary about the special-effects (15 mins); audio commentary from Raimi and Campbell; biographies on Raimi and Campbell; theatrical trailer; 4 never-before-seen deleted scenes (with audio commentary); director's storyboards;

subtitles in 20 languages.

The recent Region 2 release of *Evil Dead 2: Dead by Dawn* proved to be a real disappointment, due to the distinctive lack of extras. However, fans of Raimi's third jaunt with the Deadite hordes will find that this Region 1 release is a much more apt celebration of one of the greatest horror series of all time. Played for laughs in a Three Stooges slapstick kind of vein, *Army of Darkness* picks up the threads from the end of *Evil Dead 2*, where the series' unlikely hero, Ash, finds himself stranded in medieval England. Whilst his primary concern is to get back to his own time, Ash has to contend with 'primitive screwheads' and the undead hordes empowered by the Necronomicon. This double DVD set provides two different versions of *Army of Darkness*: the original theatrical release with a relatively upbeat ending; and the original vision that Raimi had for the film, including 15 minutes of extra footage and the post-apocalyptic ending. You can also check out the theatrical trailer (which, unlike most, is genuinely entertaining to watch); watch a documentary on the making of the special-effects; hear a hilarious audio commentary from Raimi and Campbell; read their biographies; and see the 4 deleted scenes (which also come with audio commentary). It will be interesting to see if *Army of Darkness* receives a Region 2 release, and retains the amount of extras prevalent on this Region 1 version. Whilst the film is hardly going to appeal to the mass-market, this is nonetheless another example of DVD at its best. "Hail to the king, baby!"

FINAL VERDICT

Picture ☆☆☆☆☆ Sound ☆☆☆☆☆
Entertainment ☆☆☆☆☆
Extras ☆☆☆☆☆ Value ☆☆☆☆
OVERALL ☆☆☆☆☆

BRAZIL

Price: $45-50
Supplied by: Personal import
Type of disc: Discs 1 and 2: Dual layer, single-sided; Disc 3: Single layer, single-sided
No of chapters: Disc 1: 35; Disc 2: 16; Disc 3: 21
Film format(s)/length: Disc 1: 1.85:1 widescreen / 142 mins; Disc 2: 4:3 regular / 90 mins; Disc 3: 4:3 regular / 94 mins
Audio format: Dolby Surround
Director: Terry Gilliam
Starring: Jonathan Pryce, Robert De Niro, Katherine Helmond
Year made: 1985
Extras: Scene access; on-set documentary, *What Is Brazil?*, from 1985 (30 minutes); original 60-minute doc-

umentary, *The Battle of Brazil*; audio commentary on director's cut by Terry Gilliam; audio commentary on 'Love Conquers All' version by Gilliam expert, David Morgan; screenwriters notes and commentary; production stills; storyboards for the dream sequences; commentary from composer on *Brazil*'s musical score; theatrical trailer; behind-the-scenes look at the special effects; English subtitles for the deaf or hearing impaired.

    Gilliam's tale of one man against a Big Brother-style system has not really dated, and remains as poignant now as it did back in 1985. Dark and disturbing with a suitably twisted sense of humour, *Brazil* is truly one of Gilliam's finest hours, ranking up alongside the likes of *Time Bandits*, *Twelve Monkeys* and *Fear & Loathing in Las Vegas*. Criterion has produced a landmark DVD boxset, which alone could sell even the most sceptical of VHS owners on why DVD is the medium of the future. As well as two separate versions of the film – each with their own optional audio commentaries – there are a breathtaking array of features and extras included within the 3 DVD set. In fact, the second DVD has two documentaries; a theatrical trailer; publicity and production stills; concept sketches; storyboards for Sam Lowry's dream sequences – even for some which weren't included in the final film; special effects secrets revealed; background on the composition of the musical score; and commentary by *Brazil*'s screenwriters, Tom Stoppard and Charles McKeown, about the script's development process. The film's print has been especially transferred in its original widescreen format, as well as having its soundtrack remastered in Dolby Surround. Fans of Gilliam's unique and disturbing visions will realise, with unalienable clarity, that their collections will simply not be complete without a copy of this splendid DVD.

FINAL VERDICT

Picture ☆☆☆☆ Sound ☆☆☆☆
Entertainment ☆☆☆☆☆
Extras ☆☆☆☆☆ Value ☆☆☆☆☆
OVERALL ☆☆☆☆☆

Chasing Amy

Price: $24-33
Supplied by: Personal import
Type of disc: Dual layer, single-sided
No of chapters: 25
Film format(s)/length: 1.85:1 letterbox / 113 mins
Audio format: Dolby Digital 5.1
Director: Kevin Smith
Starring: Ben Affleck, Jason Lee, Joey Lauren Adams
Year made: 1997

Extras: Scene access; video introduction to the film by director Smith; audio commentary by cast and crew members; video introductions by cast and crew members; 10 deleted scenes plus outtakes; theatrical trailer; booklet giving the background to the movie by Kevin Smith; The Askewniverse Legend: A Guide to the New Jersey Trilogy characters; subtitles for the hearing impaired in English.

    Kevin Smith has taken the old cliché about writing about what you know to a whole new level. He took his experiences behind a Quick Stop counter and planted them in *Clerks*, tipped his baseball cap towards the Eighties teen comedies he grew up with in *Mallrats*, catalogued his ruminations about faith and Catholicism in *Dogma*, and here in *Chasing Amy*, his relationship with the lead actress is aired in public. Comic book artists Holden (Affleck) and best friend Banky (Lee) are introduced to Alyssa (Joey Lauren Adams), an unabashed lesbian. Gradually, friendship between Holden and Alyssa turns into romance but neither expect the hostile, homophobic reaction of Banky or that Holden would feel intimidated by Alyssa's sexual experience. *Chasing Amy* is a daring and original romantic comedy that sees Smith return (or should that be retreat?) to low-budget indie pictures after the unjust critical and commercial once-over *Mallrats* received. It couples the effervescence of *Jules et Jim* and the cast chemistry of *Casablanca* with Smith's signature funny and perceptive dialogue. Criterion continue to trailblaze DVD production with this package. Design is strong, audio is terrific, but the enhanced picture now shows up the grain of the film. The features department is what makes the disc worth the prolonged wait. The few outtakes included give us a glimpse of Smith's on-set work practices. Far from the slacker ethos he displays in front of the camera as Silent Bob and in the numerous, entertaining video introductions, when Smith barks orders on set, everyone co-operates. More of this sort of unguarded footage would have been appreciated. Although Smith, producer Scott Mosier, actors Affleck and Jason Mewes, associate producer Robert Hawk, Miramax executive Jon Gordon and View Askew historian Vincent Pereira sit in on the commentary, it's really The Smith and Affleck Show, with occasional interjections from Pereira (to keep tangents to a minimum). Recorded in September 1997, it suffers from the absence of Adams and Lee and, perhaps because of the subject matter, it's not as much of a laugh riot as the one for *Mallrats*. Nevertheless, *Chasing Amy* is a labour of love for Smith and Criterion alike and recommended to all fans of indie cinema. Finally, a sharp and hilarious romantic comedy for the boys as well as the girls.

FINAL VERDICT

Picture ☆☆☆ Sound ☆☆☆☆

Entertainment ☆☆☆☆

Extras ☆☆☆☆ Value ☆☆☆☆

OVERALL ☆☆☆☆

CONAN THE BARBARIAN

Price: $20-24

Supplied by: Personal import

Type of disc: Dual layer, single-sided

No of chapters: 16

Film format(s)/length: 2.35:1 anamorphic / 129 mins

Audio format: Mono

Director: John Milius

Starring: Arnold Schwarzenegger, James Earl Jones, Sandahl Bergman

Year made: 1982

Extras: Scene access; *Conan Unchained*, the making of *Conan* documentary (53 mins); audio commentary by director John Milius and actor Arnold Schwarzenegger; deleted scenes; special effects; the Conan archives; theatrical trailers; soundtrack in English and French; subtitles in French.

The unstoppable flex machine had questionable beginnings in the film business, his early efforts best left unmentioned. However, from the moment the Austrian Oak lifted the sword of Conan his star status was spelled out quite clearly and he would go on to be the biggest screen hero of his day. Originally penned as the first of 12 movies by co-writer Oliver Stone (yes, Mr *JFK* Stone), *Conan the Barbarian* follows the mythical beginnings of Conan. Enslaved as a child, Conan's rise from puny servant to musclebound champion pit fighter is a fantastically entertaining one. Forged of steel flesh – not to mention being a bit handy with a bloody great sword – the story follows the gargantuan warrior on his quest for vengeance against his parents' executioner and leader of the snake-cult of Set, Thulsa Doom (Jones). Considering the film's vintage, Universal deserves a hefty pat on the back for its superb restoration, not to mention the inclusion of bonus footage. Although the sound mix remains in its original mono state, the anamorphic enhancements are spectacularly combined with crisp, clear and vibrantly stunning colour clarity. But the suits behind the disc didn't stop there, oh no. An informative look at the making of *Conan the Barbarian* features recent interviews with star Schwarzenegger, director Milius and legend Oliver Stone, among others. Unfortunately, while the documentary is interesting and informative, the audio commentary quite frankly isn't.

Schwarzenegger's mighty presence is obviously limited to visual appearances only, as the monotonous and moronic warbling of Arnie and Milius does little to justify its importation costs. Thankfully, extra special delights such as the deleted scenes, the Conan archives and special effects explanations rectify the painstaking minutes spent listening to the commentary. As an overall package *Conan* delivers a thunderous punch with both the film and special features being worthy of presence in any collection. Miss it at your peril, Arnie fans.

FINAL VERDICT

Picture ☆☆☆☆☆ Sound ☆☆

Entertainment ☆☆☆

Extras ☆☆☆☆☆ Value ☆☆☆☆

OVERALL ☆☆☆☆

FIGHT CLUB

Price: $25-35

Supplied by: Personal import

Type of disc: 1x dual layer, single-sided, 1x single layer, single-sided

No of chapters: 36

Film format(s)/length: 2.40:1 anamorphic / 139 mins

Audio format: Dolby Digital 5.1/THX EX

Director: David Fincher

Starring: Brad Pitt, Edward Norton, Helena Bonham Carter

Year made: 1999

Extras: Scene access; audio commentary by David Fincher; audio commentary by David Fincher, Brad Pitt, Edward Norton and Helena Bonham Carter; audio commentary by novelist Chuck Palahniuk and screenwriter Jim Uhls; audio commentary by production designer, director of photography, costume designer and FX supervisor; cast and crew biographies; multi-angle featurettes with commentary: Alternate Main Titles, Airport, Jack's Condo, Paper Street House, Projection Booth, Corporate Art Ball, Main Title, Fürni Catalogue, Ice Cave/Power Animal, Photogrammetry, Mid-Air Collision, Sex Sequence, Car Crash, Gun Shot, High Rise Collapse; 7 deleted scenes/alternate takes; 2 trailers; 12 TV spots; 2 'Public Service Announcements'; Dust Brothers music video; 5 Internet spots; lobby cards; press kit (mock catalogue); promotional stills; Edward Norton interview transcript; storyboards; visual effects stills; Paper Street House artwork; costumes and make-up artwork; pre-production paintings; Easter egg: *Fight Club* merchandise catalogue; soundtrack in English and French; subtitles in English and Spanish; THX EX test mode.

Telling you about this DVD breaks both the first and second rules of *Fight Club*, but it has to be done.

Something strange seems to have been introduced into Hollywood lately – intelligence. What's going on? Recently, in amongst the *Wild Wild West*s and *Deep Blue Sea*s we've been treated to films like *Three Kings*, *Rushmore*, *Being John Malkovich* and *The Sixth Sense*. More to the point, they've been successful. Maybe we're not the drooling cretins that Hollywood likes to think we are. *Fight Club* was somehow the perfect film with which to end the 20th century, a time when we'd never had it so good or so bad, simultaneously. All that money, and nothing worthwhile to do with it. The central character of *Fight Club* is Norton's unnamed narrator, a middle-management drone who rejects consumerism as a way to fill the emotional and spiritual void in his life in favour of back-alley scrapping. Meeting Pitt's anarchistic Tyler Durden on a plane one day, and soon thereafter finding the contents of his apartment propelled explosively onto the street below, the pair set up the first Fight Club, where directionless Generation X men can rediscover their identity through the primal sensation of lamping each other. But there's more to it – Tyler's ultimate plan is the mysterious Project Mayhem… There aren't many DVDs that quote negative reviews in their own liner notes. But here they are, middle-aged critics from middle-brow newspapers (including the *Evening Standard*'s Alexander Walker) hopping onto their soapboxes, puffing out their chests and accusing the film of being practically a fascist recruitment poster. The only possible response to these accusations is laughter at just how out of touch people can get; you'd have to be a grade A moron to finish watching *Fight Club* and think to yourself, "Yeah, I wanna become a mindless Space Monkey, blindly following the orders of a psychopath!" And grade A morons wouldn't even get to the end of the film – they'd have given up much earlier because it's not violent enough. It's true – for all the bare-knuckle brawling, the violence in Fincher's film is no more brutal, explicit or shocking than that found in *Raging Bull*, a film probably somewhere in the all-time top 10 of the same critics who panned *Fight Club*. It can hardly be said that it glorifies violence, either; would you want to end up looking like the dough-faced, tooth-spitting combatants on display here? Breaking the final rib of the 'Watch this and you'll sign up for the Fourth Reich' theory is the perfectly obvious fact that one of the founders of Fight Club is completely insane. *Fight Club* is a two-disc set; the first holds the film and 4 commentary tracks, the second a lot of behind-the-scenes material. Rarely has the multi-angle button been put to so much use – many of the featurettes feature alternate audio and video choices. Some of the fea-

turettes are of the one-view-only type, but all are interesting. There's also a huge number of stills and pre-production artwork, plus all the film's appropriately subversive promotional material. Details of the commentaries can be found in the 'Special Features' box – the most fascinating are the two involving director Fincher. His solo track is a detailed and wryly amusing take on the making of the film, while his second also includes the 3 leads. Bonham Carter's part of the commentary was recorded separately to Fincher, Pitt and Norton's laddish chat – had she been with them, there would probably have been much laughter at her description of Fincher as "soft and feminine". All of this extra material guarantees repeat viewings of the film – which it deserves anyway. The picture is superb, letting you spot all the subliminal secrets with ease, and the soundtrack has a THX EX option if you've got suitable equipment. There's a (no doubt intentional) irony that the DVD of *Fight Club* will fit into the movie collections of the very same aspirational consumers this black-and-blue satire mocks. But what the hell – Fincher deserves the last laugh. Buy this DVD and put it on your Swedish shelves. Just don't leave the gas on.

FINAL VERDICT

Picture ☆☆☆☆☆ Sound ☆☆☆☆☆

Entertainment ☆☆☆☆☆

Extras ☆☆☆☆☆ Value ☆☆☆☆☆

OVERALL ☆☆☆☆☆

GALAXY QUEST

Price: $18-27
Supplied by: Personal import
Type of disc: Dual layer, single-sided
No of chapters: 20
Film format(s)/length: 2.35:1 anamorphic / 102 min
Audio format: Dolby Digital 5.1
Director: Dean Parisot
Starring: Tim Allen, Sigourney Weaver, Alan Rickman
Year made: 1999
Extras: Scene access; *On Location in Space* featurette (10 mins); 7 deleted scenes (10 mins); trailer; teaser trailers; cast and filmmakers' biographies; production notes; soundtrack in 'Thermian'; subtitles in English.

Old science fiction shows never die, they just go into re-runs. As for their stars… well, the heroes of late-Seventies show *Galaxy Quest* have been reduced to signing autographs at nerdy conventions and opening computer stores to pay the bills. But all that's about to change, as the cast are mistaken by an alien race for genuine galactic warriors and beamed away to fight in a very real war… *Galaxy Quest* is, of course, a spoof of *Star Trek* and the whole anal-retentive, faux-technical manual-reading fandom it created, but it's played straight and done with enough style and cleverness to appeal to both die-hard Trekkies and those who wouldn't be seen dead watching anything involving Klingons. Allen's Shatneresque Jason Nesmith is excellent as the egotistical ham still prone to sucking in his gut and striking a pose 20 years after cancellation, but all the cast prove highly watchable (Rickman's 'ac-tor' for his reserved despair, Weaver's blonde bimbo for... well, let's just say she didn't look like that in *Alien Resurrection*). Ironically, *Galaxy Quest*'s effects were done by *Trek*'s visual wizards at Industrial Light & Magic, so it looks every bit as good as what it's parodying. The version we reviewed was the DD5.1 version; there's also a DTS available. Picture and audio are both excellent, as you'd expect from a new, high-profile title, and while the extras are maybe a little spartan, they're still appreciated. The 'Thermian' audio track, in which all the dialogue is dubbed in an alien language, has to be the weirdest extra ever! If you like *Star Trek* you can enjoy the inventiveness of the parody, and if you hate it you can revel in its mockery. Either way, you'll be entertained by this stellar DVD.

FINAL VERDICT

Picture ☆☆☆☆☆ Sound ☆☆☆☆

Entertainment ☆☆☆☆ Extras ☆☆☆☆ Value ☆☆☆☆

OVERALL ☆☆☆☆

THE GREEN MILE

Price: $20-25

Supplied by: Personal import

Type of disc: Dual layer, single-sided

No of chapters: 53

Film format(s)/length: 1.85:1 anamorphic / 188 mins

Audio format: Dolby Digital 5.1

Director: Frank Darabont

Starring: Tom Hanks, David Morse, Michael Clarke Duncan

Year made: 1999

Extras: Scene access; *Walking the Mile* behind-the-scenes documentary; production notes; theatrical trailer; subtitles in English and French.

If your name's Tom, then Hollywood is yours to rule. Cruise hasn't faltered in over a decade, and the Oscar-consuming Hanks is still revelling in his prime 12 years after *Big*. These days it's his name, star status, pay cheque and (in the role of Paul Edgecomb) double chin that all bask in the 'big' category, and allowed *The Green Mile* to somewhat soften the blow of comparison to Darabont's directorial debut, *The Shawshank Redemption*. Hanks is the chief warden on Death Row at Cold Mountain Penitentiary (the type of 'good man

in a bad place' role that Hanks could churn out with his peepers closed), who bears the responsibility of executing the gentle giant John Coffey (Clarke Duncan), accused of the rape and murder of two small girls. However, when Coffey starts demonstrating the ability to heal bladder infections, resurrect dead mice and play havoc with the lighting system, Edgecomb suspects that Coffey's guilt is a matter for debate, and that the miracles occurring on his 'mile' (a term of endearment for Death Row) cannot be caused by a man capable of murder. However, in the entire 3 hours no explanation is given for Coffey's gift, and while unusual goings-on in films such as *Groundhog Day* can be easily lost in a short movie, 3 hours may leave you feeling that you are entitled to some explanation for your patience. The other flaw, inevitably, is *The Shawshank Redemption*. When you write and direct two features, both about prison life, set in the same timeframe, and adapted from non-horror Stephen King stories, comparison can't be avoided. And in the wake of Darabont's debut, *The Green Mile* doesn't always manage to keep its head firmly above water. Its messages are not as clear, its timing is not as sharp, and it's often left failing, although not struggling, to keep up. The disc itself is a disappointment. Visually the definition is beyond criticism, and the digital 5.1 does have its moments. However, it's the special features that really don't stand up to the Region 1 norm. Trailer, production notes, featurette and that's it. It's quite likely that the movie's length ultimately foiled opportunities for a more expansive set of extras, but with just the featurette on offer to provide anything insightful, this disc only takes you a token few hundred yards down the mile.

FINAL VERDICT

Picture ☆☆☆☆☆ Sound ☆☆☆☆☆

Entertainment ☆☆☆☆ Extras ☆☆☆ Value ☆☆☆☆

OVERALL ☆☆☆

THE GUNS OF NAVARONE

Price: $25-35

Supplied by: Personal import

Type of disc: Single layer, single-sided

No of chapters: 28

Film format(s)/length: 2.35:1 anamorphic / 157 mins

Audio format: Dolby Digital 5.1

Director: J Lee Thompson

Starring: Gregory Peck, David Niven, Anthony Quinn

Year made: 1961

Extras: Scene access; director's commentary; retrospective *Memories of Navarone* documentary (30 mins); A message from Carl Foreman; 4 original featurettes in black and white; original theatrical trailer; trailer for

Behold a Pale Horse; talent files; soundtrack in English, Spanish and French; subtitles in 7 languages.

This is one of those 'classic' war films which everyone should see. It tells the story of a British team (aided by a Yank, of course – this is a Hollywood production) sent to destroy a huge Nazi gun emplacement which is dominating a section of the Greek coastline. To spice things up a little, they've only got 6 days to do it before the entire British fleet makes a drive-by! Hollywood definitely doesn't make war films like this anymore. You've got the music, the archetypal British war heroes, the plot twists – in fact, all the ingredients are here for a very enjoyable film. Not that this is any surprise; after all, it is based on a novel by Alistair MacLean, who also wrote the superb (and sadly missing from DVD) *Where Eagles Dare*. *Navarone* is an epic production, and you can see why it got nominated for 7 Academy Awards. Thankfully, the DVD does it the justice it deserves. One of the most impressive things about this disc is that the sound has been remastered for digital release into 5.1 – the sound of the big guns firing is breathtaking! In the interest of historical value you also get the original stereo soundtrack, as used in the cinemas on the film's release. The retrospective documentary *Memories of Navarone*, filmed specially for the DVD, is the most interesting of all the extras. It's basically a collection of memories and thoughts on the film decades on from a group of old men, but it is genuinely interesting, if only to hear how the entire cast developed a worrying obsession with playing chess while making the film! The most comical of the extras are the 4 original black and white featurettes. They are exactly the kind of public service newsreels which have been parodied so many times today. Finishing off the disc is an audio commentary from director J Lee Thompson. This does start out very patronising and dull, but if you hold in there it does get a lot better. Gems include why the word 'bloody' was cut out by the censors and how the Greek navy disowned them after they accidentally sank one of their ships! If you like classic war films, it's an essential purchase.

FINAL VERDICT

Picture ☆☆☆☆ Sound ☆☆☆☆

Entertainment ☆☆☆☆☆

Extras ☆☆☆☆ Value ☆☆☆☆

OVERALL ☆☆☆☆☆

INDEPENDENCE DAY: SPECIAL EDITION

Price: $20-35

Supplied by: Personal import

Type of disc: 2x dual layer, single-sided

No of chapters: 54/57

Film format(s)/length: 2.35:1 anamorphic / 153 mins

Audio format: Dolby Digital 5.1

Director: Roland Emmerich

Starring: Will Smith, Jeff Goldblum, Bill Pullman

Year made: 1996

Extras: Scene access; theatrical and special edition versions of the film; commentary by director Roland Emmerich and producer Dean Devlin; commentary by special effects supervisors; *Creating Reality* making-of documentary (30 mins); *ID4 Invasion* mockumentary (22 mins); HBO *First Look* featurette (33 mins); original biplane ending, with commentary; storyboards of 3 action sequences; original artwork; production stills; trailers and TV spots; Apple PowerBook spot; soundtrack in English and French; subtitles in English and Spanish; DVD-ROM features; 'Get Off My Planet' game; Web links.

It became fashionable – starting about 17 seconds after the movie actually opened – to slag off *Independence Day* for its corny characters, its battery of plot holes and its all-annoying 'America rules!' attitude. And you know what? Doing so is entirely justified. The characters are walking clichés, the plot holes could accommodate an alien mothership and if any more apple pie were to be crammed down the viewer's throat, it'd make you vomit. But to dismiss the film because of those flaws is to miss the point entirely. *Independence Day* was designed with one thing in mind – to provide spectacle. In this, it succeeded 100 percent. Creators Emmerich and Dean Devlin can be credited (or blamed, if you prefer) with the resurrection of the disaster movie in the late Nineties, but the likes of *Volcano*, *Deep Impact* and even the thoroughly overblown *Armageddon* couldn't match *Independence Day*'s scope. At heart, the film is just a clone of *War of the Worlds*, with DNA scrapings from *Star Wars*, *V*, *The X-Files*, *Alien* and dozens of other science fiction sources tossed liberally into the gene splicer. The world wakes up to find 15-mile-wide spaceships hovering over the world's major cities; while attempts to communicate fail, computer geek Goldblum discovers a countdown signal with the help of his faithful Apple PowerBook, and sure enough, when the count reaches zero, the aliens open fire with their monument-destroying lasers. Goldblum teams up with supercool fighter pilot Smith and Clintonesque US President Pullman to strike back against the invaders, and this unlikely trio, along with Randy Quaid's drunken crop-duster, end up saving the entire planet. It's a good job indeed that the aliens were too stupid to install a copy of Norton AntiVirus on their mothership's (Mac compatible) computer. *Independence Day* – or *ID4*, as it was mystifyingly abbreviated – may have been a cynical example of mechanical screenwriting (all the main characters, while stereotypes, have each been assigned a regulation Amusing Quirk and Emotional Hurdle To Overcome to help the audience identify with them), but nobody went to see it because they wanted scintillating dialogue or cunning plot twists. People went to see it to see stuff blow up real good. And they weren't disappointed. Four years may have made *Independence Day* rather familiar by now, but this excellent DVD transfer brings back some of the feelings of awe from seeing it for the first time. The picture is uniformly superb through the whole film, and even through a relatively modest system, the sound can rock the house – and with a full-on 5.1 surround system, blow it down. The moment where the aliens start their attack, by obliterating a Los Angeles skyscraper, has a real hammer-blow impact, and for the next few minutes it's a case of sitting there open-mouthed as LA, New York and Washington are explosively removed from the face of the planet. Of course, in amongst the cool stuff you have to sit through the cheese-stuffed personal dramas, and the Special Edition gives you even more of them. Some 12 scenes, totalling 9 minutes, have either been added or extended in the longer version of the film, and the creators originally made the right decision to remove them. Most are either mushy soap opera stuff of the kind that made *Deep Impact* so annoying, or misplaced 'comedy' bits. Like Fox's previous Special Edition winner *Fight Club*, *ID4* comes on two discs, the second home to most of the extras. There's nearly an hour-and-a-half of featurettes (some of which have been shown on TV), a batch of storyboards and design artwork, a collection of various trailers and the original biplane ending, wisely changed at the last minute. It's not as packed as *Fight Club*, but it's still pretty impressive. An all-time classic movie, it isn't. But a fantastic DVD showcase it is. If you like your plots dumb, your speakers loud and stuff blowing up real good – and who doesn't? – then celebrate with *Independence Day*.

FINAL VERDICT

Picture ☆☆☆☆☆ Sound ☆☆☆☆☆

Entertainment ☆☆☆☆

Extras ☆☆☆☆☆ Value ☆☆☆☆

OVERALL ☆☆☆☆

The Insider

Price: $20-24

Supplied by: Personal import

Type of disc: Dual layer, single-sided

No of chapters: 30

Film format(s)/length: 2.35:1 anamorphic / 158 mins

Audio format: Dolby Digital 5.1

Director: Michael Mann

Starring: Al Pacino, Russell Crowe, Christopher Plummer

Year made: 1999

Extras: Scene access; theatrical trailer; production featurette; 'Inside a Scene' deconstruction.

Those who've only heard the bare bones about this movie needn't worry. *The Insider* isn't a two-hour-plus anti-smoking campaign. Instead, it's a riveting and tense thriller that is crafted with style, wit and dynamic performances. Telling a disturbing yet true tale, *The Insider* not so much follows as clings to the struggle of veteran *60 Minutes* producer Lowell Bergman (Pacino) to air the confessions of an insider from the tobacco industry despite legal injunctions, company protests, and death threats. When Dr Jeffrey Wigand (Crowe), an executive for one of America's major tobacco companies, is fired for no official reason, he agrees to become a paid consultant for a story Bergman is producing regarding unethical practices by the tobacco industry. However, when Wigand's former employers threatened to terminate his severance pay and health benefits (which would be disastrous for his severely asthmatic daughter), he realises that this intimidation has a greater purpose, and they will stop at nothing, including smear campaigns, to make sure that he says nothing. This is undoubtedly Mann's best directorial effort to date, sacrificing much of his visual flair to actually tell a story, and a gripping one at that. His undisputed style is still present and has changed little from his *Miami Vice* days, but with *The Insider* Mann has finally figured out how to use it to tell a story, rather than just look good. Did Crowe deserve his Oscar nomination? Well, yes, he most certainly did. However, the real star of the show is Pacino. A man who has crafted shouting into a talent, he is engaging, believable and immediately empathetic for every second he appears on screen. Although not starved of extras, this is however below par for a Region 1 disc, with a basic featurette that runs for 6 minutes and has more highlights of the movie than any actual interview footage, plus a trailer. The only saving grace is the 'Inside a Scene' feature, which gives the original script, the actor, notes, and then the final filmed scene. However, this gimmick was also on the Region 2 version of *Taxi Driver*, and there you had the entire film to compare. This is one to own, but it will be the movie that will keep it in your player rather than the extras.

FINAL VERDICT

Picture ☆☆☆☆ Sound ☆☆☆☆☆

Entertainment ☆☆☆☆

Extras ☆☆☆ Value ☆☆☆☆

OVERALL ☆☆☆☆

MULAN

Price: $38-40

Supplied by: Personal import

Type of disc: Dual layer, single-sided

No of chapters: 31

Film format(s)/length: 4:3 regular and 1.85:1
widescreen / 88 mins

Audio format: Dolby Digital 5.1

Director: Barry Cook and Tony Bancroft

Starring the voices of: Eddie Murphy, Donny Osmond,
George Takei

Year made: 1998

Extras: 2 music videos, 'Reflection' and 'True to Your
Heart'; theatrical trailer; full colour character artwork;
French and Spanish soundtrack options; film recommen-
dations.

It was a huge moment for DVD when the House
of Mouse finally announced that they were unleashing
premium animated classics onto the digital format.
Then came the bad news – $40 price tags, minimal
extras and no anamorphic enhancement in sight.
Surely they were pulling our leg? Unfortunately not;
there's a bitter truth to face here, and that's that the initial 9 titles Disney unleashed into the Region 1 market
looked like little more than quick cash-ins. *Mulan* may
well have be the most impressive of the discs on offer
at that stage, but even this highly entertaining slice of
Disney hokum can't justify a price tag that converts to
around £25. So what is on offer for your money?
Firstly, the box proudly sports the seal of THX, leading
to high expectations for the picture and the sound. The
lack of anamorphic enhancement is thus an obvious
disappointment. Other than this letdown, there are no
complaints on the visual side. The choice between
standard and widescreen options is much appreciated,
as is the stirring Dolby Digital sound mix. The disc
never gets better than when you examine the audio side
of things. It utilises plenty of bass throughout the big
set pieces, and whilst not quite up to *The Prince of
Egypt* standards, still scores highly in our book. Sadly,
where the audio excels, the extras fall short. The key
attractions are two music videos and a theatrical trailer, all of which are presented in a surround sound mix
as opposed to full 5.1. The trailer is clearly the taster
version, jumbling finished sequences and pencil animation, although offered with comparably poor picture quality. The music videos are both sub-standard
and barely worth a mention. The only other bonus fea-

ture is a still image of the artwork used on the cover of
the disc. Big bloody deal. What makes Disney's
approach all the more disappointing is that it has so
much to offer, but always seems to sell the consumer
short. You really get the feeling they can't be bothered
to make any extra effort. For instance, *Mulan* is one of
Disney's better efforts of the Nineties, save for a couple
of dodgy songs. It even boasts a vocal performance
from Eddie Murphy that makes for one of the best
Disney sidekicks in years. Still, in a way it's our own
fault. It's us who like the films in the first place, and it's
us who continue to tolerate and fork out for overpriced
stuff like this. All this adds up to the fact that Disney
may well end up shifting plenty of discs, but it sure
ain't winning any new friends.

FINAL VERDICT

Picture ☆☆☆☆ Sound ☆☆☆☆☆

Entertainment ☆☆☆☆ Extras ☆☆ Value ☆

OVERALL ☆☆

NATURAL BORN KILLERS: DIRECTOR'S CUT

Price: $20-24

Supplied by: Personal import

Type of disc: Dual layer, single-sided

No of chapters: 30

Film format(s)/length: 1.85:1 widescreen / 121 mins

Audio format: Dolby Digital 5.1

Director: Oliver Stone

Starring: Woody Harrelson, Juliette Lewis,
Tommy Lee Jones

Year made: 1994

Extras: Scene access; 6 deleted scenes, each with an
introduction from Oliver Stone; the alternative ending;
trailer; documentary with interviews with the cast and
crew; commentary track by Oliver Stone; multilingual
subtitles.

It's hard to believe that *Natural Born Killers* is
now over 5 years old. Originally released in the States
back in 1994 (and has never been released on video in
the UK, despite a showing on Channel 5), this was the
picture where Oliver Stone was supposed to film a
Tarantino script but ended up significantly reworking
the movie into one of the most talked about films of
the decade. In its purest form, it follows Mickey and
Mallory Knox (expertly played by Woody Harrelson
and Juliette Lewis), a couple deeply in love who also
happen to kill people. They gain national exposure,
and much of the film explores the relationship the couple form with the media. That's only half the story
though, as director Oliver Stone mixes all sorts of film
styles to get his message across. Animation, colour,

black and white, grain and even TV sit-com style all make an entrance, as the film fills the screen with images on a constant basis (how it failed to win an Oscar for 'Best Editing' is beyond belief – it went to *Forrest Gump* that year!). With all its glorious imagery, it's a shame that Trimark failed to give us an anamorphic transfer. This is just the kind of movie that would benefit enormously from widescreen enhancement and it's a crime that we fail to get one. Mind you, that's not to say the picture quality isn't strong – this is a sharp print that looks good on the digital format. The sound does benefit from the full treatment, as a potent Dolby Digital 5.1 mix can be found on the disc. However, whilst there's a fairly wide sound stage on the track, at times you can't help feeling that it lacks a little punch. It is a commendable effort though, but just too inconsistent to be in keeping with the rest of the DVD. It's in the extras where the disc really earns its plaudits. The best on offer are the deleted scenes. Elsewhere, Oliver Stone delivers a relatively disappointing audio commentary. That's not to say it's without its moments, but for every interesting point or anecdote, there's a pause or some rambling to wade through. Sit through it on a tolerant day. The documentary is better though, running for just short of half an hour and boasting much more interesting stuff than Stone's commentary. The cast and crew get to join in on the fun, and it's certainly one of the better featurettes we've had the pleasure of viewing. Let's not forget that the film is the Director's Cut, with the restored cuts amounting to around 3 minutes of extra footage. For features then, this is a blinding disc, a genuine special edition that goes out at a decent price. As for the film itself? You're either going to love it or hate it, but it would be unwise to ignore it altogether, especially on a quality disc like this. Were the picture and sound improved upon, this would be a showpiece DVD. As it stands, there are few discs that offer better value.

FINAL VERDICT

Picture ☆☆☆☆ Sound ☆☆☆

Entertainment ☆☆☆☆

Extras ☆☆☆☆☆ Value ☆☆☆☆☆

OVERALL ☆☆☆☆

NIGHTMARE ON ELM STREET COLLECTION

Price: $100-$120
Supplied by: Personal import
Type of disc: All single layer, single-sided
No of chapters: Disc 1: 25; Disc 2: 26; Disc 3: 31; Disc 4: 27; Disc 5: 23; Disc 6: 23; Disc 7: 29
Film format(s)/length: All 16:9 widescreen enhanced /

Disc 1: 92 mins; Disc 2: 87 mins; Disc 3: 96 mins; Disc 4: 89 mins; Disc 5: 90 mins; Disc 6: 96 mins; Disc 7: 112 mins
Audio format: All discs Dolby Surround, plus original soundtrack on discs 1-3 in mono and discs 4-7 in stereo
Director: Discs 1 & 7: Wes Craven; Disc 2: Jack Sholder; Disc 3: Chuck Russell; Disc 4: Renny Harlin; Disc 5: Stephen Hopkins; Disc 6: Rachel Talalay
Starring: Robert Englund in all. Heather Langenkamp in Discs 1, 3, 7. John Saxon in Discs 1 and 7
Year made: Disc 1: 1984; Disc 2: 1985; Disc 3: 1987; Disc 4: 1988; Disc 5: 1989; Disc 6: 1991; Disc 7: 1994
Extras: Scene access; audio commentary on Disc 1 by director Wes Craven, director of photography Jacques Haitkin and actors Heather Lagenkamp and John Saxon; audio commentary on Disc 7 by director Wes Craven; cast and crew biographies from original theatrical press kit; subtitles in English; DVD ROM 'Dream World' trivia games; link to cast and crew biographies on Internet (Internet Movie Database); 'Script to Screen' interactive screenplay, allowing you to watch the film and read the original script at the same time.

Every generation has stories of a bogeyman, a monster under the stairs, an evil spirit which stalks you in the night – the threat your parents hold over you if you don't go to sleep and the reason you always asked to sleep with the lights on. For those who grew up in the Eighties that bogeyman wasn't a vague entity: he wore a beaten brown hat, had a face lacerated with putrid scars, brandished a glove garnished with blades and he had a name… Freddy Krueger. Krueger is a child killer, burned to death by a group of vigilante parents, who wreaks revenge on their unfortunate offspring when he returns from the dead. But Freddy can't touch you while you're awake, he can only hurt you in your dreams and when you die in your dreams – you die for real. Such is the fiercely original conceit of *A Nightmare on Elm Street*, Wes Craven's 1984 fantasy horror, which hatched 6 ludicrously successful sequels and made Robert Englund the first genuine horror star since Christopher Lee and Peter Cushing. The success of the first film was no fluke, Craven worked hard to develop a true story he read in a newspaper, about a child who died in his sleep after complaining of horrific nightmares. The glove, a truly vicious creation, was designed to prey on the basic primeval fear of man – the claw. And of course no one is safe – we all go to sleep. As with *Jaws*, the fear factor of the legend of Freddy is actually a good deal scarier than the fact. Englund's Krueger looks like what it is. A not particularly talented actor with a pepperoni pizza on his face. At the time however, the special effects (girl dragged bloody and screaming across ceiling, snakes writhing out of a body bag) were groundbreaking and pushed the censor to the limit in terms of gore. But *A Nightmare on Elm Street* wasn't a no-brainer, its obvious ancestors were *Repulsion* and *Psycho* (particularly when the apparent 'lead' is gutted in the first 15 minutes) and much has been made of Freddy's metaphorical significance. Is he the manifestation of guilt in a broken family? Or burgeoning teenage sexuality? You name it. But beyond all the theorising about what Freddy represents, the first *Nightmare* movie delivers on the one fundamental horror movie law – it is very scary. Sadly they chose to do it all again, again, again, and again. While this box-set is beautifully presented, the picture digitally remastered to great effect (VHS never really could cope with all those deep reds and black), the original mono sound complemented by the option of Dolby Surround and the overall extras package enticing, none of this can really compensate for the fact that all the sequels (bar part 5) are really, really rubbish. Part 2, *Freddy's Revenge* is at least packed with unintentional laughs (a psycho budgie for one) and is strangely compelling in its feebleness, but Part 3 is a humourless mishmash of teenage buddy flick and unconvincing horror. By the completely witless Part 4 you wonder if the makers are competing to see who can make the worst movie. While the original film blurred the line between fantasy and reality, the sequels hang the washing on it. Riddled with inconsistencies and shoddy special effects they reduce Krueger, who Craven originally conceived as the epitome of evil, to a cartoon character – Edward Scissorhands with a bit of a nasty temper. When Craven finally clambered back on board to direct Part 7, *Wes Craven's New Nightmare*, he introduced the convoluted but inventive 'film within a film' device, with Freddy coming to life to terrorise the star of the first movie, Heather Langenkamp. It's genuinely unsettling and by comparison, it's a masterpiece. With Parts 1 and 7 both available individually, and both enhanced by top-notch director's commentaries, if the distributers think that you should shell-out over £65 for the entire boxset then they must be bloody dreaming.

FINAL VERDICT

Picture ☆☆☆☆ Sound ☆☆☆☆
Entertainment ☆☆ Extras ☆☆☆☆ Value ☆☆
OVERALL ☆☆

PEEPING TOM

Price: $30-35
Supplied by: Personal import
Type of disc: Dual layer, single-sided

No of chapters: 27
Film format(s)/length: 16:9 widescreen enhanced / 101 mins
Audio format: Mono
Director: Michael Powell
Starring: Carl Boehm, Moira Shearer, Anna Massey
Year made: 1960
Extras: Scene access; a Channel 4 documentary entitled *A Very British Psycho* that profiles *Peeping Tom* screenwriter Leo Marks; audio commentary by film theorist Laura Mulvey; still picture gallery of rare behind-the-scenes photos; original theatrical trailer; subtitles for the hearing impaired in English.

Time and time again, The Criterion Collection has breathed new life into classic and alternative films, always going the extra mile to present the definitive version of a director's vision. It's done it once more with this forgotten masterpiece of British cinema – *Peeping Tom*. Traumatised as a boy by his psychologist father, sex, death and voyeurism become one in the disturbed mind of focus puller Mark Lewis (Boehm). To vent his anger, he skewers women with a knife-sharp leg on his camera tripod while filming his victims' shocked faces. Calamity strikes when Lewis and neighbour Vivian (Massey) get romantically close, just when the police move in. Although the concept is repugnant, Peeping Tom is a profound and incredibly original film and more relevant than ever given the recent spate of voyeuristic movies like *The Truman Show* and *EdTV*. The extra feature *A Very British Psycho* is the fascinating story of Leo Marks' life as both screenwriter for *Peeping Tom* and as one of the Allies' top code makers and breakers during WWII. The Channel 4 documentary reports on how the critics were appaled by the subject matter and condemned the film. Other extras include a thought provoking commentary by Laura Mulvey which is free of pretension. There's also dozens of rare stills which act as an interesting peek behind-the-scenes at one of the UK's finest directors. This DVD is simply the best way to watch the restored and enhanced *Peeping Tom*, an intriguing entry in cinematic history and a beautifully packaged disc to boot.

FINAL VERDICT

Picture ☆☆☆☆ Sound ☆☆☆
Entertainment ☆☆☆☆☆
Extras ☆☆☆☆☆ Value ☆☆☆☆
OVERALL ☆☆☆☆

ROBOCOP: DIRECTOR'S CUT

Price: Varies
Supplied by: Personal import
Type of disc: Dual layer, single-sided

No of chapters: 26
Film format(s)/length: 1.66:1widescreen / 103 mins
Director: Paul Verhoeven
Starring: Peter Weller, Nancy Allen, Kurtwood Smith
Year made: 1987
Extras: Chapter access; animated menus; director's commentary; storyboard-to-film comparison; storyboards for 2 deleted scenes; 2 trailers; complete *Cinefex* article.

Paul Verhoeven's first American film remains his best to date – for all the Dutchman's celebrations of the cinema of excess (*Total Recall, Basic Instinct, Showgirls, Starship Troopers*), *RoboCop* is his movie that clicks on every level. This Director's Cut is the film that he made before the American censors got their hands on it. In an unspecified near-future, Detroit has had its police department privatised by the monolithic OCP corporation. When a boardroom demonstration of police droid ED-209 goes spectacularly (and messily) awry, weasely exec Bob Morton (Miguel Ferrer) sneaks in with his rival RoboCop programme. The catch is that for RoboCop to live, a human cop has to die, and nice-guy rozzer Murphy (Weller) is the luckless test subject, blown apart by sadistic druglord Clarence Boddicker (Smith) in one of cinema's most shocking and brutal scenes. Reborn as an invincible cyborg, Murphy sets on a mission to clean up Detroit, but soon finds that his buried human memories are setting him on a course of vengeance against his own killers. In the wrong hands, *RoboCop* could have been complete tripe, as the subsequent sequels, TV spin-offs and even cartoons proved. However, the combination of blackest-of-black satire, plus Verhoeven's penchant for seeing just how far he can take things, gave it greatness. But the main story is as powerful now as it was when Ronald Reagan was in the White House. This being a Criterion DVD, it's laden with extras. The commentary by Verhoeven, along with the writer and producer, gives tremendous insight into the film-making process, as well as Verhoeven's own mind. According to Verhoeven, Murphy's transformation into RoboCop is a Christ metaphor, his death being the crucifixion. Mind you, Jesus wasn't resurrected with a huge gun to blast the crap out of his oppressors, so you have to wonder which version of the Bible he's reading. Also present are two trailers, a storyboard-to-film comparison, storyboards for two deleted scenes and 'Shooting RoboCop', which demonstrates DVD's capacity as a multimedia tool by including the entire 1987 *Cinefex* article (*Cinefex* being the film industry's special effects bible) on the making of the movie, complete with animated pictures and appropriate clips. The only downside – but one that we can live with – is that the encod-

ing isn't always up to par, with visible artifacts and graininess in several of the scenes. But the weight of extras compensates, and, best of all, it's a Region 0 DVD, meaning it'll play anywhere in the world. Buy it from the States, raise a middle finger to the BBFC and sit back to watch a modern classic – uncut.

FINAL VERDICT

Picture ☆☆☆ Sound ☆☆☆
Entertainment ☆☆☆☆☆
Extras ☆☆☆☆☆ Value ☆☆☆☆
OVERALL ☆☆☆☆☆

SAVING PRIVATE RYAN

Price: $20-22
Supplied by: Personal import
Type of disc: Dual layer, single-sided
No of chapters: 20
Film format(s)/length: 1:85:1 widescreen enhanced / 169 mins
Audio format: Dolby Digital 5.1
Director: Steven Spielberg
Starring: Tom Hanks, Edward Burns, Matt Damon
Year made: 1998
Extras: Scene access; exclusive message from Steven Spielberg; documentary *Into the Breach*; 2 theatrical trailers; production notes; cast and filmakers biographies.

This is an incredibly realistic and poignant account of the futile consequences of war. There's no bravery or overt heroism, just ordinary men who are fighting for their freedom. These are men who had no choice but to stand up to the dark oppression that existed in the middle part of the 20th century and it is this simplicity which the director captures so magnificently. Steven Spielberg goes way beyond the sci-fi fun of *ET* and the fairytale swashbuckling of Indiana Jones to create a movie that is in a sense not a movie, more a recreation of the gritty truth of war. It's a harrowing pastiche of the wasteful carnage that took 50 million souls by the end of the Second World War. This is Spielberg's gift to the generation who do not know and do not fully grasp what happened. It's also an indelible tribute so that we may never forget the price paid by our forefathers to enable us to live free in this and centuries to come. More a documentary than movie, *Saving Private Ryan* was so intense a picture that upon release, counselling was offered to some who saw it. Veterans were quoted as saying that this is the only movie that actually lived up to what took place back in 1944. The movie centres around a squad of American soldiers who land on Omaha beach as part of the D-Day invasion. Once the beach is taken, they are assigned a special mission. Captain John Miller (Hanks) must take his men behind enemy lines to find Private James Ryan (Damon), last surviving brother of 4 who have been killed in combat. Faced with impossible odds, the men begin to question their orders. The mission seems crazy. Why are 8 men risking their lives to save one? Surrounded by the brutal realities of war, each man searches for his own answer as he does his duty. The movie delivers powerful performances by all the cast. Hanks in particular proves there are huge depths to his acting talent as he struggles with the mental and physical pressures of bringing the realism of Captain John Miller to life. "On one hand, it's a grand adventure story," he points out, "but it is also a very human story". In a sense, Hanks' performance lends a sense of believeability to his character not present in his other roles. You know it's Tom Hanks the actor up there on the screen, but you become so immersed in his character, it's very easy to forget. The atmosphere and grime of the movie bring a whole new depth to acting and filmmaking. As a movie this is incredible – as a DVD, it really is a true showpiece. It's not a flick to show the family looking for fun on a Saturday afternoon, but crank up the Dolby Digital soundtrack, and on a large widescreen TV, *Saving Private Ryan* will deliver a jaw-dropping experience to viewers. Any DVD sceptics will be swayed by this movie. The crystal picture quality is magnificent. Obviously, the care, time and investment Spielberg has dedicated to the dying laserdisc format has been transferred to the DVD format with this release. The sound is incredible, delivering clear tones and thundering bass that'll rattle the ducks off the wall! The extras are pretty good, too. The one and only grumble about this disc is there's no director's commentary. Something that would have been fascinating. Instead we are 'treated' to an exclusive message, which is basically a plug for the D-Day museum opening in New Orleans. A bit tough if you live in the UK! Luckily, there's also a very watchable *Into the Breach* documentary surrounding the actual events of D-Day and Spielberg's fascination with war films. "Making a war movie isn't glamorous to me," Spielberg reflects. "My dad brought home stories of war and explained to me how unglamorous war is. What I tried to do in this film was approximate the look and the sounds and even the smells of what combat is really like." Spielberg has achieved just that and the DVD accentuates it beautifully.

FINAL VERDICT

Picture ☆☆☆☆☆ Sound ☆☆☆☆☆
Entertainment ☆☆☆☆☆
Extras ☆☆☆☆☆ Value ☆☆☆☆☆

OVERALL ☆☆☆☆☆

SCARFACE: THE COLLECTOR'S EDITION

Price: $25-30
Supplied by: Personal import
Type of disc: Dual layer, single-sided
No of chapters: 35
Film format(s)/length: 2.35:1 widescreen / 170 mins
Audio format: Dolby Surround
Director: Brian De Palma
Starring: Al Pacino, Michelle Pfeiffer, Steven Bauer
Year made: 1983
Extras: *The Making of Scarface* – 50 minute featurette featuring interviews with Oliver Stone, Al Pacino, Martin Bregman and Brian De Palma; outtakes; production notes, and notes on the cast and filmmakers; theatrical trailers; *Carlito's Way* trailer; still file; multilingual subtitles.

A remake of the more sedate 1932 version, *Scarface* pools the talents of director Brian De Palma, writer Oliver Stone and the ever-mesmerising Al Pacino in the title role. Together they have concocted a strong gangster movie, taking the standard rise and fall story, then adding plenty of trademark De Palma tension-filled moments along with an infamous chainsaw scene. The major selling point of the DVD version is undoubtedly the extras. Top of the bill is the 50 minute feature on the making of the film, worth watching for the scene by scene comparison with the original, and hilarious snippets of the 'dubbed for television' version. Elsewhere, you'll find production stills, trailers and outtakes, too (although as usual with cut-scenes, there's not much to see). Under the weight of these extras, the basics do suffer. Whilst the surround mix does a competent job (although the gunfights cry out for a full 5.1 soundtrack), the picture (not enhanced for widescreen televisions) really shows its age throughout the film. The image is still perfectly watchable, but this must rank as a disappointment on what is supposed to be the definitive Collector's Edition. Oh, and it's crying out for an audio commentary, too. It's worth the money for the production feature, and of course *Scarface* will always be the kind of movie that gets rewatched frequently. You're just left feeling that they should have done that little bit more.

FINAL VERDICT

Picture ☆☆ Sound ☆☆☆
Entertainment ☆☆☆☆☆
Extras ☆☆☆☆ Value ☆☆☆
OVERALL ☆☆☆

THE SHINING

Price: $20-25
Supplied by: Personal import
Type of disc: Dual layer, single-sided
No of chapters: 40
Film format(s)/length: 4:3 regular / 144 mins
Audio format: Mono
Director: Stanley Kubrick
Starring: Jack Nicholson, Shelley Duvall, Scatman Crothers
Year made: 1980
Extras: Scene access; English and French subtitles; *The Making of The Shining* documentary; trailer.

The most terrifying film ever? Possibly. *The Shining* is certainly up there with the likes of *The Silence of the Lambs*, *The Exorcist*, *Se7en* and *Don't Look Now* in the scary stakes. Adapted from Stephen King's novel, *The Shining* is at heart a haunted house (or hotel, in this case) story that is treated to Kubrick's trademarks of insane attention to detail and a cold, clinical camera that traps the characters in its stare like specimens under a microscope. All done at an incredibly great length. Writer Jack Torrance (Nicholson) takes on the job of winter caretaker at the remote Overlook Hotel, bringing his wife Wendy (Duvall) and son Danny (Danny Lloyd) with him. Before long, the combination of isolation and the hotel's evil aura has turned Jack into Jaaaaaack, sending him rampaging through the corridors with an axe. How will wet Wendy and psychic Danny survive? *The Shining*'s scares aren't of the 'made you jump' kind (though it does have some shock moments) but instead build up foreboding and dread over a long period to pay off the rampage at the end. Other directors would have made a much shorter film, but then unsettling moments like the two little girls and the woman in the bath wouldn't have been nearly as disturbing. So, you'd expect a fantastic film by a revered (and recently deceased) director to come on the mother of all DVDs, right? Well, expectations exist to be dashed. *The Shining* has been landed with a DVD transfer that's actually more horrifying than the film itself. The shocking lack of a widescreen version lops off Kubrick's fearful symmetry at both sides, and the picture itself is disappointing, with a lot of grain and dot-crawl. There's also a bizarre distortion at the very top of the picture that causes vertical lines (and in this film, there are loads of them) to bend inwards toward the middle of the screen. The distortion wasn't on the VHS version, so it has to be an error in mastering. The sound isn't great, either. You've got no choice but to listen to it in mono, since that's how the film was made, but you still have to crank up the volume quite a way to hear everything. The only plus points on the DVD of *The Shining* are the original trailer, which in nice contrast to modern trailers doesn't tell you exactly what's going to happen (*Sphere*, anybody?), and a 30-minute documentary made for the BBC by Kubrick's daughter Vivian about the making of the movie. If not for these, *The Shining* could easily take an award for one of the the worst DVD transfers to date. At least it wasn't a flipper!

FINAL VERDICT

Picture ☆☆ Sound ☆☆

Entertainment ☆☆☆☆☆ Extras ☆☆☆☆ Value ☆☆

OVERALL ☆☆

THE SILENCE OF THE LAMBS

Price: $25-35
Supplied by: Personal import
Type of disc: Single layer, double-sided
No of chapters: 28
Film format(s)/length: 1.85:1 widescreen / 118 mins
Audio Format: Dolby Surround
Director: Jonathan Demme
Starring: Anthony Hopkins, Jodie Foster, Scott Glenn
Year made: 1991
Extras: Audio commentary by Jonathan Demme, Jodie Foster, Anthony Hopkins, screenwriter Ted Tally and FBI agent John Douglas; 7 deleted scenes; excellent film to storyboard comparison; storyboards; FBI Crime Classification Manual (text on screen); Voices of Death: word for word statements of convicted serial killers.

To quote the package, The Criterion Collection is, "A continuing series of classic and important contemporary films." It's an achievement for any film to be selected for the Criterion treatment, and *The Silence of the Lambs*, one of the strongest character driven thrillers of the last decade, now has the honour of sitting next to the likes of *Great Expectations*, *Oliver Twist* and, er, *Armageddon*. The film itself, you should know the score by now: Foster's rookie FBI agent enlists the help of imprisoned killer Hannibal the Cannibal (Hopkins) to track down a new menace, Buffalo Bill. Add 5 Oscars to the mix and standout performances by Hopkins, Foster and Glenn and already you should be taking notice. And the good news starts here. As with Criterion's *RoboCop* disc, this is a region free affair. Furthermore, whilst you only get a Dolby Surround audio track, it suits the film well and complements the generally sharp picture. On top of all of that, the disc boasts, as you'd expect for the higher than usual price, its fair share of extras. Starting with the audio commentary, 5 of the film's personnel offer their thoughts on the same track (Hopkins, Foster, Demme, screenwriter Ted Tally and FBI agent John Douglas). There's some great anecdotes (including the fact that Gene Hackman was originally down to direct!) although it does seem a little too structured at times. One under-used option worth mentioning is the ability to flick in and out of the commentary via the audio key on your remote. There's deleted scenes too, in this case mainly extended versions of those that made the final cut. Nonetheless, they still rank as better than average. As for the rest? Well Criterion's extras are, for the money, very take it or leave it. Not many companies would be willing to produce extracts from the FBI Crime Classification Manual or dozens of storyboard illustrations, but then not everyone will be willing to plod through this material. The chilling printed interviews with real-life serial killers shows just how deep this DVD goes. A basic behind-the-scenes feature and the original trailer are glaring omissions though. Bottom line? You get a great deal on the disc, but much of it you'll only check out once. It's the definitive version of the film though, and features one of the creepiest menus since *The Texas Chain Saw Massacre*.

FINAL VERDICT

Picture ☆☆☆☆ Sound ☆☆☆

Entertainment ☆☆☆☆☆

Extras ☆☆☆☆☆ Value ☆☆☆

OVERALL ☆☆☆☆

TERMINATOR 2: JUDGMENT DAY ULTIMATE EDITION

Price: $28-32

Supplied by: Personal import

Type of disc: Dual layer, double-sided

No of chapters: 72/79/80

Film format(s)/length: 2.35:1 anamorphic / 136/153/156 mins

Audio format: Dolby Digital 5.1/DTS/Dolby Surround 2.0

Director: James Cameron

Starring: Arnold Schwarzenegger, Linda Hamilton, Robert Patrick

Year made: 1991

Extras: Scene access; seamless branching between Theatrical, Special and Ultimate Edition versions; *The Making of T2* featurette (30 mins); *T2: More Than Meets the Eye* featurette (22 mins); *The Making of T2: 3-D: Breaking the Screen Barrier* (23 mins); Data Core *T2* supplement (50 chapters including text, stills, video and commentary); Interrogation Surveillance Archives (70 video segments including interviews and behind-the-scenes information); hidden 'Ultimate Edition' version of *T2*; cast and crew biographies; 3 teaser

trailers (1 US, 2 Japanese); 5 theatrical trailers (2 US, 3 Japanese); *T2 Special Edition* trailer; *Terminator 2* original screenplay (574 still frames); original storyboard sequences (over 700); THX test signal package; audio commentary featuring interviews with 26 members of the cast and crew; DVD-ROM features; 32-page collector's booklet; Easter eggs; subtitles in English

There has always been something special about Cameron's *Terminator* films. The possibility that machine will one day take over from man as the controlling world power is an educated vision. But this doesn't mean that your microwave or toaster deserves a pre-emptive beating just yet, as the future is not set... Those unfamiliar with *Terminator 2: Judgment Day*, or indeed its pioneering prequel will be in the minority – and deservedly so! T2 sees the resurrection of Cyberdyne Systems Terminator model 101 (Schwarzenegger) – hey, it's a factory line, they all look the same – who is re-programmed to protect the future leader of the human resistance John Connor (Edward Furlong) from the deadly advances of the shape-shifting liquid metal T-1000 (Patrick). After their sterling work on *The Abyss: Special Edition*, the production team responsible was given the task of creating another Cameron DVD masterpiece. Led by creative supervisor Van Ling (who leads the audio commentary), no expense was spared to create the digital CG animated menus, which are situated within the future SkyNet compound. Featuring an amazing triple bill of editions, the seamless branching between the vibrantly coloured versions is, for want of a better word, seamless! Yet the disc also plays host to an audio bonanza of Dolby Digital 5.1, DTS and Dolby Surround 2.0, all of which tantalise your ears with stunning clarity. Labelled as an 'Ultimate Edition DVD', this bold statement is justified the moment you take a peek at the disc's special features. Three featurettes engulf you within the *Terminator* phenomenon as Cameron, Schwarzenegger and many more of the cast and crew reveal the secrets behind the film, the special edition and the MCA/Universal *T2: 3-D* theme park experience. Although familiar extras such as trailers, biographies, screenplay, storyboards and DVD-ROM features do their part to beef up the jaw-dropping lineup of features, it's the 'Data Hub' and 'Interrogation Surveillance Archives' that surpass even the most optimistic of expectations. Within the Data Core lies a virtual film school on a disc; 50 chapters in chronological order that cover the film's making in its entirety, from its beginnings on a page into full-blown motion, presenting the viewer with a unique insight into the scope and challenge of a big budget action picture. The 'Interrogation Surveillance Archives' are comprised of 70 video segments, with Cameron and crew offering their unique insight into the film's secrets and conception. Both these interviews and the aforementioned Data Core are guaranteed to require hours to digest, making this disc worth purchasing on merit alone. But combine a classic Arnie/Cameron flick with the greatest special features to grace the DVD format and you have a disc that demands purchasing. Buy it or be terminated!

FINAL VERDICT

Picture ☆ ☆ ☆ ☆   Sound ☆☆☆☆
Entertainment ☆☆☆☆☆
Extras ☆☆☆☆☆   Value ☆☆☆☆☆
OVERALL ☆☆☆☆☆

THE THIRD MAN

Price: $25-30
Supplied by: Personal import
Type of disc: Dual layer, single-sided
No of chapters: 24
Film format(s)/length: 4:3 regular / 104 mins
Audio format: Mono
Director: Carol Reed
Starring: Joseph Cotten, Alida Valli, Orson Welles
Year made: 1949
Extras: Scene access; video introduction by Peter Bogdanovich; the alternate opening voice-over narration by Joseph Cotten used in the US version; abridged recording of Graham Greene's *Third Man* treatment read by actor Richard Clarke; *The Third Man* radio shows: *A Ticket to Tangiers* written and performed by Orson Welles, and Lux Radio Theater of the *Third Man* adaptation performed by Joseph Cotten; archival footage of composer Anton Karas and the film's very famous sewer location; production history with rare behind-the-scenes photographs; original theatrical trailer; 50th anniversary rerelease trailer; restoration demonstration; booklet containing production notes and photos; English subtitles available for the hearing impaired.

British cinema has had a rocky history. It's a catalogue of triumphs, disasters, near-misses and could-have-beens, but if there is one motion picture that the UK industry can be justly proud of, it's Carol Reed's *The Third Man*. What a shame that it took an American company to turn it into one of very best DVDs ever. Holly Martins (Cotten), an American pulp fiction writer, travels to war-torn Vienna in search of his oldest friend Harry Lime (Welles) and a job. On arriving, he discovers that Lime was killed in a car accident. However, as he talks to Harry's embittered mistress

Anna (Valli) and the cynical military police chief Major Calloway (Trevor Howard) he finds Lime has turned into an unscrupulous racketeer, preying on poverty-stricken citizens. When discrepancies crop up between witnesses' statements, Martins is determined to find out the identity of the 'third man' who supposedly carried Lime's body away. Angled cinematography and *noir*-esque shadows compellingly capture the forbidding sense of fatalism that pervades the film and city. The cast are outstanding and the DVD is nothing short of a masterpiece, the Criterion Collection once again setting the standard for all DVD producers to match. For starters, the film looks and sounds better than ever! The production history is intelligently written and the introduction is thoughtfully composed by Bogdanovich, a man lucky enough to have interviewed Welles before he died. The *pièce de résistance* though has to be the two radio shows dug up from 1951. In *A Ticket to Tangiers*, Welles reprises his famous role, but this time as more of a charming rogue than the monster before. In an ideal world, all classic landmark films would be treated as reverently as this on DVD, but until that day we can enjoy this richly rewarding film on an equally rewarding disc.

FINAL VERDICT

Picture ☆☆☆☆☆   Sound ☆☆☆
Entertainment ☆☆☆☆☆
Extras ☆☆☆☆☆   Value ☆☆☆☆☆
OVERALL ☆☆☆☆☆

THE X-FILES: SEASON 1 COLLECTOR'S EDITION

Price: $110-$150
Supplied by: Personal import
Type of disc: 6x dual layer, single-sided, 1x single layer, single-sided
No of chapters: 315
Film format(s)/length: 4:3 regular / 24 x 44 mins
Audio format: Dolby Surround
Director: Various
Starring: David Duchovny, Gillian Anderson
Year made: 1993-4
Extras: Scene access; *The Truth Behind Season One* featurette (11 mins); Chris Carter interviews, about his 12 favourite episodes; 12 *Behind the Truth* making-of featurettes; 2 deleted scenes from 'Pilot'; original FX scene from 'Fallen Angel'; scenes from selected episodes in foreign languages, including Japanese and German; 10 and 20-second TV trailers for each episode; soundtrack in English and French; subtitles in English and Spanish; DVD-ROM features: Web site and links, 'Roots of Conspiracy' game, case files from Jane

Goldman's *Book of the Unexplained, Volume 1*, episode guide.

If we gave a mark for presentation, *The X-Files: Season 1* would easily get 5 stars. The packaging is gorgeous. Barely occupying more space than a VHS case, it magically unfolds to reveal no fewer than 7 discs and a booklet. Add to this the glossy (and expensive) foil-printed sleeve, and you have a genuine work of art. Do we really need to explain what the show is about? No, we don't. Suffice it to say that it's quite a shock to go back almost 7 years to find a fresh-faced Mulder and a slightly chubby (and later, quite obviously pregnant) Scully, who in early episodes favoured the Clarice Starling look. At this stage, *The X-Files* was new, different, exciting and dark, and the conspiracy stories hadn't yet collapsed under the weight of their own contradictions. Six of the discs house a total of 24 episodes between them, the seventh containing most of the extras. While the extras are worth watching, they're something of a mixed bag. The only new item is *The Truth Behind Season One*, a specially-recorded retrospective featuring show creator Chris Carter and various others, but at only 11 minutes it doesn't reveal much that X-philes won't have heard before. Some of the short interviews with Carter have appeared previously on video, the alternate-language clips are amusing (Mulder's Japanese voice is a macho, samurai-sounding one) but only one-watch affairs, and the 48 episode trailers need a lot of patience to sit through. The well-presented DVD-ROM game is quite fun, though, requiring episode knowledge and puzzle skills to crack various codes and uncover evidence. To our eyes, the picture generally looked broadcast quality, on a par with (or even better than) the episodes currently airing on Sky. A few episodes, notably 'EBE' and 'Fire', seemed grainy and over-contrasty at times, but nowhere near the point of unwatchability. Considering how dark the shows are, Fox has made an extremely good job of transferring the episodes to DVD with a minimum of artefacting. The blacks are nice and solid, and don't display any unwanted blocking effects. On the sound front, the early seasons of *The X-Files* were only made in Dolby Surround, so that's what you get here. Even so, the audio is quite effective, balancing Mark Snow's creepy music against the dialogue and occasionally letting rip with some suitably spooky effects. For fans, this is an essential purchase - it's the best package you'll ever get. As for the sceptics, the sheer amount of material should be enough to convince even Scully it's worth investigating.

FINAL VERDICT

Picture ☆☆☆ Sound ☆☆☆

Entertainment ☆☆☆☆☆
Extras ☆☆☆☆ Value ☆☆☆☆
OVERALL ☆☆☆☆

WALLACE & GROMIT: THE FIRST THREE ADVENTURES

Price: $30-34
Supplied by: Personal import
Type of disc: Dual layer, single-sided
No of chapters: *Grand Day Out*: 7; *The Wrong Trousers*: 12; *A Close Shave*: 13
Film format(s)/length: 4:3 regular / 83 mins
Audio format: Dolby Surround
Director: Nick Park
Starring: Wallace, Gromit, Gwendoline
Year made: 1989-1995
Extras: 4 early animation pieces from Nick Park; festive graphics that were used on BBC2; brief but interesting behind-the-scenes look at *The Wrong Trousers*; subtitles in English and Spanish.

Okay then, explain this one. Wallace and Gromit, the Oscar-winning heroes of British animation, huge over here, not that well known over in the States, get their debut on DVD in America, not the UK. In light of this bizarre scheduling, if you're a fan of the Plasticine duo, you'd best get your hands on this import version. Bringing together their 3 escapes – *A Grand Day Out*, *The Wrong Trousers* and *A Close Shave* – the disc offers a way for fans to get the entire collection in better condition than ever. *A Close Shave* is often labelled the best of the 3 (the sheep is a masterstroke), although with Wallace and Gromit you can't really go wrong. All 3 adventures are superb entertainment, and when you consider that it'd cost you £25-30 to buy these on video, the $34 asking price (which can usually be beaten down to around £15 through shrewd online shopping) is a glorious bargain indeed. The digital presentation is excellent. The picture is clear and framed in the original 1.33:1 aspect ratio. The Dolby Surround track is fine too, although it does lack some of the subtlety that full 5.1 can provide. There's even a few extras in the form of Nick Park's early test pieces and a behind-the-scenes look at the making of *The Wrong Trousers*. Oh, and remember the year that all of BBC2's Christmas graphics were given the Wallace and Gromit touch? They're on here too. Overall, this is a nicely packaged collection - it's great to see such quality Plasticine inhabiting the world of DVD.

FINAL VERDICT

Picture ☆☆☆☆ Sound ☆☆☆
Entertainment ☆☆☆☆ Extras ☆☆☆ Value ☆☆☆☆
OVERALL ☆☆☆☆

built in

c·o·n·t·e·n·t·s

swindon

The SWINDON WORKS

The decision to site the Great Western Railway's workshops at Swindon was made in 1841 when the Board of Directors authorised construction of 'an establishment commensurate with the wants of the company'. Isambard Kingdom Brunel and Daniel Gooch, the Locomotive Superintendent had visited Swindon in 1840 and had chosen a site at the junction of the branch line to Cheltenham and the Great Western main line to Bristol.

The area chosen was some distance from the old town of Swindon in green fields a short distance from the Wilts and Berks canal. As well as already being a railway junction, Swindon was also the place where it was planned to change locomotives on Bristol-London trains, since west of the town Brunel's railway scaled severe gradients including the 1 in 100 of the Wootton Bassett Incline and the tunnel at Box.

Men streaming from the famous 'Tunnel Entrance' of the works at the end of a shift in the 1930s.

The works opened in January 1843 but was only a repair and maintenance facility in its early years. By 1846 however it had turned out its first engine 'The Great Western' starting a long tradition of locomotive manufacture on the site.

Further expansion took place in 1868 when the carriage and wagon works was opened at Swindon. In the years before 1900 the works grew steadily, although with the turn of a new century a new dynamic Locomotive Superintendent George Jackson Churchward transformed the works into a modern factory. Old equipment was replaced, and new workshops, particularly the huge 'A' Erecting Shop were built making Swindon one of the biggest and best equipped railway workshops in the world.

After the Great War the expansion slowed, but even so, by 1935 the works covered an area of 326 acres, 73 of which were roofed. After 1945 the works took some time to recover from the demands placed on it during the Second World War.

In the Second World War the adaptability and ingenuity of Swindon staff was called on time and time again as the works produced all manner of items for the war effort. The workshops became a munitions factory, producing shell and bomb cases, but it also built tanks, landing craft, and midget submarines. The War also saw the introduction of female staff, who came into the factory to replace men drafted into the services, working in every part of the works.

Staff testing the support fixings of a 250lb bomb at Swindon Works during the Second World War. The works manufactured a variety of bombs and shells for the war effort in both world wars.

swindon

After the nationalisation of the railways in 1948, locomotives built to Swindon designs continued to be produced, but there was a gradual decline in the fortunes of the works, marked by the production of the last steam locomotive for British Railways, 'Evening Star' in 1960. In 1963 a large part of the Carriage works was closed and works activity was concentrated on the area west of the Cheltenham line. The end of diesel locomotive production proved to be the final straw, and despite some resurgence in the 1970s, the closure of the works seemed inevitable. The end finally came in 1986 when British Rail Engineering Limited finally closed the works after 143 years of operation.

A female boilersmith inside the smokebox of a Great Western engine in the Boiler Shop in 1943.

The closure of the workshops left a core of important industrial buildings, and developers Carillion have undertaken a programme of refurbishment and restoration with its partners, to give them new uses. In 1995 the old Works Managers Offices were formally opened as the Headquarters of the National Monuments Record Centre, and two years later, the old Boiler Shop complex was converted into the Great Western Designer Outlet Village, a large shopping centre set within the old railway workshops. As well as the STEAM museum, further developments are due to take place in the next few years to complete the restoration of this historic site.

A view of the 'R' Machine Shop, now the STEAM museum around the turn of the century.

The MUSEUM BUILDING

Like many buildings on the old Swindon Works site the museum has a complex history.

The entrance area, known as the 'Scraggery' to Swindon staff, was built in 1846 as part of the original Brunel works, and consisted of a two-storey machine shop. What is now the Special Exhibitions Gallery was a blacksmiths shop built at the same time. In 1865 a separate building, the 'R' Machine Shop was built, but the space between the two was not roofed in until 1872. Further alterations were made in the period 1929-1931 when the offices on

The museum building was a Machine Shop for most of its life. Staff are working on a variety of machines in this 1950s view of the workshop.

b
u
i
l
d
i
n
g

the north side of the building were added. To the south, next to the main line, an extension to the building and the adjoining 'B' Shed was made. In 1967 the workshop was gutted, renamed '20' Shop and converted into a wheel shop. After closure in 1986 the workshop was used by the restoration workshop now occupying the south extension to the museum.

The LOCOMOTIVE WORKS

The workshops at Swindon were divided into two sections, the Locomotive Works and the Carriage and Wagon Works. Each had their own character, and the staff employed there needed quite different skills in many cases.

The construction of a Great Western Railway locomotive involved a large number of staff and workshops providing component parts for final assembly in the erecting shop, where the finished product was finally built. The process began in the offices. With 12,000 staff, and many tasks and operations to manage and account for, a complex bureaucracy was required. Hundreds of clerks were employed and in many cases, information was laboriously recorded in ledgers by hand. Women were first employed in the offices during the First World War, altering the male dominated atmosphere for good. Even after the war women continued to be employed in the offices, although they were expected to resign when they married!

The inside of the original 'A' Erecting Shop in 1904, not long after its completion. Note the large gas light hanging from the roof.

One of the many women employed in the works during the Second World War, polishing locomotive connecting rods in the 'A' Shop.

At the start of the physical process of locomotive construction were the 'hot' shops. In the foundry, ferrous and non-ferrous castings were made, and in the steam hammer shop, drop or steam hammers were used to forge large items like connecting rods, or to stamp out forgings to the correct profile.

The museum building was one of a series of Machine Shops situated around the works. Here metal components could be shaped and turned to the correct size ready for fitting onto locomotives by machines such as lathes, drills, grinders, planers or slotters. Before the advent of electricity, machines were belt driven, with stationary steam locomotives situated outside each workshop to supply the power to drive them. The machine shop display in the museum features a number of belt driven machines which have been restored by the Friends of Swindon Railway Museum. The oldest, a Bevel Gear Cutter, dates back to 1887.

the works

The noisiest workshop was without doubt the Boiler Shop. Here boilers were assembled and repaired, and the din of hundreds of men using hydraulic riveters, welding machines and hammers was tremendous. No wonder most boilersmiths were deaf by the age of thirty! There were also a multitude of other specialist workshops producing parts. The familiar brass domes or safety valve covers were made in the 'K' shop, whilst the Spring Shop made both leaf and coil springs. When the works closed in 1986 the production methods had changed little in a century or more. In the 'T' Shop, whistles, safety valves, buffers and other items were made before being sent through to the Erecting Shop, where they could be fitted onto new or repaired locomotives.

The great 'A' erecting shop was a huge building dedicated to the final assembly of locomotives. Completed in 1921, it was the place where the locomotive jigsaw was finally completed, although heavy repairs were also carried out there. With the aid of two 100 ton cranes, locomotives could be easily moved around the workshop. When an engine was finally completed, it could be taken out on trial on the main line, or could be run on the Locomotive Test plant in the 'A' Shop, where static locomotives could be run up to 80mph.

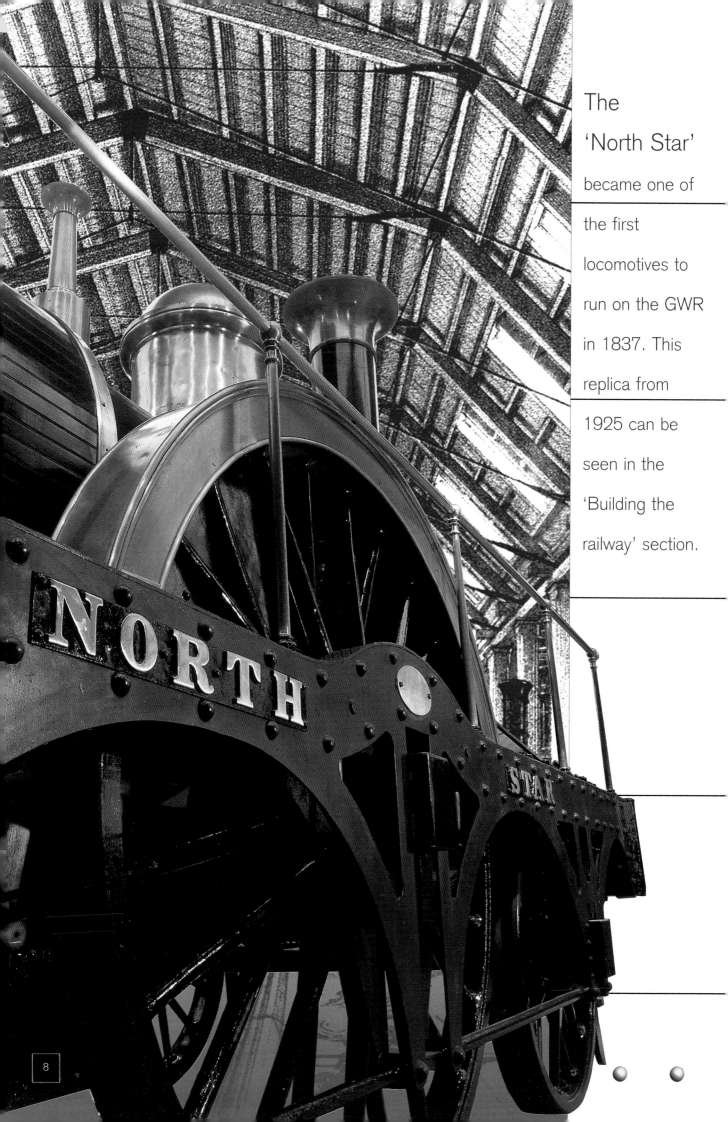

The 'North Star' became one of the first locomotives to run on the GWR in 1837. This replica from 1925 can be seen in the 'Building the railway' section.

Swindon LOCOMOTIVES

The locomotives built and operated by the Great Western Railway have always attracted great attention from engineers, enthusiasts and the general public, and there is not the space in a guide of this type to give a detailed description of the engines which made the company so famous. The locomotives on display in the museum provide a good cross section of Great Western motive power and show something of the variety of engines produced at Swindon.

Stephenson was happy to regauge them to Brunel's 7ft broad gauge. The 'North Star' seen in the 'Building the Railway' section of the museum is a 1925 replica of the engine which became one of the first to run on the GWR in 1837. Although a replica, 'North Star' does give an insight into how early GWR locomotives looked and operated.

The Swindon Engine House in 1846, from a lithograph by J.C Bourne. One of Daniel Gooch's 'Firefly' class engines is receiving attention on the traverser.

When the Great Western Railway was first planned, Brunel had intended to have locomotives for his new line built by manufacturers to specifications he had produced himself. When the company appointed Daniel Gooch as its first locomotive superintendent in 1837 he discovered that Brunel's locomotives were a disaster. Known as 'Freaks' it was reported that these engines could hardly pull themselves along, let alone a train! Fortunately Gooch was able to obtain two engines from the Robert Stephenson company which had been originally intended for a 5' 6" gauge railway in the United States. The scheme had failed, and

The high point of the broad gauge era was the 'Iron Duke' 4-2-2 express engine which was built at Swindon from 1851 onwards. These graceful engines were the mainstay of express services, and survived after rebuilding, until the end of Brunel's broad gauge in 1892.

A front view of one of Daniel Gooch's broad gauge 4-2-2 express locomotives.

One of Steam's most spectacular exhibits - King George V

George Jackson Churchward took over from Dean as Locomotive Superintendent in 1902 and produced designs for a stream of Great Western locomotives which were well ahead of their time, and were to influence GWR locomotive policy for the next 40 years. Churchward aimed to produce a complete set of standard locomotive designs from express passenger, heavy freight, mixed traffic and tank engines. As well as his famous 'Saint' and 'Star' express engines, he also introduced a number of tank locomotives including the 4200 2-8-0 class. The sole example of a Churchward design in the museum is displayed in a skeletal form in our Erecting Shop displays. No.4248, built at Swindon in 1916 was used for many years on coal trains in South Wales, as well as on china clay trains in Cornwall.

The work done by Churchward was expanded on by C.B. Collett, Chief Mechanical Engineer from 1922 to 1942. His 'Castle and 'King' designs were the benchmark for express passenger development between the two World Wars, and we are fortunate to have examples of both in our museum. 'Caerphilly Castle' was built at Swindon in 1923 and was the first of a class of over 200 express engines used all over the GWR network. No. 6000 'King George V' built in 1927 is the flagship of the Great Western Railway, and achieved fame when it

Gooch was succeeded by Joseph Armstrong as Locomotive Superintendent in 1864, and both he and William Dean who took over in 1877 designed a wide range of locomotives for both broad and standard gauge use. The oldest locomotive in the collection is 0-6-0 'Dean Goods' built in 1897. William Dean's design is simple and robust, and this type of engine was used on coal trains and other goods working until it was relegated onto lighter duties with the introduction of more modern designs. Many of the class were used by the War Department during both World Wars, although No.2516 was not taken overseas. It did have a very long working life, and was still active in the early 1950s before being taken out of service for preservation.

travelled to the United States in the same year for the Centenary Celebrations of the Baltimore & Ohio Railroad. It made such an impression that it was presented with the bell which is still mounted to its bufferbeam. The final Chief Mechanical Engineer of the Great Western Railway was F.W. Hawksworth, who succeeded Collett in 1942. Wartime shortages and the need to concentrate on war work did not give him the opportunity to design large numbers of engines in the way his predecessors had done. Most successful were his 'County' class 4-6-0 express engines, none of which was preserved.

Numerous examples of this type of engine had been used on the GWR for many years, the term 'pannier' referring to the water tanks on each side of the boiler which resemble pannier bags. After nationalisation, Swindon became part of the British Railways network, and the post of Chief Mechanical Engineer ceased to exist. Swindon maintained an independent policy on locomotive development, and tested and used two gas turbine locomotives before beginning to build diesel designs. These too used a different philosophy to that practised by other regions, since instead of constructing diesel electric designs,

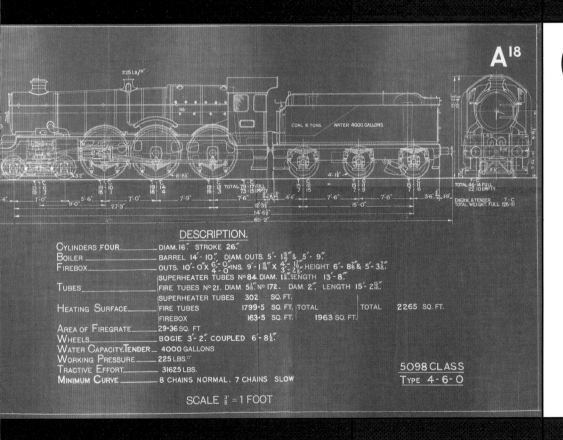

GWR
B L U E P R I N T

Castle
Class
locomotive

A¹⁸

225 LB/□″

COAL 6 TONS.   WATER 4000 GALLONS.

TOTAL 46·14 FULL
22· 10 EMPTY.

ENGINE & TENDER   T - C
TOTAL WEIGHT. FULL 126-11

DESCRIPTION.

CYLINDERS FOUR. — DIAM. 16″. STROKE 26″.
BOILER — BARREL 14′-10″. DIAM. OUTS. 5′-1 9/16″ & 5′-9″.
FIREBOX — OUTS. 10′-0″ X 6′-0″. INS. 9′-1 5/8″ X 4′-1 3/8″. HEIGHT 6′-8 5/8″ & 5′-3 7/8″.
SUPERHEATER TUBES Nº 84. DIAM. 1 5/16″. LENGTH 13′-8″.
TUBES — FIRE TUBES Nº 21. DIAM. 5 1/8″. Nº 172. DIAM. 2″. LENGTH 15′-2 5/8″.
SUPERHEATER TUBES   302   SQ. FT.
HEATING SURFACE — FIRE TUBES   1799·5 SQ. FT.   TOTAL   TOTAL   2265 SQ. FT.
FIREBOX   163·5 SQ. FT.   1963 SQ. FT.
AREA OF FIREGRATE — 29·36 SQ. FT
WHEELS — BOGIE 3′-2″. COUPLED 6′-8 1/2″.
WATER CAPACITY. TENDER — 4000 GALLONS
WORKING PRESSURE — 225 LBS.□″
TRACTIVE EFFORT — 31625 LBS.
MINIMUM CURVE — 8 CHAINS NORMAL. 7 CHAINS SLOW

5098 CLASS
TYPE 4-6-0

SCALE 3/8″ = 1 FOOT

However, an example of his 1947 design of pannier tank locomotive No. 9400 is on display in the 'Great Western Goods' section of the museum.

Swindon adopted diesel hydraulic locomotives building a number of classes of locomotive including the 'Warship' and 'Western' engines. The end of locomotive production at Swindon in the 1960s appeared to be the end for the workshops, but there was a brief swansong in 1978, when Swindon built 20 diesel shunters for Kenyan railways, a fitting finale

Opposite left: A view of one of the most famous GWR engines 'King George V' taken shortly after its return to England from the USA in 1927.

The CARRIAGE WORKS

Covering an area of over 150 acres, the Carriage Works encompassed a wide variety of trades and skills, many much different to those employed by the Locomotive Department. Once again the process of building carriages and wagons consisted of a number of smaller workshops, all producing component parts for the finished product.

The Carriage Department had its own 'hot' shops, where steam or drop hammers were employed, as well as large blacksmiths shops. Once produced, parts were taken to the fitting and machine shop where metal fittings such as axleboxes, bogies, brake gear, door handles and other fittings were made. Wheel lathes were employed in 16 Shop, where wheels were manufactured and refurbished. The metal tyres on wheels were reprofiled on these lathes, and large hydraulic presses were used to press the wheels onto axles to the correct gauge.

A carpenter at work building furniture in the Carriage Works. The GWR was in many ways self sufficient, and supplied itself with most of the furniture and equipment it needed.

Timber for the construction of carriages and wagons came from the works sawmill. Enormous logs were cut into more manageable sizes. Much of the timber used in the Great Western era is now endangered rainforest species. Mahogany, teak and other woods were used in the building of carriages. 'The origin of woods' interactive display in the Carriage Works section, shows the range and geographical distribution of timber used by the railway. In the Finishing Shop, wood from the sawmill was used to make carriage doors, windows, seat backs and other interior fittings. In the Trimming Shop, upholsterers and other craftsmen manufactured items such as seats, cushions and luggage racks, as well as towels and bed linen used by the Hotels and Refreshment Departments.

The Carriage Body Shop. A number of carriages are under repair. In the foreground is the carriage door handle exhibit now on display in the Carriage Shop section of the museum.

The equivalent of the Locomotive Erecting Shop was the Carriage Body Shop. Carriages were assembled, underframes and bogies added before being painted, lettered and varnished.

Many hundreds of hours of work were required before a carriage could be added to the company's stock. The carriage in our display is typical of those produced after the First World War. After this date carriages were built with sheet steel being attached to a timber framework, rather than the all-wood method adopted previously. In a separate workshop, the rather less glamorous task of wagon construction continued, and thousands of wagons of all types were built and repaired.

Making carriage luggage rack nets in the Carriage Works in the 1920s. Female staff were employed in many parts of the Carriage Works, particularly in areas where skill and dexterity were required, such as the Trim Shop or the Upholsterers Shop.

Below left: Staff at work in the Carriage Body Shop in the 1920s.

The Carriage Works also carried out a number of other more general jobs for the railway. In the Machine and Fitting Shop ticket machines were built and maintained, and in the Carpenters Shop a huge variety of items in general use by staff were manufactured. Hand carts, platform seats, desks, chairs and other furniture were all built, all bearing the initials branded "GWR".

Outside THE WORKS

As the railway works grew up in the fields below the old town of Swindon a whole new community was born next to the workshops known as New Swindon.

There had been little tradition of heavy engineering in North Wiltshire, so most staff for the new works came from areas where railway engineering was already established such as Scotland, the North East of England and Manchester. The old town of Swindon could not cope with such an influx, and as a result, the Great Western Railway built what is now known as the Railway Village; an estate of 300 houses for its staff. Constructed by the London J. & C. Rigby, who were also constructing Swindon station, the village grew slowly, and by 1847 only 241 houses had been built. It was not until the 1860s that work was finally completed, but the standard of accommodation was rather better than industrial houses elsewhere. Even so, the cottages were overcrowded, one two-roomed house was recorded as having eleven inhabitants, man, wife, five children and four lodgers!

railway village

A view of the railway village in the 1860s. Steam can be seen rising from the Railway Works.

cradle to grave

By the time the village was complete it was already too small, and streets of red brick houses grew up around the ever expanding railway works. The town grew rapidly, and in 1900 the population of Old and New Swindon had reached over 40,000, growing further to 65,000 in 1935.

As well as the village, a number of other organisations were an integral part of The Railway Community in Swindon. The Mechanics Institution began in 1843, as an attempt by the men themselves to set up their own library. Because of the lack of social and educational facilities in the new town, they also held dances and other events. Because they had no building, they used rooms in the works themselves, including the upstairs part of what is now the entrance to the museum. By 1855 the Institution was big enough to have its own building in Emlyn Square, and this had excellent facilities, with a Theatre, Library and meeting rooms becoming the cultural centre of the town.

In 1847 the Great Western Medical Fund was set up, initially to fund the provision of a doctor for the village and the works, since none was provided in the vicinity. With the assistance of Daniel Gooch, the locomotive superintendent, the railway funded half the salary of a doctor. The rest was raised by the workmen themselves from their wages.

This arrangement continued, and the Medical Fund soon grew up into a superb 'Cradle to Grave' medical service, with doctors, dentists, opticians, public baths and a pharmacy. The new Medical Fund headquarters built in 1892 also included two swimming pools and Turkish baths. With this standard of care it was no wonder that the National Health Service drew much of its inspiration from developments at Swindon.

Unlike some other model village schemes set up in the Victorian period, the Great Western Railway did not insist on staff attending church. Provision was made for the spiritual welfare of the men however,

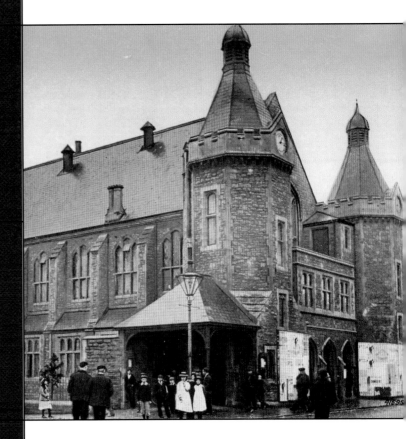

The Mechanics Institute, after its extension in 1893.

with the construction of St. Marks church in 1845. Close to the church was the GWR school opened soon after the works itself in 1843. Opposite the church was the GWR park, originally known as the 'Plantation'. It is rumoured that W.G. Grace the famous cricketer played here, although the park was better known by Swindon people as the place where the annual GWR Fete was held. Eagerly looked forward to every year, thousands crowded into the park with children receiving a piece of special fruit-cake, and tickets for two rides on the fairground which was always provided.

Building
THE GREAT WESTERN RAILWAY

The success of
early lines like the
Stockton &
Darlington Railway,
opened in 1825
and the Liverpool
and Manchester Railway, opened in 1830, played an
important part in persuading the business
community in Bristol that a rail link to London was
essential if it was to remain an important centre for
business and industry. After some discussion, a
committee was formed in 1833 to set up a railway,
and one of its first tasks was to appoint an engineer
for the new line. The man they chose was Isambard
Kingdom Brunel, a young engineer who had come
to prominence in the city by winning a competition to
design a suspension bridge over the River Avon at
Clifton.

Brunel's first task was to survey a route for the line,
and by August 1833 enough work had been done to
issue a prospectus for the new company, now to be
named the Great Western Railway. There was
considerable opposition to the railway, not least from
the Provost of Eton College, who thought that the
line would be 'injurious to the discipline of the
school and dangerous to the morals of pupils'. Two
attempts were needed to get the scheme through
Parliaments, but on 31 August 1835 Royal Assent
was finally granted allowing work to begin.

A reconstruction of the
opening of the GWR in
1838 when the London
to Maidenhead section
was finally completed.
This reconstruction took
place in 1935 for a film
made to celebrate the
company's centenary.

Work began almost immediately in the autumn of
1835 on construction of the 112 mile line, which it
was estimated would cost £2,500,000. Brunel had
a very strong idea of the railway he wanted.

A plan of the original
GWR line, from the
company prospectus,
issued in 1834.

It would not be a copy of schemes already built or under construction but would be a whole railway system, with its own unique buildings, track, track gauge and motive power. Working long hours, Brunel superintended almost every aspect of the project, producing drawings and specifications, meeting with landowners and contractors, and checking work as it progressed.

The construction of the railway was divided into numerous contracts, for particular stretches of line or structures like bridges, each carried out by a particular contractor who employed gangs of navvies to do the construction work. Unlike today, railways like the Great Western were built largely by sheer physical effort, and railway builders had few machines to help them. The navvies were without doubt a tough breed, who worked hard for relatively poor pay in bad conditions. Many lived in tented shanty towns dotted along the route of the railway, and their drinking and behaviour struck terror in the hearts of local communities.

The route of the railway between London and Bristol ran along the Thames Valley from London to Reading, crossing the river a number of times, most notably at Maidenhead, where Brunel's graceful bridge caused much controversy due to the shallowness of its arches.

The interior of Box Tunnel in 1846.

From there to Swindon the line runs along what is now nicknamed 'Brunel's Billiard Table' because of its easy gradients. After Swindon however, the railway is forced to cross a far more hilly landscape, and the route includes some ferocious gradients of 1 in 100 at Wootton Bassett and through Box Tunnel. The tunnel at Box was another cause of controversy, burrowing through two miles of Cotswold limestone, it was one of the last sections of the railway to be completed, and only one track was ready for use when the Great Western Railway finally opened throughout from London to Bristol on 30 June 1841.

Brunel

Born on 9 April 1806, Isambard Kingdom Brunel is perhaps one of the most famous and flamboyant of the Victorian engineers. His father, Marc Isambard Brunel was also a distinguished engineer, and from a young age IKB showed a precocious talent for drawing and mathematics. He first came to prominence working with his father on the construction of a tunnel under the river Thames in London in 1827. Badly injured in an accident during the construction of the tunnel, Isambard was sent to Bristol to recuperate, and it was here that he heard of a project to design a suspension bridge over the River Avon at Clifton. Brunel eventually won a competition to design the bridge, and although it was never completed in his lifetime, it was a springboard for his career. Whilst in Bristol he heard of plans to build a new railway from London to Bristol, and in 1833 he was appointed as engineer of the Great Western Railway.

He also designed many other railways including the Bristol & Exeter, the South Devon, South Wales and the Cornwall and West Cornwall Railways. Some of his drawing and surveying equipment can be seen in the showcase near to the tunnel.

Not all Brunel's work was entirely successful. The use of the controversial 'Atmospheric' system in the construction of the South Devon Railway was one of his more conspicuous failures - George Stephenson called it a 'humbug' and the system never really worked, leaving the shareholders of the railway with a large loss. The timber viaducts he designed, many of which were used in the West Country were cheap to build, but had a short life span, and eventually had to be replaced by the GWR at considerable cost.

famous and flamboyant Victorian engineer

A model of Ponsonooth Viaduct near Truro is displayed near the 'North Star' locomotive. Elsewhere however, many of Brunel's successful railway accomplishments survive - Paddington station, the Maidenhead bridge, Bristol Temple Meads Station, and perhaps his most greatest achievement, the Royal Albert Bridge over the River Tamar at Saltash, opened in 1859.

Brunel was also an accomplished marine engineer, and designed three steamships; the 'Great Western' launched in 1838 was a conventional wooden hulled paddle steamer, but its successor, the 'Great Britain', was revolutionary in many ways. It was the first iron-hulled, screw propeller driven Atlantic liner, and but for an unfortunate wreck some years after its launch in 1843, would have been a great success. The Great Western Steamship Company, who had built the ship, ran out of money, and the 'Great Britain' was sold, being rebuilt to transport passengers to and from Australia for many years. Brunel's third ship, the 'Great Eastern', launched in 1859, was a far different proposition. This huge ship, designed to sail from England to Australia weighed more than 18,000 tons, and its construction and launch were fraught with difficulties, hastening the death of the great engineer in the same year. Brunel also designed a prefabricated hospital for the Crimean War, assisted in the Crystal Palace exhibition of 1851, and worked on many other projects besides.

A cartoon from Punch marking the end of Brunel's broad gauge. Brunel's ghost haunts the scene.

Cartoon from 'Punch' 1892.

Navvies at work converting Brunel's broad gauge at Saltash bridge.

The GROWTH OF THE NETWORK

Brunel's original Great Western railway was to link the two cities of Bristol and London, and the company coat of arms reflects this, incorporating the arms of both places. But before the Great Western had opened, connecting railways were already being planned by other companies, to link it with Exeter in the west, and Cheltenham and Gloucester via Swindon. Brunel's aim was not just to build a railway line, but to create a new railway system. The Railway Mania of the 1840s and 1850s saw the British railway network expand rapidly, and it was estimated that in 1845 over 200,000 people were employed in the building of railways all over the country.

By the time of Brunel's death in 1859, the GWR and associated companies stretched from London to Penzance in the West, and also into West Wales through the South Wales Railway of which he was also the engineer. The purchase of the West Midland Railway in 1863 brought the company into the West Midlands. By 1866 the company owned or worked 592 miles of Broad Gauge track, 240 miles of Mixed Gauge and 462 miles of Standard Gauge.

Although the railway had steadily grown in the nineteenth century, after grouping in 1923 the Great Western acquired large numbers of railways, particularly in South Wales. When the "Big Four" railways of the Great Western, the Southern, The London Midland & Scottish and the London & North Eastern Railways were created the G.W.R. was the only one of the new companies to keep its original name, making it one of the biggest and most prosperous railway companies in the world. During the Second World War the "Big Four" railways and London Transport had been under the control of the Railway Executive. After some debate, this arrangement was made permanent and in 1948 the Great Western Railway became part of British Railways when all four main line railway companies were nationalised by the government.

In the years after nationalisation, British Railways (Western Region) retained much of the character and traditions of the old Great Western. Much changed with the Beeching Report of 1963 which recommended the closure of many small stations and lines and reduced the size of the network by over 40%. Many staff lost their jobs, and small communities lost railways linking them with the rest of the country.

In recent years the privatisation of British Rail has seen a return to a railway network run by many different railway companies. Today the track, stations and signalling of railways is looked after by Railtrack, and most of the train services on Brunel's old main line are provided by First Great Western, reintroducing the old name once again.

BRITISH RAILWAYS

Brunel's Paddington Station more recent years showing high speed train in BR West region livery. Since privatisa the trains have been repaint in a new livery to reflect the ownership of First Great Western, who now run mos the services from the station

Wartime conditions at Birmingham Snow Hill station.

Above right: The 'Lion & Wheel' totem adopted by British Railways immediately after the nationalisation of British railways.

character and traditions

Operating THE RAILWAY - The Driver

Until recently, to be a locomotive driver was the ambition of many youngsters, and the job of engine driver was seen as the top job amongst railway staff. To become a driver of a large express engine like 'Caerphilly Castle' or 'King George V' did not happen overnight; years of experience were required before taking the reins of such an important locomotive. The bottom of the ladder was the job of engine cleaner, and boys wishing to become drivers started here. Steam engines were dirty and oily and it was the job of the cleaner to not only keep the engines sparkling, but also to shovel out all the ash and clinker from the locomotive ashpan at the end of the day. It was also the job of the most junior member of staff to go from the shed early in the morning to knock on the doors of drivers to ensure they got to work on time! Drivers then worked their way upwards, starting as drivers on shunting engines, gradually working on more important services as they gained more experience.

Great skill was required to both drive and fire steam locomotives - there are two hands on exhibits near this engine which show that skill - the 'Train Driving' simulator and the coal shovelling exhibit.

pride in the job

and timetables to keep the train running correctly and lamps and detonators to warn other trains in an emergency. Until more recent times, guards vans were a familiar sight, attached to the end of long goods trains as they made their way along the line. With the advent of continuous braking systems, brake vans have become obsolete and with them the job of goods guard. The brake van seen here is a typical GWR design, built in 1946 known as a 'Toad' - all wagons used by the railway were allocated names to allow them to be identified in paperwork and telegraph messages. The wide veranda not only gave the guard a good view, but

One of the most important jobs of a guard was to check the lamps on the train. The lamps shown here are from a slip coach, used on non-stop services like the Cornish Riviera Limited.

The work of a guard was far more difficult and dangerous at night.

The Guard

Another significant although more humble job on the railway was that of the guard. The tasks done by passenger and goods guards were different, although the safety, security and correct operation of the train were the most important tasks to both. Guards were responsible for the whole length of the train, except the engine itself and details of every trip were kept and sent to divisional headquarters. Many guards came to know the sounds a train made as it passed under bridges or climbed hills, so they could tell their position on the route exactly. Guards carried special instructions

lonely hours

also housed the brake handle which was used by the guard to control the speed of the train where required. Inside the van as well as emergency equipment, the guard also had a stove, very useful on long winter nights when guards could spend lonely hours as the train made its way from station to station.

The Signalman

The signal box displayed is a replica of a small GWR signal cabin, which has been equipped with some of the original equipment a box of this size would have carried. The lever frame, which was used to change points or operate signals, came from Ladbroke Grove just outside of Paddington. The frame was modified by London Transport who took over the box, which is why some of the original GWR features are now absent. In small signal boxes the signalman had a solitary life. Inside the box there were few facilities, often no running water or toilet, and only a small stove and kettle. Meals had to be taken during a break in the traffic. The floors and brass fittings were kept beautifully polished but no armchairs or newspapers were allowed in case the signalman was distracted or fell asleep.

A view of the large signal box at Reading East around 1914. Most signalboxes had far fewer levers than the one shown here and (below left), an example of one of the electromechanical signal boxes introduced to replace the old style boxes in the 1930s.

Outside the box a variety of GWR signals are displayed, including a selection of the original signals from the broad gauge era - including a fantail and disc and crossbar type, unique survivors of Brunel's railway.

The signalman had to know his systems exactly and be able to work under pressure, because a small mistake in signalling or controlling points could lead to disaster. In the early days of the GWR long working hours and lack of sleep led to many accidents, but the Company resisted the use of mechanical aids, because they were supposed to lead to lack of concentration. From the 1860s to the 1880s, new safety devices were at last introduced. These prevented the wrong lever being pulled by mistake and sent messages by telegraph or bell to allow only one train to travel on the line at a time.

Signalmen needed intensive training, learning much on the job, and regular examinations were taken to ensure staff were up to scratch. Modern signalling uses electronic switchboards, which have greatly increased comfort and convenience, and many manual signal boxes have now been removed. There are many more fail-safe systems but accidents can still occur.

a solitary life

Great
WESTERN
GOODS

Although thousands of passengers were transported by the Great Western Railway each year, the task of moving goods from place to place was equally important to the company. Although much less goods traffic travels by rail today, it remains an important mode of transport for heavy or bulk goods such as coal, stone or oil. In fact goods traffic on railways has increased in recent years. Today there is far less variety in the items transported by rail. The huge pile of goods displayed at the beginning of this section of the museum illustrates the huge number of different items the railway did move in its heyday.

The work of the Shunter in the Goods Yard was a highly skilled one - wagons needed to be sorted into the right order and couplings hooked up and unhooked. The dangers lurking in a goods yard were considerable - shunters could be knocked over by wagons as they were propelled into sidings, or crushed between the buffers of wagons if a driver was not concentrating on what he was doing! Although in smaller goods yards horses were used to move wagons around, in larger stations small tank locomotives such as this one, 'Pannier Tank' No. 9400 were used to do the work. The wagon next to No. 9400 is known as a 'Shunters Truck' and was used by shunters to ride around larger goods yards in safety. The tool box on top of the wagon was used to store spare couplings and shunters' poles, the 'tool of the trade' for shunters - the character figure between the buffers is holding one of these too. As well as moving goods from station to station, the Great Western and British Railways also ran a service to deliver goods from the station to the customer. Once unloaded from the goods wagon, the goods could be stored in the Goods Shed in the station yard. Once the paperwork had been

The scale of the coal traffic handled by the GWR can be seen in this view of one of the many goods yards in the South Wales area.

completed, goods could either be collected by the customer or delivered by the Great Western's own staff. From the earliest days this was done by horse-drawn vehicles, and the dray seen here was used in the Bristol area for many years. Horses were cheaper to run than lorries for short runs where much time was spent waiting around. This is why 500 GWR horses still worked in London as late as 1937, even though the first lorry started work in 1905. The new lorries could do in 8 hours what horses had done in 14 hours. From 1933 express parcel vans were introduced in London. They carried cream, fish, live animals and food which would not keep, very useful in the days before freezers. Fresh Cornish fish which arrived at Paddington Station at 4pm could be delivered to a restaurant, in time to be served the same evening.

The 'mechanical horse' on display here is typical of many used all over Britain in all manner of locations, and although it was not originally owned by the GWR, its livery has been carefully researched to illustrate the type carried by other GWR vehicles of the period. The GWR goods wagon is a 'Mink' wagon used to carry general goods and produce. Other specialist wagons were used to transport things like fish, bananas, milk and grain and all had weird and wonderful names like 'Bloaters', 'Micas' and 'Mogos'!

A goods porter at work at Paddington Goods Depot in the 1920's.

Fish traffic being loaded at the South Wales port of Neyland. Rail travel allowed fresh fish to be rapidly moved around the country.

The wide variety of wagons used by the GWR can be seen in this view of Acton Yard, taken to mark the testing of the first 100 wagon train on the Great Western in 1904.

A view of Paddington Station with passengers awaiting the departure of the Cornish Riviera Limited Express, which left the station at 10.30am.

stations all over the GWR network, whose humble appearance contrasted with the grand stations like those at Paddington, Birmingham Snow Hill and Bristol Temple Meads.

Today buying a ticket at a railway station is very simple - you can even buy tickets over the phone or the Internet! In the golden age of steam, passengers were required to buy their tickets at ticket offices like this one in our station. The booking clerk sat behind the wooden partition, surrounded by racks containing all the numerous tickets he might require. Depending on what sort of journey you might take, or what type of passenger you might be, there were hundreds of different tickets - First, Second or Third Class, Single or Return, Excursion or Day Return. There were tickets for the transport of dogs, and even if you were a shipwrecked sailor there was a ticket for you! Tickets were also required if you wanted to stand on station platforms - until the introduction of 'open stations' you needed a platform ticket. Why not try out one of our platform ticket machines?

One of the Ticket Offices at Birmingham Snow Hill station in 1913.

Passenger TRAVEL

Thousands of people travelled on trains across the Great Western network each day. Some journeys were business, others for pleasure, with many using the railway to visit the seaside for their annual holiday.

Today, far fewer people use trains, but the number is again increasing. Although they are no longer hauled by steam locomotives, modern trains are faster and more comfortable than they were. With the introduction of services such as Eurostar, fast international travel is now possible.

The station building on our platform is a replica, based on a number of real locations, including Eynsham in Oxfordshire, Culkerton in Gloucestershire and Banbury in Oxfordshire. It is typical of the smaller

Many of the jokes about curled up railway sandwiches date from the early days of railway catering! Before the Great Western ran its own refreshment rooms, it leased them to private companies who did not always treat passengers well in those early days. The Swindon refreshment rooms were no exception, and there were many complaints about the standard of food served. Brunel complained about the coffee, and you can hear his letter of complaint in this display. Things were so bad that Swindon was nicknamed 'Swindleum' by irate travellers who only had 10 minutes to eat their refreshments. Happily in later years things improved, and passengers could take refreshment from a variety of sources - refreshment trolleys like the one shown here, refreshment rooms, and buffet and dining cars on trains themselves.

Today thankfully the standard of food served on trains and at stations is rather better than in the past - usually!

The coming of railways also brought a revolution in the way in which we tell the time - before they were introduced, every town and city relied on its own local time, and there was a wide difference between one side of the country and the other. In order to run trains to a timetable a standard time for the whole country needed to be introduced, and largely as a result of pressure from railway companies, Greenwich Mean Time was introduced. Clocks were a feature of all GWR stations and offices, and a time signal was transmitted by telegraph once a week to ensure that all clocks told the same time. The Railway had a clock workshop at Reading Signal Works which maintained all the thousands of clocks and watches used by the company and its staff, some of which are on display in the showcase.

Reading Refreshment Rooms c.1914.

The Clockmakers workshop at Reading Signal Works. All clocks and watches used by the Great Western apart from those at Swindon Works were maintained here.

Refreshment Rooms at Exeter St Davids Station in the 1930s.

August 1935 -
halcyon days
on holiday

Speed
TO THE WEST

From the end of the Victorian era onwards, more and more ordinary people could afford to take a holiday or day trip by rail. The Great Western Railway responded by successfully promoting itself as 'The Holiday Line'.

No other railway company matched the quality and output of the Great Western's publicity material. Their historical books, popular guides and striking posters offered people a compelling and romantic image of the company's holiday regions. For the manual workers, craftsmen and huge new class of office workers in Britain's congested and smoky towns, 'Smiling Somerset', 'Glorious Devon' and the 'Cornish Riviera' seemed full of promise.

In order to attract passengers during the quiet season the GWR went to great lengths to promote Cornwall as a winter holiday resort. One publication noted "The blessings of warmth, sunshine and a mild climate may be found during the winter months without crossing the channel or the continent or incurring the toil and expense of a sojourn in Egypt, a visit to Algiers or even a trip to Nice or San Remo". GWR tourism had an enormous impact on the once remote regions of Devon and Cornwall. The influx of thousands of visitors every year quickly

turned Torquay, Newquay, Penzance and St.Ives into prime resorts, with many other towns to follow. In 1906 the 'Daily Telegraph' reported 'scarcely a place on the coast untouched by the ramifications of Brunel's famous line'. Passengers taking advantage of tourist-rate tickets flocked to the beaches while shops and businesses sprang up to cater for this new wave of holiday makers. Local people took in lodgers during the holiday season and the GWR opened its own prestigious hotels and rented out camping facilities in old railway carriages for those on a tighter budget.

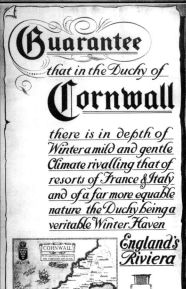

The Bookstall at Paddington station. GWR books and pamphlets are much in evidence in this 1913 view.

The Great Western used buses to advertise its services. Many travelled huge distances. In the period before 1914 buses were sent to Scotland and the North of England, deep into the Heart of their rival's territory.

Holidaymakers arriving at another popular GWR destination, Weston-super-Mare.

After nationalisation BR Western Region continued to produce posters for the old Great Western resorts but despite their efforts the number of people taking holidays by train steadily decreased. The rise of car ownership was the single biggest factor in that decline. The car allowed families a sense of freedom, flexibility and privacy which seemed unanswerable. Packed holiday trains were increasingly replaced by busy roads to the coast. Today the popularity of English resorts has faded like the holiday trains before them. Many of today's holiday makers head for the airport and resorts overseas.

Speed, comfort and glamour were the hallmarks of the Great Western's holiday express trains epitomised by the 'Cornish Riviera Ltd.' and the 'Torbay Express'. Whether you were taking a third class ticket on a packed excursion train to Weymouth or travelling first class on the 'Cornish Riviera', the GWR aimed to

Opposite right: A view of one of GWR's hotels and an example of one of its rooms.

provide as fast and as comfortable a service as possible. Extra trains were laid on to cater for the increasing numbers of holiday makers and day trippers taking advantage of the GWR's cut price Holiday Season Tickets. Improvements to the old main line between Paddington and Penzance meant passengers for Devon and Cornwall could expect to reach their destination in record-breaking time.

The 'Cornish Riviera Ltd.' was the GWR's most prestigious holiday train. Introduced in 1904 the train provided passengers with a faster, more comfortable and convenient service than ever before. The 'Torbay Express' began its historic runs from Paddington to Torbay in the 1920s. In peak periods by 1938 each train could carry over 1000

shows, donkey rides, brass bands and boat rides. Dances and concerts in glamorous pavilions all added to the holiday fun. Those who preferred a more peaceful time could opt for the smaller bays and fishing ports served by the GWR's branch lines and motor buses.

people to the resorts of South Devon. In August Bank Holiday weekend of that year 20,000 people arrived in Torquay alone from London, Wales, Bristol, and the Midlands. With the trains so packed not everyone was lucky enough to get a seat.

Day trippers and holidaymakers stepping down from packed Great Western Trains expected to enjoy a more active holiday than many people choose today. Early trippers arrived at the seaside laden with coats, umbrellas, buckets, spades and baskets of food.

By the turn of the century big resorts like Torquay and Weymouth entertained the crowds with side

In the 1920s and 30s GWR literature recommended sightseeing, rambling, cycling, and golf as alternatives to the big seaside resorts. Although many holidaymakers could only afford to stay in boarding houses or lodgings, the better off could stay at one of the company's own hotels. As well as the prestigious Great Western Hotel at Paddington, the railway also owned three others, all providing a very high standard of accommodation.

Swindon Trip Holiday

Every year the Great Western Factory closed for ten days and the company ferried its employees and their families to their chosen holiday destination. It was a massive operation and by 1912 it involved moving almost 25,000 people on 23 different trains.

In order to dispatch all the trippers promptly, the long haul trains bound for Cornwall left Swindon on the evening the factory closed. Early next morning Swindon trippers poured onto the sidings, walking along the railway tracks to where their trains lay waiting.

One publicity campaign run by the GWR was that Cornwall was warm enough for 'Bathing In February'.

Trip tickets could be used to travel almost anywhere on the British railway network, although many Swindon families chose familiar destinations such as Weston-Super-Mare and Barry Island. Most popular of all were the trains which ran to Weymouth where the influx of railway families was so great the town became known as 'Swindon-by- the-Sea'. With its workforce gone, Swindon itself was left strangely empty, and many other businesses in the town closed during trip week since trade was so poor. Everyone knew that money was tight after Trip Week. Until 1938 holidays were unpaid, so many Swindon families came home early or spent just a day away.

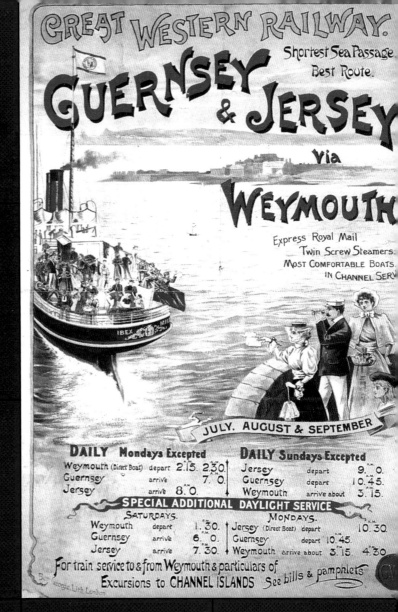

S w i n d o n - b y - t h e - S e a

Many children had happy memories of travelling by train to the seaside.

The WORKSHOP

This part of the building was added in 1929 and 1930 when part of the original Brunel workshops were demolished and both the building now the museum and the old 'B' Shed next door were extended. The new brickwork can be clearly seen on the old 1872 stone wall. This space is now occupied by Swindon Railway Engineering Limited, a small company who are maintaining the skills practised by generations of Swindon workers, and are restoring locomotives and rolling stock for preserved railways.

On the back wall of the gallery is the Swindon Works Wall of Names - this is a tribute to the many thousands of people who worked for the Great Western in the Swindon area, and each name has been pledged by members of their family who have contributed to the Swindon Railway Heritage Centre Trust. If you would like to nominate someone for the Wall of Names, ask at the museum information desk for a form.

A viewing gallery onto the main Bristol to London railway is next to the Wall of Names, giving views of modern rolling stock on Brunel's original Great Western line.